I0641120

ALSO BY ELLIS KROSS

The V Trilogy
Freeze Vol. 1: A Week With Mr. Hopkins
Freeze Vol. 2: Final Days
Joshua'z Tree
The March to Sundown
FRANKIE
Spell of the Eye
A Tear That Ripples Across The Pale Sky

ALSO BY DALIVIA PLAUT

<u>The *Midnight World* Anthology:</u>
Cut From Darkness
Wrapped In Darkness
Possessed By Darkness
darkness_4.0 OS V.2.1
Down With Darkness
1-800-Darkness

Rare Breed
House of Drenelle
Cracked

ALSO BY RICKIE TRACE

Transfer of Power

SECONDS TO NOWARE

"NIGHT HANDLER"
by
DALIVIA PLAUT

"COLD BY NATURE"
by
ELLIS KROSS

"DEEP FREEZE"
by
RICKIE TRACE
DALIVIA PLAUT
&
ELLIS KROSS

First Edition, November 2023
Story by Ellis Kross
Edited by Sidonie Lailler

Copyright © 2022 Universal Computer, Ellis Kross, Dalivia Plaut, Rickie Trace

"Night Handler" written by Dalivia Plaut; "Cold By Nature" written by Ellis Kross; "Proximity to Power" written by Rickie Trace

PUBLISHED BY SHADOW MOUSE

ISBN: 978-1-7344831-8-5
Seconds to Noware
I. Title. Science Fiction. Thriller

ISBN: 978-1-7344831-8-5 pbk.

Book design by Izzy
Cover artwork by DKosig (istockphoto.com)
Interior artwork by 3quarks (istockphoto.com)

This is a work of fiction.
Names, characters, places, and incidents are the products of the author's imagination.
Any resemblance to actual persons, living or dead, is entirely coincidental.

Printed in the United States
10 9 8 7 6 5 4 3 2 1

"How many times does one have to tell a lie in order to believe it as truth?"

— Timothee Chu, author of *The Shepherd's Gambit*

"Both artists and laborers are the glue to society bound by a common structure in that each craft or skill carried out through the invaluable tools we possess, either between our ears or before our very eyes, keeps the wheels greased and spinning, physically and mentally, and neither one is anymore vital than the other."

— Stanley Pruitt, author of *A Prelude to Darkness*

"Fib, flap, the King (above) *has no cap."*

— P.B. Jacobi

Snap!

Deal Gone Dark

Ellis Kross

Deal Gone Dark (Take it and Run)
E-mailed by Ellis Kross

COMPOSE

MUTY dangles a small baggie of VP-23 before the junkie.

Craving a small taste of that "sweet 'globin," the crème de la crème of nose candy, that pick-me-up-before-you-go-go, the junkie's blood-shot eyes swell as round as quarters while licking his leathery-chapped lips in a staticky state of arousal.

Muty holds up the baggie in a flickering light cast from a floodlight above, showing his potential buyer the many rare crystals among that red powder, which sparkles like glitter when held into the light.

The junkie takes a whiff of the metallic-like scent that emits from VP-23, as Muty waves the plastic baggie in the air, as though he's not only teasing the junkie, but he's also bringing out the unique smell the same way a cook would rub the leaves of a herb together, like basil, in order to awaken its aroma or similar to how a wino would twirl around a glass of wine in order to awaken a medley of fruit and woody magic. The junkie's senses are still heightened from the last hit before his stash ran out. Either way, he is interested in what Muty has to offer. He most definitely digs.

"*First*," he says fiendishly, "a bump. Got to know if it's the real deal, you feel?"

The VP-23 has already highjacked his body and each word that comes out of the junkie's mouth has a desperate tinge to it.

The once crooked smile flatlines along Muty's gray, deformed face, which remains tucked in the shadows of a damp black hood.

"You don't trust me?"

"Nobody *trusts* a mutant," the junkie says snappishly.

While Muty absorbs the insult, the jittery junkie makes a half-ass attempt to snatch the baggie of VP-23 from Muty's three-fingered grip.

Muty pulls the baggie away.

"Right you are, *Vermin*," he says, his voice raspier like the voice of a lifelong smoker. "But where else you gonna buy the finest vamp blood in the city?"

"Just a bump," he pleads with Muty, who, in return, relishes in the junkie's desperation.

The junkie is incredibly irritable and paranoid, as he looks around the alleyway, scanning not for cops, but for other mutants.

Muty is aware of the harsh withdrawals from VP-23, and the junkie, whom Muty thinks comes from wealth based off the expensive clothes that he is sporting, as well as an aura of entitlement that he projects whenever he opens his mouth, that sort of windy and stretched out drawl like he'd hear during his days in the Valley, is displaying the classic symptoms, one of them being the most transparent: the shakes, a wickedly erratic tremble that fed off the waves of hungry and thirst.

"Curious," Muty says, teasing the potential buyer, "having trouble in the sack? Can't get 'it' up?" He asks, leaning closer, "Or, are you feeling a little down, my clown?" Muty acknowledges the junkie's expensive black suit (the only part of the junkie's attire that hints at his needy state, except for the dark bags underneath his crimson eyes or the pale complexion or gaunt face, the worn and wrinkled collar of his white dress shirt, which is speckled with brownish droplets of blood and drenched with sweat). More closely, Muty says, "Based on what you're wearing, you look like a man who comes from Above The Clouds." He points at the modern skyscrapers that tower over Kingsport. The tops of the buildings vanish into a newspaper gray that blankets the skyline like a pillowy canopy. "Has the apple fallen far from the tree?"

"And do you know what tree that is, *mutant*?" says the junkie.

Muty thinks for a second.

"Gee," he teases, "is it the Almighty Himself?"

"Does the name 'Coney' *clink* your bottle?"

"Coney *Coney*?" says Muty. "The same Coney on the building façade on 42nd Street?"

"Now you know who you're dealing with, *mutant*," says the junkie, Dilbert "Bert," youngest son of Edmond Coney, a businessman who made his millions from his chain of luxurious hotels.

"Well," Muty says with a mischievous grin creasing over the corners of his gray face, "isn't this a surprise? Surely, Prince Vermin has many friends who have a crazing for vamp blood?"

Irritated by Muty's inquiries, the junkie, Bert, suddenly reaches his hand into his pocket and brandishes a butterfly knife and threatens Muty to hand over the VP-23.

Muty cracks open the flap of his raggedy dark green overcoat, exposing his left nipple behind a torn hole in the black hoody worn underneath.

Before Bert can grab the baggie of VP-23 from Muty's hand, a gray tentacle shoots out from the nipple, grabbing the knife from Bert's hand.

With his free hand, he reveals the inside of his overcoat: a vast collection of knifes and other weapons, including handguns and pistols, dangling like hooked ornaments on the interior side of the over-coat, which Muty holds outward like the *muleta* of a matador.

"You gonna play nice?" says Muty, as he hooks the butterfly knife to a ringed-loop attached to the interior of the coat.

Muty closes the overcoat.

"A'ight," Bert says, holding up his shaky hands. "Your turf."

"Right you are, *Vermin*," Muty says. "*My* turf. *My* rules."

"So, are you going to make a deal or what?"

"How much you got?"

Bert reaches into his pocket—"slowly," as Muty warns—and pulls out a hundred-dollar bill from his leather wallet.

"Normally, it'd cost you twice as much," Muty says, "but since you threw in the knife, I'll make an exception."

The two make the exchange, Bert handing over the hundred (Muty inspects in the beam of a floodlight flickering above) and then, after pocketing the cheddar, Muty handing over VP-23.

"Now, off you go, Prince," Muty says, as Bert shakes his head in disgust and walks from the alleyway.

From the shadows behind a dumpster emerges a skittish stray named Low-Key, probably no older than fourteen years old, maybe more (he doesn't know his age). Some years ago, around the time of the economic collapse, Low-Key was abandoned by his parents, who lost their jobs to robots, his father, a former claim adjuster who was canned after AI stole his job, and his mother, a former bank clerk who lost her job to a toaster oven, and like many around Low-Key's age (?), left on the streets to fend for himself.

Low-Key says from behind, "Who's your friend?"

Recognizing Low-Key's voice, Muty says, "Look who decided to crawl from his hole."

"Who was that?"

"Customer."

"So, what's his poison?" asks Low-Key.

"Red Death," he says. "Vermin has himself a sweet nose." Falling into a state of reflection, Muty brings up a story about VP-23, a cautionary tale that another mutant told him when he first entered the service industry. He says, "Reminds of a guy I once heard about through lore: A music man, once famous before he lost himself a screw, his brain with as many holes as a slice of Swiss cheese, who flew too close to the sun but never got himself burned until one night when he decided to dance with the devil."

"Music man, huh?" asks Low-Key.

"You remember that pimp, Limou, who was dropped from the top of the hotel off 42nd?"

"How could I forget?" says Low-Key. "It took the city forever to scrape all of those bits and pieces of body from concrete. You can still seen bloodstains on the sidewalk—"

"*Like him*," Muty says, "only instead of pimping out fish flies, he pimped out musicians and made himself quite a reputation. Those who roamed his circles called him 'Hit Man.'"

"Hit Man, huh?

"Never did he expect for such a nickname to take on another meaning of its own. *BANG!*" Muty shouts out while shaping his three fingers like a handgun, one finger like the gun's handle, the middle finger a barrel, and the third and smaller finger a hammer, then placing the fingered-barrel against the side of his temple and closing his third finger, emphasizing a gunshot straight to the bone dome.

Low-Key flinches from the invisible gunshot.

"*BANG, Hit Man!*" he shouts once more, "only not the kind of hit *HIT* Man expected."

"Hit?"

"Several months before the massacre," Muty says, his energy revs up by the legend, "*HIT* Man got his hands on this new drug on the street. The drug smuggled across the border—" from the corner of his mouth, he says, "—and I ain't talking about *that* border."

"You mean the place you don't speak of."

"Right you are," Muty says. "A place filled with monsters that would eat you whole and use those bones of yours as toothpicks."

"Sounds like a friendly place," Low-Key says foolishly. "When can I visit?"

With a sniffling laughter, Muty says, "Funny guy, you are. Can't say the same about our guy *HIT* Man. Little did he know this new drug—'red dust,' as the uprights called it at the time—wasn't thoroughly inspected when it was cut before it wound up on the streets. The legend goes: A shard no larger than a grain of salt was accidentally chipped off a protective armor of the Annexus tribe called E'Raknish during the process of packaging up what you now know as VP-23."

Low-Key furrows his brow and stares at Muty's face the same way he looks at it whenever it isn't masked with shadows.

"Wait a sec," he says, confused. "Annexus? Who's that?"

Frustrated by the stray's interruption, Muty says, "Annexus is a group of. . . likeminded folk, said to be the former guards of the High Order, who hunt down vamps, gut 'em, hang 'em out to dry—literally—and sell their blood to suppliers, who make their living off people like *HIT* Man. In this particular case, Annexus wrangled up themselves a century-old vamp, Head of the Leatherwood Family, blood as sour as stomach bile, shall I say, a 'potent' batch of red dust that would knock the socks off any powder king. Any other *quest*-ions? Or, can I finish the story?"

Low-Key makes a face and says more impatiently, "By all means. . ."

"After months of getting high off vamp blood—but not just any vamp blood, the Head of the Leatherby Family vamp blood—our *HIT* Man is a complete wreck. Unaware of the shard that he ingested into his body, he starts hearing voices in his head, ghosts of the very armor that has protected Annexus since the First Hunt, guiding him, manipulating him, controlling his every single thought. As *HIT* Man's stash starts to run out, he decides to cut it with a little bit of white powder courage, not only to preserve the stash, but also, in a desperate attempt, to try recapturing that same godly high he first experienced when sampling what would come to be VP-23. So," Muty says, as he can hardly contain his excitement in the telling of the story, "one night at a nightclub in Fog City, while high off a strawberry swirl of vamp blood and coke, *HIT* Man empties out his remaining stash onto a table in the back of the V-I-P and takes a massive *HIT* straight to the bone dome, a *HIT* that'd soon turn him into a monster of all monsters. *HIT* Man goes straight up Berserker! *BANG!*" He points the three-finger handgun to the side of his head once more, pulls the finger-trigger once more. "*HIT* Man goes on a killing spree, claiming the lives of eight people. Cops arrived and managed to subdue him before he turns the gun on himself."

Not only amazed by the story, but also Muty's wild and exaggeration animation while sharing the story, Low-Key asks, "What happened to this Hit Man?"

"After his sentencing, he was sent to an insane asylum," Muty says to Low-Key. "As for the E'Raknish armor, nobody knows what happened to it, if it was buried with our *HIT* Man after he died, or if it managed to crawl out of his body and seek out a more appropriate user."

"And is that what you sold that guy?" asks Low-Key.

"That guy" being Bert Coney.

"That?" says Muty. "That was just cayenne pepper cut with pulverized muh-sakel dandruff and a dash of blood drawn from a vamp toy to give him the illusion he's snorting pure VP-23."

"Muh-sakel?"

"It's like a rodent, only far more aggressive," Muty says. "Where I come from we call it the 'devil rat,' pesky as hell, hard to catch. According to what you call in your world an old wives' tale, the devil rat's blood is said to be an aphrodisiac. Our pal Bert won't know what *HIT* him—that is, if the mood should strike him. You dig?"

Muty slightly tilts his head from the sound of approaching footsteps on the sidewalk outside the alleyway. He looks to the end of the alley and sees the shadow shrink and take a shape along the sidewalk. The footsteps stop to a deafening silence. At the end of the alley stands the lanky silhouette of a middle-aged woman.

"Are you Muty?" asks the strange woman.

"Depends on who's asking. . . "

Muty squares himself to the dark stranger.

"I was told you could possibly help me out with a certain situation."

"Depends on the situation. . . "

"I need protection."

"Well," Muty says, waving the stranger into the alleyway, "step into my office. . . "

He shoos away Low-Key, who scurries away.

Hesitant at first, the stranger approaches Muty.

"So," Muty says, grinning, "what kind of protection are we looking for tonight?"

"I need a gun," she says and partially steps into the hazy light, revealing the name "Sᴜᴇ Lɪᴜ" on the nametag, which is pinned to the upper right breast pocket of her silk burgundy blouse.

"I think I might be able to help you out. . . " Muty reads the nametag, ". . . Sue Liú."

The woman, Sue, pulls out a billfold from her purse and asks, "How much?"

"Like I've said before, depends on the situation."

"Something small, handheld, easy to use."

"You have any experience handling firearms?"

"Once," Sue says with rehearsed calmness, "when I was younger. My first husband used to take me to the shooting range."

"Sounds like a man who knows how to show a lady a good time."

"He was a pathological liar who slept around with other women behind my back."

"And excuse me for prying: Do you plan on using a gun on this. . . man you speak of?"

"It's none of your business who or what I use my gun on," Sue snaps.

"Fair point." Muty says, leaning closer, "But it ain't your gun. . . yet."

"So, what do you got?" Sue asks in a pushy manner. "I'm going to be late for work—"

"Small, handheld, easy to use, right?"

Sue nods *correct*.

Muty cracks open his worn overcoat as he did before, revealing that vast collection of weapons hanging along the interior of the flap. He grabs a snubnosed revolver and unfastens the hook clipped around the trigger guard. Once the revolver is free, he displays it for Sue.

"This is what's called a 'belly gun,'" Muty says. "Small, as you can see, handheld," he then pulls back on the hammer and dry-fires at a rat scurrying behind Sue, "easy to use."

"Why do you call it belly gun?" asks Sue.

Muty displays how to carry and conceal the revolver, best carried underneath a waistband or "close to the belly." Then, as an example, he turns to the side away from Sue, draws the revolver from his waistband and fires from the hip.

"The perfect weapon to provide you with plenty of *safe* space."

"How much?"

"For you," Muty says, looking over Sue's attire, the nametag suggesting that she is in food or retail, "a fellow service member, especially in this economy, I'll do two-fifty. I'll even throw in a box of ammunition, no charge."

"Deal," Sue says over a rehearsed pause, as she tries not to give away her cover.

She pulls out two hundreds, two twenties, and a ten from a billfold, and hands the crisp bills to Muty.

After the two make the transaction, Muty says to Sue, "*She who handles the torch will own the night.*"

"I'm sorry," Sue says, confused by Muty's comment.

(*She who handles the torch will own the night*)

While looking her over with suspicion, Muty says curiously, "How'd you hear about me?"

As Sue begins to load ammo into each chamber of the revolver's cylinder, she says the name in a suspicious manner, "Mr. Dukes."

"Dukes, huh?"

"You know him?"

"He was one of my most loyal customers—"

Halfway through loading the revolver, he tells the lady to load the revolver somewhere else.

Once the revolver is loaded, the cylinder shuts close, Muty puts the two pieces of the puzzle together: the lady in need of a weapon and the batch of shvak urine disguised as CBD oil that he sold Dukes last week for a discounted price.

Before Muty opens his coat and reveals a tentacle underneath, Sue raises the revolver, points the barrel to Muty's head, and shoots him directly between the eyes.

Low-Key, who witnesses the entire transaction, which leads to the killing of Muty, suddenly makes a noise, causing Sue to turn the revolver on the dark figure cowering behind the dumpster.

With his hands raised, Low-Key rises from the shadows and says submissively, "I didn't see anything. Please. I'm no nark—"

"Good," Sue says over the stray and walks away.

Low-Key checks on Muty, who is dead. His brains are like a can of worms, both splattered on the building, as well as dripping from the hole in the back of his head.

Carefully, Low-Key reaches inside his coat and grabs a handgun from Muty's collection of weaponry. He finds the right ammunition in another pocket.

Armed for the night, Low-Key cautiously exits the alleyway and ventures out into the city of Kingsport, ready for whatever the night has in store for him.

SEND

NIGHT HANDLER

DALIVIA PLAUT

BOOK ONE

THE BL@CKOUT by Stanley Pruitt
MAY 30, 2030
NEW ORLEANS, LOUISIANA

SUSPENDED over the author's table, a black banner reads in bold white lettering:

THE BL@CKOUT

The author, Stanley Pruitt, shakes hands with fellow writing pal, Arty Zine, charged hair and wired eyes, a beatnik reincarnated, whom he hadn't seen in ages, before his bubbly handler, C.J., escorts him to the black-clothed table inside Booth #37.

In front of the booth, which is decked out in all things BLACKOUT: a line of stoked Luminatis (loyal readers of Pruitt, the name branded by Pruitt himself during an off-the-cuff comment in an interview with *Gateway Books*) stretches from the red letter **X** taped on the floor in front of the booth's table, which indicates the spot where the reader must stand while meeting the author, to beyond the packed convention center.

On the glass holder perches a translucent eTablet with a digital copy of Stanley's latest novella, *Just Another Blackout Story*, a very Meta, very self-indulgent, very anticlimactic sequel to the best-selling hit *In the Wake of Darkness* (BOOK ELEVEN).

Stanley's previous title, not necessarily considered a major flop but more or less an exercise in experimental storytelling done in the format of a quasi-social commentary called *A Prelude to Darkness*, a sort of "told-you-so" rub job written as an origin story for the controversial *Blackout* series, was such a divisive outing—created lots of irrelevant headlines and slam articles and way more press than its intention, as well as a word-of-mouth throughout the public, what folks in the industry once referred to as a "water cooler" because most conversations, let's say, about *A Prelude to Darkness*, happened in front of the water cooler inside the break room of an office, a place where employees often mingled, socialized, or yapped away about the hottest bullshit ("coffee machine" was probably a more up-to-date expression), even though half the people who gossiped about the book never actually read the book—Stanley's agent, Rod Cloverfeld, got down on both knees, pleading with his most favorite author to write another story, told him to grab that pickaxe of his and unearth one more gem, not only because the fans were dying to learn what happened after, as stated by the publisher in a misleading marketing campaign, Stanley's "final" *Blackout* novel, which left many fans divided about the deus ex machina ending, one so gapingly open and ambiguous that Stanley received many death threats (once, a fan of Stanley's attempted to assassinate him while he was giving a speech on the importance of "Creative Writing" at Dapper University), but also because of the most obvious reason: of all the authors Rod represents, Stanley Pruitt is his most successful author, and you couldn't scroll through a single page on a news feed without reading the author's name in an absurd headline or clickbait, and Rod, who'd say he's as loyal as a Jack Russell, certainly prefers living with a roof over his head, even if it means whispering sweet nothings into Stanley's rabbit hole of an ear, a dose of confidence boost for a writer whose many characters have overstayed their welcome inside his head, just "one more" Stan the Man, "Who's your bad agent?"

After taking photos for their digital copies, as well as signing them with a stylus pen for his Luminatis—some of whom don't hold back any emotion while expressing their likes or dislikes or even grievances with *A Prelude to Darkness*—Stanley can't help but notice the paperback in the hand of the reader who's next in line, not a Luminati, clearly, he can tell, not only by his mild mannerisms and lack of fanboy attire, but also the physical book he's holding under his armpit. Luminatis have never read the book nor have they shown interest in his past work, pre-*Blackout*. Stanley knows these things because not one single Luminati, either online or in person, has expressed views or opinions about the book, not one peep.

Stanley signs a copy of *Just Another Blackout Story* for the uber-excited fan, who, after the head Luminati, King of Light himself, verbally offers his consent, takes a selfie with the author.

As he places his black gloved hand over her shoulder, the fan politely asks if he can remove his hand—better yet, switch sides with her—not because the author's left hand, which, for years, has been cloaked in rumors, makes her uncomfortable or invades her personal space, but because the alleged disfigured appearance underneath the black glove may take away attention from herself.

Rumor has it a majority of muscle and tissue had been ripped away in what the author previously alluded to a car accident, which nearly killed him. Results of flesh and bone caught in hot twisted metal, which, over time, gave the appearance of thin, papery skin tightly shrink-wrapped around bone. This, of course, is hearsay, despite the author's allusions, and claims aside, not one Luminati has actually seen Stanley's hand.

Other rumors suggest that the author is wearing a prosthetic, hence a lack of mobility in the hand. It wouldn't be a first time the hand has disturbed fans, especially Stanley's younger ones, in fact, over the years a legend has grown around Stanley's hand (the black leather glove that he never removed in the public eye only enhancing suspicion), some fans claiming it was the result of the King of Light plunging his hand into a running garbage disposal after the death of his second wife, while others taking the claims a step further, saying he stuck it in much darker places, for instance, the burrow of an Inland Taipan whose venomous bite caused the flesh of his hand to melt away like ice-cream underneath a hot afternoon sun.

Rumors about Stanley's hand are merely the spittle of trivial gossip compared to the strange marking on top of his head, the marking covered up by a solid black baseball cap that he always wears. As with the black leather glove, which Stanley wore on his left hand, Stanley never removed the baseball cap while he was in the public eye, except for a few times when he was seen without the cap in rare photographs, which were taken from a distance by either paparazzi or one of his Luminatis and each one gave off heavy stalker vibes: one photo taken outside the cabin in the Blue Ridge Mountains where Stanley was known to vacation, and another, in the small town of Simpson, Colorado, where a sudden gust of wind had blown away the ball cap—in the photograph Stanley is spotted chasing after the hat on a sidewalk along Main Street. In each one of the photographs, however, that pinkish scar on top of his head, shaped like a large starfish, like the hand, has created a greater legend amongst loyal fans, all of it aided by the elephant in the room, which is Stanley's bald scalp. Stanley, who should've been called "King Deflector," once stated in an interview that the hairstyle was done as a means of "convenience." In other words, according to the author, the easy hairdo, which required him a few extra minutes out of his week to extend his shave from his face to his head, allowed him to, as quoted, "spend more of his time focusing on writing," opposed to maintaining "presentable hairdos." The past comment put aside any rumors of Stanley fighting a bout of cancer. The baldness or at times, twice during Halloween, the wearing of over-the-top wigs, gave off impressions to recently knighted Luminatis that the author was dealing with his share of health issues.

Whatever the case may be about Stanley Pruitt, the fan's comment hardly carries a sting; in fact, on the contrary, it makes him feel taller and more powerful.

The next reader, sweaty pits, makes his way toward Stanley.

He places the damp book on the table.

With his good hand, Stanley picks it up and reads the title, *"The Song of Summer."*

Stanley looks over the worn, wrinkled book and despite its shabby appearance—which, on the contrary, only exemplifies the many miles the book traveled, as well as the many hands and eyes and hopefully, hearts it touched—the sight of the book brought Stanley comfort, like a hug, as warm and nourishing as two souls intertwining.

So many years it has been, he thought. *So many tears shed.*

With eyes blanketed in nostalgia, he says to the reader, "I wrote this book on a vintage typewriter that I bought from a pawnshop."

"A Stanley and Sons, right?"

"You've done your research."

The reader says, "I heard you bought it because of the name."

"Sadly," Stanley says, turning over the rare paperback. "That's as true as the color blue."

The reader doesn't know what to think of the comment.

"Didn't know this book still existed," Stanley says, admiring its age.

Stanley looks up at the reader, who, if he guessed, is in his early thirties.

"They don't," the reader says. "I bought it through a private seller on Book-Rat. Wouldn't believe how much I had to pay for it."

"I don't want to know," Stanley says, "but it must've been worth a pretty penny."

"It helped me through a tough time," he says awkwardly.

"I'm glad I could help." Then, avoiding the subject, Stanley asks before the reader can follow up with a question, "Is this your first time at LitCon?"

"It is," he says, looking around like a stiff puppet. "Not what I expected."

Stanley smiles and opens the book to the first page.

C.J. swoops in and hands Stanley a pen, a real one that is, loaded with rare black ink.

"Your name?"

"Jacob," he says, his voice rattling, his movements mechanical.

"Nice to meet you, Jacob."

Stanley signs the inside of the book: *"To Jacob, Keep Shining - Stanley Pruitt."*

"Keep shining," he says and hands the book to the reader, Jacob.

A tense, and yet, another awkward pause develops over the conversation.

"The character in the book," Jacob says, speaking more freely. "Donnie," he clarifies. "If you would please forgive me for being so intrusive, but. . . did you know the character?" Before Stanley can answer, Jacob once more clarified, "The reason I ask is because, the way you wrote about him—I apologize. Forget I asked."

Stanley is hesitant to answer. His handler, C.J., attempts to patiently guide the reader, who's backing up the line, away from the table. One of the security guards steps forward, ready to take action.

"Again, sorry," Jacob says. "Didn't mean to—"

"Yes," Stanley says over Jacob. "As a matter of fact, it was."

Another pause, this time heavier.

"I, too, lost my wife and son," Jacob says to Stanley. "Similar situation, except for your son. Sorry to bring them up. I don't know the full story about your son, but whatever it's worth, I'm truly sorry about what happened."

Stanley smiles, both lips pressed together, which, in a way, confirms that he is, in fact, the real life Donnie. He holds out his hand, signaling C.J. to back off.

"No," Stanley says, more tenderly. "I'm sorry for your losses. When was this?"

"Last year," Jacob says. "A few months ago, I came across your book. . . " he holds up *The Song of Summer*, ". . . this book while browsing through your catalog. After reading the synopsis of the book, I was immediately drawn to it. It was almost as if they were guiding me to it, knowing that it'd help me move on."

"What were their names, your wife and son?" asks Stanley.

"June, my wife," he says. "Our son, Dylan."

"Sorry again to hear about your loses," Stanley says, looking into Jacob's teary eyes.

After recognizing how much those words impact Jacob, Stanley gets up from the seat, walks around the table, and stands face-to-face with the reader.

While looking Jacob in the eyes, Stanley reaches out his hand, the gloved one. He removes the glove, revealing the gnarly-looking hand covered in scars and tragedy, everything that Luminatis assumed about the hand.

Jacob looks down at the disfigured hand and eventually, shakes it.

In the line behind Jacob, Luminatis pull out their phones and take photos, as well as videos of the rare exchange. For those in line wearing black face masks, some masks sported with Luminati decals, their gawking, though concealed, spreads to their wide even more expressive eyes. The eyes don't lie. Ever since the *Blackout* series was launched and met with critical reception, most of it being praise, Stanley's most loyal readers have never seen anyone touch his left hand, the right, for sure, but never his left, let alone without a glove. For years, it was sort of off limits and only supported whatever rumored legends existed in the ethos.

A couple in their late thirties who are wandering through the convention center stop in front of Booth #37 and while witnessing a warm, human embrace before their eyes, consider buying a subscription from the compassionate author, who, at times, may come across as incredibly self-centered, merely a lap dog for the limelight.

What draws the two in is the "free download" of Pruitt's latest novel, *Just Another Blackout Story*.

One of them says playfully, "Who doesn't like free downloads?"

"Nothing's free," the grumpier, more cynical partner says.

"Maybe you're right, but I'll buy you a sub if you're interested."

The grumpy one shrugs and says, "I'll wait for the movie."

THE BOYFRIEND'S CHARM
JULY 23, 2046
KINGSPORT, MARYLAND

EMMA waits for the rowdy group of black clad vandals to stroll past by their apartment complex before she opens the door and sets her sights on Rowan's 2023 glittery gunmetal gray Lunarian parked next to the sidewalk.

With one side of her body weighed down by a purple suitcase filled with everything that she owns, Emma drunkenly sprints to the car. Her right leg heavy and awkward and dragging behind one side of her body from carrying that extra weight.

With a round moon fob dangling from the key chain, Rowan aims the remote at his Lunarian and presses the unlock button, resulting in the vintage car to let out a *beep-boop* sound, as well as a flicker of headlights, which act like a beacon for his girlfriend. She tosses the suitcase in the backseat and quietly closes the door behind her in fear of drawing any unwanted attention, more specifically, the black clad vandals. As though by command, the city suddenly screams all around Emma as she swings open the passenger door. She can feel the rage, as steaming hot as the devil's breath, pressed against her flesh, as if at any moment that devilish night darkness is going to spawn from the liquid asphalt, reach out its shadowy hand, and pull her into its mouth of shit and horror.

Not too behind Emma is Rowan, both of his arms full of luggage, including the one item that Emma couldn't fit in a suitcase—an expresso machine, which feels as if it weighs a ton, passed down to her by her momma, who was a collector—and pretty much everything that the two will need to stay comfortable for the next few months until they can find a safe place somewhere outside the city to settle down and gather, as well as stock enough supplies, including food and water, to survive the dark summer when even the dogs have uncanny ways of mistaking themselves as wolves.

At the nearest intersection, the stoplight, once flashing yellow, goes dark. For the past week or so, the lights have been shutting off at random times of the day, then coming back on, but only for a few seconds at a time before the city falls back into total blackness. Rowan once compared the city of Kingsport to a living, breathing, constantly evolving—or devolving—entity. Lately, despite Rowan's past wrongdoings, he feels as though the city has turned into a three-headed monster due to, not only the spike in crime, but also the nature of crime itself, murders becoming more violent and gruesome (the police have seen an uptick in cases of cannibalism, as well as public shaming by way of criminals leaving victims for public display, stripped, violated, and at times, hung from overpasses, gutted), as well as this overall sentiment of lawlessness, easily contagious, contributed by the erosion of corrupt public institution. For many of those, like Rowan and Emma, who have lived in one of the three boroughs of Kingsport, who once called Kingsport home, it's become evident that the city is dying and some would even say that Kingsport died when Mayor Shepard was elected into office and then came back haunted when Mayor Shepard was reelected into office, and the deterioration is nothing more than proof of a collapsed city that slowly consumes the very parasites it produces without maintaining order. Civilians who partake in civility fear that the lawlessness that has metastasized throughout the city is no longer curable. For months, those who lived in all major cities, like, for example, Kingsport, were warned about frequent blackouts. Rumors also spread about the "Big One," as insiders called it, a complete shutdown of the electrical grid, which would not only affect major cities, but also the entire country, and it'd crush all progress made over the past twenty years and send humanity into the Dark Ages. Of course, nobody listened.

Despite the loss of visibility, after sprinting from the doorway, Rowan manages to catch up to Emma and closes the door behind her.

From a block away, the two hear glass shatter.

The same group of vandals from earlier have gotten their hands on Molotov cocktails. They set fire to a local bodega, the rising flames, a tragedy, nonetheless, provide Rowan with enough light to finish loading the car.

More riots erupt a few blocks away.

Startling sounds of glass shattering randomly crescendo throughout the city.

Not too far away bricks act like beaters against high hats in an impromptu jazz session.

The shatter of each window startles Rowan and Emma, in particular, Rowan, who struggles to watch his neighborhood burn.

The riots intensify, the looting spreads like a virus; and those in the vicinity, even those who have rejected a life of criminality, catch the bug.

More destruction means more opportunities.

So close, the opportunities are, you can reach out and touch them.

"Hurry, Rowan," Emma says, out of breath.

Like Emma, Rowan can feel that rage strengthening all around him and soon, it will swallow the entire block.

They were warned.

This is now the rule of the land: survive by any means necessary.

And if it comes down to it: Kill or Be Killed.

As Rowan hurries inside the car, he turns on the ignition and puts the gear in drive and just as he's about to drive away, he extends his scarred right hand toward his girlfriend, his sweet and lovely Emma, a beacon, a light. Part of his right palm pieced together like a warped jigsaw puzzle with skin fragments taken or better yet borrowed from his thigh. Two of the fingers, a middle and ring finger, barely intact, skin thin and soft, like cellophane. Apart from using a thumb, index finger, and pinkie finger, which acts no differently than a claw in a crane vending machine to pick up items, a significant portion of his gnarly right hand is unable to perform tasks that once came natural to him for a majority of his life, especially during adolescence.

Rowan glances down at a latticework of pale-pinkish scars, the doc's mosaic. Right before Emma grabs his disfigured hand, he turns to Emma. His face, worried; eyes riddled with regret.

"Lock the doors," he says and steps outside while keeping the engine running.

He leans back inside and unhooks the apartment key from the keychain.

"Where you going?" asks Emma.

"I forgot something. . . "

"Serious Row?"

"It'll only take me a sec," he says and pulls out a loaded revolver from behind his waistband. "Here. . . "

Emma's hesitant about grabbing the pistol.

"Take it," Rowan says, pushing it closer.

Emma takes it.

"If anyone approaches the car," he says, pulling back the hammer, "point and squeeze, like in those ridiculous video games you play."

"But *Rowan—*"

Her eyes snap toward the growing violence ahead. Flames rising higher, touching skyline.

"Just a sec, okay?"

The blank expression of Emma's face hardens. Her eyes sharpen and narrow.

"One, two, three. . . " she counts with a tremble in her throat.

"I'm fast, but I ain't that fast," Rowan says, half-grinning. With his good hand, he redirects Emma's head. Her eyes eventually find Rowan's and when they do, they stay on him, studying each and every tiny detail of, not only his eyes, but also his face. It may be the last time she sees it. She wants to remember it. She relishes it. She wants to riot in his flesh. *I fucking love you more than you'll ever know*, Emma is tempted to say to Rowan, but she doesn't want to give him any distractions. "Count to a hundred," he says. "By the time you reach seventy-eight, we'll be long gone from this hellhole."

Emma's glossy eyes swell with tears.

"How about seventy-seven?" she says, her face long and pouting.

"Is that a bet?"

"Maybe."

Rowan wipes away the tears from underneath Emma's eyes and kisses her on the lips, then closes the door behind him while Emma starts to mentally count to seventy-six.

After entering the apartment complex, Rowan uses the flashlight on his smartphone, which is the only feature that works properly, and races up eleven flights of stairs before he reaches his

DALIVIA PLAUT | 13

level. The tenants, his fellow neighbors, remain surprisingly quiet inside their apartments. Some of them have already left the city. Earlier, in fact, right before he and Emma decided *not* to wait out the blackouts, he witnessed a couple of his neighbors scramble past his apartment. From the peephole, he saw them in a similar state: carrying everything that could manage, the panic worn like a thick ghostly cloak over their aura.

He hears a sudden racket coming from down the hallway. Objects crashing to the floor. He presumes it's luggage. People in a similar situation. People who just want to get the hell out of this hellhole. Then, once he hears the shrieks of horror atop quaking *thuds*, some strong enough to shake the floor of his level, the blood in his veins runs cold and icy.

"Fifty-three," he counts.

As the noise grows louder and closer, he uses the key to unlock the door; and once he enters the apartment, which is lit up by the beating glow of firelight, Rowan heads straight to the bedroom where he opens the top drawer of the chest. He pulls out a rag covered in dried blood from inside the drawer. He unfolds the rag, frayed at the ends, revealing a strange metallic device, or artifact, shaped like an eight-point asterisk. The arms—or legs— eight of them, each three inches long and curled inward like a dead spider. The ends are as sharp and pointy as a sharpened pencil and covered in Rowan's blood, which appears a brownish-black from being exposed to air. The center of the artifact is circular and roughly the size of the cap of a medicine bottle with an ancient symbol of a mantra, which is shaped like the letter E, the three lines veining outward like the branches of a tree:

As Rowan pockets the artifact, he hears a young woman screaming his name outside. Her voice cracked, her shrieks sound like crushed gravel.

Emma?

Startled by the sound, Rowan rushes to the window where he witnesses a bloody Emma lying helplessly on the street. Pulled out from the driver's side window, which appears shattered. Candy-sized pieces of glass are scattered over the pavement. He counts at least six of them, each one wearing werewolf masks and brown leather circling around Emma. Two of them undressing her, another pinning down both of Emma's arms and shoulders to the pavement. She attempts to kick the two off, but she's clearly outnumbered and overpowered. One of them isn't wearing a mask and left exposed in the distant firelight is his waxy bald scalp. He fumbles the mask in his hands before placing it over his head, concealing his identity; nonetheless, giving Rowan a tease. *Here am I boy*, Baldy says, *come and get me. . .*

In that split second, all Rowan sees is the back of that man's baldhead and part of his profile: high cheeks with a wide flat nose. Each feature, Rowan tells himself as the blood rushes through his veins, soon to be split open and held on display, a precise surgical operation carried out in the public square for the entire world to see. Rowan takes a mental snapshot of the attacker's face—for later use.

As the second passes, Rowan races from the apartment.

While running and at times, his heels sliding down each flight of stairs as though he's gliding down stairs, he attempts to place the artifact over the top of his hand despite the ramifications of wearing it; however, the stinger-like needle, which erects upward from the center of the device isn't working. Hoping that maybe it's asleep, he bangs on it a couple of times.

He receives neither a prick nor a sting but rather the bolts of pain that shoot up his arm from the unearthly metal banging against bone.

Once Rowan reaches the first floor, he pockets the artifact.

He charges at the door and violently kicks it open for the entire block to hear—so hard that he breaks two of the hinges. While racing toward Emma and her attackers, he's startled by the bright flash of a gunshot coming from below the car. The sound makes a fire cracker-like *pop!*

Despite the gunshot, Rowan doesn't break pace.

Halfway toward Emma, a masked attacker rears back his leg, which is shaped like a slanted letter V, and holds it high against his chest, a soon-to-be deathblow.

Emma can barely hold the pistol above her waist for she is too weak.

She fires from the hip.

Right before the attacker stomps on Emma's head, two more gunshots ring out!

Pop! Pop!

Two of the wolves, including the stomper, suddenly flinch and stumble backward, backpedaling from Emma. One grabbing his shoulder, another his belly.

One of the masked attackers, in fact, the same bald-headed one, flees the scene and vanishes into the shadows across the street.

The other five jump into Rowan's Lunarian.

One of the attackers—the one shot in the belly—is helped into the back of the car.

As soon as Rowan reaches Emma, who manages to fire off a couple of shots at the Lunarian, one round hitting the back windshield, shattering it, the attackers speed away with the backdoor wide open and leave behind a cloud of smoke so thick in the air that it temporarily masks their speedy getaway. Emma drops the revolver to the ground. One round left in the chamber.

Rowan cuts through the smoke and keeps up with the Lunarian for about twenty yards or so.

In that short distance, Rowan manages to catch yet another attacker's face as he removes the sweaty mask from his head. The same attacker who was on top of Emma. Shot in the shoulder but nothing life threatening. Like the other one, he has a bald scalp, the sweat making it appear shiny. The expression on his face is one of great amusement. Rowan tells himself that he'll use it later, as fuel to drive Baldy into the depths of hell. Before the Lunarian gains more distance from Rowan, he spots a tattoo on the side of the smirking man's neck, and it looks similar to a swastika. Before Rowan can make it out in its entirety, the driver increases the speed of the Lunarian, leaving Rowan no other choice than to return to Emma.

Pushing through exhaustion, Rowan races back to Emma and tends to her. Both her arms, as well as her legs are covered with cuts from the broken glass. The clothes have been ripped from her body. The sight alone of Emma and what was done to her, both physically and emotionally, causes Rowan's insides to twist in knots. The rage, like oil in a glass of water, slowly surfacing through the despair and settling on the top, and Rowan can feel the grip of the rage against every inch of his body. He grabs the revolver from the ground, checks the chamber; then once he finds only one round left, he closes it and slips it back underneath his waistband.

As he carefully picks up Emma, the pressure from his hands causes her to cry out in agony. Rowan removes his hand from her abdomen and holds his hand up to his face. It's dripping wet with blood, not his blood but Emma's. It's way too much blood, more than what you'd get from a cut. He lays her back down and checks her wound and finds a deep incision from a blade, deep enough to penetrate major organs or main arteries.

The chaos builds around them.

More shadows, as hungry as hyenas, close in.

Rowan looks around the dark streets and finds opportunists turning their firelit eyes toward their direction, as if, in a way, they're drawn to the blood, as if they could smell it and it's more precious than water.

Despite Emma's pain, Rowan helps Emma to her feet. She tries to walk but only makes it a couple of steps before the pain settles in like an unwelcomed visitor, an incredibly fragile, sensitive thing that aggressively responds to Emma's every-movement.

With threats circling them, Rowan carries Emma back to the apartment complex where the two seek shelter. He only makes it three flights before Emma starts to lose consciousness.

Rowan rests Emma along the stairs, places a hand around the back part of her neck in order to support her head, and with his hand, applies pressure to the wound. He tries to stop the bleeding, but the blood manages to slip through the cracks of his fingers. In the back of his mind, he knows Emma's dying, and there's nothing he can do to save her, except for this very moment, as he holds her and watches her fade away into oblivion. The pain has overtaken her and strangely, leaves her in a tranquil state as she succumbs to her pain, her crutch, her savior.

As Rowan stares into her tearful eyes, he cradles to the life, once brilliant, now dull and docile, vanishing inside them. A life, nonetheless, that he was so damn grateful to be a part of—and if he had one wish right now, he'd wish to swap places with Emma. He'd suck out her pain and carry it for her, not as a burden to be lugged around but a prize to be showcased, because when you're madly in love, you'd do pretty much about anything to take away your lover's pain, even if it means inflicting pain on one's own being.

The two met thirteen months ago at the hospital. Love at first laugh. She was a visitor, who often spent her time between visiting hours roaming through the stale, lifeless hallways. Daughter of an elderly patient, Theodore Ambrose, admitted three days before Rowan was dumped off at the ER like a UPS package. Her father's illness: Cirrhosis of the liver. "Teddy," she called him, didn't have long to live. His liver was failing and even if he received a transplant—Teddy was one of many on the list—there was the possibility that his body would reject it. The two ran into each other in the elevator. Rowan snuck out of his hospital room. A late night excursion through the maze of Macy Memorial. His right hand bandaged up like a mummy. He clung onto the IV pole with his other hand as if it was an extra appendage. An invisible sign worn over his chest that said, *"Lost and Lonely,"* underneath the clearly visible wear and tear of corruption. Emma, also somewhat lost and lonely, anything but corrupted—she would say she liked being alone but never considered herself to be lonely—cracked a joke about Rowan's gown, which swung open like a door behind him, exposing his butt. Both cheeks. At the time, he was so constipated from the medicine and a lack of movement that even the slightest laugh caused him abdominal pain. But Rowan did laugh, from both ends. With his face clouding red in embarrassment, he shrunk in the corner of the stinky elevator. Emma laughed at Rowan's dispense, releasing any tension between them; and from that moment forward, he was hers; and in time, she was his. Rowan saw her once more in the hallway the next day and decided to *verbally* talk to her. He rehearsed several lines in his head, had a few good ones that he drafted after he first laid his eyes on her. He never used those lines. Didn't need to. He had already made an impression on Emma and there was no need to further win her over. The two talked for what felt like seconds to Rowan but was actually forty-three minutes—but for Rowan, who was counting? She stated the reason why she kept coming back to the hospital. Part of the conversation centered around Emma's father, whose skin had turned yellow. Her father, despite a grim diagnosis by a doctor who was as pessimistic as a bitter old lady who owned a dog named Scram, had quite a sense of humor about it and said he looked like a fucked up-looking banana. Emma smiled whenever she mentioned Teddy's name, but Rowan knew that she knew her old man was dying and she was okay with it. As for Rowan's reason for his extended stay in the Macy Memorial Inn, he was being treated for a hand injury. Nearly lost it. However, the doc was one helluva artist. The injury, the story leading up to it, all of it based around a white lie. He told doctors that he got it caught in a wood chipper and he knew if he told anyone the truth, including Emma—later, she'd find out about the artifact and how Rowan didn't need it anymore—the entire world would be after him and the artifact that he possessed. Eventually, Doctor Michelangelo managed to piece Rowan's hand back together and during his recovery, including some rehab in the facility next to the hospital, he found time to see Emma. He kept seeing her again and again, reaffirming his love for her. Made it his mission in life, to go out of his way, even if it was to catch a glimpse of her. She was a window, *his* window; and each time he saw Emma, this window, she'd crack it open wider than the previous time before, wide enough to let the light escape. Over time, Rowan poured a little bit of himself into the window, each time shedding a piece of himself to Emma until he had absolutely nothing left to prove but everything to give. Once he made his peace with a world designed by the very machine that conjured him, Rowan, ready to embrace the unknown, decided to step through that window; and once he did, he was shown a world that he had been hiding from for so many years, a world opposite to the mirrors that consumed his daily life. In this old yet new world, there were no more reflections, only windows, and bursting from those windows, was a light so brilliant and enticing that it lured in each willing participate. Emma was Rowan's window, "his light," he once told Emma during a romantic picnic in the park, and without her, he'd be nothing more than the faint odor of a fart that eventually dissipated in the air.

Emma's eyes remain still and as that once radiant life lifts from her lifeless body, Rowan holds her in his arms as though begging her to stay. In that pulsating calmness, as the remaining blood and gas move underneath her cold flesh, a hot army of rage bubbles inside Rowan, leaving him with no other choice than to give in to its unified parade. He does everything in his power to contain it, the rage, and keep it at bay until after he carries Emma's body back to the apartment and lays her in bed. The rage rises up inside Rowan as he tucks her body underneath the covers. The sorrow he feels is like water washing over a bed of hot coals and the more pain he feels, the angrier he feels. He can no longer reject these feelings. For years, he had cast them out, shunned them; and if they ever surfaced, he made sure to lock them away in his own Hall of Mirrors, never to see the light of day.

Rowan pulls the blanket up to her chest, covering the wound. Lastly, he closes her eyelids.

With every nerve in his body as tight as a coil, he walks to the window and watches the fire growing outside. Flames rise from nearby buildings and spread to other buildings, casting more light into the dark bedroom. Rowan surrenders to the flaming chaos before him, and the more he stares into the fire, he feels the fire staring, not only at him, but also into him, as if the two share an unequivocal bond forged by time and space.

In that trance-like moment, he witnesses a woman and a boy being consumed by flames: two moments, one of poison, corruption, and politics; the other, a horrific accident brought on by the grief of a loving husband. These two are the wife and son of an engineer and soon-to-be author, who, in order to cope with the tragedy of losing everything that he held dear to his heart, wrote a novel called *The Song of Summer* in which he expelled the burden of seeking retaliation against those who poisoned his wife, who traveled to Tijuana, Mexico, in order to find a cure for Stage 4 breast cancer after her current treatment wasn't working, only to wind up dead in a sleazy hotel room after ingesting an experimental cancer drug laced with fentanyl. After the husband character—the engineer—tracked down the source of the tainted cancer drug to a local cartel, he was faced with a life altering decision that would change his life forever. He rejected the violence— wasn't in his nature but he knew it was there to access, if he needed it—then decided to redirect and channel his vengeance through the pen or in this case, a typewriter, the corrupt pharmaceutical company, Coklin Corp, in the novel being inspired by the cartel, La Cuchilla. Rowan doesn't know this man, this engineer turned novelist, has never seen his face before; yet, as he witnesses the past tragedies (first, the death of his wife, and then his son, months later after the death of the boy's mother, drowning in the backyard pond after his intoxicated, grief-stricken father failed to watch over him) unfold right before his eyes, he feels as if he carries the memory of not only this man, but also the memories of many like him, including a disturbed boxer with boss-level rage, whose single right hook could punch a hole in the fabric of the universe.

Rowan ignores the chaos around him, the flames, and focuses on this one particular man, the author, and the tragedy that defines him.

With just a few thousand copies sold, the novel *The Song of Summer* never reached the level of its desired recognition. Yet, for the readers it *did* touch, including one particular reader, who, similar to the author, lost his wife and son, like the author's wife, from an experimental drug—in his situation, an emergency vaccine forced onto the public in order to fight against a new, deadlier strand of coronavirus that contained the polyether compound called polyethylene glycol, also known as "PEG," which his wife and his son were allergic to, however, were uninformed by the family doctor about the potentially harmful ingredient in the vaccine (his wife, in particular, being picky about reading the labels on the back of each product they purchased, being that PEGs were also found in everyday items and since they were on a tight budget and couldn't afford epinephrine for it sold for twice, sometimes, triple the monthly car payment, must be avoided at all costs) and only hours after the vaccine was administered into their bodies, both his wife and his son went in anaphylactic shock, his wife first, then their son, ultimately resulting in their deaths, the cause later concluded by a private coroner as a delayed yet rare side-effect of the vaccine—it made the pill of loss easier to swallow.

For this man, this troubled author who had spent his youth struggling with his masculinity, it was never about money—in *The Song of Summer* the protagonist Donnie burned, not only all the money that he won during the settlement with the pharmaceutical company, but also everything that reminded him of his wife and son for the memory of the two were too painful to bear—but rather the purge of loss, a violent expulsion, if you will, where the only function was total cathartic liberation. His way of eradicating each and every member of La Cuchilla in order to regain a sense of control over his life while, on the contrary, sacrificing the one privilege that the job had been taken away from him: privacy.

As Rowan pulls himself from the trance, everything about him changes.

His eyes, demeanor, posture.

That famished rage breaking through his flesh.

Everything about Rowan is sharp and deadly, nocturnal.

He uses Emma's death, like an artist's tool, to go after the one attacker who fled right before his fellow wolves sped away.

Rowan doesn't have a hard time tracking him down.

After walking three blocks, he locates Baldy inside the laundromat on Delaney Street where parked cars have been flattened, destroyed, some overturned, nonetheless, torched by Molotov cocktails, each vehicle tamely burning like primitive nightlights, providing enough light on the deathly quiet street.

His senses are locked in, strangely, enhanced as if these tools are built into the human body or perhaps the lasting residue of the artifact, which once consumed every inch of him.

In yet another attempt, he applies the artifact to his right hand, even tries his left as well, but it's neither activating nor sticking to him; and whenever he attempts to forcibly wear it on top of his hand like an apparatus, it slides off and collapses. Each metal leg loosely droops like a damp rag. Rowan is convinced that it's his blood, even though the thing looks as if it's broken. It has no taste for his blood, he believes, nothing to activate a response. He pockets the useless artifact and channels his anger, focusing it directly on the people responsible for Emma's death. He tells himself that he doesn't need the artifact—not anymore.

With only one round left in the revolver, Rowan stands in the shadows of a narrow alleyway and watches the bald-headed man, who looks fidgety and freaked out as he unsteadily paces back and forth inside the laundromat, which has been untouched by riots. The bluish pale glow of the smartphone lights up the bottom part of his sweaty, ghostly face, like a storyteller in a campfire story. He doesn't expect the phone to work. Most cellular service has been down ever since the blackouts, meaning text won't work either, and all that remains in way of long distance communication is SOS via flashlight. But it doesn't stop the silly rabbit from trying to send out a text.

Rowan finds an opportunity when the man turns his back toward the side door.

Concealed by the blackout, he creeps inside the laundromat. The sound of his shoe stepping on an overturned box of detergent on the floor makes a noise loud enough to startle the man, who then rotates around, only to find Rowan stalking through the dark laundromat.

Hanging loosely from the right pocket of his black hoody is the same werewolf mask. He's a heavyset man who eats at least four square meals a day, not ripped but rather big boned, weighs at least sixty pounds more than Rowan; however, size doesn't play a factor when it comes to purpose. Just look at those eyes. The man's already lost before the fight even begins.

Immediately, he drops the phone to the floor.

From the inflation of his chest and shoulders, it appears as if he's not going down without a fight, and that's all right by Rowan.

As Rowan approaches, the man pulls out a knife, unfolds the blade, then shows it to Rowan.

Before the man has a chance to use it, Rowan pounces, leaving the man absolutely no room for him to rear back or maneuver the blade.

With both hands, Rowan grabs the man's wrist, pulls it into his body, and with the very top part of his forehead, head butts the man on the bridge of his flat nose, causing it to split and burst open. Blood sprays upward like a geyser. The man's head bobbles around for a moment, leaving his entire body vulnerable for an imminent attack. He disarms the dazed man by twisting and pulling back on the man's wrist, nearly breaking it. Like the phone, the pocketknife drops to the floor. Rowan kicks it across the laundromat, far from the man's reach.

The man frees himself from Rowan's grip and throws a right hook.

Rowan dodges the wild punch, grabs the man's right forearm, and then while the man's arm is extended outward, he returns a vicious blow directly to the back of the man's elbow, this time bones break, in this case, two of them, the ulnas and radius, each one shooting out from the skin at the bend of his elbow. The man cries out, his eyes go wide and dark.

As though given a burst of energy, the man tackles Rowan and starts whaling at him with his left fist and elbow, mustering all of his strength into each blow. The only issue: He's incredibly wild and reckless and exhausts that sweet adrenaline in a matter of seconds. Rowan takes each blow, in a way, absorbs them, most of the blows shielded by his arms. The man, however, lands a couple of blows that leave Rowan dazed and dumbfounded.

Once the man poops out, his good limb slow and heavy, Rowan finds a weak spot in the upcoming blow as the man strikes downward. Rowan catches the man's arm and yanks it downward into his body where Rowan grips the man in a bear hug, wrapping both his legs around the man's torso.

Using every tool at his disposal, Rowan bites the man in the neck. His teeth, especially his canines, dig into flesh, drawing blood, lots of it. Considering he was raised by an overprotective mother who always overcooked whatever slab of meat for dinner—as once described to Emma, Rowan explained that she'd nuke, for instance, a cut of sirloin until it was as tough as a fucking tire—in fear of her child ingesting any harmful bacteria, it's no surprise that Rowan's teeth break through the skin.

With a grip of flesh in his mouth, he pulls back, ripping a mouthful of flesh from the man's neck. Blood squirts all over Rowan's face. Rowan spits out the flesh.

The man's body goes limper, giving Rowan enough maneuverability to roll the man off his body. They wrestle, briefly. The man gets creative by using the broken arm bone to stab Rowan in the shoulder.

Somehow, the man finds himself back on top of Rowan. He wises up and decides to use the sharp bone as a weapon by attempting to stab Rowan in the neck with it.

Rowan grabs the man's arm.

The man pushes through the pain, as he pushes the jagged bones closer to Rowan's neck.

As the bones inch closer to Rowan's jugular, Rowan uses his other hand to pull out the revolver from his waistband.

One shot left, he tells himself.

He moves the revolver up to his chest, aims the barrel directly underneath the man's chin, and then pulls the trigger.

The gunshot blows the man's brains from the top of his head.

His eyes roll back in his head, mouth gaping open like a death yawn.

The upper part of his body falls forward, dropping onto Rowan.

Using whatever strength he has left in his body, Rowan pushes away the dead man.

Before Rowan can even catch his breath, he catches a beam of headlights cutting through the laundromat.

He sits upright and focuses in on the headlights.

The Lunarian—*My Lunarian.*

Must've heard the gunshot, Rowan tells himself as he once more checks the chamber of the revolver, hoping to find one more round inside.

Empty.

"Damn it."

He looks back up and after his eyes adjust to the brightness of the headlights, confirms that the car is, in fact, his Lunarian, recently stolen by a gang of monsters dressed as monsters; however, he only counts four heads, not five. One of them is missing, potentially dead.

The driver parks the Lunarian in front of the laundromat.

Two unmasked men rush from the car; and as they enter the laundromat, Rowan makes a run for it. He exits via backdoor and cuts through an alleyway, which is about the width of the Lunarian. The two men chase after Rowan. The driver pulls the car into the alleyway and picks up the two men, who give up on their pursuit. The alleyway is so tight and narrow that the doors hit the sides of the buildings; however, the two men are able to squeeze inside.

Once safely inside, the driver takes off.

Rowan exits the alleyway and barely manages to escape the Lunarian, which runs over every obstacle in its way, including two homeless men sleeping on a bed of cardboard. From behind, Rowan can hear the howling laughs over the roar of an engine after they potentially kill two people, not including Emma. How many others have they killed tonight?

For the next hour, he does everything in his power to shake Emma's murderers off his tail—for instance, he cuts through abandoned buildings; he hides inside a dumpster as they cruise by yet another alleyway; he dashes into a construction site after they spot him leaving the Historic Art District, which was one of the first locations in Kingsport to be leveled by riots.

Finally, after an hour of the cat and mouse chase, they catch up to him inside an abandoned warehouse along the Walabique River.

Exhausted and barely able to stand, Rowan removes a loose brick from the side of the building and hides the artifact securely inside. He takes a mental note of the exact location. Above is a crooked sign next to a boat ramp, the letters "OR" of the word *port* still lit, the remaining letters dead and dark.

As the Lunarian creeps through the industrial park without its headlights still lit, Rowan decides to take the fight inside the warehouse.

No more running or hiding.

The car parks outside the warehouse.

Five men exit the car, blood in their eyes, their appetites bottomless.

With a tire iron gripped in his good hand, Rowan seeks cover in the shadows behind a network of rusty pipes and waits for his bloodthirsty opponents to enter the warehouse.

The memory of Emma forces Rowan to remember the words he had spoken to her the moment in the park, more or less, a promise, not only to himself, but also Emma. He lost himself in her eyes while they told jokes and snacked from an array of fruits and cheeses, pairing them together with a bottle of aged Pinot Noir that Emma had been saving for a special occasion. The sun poke through the clouds above and a ray of light shined on Emma's glowing porcelain skin. Emma fed Rowan a cracker with sliced prosciutto and Gruyére cheese and told him a story about a long dirt road that was lined with maple trees behind the ranch-style house where she grew up and how, during autumn when those maples changed colors, she'd take these walks with her dog, Luscious, and marvel in the colors and calmness. The road was many centuries old, and settlers had used the road to travel into town. Nothing grew on the road. Yet, it was worn down, barren, except for the maples, which flourished every spring before their leaves fell and covered the dirt road like a blanket that crunched and rustled underneath Emma's feet. Emma described how she felt so little and so insignificant while taking those long walks, a speck on this giant rock and yet, despite feeling so little and so insignificant, she was perfectly at ease as she absorbed her natural surroundings and warded off whatever inside world that awaited for her when she returned back home. One day while she was on one of her walks with Luscious, the world yet again reminded Emma of her very existence. She found the man lying facedown on the side of the road. He was much older than her father and from time to time, she had seen his face in town. He never spoke to anyone. He was an unfriendly man whose gaze could penetrate even the weariest of men. In hopes of waking the man, she kicked the side of his leg, but when he didn't respond, she knew he was already gone. She couldn't find any marks on his body that would suggest foul play. From the looks, the man appeared as if he had died of natural causes. In those eerie moments, she tried to imagine his final moments. At that young age, she didn't know it at the time but it came to be one of the greatest pleasures that many her age never experienced. The uncanny ability to devour with one's eyes and strangely, appreciate what came before.

It was at this very moment at Bluth Park when Emma stole Rowan's heart.

THE BOOLE SISTERS
MOMENTS AGO
SAME HELLHOLE

STARTLED by the booming sound of a gunshot coming from outside, Violet stops midway while emptying out the entire drawer of clothes into the pink luggage on the bed.

Three times in the past hour gunshots have rung out, most of them sounding like firecrackers at a distance. This one is much closer to home than the others, and it leaves Violet more startled than the shots before. She redirects to the mounting frustration toward her younger sister Misty, who hasn't moved an inch from the couch ever since the blackout. Her round face glows from the screen of the smartphone, as once again she attempts to send out texts through the group chat of friends, some of whom have already left the city, but every time she receives an alert message informing her that the text failed to send.

Growing annoyed by Misty's hard-headedness, she says with a big sister's tone laced in her voice, "*Seriously*, Miss. Move it or lose it!"

The only parts of her younger sister that budge are her fingers as she attempts to send out yet another text but receives the same "failed" message. Violet grabs a lit candle from the top of the dresser and out of curiosity, breaks the one rule that she had been enforcing all night: She checks the window where she sees a dark figure running from the laundromat across the street.

The figure darts into the alleyway.

A car filled with rowdy passengers drives after the figure, which Violet identifies as a young man.

Violet pulls herself from the window.

"Misty—"

"What?" she snaps. "Have you not checked the latest feed?"

"How can I, Miss?" Violet snaps back while she returns to throwing in as much of her belongings as she can fit into her luggage. "Service is down, has been down for hours, and whether you like it or not, we have to assume that it's not gonna work anytime soon."

"Not mine," Misty gripes. "Last I checked it the bridges were blocked!"

Violet stops packing and says over her sister, "How many times do I need to tell you, Miss? We're not taking the bridge. We're going to meet up with Quincy, remember? Besides, why are you not packing?"

Again, Misty doesn't budge. Yet, she continues to sit on the couch, staring at the phone as if any moment the phone is magically going to work (It's not, won't, the blackout disabled most, if not, all of the phone service in the Kingsport area, rendering phones useless, except for the trusty flashlight feature, which, depending on the circumstances, may come in handy).

"I thought you were joking."

"Do I look like I'm joking?"

Misty remains silent, her burning glazed eyes glued to the screen.

Tempted to yank Misty off the couch, Violet finishes packing. The frustration causes her to miss certain items, like a toothbrush and toothpaste, hand sanitizer wipes, as well as several important toiletries to maintain proper hygiene, as she scrambles through the bedroom.

After she uses the zipper to close the luggage, she moves her way into the living room in a hurried manner. Violet's presence alone, like an invisible kick in Misty's rump, causes her sister to get up from the couch and begin packing, which, again Violet reiterates, she should've done twenty minutes ago when she was first asked by her big sis.

"Our window's closing—" Violet says urgently, as she grabs Misty's luggage from the hallway closet.

"I can reach it!"

Since Violet is much taller than Misty, Violet has no trouble grabbing the luggage from the top shelf. In a careless package handler manner, she dumps the luggage into Misty's arm, and in return, Misty, who displays a sour look on her face, carries the luggage to her bed where she begins to pack clothes. Again, since time is of the essence and Misty's moving rather sluggishly, her sister steps in and helps her pack.

Misty uses that flashlight on the phone to help her see.

Violet immediately snatches the phone from her sister's grip and tells her that she's going to waste the battery and in return, hands her a candle.

"Like the phones, we have to—" she takes beat, "—we *must* assume the power isn't going to come back on for a long time. A'ight?"

"But can't we just stay here and. . . "

"And what? Have you heard what's going on out there?" asks Violet, more concerned. "It's not safe here anymore."

"But we can stay another night—"

"We can't," Violet says, her patience thinning.

"Why do we have to go with Quincy?" Misty asks and places the candle on the nightstand.

"Daddy said we can rely on him if anything bad were to happen," Violet says. "*This is happening.* Accept it. We're in the bad now, smack dab in the middle of it, sandwiched in like condiments, and Quincy's boat is our way out of the bad."

"Didn't I tell you this would—"

"Don't even!" Violet says before Misty can finish her sentence.

Those words or similar words, *told you so*, which Misty used every now and then whenever she made a predication, stirs a feeling of anger inside her.

"Sounds more like a gravy boat to me. . . " Misty trails off.

A sense of relief washes over Violet, if only for a brief second.

"You know what I mean," she says, her head slanting.

"So, you're like barbeque sauce," Misty says. "What does that make me?"

Violet half-grins.

"We all know you got a little bit of Sriracha in you."

"I was thinking more like a Lil' Pomp and a Lil' Power."

"What's that?"

"My stage name," Misty says, more upbeat. "Like it?"

Violet rolls her eyes.

After the two sisters share a moment, they finish packing.

Last but not least, Misty grabs a two-in-one device called "CaMMDoc," which has become a popular multi-purpose camera over the past decade. The rectangular shaped device, similar to an eTablet, only surprisingly much smaller yet thicker, bulkier, and more durable, allows aspiring, as well as professional photographers to edit photos in real-time using AR technology, also comes with an attachment to connect to a VR headset. On one side of the device: a touch-screen where users can edit or doctor a photograph. On another: a lens. On either end of the camera are two handles used to grip the device, which can come in handy while on-the-go, also helps stabilize the camera to create "The Perfect Shot." The device comes with a mount, which attaches to the bottom of CaMMDoc, but for the past few months, there's been a supply shortage and trying to track down one of these rare mounts is like searching for an eyelash on a sidewalk after blowing a regretful wish. In Misty's case, she's using an anamorphic lens. Attached to the device is a heavy-duty strap cushioned around the neck, which allows her to use the CaMMDoc, hands-free. Of course, knowing Miss On-The-Fly, she jerry-rigged her own mount instead, scraped together discarded tripods, used various parts from each one, and then tweaked several screws to fit into the device. When people ask Misty about the mount, she likes to say it has a "vintage"-feel to it, similar to a photographer back in the day holding up a large bulb to snap a shot.

Violet hesitates to warn Misty about the CaMMDoc. Clearly understanding her sister's passion for photography—she'd say there was nothing else that she'd rather do and Violet knew she certainly couldn't take that away from her sister—Violet remains concerned about Misty bringing along the device.

"Leave it, Miss," she says. "We can't afford the distraction. Sorry—"

"Over my dead body," Misty says over her big sis.

"If people see you with that thing, we'll have a target on our heads."

"You said we're not coming back here. So. . . "

"I don't know for sure, but—"

"But a'ight. Then what's the problem? I'm not going anywhere without it."

Misty throws a "Sorry" back into Violet's face.

Violet clenches her teeth.

"You have to promise me that you keep it hidden," she says in a motherly way. "Some people would kill for one of those."

"What are people going to use with a CaMMDoc, especially when the world is falling apart? The CaMMDoc is the last thing people need right now—"

"Why do you feel the need to bring it then?"

"Because it's mine," she says, more defensively. "That's why."

"It stays hidden," Violet says again. "*Deal?*"

"Fine," Misty says sharply and secures the CaMMDoc in her satchel.

Once the two sisters are packed and ready to head toward the dock, they cautiously step out of the apartment. Since the elevators aren't working, the sisters take the stairs.

Before making the trek down the stairs, Violet leans over the railing and watches the couple below them, Tee and Gillian, she thinks, based off the sound of their voices, however, she's not entirely sure considering she can hardly see her own hand in front of her. The couple, both guided by flashlights, hurries down the pitch-black flight of stairs, unscathed.

On a whim, Violet calls to Tee and Gillian but the couple doesn't answer.

"Come on, Miss," Violet says to Misty. "Let's get this over with. . . "

"Serious—"

"Quit your fussing!"

The two sisters, especially Misty, being incredibly out of shape and overweight, who's been relying on an elevator to transport her to her floor, have no other choice than to walk ten flights. Misty has a near panic-attack from the sight of the stairs spiraling downward in a wicked-looking square. While living in the city with her big sis, she had only made the trek once, last year, as a matter of fact, when the power went out and she was desperate to make a food run. Violet was away for the night, with a "friend" from work, and she wasn't expected to show until the next morning. By the time Misty made the trek down, grabbed food, then made the trek back up to her floor, she was so damn tired and exhausted that she couldn't even eat.

With their arms full of luggage, Misty feels the pressure of each step.

Out of breath, the sisters manage to make it to the first floor, Misty clearly being affected the most by the walk down. Before her sister has a chance to rest or catch her breath, Violet emphasizes the severity of the situation. Life and death. And if they don't make it to Quincy's boat in time, then that persistent bitch of a needle inches closer to death. The words of her big sis act as fuel. She gathers herself, takes in a deep, stuttering breath, and hurries alongside Violet through the parking lot where an ambience of violence swallows the scene: Distant screams and shouts and shrieks of horror, as well as more of those startling firecracker-like *pop-pop-pop* of gunshots followed by high-pitch crashes of glass shattering.

In a matter of hours, the violence has gone from a wave of petty theft and robbery to full-on murder.

In the corner of her eye, Violet peers past a row of cars and witnesses a young man, probably no older than her younger sister, being gunned down in the middle of the street. Two shots directly to his chest. Then, after he collapses to the ground, one more straight to the head. Brain matter splatters over wet pavement like pumpkin guts. Flashes of gunfire light up the shooter's face, as well as the horror below him. The black clad shooter, as dark as a silhouette, searches through the dead man's pockets. Several onlookers—or shapes—duck behind cars and hide.

Violet tells Misty that once they reach the car, they'll be safe.

When they finally reach their car with the help of Misty's flashlight, they throw all of their belongings inside the trunk.

Violet, who wastes no time locking the doors, takes the steering wheel. Misty rides shotgun. Violet turns on the car, which only has about a third of battery left, more than enough to make it to the dock; however, the two sisters can't afford to take any detours.

Misty checks the percentage of battery: 33%

"Thought you charged it last night," she whines.

Pissed off at herself, Violet redirects her anger toward Misty: "I forgot, a'ight!"

All of a sudden a massive explosion erupts behind them, startling the two sisters!

In the rear view mirror, Violet watches the ball of fire rising from the police cruiser parked across the street.

Breathing heavier, Misty asks Violet, "What are you waiting on?"

As Violet puts the car in drive, she witnesses a dark figure in the corner of her eyes. A hand reaches for the door handle, attempts to open the door. She looks to her left and sees a man rearing back an aluminum baseball bat over his head. He strikes down at the car, the bat shattering driver's side of the front windshield.

With Misty screaming in her ear, Violet speeds away.

The front of the car clips the side of the slugger, causing him to roll over the hood of the car like a stuntman before landing on his neck.

Violet drives through the hellscape, weaving around wreckage, as well as a horde of rioters, who have completely overrun the city. Being the opportunists that she is—after all, someone has to document what's going on and it certainly isn't the news—Misty pulls out the CaMMDoc and begins taking photographs of the chaos all around her.

"Would you put that away?" asks Violet.

Misty continues to photograph the rage on display.

Ragers raging in the streets.

Looters, with armfuls of merchandise, slipping through shattered store windows before rioters burn it down to the ground.

"Be careful who sees you with that!"

That, referring to Misty's rather pricey camera.

As ordered, Misty slouches down in the seat and takes more discreet photos.

The eyes.

She searches for the eyes.

Even that word *eye* carries enough weight not to go unnoticed.

The summer blockbuster, *The Eye Thief*—the letter "y" in the word *eye* crooked and hanging and about to fall from the marquee, which is lit up by the glow of firelight—steals Misty's eye as Violet drives by the trashed twin theatre.

Misty snaps photos, experiments with different filters, decides to use a black and white filter on it, makes a few edits using the touch screen, finalizes it, then dollars bill y'all!

After each photograph, she pulls the CaMMDoc away from her face and holds it from view of those primitive eyes.

Eventually, after taking one minor detour around a blocked road, the two sisters arrive at the docks where Quincy, a local fisherman and a close friend of their father's, as well as his son, Michael, who's a couple of years older than Misty, dropped out of college to help out with his old man, are loading up the boat with supplies.

As soon as Violet parks, Quincy orders Michael to help the girls. He rushes toward their car and helps them with their luggage.

Quincy tells them to hurry up, says he heard chatter on the radio about how the Main Docks have been overrun—which, if true, is going to be one helluva major problem for them considering they have to sail past the Main Docks in order to leave Kingsport.

"Can't we not just take an alternate route—"

"What? And wind up in the Atlantic?"

Michael reassures Violet, "Once we make it out of Kingsport, it should be smooth sailing."

With the blood pounding in her veins, Violet fires a series of questions at Quincy: "How you know? What makes you so certain that it's better outside the city? If you saw what we just saw, you wouldn't be as calm as you are right now. . . ."

"Don't worry, girls," Quincy says to not only Violet, but also Misty, who doesn't appear as rattled as her big sis from the chaotic drive. "I'll cut off the lights. We should be fine."

Violet is tempted to protest once more, but she realizes there's no getting through to Quincy. He's already made up his mind.

Once the boat is loaded up, the two sisters board. Misty can't help but point out the smell in the water. She shines a light on the river below, which is heavily polluted. The sight of the light causes a reaction from Quincy, who goes straight from zero to ten on the rage scale and gives her a stern warning about the light and how, once they take off, there's to be absolutely no electronic devices turned on. We're nothing more than shadows, remember?

"Can't believe you actually fish in these waters," says Misty.

"Don't," Quincy says, as he remains cool despite the dangers ahead. "Michael and I stopped a while back. You eat food out of these waters and you're destined to wind up as sick as a dog."

Michael removes the rope from the dock and is last to board the boat.

Before Quincy departs from the dock, he grabs a life vest from a rack and hands it to Misty.

"Got one left," he says, not taking "no" for an answer. "Put it on."

Considering Misty can't swim, she doesn't argue with Quincy.

She puts on the vest, no questions asked.

After about ten minutes in the trip, Quincy warns everybody to remain absolutely quiet and keep a lookout as they approach Lockette's Bridge. He maps out a route along the river, making sure the path is cleared before he temporarily cuts the lights.

"Heads up," he whispers to Michael, who relays the message to the two sisters.

As Misty stated earlier, Lockette's Bridge is blocked with vehicles. Bumper to bumper.

Most of the vehicles appear abandoned, others wrecked.

A couple of vehicles have caught fire and the hot metal burns like ambers.

Misty hears a couple of *thuds* below!

Without Quincy looking, Misty briefly shines the flashlight on the water and realizes the objects banging against the hull of the boat aren't logs, as she first suspected, but human bodies—at least dozens of them, their bloated bodies facedown in the water.

In the corner of his eye, Quincy catches the glow of a phone.

"Cut off that light," he whispers loudly while cautiously steering the boat under the bridge. "Do it! Now!"

Violet hits Misty on the arm, forcing her to turn off the flashlight.

Misty sits back down on the bench while Violet grabs her by the hand and tells her that everything is going to be all right.

"What if it's not, Vigh," she says quietly. "*What if* this is the end?"

"Maybe it is for them," she says in a similar quiet tone, talking about the people in the city, "but *not* for us. Once we reach Gee-Gee's, we'll be safe." In the pitch black, a flicker of a smile flashes on her face. Her glossy marbled eyes are pinned on the bright night sky above. "You 'member that one time when we were kids, we were spending Christmas at Gee-Gee's, we got snowed in? Gee-Gee got you that skateboard—"

"How can I forget?" Misty says, thinking. "I also remember you nearly catching the house on fire with that ridiculous drone."

"You were eight, I think, maybe nine."

"Nine," Misty corrects without missing a beat. "That was the year I banged the side of my head on the bathtub, remember? The doctor said I was lucky to survive. Said I had nine lives. Used up one of them in the fall."

"If that's the case, then you must have at least thirty lives," Violet says playfully.

Misty elbows Violet, who turns more serious.

She says, "I r'member you couldn't ride that skateboard worth shit. I think you gave up after your first attempt."

"Never was the athletic type."

"Yeah," Violet says and looks into her sister's dark eyes, "you weren't. But when it comes to survival, you don't have to be athletic. You just have to access the special part inside you that gives you the right tools to survive. In your case with that skateboard, your willingness to listen to your body and focus."

"Well, if I didn't know any better at the time, I swore you were trying to kill me."

"I tricked you into going with me to that hill because it was the only way you'd learn how to ride."

"Yeah but you didn't have to push me, though."

"It worked, didn't it?"

Misty struggles to nod her head.

"It's one of the rare qualities humans possess," Violet says, "that thing inside you that kicks on, like a switch, when faced with the threat of death. And you have it inside you. I saw it then when you first learned how to ride a skateboard. I see it now as you sit right by my side, ready to leave this place behind."

"I see it now," Misty says, as the car ride to the docks woke up a part of herself that she tried to ignore. "This place *is* death. We should've—"

"Don't go there," Violet says over Misty. "We're still here and we must keep our heads up, every step of the way from this point forward, got it? Otherwise, we'll never make it out of here alive."

All of a sudden, the boat runs into an object—possibly another body—and makes a thud so loud that it startles the two sisters.

"Damn it," Quincy says. "I don't how much longer I can ride blind like this. . ."

Before Misty has a chance to shine the flashlight over the object, Violet grabs her by the arm and tells her to look alongside the river.

A massive bonfire highlights the horde of ragers, howling in the night darkness, hundreds of them at least, gathered along the edge of the river, waiting for passing boats, doing what they do best, raging against the machine. Firelight reveals at least a dozen ragers clinging to what looks like an overturned fishing boat. The boat much smaller than Quincy's. Several people struggle to stay afloat as they thrash their arms through water.

A thought comes to Misty, who grabs the CaMMDoc from her bag, secures the strap around her neck, and views the dark river through a night vision filter. Each rager, each body, appearing like a negative of a photograph. Each one appearing a bluish-white color, the filter bringing out each act of violence being committed along the river. Through the CaMMDoc, Misty witnesses a man being butchered to death.

With the CaMMDoc, Misty is able to spot obstructions ahead of them, one being a jagged metal beam protruding from the water, perhaps part of the bridge; nonetheless, it's long, sharp, and sturdy enough to pierce the hull of the boat if Quincy doesn't maneuver fast.

Misty indicates the obstruction, tells Quincy to steer to the right.

At the last second before impact, Quincy trusts Misty and makes a hard right; however, part of the boat catches the end of the metal beam, resulting in a harsh nails-on-chalkboard-like noise to blare throughout the river.

"Good thing you brought the CaMMDoc," Violet says, impressed by Misty's thinking.

Misty turns the CaMMDoc toward the riverbank.

"We got trouble," she says, panic in her voice.

The previous noise is sharp and resonant enough to grab the attention of a nearby group of onlookers. Holding torches in their hands, the onlookers point toward Quincy's boat. Commotion erupts from the group. Splashes of bodies hitting water catches Violet's ear. She tugs on Misty's arm and then points toward the sounds. Misty, in return, redirects the CaMMDoc toward the other side of the bank where she sees people jumping into the river. First, she spots only a couple of ragers; and then, as she gradually pans the CaMMDoc alongside the entire bank, Misty spots more people, more of these ragers. Dozens upon dozens of bloodthirsty ragers, all swimming directly their way.

"Quincy!" Misty shouts out. "We have company!"

"Fuck it," Quincy says and switches on a spotlight, revealing more people than Misty originally spotted through the CaMMDoc.

As Quincy accelerates, several ragers manage to climb up onto the boat.

Violet picks up an oar hanging on a mount and uses it to beat away the desperate hijackers. In those moments, right before she uses the end of the oar to strike each hijacker in the head, she witnesses the madness in their wide, craze-laced eyes, inhuman almost, controlled, primitive.

The sight alone of their eyes reinforces how vital it is that not one of these creatures step foot onto the boat. One of them manages to grab Misty and pull her overboard. This minor distraction forces Violet to the other side of the boat, which allows several hijackers to board. Michael steps in and tries to fend away the hijackers, but they end up overpowering him. In a matter of seconds, the boat has been taken over by hijackers: people whom you'd least expect, everyday folk, laborers, neighbors who'd pass you in a grocery store. Quincy ends up locking himself in the cabin. The hijackers use whatever objects they can find on the boat to break through the cabin while Violet has no other choice than to abandon ship.

As more and more bodies pile onto the boat, Violet swims to Misty, who's clinging onto the CaMMDoc as if it's her own child. The life vest manages to keep her afloat, as she uses her free arm to doggy paddle. The cabin suddenly catches fire. Quincy still inside. Both Misty and Violet watch on helplessly. Eventually, the boat starts to tilt from the weight of bodies.

As the boat begins to overturn, the two sisters swim away.

Halfway toward the bank, the boat suddenly explodes behind them!

Fighting off the tears, Violet helps guide Misty, who's mostly splashing around, to the bank.

"Kick your legs, Miss," Violet instructs.

"I can't. . . " she says, struggling to keep her head above the polluted water.

Violet cries out, "You must!"

She ends up swallowing a couple mouthfuls of water and it runs down her throat like slime. The feeling alone of being submerged in pollution activates that so-called "switch" inside Misty, the one Violet recently mentioned just moments ago.

After the sudden burst of energy, she pushes away Violet's hand with her free hand and together, the two sisters swim to the shore where not too far away is an industrial park.

After crawling onto dry land, the two sisters rest and catch their breaths.

"What about. . . Michael or. . . or Quincy?" asks Misty.

"They didn't make it," Violet says, sitting up.

"How'd you know?" Misty asks while lying on her back.

More visibly frustrated, Violet ignores Misty's question and stands to her feet.

"Come ahh'n," she says, using her big sister tone.

Before leaving the muddy shore, Misty checks the CaMMDoc for any possibly damage, first by inspecting the hardware.

Violet asks, "Is it broke?"

The CaMMDoc is waterproof, according to the literature in the online manual; however, not once has Misty even thought about testing it out to see whether or not the manual is full of shit, for she feared the results may be devastating. Surprisingly, the CaMMDoc still works.

"Nah," Misty says, relieved. "Thank you, Jesus. Thank you. . . "

Once the CaMMDoc is secured, she follows Violet toward the industrial park where the two sisters walk past a boat ramp. Misty glances up at a crooked sign above, the letters "P" and "T" of the word *port* are burned out, leaving only a flickering "OR."

Wondering how the sign is still lit up, Misty spots the small solar panel attached to the top of the sign, potentially generating enough stored power to barely keep the sign lit.

"Where are we going?" asks Misty, as she struggles to keep up with Violet.

"We need to find ourselves a car," she says, "one that we can hot-wire."

"*Good luck with that. . .* " Misty trails off.

"Well, you can walk all the way back home. Me," Violet says, "I'd rather drive."

Misty stops walking, then asks with both her shoulders held in a fixed position, "What about Aunt Gee-Gee's?"

Violet stops as well, rotates around, and faces her sister.

"We need to regroup and come up with a new plan," she says and looks around the sketchy industrial park. "In case you forgot, all of our supplies were on that boat."

"Gee-Gee's *is* the plan."

All of a sudden, another explosion erupts from the river. The sound startles both the sisters.

"It's not safe, Misty," Violet says, more urgently.

Using a flashlight, not the one on Misty's phone, which Violet specifically instructs her sister to preserve, but a flashlight with a D-battery, Violet walks toward an abandoned warehouse, and Misty has no other choice than to follow.

Along the way, a car drives by, forcing Violet to turn off the flashlight.

The headlights of the car briefly cross the side of the warehouse. Violet follows the beam of light and in that oscillating-like passing of light, notices a body lying on the ground.

Eventually, the driver of the car, either lost or like the two sisters, trying to find a way out of this place, drives away.

As the two sisters reach the warehouse, Violet is first to point out the body. With the flashlight drawn, she carefully inches closer to the body, a young man she can tell, lying facedown in his own puddle of blood. With the toe of her shoe, she taps the young man's arm but doesn't receive any response.

"Is he dead?" asks Misty.

"Think so," Violet says and removes the wallet from the young man's back pocket.

As she kneels down, she passes the flashlight to Misty in order to free up both her hands and then turns the young man over on his back.

The young man is, in fact, dead. His blue-purplish face swollen with blood and marked with dozens of deep gashes and cuts. From the freshness of the wounds, except for his hand, which is covered in old scars, Violet can tell that his death was recent, happened maybe an hour or so ago. She opens the sticky leather wallet, skims over his driver's license, and then hands it to her sister, who reads the name: "*Rowan* Oxley."

Misty hands the flashlight back to Violet. She shines the light on the dirt road and follows the footprints circling around the body.

"From the tracks everywhere," Violet says, as she investigates the scene, "our friend, Rowan here, was outnumbered, jumped. Must've been at least six of them. Maybe more."

"Doesn't take a genius to figure that out," Misty says sarcastically and uses the flashlight on her phone. While towering over his body and staring at his face, she can't help but notice: "He's cute."

"What'd I tell you about wasting your battery?" says Violet.

"We may be able to find something we can use to help us," Misty argues, as she rummages through Rowan's wallet.

Violet shines the flashlight on Misty's face.

"Save your battery," she says, dead serious.

Misty switches off the phone, as instructed by her sister, and decides to use that night-filter on the CaMMDoc in order to see more clearly in the dark.

Violet hears a rat-like *squeak* coming from deep inside the warehouse.

With a flashlight in hand, she checks out the noise

Misty hears Violet trailing away from her and aims the CaMMDoc in Violet's vicinity, only to see a strange object on the side of the building. As with Violet's body, the object is also lit up in a soft whitish light; and for a second, Misty believes it to be some kind of small rodent, possibly that rat inside the warehouse. She looks closer and based on its many legs, realizes it's not a rat, but rather a beastly-looking spider perhaps. As she reaches the warehouse, she removes the loose brick from the side of the building and out falls the creature, which, after Violet shines a flashlight on it, is neither a rat nor a spider, but rather the artifact that Rowan once wore on his hand—at least, tried to wear.

"What is it?" asks Violet.

"Whatever it is," Misty says and kicks at the metallic artifact, "it lit up in the filter."

"Strange, but I thought. . . "

Misty says over Violet, "Must be important."

She further inspects the metallic apparatus—the artifact—partly wrapped in a rag covered in Rowan's blood. As she stares at her distorted face in the reflection in the mirror-like metal, she finds herself drawn to it as it pulls her closer and closer, like a whispered spell.

"You think it belonged to the cute guy?" asks Misty.

"Dunno," Violet says and shrugs. "Maybe—"

Misty reaches down to pick it up.

"What'r you doing?"

Misty looks up at Violet, who shines the flashlight on her face.

"What does it look like?"

"You don't know what the fuck that is—"

"Uh, it may come in handy, Vigh."

"How so?"

"It could be worth a lot of money."

"You honestly think money is going to help us right now?" Violet argues. "We need to find a ride—"

"Money can buy resources, Vigh," Misty argues back. "In case you didn't realize, we have nothing but the clothes on our backs. So, yeah, I'm taking this. . . "

"Misty. . . " Violet says with more urgency, ". . . Are you trying to get yourself killed?"

Misty doesn't answer her big sis. Against her orders, Misty carefully picks up the strange-looking artifact and as she slips it into her damp satchel, she feels a sudden pinprick sensation on the tip of her finger.

"Ouch!" Misty wags her finger and it's not until Violet shines a light on her finger that she realizes the artifact drew blood. A drop of Misty's blood dribbles into the center of the artifact, thus causing it to stir for a moment; however, Misty confuses the subtle movement of the artifact as merely its parts shifting around as she readjusts the satchel's strap around her shoulder.

"See? What'd I tell you? Good way to get yourself rabies."

"You mean tetanus."

"Whatever," she says, her voice trailing off into a heavy sigh. "Already dangerous enough for you walking 'round with that fancy camera. Now you just made the target on your back even bigger."

"Did that guy have a target on his back too?" asks Misty.

"You don't know his story?"

"Maybe not," Misty says. "But I know people."

"You do?"

"Some people aren't interested in. . . " Misty holds up the CaMMDoc, ". . . so-called 'stuff.' Some people just like messing with others. Because *now*, they can. And there ain't nothing anybody can do about it."

Violet steps closer and says more clearly, "Which is why we need to get the hell outta here!"

Misty starts walking toward the main road.

"Where you going?" Violet says from behind.

"Getting the hell outta here," Misty says.

For the first time in her adult life, Violet finds herself following her younger sister.

Making sure to preserve the batteries, not only in the smartphone, but also the flashlight, the two sisters walk down a pitch-black road.

Misty picks up a distant light ahead.

"See what I'm seeing," she says to Violet. "Up ahead. . . "

"Yeah," Violet says. "What could it be?"

"A car maybe."

"Use your little camera-thingy."

"Good idea."

Misty pulls out the CaMMDoc, switches the filter to night-vision, and holds the device up to her face. Through the lens, she witnesses what looks like yet another body hanging from a dark object. The two tiny red lights seen without the CaMMDoc suggest a car.

"What'd you see?"

"I think a person," she says, looking back into the CaMMDoc. "Not moving."

"I don't like this, Miss," Violet says and grabs hold of Misty's arm. "We should try our luck back in the city."

With her eyes narrowed, Violet searches for buildings that she can recognize. She spots the silhouette of a familiar structure not too far away, barely visible in the smoky night sky. She believes it to be the pharmaceutical company, PPP, but she's not a hundred percent certain.

"I think we're good," Misty says, looking through the CaMMDoc.

"It might be a trap, Misty."

"It might, but it beats going back into the city."

Misty continues to walk toward what she identifies as a car, which is parked in a ditch. The overhead light remains on, highlighting the horror inside the car. The closer they inch their way toward the car, the more details emerge and become clearer. Both car doors are open. A lifeless body hangs from the passenger seat, half of her body held up by the seat belt. A woman, Misty points out to Violet. A dead woman. Her throat has been slit open. She wears blood like a mask over her face. The driver seat, however, is empty.

As the two sisters inch closer to the car, Violet is the one who finds the driver on the driver's side of the car. It appears as if he has been dragged out of the car. He's not wearing any clothes, except for his underwear. His body is covered with fresh cuts and bruises and as with Rowan Oxley, he appears as if he has been beaten to death.

"Must've just happened," Misty says, as she secures the CaMMDoc and checks the vitals of the woman hanging from the passenger seat. As she suspected, the woman is dead. Next to grab her attention is the set of keys dangling from the ignition. "Vigh," she whispers, "come quick!"

After inspecting the driver, Violet rushes over to the driver seat and follows Misty's eyes.

The key in the ignition.

"Talk about luck."

"Why wouldn't they steal the car?"

"Maybe *they* aren't trying to leave the city."

Misty thinks for a moment about Violet's loaded comment.

After everything that she recently witnessed—*who in their right mind would want to stay in this death trap?*

Reeling back her sister's attention, Violet says, "Which is all the reason why we need to get the hell outta K-Port."

"Amen," Misty *finally* agrees.

Violet helps Misty move the dead woman from the passenger seat. They drag her body next to the driver, whom they believe to be her partner.

"I feel bad," Misty says, as Violet shines a flashlight on the couple, "leaving them here like this."

"Sorry, Misty," Violet says. "There's nothing we can do for them."

After Misty and Violet leave the couple behind, the two sisters make their way back to the car. Misty peels away the floor mat and uses it to cover up the blood-soaked seat before taking a seat while Violet, with her fingers mentally crossed, turns the key in the ignition.

The car engine starts!

Violet manages to drive out of the ditch.

Relieved, Misty switches off the overhead light, and together the two sisters ride away with nearly a full tank of gasoline.

Since the three bridges on the Walabiquc River are too dangerous to cross, each one blocked with vehicles and completely impassable—one of the bridges, the seventy-five year old Warren Beasley drawbridge on the Southside of the Kingsport, has partially collapsed into the river—the two sisters have no other choice than to brave the Interstate west of the city. The last time Misty checked a traffic update on her smartphone before it had been reduced to a glorified glow stick, the Interstate was entirely backed up, more than likely due to an automobile accident or vehicles that either ran out of fuel or battery; however, the only route toward the Interstate is through the heart of the city, in New Triad, where most of the fires are blazing and lighting up the crime-infested district like a collective bonfire.

As Violet weaves around destroyed vehicles, some of which have either caught fire or been set on fire by the local ragers, in-

cluding an overturned police cruiser that forces Violet to mount a
curb and cautiously ride onto the sidewalk in order to stay on
route, she spots a dark figure in the corner of her eye.

The figure races from the alleyway and makes a move directly
at the car.

First, Violet witnesses the whites of the figure's eyes, then the
desperation swimming inside them.

Next are his hands and each one is covered in blood, both
held up in surrender. His bloody hand presses against the driver's
side window of the car and leaves behind a red streak as though
begging for Violet to help. . .

OFFICER ROSE AND DARWIN
EARLIER THAT NIGHT
THE K PORT

INSIDE a nearly empty Moongate Café, Officer Cashel Rose and
Darwin "D-Win" Acosta, a fourteen-year-old delinquent from Sky
Hill, one of the most dangerous neighborhoods in Southside, sit
at a booth at the front of the restaurant.

The police officer, who's seated directly across from Darwin,
watches with a stupefied expression as the angsty-faced kid
scarves down yet another plate of egg rolls.

Once more, he attempts to wrap up his argument about the
once-favorable Kings and why the team isn't worth a darn this
year and more than likely aren't going to make the playoffs next
year, but the sound of each distracting *crunch* made by Darwin as
he munches on the greasy egg roll drowns out the officer's words,
which end up fizzling out like a deflated balloon.

Five egg rolls down Darwin's hatch.

Straight into Darwin's black hole of a stomach.

Darwin grabs the last egg roll on the plate and eats it with a
similar manner as the first one: fast and furious. Three or four
bites—no more than four—with very little chewing, occasionally
chasing a bite with a slurp or two of filtered water, then down the
hatch it goes.

"Geez, Little D," Officer Rose says, sipping from the mug of
steaming hot coffee. "When's the last time you ate?"

"Yes'r'day," he says from the corner of his mouth.

Darwin cleans his plate, even uses the tip of his greasy index finger to pick up each remaining crumb on the plate.

As he presses his finger against the flaky crumb as if he has adhesive spider fingers, Officer Rose reaches over the table and pulls away the plate.

"That's enough," he says. "You're going to make yourself sick."

"You got room to talk. . . *Orange Bucket*."

Officer Rose bites his tongue, as his eyes narrow sharply from the sound of hearing the nickname, which he earned on the streets after a hooker from Sky Hill witnessed the ill officer puke orange chunks behind the cruiser after ingesting tainted food while on duty.

After Darwin washes down the pieces of leftover food stuck between his teeth with a sip of filtered water, he lets out a violent, almost excruciating belch.

"Excuse me," he says, grimacing.

"You see, Little D," Officer Rose says, amused, "your body's telling you that you're full."

"Or it's just telling me that it made room for more."

"That's one way of looking at it. After three plates of egg rolls, you still want more food?"

Darwin shrugs.

"Fast metabolism."

"How about some hot chocolate?" the officer suggests. "I can get Sue to make you a cup."

Again, Darwin shrugs.

"M'kay."

Officer Rose waves down Sue, who's working on a short list of supplies. In the corner of her eye, she notices the officer's hand rise from the booth like a flag. She holds up her index finger, indicating to the officer that she needs a second as she finishes a math problem in her head. Once finished, she moves from behind the cash register and glides over to the booth and moments before she checks on Officer Rose, the lights on the ceiling suddenly flicker.

With his eyes trailing upward at the flickering lights, the officer says to Darwin, "Looks like we might take a rain check on the hot chocolate."

"That's twice tonight," Darwin points out. "I heard it might be the Russians trying to hack into our power grid. According to the chatter on Lo-Ro's feed, it's only a matter of time before the Russians clap back."

"You don't know it's the Russians," Officer Rose says, not drawing any reaction from Darwin. "And I'm glad you brought him up. You need to stop hanging around clowns, like Lo-Ro. Man's nothing but trouble."

Darwin smacks his gums and fires back: "Whatever." He ignores Officer Rose and changes the subject, "What makes you so sure it's not the Russians?"

"It's extraterrestrials draining our natural energy resources. Didn't you hear?"

"What?" Darwin tilts back his head and looks at the officer as if he's been smoking something. "That's IN-sane! Where'd you hear that?"

"On The Feed, of course."

"Thought you cops were too busy *eating* the feed."

The officer says with a striking glint in his eyes, "You'd be surprise how many clowns, like, for instance, Lo-Ro, incriminate themselves with a single post. In my world, it's not about going after the little fish that swims just below the surface of the water, doing the bidding of much bigger fish, like the shark swimming below, the one lurking in the dark, where no one can see, occasionally poking its fin above water to show us little fishes that he, in fact, exists, that the threat is, in fact, real." Officer Rose pauses and reflects inward, hesitant whether or not to share the trade secret picked up by police officers, like himself, over the years, especially in a digital age where criminal activity is driven by an all-important LIKE posted onto one's own feed. "Let's just say: 'Sometimes, you have to swim with the little fish in order to get a whiff of the shark.'"

Darwin remains baffled by Office Rose's comment and makes him think twice about following the popular trend of posting videos of a new dangerous and at times, deadly game, "Whack-A-Mole"—the mole, in this particular case, being a bystander.

Despite Officer Rose's indirect warning, Darwin feels the need to ask: *Does a fish have nostrils?* And if so, *can they smell?*

After the sudden yet brief power outrage, Sue arrives at the booth.

"Sorry about the power, Cashel," she says.

With one side of his mouth curled in a smile from Sue's presence, Officer Rose says, "I was gonna ask if you can make D here some hot chocolate, but—"

"Not a problem," Sue says over the officer. "We have a portable propane grill for this kind of situation."

"It's no trouble?"

Sue smiles, her face cutting in and out of blackness due to yet another brief power outage.

"For my two favorite customers, it'd be my pleasure."

"You're the best, Sue."

Eventually, the power kicks back on.

The last remaining customers exit the restaurant.

While Sue returns to the kitchen to make Darwin a cup of hot chocolate, Darwin nods at the officer.

"She likes you," he says, "and she's not just being polite because you're a 'customer.'"

"Well, I like her."

"I'm not talking in that kind of way."

The officer makes a noise with his mouth.

"She's got a kid," he says. "I don't mess with women with kids."

"I know hombres who'd say single mothers are the best catch."

"I bet you do," the officer says, trailing off.

"They already did all the hard work, with raising the kid and all."

"The work *never* stops," he says. "Believe me."

"So, when you ever gonna settle down. Huh, Cash?" asks Darwin. "Most men your age are already married and have families—and don't say it's cuz you a cop."

"I ain't that old," he says. "In fact, I bet I could run circles around you all day."

"You'r crazy."

"I just turned forty," he says. "Forty's like the new twenty."

"That's like ancient, you know?"

"I guess to a fourteen year old, it is."

Darwin asks again, "So, what's your excuse?"

"My excuse?" Officer Rose recoils at Darwin's question. "The day I stop attracting Crazy: that's my excuse."

He speaks about "crazy" women as if they're in their own separate category of women.

"Aren't all women crazy?"

Officer Rose laughs at the question.

"How 'bout Judy's friend?"

"Amber?"

"Yeah," he says. "Am-*purr*."

"Krazy spelled with a K."

"She don't look crazy to me."

"That's because you're fourteen years old, *D-Win*."

Officer Rose lifts up the mug of coffee, takes a sip, places the mug back on the table, then, afterwards, grimaces from a sudden pain in his knuckles. He pulls out a bottle and pops a small white pill that the doctor gave him to treat his arthritis, and then washes the white pill down with another sip of coffee.

"The hand again, huh?"

"It's nothing," he says, shaking off the pain.

Over an uncomfortable silence, Officer Rose asks Darwin a question that's been on his mind all day: "Talked to L-Train the other day and he told me he saw the Armadillo yesterday hanging around the Deadstreet Boyz on 7th." A tense pause develops over the conversation. "You know what L-Train is talking about?"

Darwin moves his attention back to the plate where he focuses on cleaning each crumb from the plate.

Once more, Officer Rose slides the plate farther across the table until the plate's no longer within Darwin's reach.

"D?"

Darwin shrugs, head down.

"A member of Deadstreet was involved in a double homicide last night. Tomb. You know him?"

Darwin doesn't answer.

"Listen, Darwin," Officer Rose says, more patiently, "I'm not trying to shake you down. I just thought you were done crossing paths with those people—"

"They don't consider themselves people. You know that, right?"

"Of course," the officer says with mild sarcasm. "*Dead*-street," he says, emphasizing dead. "Despite what they may think of themselves, they're very much alive, Little D. And so are you. But you won't be, if you continue to make deals with the Dead-street Boyz—"

"I just needed some extra bread."

"Were you involved in what happened last night? Be honest—"

"No," Darwin says without missing a beat.

"Okay," Officer Rose says. "I believe you." Then pauses. "So how much? And for what?"

"Two-K, to answer your first question," Darwin says. "And as for your second question, it's none of your business."

"What in the hell does a fourteen year old need with two thousand dollars?"

Hesitant to answer, Darwin says, his voice trailing off: "A new system. . . "

"What about that one I got you last year?" asks Officer Rose.

"It broke."

"What about the warranty?"

"Expired."

The officer takes a deep breath.

"Be real with me, Darwin."

"I am being for real," Darwin says, more agitated by the officer's questions.

"I've looked after you, haven't I?"

Darwin shrugs.

The officer answers for Darwin, like an overbearing parent.

"Yes," he says, nodding his head for Darwin as if he expects the kid to nod along with him.

Once Officer Rose realizes how strong he's overstepping his authority, he leans back in his seat and studies Darwin's upper body slumped in a deflated pose.

"You could've at least told me about this before going to the Deadstreet Boyz. If you're in some kind of trouble—"

"I can handle my own," Darwin says, looking up at the officer.

The officer witnesses a sudden darkness in the kid's eyes.

The Armadillo.

He takes a sip of coffee and savors it before asking Darwin: "How bad?"

"It ain't good," Darwin says and switches subjects. "In these past couple of years of getting to know each other, you never asked me why they call me the Armadillo."

Officer Rose says, "Sure I did. Because you once ate an armadillo when you were on your own in Texas. You're a brave soul, D. . . "

The officer recalls Darwin's story, the vivid details of it when Darwin first told him in this very booth exactly two years ago, when the two started this sort of father-son relationship. Darwin traveled with his older sister all the way from Sierra Madre del Sur to the US/Mexico Southern Border in hopes of fleeing civil unrest. Darwin eventually made it to the border. He lost his sister, Carolina, along the way. She drowned while swimming across the Rio Grande.

While Darwin was being transported into the States in the back of a cargo truck, Darwin was pushed off the truck by one of the immigrants during a scuffle. For weeks, Darwin survived on his own. Alone in Texas with no food or water. During that time, Darwin saw visions of his sister, whom he swore was still alive in spirit and not a mirage or a hallucination. *She* guided him through the deserts and the harsh, rugged landscape of Texas. *She* guided him toward safety and eventually, food. An armadillo, which he cooked over an open fire. The meat gave him enough strength to survive his journey and find a ride into the nearest city where he was picked up by a showy arms runner named Julio, who was returning from a job in Tijuana.

In the next couple of weeks Officer Rose learned of the Armadillo Story and bits and pieces of Darwin's backstory, but mainly about his mother, his *madre*, or what Darwin referred to as a "*bruja*," who, knowing the rapid maturity of Darwin, was desperately clinging onto control over her son, as well as his spirit. Each day spent in her company drained his spirit, corrupted it and through rigorous means of conditioning, despite her having little interaction with society, except for nibble-sized engagements with those who mean to serve her and her interests, forced Darwin and his sister to believe that people carry little-to-no good inside them and society is a diabolical trap and no place for her children, especially her boy. Each day she planted that seed of despair, persuading Darwin into believing that life in *all* forms beyond the quarters of their home was a disease and if Darwin should step out into the nasty, contagious world, then he'd be infected; and once he was infected, he'd be damned to hell. These admissions about Darwin's mother and her wicked ways of dehumanizing her son emerged through conversations Officer Rose and Darwin shared. The constant abuse, both verbal and physical—in the case of Darwin Acosta, the verbal being way *more* damaging than the physical. According to Darwin, his poor madre wasn't only oppressive. She was the devil's apprentice. Each act carried out with intention. Each word strategic and meant to redirect her son. Words like the flame along a running fuse: "(*Heard from the neighbors that street rat, Miguel, likes to stick his pecker in goat holes and if I catch you hanging around him, you'll be grounded for a month*)." As far as Darwin was concerned, Miguel never stuck his pecker inside a goat, despite so-called hearsay, had a new lady hooked around his arm every other week and from what Darwin gathered during their time together, showed no interest in goats. Darwin brought up his mother on more than several occasions, the good officer playing an unassuming and surprisingly unwanted role of therapist, whose only charge involved not only the kid's presence, but also his attentiveness—which brought into question Officer Rose's motives for specifically focusing on Darwin (regret played a major factor).

During their conversations, Darwin talked about his mother with a great deal of emotion—never would he dare speak these words to her. Not only was it religion, but it was also a sort of unspoken law to talk back to one's elder, especially one's parent. His mother's name was María, a loyal and obedient apparatus of the State. Over the course of four years, two of those years his mother bouncing from one job to another and unable to maintain any stability due to a weakened economy, she became obsessed with a popular TV personality, Jesús De León, after she first discovered his late-night show while flipping through channels to help her fall back to sleep. When she first saw him and heard him talk about current politic climate that was eroding the very fabric of society, she was hooked like a dope fiend. His words like a shot of dopamine. She needed Mr. De León as much as he needed martyrs, like María or other women like her. Mr. De León was incredibly charismatic and full of bravado, and his followers actually believed he was the reincarnation of Jesus Christ—some of them, at least. Darwin knew Mr. De León was a con artist, one of those fly men selling "get-rich-quick" schemes—instead of the promise of money, he was selling red hot rage and if you listened to him long enough, you'd be surprised how easy it was to fall into his trap. But it wasn't María's fault, Darwin discovered after she heard Mr. De León's words escaping from her mouth. Darwin knew Mr. De León was exactly whom his many adversaries claimed he was, a "false prophet." If there was such a thing as a devil, *el diablo*, he was perched on Mr. De León's shoulder, whispering truths into his very ear, then broadcasting it like a swirly-eyed influencer. Not only selling rage, but also spreading lies and division and often conspiracies about the opposition, a bloated bloodsucking regime of baby eaters who plotted inside their private penthouse suites at the top of skyscrapers or carried out their fiendish perversions inside underground dungeons on their gated properties while the rest of the country below or outside the comfort of their secured bubbles languished in a manufactured poverty plagued by viruses. Over a span of four years of being on television, Mr. De León created that sort of "Us" versus "Them"-like mentality among those who hung onto the breath of each one of his words, as vile as they could be at times. Mr. De León had awakened something inside Darwin's mother, something that had been buried deep among the skeletons. Mr. De León swooped in at the right moment and took a tiny chisel to María's special something and gave it a sturdy tap, just a crack, but long enough to spread and eventually, burst wide open. María was Mr. De León's most loyal follower, wore his flashy, colorful swag with great pride, and opposition was unacceptable, never allowed in her household; and if such dissent should arise, it was treated like blasphemy. María met Mr. De León once after one of his many TV shows, this one being "*Luchador de la Verdad*," which was filmed at a local studio, Épico. Most of the audience was older. He often targeted the vulnerable, including the elderly, which was most of his fan base.

After four years of watching his mother turn—or transform into an overly spiteful, vengeful, highly manipulative and often-paranoid woman, who, after her party, same one Mr. De León had been frequently pushing his followers toward each night, was elected into office, became as loyal as a lap kitty, a long paw for the State—Darwin had no other choice than to zero in on the source of her infection, cut it out, and remove it before it consumed her.

Darwin was eleven-going-on-twelve when he botched an assassination attempt against TV personality, Jesús De León. It went down while Mr. De León was leaving the studio in the middle of the night. In the parking lot, Darwin dowsed a random car with gasoline and set it on fire in order to distract the two bodyguards, who were protecting Mr. De León. As soon as the two were distracted by the fire, Darwin snuck up behind Mr. De León and attempted to stab him, but instead of stabbing Mr. De León in the side, he stabbed Mr. De León's look-alike, whom he frequently used as a decoy in public for these kinds of circumstances, while the real Mr. De León exited with his handler, a controversial rage whisperer named Toupee whose hand stayed close to the pulse of the country, through the back of the studio.

The look-alike, real name "Marco Fernando," was later transported to the nearest hospital and despite several stitches and a sore mid-section, managed to survive the attack. Darwin fled Sierra Madre del Sur with his sister, Carolina, who, like Darwin, was anxious to leave the mountains, but for her own reasons that included the one-size-fits-all package of a better, more glamorous life in America, and later sought cover inside a caravan until he reached the border. Having been raised by a single mother, Darwin never had a father figure in his life, except for a lowlife drug dealer, a street rat, who had a good heart but was always getting caught up in trouble. Darwin met Officer Rose several months later after crossing the border and only after a couple of conversations, confessed the reasons why he fled his home in Mexico—if anything, Officer Rose admired Darwin's tenacity. He didn't kill the man, but he made quite the effort. But the officer, having heard stories about the controversial TV personality and his cult leader-like aura, knew that if you killed a man like Mr. De León—because that's all he was, a man—then another Mr. De León would manifest in his wake and he'd be much stronger and far more dangerous; however, ever since Darwin admitted to the crime, the officer never brought up the confession.

Darwin's confession was their own little secret.

Their bond.

Over the building tension, Darwin finally says, ". . . That's only half the story."

"Well," Officer Rose says, "enlighten me. And you have around. . . " the officer checks his wristwatch, ". . . around ten minutes, no, nine minutes before I leave for my shift and I must say, based on how tonight's going so far with the power outages and all, it's shaping up to be one helluva night." He makes himself comfortable in the seat by placing both his hands on the table, his body open, that flawless instrument between his ears ready to absorb the rest of Darwin's story. "So why do people call you the Armadillo?"

"You know the story about how I wound up in Kingsport, how I had no other choice than to kill and eat an armadillo when

I was on my own after crossing the border," he says, moving his eyes from his hands to the officer's eyes, "but that's *not* why they really call me the Armadillo."

Officer Rose says more casually, "I once read that back during the First Great Depression, it wasn't uncommon for folks who were starving to death and struggling to make ends meet to eat armadillo. Back then, they called it a 'poor man's pork chop,' or '*Hoover* hogs,' named after the current president of the time, President Herbert Hoover, whom folks believed was to blame for the First Great Depression."

"*Blame?*"

Officer Rose furrows his brow in confusion.

The word not only sounds foreign to Darwin, but it also sounds forbidden once it leaves the officer's lips.

"It's when one owns up to one's wrongdoing."

Darwin isn't at all interested in a word like *blame*, since such a word no longer exists in society and the once stewards of the word, like, for instance, police officers and the Gestapo-esque Health Compliance Administration (HCA), are less likely to withhold and properly maintain its existence in a place where crime is like a merry-go-round.

"Can I finish my story?" asks Darwin.

Officer Rose checks his watch yet again.

"The stage is all yours."

Right before Darwin is about to tell his story, Sue returns to the booth with a cup of steamy hot chocolate. She places the warm mug on the table before Darwin.

Officer Rose smiles at Sue and waits for Darwin to respond.

He doesn't.

The officer asks Darwin, "What do you say?"

"Thanks, Sue," Darwin says after a blank-faced pause.

"You're very welcome, Darwin," she says. "Anything else I can get you?"

"That will be it," Officer Rose says. "Thank you. By the way, I was meaning to ask you," he says before Sue walks away, "how's the little one?"

"Jack?"

"I haven't seen him around. . . "

"He's at home recovering. My sister's watching over him."

"Is he feeling any better?" Officer Rose asks.

"He's still having the episodes," Sue says to the officer, "but they're not nearly as bad as last week. We've tried everything, but nothing seems to help."

"How about the oil?" asks Officer Rose. "Thought it was helping with the seizures."

Sue hesitates.

"It was," she says with a slight stutter. "But it's hard to find, you know?"

Officer Rose says despairingly, "What isn't these days?"

"And then there's the cost," she says, awkwardly. "You know how it is."

"Poor kid," he says. "He's been through a lot. Tell him I said hi, will you?"

"Sure thing, Cashel," Sue says and touches the officer on the shoulder.

Sue leaves the booth and makes her way back to the kitchen.

Darwin gives Officer Rose a look and before he can open his mouth, the officer holds up his finger and says, "Don't!"

Pushing aside the thought, Darwin finishes his *other* thought.

"Do you remember when you found me after The Portside Massacre?" asks Darwin.

"How can I forget?" Officer Rose says, as the pictures return to his head.

He received the dispatch right before his shift ended. Actually thought about ignoring it, but he was only a couple of blocks away from the warehouse, which was run by the head of K-Town Mafia. He was one of the first cops to arrive at the scene. Images such as the ones that he saw in the warehouse would stay with him until the day he could no longer draw a breath: Bloody bodies piled up on one another, blood puddles like tiny ponds all over the floor, bullet casings scattered everywhere. The only sign of life came from the back of the small boyish figure between two bodies. With his gun drawn, Officer Rose told the suspect to show both his hands, and out emerged a twelve-year old boy dripping with blood.

Not a single scratch on his body, except for his palms, which were red and blistered.

With his mind painting pictures about dead gang members of what used to be Chupacabras and K-Town Mafia, Officer Rose finishes, "And don't mind me saying, not one of them will be missed."

"I agree, but it's how the shootout was started that earned me my nickname."

More serious, Officer Rose leans closer and places his elbows on the table.

"One of the runners, Carlos, returned from California after making a drop. The Chupacabras and K-Town were celebrating after a successful. . . "

"Transaction," the officer says for Darwin.

"Yeah, something like that," he says and warms his hands along the mug.

"Thought I'd never live to see the day when the Chupacabras teamed up with K-Town. But then again, criminals tend to flock to their own kind."

Darwin gave him a look again, both of Darwin's eyes piercing right through him.

"Of course," the officer says, realizing his comments are preventing Darwin from finishing his story.

"Every time I saw Carlos, I had this tension inside me, not like in a big brother kind of way, although I wouldn't know how that would feel considering I've never had a big brother, but I can only imagine the feeling. It was more like a feeling you get when you're around a bully. But the bully is on your side. Yet, it feels like he's not on your side, if that makes any sense—"

"You were threatened by his presence?"

"In a way, yeah," Darwin says, holding his head down for a second. "I think it was because he saw a lot of himself in me. That's why he was always ragging on me in front of everybody else. He said he brought me a gift from Cali. Had it boxed up and everything. He gathered everybody around, including KTM. He opened the box and inside was a dead armadillo. It looked like Carlos scraped it off the side of the highway. The thing reeked worse than anything I have every smelled. Everybody started laughing. As the laughter builds, I guess I just. . . snapped."

Officer Rose remembers the condition of Carlos's body when investigators found it and how it didn't match the others, who all died from gunshot wounds.

"I grab the tail of the armadillo and I beat Carlos to death with it," Darwin confesses, both of his eyes pinned on Officer Rose.

"Why didn't you tell investigators this when they questioned you?" asks Officer Rose.

Darwin shrugs.

"You know how much trouble you can be in right now?"

Darwin doesn't answer. He attempts to take a sip of the hot chocolate. The officer grabs the mug from Darwin's hands and slides it to the other end of the table.

"Why'd you do that?" Darwin asks, more upset.

"What happened after you killed Carlos?" the officer asks, but strangely he feels as if he already knows the answer.

Hesitant to answer the officer's question for his next words may further incriminate him despite the previous confession, Darwin says, "Before the celebration, I made friends with a couple of cats in K-Town. Once they saw what the Chupacabras were going to do to me after my—"

"Misunderstanding," the officer says for Darwin.

"Yeah," he drawls. "Right." Then finishes, "They didn't like it, so they came to my defense. One thing led to another and before I know it, I'm in the middle of a shootout. So, I did the only thing I knew how to do."

"What's that?"

"I hid," Darwin says, forcing a pause in the conversation.

The officer chews on Darwin's story, the nickname that he earned, which could've very well come from a defensive tactic of burrowing himself between dead bodies, even though the officer knew the name came from the weapon of choice used on Carlos Reyes—he recalls investigators having a hard time trying to identify the armadillo, some thinking it might've been a large rat.

Finally, Officer Rose says to Darwin, "I'm not upset at you for what you did. I'm upset with you for what you didn't do."

"Believe me," Darwin says over the officer. "I was gonna tell you."

"Carlos Reyes was a murderer and frankly, the world is a better place without him."

"But—"

Darwin makes an attempt to further plead his case, but the officer interrupts and takes control over the conversation.

"Let me finish," he says sternly.

Darwin turns quiet, listens.

Officer Rose pauses once more, collects his thoughts, and says, "Forget about it—"

"I'm sorry, Cash," Darwin says. "It wasn't like I was trying to. . . you know."

"If it wasn't you, Little D, then it'd be someone else," Officer Rose says. "Guys like Carlos Reyes have an expiration date."

"So, I'm not in trouble?"

"For now," he says. "No. But this conversation isn't over. Understood?"

After checking the time on his watch, the officer slides out of the booth.

"Well," he says in a fatherly way, "I have to run. I'll drop you off at Judy's."

"I'm good," Darwin says. "I can walk home—"

"Absolutely not," Officer Rose says. "It's too dangerous out there."

"Cash?"

Officer Rose stands to his feet.

Looming over Darwin, he says, "Let's go. Now."

The officer pays for the meal, leaves behind a tip for Sue much larger than what he normally tips, and says his goodbyes to Sue, and with Darwin by his side, leaves Moongate Café.

Right before stepping into the police cruiser, he hears Margarine from Dispatch over the radio. He checks his watch, reads the time, and then turns to Darwin.

"What time do you got?" he asks, tapping the touch screen.

He shrugs.

"Don't know."

Frustrated, Officer Rose enters the cruiser. Darwin follows and takes a seat in the passenger seat.

After the officer starts the cruiser, he checks the time, which reads a different time.

"8:37," the time on the dashboard reads, unlike his smartwatch, which is twenty minutes off.

"Great," he says, more frustrated.

Officer Rose responds to the dispatch.

"Looting in progress on Wilmore Avenue."

Officer Rose turns to Darwin.

"Buckle up," he says.

Darwin does as he's told.

Officer Rose puts the gear in drive.

"Are you going to drop me off at Judy's?"

"Don't have time."

Darwin protests, "What do you want me to do? I can't be seen riding with you?"

"Then do what you do best, kid?"

The comment weighs heavily on Darwin, as he contemplates whether or not he should jump out of the car before the officer speeds away.

"After all," the officer says jokingly, as he begins to drive, "you are what you eat?"

Darwin, whose sensitivity can be at times as thin as glass, lets out a deep sigh of frustration.

Officer Rose's laugher eventually draws reaction from Darwin, who, despite the recent confession, can't help but bring himself to laugh as well.

THE MARK OF E'RAKNISH
BACK TO THE SISTERS
SAME SHITSTAIN OF A CITY

THE bloody hand slides from the driver's side window, revealing Officer Rose's colorful, disfigured, badly swollen face covered with lacerations.

Violet slows down the car.

The badly injured officer once more cries out for help while Misty yells at her sister to keep driving.

"Don't stop!" Misty shouts out, as the car creeps to a near stop.

The officer slides off the car, staggering and then eventually falling to the ground.

"I can't leave him out here," Violet says to Misty. "He'll die—"

"Then so be it!"

"Misty. . . " Violet, disappointed by her sister's words, says with a sharp tone.

Violet cracks the window.

While clutching his side, the officer crawls away from a fetal position and manages to stand to his feet after using a fire hydrant for support. He stumbles to the car where he shows the two sisters his badge.

"Please," he says, out of breath as he leans against the side of the car, "I need your help. . . "

Vexed by her sister's gullible nature, Misty leans past Violet and asks with a hint of sarcasm in her voice, "What seems to be the problem, Officer?"

Violet hits Misty on the leg.

"Stop," she whispers to her, then redirects her attention to Officer Rose. "What happened?"

After Officer Rose catches his breath, he says, "There's no time to explain." He looks over his shoulder, into the darkness of the alleyway as if he's anticipating someone—or something—to emerge, then rotates back around. His eyes are wrapped with the terror of a thousand horror stories left untold. Finally, he says, "Can you help me out or not?"

"Where'r you going?" asks Violet.

"Anywhere but here."

Violet thinks for a moment.

Misty rebels.

"You can't be serious. . . "

"Miss," she says again for she is unable to give Misty a proper reason to help out the officer.

He removes his bloody hand from his side, revealing his empty holster.

"Please," he begs. "I'm unarmed."

Misty recognizes the shock stick on his belt.

The officer follows Misty's eyes.

"Here," he says, as he unclips the shock stick from his belt and extends it toward the sisters. "If it makes you feel more at ease. . . I just need a ride out of the city. . . "

Violet asks, "Are you in danger?"

"Please," he begs once more. "No time to explain. I just need a ride. . . Please. . . "

"Violet," Misty says in her other ear, "talk about a target on our heads. We'll have a HUGE sign on our backs saying 'KILL ME.' Is that want you want?"

Violet absorbs her sister's comment as she peers into the officer's bloodshot eyes and again recognizes that raw terror accompanied by desperation, a pair whose relationship is complex yet, at times, necessary in order to survive. She knows that exact look on his face and the feeling behind it, often misinterpreted as a feeling of little to no self worth, for she herself had felt it many times before while struggling to make ends meet in a city where only the strong survive and the weak are left to rot away on the streets, an everyday example of showing Violet what awaits her if she doesn't pay rent or stay hungry, that natural rot, created by a lack of guidance or love, dangling right in front of her face, so easy to smell and even easier to touch; and yet, despite having seen that look on a daily basis whenever she drove past The Traxx on the way to work, she'd never wish that feeling on anyone, no matter who they are, what they stand for, or if they share a different point of view from her own.

In that moment, Violet thinks about what Gee-Gee would do.

Without giving it any more thought, she unlocks the doors.

Before the officer can make an attempt toward the backdoor, Misty reaches over Violet and grabs the shock stick from Officer Rose's hand.

The officer opens the backdoor. His body flops into the backseat.

Misty aims the end of the shock stick at the officer's face.

"If you try anything. . . "

Officer Rose, relieved by Violet's generosity, holds out his bloody hand.

"You have my word," he says to Misty.

Violet drives away and adjusts the rear view mirror, positioning it directly on Officer Rose, who closes his eyes and rests.

In the side view mirror, she witnesses at least a dozen shadowy figures emerge from the alleyway. Highlighted by a distant firelight, the mob-like crowd becomes smaller and smaller the farther she drives away. She pulls her eyes back to Officer Rose.

"So. . . what'd you do?" she asks the officer.

Officer Rose drunkenly cracks open his eyes.

"Looks like you made a lot of enemies," she says.

"Wouldn't be the first time," he says, grimacing.

"So what did you do?" Violet asks again.

"They're not after me," he says. "They're after this kid."

"Kid?"

"He was someone I was supposed to be looking after."

"And why aren't you looking after him?"

"We got separated after the blackout," he says, removes his hand from his side, and inspects the stab wound. A trail of blood pours out of the wound, forcing the officer to apply more pressure to it. "He's not exactly what you call a good kid. But. . . I guess I saw potential in him."

"You can't save everyone," Misty says, her eyes sharp and locked on the officer. She readjusts her grip along the handle of the shock stick, ready to use it on Officer Rose.

Violet asks, "Where is he, this kid?"

"Knowing Darwin, he's probably hiding out somewhere," he says. He nods at Violet's reflection in the rear view mirror. "I'm Cashel."

"Violet," she says and points at her sister. "This is—"

Misty says, "Don't!"

"My sister, Misty," she says, ignoring Misty's paranoia.

"Thanks for helping out," Cashel says and removes the badge from his uniform.

"I can't take you with us," Violet says. "The farthest I can take you is Bluth Park."

"Yes," he says. "Thank you. Anywhere but here."

To reassure Misty that he means no harm, Officer Rose shows the badge to her but lets her know that he's off-the-clock; however, considering the city of Kingsport has gone tits up, Cashel Rose is no longer a police officer.

"If it makes you feel any better. . . "

"It doesn't," Misty lies.

Office Rose eyes her and clearly senses the discomfort in her from his presence. The fidgety movements, heightened senses, shortened and at times, labored breath, or an inability to remain steady: these are just some of the many tell-tale signs that the officer observes.

While holding the badge in his hand, Officer Rose considers pocketing it—after all, he had worked so hard to earn the badge, spent over eight years of devoting his life to it, wearing it, not with pride, but with honor as he selfishly tried to carry out his job of maintaining order and keeping others safe after years of training and hard work and molding his body into its peak condition in order to handle whatever was thrown his way. But instead, to publicly display his resignation from the law, he decides to toss the badge out the window and rest until the two arrive at Bluth Park, which is about a thirty-minute drive across town.

After a few minutes into the drive, Misty lowers her guard while Cashel uses the time to rest from his wounds.

Misty places the shock stick aside, close within reach, and uses the little downtime they have to document the collapse of Kingsport with her CaMMDoc. Through the passenger window, she takes strikingly vivid photographs of ruined buildings, destroyed vehicles, gutted stores, as well as dead bodies on the street. The various night filters on the CaMMDoc acting like a new pair of eyes in the dark.

"Crazy how fast it all came crashing down," Violet says, absorbing the chaos all around her. "One minute, everything seemed, dare I say, normal. And then just like that, in the flip of a light switch, everything reverted back to the freakin' Dark Ages."

"It's in us," Cashel says tiredly, as he stirs in his own sticky pool of blood. "That camera of yours, phones, *sports*, movies: What do you think would happen if you remove all those distractions?"

The two sisters don't answer the question.

"*This* would happened," he says, more cynically.

"People are good by nature," Violet says, still hopeful despite Cashel's despair.

"True," Cashel agrees, as he turns his soft eyes toward the rear view mirror. "*They are.* I've seen good, even in the eyes of those who have committed the most unspeakable acts of violence. A regret of not being good and how something as sudden as emotion got the better of them. We can be incredibly emotional creatures, especially in the face of instability. But do you think people would still be good if accountability no longer existed?"

"Everybody is accountable," Violet says, her gaze sharpening over Mr. Soapbox in the backseat.

"I'd like to think so, Violet," he says. "But I just don't know anymore."

Violet turns onto a quieter, less active street where she drives past a super mart. She slows down the car and turns to Misty, who seems confused as to why Violet is slowing down.

"We need supplies," she says, as she instructs Misty to look through her CaMMDoc.

Misty looks through the night filter and doesn't see any movement coming from within the store.

"I don't think this is a good idea," Cashel says, more alertly.

"No offense, Cashel," Violet says over Cashel, "but we *need* to stop. We have no food, no supplies, no clothes, except for the ones we're wearing. This may be our only opportunity before we leave K-Port."

"I don't think right now is the best time to go shopping—"

"No offense, Cashel, but it's not your decision."

"Good luck trying to find supplies in there," he says disparagingly. "Surely, a place like that has already been ransacked—"

"We have to at least try," Misty says.

"I'm telling you you're wasting your time."

"Misty's right, Cashel," Violet says, more directly.

"You're going to get yourself killed."

The two sisters remain determined.

Two against one.

Majority wins.

"Here," Cashel says and while letting out a grunt, lifts his leg over the center console.

With confused expressions, the two sisters look at one another.

"There's a gun on my ankle," he says. "Grab it."

Carefully, Violet pulls back the bottom of the damp pant leg and removes the compact pistol from the ankle holster.

"The Force isn't aware of the gun," he says. "It's what I call my own little 'Backup.'"

"Well, you don't have to worry about them anymore, right?"

"Thought you were unarmed."

"I lied," he says.

"I knew he couldn't be trusted," Misty says under her voice.

"You ever used one?"

"Once," Violet says and struggles to look Misty in the eyes.

Misty says, "Oh yeah, G.I. Jane? When was this?"

"When I was dating Roscoe," she says. "He took me to a gun range once."

"Some date."

"Are you gonna come with us?" asks Violet, as she checks the safety on the side of the pistol. "Or, are you gonna stay here and bleed?"

"Bleeding sounds better."

Violet rotates around and says more directly, "We can use a hand."

"That depends," Cashel says suspiciously. "Are you gonna leave me the car keys?"

"That'd be a NO, in all CAPS."

"No harm in asking," he says, trailing off. "On that note, what other choice do I have?"

Like his words, Cashel eyes trail downward onto a tote bag on the floor. He shines a flashlight on the contents inside the bag:

Clothes, a hair dryer, a handbag of toiletries, and then, lastly, an ID.

"I reckon this isn't your car," Cashel says over the silence.

"What gives you that impression?"

Grimacing from the pain, he removes his leg from the console and leans forward and picks up the driver's license from the bag.

He reads the name.

"Either you recently got plastic surgery or you're a shape-shifter. . . Mrs. Taurus."

Violet fully rotates around and asks Cashel, "Are you gonna to arrest me?"

"I would if I was a cop," he says. "But I resigned ten minutes ago."

More relieved, Violet asks, "You coming with us or what?"

After Cashel agrees to brave the store with the two sisters, he removes his bloody shirt and changes into a loose-fitting designer T-shirt with holes, which easily slips over his body.

In those brief moments when Cashel exposes the ripped white undershirt drenched red with blood underneath the police shirt, Violet's able to see the extent of his injuries. Stab wound two inches below his ribcage. More than likely, the knife didn't hit any major organs. But it's clear to her that he needs to stop the bleeding. Not only that, if Cashel doesn't treat the wound, it has a greater chance of becoming infected.

"We need to close that wound up," Violet says.

"Got anything for it?"

"No," she says. "But they *will* inside."

He looks down at the new attire.

"When did dressing like a fucking bum become the latest trend," he says to himself. Then to the sisters, more specifically, Misty, "Looks like you're not a target anymore."

Cashel grabs the bag from the floor, empties the contents, and hands it to Violet.

"Could come in handy," he says.

"Good thinking," Violet says, surprised by Cashel's generosity.

As the three prepare to step outside the car, Misty grabs the strange-looking artifact from the glove compartment. Part of the artifact is exposed enough to grab and hold Cashel's attention.

Without uttering a word about the artifact, he carefully watches Misty as she places the artifact inside a satchel. Misty looks up, only to catch Cashel staring at the satchel.

The two lock eyes.

"Problem?"

"No," Cashel says in a similar tone and gesture used by Misty when she was asked if she felt more comfortable about Cashel removing his badge.

Misty, who hasn't been around enough people to sense or pick up on a lie, ignores Cashel—and his interest in the artifact—and after receiving the go-ahead from her big sis, steps out of the car with the CaMMDoc worn like a heavy pendant on a rather bulky necklace around her neck. The cushioned strap helps relieve some of the pressure of the device, despite being lightweight.

With Cashel trailing behind the sisters, the three cautiously enter the super mart store, Your Market. The front windows of the store are shattered and leftover debris and projectiles, such as bricks or street signs, are strewn about and the entire scene appears as if a bad storm recently swept through the area. Violet dumps out the remaining trash from an overturned trashcan and hands the garbage bag to Misty, telling her to fill it up with only essentials.

Mindful of the broken glass all over the ground, both Violet and Cashel watch their steps as they shine their lights into the store, Violet's flashlight being much brighter opposed to Cashel's pocket-sized flashlight. The store appears devoid of rioters, looters, and ragers; however, Violet doesn't take any chances as she brandishes the pistol in her other hand.

"Make sure the safety's on," Cashel says and watches Violet's hand, more specifically, the barrel of the pistol as it crosses his path.

Violet turns the pistol sideways and shines a light on it.

"On," she says.

"I think we're all clear," he says and scans the store for life.

Most of the shelves are empty, as they anticipated; however, several items still remain on the floor, such as clothes and blankets and some canned food. Misty starts filling up the garbage bag with as much items as she can find.

"So, this kid who you're supposed to be looking after," Violet says, making sure to keep her voice down despite the "all clear" sign from a former police officer, "you think he's still alive?"

"Darwin," Cashel says with a similar volume. "His name is Darwin. And yes, he's alive."

"What makes you so sure?"

"The kid's probably hiding somewhere safe, waiting for all of this to blow over."

"Smart," Violet says.

"When it comes to being street smart, the kid's a genius," he says and makes his way toward the pharmacy aisle.

"If that's the case, then there should be nothing to worry about," Violet says, as she nods at Misty who's off on her own filling up the garbage bag with canned beans and fruit that have fallen from the shelf and rolled underneath a wing-stack. "It's those book smart folks that should worry you—at least, worry me."

"How's she holding up?" Cashel says, quieter.

"Fine so far," Violet says. "I know on the inside she's freaking out, but she's not showing it yet."

"Your sister's not the only one."

"You have any kids?"

"Nope," he says. "Darwin's probably the closest I have to a son."

"You two sound close."

"Sure," he says. "Kid's been through a lot. It's the least I can do—"

The two redirect their attention to a sudden *thud* coming from one of the middle aisles. Violet switches off the safety from the side of the pistol and with a steady aim, inches toward a small rustling-like sound in the cereal aisle. Staying close to Violet, Cashel shines a light on the overturned cereal box on the floor. A rat suddenly pokes out its head and then scurries underneath a shelf.

"Just a rat," Cashel says, as he places his hand on top of Violet's and helps lower the pistol. "Completely harmless."

Violet switches the safety back on and takes a breath.

Misty rushes over to the two.

"What was that?"

"Rat," Violet says.

As the three leave the aisle, Violet comes across a stick of superglue near the checkout aisle. She brings it to Cashel and hands it to him, as if it's a gift.

"Lookie here what I found," she says.

"What's the glue for?" asks Cashel.

"It's for you, genius," she says sarcastically and points at the stab wound. "Your wound."

Leery about the glue, Cashel says, "I need to find some stitches—"

"Already looked," Misty says, the comment surprising Cashel. She pulls out a pack of bandage wrap from the garbage bag, as well as a pint of whiskey. "Found these, though," she says. "You'd be amazed by what you can find underneath these shelves."

"Folks in a hurry, accidentally kicking goods around. . . " Violet acknowledges Misty's keen awareness of the situation, then compliments, ". . . good thinking, Miss."

After Violet helps clean the stab wound with alcohol, she closes the wound with the superglue by first pinching the laceration shut and then, with her thumb and index finger pressing the two ends together like a pair of lips, running a line of glue along the laceration, then, lastly, holding it close until the glue dries. Lastly, she wraps the sealed-up wound with clean bandages.

The three continue to gather supplies throughout the store. Misty, as before, goes off on her own.

Driven by the growl of her stomach, Misty tries to collect as much food as possible, finds a pack of chocolate pretzels, eats the entire bag, including the leftover crumbs.

Despite the empty shelves, Misty manages to scrape together nearly an entire garbage bag full of items, mostly ones that looters glossed over, canned items or seasonings or condiments, as well as boxed rice and grains—*How in the hell is one supposed to heat a pot of rice without any power?* The good stuff is rather scarce, bread, gone, fruits and vegetables, gone, all of the thick cuts of meat cleared out. She starts to think outside the box, no pun intended, or inside the box, depending how one looks at it, and returns to the aisle where she collected the bottle of alcohol. With her body flat on the floor, she reaches underneath the shelf and grabs as many bottles as she can. Alcohol is flammable. Next on her Back-to-the-Basics list: A box of matches, the quintessential tool for making fire.

While using the CaMMDoc's night filter, she locates the outdoor section in the back of the store where the shelves have been nearly gutted; however, the section appears more in shambles than the other departments, including the Food Market, as well as the neighboring sports department, which, unlike the previous departments, has been neglected by looters. In fact, some aisles appear untouched, except for the baseball aisle where nearly every baseball bat has been swiped from the racks.

In the camping section, Misty comes across a fireplace lighter but no lighter fluid. She bags the lighter and then locates a full box of matches in the very back of the shelf, which is too far to reach with the satchel worn over her shoulder, preventing her from squeezing her body farther into the shelf. She sets aside the satchel on the floor and climbs into the shelf to grab the box of matches, first clawing at it with the tip of her finger until she's able to get a whole finger around it and slapshot it closer. When Misty slithers out of the shelf after grabbing hold of the matches, she blindly feels for the satchel on the ground but comes up empty. The satchel is gone!

She frantically holds the CaMMDoc up to her face and as she peers through it, she witnesses a blaring white-bluish figure before her eyes!

Startled by the figure, Misty reaches for the shock stick.

Suddenly, a blinding light blooms from the waistside of the figure, forcing Misty to pull the CaMMDoc away from her face.

With the shock stick gripped in her other hand, she does a double-take at the figure, the glare of a flashlight shining over Cashel's shadowy face. He shines the light into the satchel, digs out the artifact—Misty's artifact—and stares at it with both awe and horror.

"What you doing?" asks Misty.

Misty spots an object tucked underneath his waistband—the pistol.

She asks more suspiciously, "Where's Vigh?"

"She's fine," Cashel says.

"That's not what I asked you," Misty says, her voice louder and more upset.

He secures the artifact by tucking it underneath his armpit on the opposite side of the wound, pulls out the pistol, and aims it at Misty before she can make the first move.

"Easy, Misty," he says, struggling to hold up the pistol for the pain weighs down his arm. "I don't want to hurt you."

"Where is Violet?" says Misty, her body shaking with fear.

"I left her next to the freezers," he says. "She's fine. Trust me."

Misty asks, "Why are you doing this?"

"You and your sister have every right to be upset with me," Cashel says, as he starts backpedaling away. "But trust me when I tell you this: I'm doing this for your own good."

The anger rises up into Misty's face.

She seethes, "Why should I trust you?"

"You're still alive, aren't you?" Cashel asks.

Misty doesn't answer.

"Grab all the supplies you need and get the hell outta here," Cashel urges. "There's nothing for you here—"

"Fuck you, man!"

Cashel ignores Misty and the temporary emotion that currently drives her.

"Good luck," Cashel says and puts away the pistol.

As Cashel leaves the store, she attempts to chase after him but the thought of leaving all of the supplies that she recently collected, including those matches—which she had a hard time acquiring—forces her to remain idle. Not only that, the thought of her big sis: Was he lying about what he said about her?

Misty picks up the satchel, as well as the garbage bag of supplies from the floor, hoists them over her shoulder like Saint Nick, the satchel worn across her chest.

Using the CaMMDoc to locate the freezer aisle at the other end of the store, Misty follows the muffled grunts and groans until she tracks down Violet, who's tied to the leg of a shelf with a pair of zip ties. Violet's unable to mouth any words to Misty for Cashel used a torn strip of the bloody police officer shirt that apparently he secretly kept in his possession to use as a gag. She removes the shirt from around her face and then checks the bag for a sharp object she can use to cut through the ties.

"Are you hurt?" asks Violet, more worried about her sister's well being than her own.

"Nah," she says and then once she realizes her big sis is all good, releases a sudden burst of anger. "I knew we couldn't trust that fool—"

"Did he take the device?"

"What device?"

"That thing you stole back at the warehouse. . . "

"Yeah," she says, trailing off. "Why?"

"He kept going on and on about it, how dangerous it was to have it in your possession, saying it was used to. . . I dunno. . . " she catches her breath, ". . . murder a whole bunch of people."

Except for a can of beans, which for a second Misty thinks about stomping on with her heel and using the metal lid to cut through the ties but realizes how essential the beans may be days or even weeks from now, she comes up empty.

As she disappointedly sets the bag aside, she remembers those shards of broken glass by the entranceway. Her eyes light up, as if she's discovered a cure for old age. She tells Violet she'll only be a sec and while securely holding onto the CaMMDoc to prevent it from banging against her chest, rushes to the front of the store where she sorts through glass and picks out the largest shard of glass from the floor. She finds a shard roughly the size of a switchblade.

Once she's acquired the shard of glass, she hears a commotion coming from the parking lot outside. She grabs the CaMMDoc worn around her neck and lifts it up to her face and counts at least four gangsters making their way toward Your Market.

Through the CaMMDoc's filter, each one of the gangsters appears clear and visible, highly detailed; their expressions vary in emotion. Misty removes the CaMMDoc from her face and all she sees are silhouettes as dark as shadows, more or less, moving bodies that blend with the night darkness.

Mindful of the broken glass all around her, Misty slowly and quietly backpedals away until she's clear of the glass. Then, once she's clear, she rushes back over to Violet and uses the sharp glass to cut through Violet's ties.

"We have company," she whispers to Violet.

"How many?"

"Several," she says, out of breath.

She finally cuts away the last zip-tie, freeing Violet's wrists.

The sisters gather all of their belongings, including the shard of glass, which Misty keeps for later use, and leave the store through the back exit while the four gangsters linger around the entranceway, breaking and throwing things and making a racket.

Once outside, they hurry to the edge of the building and peek around the corner where Misty spots the car, still intact, with the CaMMDoc.

"I say we make a run for it," Violet says over Misty's shoulder.

"You won't make it."

"*What if* I distract them?" Violet suggests. "You can grab the car and pick me up—"

"There's too many, Vigh," Misty says. "What if we just wait here? Wait till they leave?"

Violet says, "Who in the hell knows how long that's going to be?"

The two suddenly hear the grating sound of grit moving underneath the sole of a shoe. The footstep is light yet heavy. Violet rotates around, only to find one of the gangsters creeping behind her.

The gangster, who's wearing a pair of night vision goggles, grabs Violet by the hair, causing her to scream out to Misty. The green-eyed gangster pulls out a handgun from his side, presses it against the side of Violet's temple, and tells Misty to back away.

"Shoo fly," he says, flicking the barrel of the gun like a wave of a hand before pressing the barrel back to Violet's head.

Misty holds out both her hands and backs away from Violet while the gangster hollers out to the other four gangsters. In that blink of a moment, when the gangster is distracted, Misty makes sure to tuck the CaMMDoc underneath her shirt, hoping the night will conceal it from the other gangsters, despite the bulky protrusion along her chest.

One of the gangsters uses a road flare that he stole from the back of a police cruiser to light up the front of the store.

The burst of light from the pinkish-red road flare forces the other gangster, whom his fellow gangster buddies refer to as "Deco," to remove the night vision goggles from his face.

"I see you brought gifts," says one of the gangsters.

"Easy, Smoothie," the incredibly muscular gangster, whom the others call "Rimes," the head member of the gang, the alpha, says to the shorter, weaselly gangster.

"What'd you rocking there, Deee-cooo, my man?" asks another.

"Night vision, Baby," he says, her pearly whites like a crescent moon. "Found 'em inside a wrecked RV."

"Where?"

"Off 7th," he says.

"The people inside were all dead," he says. "They had a lot of bread from what I could tell."

"Let's find out where they live!" Smoothie says, growing more excited about the possibility of becoming wealthy. "What you fools waiting on? Let's hit 'em up!"

"Enough, Smoothie," Rimes cuts in, silencing Smoothie. "That bread ain't worth shit now." He nods at Deco, "Who the fuck are these two?"

Deco pushes the barrel of the gun into the head of Violet's head, forcing Violet closer to the gang.

"I'm Violet," she says, her voice trembling, head slightly lowered in submission. "This here is my sister, Misty. We're not trying to cause any trouble or anything. We're just trying to leave the city. That's all."

"Where'r you two from?" asks Rimes.

"Silver Heights," she says.

Rimes knows the area, has a nana who's been living in Silver Heights ever since he was just a young buck.

"Let's lights things up around here and have a better look at what exactly we're dealing with here," Rimes says, as the flare starts to fade. "Yo, Count," he says to the tallest and lankiest one of the gang.

"There's no need for that," Violet interjects, her body shaking, not with anger but with great terror. "We'll be on our way. . . Please. . . "

While the other gangsters are distracted, Misty, who surprisingly remains cool and collected despite the gangsters' intentions, carefully reaches for the concealed shock stick holstered underneath the waistband behind her back.

As commanded by Rimes, Count holds the flame of a lighter under the damp rag of a Molotov cocktail and right before he lights the rag on fire, Smoothie hollers out, "What about the loot inside? I'm fucking hungry. . . "

"Trust me, Smoothie," Deco says, shoving Violet. "They'll be plenty of food to go around."

Another gangster, Shaman, returns from his survey inside Your Market.

"Any luck?"

"The place is gutted like a Thanksgiving turkey," says Shaman, "You ain't gonna find shit in there."

Smoothie draws his dark yet glossy firelit eyes toward the two sisters and says while rubbing himself, "Speaking of turkey, I got some stuffing for these two c'here. . . "

"Cool it, Smoothie," Rimes says to Smoothie, then Deco. "Same goes for you, D."

The comment alone emphasizes the severity of the situation, forcing Misty to mentally plot a course of action—first, go after this Deco fellow, shock him where the sun don't shine, then steal his gun, pull and squeeze and hope for the best, allowing enough time for Vigh to make a run for the car.

Deco kneels down and with a glance through the night vision, takes a look at the contents of the garbage bag. He decides to dump out the supplies, including food, onto the pavement.

"Looks like these ladies made it a lot easier for us," Deco says, referring to the supplies that Misty gathered inside Your Market.

"Count," Rimes says again. "Light it up!"

Once more, as commanded, Count throws the Molotov cocktail inside the front entrance of the store. The first checkout aisle catches fire and spreads to other aisles, providing enough light in the parking lot for Rimes to see the two sisters' faces. Struggling to make eye contact with the other gangsters, Violet moves her eyes down at the supplies below and among those supplies is a shard of glass, same one that Misty used to cut away the zip ties around her wrists.

Deco grabs hold of the back of Violet's neck and pushes her closer to Rimes, who looks her over the same way a predator looks over its prey right before it consumes it. She looks up and makes eye contact with the gangster. His firelit eyes, both sharp and menacing, as he breathes in Violet's scent. A variation of smells, from body odor to the synthetic pungency of Walabique River to the hint of fruity shampoo: each smell arousing Rimes.

Before the gangster can make a move on Violet, she makes it easy for him and gets down on her knees.

Other gangsters circle around Violet, as she falls into a submissive position.

Smoothie breaks away from the others, creeps over to a vulnerable Misty, and in his smooth voice, whispers into her ear, "Ain't nothin' to worry about, gurl."

He kisses her on the side of the neck and moves his way toward her lips.

With her head lowered, Violet carefully reaches for the shard of glass lying next to a can of pinto beans; and as soon as Rimes unzips his fly, she grabs the shard of glass and stabs him directly in the gut!

She turns the shard of glass in a clockwise motion, the jagged glass cutting and twisting his insides.

On cue, Misty clamps down on Smoothie's tongue with her teeth and bites so hard that she ends up biting off the tip of his tongue. She spits out his bloody tongue while Smoothie falls to the ground, screaming and grabbing his face. Strings of blood dribbled from the cracks between his fingers. She pulls out the shock stick from behind her back and does exactly what she originally planned, except for sticking that shock stick where the sun doesn't shine. Instead, she takes it one step further and as soon as Deco aims the gun at Misty, he shouts out to the others. In that small speck of a window where the gangster mouths the first syllable in the word *bitch*, she jams the shock stick straight into his throat, as though she's plugging that noisy sound machine of his mouth. The sudden shock causes Deco's eyes to roll in the back of his head.

Deco is down for the count, unconscious, maybe dead; the gun is lying on the ground. The shock stick, which is lodged in the back of Deco's throat, loosens from Misty's grip. She tries to cling onto the handle, even yanks on it several times during his stagger; however, the shock stick is so deep in his throat that it appears stuck.

Desperate for a weapon, Misty finds one, the most obvious one: Deco's handgun.

Before the others can make a move, Misty darts toward the gun, grabs it off the ground, then opens fire on the other gangsters. Missing each one, except for Smoothie, who she shoots in the shoulder, although, only a graze but jolting enough for the tongueless gangster to violently spin him around like a top; both Rimes and Smoothie, despite their injuries, are still able to dodge the remainder of gunshots. Smoothie recovers and seeks cover behind a concrete post and while he hides, he spits out gobs of blood from his mouth.

Misty drunkenly empties the entire clip.

Despite a valiant effort by the two sisters, Count lands a blow to Violet's face, his knuckles connecting with her chin. The blow dazes Violet, causing her to fall back to the ground.

As both Shaman and Count turn their sights on Misty, who's now defenseless, Misty backpedals away. She shoots a glance at a wobbly Violet, who's still shaken up by the startling blow and can hardly stand on her own two feet.

"Come on, Vigh," she cries. "Get up!"

Violet reaches for the car keys in her pocket and as she grabs hold of them, Rimes stomps on the back of her shoulder, forcing her back to the ground.

While backpedaling away from the two gangsters, Misty spots a dark figure in the corner of her eye. She rotates around, only to find Cashel stepping out of the shadows.

Worn loosely over his hand is the artifact.

"Stay behind me," Cashel instructs, as he steps in front of Misty, who, despite the sheer horror of the situation, is left in awe by the artifact and how Cashel is able to wear it on his hand like a glove. Which makes her wonder about those people who were apparently killed by the artifact and if Cashel played any role in their deaths.

Cashel distracts the gangsters long enough for Misty to help a dazed Violet to her feet. The two flee, both Misty and Violet, Misty's arm wrapped around the body of her big sis, doing most of the heavy lifting by dragging her from the scene, while Cashel stands his ground and puts up a fight.

Wanting first dibs on Cashel, Shaman steps forward.

Cashel throws a right hook, the artifact catching Shaman's chin. Metal clashes with bone—on both ends, the bottom of Shaman's chin and Cashel's fingers, as well as knuckles, resulting in the bone, including all of his teeth, to shatter like glass. He grabs the bottom half of his face, the bruised skin along his chin holds the crushed bone like a tiny pouch of gravel. His entire chin is destroyed, shattered, the impact of blow so violent that it resonates up his entire face.

With his face fragile and painful to touch, Shaman spits out crushed teeth, which have been reduced to sand-like grains, from that swollen hole of a mouth.

As for Cashel's right hand, it's completely broken, nearly every bone in his hand, like Shaman's jaw, shattered, for two reasons: the first and most obvious, Cashel's not properly wearing the artifact; and the second, the artifact doesn't recognize the body of its wearer—in other words, the former police officer's blood, which means the artifact is currently connected, *bound*, or better, linked to Misty Boole, who, if you remember, cut her finger along its mouth when she first discovered it back at the warehouse.

Clutching the wound in his gut, Rimes pulls out a gun with his other hand and before opening fire on Cashel, Cashel pushes through the pain and knocks the gun from his hand at the last second and lands yet another crushing blow with the artifact; however, the artifact ends up breaking Cashel's hand for good, this time every single bone in his hand—all twenty-seven—shattered like glass.

Unlike the previous blow to Shaman's face, the blow isn't as damaging to Rimes's face; and yet, it sends him a few feet back, causing him to stagger and take a beat to regain his composure.

Surprised by Cashel's strength, as well as the pair of jacked up brass knuckles he's wearing, Rimes shakes off the blow with a laugh and asks Cashel, "What the fuck is you rockin', boy?"

Cashel doesn't respond, too much in agony, his posture weak.

The artifact, Cashel realizes, is making the pain more intense as it radiates up his entire arm, and he has no other choice than to try to remove it.

While attempting to remove the artifact, one of the metal fingers unfolds like a claw, revealing a dagger-like blade. As Cashel peels away the artifact, it releases the blade between his ring and middle ring, causing his hand to split in two halves.

Left in excruciating pain, Cashel cries out as the artifact dangles from his V-shaped hand.

"Gimme that," Rimes says greedily to the remaining gangsters: Smoothie, who's in pain and yet incredibly pissed, rising from his cowered position behind the post, then Count. Deco's still down, possible dead from taking over fifty thousand volts straight to the dome, and Shaman can neither speak nor hardly hold his head up for the bottom half of his face has been rearranged like a mosaic painting. "I want what's on his hand," Rimes demands while pointing at the glistening artifact. "Gimme that shit! Right now!"

As the two sisters arrive at the car, Misty helps Violet, who's still out of it, to the passenger seat, closes the door behind her, and then rushes around the car; and as she's about to enter, she watches the gangsters beat Cashel senseless.

Rimes towers over Cashel, who's slumped over on both of his knees, picks up the gun from the ground, and shoots Cashel directly in the head, execution-style.

Misty gasps, covering her mouth in horror.

Once the gangsters turn their sights back to the sisters, Violet calls out to Misty, who hurries inside the car. She starts up the ignition and speeds away from the scene.

Back to Rimes, who brushes off the two fleeing the scene and redirects his attention back to the artifact.

As Rimes pulls the artifact from Cashel's split hand, the blade flicks outward and erects all on its own, startling Rimes, as well as the others.

Before Rimes can step away, the artifact suddenly springs upward and grabs hold of Rimes's face, crushing it like a soda can. The artifact leaps from Rimes's face—or what's left of it—and ends up killing Count by shooting directly through his body, leaving him with a gaping hole inside his chest cavity. Smoothie makes a last-ditch effort to flee from the scene; however, the artifact finishes him off, grabbing hold of his spine from behind and ripping it from his body as he runs away!

Back to Misty, who's left in a state of shock after witnessing Cashel being executed before her eyes.

She's driving fast and reckless, the adrenaline like a drug.

"Slow down," Violet groans.

Misty doesn't listen to her sister; in fact, she does the opposite of what Violet utters.

"Goddamn it, Misty!" Violet cries out, using whatever strength she has left. "You're gonna get us killed!"

Eventually, Violet talks some sense into Misty and she pulls over on the side of the road and breaks down in tears.

After the two settle down, Misty continues driving. They make it to the highway, which is partially blocked with abandoned cars, but passable. As Misty drives out of Kingsport, she looks in the rear view mirror.

"Don't look back, you got me?" Violet says. "It's time we put this place behind us."

"How?" asks Misty.

"One day at a time," Violet says, her words comforting Misty.

As the night rages on, the two sisters drive south for about an hour until they finally run out of gas in front of an old, dilapidated bridge that locals call "Raven's Beak," where the Walabique River fingers outward into a web of five other rivers, one of them being Vermillion River, which runs through their father Dante's hometown, Paige. Misty puts the car in neutral, then helps Violet push the car from the highway to the woods where they hide and camouflage the car with tree branches.

The two sisters contemplate taking shelter under Raven's Beak, which Violet concludes will be much safer than sleeping inside the car. In the back and forth debate, Violet's argument holds the most footing: "Options," she emphasizes for Misty.

Locked—or better yet, trapped inside a car, they have very little options, including the most vital one, which is the ability to run away, if any threats should arise or worse, if they should be ambushed while being stuck inside a car surrounded by glass that can easily be broken.

After Violet makes her case to Misty that the bridge is a safer option to spend the night, she wins the argument.

Misty follows her sister down a hill toward the riverbank, and the two seek shelter under the bridge.

While trying to find a soft spot on the rocky soil but failing to make herself comfortable due to the blaringly loud quietness surrounding her, Misty asks Violet about a next course of action.

"For now," Violet says, "rest." She hands Misty a wool sweatshirt from Mrs. Taurus's bag and tells her to stay warm—it's going to be a long night. "I'll take first watch while you sleep."

She touches the material.

"Allergic, remember?"

"Right," Violet says, her voice trailing off. "How could I forget?"

"Well, considering everything that just happened, I'll give a free pass. Besides, I'm way too hot and wired to sleep."

"Just try."

"No way."

"Fine," Violet says annoyingly. "*You* keep watch. And wake me up in about an hour. You got it?"

"Sure thing, Queen Vigh," Misty says in a whimsical manner. "Lil' Pomp and Lil' Power at your service."

"No playing, Miss," Violet says, that big sis tone returning to her voice.

"I got your back," Misty says, more annoyed. "Sleep."

"When morning arrives, we'll come up with a plan."

Violet closes her eyes and rests against the side of a concrete pillar. The sound of the river lulls her to sleep.

On the lookout for nocturnal animals in the woods, including the human kind, Misty ends up mentally wearing herself out after forcing her eyes open while scanning her surroundings.

For many years, in fact, as far back as Misty can remember, she has spent the nights among the sounds of her manmade environment, whether it be from the white noise-like sounds of an air condition running to the sleep app on her phone to a bumpy, metronome-like *tick*, *tick*, *tick* of the rickety ceiling fan spinning at the highest speed to brutal street ambience outside her bedroom window, yet strangely, despite the inconsistency of these very sounds or noises, from mechanical to violent in nature, Misty found comfort in them. Now, with all of those sounds gone, the sound of the natural world feels almost deafening and causes her ears to almost radiate.

Despite her eyes adjusting to the night darkness, Misty's eyelids eventually grow heavier by the minute. She sits for about thirty minutes next to Violet, who's sound asleep; and by the time she hits the forty-five minute mark, she's drunk with exhaustion. The constant sound of the river drowns out smaller noises, including footsteps, which leave her in a heightened state of paranoia.

After an hour of mentally draining the energy from her body, she lies down on her side and drifts into the constant flowing sound of the river, which, after awhile, begins to sound more and more like the AC back at home, only amplified by ten.

Misty's ear catches one of those smaller noises underneath the fleeing water, this one being the sound of gravel moving. Her head turns toward the noise and while searching for the source of the noise in the darkness, her eyes open and close, like the shutter of a lens.

As Misty drifts back into a deep sleep, the artifact climbs up her leg and crawls like a spider onto her hand.

A stinger-like needle shoots outward from the center—or mouth—of the artifact and injects itself into Misty's flesh. Misty doesn't budge an inch and remains completely unaware of the jab due to the past events, which have left her drained of energy despite being wired only a thirty or so minutes ago.

After acquiring a taste of, not only Misty's blood, but also her deepest desires that drive her, including the words that inspired Misty's love for photography, in fact, it was Violet's words that helped nurture her sister's pursuits, Violet telling her in the wee hours of night after she returned home from a second job as a delivery driver, *"Your eye is your voice,"* the artifact suddenly releases the needle from Misty's hand and crawls up her body until settling around the right side of her face. The animated metal fingers connect to one another like a mechanism, then fold, form, and finally, fit around the upper part of her right cheekbone, as well as her eye in the shape of a letter C. The artifact, which has shrunken to the size of a silver dollar, once more jabs the soft and fleshy part underneath Misty's eye with the same needle, initiating a process known as "coupling."

Misty wakes, only to find herself sitting in a creaky wooden chair inside a dark office.

"Vigh?" she says, searching for her big sis.

While anticipating a response from her sister, Misty feels a weight, as heavy as bruise, along the right side of her face, irritating enough for Misty to pick at yet growing increasingly numb the more she becomes aware of its presence.

With her fingers, she touches the metallic artifact on her face and tries to make sense of it. She doesn't know what it is or how it ended up on her face. She suddenly panics, as she begins to touch the rest of her face with her hands; and as she begins to feel each groove of the artifact, each bump, each narrow trench along its archaic design, the right side of Misty's face goes completely numb. Once more, Misty feels for the artifact but all she feels is smooth skin along her face, no artifact; instead, the artifact dupes her into believing that nothing is on her face when, in fact, the artifact has already coupled with her body by means of tapping directly into her nervous system, a puppeteer, a certified expert in hypnosis, both pulling its user's nerves like the strings of a puppet while, at the same time, subjugating its user into believing "There is nothing to see here," a sort of swirly-eyed parlor trick cast by a power as old as time itself.

"*You don't find it*," a voice says in the dark. "*It* finds you."

Inside the office, objects start to materialize, first a desk and then a bookshelf, then, finally, a strange silhouette of a man standing in the corner of the room. The man dressed in a beige cardigan over matching black attire and a black baseball cap steps from the shadows, revealing himself to Misty.

The author.

Stanley Pruitt.

With a spotlight shining down on him, he says more directly to Misty, "Which means it saw something in you that it could use to its advantage."

Bewildered, Misty says, "It? What's it?"

"Annexus," he says, "The Ancient Ones of Mt. W'ki, short for D'onwake, call it the 'Hand of E'Raknish,' the very thing you've been holding onto all night."

"So, this is a dream, right?"

"Does it feel like a dream?" asks Stanley.

Misty looks around the dim office.

"Honestly," she says, furrowing her brow. "That's weird." She looks down at her hand and says, "What is this?"

"I was once in your exact same predicament, Misty," Stanley says and steps closer, the spotlight following his every movement. "Only for me, it saw my need for vengeance after I lost my wife and son."

Out of curiosity, Misty feels the right side of her face once more.

"Don't bother," Stanley says. "It's already done."

"What does it want?" asks Misty.

Stanley returns with a question: "What does every living thing want in life?"

Misty shrugs, says more straightforward, "To be loved, I guess. . . "

"I wish that were true, Misty."

"Then what—"

"*Control*," he says. "And it will give it to you, if that's what her heart desires."

"I just want people to see me," Misty says.

Stanley smirks at the comment and takes a beat.

"After my thirst for vengeance eventually lessened, I felt the same way. Like you, I wanted people to see me. To *listen* to what I had to say. To *read* what I had to write."

"And did they?"

Stanley pauses, another beat.

"They did," he says, his once mellow eyes sharpening. "And my words were deafening."

"So," Misty drawls, "it's like some kind of an enhancement or something. . . "

"That's one way of looking at it, although. . . " Stanley tilts his head to the side in thought, ". . . for some, it can bring out the very worst in humanity."

The spotlight cuts off, revealing a projector-like screen behind Stanley, the walls displaying the images of a serial killer, a former lightweight boxing champion turned psychopath, using the E'Raknish to murder his victims by means of punching their souls from their bodies. The serial killer uses the artifact, E'Raknish, as though it's a glove, providing him with three extra fingers, one next to the index, one in the middle, and another next to the pinkie.

Then, the aftermath, investigations into the serial killer known as "TKO," originally dubbed Kayo, or "KO," before the media changed the name for more "punchy" headlines.

Among the investigations into TKO, the seasoned police officer turned detective, Detective Dat Kneemo, Cashel's former partner and mentor, obsessed with TKO, disobeys orders from his sergeant and consumes his hours while off-duty to track down and catch the notorious serial killer but, except for the surveillance footage of a man wearing an artifact on his hand while exiting a shady nightclub, comes up empty-handed—or does he?

"For others. . . " Stanley says, as each story of each previous user unfolds behind him, ". . . it can save a life."

The screen displays a young man who Misty also recognizes.

Rowan Oxley.

Images of Rowan using E'Raknish to manipulate or trick women into having sex with him. The touch of the rare unearthly metal on each woman's perspired flesh causing them to fall into a trance-like spell, which wields them against their will. Lastly, after being overwhelmed with the guilt of having taken advantage of vulnerable women, images of Rowan forcibly ripping the artifact, E'Raknish, from his hand, resulting in Rowan's hospitalization where, during his recovery, he meets a fiercely attractive young woman—"Emma," she says to Rowan. "Emma Ambrose."

The screen fades to black behind Stanley, who steps closer to Misty.

He says closely, "You're inside an ancient jigsaw puzzle that stretches back to the beginning of time. And you, Misty, *you* are one of the final pieces of the puzzle."

"You mean," she says, "after this thing is done with me, it will find others?"

"Yes."

"How many?"

"I'm afraid that's not for me to decide."

As Misty stares into Stanley's now metallic eyes, she once again touches the side of her face and as her hand falls below, asks, "Who are you?"

Wearing a similar smirk as before, Stanley grabs hold of the darkness behind him, then pulls it down, like a curtain, revealing the belly of a fiery volcano, as well as the members of a darkly dressed tribe, Annexus, standing next to a stream of hot lava. Members of the tribe break down a suit of armor, E'Raknish, from a knight of the High Order after dumping his body into a pool of lava. The once-knight in shining armor now stripped bare screams out as his body ignites into a glaring spark before melting into a puddle of flesh and bone.

Tribe members divvy out the pieces of armor to one another, each one fitting accordingly to a part of their bodies, one member wearing a template on a hand while another member, for example, wearing it on a foot or even head, depending on the area or extremity of each user's deficiency, or, on the contrary, a part of the body that, in Misty's simplistic observation, requires enhancement.

She looks around her surroundings, the office gone. She moves her eyes downward and realizes she's standing inside a volcano. The heat of the lava, like nothing she has ever experienced before, presses against her face. Misty follows Stanley down a rocky black hill, the ground below her as hot as coals. The two arrive at a flat area along the lava stream where Stanley walks her over to the Annexus tribe. Each member flanks the two until they find themselves circled by the tribe. She can't help but notice their red, coarse-skinned faces, some blistered, others tumorous, hideous and hard to hold a stare. She turns to Stanley, who's no longer dressed as Stanley Pruitt, the author, but rather a member of the Annexus tribe.

The tribe member walks up to Misty, then touches her on the right side of the face.

"Embrace us," he says, his voice deeper and throatier.

In the background, the other shadowy-faced members repeatedly hum the words "*Whesh'a, wash'a, umm*" as though it's a strange chant.

Again: *Whesh'a, wash'a, umm.*

The hums seep into Misty's ears, into her brain.

Without Misty putting up much of a fight, the tribe member reaches his red, raw fingers into Misty's right eye. Those warm raw fingers push further and further into her eye socket, pushing aside Misty's eyeball until he's hand-deep inside her head. He readjusts his slippery wrist and twists it slightly before he pushes his hand further inside her head, now elbow-deep. Her knees suddenly buckle from the weight of his body. She staggers and then sways back and forth. The tribe member softens Misty's landing as he wraps his other arm around her upper body and helps ease Misty to the ground where he forces his entire arm into her head.

With his other hand, he pulls open her stretched-out eye socket as if it's a door made out of rubber and then climbs his way into Misty's head.

THE MARK OF THE ARMADILLO
AUGUST 22, 2048
FISHER'S NECK, VIRGINIA

PISSED drunk off illegal booze, Edgar, former owner of a family-owned grocery store before the store went out of business and was unable to compete with the other major retailers during the last pandemic, rips the worn sign of President Lockhart's upcoming bid for the 2048 reelection from the side of the building and urinates all over his doctored face.

"Fuckin' crook," Edgar slurs, as he sways back and forth. The drunken anger grips him and the very thought of what Lockhart has done to a once great and well-respected country, including crippling the economy and leaving millions of hardworking Americans without a sustainable income, drives his rage. "Fuckin' spawn of Satan. . ."

"Hey," one of the security guards monitoring the nearby gallery calls out to Edgar, "get lost, bum!"

"Fuck you!" Edgar cries out, as he almost trips over his own two feet. "I have every right to be here! You get lost, you nihilistic azzhole!"

"Try me, old timer," the guard says to Edgar. "I make one call and you disappear."

"Oh yeah?!?"

"This is your last warning."

With one eye squinted, Edgar peers at the fancy man with his good eye, realizes the power he wields, and how that power can very well make him, as claimed, disappear, not only from the alleyway, but also from existence. Has several buddies, as untrustworthy as the very system that they claimed destroyed their livelihoods, who went missing some months back. Vets, as well as laborers and retail workers whose jobs were stolen from a robot: each one has a different narrative yet carries a similar theme. After living off the streets for two years, Edgar has created his fair share of both friends and enemies. Regardless of how he may feel about his territorial rivals, he knows that they wouldn't go out without a fight. Mouthy sons of bitches who'd put even the toughest wise guy flat on his ass if he looked at them funny. Despite how a modern day society, including the ruling class, may feel about Edgar, what has become of him, and the many others like Edgar, it's not a hard sell for an average man, who can barely afford a roof over his head, to have respect for another fellow man who takes the responsibility in defending, not only his pride, but also his name, even if he has been stripped of it.

Edgar squares off with the guard, tempting to make his stand.

As the weight of these past two years overwhelms him, Edgar shouts out, "FUCK YOU, you FUCKIN' SATANIC NAZI-ASS TURD! GO FUCK A GOAT!"

Nearby, several of the guests waiting in a line outside the art gallery turn toward the commotion across the street.

The hostess opens the doors and welcomes the next couple in line into the gallery where the legend herself, Misty Boole, the artist informally known as "Miss T," makes her rounds through the packed crowd, circulating from one fat cat to another, thanking the patrons for their support.

Many celebrities among the crowd, including famous athletes, actors, activists, influencers, techies, who traveled all the way from Silicon Valley, as well as D.C. lobbyists and local politicians: all of them gathered shoulder-to-shoulder inside a renovated building, which used to be a Methodist chapel on 5th and Market Street.

The entire building gutted, the wooden columns removed, walls replaced. The façade, once brick, has been torn down and replaced with glass.

The nicely dressed couple provides their names for the hostess, who checks the list of guests on her eTablet before allowing the two to enter the gallery.

"Welcome to *Escape from Kingsport,*" she greets the couple again as if the previous greeting was all for show.

Above the mouth of the entrance is a graffiti style flame logo with the words:

"ESCAPE FROM KINGSPORT"

The couple enters the gallery where high-definition photographs of Misty's perilous journey in the city of Kingsport during the infamous blackouts hang on the white walls.

Misty's assistant, Tameron, notices her boss picking at the piece of golden jewelry worn on the side of her face, the piece being E'Raknish, which has taken a brand new shape but her assistant only recognizes it as part of Misty's act: "Bothering you again?"

"No," Misty says, forcing herself to remove the glittery nail from her face. "Just an itch."

Commotion arises at the entranceway of the gallery.

Two people, bystanders, wearing the street on their worn clothes, try to sneak into the event.

Two sisters, Misty recognizes, as she makes her way to the front where the curator, Roslyn, is ordering security to remove the disrupters.

"We just want to see Miss T," says one of the sisters.

Misty steps in front of security before they handle the two sisters.

"Just let 'em stay," she says and turns to the sisters. She asks, "They're not gonna cause any trouble, are you?"

"Of course," the other sister says. "We couldn't buy a ticket."

As Misty offers to let the two enter the gallery, Roslyn once more orders security to remove the two nuisances.

"Roslyn," Misty says over the disturbance, "they mean no harm."

"This is a special event, Misty," Roslyn says, more closely. "And I'm not going to have the *public* come in here and ruin everything for everybody."

"You win," Misty says in defeat, as security looms behind her, ready to take action.

As security escorts the two sisters from the gallery, a friend of Misty's, Axious, an art critic from New York, approaches her, smartphone raised in frustration.

"What is up with this town?" he asks in a sassy voice. "Haven't got a signal in like an hour. Can you, like, call up the mayor?"

"I wish," Misty says, brushing off Axious's concerns. "I always receive bad service whenever I'm here. I talked to Ron about it and he says it has something to do with the materials the builders used. Compared it to a Faraday cage."

"More like a dead zone," Axious utters from the corner of his mouth.

"Don't you worry, Axious," Misty reassures Axious. "Take a look around the gallery. *Embrace* the story before you."

"Too nostalgic for my taste."

Misty rolls her eyes.

"Well, dear, think of tonight as an exercise in self-control."

"Who do you think you're talking to? If I had any ounce of self-control, I would've stayed clear from The Greek. Besides, why'd you invite him? You know our history."

Misty follows Axious's eyes toward The Greek, the young model wearing the black blazer, no shirt underneath, chest exposed, flirting with other guys.

Caught off guard by the mistake, she points to her assistant.

"Blame Tameron," she says jokingly. Then touches Axious on the shoulder. "You want my advice, Axious?" Axious holds his head up, eyes wide, listens. "Chill the eff out. . . "

Misty wanders off. Only a few steps in her stroll she spots the photograph of her older sister. In the photo, Violet is driving through the night. The night vision filter highlights a pensive expression on her big sis's face as her eyes focus on the road ahead. Misty specifically remembers that exact moment when the photo was taken: right after they came across that dead couple on the side of the road. The Taurus's. The mood in the car was incredibly tense and filled with uncertainty, Misty recalls, yet there was a brief sense of relief for discovering the ride.

A hand touches Misty on the shoulder.

A voice in Misty's ear: "*She would be so proud of you.*"

Misty rotates around where another socialite named Doug, sweet yet clingy, spawned from wealth, son of a current sitting Senator, is standing before her, congratulating her on her success, in particular *Knights in Kingsport*, the first gallery that helped launch her career, turning her into a force in the industry for her startling and at times, breathtaking photography, despite all of the controversy surrounding the first showing in New York, most—if not, all of the shots in *Knights in Kingsport*, in fact, captured by her older sister, Violet, after Misty was abducted by a colorful group of marauders who were on their way to Kingsport when they stumbled upon two famished sisters hiding out in an abandoned house alongside a back road. Using Misty's CaMMDoc, Violet tracked down the marauders, found her little baby sis, and after a daring rescue attempt, ended up escaping Kingsport for a second time with Misty; however, sadly, Violet died from her injuries, leaving Misty to trek the wilderness alone until power was eventually restored.

"Thank you, Doug," she says, slightly choked up from the photograph. "Without Vigh," she glances around, acknowledging the money in the room, "my dream never would've come true. I dedicate all of this to her."

Before the emotion can overwhelm her, Misty continues to make her rounds, stopping by yet another duo, two visual artists, like Miss T, collectively known as Shutter/Bug, the purple-haired gal with a tatted up face being Shutter and her lanky partner dressed in Goth getup, Bug, who are talking about "*Midnight Magic*," Miss T's previous project, a series of negative photos that depicted the day in the life of a stray cat named "Blue" and her adventures throughout the outskirts of the ruined city, Kingsport. She won several photography awards for the series.

Hearing her name over the chatter, Misty sneaks up behind Shutter and welcomes the two to the gallery.

Shutter addresses one particular photograph on the wall.

"I like this piece here," she says to Misty, then Bug, "It's got a dash of *Knights in Kingsport* vibe, doesn't it?"

Shutter is referring to the photograph captured by Misty's CaMMDoc.

"Only more amateur," Misty teases her own work.

"Anything but," Shutter says, admiring the photograph while emphasizing, "Miss T. The T must stand for '*Trending*' because it seems like you're trending everyday."

Misty waves off Shutter's compliment.

"Stop it already," she says, humbled.

In the photo is the downtown street of Kingsport. Some of the buildings alongside the street are on fire, also overturned cars, including a police cruiser.

"The use of natural light is exquisite, don't you think?" Shutter says to Bug.

"Can't believe you captured all of this on a CaMMDoc," Bug says to Misty.

"Whatever works, right?"

She leaves the duo to pick apart the piece and runs into yet another socialite, the photograph before her taking place farther down the timeline of the story, "*Escape from Kingsport.*"

In the photo is the head gang member, Rimes, shooting Cashel in the head. The flash of the gunfire highlighting the gangster's face.

"Truly transcendent," she says to Misty.

After thanking the socialite, she moves to other pieces where other guests analyze and pick apart each and every detail of the photograph; nonetheless, each one pulling the star of the show aside to shower her with warm accolades until Misty lays her eyes on one guest in particular.

"Her again?" says Misty.

She motions Tameron over.

Once Tameron acknowledges Misty, she glides her way to Misty.

"What's a matter?" asks Tameron.

"Her again," Misty says and subtly nods at the guest.

"Oh," Tameron says, her voice lowered. "Her. Just be nice—"

At the last second, Misty catches the guest's eye.

Shooing away Tameron, Misty walks over to another piece and follows another guest's hand as he points to an area in the photo that she hasn't seen before—or at least, missed when she was mapping out the complete story: the initials, F.S.G., engraved at the bottom of an expensive gold wristwatch worn by Smoothie, one of the gangsters who was beats away from assaulting Misty, the action-like shot, purposeful or accidental—Misty doesn't quite remember much details considering the chaos of the moment—taken right as she was falling to the ground. The CaMMDoc switched to video instead of photo, which captured the moment in front of Your Market. During the editing process, she collected the best still to use, still somewhat blurry but it was the blurriness, which only made the photograph even more mysterious.

Mindful of that one particular guest, Shaolin, Misty carefully watches her eye as it lands on the piece.

Shaolin is a philanthropist from Silicon Valley, was part of the creative team behind MyCircle when it first launched, gathering millions of accounts and becoming one of the most popular social media platforms thirty years ago. Her husband, currently separated from Shaolin, is Franklin Sawyer Gunnar, and it doesn't dawn on Misty that he bears the same initials—F.S.G.—until she eavesdrops on her conversation about Frank, the former police commissioner of Kingsport before it went tits up, and how he'd have himself a heart attack if he saw these images, which act as a stark reminder of how fast a once beautiful city can fall into darkness when placed in wrong hands.

In a side thought, she says with resentment, "Especially in the thin-skinned hands of a slimy weasel like McGovern."

"What a nightmare," one of her handlers comments.

"For me," Shaolin says more gleefully, as she reaches over and pulls Misty closer, "I absolutely can't get enough of Miss T's work. Such a young talent, she is. Such a *raw* eye, she has."

"Thank you," Misty says, shyly. "But let's put the politics aside for one night, shall we?"

"Nonsense, Misty," Shaolin says and hands Misty a glass of champagne.

Misty declines the drink.

"Not old enough," she says.

The comment draws a few laughs from Shaolin's entourage.

Misty swallows her frustration and finally accepts the drink.

Shaolin and her friends make a toast to Misty and her outstanding work.

"Your work is political, dear," Shaolin says to Misty.

Caught off guard by the remark, Misty says, "I never looked at it that way, I guess."

"Serious? Your work screams politics."

"How so?"

Shaolin laughs off Misty's innocence.

"But of course your work not only exemplifies the ramifications of bad policy, but I'd like to think that it also brings to light—no pun intended—the collapse of a society that is dependent on everyday distractions and when having those distractions stripped away, the whole system collapses, leaving the very people who were once dependent on the system in a primitive state—or one may also like to think, their most *natural* state." She leans even closer. "Believe me when I tell you this: 'There's nothing in this world more entertaining than watching a man's head being blown off.'" With much exaggeration, she cups her mouth and whispers loud enough into her handler's ear for the others to hear: "Don't tell Frank."

Billows of laughter and stentorian *ha-has* erupt from the crowd that gradually forms behind Misty. Each guest and patron is left in awe by Shaolin's bluntness.

Left in a state of discomfort by, not only the philanthropist's comment, but also the overly chummy reaction to the comment, Misty politely excuses herself and as she's about to make her way toward the restrooms, she passes one final piece in *Escape from Kingsport*: a close-up shot of the side view mirror of the car as she and Violet are riding away from a fallen Kingsport. The photo was taken while Misty was driving, moments after witnessing a courageous police officer, Cashel Rose, being executed before her eyes. The images in the side view mirror were shocking at the time she documented them and worthy of capturing, regardless of the recent trauma: The silhouette of a fiery skyline shrunken down, displayed in the mirror, more or less, a thought piece filled with symbolism and the right amount of detail to sprinkle over a critic's own imagination. Misty forces herself to look away from the piece as the white wall behind it starts to crack and chip.

After taking a step closer, Misty follows the crack up the wall and as she runs her index finger over the crack veining upward, Tameron says from behind, "You all right, Misty?"

Misty pulls her finger away, turns to Tameron, then redirects her attention to the wall where the crack is nowhere to be found.

"Give me a sec, will you?" Misty asks, as she excuses herself.

Concerned, Tameron decides to follow Misty into the restroom.

"Misty," she says, entering the restroom behind Misty, "are you sure you're all right?"

"Must be a floater," Misty says and inspects the jewelry on the right side of her glossy face.

More visibly concerned by Misty's well-being, Tameron says in all seriousness, "You can't remove it, can you?"

Misty holds down her head.

"No," she says depressingly. "I can't, even when I try. It's like every time—"

"Hold that thought," Tameron interrupts and checks underneath each stall for any unwanted listeners. In the last stall, she finds two with thirsty noses doing pencil-thin red lines of modified VP-23. The two look up at Tameron, deer in headlights, gotcha.

"Out," Tameron orders. "Now!"

Once the VP-heads leave the restroom, she locks the door behind her for added privacy.

She asks Misty, "Have you been to a doctor?"

"They can't do anything about it." She looks up in the vanity mirror and says to Tameron's reflection, "I never wanted any of this, you know? It's all for show. I have absolutely nothing in common with these people."

"We both knew how hard this was going to be, to take a trip down memory lane."

"I'm just tired," Misty says. "I'm tired of pretending like this is normal. These people," she says, referring to the guests at the gallery, "they don't give a flying rat's ass about me, who I am, or where the hell I came from. They're vultures and I'm the carcass, and soon they'll discard me once I'm of no use to them." She reflects on a brief career as an outstanding photographer while Tameron once again reassures her that it's only natural to feel upset and these feelings will pass. In deep reflection, Misty says, "When I first started this venture, I wanted them to see me. The people. *My work*. Before this, before the fame," she glances down at her sparkling golden dress, "before all the fancy things that came with fame, I did it all for myself and I didn't have a care in the world. In a way, I was at peace. *My work* gave me peace of mind, dare I say, happiness, and my only fan was the one person in my life who saw me—me—" Misty pointed at her chest, her finger jabbing her left breast, "—for who I was. But after the positive reaction I received in New York and now, it's like I don't wanna do this for them anymore. I *don't* belong to them—"

Tameron says, "Don't talk like that, Miss. It's been a very long week. I've seen how overwhelming it can be for you." She pauses, thinks more about her words, and chooses them more carefully. "You know what? You're a hundred percent correct, Misty. This is *your* work. Not theirs. *Yours*."

She steps forward and hugs Misty.

"I say 'Fuck these elite assholes,'" she says. "Who the fuck are they? What the fuck makes them so special?"

Misty smiles and says more mindfully, "You're right. Fuck 'em."

After the short pep talk, Misty and Tameron exit the restroom.

Misty returns to the main floor to make her rounds, internally marveling at those who suck up to her and try to win over a piece of Misty—in essence, take a bite out of her through means of snapping a photo with the legendary "Miss T" or spuriously picking at Miss T's brain or even buying a piece from *Escape from Kingsport* for six or seven figures—name your price—only to later make a post about the recent purchase all in the name of "support" before inevitably Misty's piece winds up in a dusty attic space—but really, in the back of Misty's mind, all they receive in return is shit, great big blobs of figurative shit all over their filthy noses from having them stuck so far up Misty's ass. The thought alone of not only watching all of these insecure, smelly-nosed narcissists go out of their way to impress Misty for validation and cultural points, but also listening to each and every one of them praise her with insincere compliments while displaying a hidden sense of desperation, an eagerness to win her over so later they can control her, fills her with disgust so filmy and sticky that it feels as if she has walked through a kind of translucent membrane and now, her entire body is covered in it, making her so damn sick that she no longer looks at them as humans or even humans who bare similar characteristics as vultures, but rather these soulless miniature-sized figurines small enough to hold in the palm of her hand but make a damn mess of everything with all of their phlegm and wasted spittle.

As the event starts to wind down, Misty excuses herself from the figurines and redirects her attention toward the street outside where she spots several locals of Fisher's Neck, dirt poor and struggling to get by, salt of the earth and yet salty as ever as they should be after sitting on their hands and watching the rich become richer and more powerful after the spell of blackouts, which left nearly the entire workforce, the backbone of a nation built by callused hands, struggling to survive and make ends meet.

Among the locals on the sidewalk stands a young man, Darwin, who picks up the President Lockhart flyer off the side of the curb.

Alongside the tattoo of an armadillo on the fleshy area between his thumb and index finger, each one of his fingers above his worn and crusty knuckles is tattooed with a letter, altogether the letters spelling out the name "G-E-N-I-E." After looking over the flyer with disdain, he crumbles it in his hand. Misty picks out Darwin in the crowd, can't look away. It's his eyes and the fire in them. She has never seen him before, but she recognizes those eyes and the expression that surrounds them. She moves her eyes downward, toward Darwin's gold wristwatch.

With a sudden clarity, Misty draws her eyes back up to Darwin's eyes, and at that moment, everything starts to click.

The next morning, Misty wakes up with E'Raknish gone from her face. A weight has been lifted from not only her face, but also her body, especially her chest and shoulders.

Surprised and yet at the same time, relieved by the disappearance of E'Raknish, she touches her face, only to map out the lines, marks, and speed bumps next to her right eye in what appears like a pair of wicked crow's feet. She rushes to the restroom where she looks into the mirror and examines the change of color in her once black pupil, as well as the markings on the side of her face, not a scar but rather a deep imprint that she knows will only heal and eventually return back to normal over time.

Misty thinks out loud: "*Is the dream over?*"

The first thing Misty does after E'Raknish has left her face: She splashes her face with water over the sink. The feel of cool water against her face brings great relief.

She cancels a meeting with her agent, texts Tameron about taking the day off, and decides to spend the day all to herself. She puts on a pot of coffee and after the short brew, makes herself a cup of coffee, just the way she prefers: Very strong and very black.

While enjoying the rich and bold brew, Misty takes the cup outside where she stands behind the railing of the balcony of her condo overlooking the bay and watches white egrets majestically soar above the water. The reflection of the rising sun glares off the surface of the water, creating a sparkle-like effect.

After scrolling through her feed that consists of compliments from Miss T's loyal fan base, as well as comments, both positive and negative, from her most vocal admirers and haters, Misty closes the phone and without putting any extra thought into the matter, flings the phone into the bay. The phone makes a *plopping* sound as it hits the water, making a tiny splash.

Misty sits back in the chair and finds pleasure in the sight of the water, as well as the natural world thriving before her, and never has she felt more alive.

Another account

Cumshoe

Sign in

dalivia_plaut

Password

Login

☑ Remember me   Forgot password?

Create Account

Knot Town (Break a leg!)
Forwarded by Dalivia Plaut

NIKOLA Olívia Rose was seven-going-on-eight when she went missing. Her mother, Hilda Dulík Rose, a ninth grade Algebra instructor who taught at Plymouth High, knew that her sweet Nikola was in trouble when she never turned up after school. Nikola was like clockwork, a trait that she picked up from studying her old man's movements, as well as his patterns throughout the house. Like Hilda, he too was a creature of habit, driven by a strict diet of obedience and routine: from making the morning pot of coffee to ironing his shirt to turning off each light inside the house or inspecting the knobs on the gas stove before leaving to work, he was as predictable as the rising sun. The two schools, Plymouth and Nikola's school, Lincoln Elementary, slightly varied in duration (a typical school day at Plymouth ending an hour and a half earlier than Lincoln). After the last period was dismissed, Hilda would spend the quiet time tidying up the classroom or exhaust twenty-five minutes or so grading papers, quizzes and whatnot, before packing up her bag and calling it a day. When Hilda arrived home from school, the bus would drop off Nikola at the front of the neighbor-hood around three forty-five in the afternoon. She'd spot her daughter and the neighbor, Tiffany, walking down the hill before the two parted ways and said their goodbyes. Like Nikola, Tiffany was exceptionally quiet and kept mostly to herself. She enjoyed Nikola's company; yet, despite living on the next street over, Nikola felt as if she and Tiffany were worlds apart.

On the day of Nikola's disappearance, which was a Tuesday, Hilda checked the front dining room window where she saw Tiffany making her way onto her street.

As she watched the minutes pass, the mother's instinct grew stronger and stronger until, eventually, the thought of a worse case scenario consumed her. Thinking—in fact, praying—maybe Nikola stopped by Minnie's house to play with Minnie's pug Buggy, who was named after her ex-husband, Bugsy, Hilda gave her daughter till five before taking action.

Ten minutes after five, a feeling of dread washed over Hilda. The feeling, or rather, instinct, forced Hilda to search for Nikola, first stopping by the next-door neighbor's house where Minnie informed Hilda that she hadn't seen Nikola; in fact, she told Hilda that she never saw her daughter walking home after the bus dropped off the children.

Hilda then drove to Lincoln Elementary where she interrogated her daughter's teachers, including Nikola's Language Arts teacher, Ms. Wright, whom Hilda respected as a fellow teacher herself, but never saw eye-to-eye with her due to the rumored past affiliation with the Black Panther Party. Despite their strained relationship, Ms. Wright informed Hilda that Nikola was acting unusual in class—"Quieter than her normal self," Ms. Wright explained to Hilda.

After talking with Ms. Wright, she desperately continued the search for Nikola by stopping at each hangout spot in Bluefield. Being a small town and all, there were only a few of them: the playground and surrounding ball fields at Poet's Park; then, a popular candy shop, Candy Castle; the Town's Place Mall; the abandoned Mawk Daavy bridge, a seedy spot plagued with tetanus, where the older children played; then, lastly, Black Rock, said to be a meteor from outer space, a massive boulder about the size of a two-story house where high schoolers from Plymouth hung out, smoked dope, drank stolen beer, or rounded second base with chicks. Black Rock was specifically "off limits," and numerous times she warned Nikola, as well as Nikola's sister, Milo, to keep clear from the location and if she ever caught either one of them hanging out at Black Rock, they'd be grounded and forbidden to leave the house until they reached the age of reason.

Hours went by, and Nikola was nowhere to be found.

As day turned into night, word of Nikola's disappearance spread throughout Bluefield—fast, too, like a wildfire on a windy day—first stirring up at the local pub, Lucky's, where the drunks were spiced up at the very notion of being the one to rescue that Rose girl, the sound of a savior carrying a nice ring to it, where the newly knighted title of "hero" in a town that, on the contrary, wanted little-to-nothing out of them, except for their minor contribution in making sure the gears of a functional society remained greased, was like a gift from the heavens, their redemption, their moment to shine and prove and even exceed their own worth.

Nikola's father, Victor Cashel, a renowned doctor who once practiced in Philadelphia before opening up his own medical practice in Bluefield, contacted the sheriff's office, who then began an investigation into his daughter's disappearance.

Two days passed.

For those who knew Nikola best as "Knitty," a sickly girl who had quite an interest in playing with spools of yarn, they feared the worst had happened to Nikola, including Milo, two years Nikola's elder, and Nikola's only friend.

After the third day, Nikola's disappearance turned into the talk of Bluefield, a town west of Philadelphia where, like most small towns, everybody knew each other's business, including the business of Reginald "Reggie" Pelisse, a sex offender who was released from

Rhine Penitentiary in Mote County after serving a five-year stretch for exposing himself to minors at a drive-in theatre. Pelisse was the first one questioned by police, not only to squash hearsay, but also to tame a growingly angry mob with itchy trigger fingers and prevent it from turning up on Pelisse's front doorstep. Despite how much the police wanted Pelisse to have a hand in Dr. Rose's seven-year-old daughter's disappearance, Pelisse had an alibi: "Out of town, visiting his sister over the holidays." Reggie's sister confirmed to the police that her little brother was in Blankinton, Kentucky, on the day of Nikola's disappearance.

On the fourth day, as determined search parties continued to fight against the bite of winter and combed through every inch of the town, one of the members of the search party discovered a scarf in the woods. After the search party was called to the location, it was like following a trail of bread crumbs: first, a beige knit cap underneath a bed of leaves—Knitty's knit cap, Hilda concluded—then two beige mittens, same ones that Nikola wore. The rest of Nikola's bloodstained clothing was discovered close by. The sleeves and the pant legs were precisely cut by a blade of some kind. Sheriff Fisk ordered the deputies to clear the area. Deputies escorted the rescuers of the search party, including Victor, from what they were calling a "crime scene."

Deputy Collins, only two months with the sheriff's office—"Oh! Georgie Boy," his superiors called him, emphasizing the *Oh!*—discovered the body after following the trail of blood from the torn clothes to a burrow underneath an overturned tree.

Nikola.

"Knitty."

The girl who liked playing with yarn.

The body appeared as if it was turned inside out, and the very first thought that ran through the deputy's mind was perhaps an animal had gotten to it.

But the more Deputy Collins tried to wrap his head around the discovery—the notion alone sickened him to his core—he couldn't think of any animal out there of inflicting so much horror to a human body.

From what he gathered, the bones were nowhere to be found and all that remained was flesh and internal organs.

The entire skeleton, including the skull, missing. . .

Deputy Collins could barely contain himself as he cried out to Sheriff Fisk, who rushed over to the deputy.

Word of a body being discovered spread to the rescuers, who were waiting at the edge of the woods.

Eventually, the word found its way to Victor's ears.

The sheriff immediately ordered the deputies to keep Victor away from the crime scene.

Victor, who was surrounded by deputies as he struggled to hold himself together, managed to squeeze a word out of one of the deputies, who told Victor that a body had been, in fact, found.

But they still didn't know for sure if it it was Nikola.

The coroner was baffled after examining the body and after twenty-plus years of working in the morgue, hadn't seen anything like it before.

Sheriff Fisk brought in both Victor and his distraught wife, Hilda, to the morgue where they were guided to a table covered in a white sheet in the back of the morgue. The coroner slightly lifted the top part of the white sheet, revealing one half of the dead girl's face for her entire face had been ripped down the middle.

Once Victor and Hilda were shown the face—Hilda could barely bring herself to look—they identified the body as Nikola, their sweet and shy Knitty who possessed the power to brighten up any rainy day with a laugh or smile, despite how achy she was or how sick she felt.

After the coroner brought in a colleague, his mentor, a forensic pathologist from Chicago, to help out with the autopsy, the two found *no* blunt force trauma to Nikola's body nor any sign that foul play was involved, no defense wounds, not a single scratch, except the cuts along the arms and legs, as well as the standard Y-shaped incision, which connected with the other cuts along the arms, starting from each shoulder, then vertically running down the middle of Nikola's chest and abdomen until the incision continued past the pubis bone, then connected with the other cuts along the legs, appearing as if, in a way, the cuts traced Nikola's entire skeletal structure. What made these perfect, surgical-like incisions even stranger and more startling: The cuts were made from the inside of the body, not the outside!

Sheriff Fisk first started with Nikola's parents and questioned them about their relationship with Nikola. Each answer the two parents gave to the sheriff wasn't at all a surprise.

After the sheriff spoke with Victor and Hilda, he immediately ruled the two out as potential suspects.

Weeks turned to months.

No suspects.

No witnesses.

The mood of the town changed, bizarre rumors spread of Nikola's death, some including her killer being a doctor but more specifically, considering his background in medicine, Nikola's father, Victor, who lost many patients after the death of his daughter.

If it wasn't for hope of one day Nikola's murderer being brought to justice, then the thought of what happened to Nikola could've very well destroyed the spirits of the townspeople.

Eventually, Nikola's case went cold, like a lot of things in the small town of Bluefield.

SEND

COLD BY NATURE

ELLIS KROSS

BOOK TWO

THE GIRLFRIEND'S PLIGHT
NOVEMBER 20, 2048
PADADOCK, PENNSYLVANIA

AFTER returning home from a late afternoon doctor's appointment, Lacey wheeled her daughter, Selena, through the front doors of their two-story house and into a pitch-black living room.

Still somewhat groggy from a pain pill that she took before the doctor's visit, she groaned to Lacey, "More freaking blackouts? Serious, Mom? I thought they fixed the power. . . "

"I thought so too," Lacey said suspiciously.

The lights suddenly flicked on, revealing smiling heads surfacing from behind the furniture like gleeful gophers, as well as a pink banner suspended over the fireplace mantle, which read:

HAPPY BIRTHDAY, SELENA!!!

"Surprise!"

Startled by the sudden welcoming of what felt like a hundred voices yelling at her, Selena's heavy eyelids widened.

Her mouth opened like a yawn, briefly letting out a faint gasp.

Lacey touched her daughter on the shoulder before rubbing her back and telling her, "Happy birthday, Selena."

With a stunned look on her face, Selena said, "Did I miss something? My birthday was last month."

"I know, Selena," Lacey said. "With you in the hospital, we didn't have the chance to properly celebrate your birthday."

"Wow. . . " she said depressingly and flashed a drunken smile on her face, ". . . thanks. . . I guess."

Once the excitement wore off, Selena's friends, as well as the rest of the Barbarys, including her stepfather, Dean, her eighty-three year old nana, Eleanor Barbary, who moved into the house last year after her husband died from a sudden cardiac arrest, and her younger brother Bret, who turned seventeen over summer and had grown a few sprouts of hair along his dark milk mustache the last time Selena saw him before he took a week off from school to compete in a high-stakes video gaming tournament in Austin where he won over ten thousand dollars in prizes, revealed themselves behind their hidden positions in the living room. Also in attendance were four of Selena's closest friends from the team who, except for her boyfriend John, whom Selena had been dating since her junior year at Del Soaka Falls, carpooled together from Brighton University to Selena's hometown, which, according to GPS, was roughly a two and a half hour drive.

"Far enough to keep Mom away," she'd say about her mother who had a knack for sticking her head in places where it didn't belong, mainly a decked-out bedroom of an eighteen-year- old high school senior who cherished space or what little *space* she had inside a nest that felt as if it was getting smaller and smaller by the minute. Selena, who recently turned nineteen three weeks ago, was planning to stay in Padadock for the duration of her recovery while she took a semester off from school. Selena had no other choice in the matter. A dormitory filled with tempestuous young folks was no place for "special accommodations," and yet, if she did change her mind and wanted to go back to Brighton (Strangely, despite random urges that crept up throughout the day, especially living with two parents who, at times, could be as annoying or as intrusive as a gnat, a part of Selena didn't want to return, at least not until her leg was a ninety-nine point nine per-cent better, most of her doubts centered around sleep or a lack of sleep she'd receive in a dorm room), her mother wouldn't allow Selena to return back to school in her current condition.

Selena's nana was first to make a comment about her grand-daughter's condition, poking fun at the wheelchair, telling Selena that the two could ride around the neighborhood, Selena on her wheelchair, Eleanor on her motorized scooter. The comment alone fleshed out a previous argument between Selena and Dean, Selena being more upset at Dean, rather than her doctor for not prescribing her with an electric wheelchair (She had her eye on one of those fancy wheelchairs with all the bells and whistles: a joystick and heated seats and stereo). However, considering the cost of the surgeries, the wheelchair didn't meet Selena's insurance deductible.

After Selena made her case, the other four from Brighton, who hadn't seen Selena since her second surgery, stepped forward to greet her.

Two of the four girls were stopping by Selena's to wish her a speedy recovery right before heading to the airport to catch a flight back home for Thanksgiving. The other two were going to spend Thanksgiving in Virginia with Mazzy's family.

Among the four to show their support for Selena were Kellie, who held the school record for the most wins in hurdling, Mazzy, a long jumper who was admitted into Brighton under an athletic scholarship, Whisper, who was one of the fastest runners on the team and also won 1ˢᵗ place in the hundred meter dash last year at State Finals, then, lastly, Azalea, who excelled at the javelin.

Her friends admired the pink scars from the screws and plates along Selena's right leg. Kellie made a comment on how the leg no longer looked like Frankenstein's monster.

Then, another teammate pressed on her leg, trying to feel the screws, altogether nine screws, as well as two plates, holding Selena's femur and tibia together, three screws and a titanium rod, Selena said, in her femur, which suffered from a comminuted fracture (which was when the bone broke into three or more pieces), then her tibia, which suffered from the worst and possibly most gruesome break, an open (compound) fracture, requiring six screws, the two breaks said to take three to twelve months to fully heal; however, Selena and her mother's only concern was the risk of yet another infection. On a lighter note: She said that she was looking forward to "screwing" with TSA agents whenever she'd "pass through metal detectors."

According to Selena's mother, it was a miracle that Selena was able to keep the leg, considering the severity of the breaks and the infection that developed after a second surgery; and with impulse, Lacey was tempted to remind her daughter of a higher power, "*The*" Higher Power that saved Selena. But with Selena's friends here to show their support, she knew that it was best to keep her personal beliefs to herself for she felt as if it wasn't the appropriate time to explain why Selena still had her leg or based on the inevitable reaction she'd receive from Selena—a natural response of a growing young woman pushing back against the "told you so," mother-knows-best mentality that Lacey often shoved down her throat—rehash a traumatic event. The main reason Lacey decided to bite her tongue was that everybody who was at the Fall Classic, which was held the following weekend after the first day of autumnal equinox, except for Lacey's mother, who was at home baking a vanilla cake, and Bret, often referred to as his black hooded avatar "Bet," who was playing a co-op with gamer heads, could hear her bones breaking throughout the indoor arena.

One couple, Sonya and Jonah, who were "chilling out" in the upper bleachers, told Rella, a teammate of Selena's, they could hear the break as well, which Sonya compared to the sound of a firecracker. The alarming *crack* of Selena's bones breaking reverberated across the track, some attendees even mistaking the sound for a gunshot, prompting momentary panic. Selena's doctors weighed several options and one of them, according to a specialist, included amputating the leg. For Selena, that option was clearly not on the table.

"The girls told me the hospital lost power during your surgery," Mazzy, who hadn't seen her teammate since the accident, said to Selena.

"That's what my mom told me," Selena said, still somewhat upset at Mazzy for her excuse for not seeing her during her temporary stay at the hospital.

"It also went out again right before we were about to leave the doctor's office," Lacey said with frustration, as Selena wheeled herself into the living room. "I don't know what in the world is going on—"

Those in Selena's vicinity made sure to steer clear from the leg, which was held outward in a secured yet stiff and fixed position along the leg rest.

"I would've been so freaked out," Whisper said, recalling a previous conversation she had with Selena during the first outage. Mazzy, who had taken the accident the hardest and was unable to stomach visiting Selena during her recent hospital stay(s), was brought up to speed about Selena's terrifying experience when the hospital lost power—according to Lacey, twice now.

Then, Azalea: "I never lost power."

"That's because you live out in the county, gurl."

"Did your parents lose power?" Azalea asked Mazzy.

"Just for like thirty minutes," she answered.

Azalea, who was going to be spending the week with Mazzy in Virginia, was relieved by her response.

"It's a good thing I charged up all my devices; otherwise, I'd lose my mind—"

"You hear about Marty World?" asked Whisper.

The others didn't, except for Lacey.

"I heard," she said, more youthfully. "They said eight people were injured."

"What happened?"

"Apparently, Marty World lost its power during Black Friday—"

"Thought Black Friday was next week."

"It was pushed up a week due to rumors of potential blackouts," Whisper said, showing the headline about Marty World on her phone to other teammates, who seemed rather uninterested. "Registers stopped working. It was a freaking mad house. People just walked out with armfuls of merch. Their servers were also down. So people couldn't buy online."

"It's gets worse and worse every year, doesn't it?"

"Wait till next week."

"I can imagine," Lacey said with a growing hostility in her voice, as though she was luring a gullible Whisper into a soon-to-be, same ole-same ole tirade about the decay of civilization and how selfish Americans had become over the past decade. Unfortunately, Kellie made a mistake of bringing up a triggering subject such as Christmas when Selena first introduced Kellie to her mother during the off-season practice in early September before the Fall Classic. Being a strong supporter of the holiday, as well as its tradition that came with it, Lacey, as though set off by the word *Christmas* but more specifically, "last year's Christmas," went off about the city ordinance, which limited residents from using electrical Christmas decorations or lights due to the apparent "strain" it'd cause on the already overloaded electrical grid and required "rolling blackouts" in order to alleviate the current workload. For a second, Kellie thought that she witnessed Selena's mother turn a bright glowing red. "Yesterday," Lacey said, more agitated, "I tried ordering this nice pair of garden shears and the website kept freezing on me. . . "

Selena shot Lacey a glare as though warning her mother to tone it down.

On cue, John, whose heard Lacey during one of her tirades, tended to Selena.

"I want to show you something," he whispered in her ear.

Selena cracked a smile, this time a closed and tranquil smile.

"Be careful," she whispered back. "I'm fragile."

John pushed Selena toward the guestroom where she was staying while she was recovering, since her former bedroom was located on the second floor and Lacey and Dean didn't have any way of transporting Selena upstairs. Dean, or "Lean Dean," as Selena called him after he shedded over twenty pounds from a new diet over the summer, moved most of Selena's belongings to the guestroom after the first surgery. Her nana, Eleanor, who was staying in the guestroom prior to Selena's injury, currently occupied Dean's office where Lacey had set up a cot for her to sleep on, and said that she didn't mind playing musical beds while her granddaughter fully recovered; in fact, anytime spent with her granddaughter was considered a blessing and if she had no other choice, she would sleep on the couch, if it meant spending more time with her precious Selena.

After wheeling Selena into her temporary room, John closed the door behind him.

"I must say: Timing has always been your strong suit," Selena said, as John was opening up a drawer behind her.

Selena tilted her head to the side as John began to make clattering sounds from his rummaging.

"You okay over there?" asked Selena.

"Don't turn around," John ordered.

"Okay," Selena said with a smile growing along the corner of his face.

During the wait, Selena, who bored easily, occupied her time by walking her two fingers—both her index and middle—along the armrest of the wheelchair. As she strolled her fingers to the end of the armrest, she decided to turn around. Halfway through rotating herself around, she said more playfully, "I'm still a little doped up from the last pill, so please don't take offense if I doze off—"

As Selena fully turned toward her rascal boyfriend, he was standing directly behind her. In his hand he was holding a round present in a red and white snowman patterned gift-wrap.

"Christmas isn't until another month," she said, surprised.

"It's not really a gift," he said hesitantly. "It's something that I've been working on while you were away at college. I wanted to finish it before Winter Break, but considering your—you know—injury, I sort of had to put a rush on it."

"You didn't have to do this?"

"Well," he said with a shrug, "I wanted to."

"So, that's why you've been avoiding me these past couple of weeks."

"Not avoiding," he said. "Working."

"Okay," Selena said with anticipation, as she ripped through gift-wrap paper, "let's see what was so important. . ."

Selena opened the present and in her hands she held a snow globe, which he made using local materials, except for the house that he carved from beach wood collected from Jeffery's Isle. He told her that it took him three months to construct, the house taking the longest.

With her eyes lit up in a child-like wonder, Selena couldn't express how much she loved it. The detail was spot-on—her "Dream House," as John called it. Behind the house, a garden filled with fresh tomatoes and herbs. On the side of the house, a chicken coop. There was also a small doghouse with the word *Max* written above the doorway. The house was decorated with Christmas lights. John instructed Selena to flip the snow globe upside down and hit the switch underneath, which resulted in the lights turning on.

"Now, you don't have to wake up in the middle of the night to turn off the light," John said. "Think of it as an elaborate night light."

"I will admit," she said, still impressed, "you are good with your hands."

"Well, sometimes I wish I had an extra pair.

Selena rolled her eyes at the remark.

Carefully, she flipped the snow globe upright, stirring the bed of fake snow.

Once more, the sight of the colorful house left her in a state of awe.

"I know how hard these past couple of months have been on you and your family," he said to Selena, who couldn't remove her eyes from John's gift.

"Thank you," she said and once more, couldn't express how much she loved the snow globe.

The two embraced, locking lips and holding one another in each other's arms.

As the snow globe started to slip from Selena's hand, John suddenly grabbed it and placed it on Selena's desk, which was covered in printed out "blog entries," "forums," as well as "articles from medical journals," and other health websites about a popular antacid drug, *Elimidine*: all of which Selena compiled from the Internet. Dozens of papers with headlines such as "LONG-TERM USE OF ELIMIDINE RESPONSIBLE FOR BONE FRACTURES" or "A LAWSUIT PENDING AGAINST MAKERS OF ELIMIDINE."

John found a page on the makers, the pharmaceutical company Neuvak.

He held up one of the printed out articles.

"What's this?" asked John.

"It's nothing," she said, defensively.

He read more headlines.

"Woman says Elimidine was to blame for her broken leg," he read out loud.

"That's none of your business, John!"

"I thought you said you stopped taking this drug."

"I did," Selena said, her tone switching from pleasant to pissed.

"What?" John said, almost amusedly. "You think Elimidine is to blame for what happened? Selena, your leg broke because you fell—"

"Thanks for reminding me."

"Sorry."

"And what makes you so sure?" Selena snapped.

"Sure?" John looked at Selena with a more confused expression. He said more slowly and carefully to her, "Selena, unless you have superpowers that I'm not aware of, anyone who landed the way you did would've wound up the same way as you. It was a freak accident."

Her eyes narrowed, lips tightened.

"A freak accident?"

"I'm not trying to fight," he said, holding up his hands. "All I'm saying is that it takes a lot of money and resources to go after a company like Neuvak. David versus Goliath."

"Yeah," Selena said. "And last I checked, David *slain* Goliath. Did he not?"

"You win," he said and made amends by reaching out his hand. "Sorry for being so snoopy. It's not my place." Selena, who wanted to be mad at John for sticking his nose into her personal business but couldn't find the strength to stay mad at him for he, in all the years she had known him, was considered the perfect boyfriend—she'd even go so far to call him "Mr. Right," despite all his faults, like the fact that he sometimes farted while in her presence. One day, perhaps after she graduated, she was going to give John her hand in marriage. "Whatever you're planning on doing," he said over a long silence, "just remember I got your back. All the way. *But*," he stopped, his eyes meeting Selena's as he emphasized another pause, "just please be realistic. That's all."

"Yeah," Selena said, more hurt. "I know."

John asked Selena if she wanted him to stay for the night.

As much as she wanted to sleep in John's arms, she said that she needed some rest and that she wasn't in the mood.

"But tomorrow," she teased.

John read Selena's face.

"Is it because. . . "

Selena, fully aware of what John was about to ask, nodded her head.

"Yesterday was *the* Thursday."

On the inside, John laughed not only at himself, but also that particular day *"Thursday"* and the trendy adjective that often came before it.

Grinning, he said, "I swear you're like clockwork."

"Welcome to a day in the life of a woman," she said.

"Sucks being a woman."

"It's only a couple of days out of the month."

"Still," he insisted, as he held Selena's hand, "it doesn't mean we can't, you know. . . I mean it wouldn't be the first time I got *blood* on my hands."

Selena pushed John's hand away and hit him on the shoulder.

"When'd you get to be so bad?" asked Selena.

John shrugged.

"I've missed you."

"Tomorrow. . . " Selena said, her eyes wide and pinned on John.

Based on John's deflated state, Selena knew that she wouldn't have to tell him a third time.

Most of the time it only took two times to tell him before he got the picture.

HOURS after everyone left the house, the pain, which had been coming in hot waves over the past two months, returned with a vengeance, radiating throughout Selena's body.

While resting in Dean's recliner in the living room, she closed her eyes and tried to ignore the pain by imagining herself back on the track, her church, her canvas, a place that she rightfully called "safe." The bleachers were faded into the background, the attendees as dark as shadows. Everything around her was dark and unlit, except for the main stage before her. Selena chalked up her palms before grabbing hold of the pole and as she prepared to vault over the high bar, the pain resettled in her leg, heavier than before, and it felt as though she was carrying around an extra appendage. The high bar suddenly stretched out, higher and higher into the jet-black sky until Selena could no longer find it in the blinding glare of the stadium lights that loomed above. She shelved the pain and ran (The thought of running brought her great comfort). The faster Selena ran, the quicker that pain deepened, like a subterranean creature burrowing deeper into her body. Right before she planted the end of the pole into the vault box, a stabbing pain shot up her leg, biting at her, forcing her to open her eyes before the pain swallowed her whole. Selena stirred in the seat, her body movement causing the paperback, *Raven The Wise* (a body of work inspired by her favorite author Edgar Allen Poe), to fall from her chest.

Selena cried out to Lacey, who surfaced from her bedroom in the room closest to the kitchen where she and Dean were watching a reality TV show that started with *Romance*—

"What is it?" Lacey asked, as she hurried into the living room.

Sweating profusely, Selena begged her mother for more pain meds.

Lacey, who was monitoring Selena's prescription of painkillers by keeping a digital journal that documented the time her daughter took a pill, insisted that Selena watch a movie or try her meditation or anything to take her mind away from the pain since she wasn't due the next pill for another two hours. Eventually, Lacey caved into Selena's demands and gave her a pill from the locked medicine cabinet where she was storing Selena's prescription.

Once the medication kicked in, Selena put the paperback aside, switched on a shoot'-em-up movie, and drifted to sleep.

Minutes or hours later, Selena woke to the dead silence. Both the white noise-like sounds of an air purifier, as well as the sound of ocean waves on the alarm clock with nature sounds which helped lull her into a deep sleep, were without power.

In a slight wave of panic, Selena sat up and checked the time of the clock, both the minute as well as the hour hand stuck on "12:00 AM."

She surveyed the pitch-black living room and despite the limited visibility, couldn't find any source of light, not from the TV mounted on the wall or the time on the microwave in the kitchen behind her. The silence was deafening. She called out to her mother. Being a light sleeper who could properly function off two or three hours of shuteye, Lacey woke from sleep and as soon as she realized what happened, blindly reached for her smartphone on the nightstand and used the phone's flashlight to check on Selena.

In the corner of her eye, Selena caught a pale blue beam of light. A heavy hand grabbed her on the arm. The hand was not her mother's but rather the cold, chrome hand of what felt like the thorny touch of a demon. In the pale glow of light, Selena followed the hand up the arm, which evolved or better yet, devolved into flesh. Her eyes drifted upward and behind the pale light, she witnessed her mother's face.

Relieved, she moved her eyes back down at that strange hand, only to find her mother's.

"Didn't mean to startle you," said Lacey.

"No," she said in a state of shock. Her voice then trailed off, "It's just. . . " she paused and debated whether or not to ask her mother if there were any harsh side effects to the meds, hallucinations being one of them, ". . . never mind."

"Power's out."

"Yeah," Selena said, as she was one response away from turning into one helluva grumpy old hag. First, it started out with a hint of sarcasm: "Thanks for waking me," she said, her tone laced with bitterness. Then, a sharp "Geez!"

"I'm sorry," Lacey replied, her tone much softer. "I'm sure the power company is working on it as we speak. For now, try to get some sleep."

"Well, I *was* sleeping," Selena said, more hag-like.

"Okay, okay," Lacey said, stepping away. "Go back to bed."

Lacey returned to her bedroom.

Selena closed her eyes and considering the drugs that were still in her system, didn't have a hard time falling to sleep. She dreamt that she was waking up from the recent surgery, a similar dream that she had been having ever since the second surgery on her femur. The lights inside the operation room were a hazy red. The room was empty, except for a couple of shadows along the floor from where two tall figures were standing inside a smaller room that was lit up by a bright bluish white light. She glanced down at her leg, which appeared normal, no screws or plates, no stitches or staples, no scars.

As the feeling returned to her lower extremities, Selena rolled from the operation table and made her way toward the two dark figures in the other room. The hallways, which could be seen from the windows of the door, were also lit up by a soft, hazy red light, possibly powered by the emergency generators inside the hospital.

Selena reached another room where she saw two people dressed in white coats, doctors perhaps, standing in front of a lit-up view box.

On the box were several X-ray sheets of sections of a leg (Selena's leg?).

One examined the metal drilled into the femur while the other one examined all of the metal, including the long screws, drilled into the tibia. As Selena peered closer at the metal attached to the femur—possibly her femur—she saw what looked like a circular engraving in a metal rod.

The LED of the view box suddenly grew brighter and warmer and the red light from the operation room bled over the light.

As the two masked doctors looked over their shoulder, each one made eye contact with Selena.

Their eyes were big and black and glossy, like those of a raven's eye.

One of the doctors squared himself to Selena. Apart from his black eyes, his facial features were striking familiar, at least the ones that weren't covered by the mask: First, his unibrow that was as thick and dark as the end of a paintbrush; and second, his eye sockets, which were sunken in as if he was suffering from severe dehydration.

SHE gradually woke from the dream, which lasted longer than the previous dreams and brought forth newer detail, especially more description of the doctor's face.

Her body was warm, almost feverish.

The loose clothes she was wearing were drenched with sweat.

Rays of sunlight washed over her closed eyelids.

As the images from the dream blended with the red, veiny flesh of the backside of her eyelids, Selena cracked open her sore and incredibly sensitive eyes.

The sunlight, which poured in through the living room window, was blinding and forced her to shield her face. Other senses returned sharply, as the pain meds wore off. Her sight first, then her hearing. Following that ache of light was the *rustling* of bags, as well as the dull *thuds* of the refrigerator door opening and closing inside the kitchen. Each noise—or lack of noise—sounded amplified.

Sporting bags underneath his eyes from an apparent lack of sleep last night, Selena's stepfather clumsily transported food from the fridge to paper bags and water coolers, which he planned to store in the garage in order to prevent food from spoiling.

Currently, the temperature outside was thirty-three degrees, only a few degrees off from the set temperature inside their fridge, and most of the sun they received during the morning came from the other side of the house, opposite the garage. According to a latest forecast before the power outage, the temperature's high was going to reach the mid to upper thirties.

Dean, who was selfishly wearing the title "Mean Dean," slammed the fridge door, startling Selena.

"Can't you see I'm trying to sleep here," Selena griped.

She removed the thick comforter from the lower half of her body as she was struck by a hot flash.

"Sorry, Selena," Lacey said from the edge of the kitchen, as Dean carried paper bags filled with condiments into the garage. "We were going to wait till you woke. But Dean wanted to do this while it was still cold outside." Dean returned to the kitchen and grabbed more bags to carry into the garage. She said indirectly to Selena, even though she was staring directly at Dean when she spoke, "We'll try to be as quiet as possible."

"You're the one who wanted this done," Dean said with restrained anger.

"Someone's mode is dialed to *diva* this morning."

Selena's words drew more reaction from Dean, as he poured his emotion into emptying out the fridge.

Fed-up by the racket coming from Dean, which Selena thought was deliberate, she reached out over the armrest of the recliner and pulled the wheelchair closer.

Lacey rushed over and attempted to help but Selena shooed her away.

"I can handle it on my own."

"You sure?"

"Yes."

Selena struggled to lift herself from the recliner.

Driven by Mean Dean in the kitchen, Selena managed to successfully slide her body into the wheelchair.

Once she was settled, she wheeled herself to her bedroom.

Lacey followed and asked if she needed any help getting in bed.

Then reminded her that she needed to keep her leg elevated. Doctor's orders.

Somewhat exhausted despite having slept over eight hours, she wheeled herself to the bed and while ignoring Lacey's help once more, gently hoisted herself into bed.

"Space please," Selena said shortly.

Lacey threw her hands up in surrender and exited the room.

"Door!" Selena shouted out.

Lacey returned to the room and closed the door to Selena's room.

The two didn't utter a word to one another about the power for the mother and daughter had an unspoken understanding— based off Dean's chippy behavior—that the power wasn't going to return for a while, maybe even days.

As she propped up her leg with a couple of pillows, she sat back in bed and tried to get some rest. She was already up, not physically, but mentally; and despite the returning pain, the thought of what they, those snakes, did to her inspired her to roll out of bed and finish what she started.

While looking over the research that she printed out after the first surgery, Selena was struck by a feeling of insecurity. John's words from last night, as grounded in reality as Selena felt they were, rattled inside her mind until eventually those levelheadedly spoken words began to pull her from the storm clouds above and ease her back down to earth where even the sunrays that poked through the heavy grayness were stark reminders of the environment surrounding the world between the gateways of her ears and windows of her eyes. Doubts consumed her world like a virus until the debilitating thought of failure filled her head and weighed down each fantastical notion, her own castle in the air where she'd nuke Neuvak from orbit, opposed to the more realistic approach, from the ground-up, like talking to employees of Neuvak and gathering intel that could help expose and ultimately, destroy the company for good. Each and every story from each and every user of Elimidine was her own ammunition to take legal action against Neuvak. But who would listen to a woman whose own story would work against her in a court of law?

Out of curiosity, Selena checked her phone, which she forgot to charge last night before the power outage. The video was still up; in fact, all she had to do was Gumshoe the words *girl pole vault* into the search bar and the line "girl pole vault meme" appeared. In the results, she clicked on the first link, which sent her to an "11 sec." video of Selena breaking her leg at the Fall Classic.

As much as she wanted to watch the video again, she couldn't bring herself to relive the pain for it was, by far, the worst pain she had ever experienced.

She scrolled down the video and read a couple of comments below.

Some were positive.

Most were negative, degrading, and insulting.

Trolls had a field day with her.

She read the bad, trollish ones.

One commenter even posted a still from a close-up of Selena's face the moment her leg was broken. Selena was screaming in horror. Tears flooded from her bloodshot eyes. The corners of her face were pinched together, making her look twice, even thrice her age.

In the MEME was written: "The moment you find out Prince Samuel got divorced."

With building rage, Selena closed the phone and chucked it across the room.

The top of the phone hit the bottom corner of a poster, leaving a dent in the drywall underneath. She drew her eyes from the mark in the wall to the poster of the famous track and field three-timed Olympic gold medalist, Angelina "Geaux" Campbell.

The sight of the star athlete sparked a mixture of emotions, from envy to anger to great anguish, making whatever physical pain she was experiencing in her leg seem dull, even tolerable.

She wheeled herself to the window where she witnessed more than usual activity.

The entire neighborhood was without power, she could tell as she looked out the front window. A neighbor across the street was running a generator. Two other neighbors were gathering around a portable fire pit in front of their driveway.

As the emotions eased off, she wheeled herself into the kitchen where Dean and Lacey were finishing up with the exodus of the food.

Before Selena could ask, Lacey brought out the bottle of kefir from the garage.

"Don't worry," she said. "Saved your kefir. Know how you like to drink it every morning."

Eleanor, who was working on a puzzle of legendary saxophonist Mr. Vortex on the kitchen table, said good morning to Selena.

"So, how are you feeling?"

"Still sore."

"Still?"

Selena nodded.

Lacey chimed in, "Well, you have a long road ahead of you, kiddo."

"Thanks for reminding me. . . again."

Selena, who wasn't completely useless, grabbed a cup from the dish rack and poured herself a glass of strawberry-flavored kefir, a drink, which three years ago she incorporated into her diet, along with yogurt, which helped curb her GERD.

Selena asked Lacey if they ("they," as in the power company) had any answers as to why the power was out.

"The word is that they're claiming it's due to the rolling blackouts," Lacey said, "but usually in the past, when they did these rolling blackouts, the power would only be out for around thirty minutes, three hours tops. Not this long, which makes me wonder if there's not something else going on. Also, don't get your brother started on what he thinks is going on."

Selena asked, "Why's that?"

"You know how he is with his conspiracy theories and all," Lacey said with a quieter tone.

More intrigued, Selena asked, "What does he think it is?"

"He's heard rumors—"

"What? On the Internet?"

"Maybe, I don't know," she said. "He's heard that whatever happened two years ago was only a shape of something bigger to come."

"Bigger? Like what?"

"Like big-big," Lacey said, emphasizing the word *big* in a quirky manner, a sense of humor, which she often used as a coping mechanism to deal with the death of her husband, Selena and Bret's father.

"How big? Apocalyptic-big?"

She used her hands, as well as her over-the-top facial features to exaggerate the word *BIG*.

Then, Lacey finished, "Like us returning back to the prehistoric days where we hunt for food and huddle around campfires to stay warm—"

"Enough already," Selena said, frustrated by how easily her mother could be manipulated by a seventeen-year old. "Not in the mood."

"Well, I just can't stop thinking about what all those people who were planning on traveling this weekend are going to do. How about Kellie and what's her name—"

"Whisper," Selena said.

"Have you talked to them?"

"No."

"The last I heard is all flights in the Northeast have been temporarily grounded," Lacey said. "I just can't help but think: *What if* Bret is right—"

"Enough," Selena groaned. "Geez!"

With wide eyes, Lacey held up her hands in surrender and walked from the kitchen.

"Reminds me: Dean has a surprise for you," she said more suspiciously and from the dining room window, spotted Dean returning from the neighbor's house.

Selena asked, "What kind of surprise—"

Before Lacey could answer, Dean entered via the garage door with a tray covered in aluminum foil. He placed the tray on the kitchen countertop and removed the foil from the bowls and plates. Steam rose from the hot food, along with an assortment of smells, from savory to sweet.

"All thanks to Frankie's generator, we have hot breakfast," he said.

On the tray were plates of hot scrambled eggs, fried potatoes, four bowls of warm oatmeal, and finally, several warm pastries and sweets, including homemade donuts that Mr. Toto's wife, Mage, made for the neighborhood.

Last but not least: A T-bone steak, cooked the way Selena preferred, medium rare.

"And for our new carnivore," Dean said, placing the plate of steak in front of Selena.

Both Selena and Lacey were blown away by the spread.

"This looks amazing," Selena said, eyes wide, glad. "Thanks, Lean Dean."

Lacey eyed Dean, expecting a reaction.

He shrugged and said to Lacey, "Beats Mean Dean."

"Dean, can you go check on Bret?"

Lacey said, "Be careful. Thought I heard some strange noises coming from up there."

"He's probably still sleeping."

"Who knows what he's doing?" Selena said. "Honestly, I don't wanna know."

Dean said to Selena, "After you finish up with breakfast, you should go over there and thank the Totos. They were asking about you."

"Maybe I will," Selena said, grabbing a plastic knife to cut through the steak. "I like Mage. But Mr. Toto not so much."

"Frankie's sweet, and you be nice to him, especially with everything he's been through. . . "

Selena said with a trace of sarcasm, "What has he been through?"

"Before you left for Brighton, his house was broken into—"

"That's right," Selena recalled the story when Lacey told her over several phone calls when she was getting settled into the new college-lifestyle. "I remember you told me something about that." Then, added: "But I thought they didn't steal anything?"

"Just a few items," Dean said. "But it's just the thought about it happening so close to home that gets me."

"Cops didn't catch whoever did it?"

"Nope," Dean said shortly.

"So, that's why you changed the door locks."

Dean gave Selena a look that said "Enough already."

"Well, I caught him once checking me out."

"You're an attractive woman."

"Mom, the guy's twice my age—"

"Would you like some eggs with your steak?" Lacey asked while ignoring Selena's concerns about Mr. Toto, the neighbor who lived in the lime green house across the street.

Selena asked foolishly, "Got any War. . . chess. . . er. . . shire sauce?"

AFTER Selena finished her steak and egg breakfast and moved her way to a bowl of oatmeal, she listened to Dean rage about their Internet service, which had been dropping in and out after the power outage. Dean, who heavily relied on maintaining a robust Internet connection to monitor and make daily adjustments to a website for his company, Sportica, a retail store that specialized in sporting equipment, made yet another attempt to reach out to their service provider.

Pacing around the kitchen, Dean said, "We pay all that god-damn money each month to keep the Internet running and this is how they treat us?"

"I got a connection earlier," Selena said casually, as she took a bite of a spoonful of lukewarm oatmeal. "Seemed to work fine—"

"School related, I hope," Lacey said in a stern manner, as she recalled and at the same time, reinforced the words her daughter told her prior to the injury.

The Internet was one of the main reasons why Selena lost most of her high school friends—a majority of them skipping college to focus on creating various content on the Internet.

As Selena redirected her attention back to breakfast, she didn't even realize it at the time but with her plastic spoon she scribbled an odd-looking symbol in the oatmeal.

The symbol was detailed and brought forth more clarity to that image in her dream.

The one engraved along the metal rod, which was holding her femur together.

She tried to think back to where she encountered such a symbol, if she had seen it in a movie or TV show or saw it on a sign when she was a little girl and perhaps the symbol got lodged deep in her subconscious and somehow, the pain meds jiggled it free.

And if she had seen it before, she couldn't remember where.

AROUND midday, while spending the power-free time to catch up on reading the rest of Chapter 11 from *Raven The Wise*, Selena was drawn to the ceiling where she heard—and felt—stomping coming from Bret's bedroom, which was located above the guest-room. Selena called out to Lacey and asked if she could fetch Bret for her.

Hesitant about disturbing her son, Lacey called out to Bret after she was asked once more.

Eventually, Bret made it downstairs to the guestroom where Selena asked him to join her. He was sweaty and out of breath and when Selena asked him what he was doing up there, he told her that he was playing VR for his subscribers (Bret had over *ninety-thousand* subs, not bot accounts, but actual real-life eating, breathing, shitting people who watched the one and only "Bet" on his Streamerz channel), which she knew was a lie based on his inability to make eye contact with her. She reiterated that Bret chill with her, which he thought was strange of Selena to ask and considering they *never* chilled, questioned if she had a screw loose, not in her leg, but in her brain.

Since they never got a chance to talk earlier, with everything going on, the injury, as well as the two surgeries, Selena decided to take advantage of the free time and chat with Bret, starting with Del Soaka Falls, asked him about his friends, if he was seeing anybody (girl or boy?), then, when Selena hit a dead end, turned her attention toward Padadock, if anything exciting happened while she was away at college.

As usual, he kept his answers relatively short, mainly answering in one-word responses and body movements.

When Bret failed to mention one name in particular, like the mystery girl from the other day, Selena said, "Who was that girl I saw you talking to outside the Shag and Tag."

"You mean Kourtney?"

Bret blushed and shrugged his shoulders.

"I don't know her name, but she looks familiar."

"She has a sister."

"What's her last name?"

"McCormick," Bret said hesitantly.

"You mean Jorgina McCormick?"

"Who?"

"*Who*, Bet!" she mocked Bret, *Owl The Boy Who Goes Who, Whooo!* "Jorgina McCormick. Short hair. Looks kind of like the actress Eliza Kirby."

"Yeah," Bret said, grinning. "She sort of does, right?"

Selena said, "She went to The Soak Machine with me. Brilliant girl. Think she went to law school." Selena said from the corner of her mouth, voice trailing off, "I don't remember much about her little sis. Although," she paused, "now that I think about it, I remember she was wild." She warned, "Be careful."

Bret waved off Selena.

"It ain't like that," he said, his cheeks red as hell.

"Sure," Selena said, studying her brother's telling face.

Bret ignored Selena's evasive remark; in fact, he started to get agitated by Selena's interest in his "interests," more specifically, Kourtney McCormick. He pulled out his smartphone while Selena, aware that Bret didn't want to talk about Kourtney, changed the subject to "Jillian From Down The Street," and how their mom talked to Jillian's mom, and Jillian's mom told their mom that her daughter, a senior, one year older than Bret, died from an overdose last week.

The comment drew the most reaction from her brother. Selena had her ways of getting him to talk, even if it was about anybody but himself or his sacred Streamerz channel where he spent most of his time whenever he wasn't at school or now, based off a blushing face that her brother displayed whenever she brought up Jorgina's younger sister's name, possibly with or more realistically, based off Bret's lack of game, fantasizing about Kourtney—Selena leaned more toward the latter.

"Massacre was obsessed with her."

"Massacre? Which one's this?"

"Trip."

"You boys need some new names, you know that?"

Bret shrugged off Selena's comment.

"Massacre wouldn't shut up about—"

He suddenly stopped talking, causing Selena to pay closer attention.

"What is it?"

"He thinks Jillian was murdered."

"Serious?"

"She wasn't depressed or anything."

"People get depressed," Selena said. "It's part of life."

"Yeah, but she wasn't into logging."

"How you know?"

"I've seen people who log and she wasn't the type."

"You don't touch that stuff, do you?"

"Lo-ro?"

Selena nodded.

"Nah," Bret said. "That stuff messes with your head."

He returned to his phone and scrolled through the recent headlines, which, unlike most teens his age, was considered a pastime whenever he wasn't playing video games. He saved one particular headline from Padadock Daily. Under the headline was an article about Blaire Tudor, as well as a photo of the "MISSING" fifteen-year-old.

"Massacre says Jillian's death may be related to Blair's disappearance."

"Don't get me started her," she said dismissively. "Mom wouldn't shut up about the girl last night. Blaire Tudor! Blaire

Tudor! And the whole rant about your *cat* killer somehow involved in Blaire's disappearance. She practically scared off my friends."

"If you only saw what I saw," Bret said, referring to the dead tabby that he found in front of the hospital two months ago when he was riding his bike through town and how the cat had been, as Bret stated to Lacey, who adored cats, "turned inside-out."

Selena said, "I told you, Bret. An animal probably killed it. Probably an *owl* grabbed it and dropped it from the sky. Even better. . . " Selena had a glint in her right eye, as she mocked her brother, "it might've been from the one and only *Gray Scorpion*! Besides, of all people, why are you coming to Mom's defense?"

"She's just being protective," Bret said, bashfully. "Can't blame her."

Bret showed Selena the article on his phone, not the one regarding the trendy #GrayScorpion or a supposed highly detailed *map* that one of Bret's followers constructed during his free time, but rather the article on the "missing fifteen-year-old, Blaire Tudor."

To keep the conversation moving along, she grabbed the phone from his hand and skimmed through the article.

"So," she said, thinking back to what Bret said moments ago, "why does your boy 'Maniac' think they're connected? Nothing in this article mentions anything about lo-ro—"

"You mean Massacre?"

"Whatever," she said. "Does he think Blaire was into logging?"

"No," Bret said. "He thinks there's a serial killer out there drugging girls."

Selena laughed.

"You've been reading *way* too much news," she said, annoyed by her brother, as well as the thought of his gamer pal's theory. "My advice: I say you stop chilling with kids named Massacre. Does he actually think that name's cool?" She answered her own question: "Cuz it's not."

"Massacre's harmless," Bret paused and with a mischievous expression on his face, said, "in the real world, that is."

"By the way," Selena said in a side thought, "how are you getting a signal?"

"I'm piggybacking off the neighbor's wi-fi."

"Mr. Abrams?"

"Why does it matter?"

"You know he'll kill you if he finds out."

Bret waved off his sister's comment.

"I like to see him try," he said with a dark and sinister look on his face.

AFTER a light lunch, Selena took a nap and dreamt about the accident at the Fall Classic. Echoes of that awful pain could still be accessed, as if Selena had collected the pain and shelved it aside, like a hardback with edges that wore and tore over time but still remained intact, that pain itself leaving behind a wicked signature, although frayed and faded but still accessible, and if she ever felt the need to open up that book of pain and relive the experience, if only for a line or two, she could at *any* moment. The images flooded her mind. The pain in her leg intensified, as she propelled her body upward with the pole. While attempting to hurl her body over the high bar, the pole suddenly bent sideways, forcing Selena from her initial trajectory. Her body flipped backward, several feet from the landing mat, and plummeted toward a hard surface on the track where her right leg was about to bear the brunt of the fall.

Upon violent impact the upper part of Selena's body was thrust through the front windshield of a car, which overturned on its side. As the car came to rest, Selena, who was lying in a bed of broken glass, managed to crawl from the smoky car, which caught fire. She could feel the shards of glass beneath her palms. Each shard dug into her flesh.

As the flames grew closer and closer, the pain radiated up Selena's body.

She lifted her bloody hands to her face, and they felt foreign to her, as though the hands belonged to someone else.

Sweating profusely, Selena woke and called out to her mother, who rushed to her aide with a pain pill and a glass of water.

Hours went by, and after the pain eventually melted away, Selena received a text from John, who was thinking about her and wanted to see her.

Surprisingly, the phone, which had been fully charged to a 100% using her car's battery, still worked, despite being treated like a discus earlier that day. The upper part of the screen, which was protected by a case, was partially cracked.

Ignoring the damage, Selena texted back: Let's chill. I'm not going anywhere.

* * *

THAT night, after John left the house, the power was still out throughout the town of Padadock, and worse, the temperature was dropping well into the twenties, leaving thousands without heat.

Dean grabbed three battery-operated space heaters from the garage, one he set next to Bret's bedroom, another one inside the master bedroom where he helped Eleanor move the cot on the other side of the room until the power issue was sorted out—which, despite his candor with Lacey about having a gassy old lady, whose snoring sounded like elephants stampeding through the Serengeti, sleep in the same room as them, Dean forced himself to put on a happy face—finally, the last one was placed inside the guestroom where Selena slept or at least, tried to sleep.

As Selena bundled herself up with blankets, she turned on the snow globe that John gave her and with the multi-colorful light providing enough light for the book, read a few chapters from *Raven The Wise* before eventually dozing off.

She dreamt that she woke up to the power returning.

The lamp flicked on, as well as TV mounted on the wall.

The burst of an anchor's voice from a morning TV talk show startled yet comforted her.

Other sounds returned: the air purifier, which hummed with a soft rattle; the relaxing sounds of ocean waves crashing into shore on the sleep machine; the AC kicked on, the heat warmed up the room, shaving off the chill, an entire world of manmade sounds and comforts filling her own designated space.

Relieved by the sounds filling the guestroom, Selena rolled out of bed.

The pain, which had been coming in waves, was gone. So was the memory of pain.

Her leg felt much better and to her surprise, she could apply more weight to it. She grabbed the crutches and skipped her way from the guestroom and into the kitchen where Dean was roasting a turkey in the oven. The morning flew by, as Selena filled the time on her fully-charged devices: first, her e-tablet where she played the highly addictive mobile game *Toss-A-Tomato*; then, after she broke the highest score, she messed around on her smartphone where she watched latest GIFS, MEMES, and video clips of people's experiences with the latest blackout.

When lunchtime arrived, Selena worked up an appetite after indulging in the latest viral content that Internet had to offer.

Before Dean began plating the turkey, she beat Bret to the drumsticks. Her brother threw a tantrum. Selena laughed and marveled at his behavior before she shared one of her drumsticks.

While eating from the drumstick, the bone protruded from the crisp fatty skin. The sight of the bone sticking out reminded Selena of the previous injury. The horror slowly manifested itself, like a thief in the night climbing its way up inside Selena, stealing each pleasant thought and replacing it with reality. A flash of her own bones protruding from her skin came to her, the tibia bone especially, as it stuck out from her leg like a branch that snapped from a tree. She ignored the graphic images and continued eating; and the more she ate, the quicker those images receded back into the recesses of her mind.

After lunch, Selena used the crutches to walk back to the guestroom where she grabbed the composition notebook from her desk and began drawing those strange symbols that she had been seeing lately, both in her dreams, as well as in her daily life, for instance, earlier that same day, when she saw the symbol in a gimmicky TV Ad before she and John left Knife and Fork to catch up on the latest small town gossip.

The Ad was for a brand new state-of-the-art kitchen knife that could cut through metal. The showy salesman used the knife to cut through food like cantaloupe, watermelons, and pineapples, as well as various items of metal, like, for instance, a manhole cover, which the salesman lugged onto the kitchen countertop. The sound of the manhole cover falling onto the countertop, nearly cracking it, caused a startling *thud* against the granite. Selena couldn't help but express to John how she preferred her manhole well done, even though, lately, she liked her meat cooked on the medium-rare side—a "little pink in the middle," she'd say.

As John opened the door for Selena, she saw the symbol in the corner of her eye. The symbol was engraved in the bottom of the blade, right above the handle.

With the image in mind, she sketched the symbol on the paper, trying to replicate the same image that she saw on TV.

With her hand sore from all the drawing, she used the hallway bathroom to freshen up.

She relieved herself and afterwards, while washing her hands in the sink, saw a young Hispanic kid standing in what looked like an alleyway in the mirror's reflection.

Shocked, she touched her face.

In the reflection before her, the kid touched his face.

Selena rotated around, only to witness the towel hanging from the rack on the door.

When she rotated back around toward the mirror, she was standing in the same gritty, grimy alleyway.

She glanced down at both her hands, which were coarser and more callused and not to mention, smaller, in fact, not her hands, but rather the hands of a young Hispanic kid.

There were several tats on his hands: One of an armadillo; and the other, a name, "GENIE," tattooed above his knuckles, a letter for each finger.

To the right of her was an oil drum where a tame fire burned. She walked over to the drum and inside were various articles: picture frames with black and white photographs of a heavy set man and his family, as well as a black garbage bag full of clothing stained with blood. Each item blackened and curled to ash.

As the heat of the fire intensified, Selena suddenly woke up from the vivid dream. Her body was hot yet the pain in her leg was greatly lessened.

The power was still out, which, despite the progress in her leg, made Selena feel rather depressed and hopeless and incredibly cranky throughout the morning.

Later that Sunday afternoon, the 22nd of November, while Dean was, as he claimed, "searching for gasoline" in surrounding towns, Selena was overwhelmed by a sudden rush of panic after she found a black and white speckled composition notebook lying underneath the bed while she was tidying up the guestroom. She cracked open the notebook, only to find those same symbols covering the pages like a wicked mosaic. Hundreds of these circular symbols, sketched in varying shapes and sizes.

Once she calmed herself with easy breathing tips that her high school coach showed her, she tried to think back as to when she drew the symbols. She remembered fragments of a dream.

"But it was only a dream," she convinced herself. "Right?"

THE power was restored Monday morning before shutting back off the next day, which created a frenzy all over the Internet, sparking rumors of potential doomsday, the "calm before the storm," the all-knowing cosmos telling people to stock up and take full advantage before the country fell into total darkness.

From what Selena learned, the outages were not only happening throughout the Northeast, but also many areas of the country, creating a domino effect throughout major cities; cyber attacks seemed more likely, but other culprits weren't ruled out, such as what experts initially claimed, which was due to a strain on a compromised electrical grid.

Due to a surge on Monday, the suppliers were running empty on gasoline and it was becoming harder to track down not only fuel to power up portable generators, but also propane tanks.

Lacey and Dean, who both took off from work, Lacey at her real estate job that covered the three surrounding counties (frankly, work was slow and nobody was buying houses at the time—and none of it had to due with the blackouts), and Dean, with the servers for his online store still being down, were able to beef up their supply on the essentials, such as food and water.

Dean managed to find a "gas guy," who, for an extra buck (Dean wouldn't say how much he was paying his gas guy), hooked him up with enough gas to last them for another week or more. According to word-of-mouth around town, there had been an uptick in break-ins, as well as car wrecks (John said he witnessed a wreck the other day: a woman flew through an intersection and T-boned a car, killing the driver, first responders didn't arrive till hours later, and the body sat in the car, dead and bloody).

Also, Selena struggled to find decent reception on her phone since the cellular towers, despite running off a backup power supply, were being overloaded. Finding service was like playing a rigged slot machine. The more people tried to use their networks, the more the service was greatly reduced. Eventually, some people, Selena being one, gave up on using their phones, and were better off without them.

When Thanksgiving arrived, the power was still out.

The neighborhood came together and prepared a potluck dinner.

Dean's parents, who normally drove up from coastal South Carolina to spend Thanksgiving with the Barbarys, decided to stay home. Also, Dean's mother, who recently fought off a case of the shingles, had what she called a "little ole cold," and she didn't want to pass it along, especially to Selena, who was still recovering from her injury.

* * *

THE Saturday following a slow and uneventful Black Friday, more news broke around the neighborhood about yet another missing person, this one being a junior from Del Soaka Falls who was recently reported missing.

Her name was Ashleigh Reap, and she was seventeen years old and apparently, according to the sheriff's office, went missing on Thanksgiving night.

Bret, who was in the same grade as Ashleigh, didn't have a whole lot to say about her, only that Ashleigh was shy and didn't talk to people and had little-to-no friends at Del Soaka Falls.

As far as being a user of lo-ro—the question came up based on an absurd theory regarding the recent disappearance of Blaire Tudor—Bret couldn't say whether or not she dabbled with the popular drug, although he didn't know much about Ashleigh other than she came from a troubled home.

WHEN Sunday arrived, the power was *still* out and most, if not all of the schools throughout the county were canceled, including virtual learning. Bret, who should've been amped up about the news given that he wasn't fond of academics, stayed in his bedroom and kept mostly to himself throughout the morning and not once showed any emotion about the school cancellation.

Since John was in the area, he stopped by Selena's parents' house to see how she was doing, especially given the recent news about the latest missing girl, Ashleigh Reap. Selena, who was still trying to adapt to her current situation, wheeled herself outside instead of relying on John.

"I don't mind, you know," he said, as Selena wheeled herself into the driveway. "Don't you start thinking that your situation is a burden, because it's not."

"You like me this way, don't you?"

"Of course not—"

"Now, you don't have to worry about me straying too far from your sight."

"Selena, you know I didn't mean what I said before," John, who was caught off guard, struggled to find the right words to say without offending Selena, "All of this. . . "

"And what is this, John?"

John said more clearly, "A test."

Selena sighed.

"Got that right."

"How's your physical therapy going?" asked John.

"I'm able to put weight on my leg."

"That's good—great, actually!"

Right before awkwardness settled into the conversation, the neighbor from across the street, Mr. Toto, stepped outside to throw away a bag of trash. He walked from the garage to the edge of the driveway where he waved at Selena.

"Hey, Mr. Toto," she said. "Thanks for letting Dean use your kitchen. . . again."

"You keep supplying the juice. I'll supply the power."

"*Juice?*" John whispered in Selena's ear.

"No problem, Selena," Mr. Toto said and welcomed Selena to use the kitchen whenever she pleased.

Selena thanked him once more for the nice gesture.

Mr. Toto asked how Selena was doing, health-wise.

With the thought of Mr. Toto staring at her ass the last time she talked to him, she said more bluntly, "Constipated from all the drugs I'm taking. But other than that, I'm feeling better."

She watched Frankie somewhat cringe from the comment, which came as a surprise to him.

He said his goodbyes and left Selena and John alone.

As Mr. Toto stepped back into his house, Selena glanced up at John and said, "My dad has a gas guy."

"That's gotta be nice. How'd that happen?"

"He knows a guy who knows a guy who's been hoarding gas."

"Your step dad knows a lot of people."

"I guess working in the retail business has its perks." Then, she said in half-truths, "For the record, I'm not constipated. I only said that because Mr. Toto has a strange way of mistaking my ass for eyes."

"Still an ole horny perv, huh?" John teased, "I don't blame him, though. If I was him I'd be checking you out too."

Selena's lips slightly curled into a half-smile.

"Serious," he said, widening his eyes with exaggeration. "I'd be King Creep."

"Stop, you creepo," she said playfully.

"That's right," he said. "I'd always be standing at my window. Waiting for you to leave the house. He's probably even watching you right now, as we speak."

"No he's not."

After John was finished ragging on Selena's neighbor, he asked Selena if she'd like to go on a walk through the neighborhood.

With the same smile crawling on the side of her face, Selena eyed John closely.

"Yeah," she said. "I'd like to go for a *walk*."

As John walked alongside Selena, the two talked about the current situation, not Selena's, but the most obvious one: the power outage, which people were officially calling "The Blackout."

"My little brother thinks the blackouts are deliberate," Selena said.

"He told me the other day."

"As much as I'd like not to agree with Bret, I'm starting to think that maybe he's right."

"In an age where information is constantly shoved in our faces," John said, "it's hard to believe fact from fiction. People are saying it's similar to what happened two years ago, only expected to be ten times worse."

"Wasn't that caused by a cyber attack?" asked Selena.

John shrugged.

"They still don't know." He paused. "Me, personally, I'd like to believe these blackouts are reminders."

"Reminders of what?"

John made eye contact with Selena.

"To cherish the people in our lives."

"That's sweet," Selena said, smitten by John's words.

"I mean, think about our ancestors," he said, provoking an idea possibly inspired by a recent conversation with her brother. "How'd they survive in the past without all of this technology we now possess at our fingertips? We have evolved with this technology that has been given to us, but with it, are we better than our ancestors? Isn't that the whole point? To learn from their mistakes, which, at the time, I'm sure our ancestors didn't look at it as mistakes, but rather a means of survival?"

"Clearly, we didn't learn anything from two years ago."

"I mean. . . I don't even know how to build a fire."

"That's why we invented lighters."

John asked, "But what happens when there are no more lighters?"

"Well, then, you'd have to *learn* how to build a fire," she said over John. "People adapt."

"Yeah," John said, "but what they're adapting to is what bothers me."

A pause, one of comfort, developed over the conversation.

John noticed Selena's arms getting sore from several brief rests while rolling the wheels. He decided to step in and push Selena.

"Thanks," she said. "Still trying to get use to this POS."

"Well, don't," he said. "The quicker you can get out of it, the better."

Selena sighed.

"Don't get me started," she said. "I can't tell you how much I miss an afternoon jog."

"It takes time."

"*Time*: Never thought I'd loathe such a word."

"They should've given you one of those fancy exoskeleton suits."

Selena furrowed her brow, as she glanced up at John.

She asked, "What was it about technology that you were talking about just seconds ago?"

John brushed off Selena's comment.

Another topic came to mind.

"Any word about Conner's sister?"

"None so far," John said. "He's put flyers all over the town." He then asked, "Did I tell you I talked with him the other day?"

"I haven't talked to Conner since, I guess. . ." Selena thought back to the last time she saw Ashleigh's older brother, ". . . graduation. Last I heard he got arrested for possession of loro."

"The sheriff was easy on him," John said. "Believe it or not, he actually cleaned up his act."

"I'm sure he's devastated about what's happening," Selena said, thinking about Ashleigh's brother and how he was always nice to her. "He's like a father to Ashleigh."

"Ashleigh is nothing like him."

"I never knew her," Selena said. "Saw her briefly when I was at The Soak Machine."

"He thinks that she's having an episode."

"Holidays can do that to some people," Selena said simply. "Throw in a blackout. Bad recipe, I'd say."

"I'm wondering what will happen when Knife and Fork runs out of fuel for the backup generator," John said. "Maybe Dean can put in a word to his gas guy."

"I'll try, but you know how he is."

"You're lucky you have neighbors with generators. Some folks would kill to have a generator right now."

"Let's not go there just yet."

"Well, if this keeps up, you'd be surprised what some people would be willing to do—"

"The power will come back on, John."

"And *what if* it doesn't."

"Then, it doesn't."

"Well, if that's the case, then I need to hone up on my fire-making skills."

"Shouldn't be a problem for you. Once you set your mind to it. . ."

She looked over her shoulder at John, grabbed a fistful of his sweatshirt, and pulled his body down until his lips were touching her's in a kiss.

Selena suggested that they stop by Knife and Fork.

"I haven't been there in a minute," she said. "I remember Tom used to make one of the best peppermint milkshakes."

"It's too cold for a milkshake."

"It's *never* too cold for a milkshake."

There was a joke somewhere in Selena's comment.

John thought about using it.

Then, again, he thought that perhaps it was a joke best kept to himself.

Inside he was laughing.

And in a way, so was Selena.

THE diner, Knife and Fork, was unusually packed for a cloudy Sunday afternoon, which mostly attracted a wicked mix of churchgoers and high schoolers from Del Soaka Falls, who were still battling hangovers from parties the night before with greasy food and Tom's discreet remedy, a shot of pickle juice. The parking lot was full, which was strange, considering church service was canceled due to the blackouts; although, the thought alone of a bunch of churchgoers worshiping in pitch-black intrigued her. From what Selena gathered, most of the cars belonged to a variety of townspeople inside the diner, which made her breathe a little easier, knowing her chances of running into any old faces dropped drastically.

Before entering the diner, Selena spotted two teens, a few years younger than Selena, probably sophomores, who were high off the street drug lo-ro. Their eyes rolled over white, as the two gawked at the overcast sky.

"Leave 'em alone," said John, who touched Selena on the shoulder.

"They look like these other kids I saw yesterday loggin' outside the doctor's office."

"You can't help 'em, Selena," he said. "Nobody can."

Selena's eyes moved away from the teens and landed on an oil drum next to a garage dumpster next to the back door of the diner. She fell into a sudden trance for she couldn't remove her eyes from the old and rusty metal drum with the brim caked with a hardened liquid that had overflowed from the inside, which was covered in black char.

A flash of raging fire inside a deep and dark pit filled her mind. The fire was loud and roaring and when the flames crackled, they sounded like a thousand tiny voices screaming out in horror.

John touched Selena on the shoulder.

Startled by the hand, she flinched.

"You all right?" asked John.

Selena pulled her eyes back to the drum.

Before she could find herself in another trance, she looked up at John and said, "Fine. Now, how about that milkshake?"

They entered Knife and Fork where most of the patrons were hardly touching their food. All of their attention was directed toward the BREAKING NEWS report on each of the four televisions mounted above the counter. On the screens, the local news reporter from PKWY11 was standing on the front porch of Ashleigh Reap's house, interviewing Ashleigh's mother, Aileen, who, from the slight slur in her voice and the way she easily lost her train of thought whenever the reporter asked her to further elaborate on an answer, sounded as if she was intoxicated or hungover or possibly both and Selena couldn't help but wonder if the reporter, knowing Ashleigh's mother's current state, as well as her clownish appearance (she was wearing heavy shades of makeup, the edges of movie-blood red lipstick smeared, along with the clumpy black mascara, and dressed in a purple bathrobe), deliberately chose to interview her. Aileen mentioned that she was cooperating with the sheriff's office after new details emerged in the missing case. According to an eyewitness who came forward yesterday, Ashleigh was last seen the afternoon before her disappearance. After having spoken with the sheriff's deputies, the eyewitness, owner of an antique shop called Pawp, which Ashleigh normally frequented, was interviewed earlier that day. The news played the clip from the morning broadcast: In the clip, Pawp told the reporter he saw Ashleigh walking along the street and she was acting paranoid and didn't appear like her normal self and Pawp mentioned she might've perhaps been in "trouble" or that someone might've been "following" her, based on his observations.

More news caught Selena's eye, which the anchor didn't specify whether or not the two incidents were related: "Kourtney McCormick" and "Billie Idlewile," two juniors from Del Soaka Falls High, were both reported "MISSING" yesterday afternoon. The two were last seen on Friday. Both of the girls' photos were displayed on the TV, and the anchor insisted that if anyone should see the girls then to contact a 1-800 number at the bottom of the screen.

One of the names immediately grabbed Selena's attention.

"That's Jorgina's sister," she said to John.

After stopping to listen to the rest of the report, John wheeled Selena to the back of the diner where he parked the wheelchair next to the one of the few booths that wasn't full.

"Dude," she said to John, "what the hell is going on around here?"

"I don't know," he said, downplaying the report. "Nothing in the report said that foul play was involved. It could be that the two are out on a bender or something."

"A bender?"

"It's happened before," he said more foolishly.

"John, they're seventeen years old."

"Maybe the power outage did something to their heads."

Selena said, "That's what I worry about."

A chatty waitress stopped by and asked how Selena was doing, mainly, Selena's leg.

Selena gave the same response—or statement—as she had been giving ever since the injury, as if she was reading from a script.

Then, after pushing aside the superficial inquiry, ordered a peppermint milkshake.

John ordered a cup of hot green tea.

After the waitress tended to their orders, Selena asked, "Green tea, huh?"

In a more studious manner, John lowered his head as he closely eyed Selena.

"What?"

Selena tried to hold back laughter.

"I read that it helps lower stress levels."

"Stress?" Amused, she said, "You're stressed?"

John shrugged.

"Lately," he said shortly. "Yeah. Who isn't?"

"About what? The blackout?"

Somewhat bashful, John was hesitant about answering.

"All I'm saying is you don't seem stressed out to me."

"Well," John said, trailing off, "it's just—I dunno—I've been thinking more about what you said before, you know, and maybe you're right. Maybe it's time for me to finally put this place in my rear view mirror."

"Where's all this coming from?" asked Selena.

"Things feel different."

"How?"

Before John's response, Selena couldn't help but turn to the TV.

In other breaking news, as though on cue: A latest update on the president-elect's condition, Lockhart, who was released from Walter Reed in October, and was currently spending the weekend at Camp David; and according to his doctors, he planned to make a full recovery after being shot in the face on September 8, 2048.

An image of the shooter, who attempted to assassinate Lockhart during a campaign rally in California, could be seen on the TV screen.

The shooter, a twenty-four year old "nationalist" named Jared Flack, whose scruffy face had been plastered over every news channel for the past two and a half months, was recently transferred to the hospital after experiencing severe chest pains.

Strangely, as Selena looked closer at Flack's face, she somehow knew the anchor was lying. As though in secret, most people knew about a conspiracy theory on the Internet, which involved Flack not being the real shooter but rather a "fall guy." The longer Selena stared at Flack's face, the more Selena began to think maybe that conspiracy theory was *not* a conspiracy, but rather the cold hard truth.

She couldn't help but overhear two locals sitting in the booth next to theirs: "*Man gets shot in the face, and his poll numbers skyrocket so fast you'd think he was more popular than Henry the Fif. When was the last time a sitting president turned California burgundy?*"

His friend replied: "*I think they said not since 1988, before the whole, you know, switch.*"

"That long, huh?"

"That's what they said."

"I see why the Halloween Party is obsessed with him."

"Too much jelly on their toast, I'd say. Wish they had a Lockhart on their side."

"Those orange bozos can never figure out whether they're a Unifier or a Divider—"

"The man's a snake in the grass. He'd fit right in with 'em."

Then, a retort from his friend, an vocal admirer of Lockhart: *"Snake or not, Americans like a SOB who's tougher than Maggie's meatloaf."*

A follow up: *"Maggie'd have your balls in a jar, if she heard you talking about her meatloaf that way."*

John followed Selena's eyes toward the TV screen where he witnessed the grainy still taken from surveillance camera footage outside the waterfront where Lockhart was holding a rally.

"Take a look around," he said, excluding the two friends who started arguing about a woman named "Maggie" and her god-awful cooking. "People are acting suspicious of one another. You think what happened to Lockhart would bring the country together. I mean. . . " he backtracked, ". . . it did. Yet, it didn't."

She looked around the inside of the diner at the townspeople whose eyes were glued to TV screens above the front counter.

"All looks the same to me."

"This used to be a place where people looked out for one another."

"It still is," Selena said with her brow furrowed. "I've been gone for not even a month and it still is your typical boring ole town."

"All I'm saying," he said, repeating Selena's very words, "maybe I can do better elsewhere."

"You can," Selena said, more upbeat. "And you will. You can't work at The Shop forever."

The waitress arrived with the drinks, a peppermint milkshake for Selena and a steaming hot cup of green tea for John.

They thanked the waitress, who, in return, asked if they'd like anything to eat.

"Just the milkshake," Selena said. "Although," she said to John, "the smell of hamburger is making me hungry."

She'd tell John that she was craving red meat as of lately.

As for John, the smell of the milkshake compelled him to order a slice of pumpkin pie.

With a flirty look in her eye, Selena said to John, "Nothing more stress-reducing than a slice of warm pie."

Both of John's shoulders deflated from what he thought was his girlfriend's half-ass attempt at a sexual innuendo, more or less, her attempt at showcasing her power over him, like a person dangling a treat over the snout of dog, slow close but too far from reach, and in time, if he was a good boy who didn't misbehave, he'd have his treat and then some.

Staring Selena in the eyes, he said, cracking a smile, "Now, you're just being cruel."

Selena gave him a shrug of the shoulders.

"Who doesn't like warm pie?" she asked but didn't receive a reaction from John.

The two sat in silence and drank from their drinks and enjoyed each other's company.

ON the following day, a Monday, Selena's physical therapist, Carly Schneider, made a house call since the rehabilitation center was closed due to the shortage of power.

During her session with Carly, she was able to walk from the guest bedroom to the edge of the kitchen without the physical therapist's assistance. Carly was at a loss of words and couldn't believe how much progress Selena made during the past week and had never seen such a speedy recovery, especially in a break as horrific as Selena's.

Carly worked on range of motion exercises with Selena. She also showed Selena a series of small workouts, as well as stretches and poses that Selena could work by herself, considering the uncertainty of the blackout, as well as the gas shortage. Carly was unsure whether or not she was going to be able to visit with Selena. The same went for Selena's orthopedic surgeon in Dumar, as well as her primary care doctor, whose offices were temporary closed. Last Selena heard: her doctor was making Cam-Calls with patients during the blackout. But like most people, she reckoned it was only a matter of time before they lost complete access from the Internet.

AFTER a strenuous yet productive day, Dean treated Selena to a warm bath after making two trips with a large pot of boiling hot water from Mr. Toto's house to the guest bathtub where he helped fill half of the bathtub, the remaining half Selena filled with cold water.

Once the bath was ready, Selena used a lantern to light up the bathroom and sat on the toilet, hesitant to step into the warm water. She pulled out her cracked phone and scrolled through the several photos of her leg after the surgery. She pinched her fingers over the screen and zoomed in on the incisions, the first photo taken after the first surgery and the second taken after the second surgery. Her swollen leg stitched and stapled up, as Kellie best put it when she saw her during her belated birthday surprise, "Frankenstein's monster."

She closed the phone and placed it on the edge of the vanity and contemplated taking a bath. She couldn't bring herself to step into the bathtub for an overwhelming fear of water left her in a crippled state. Never had she ever felt so scared of something as basic as water.

After twenty minutes passed, Selena drained the tub.

She told herself that the water was already too cold.

But she'd wet her hair and later thank Dean for the nice gesture.

THE CURIOUS *CASES* OF ROSES
DECEMBER 1, 2048
PADADOCK, PENNSYLVANIA

THE next day, a Tuesday, which marked the first day of December, Dean surprised Selena with a present: a full leg brace given to him by a close friend of his, "Roge," who worked at a medical supply store. The brace wasn't covered by their insurance—despite his daughter's desired and at times, sacred independence, Selena was still on Dean and Lacey's policy. Normally, the special leg brace would cost a couple thousand; however, Keen and Anything But Clean Dean managed to score the brace for nearly a quarter of the original cost, which didn't effect the payments of the monthly bills or force Dean and Lacey to make adjustments to their daily expenses. Dean was already one step ahead for he had an uncanny knack for, not only smooth talking his way into a good deal, but also foreseeing benefits of handing out certain discounts at his own store in hopes of one day finding himself or his loved ones in the good graces of one of his customers who was willing to reciprocate, for example, last year, Dean hooking up

Roge with a sweet deal of camping gear for Roge and his family, Roge promising Dean that one day he'd repay him. Despite his many titles, Dean the Scheme was said to be one of the "best hagglers on the planet," according to Lacey, a skill he picked up from working many years in retail.

When Selena finally tried on the brace for the first time and gave it a test drive with the help of crutches, she described it as "walking on air."

After sporting the new brace around the neighborhood, Selena wore herself out and decided to remove the brace and take a break.

While airing out the brace, she was drawn to the poster on the wall, the one of the Olympian Angelina "Geaux" Campbell, as well as the rip along the bottom part of the poster. She sat on the bed and questioned whether or not to remove the poster from the wall, but ultimately, after several minutes of contemplation, ended up keeping it on the wall.

Around midday, when Bret was said to be at Massacre's house, Lacey and Dean went on a walk through the neighborhood, allowing Selena enough time to take advantage of a quiet house and snoop around Dean's office, particularly, his impressive library where he had a vast collection of books on SPORTS, as well as autobiographies on various athletes, from José Santiago, the renowned baseball player who won the World Series for the Atlanta Hellhounds in 2029, to Marcie "Low Blow" Styles, the first woman to play professional football—also, by far one of the most talked about athletes of the decade due to the controversy that surrounded her.

Next to Marcie Styles' autobiography was a book called *Modern Amazons: The Trailblazers Who Paved A Way For Future Generations.* The book, which Selena thought about reading multiple times whenever boredom set in throughout the day but was always intimidated by its size—over a thousand pages—highlighted the achievements of women in sports.

She sat down in Dean's comfy chair and skimmed through the book until she came across a photograph of a soccer player, Milota "Milo" Rose, who, several years prior to her death in 2023, was accused by a trainer of taking "sports enhancement drugs" and ultimately, was rejected from the Women's Soccer Hall of Fame. The reason Selena was drawn to Milo: the strange tattoo on her neck.

More intrigued by Milo, Selena flipped to the next page where she came across a gallery of photos, all of which were taken throughout the span of Rose's tumultuous career.

Among the photos, Selena found a better, much clearer image of that tattoo, which was the same symbol from her dreams. The action-like photograph was taken during a final match in the 2007 World Cup, which was held in China. In the photo Milo was kicking one of the three goals scored by the United States, who later went on to defeat Germany in a nail-biting shoot-out that ended with goalie Kylie-Joe Bryan blocking the fifth and final shot by rival Randilyn "Rampage" Müller. She read more about Milo's background and all of the records she broke during her professional career. Selena started at the beginning with Milo's hometown, Bluefield, Pennsylvania, which was where Milo was born.

Considering the town was only a few miles away made Selena even more interested, in fact, obsessed with learning about Milo Rose.

As Selena skimmed through Milo's bio, her finger ran across several words that caught her eye: "*Death*," read one of the words, another, "*Poisoned*," then, lastly, "*Murdered*."

Returning back to the top of the paragraph, Selena started to read about Milo's death, which in the fall of '23 had become a national spectacle.

While reading, Selena heard a *rustling*-noise behind her, forcing her to rotate her shoulder where she saw her nana grabbing a puzzle on deep-sea creatures from the corner of the office.

"Don't mind me," Eleanor said, trying not to disturbed Selena. "I'll be out of your way—"

"I was just browsing," Selena said and closed the book.

Eleanor eyed the thick paperback in Selena's hand.

"I see," she said, placing the puzzle aside. "I'm sure your stepfather won't mind. Ever since I've known the man, I've never seen him with a book in his hand. I often wonder if all this. . . " she glanced around Dean's library, ". . . is for show."

"You know what?" Selena said amusedly, as she tilted her head in thought. "I've never seen him read either."

Selena laughed inside and whatever bit of laughter that broke through manifested in the flick of a crooked smirk on her face.

After the amusement faded away, Selena hung her head with melancholy.

Eleanor, who had quite an eye for reading people, picked up on her granddaughter's vibe.

"What's a matter?" asked Eleanor.

Selena shrugged her shoulders and after a pause, said, "Lately, I've been thinking a lot about school and whether or not I should return."

"What about track?"

"I dunno," she said depressingly. "I don't feel as driven to compete as I once did, before all of this."

"You experienced a traumatic event, Selena."

"I feel that sports was always my way out of here. But now, I fear that I won't be able to get back to the way I was, physically. And even if, by some miracle, I do, I don't know if I'll ever recover, mentally. I just don't want to experience that pain again."

"When you get to be my age..." Eleanor said, similarly amused as her granddaughter moments ago, "... you become best friends with pain. It's a sort of love-hate relationship."

"I never want to get old." She paused, realizing the recent slip of her tongue. "No offense."

"None taken, Selena," Eleanor said, more wittingly. "I know I'm old. Except for death, it's the one thing we all have in common. *Getting old.*" She let out a sigh. "You certainly can't run away from it, although—" she said from the corner of her mouth, "—with the advances in modern medicine, drug makers have created a pill to expedite the process. Can't believe such a drug was even approved."

"Equanimity," Selena said, thinking about an Ad for the new drug that she recently saw being promoted on her feed before the blackout. "They call it Queuc."

"Who's *they?*"

"People on the Internet."

Eleanor waved off the Internet, as if it was no different than an imaginary place where truth was as hard to find as a cave diver searching for light.

Once considered a handy tool meant to educate before it turned into a place of manipulation and corruption.

Whose mere existence was to enslave those who access its very presence.

Tempted to tell Selena how she truly felt about the Internet, she pushed aside her complaints for they weren't even worth her time or Selena's, considering Selena wasn't a part of the whole social media scene—Why preach to the choir?

"Sure," Eleanor said, "you can fight it off for as long as you can. The pain. Eventually, you wake up one day and realize the fight's over. Ultimately, the pain wins. But just know, Selena, there are monumental consequences for the actions you make in your life, cause and effect. *'The Earth giveth, The Earth taketh away.'* So, you must decide which fight is more important to you: your dreams or your health. Or the trickiest fight: Are your dreams worth risking your health?"

Selena started to think that maybe her nana had been snooping around the guestroom whenever she wasn't home or maybe Lacey, who spent her days off work scrapping together photo albums in fear of losing all of her photos on all of her digital devices, informed her mother about Selena's beef with Neuvak—how a pharmaceutical company being responsible for the accident was a strong possibility, even though she didn't have any concrete proof to back her claims.

Unsure, she said, "I've been thinking about traveling."

"I don't blame you," Eleanor said. "If I was your age, I'd get as far away as I could from this place. You're so smart, Selena. You possess a keen awareness that many your age lack or fail to appreciate, given the current nature we live in. You're still young," Eleanor reassured her granddaughter. "Embrace your youth while you still have it. Otherwise, you'll spend the rest of your life thinking 'What if?' And that's certainly no way to live."

"Say," Selena said with a slight tremble in her voice, as she looked down at the book in her hand, "by any chance, did you know a woman named Milo Rose?"

Eleanor's face slackened, her breath grew heavier.

"Of course," Eleanor said with a stutter, which Selena thought was unusual coming from a lady who carried herself with grace and confidence. "I knew Milo, like most folks my age, considering she grew up in Bluefield. She was quite famous, tragic story, though. Why do you ask, Selena?"

Selena showed Eleanor *Modern Amazons*, as well as the photograph of Milo Rose inside the book.

With a startling awe on her face, Eleanor stared at the photo.

The awe soon fell into reminiscence.

Selena watched Eleanor, her face, like a sad story slowly unraveling.

"Was she one of your students?" asked Selena.

With tears in her eyes, Eleanor said, "She was."

Eleanor looked over the other photos of Milo while Selena kept her eyes on her nana.

"What were things like," Selena said curiously, "when you were my age?"

"Unfortunately, not so different."

"How so?"

"Except for the whole, you know, *Internet* stuff, people still acted the same, still acted out; however, regardless of people's antics and whatnot, there was still a level of respect for one another that doesn't exist nowadays, a sense of community." She sat down on the couch and tried to compose herself, as she told her granddaughter about the missing case that she had been thinking about ever since she heard about those four missing girls from Del Soaka Falls (Blaire Tudor, a freshman, and the three juniors, Ashleigh Reap, Kourtney McCormick, and Billie Idlewile) in the news.

"I guess they rehashed some old memories," she went on to say. "Back when I was young, a few years older than you are now, a girl, Nikola Rose—'Knitty' was what everybody knew her by— was brutally murdered in Bluefield."

Nikola Rose?

Selena immediately put the two together.

"Was she related to Milo Rose?"

Eleanor paused, looked over her granddaughter.

"She was Milo's sister," she finally said.

"I've heard stories about it, not the girl, but Bluefield and how it went straight downhill after the steel factory was shutdown in the early Nineties."

"The reason why the steel factory was shutdown had a lot to do with Nikola's death, not the crisis."

"What happened?"

Eleanor took yet another deep breath and said, "One day, she just went missing. Days later, her body was discovered in the woods. Her death was disturbing, to say the least, and it's probably best I spare you from the details—"

"Seriously?" Selena said, surprised. "Trust me. I've heard about much worse—"

"Her bones were missing," Eleanor said with a rather solemn tone.

"Bones?" Her voice trailed off, "How does that even happen. . ."

"The person responsible for Nikola's death was never found," Eleanor said. "Some believed it might've been from an animal."

"What kind of animal eats bones?"

Shaking her head, Eleanor said, "None that I've heard of. According to the coroner, the cuts on Nikola's body were done by a professional."

"You mean like a hit man?"

"More like someone in medicine."

"Like a doctor?"

"Yes," she said. "That was one theory."

"I can't imagine what her parents went through," Selena said tenderly.

She studied her nana's face, as the sound of Nikola's parents forced her nana to once more compose herself.

Before the emotion could take over, she sighed and regained her composure.

"It was a complete mystery," she said to Selena. "Several years went by, and the ripple effect from Nikola's death spread like a virus through the town, as well as the surrounding towns, including Padadock."

"You're talking about North Tryon," Selena said, thinking about what used to be Padadock's old downtown.

"Padadock never had much of a downtown," Eleanor said bluntly. "I've heard that developers wanted to revamp North Tryon, but I'm sure once they found out about its morbid history, I reckon they had second thoughts."

Engrossed by the story, Selena asked, "What kind of history?"

"Once word spread about what happened to Nikola, her death resulted in more deaths—self-inflicted, deadly disputes, murder, rape, robbery, unrelated yet *very much* related. People turned on one another. They simply lost all hope in humanity. I guess, people were blind of man's capability, and when people realized what man was capable of, especially what it can do to even the most innocent of life forms like a precious young girl, like Nikola, some people. . . " She said more directly to Selena, ". . . broke."

Thinking about her nana's comments, Selena said, "I wish someone would come in and redo the old downtown."

"Don't get your hopes up, kiddo," Eleanor said pessimistically.

AFTER an eye-opening conversation with her nana about Nikola Rose and her older sister, Milo, as well as Milo's high-profile death, which shocked, not only the country, but also the world, Selena went back to her room where she reflected upon her own life and whether or not a future in track was going to play an important role in her life. The more Selena thought about her life, the more she thought about Milo's. Her eyes trailed up to the partially ripped poster of Geaux on the wall. In a sudden fit of anger, Selena removed the poster, rolled it up, and tossed it in the closet.

Once the anger settled, Selena focused on Milo and her story; and right then, Selena figured out what she wanted to do during her time in Padadock. Call it what you will, a personal project or Selena whetting her own curiosity, Selena found a purpose—or at least, thought she did.

After she finished reading about Milo and her career as a professional soccer player, she was hungry for more.

She pulled up the Internet on her phone—the wi-fi signal was weak but she was able to find results on the search engine—and continued her research into Milo through Wikipedia and other informational sites or forums. She learned more about Milo's parents, her mother being a ninth grade Algebra instructor at Plymouth High and their father, a doctor who practiced in Blue-field, originally questioned about Nikola's death, considering the condition in which her body was discovered, but in the end, ruled out by investigators as having any part in the death. Selena's interest were directed toward the mother, Hilda, who, after the death of Nikola, ended up leaving her position at Plymouth to pursue a career in art, which, according to a grainy screenshot taken from a rare interview inside an art magazine, in her own words, *"was a coping mechanism to deal with Nikola's death."*

She pulled out pictures of Hilda's abstract paintings, and there they were, symbols. In all of Hilda's artwork, the same symbols from Selena's dreams were incorporated into each piece, either plain as day or disguised within a shape or pattern, nonetheless, present in Hilda's artwork.

With the recent discovery in mind, Selena sought out Eleanor, who was taking a nap in her parents' room. She asked her nana if she knew Nikola's mother, Hilda. She told Selena that the two both taught at Plymouth together. At the time, her nana taught English Literature. Despite having worked at the same school, the two—according to Eleanor—were *not* close (a part of Selena, for some reason, felt as if her nana wasn't being totally honest, especially when she added with clarity that whenever a child died, part of that parent, in a way, also died, at least a part that mattered the most, in this case, Victor and Hilda).

Selena decided to leave her nana and let her get back to her nap while she grabbed her phone and continued her research into Milo Rose.

WHILE digging into the unsolved murder case of Milo Rose, the signal from the neighbor's wi-fi dropped, prompting the irritating "No Connection" message on the true crime site. She refreshed the page, only to wind up with a blank screen. She tried to reconnect to wi-fi, but it was down.

Frustrated, Selena called out to Bret, whom she soon realized wasn't home; in fact, she had hardly seen him around the house for the past couple of days. Which made her wonder if he was going through a kind of withdrawal from not being able to play VR.

After Lacey and Dean returned from their walk, Selena decided to sneak into her brother's bedroom by using the railing on the side of the staircase to climb up the steps.

Once Selena reached the upstairs, she used the wall and with one leg, hoped her way into her brother's bedroom. She searched for his phone or any device that had a connection, like a laptop or tablet. All she found was a portable mp3 player, which had various apps, like a web browser, but she needed a password to access the device.

Then, she checked the desktop computer but had no luck.

Lastly, Selena checked the desk drawers where she found two items that grabbed her attention—a damp, raggedy toboggan that reeked of shit and the other, a SOG knife, both the handle, as well as the blade caked with what looked like blood.

On the very bottom of the handle were the two initials "FT."

With the tip of her shirt, Selena picked up the old knife and studied it closely and wondered what her brother was doing with the knife and most importantly, why was it covered in blood.

DETERMINED to find out more about Milo Rose, Selena continued her research at Knife and Fork where she used a hotspot to reconnect to the Internet.

John, who never saw Selena at the candlelight vigil for the girls, which was held last night at the garden in front of Town Hall, stopped by the diner, only to find Selena sitting in a booth with notes on Milo Rose scattered all over the table.

Considering the delicate situation, Selena gathered her notes and told John that she'd explain everything to him but somewhere else. She couldn't help mention John's body odor and how he smelled, which, in John's defense, he claimed that he wasn't a fan of cold showers. Also, he was sort of running out of clothes to wear—hence why he was wearing the same blue flannel that he was wearing the day before.

Stink aside, the two left Knife and Fork. John carried Selena's notes while Selena, with her new brace, used the crutches to walk out on her own. As the two walked back to Selena's house, Selena explained the reasons for her "new project," first by handing her phone to him and showing him the screenshots that she took of Hilda's artwork, as well as the tattoo on her daughter's neck.

Then, after John asked why he was looking at these symbols, came the difficult part for Selena: "I've been seeing these same symbols in my dreams."

"Serious?"

"*Dead* serious," she said with a straight face.

"What are they?" John asked, as he scrolled through the photos on Selena's phone.

"According to Hilda Rose—"

"The mother of the dead girl?"

Selena furrowed her brow with confusion.

"You know her?"

"Not personally," he said. "But yeah... everybody around here knows her, and I'm sure as hell they wouldn't appreciate you dredging up the past. Did you ever stop to think maybe these 'visions' you're having could be associated with the medication you're taking?"

"I'm not on any medication," she said clearly. "The pain's gone."

She demonstrated her lack of pain by bending her knee.

"See," she said and suddenly grimaced from a bolt of pain shooting up her leg.

"You should be home resting, Selena."

"I'll be fine," she said shortly. "I think I put the brace on too tight. Anyway, like I was saying," she said, ignoring the pain as if it was no different than an itch, "I think these cases are connected."

"Cases?" John stopped in front of Selena. "You're talking about the four who're missing?"

"Nikola Rose's body was found January 16, 1988," Selena said. "Badly murdered."

John asked, "Is there a good kind of murder?"

"I'm talking like NC-17-type stuff—"

"I know what happened, Selena," John said flatly. "But thanks for reminding me."

"Her older sister Milo was murdered thirty-five years later."

"How do know she was murdered?" asked John.

"According to researchers who followed her case, she was poisoned."

"And I'm sure you know that, before her death, she was diagnosed with cancer, right?"

Selena didn't respond to John's comment.

"Bone cancer, I believe," he said, trying to think of the cancer. "Osteo. . . "

"Osteosarcoma," Selena finished John's thought. "I read about that, but she lived with it for years. Like eight years or something like that. . . "

"All I'm saying is nobody knows what really happened to Milo Rose," John said, shrugging his shoulders. "People can speculate all they want, but the fact of the matter: People die, Selena. It's part of life. Unfortunately, some of us go out sooner than others. Yet, I dunno, sometimes, it feels like the good ones always die young."

Selena clenched her teeth and swallowed the retort, her main grievance being the "way" the two sisters died, mainly Nikola, which was unthinkable.

More calmly, she said, "I've been reading about her, about Milo. She's a fascinating person. Married twice. One year before winning the World Cup in 2007 she had a son. She was twenty-eight at the time and a lot of haters thought she was washed up and didn't deserve to play for the US. Milo proved them wrong. Later, she went on to play professionally for ten more years until the League decided to give her the boot—some kind of doping scandal that turned out to be all bullshit. Sports enthusiasts believe it was the League's excuse for getting rid of Milo. After her second divorce, she went back to using her maiden name. Her son, Cashel, ended up becoming a cop and from what I read on the Internet, the only reason why he joined the Force was to find the person responsible for his mom's death."

"That's actually pretty cool, despite being kind of cliché, though," John said with sincerity.

"Get this. . . " Selena said, more excitedly, ". . . he, too, was murdered two years—"

"Let me guess," he said sarcastically, "by your so-called 'mystery killer' who, by the way, if my math is correct, would make him like a hundred years old."

"It wasn't *that* long ago, if you stop and think about it."

He handed back Selena's phone.

"Happened during the blackouts in Kingsport."

"I remember hearing about it," John said. "Lotta people died."

"In an interview, I read that Milo would play for free, if she could do."

"Why?"

"She loved playing soccer," Selena said. "After her sister was killed, she found an outlet in the sport. For Hilda, it was painting. For Milo, it was kicking around a ball. As for Nikola and Milo's father, well, that's a whole different story."

John asked, "What kind of story?"

"Apparently, there was this author from London," Selena said, more carefully, "Henry Jaub. From what I've read, he wrote a pretty compelling book about Nikola's case. I was only able to read an excerpt online, but from what I've read, it digs deeper into Nikola's father's past, and in particular, a former colleague of his who, let's just say, has a bizarre background."

"Bizarre?" John squared himself to Selena. "What's going on with you?"

With her eyes pinned on John, she said in return, "What do you mean?"

"You're doing it again."

"Doing what?"

"First, you had your mind set on Neuvak," he said. "Now, the Rose family—"

"I truly feel that there's some kind of connection."

"Maybe you saw these. . . " John trailed off, as he searched for the word.

Selena filled in the blank: "Symbols."

"Maybe you saw them when you were younger," he said, "and now, perhaps, because of the recent trauma you experienced, it's all coming back to you."

"I don't think that's it."

"Then what do you think?"

Selena didn't answer, not immediately.

John waited.

"I think. . . " Selena said, struggling to find the right words to say to John, ". . . I think this is what I'm supposed to be doing right now. Why?" Selena asked aloud, not to John, but to herself. "I don't know why. I just know, in my gut, that something, I don't know what, but *something* is drawing me toward Milo. I just need to know. And if you're not okay with that, then please get out of my way."

"But Selena, this is schizo!"

"I know how this all sounds," she said over John. "But if you truly care about me, like you say you do, then prove it."

He studied Selena's face and observed how serious she was about the Rose family and pursuing the truth behind Nikola's death.

Eventually, after collecting his thoughts, he said, "What's the plan?"

THE plan wasn't so easy, as Selena pointed out, and it required extra legwork from John.

After Selena convinced John to do her bidding, John, whose only crime throughout his nineteen years of existence was doing the occasional rolling stop at stop signs in empty intersections, agreed to ignore a ten o'clock curfew issued by Mayor Benkins and break into Mrs. Applegate's bookstore in Midtown to steal two books: the first being Henry Jaub's true crime novel on Nikola's gruesome death, *When The Sun Stopped Rising*; the other, a copy of the book *MACHINE: The Life and Death of Milo Rose* written by admired sports journalist Ralfe Lagilio, who died a month after the book's publication in October of 2029, six years after Milo's death.

While Selena concealed herself behind a trashcan across the street, John used a brick, which he wrapped with an old, raggedy T-shirt, to partially shatter the glass of the front door, making a hole large enough to stick his hand through to unlock the door from the inside of the store.

He unwrapped the dirty tee from the brick and shook away the shards of glass onto the sidewalk before placing it back in his bookbag and entering the store.

He stepped over the glass along the entranceway and pulled out a flashlight.

After scouring through the store, John managed to find both books.

He returned to Selena and showed her the books that he had stolen.

"Did you leave the note behind?" asked Selena.

John quivered at the very notion.

"Well, did you?"

With a sharp whispered, John said, "You know how much trouble we can get into?"

"It's the right thing to do, John," Selena said. "Besides, I know Casey. She won't tell your Dad."

John's eyes trailed downward in thought.

While he debated whether or not to leave behind the note, which, in it, consisted of a sincere apology for the broken window that John and Selena would repair, as well as the two books that were stolen, which would be returned ASAP (Selena drew a ☺ at the end of the note as her way of reassuring Mrs. Applegate that there was no reason to be upset for the damage to her business when, in secret, it was Selena's way of begging Mrs. Applegate to please reconsider taking any legal action against the two book-worms who desperately needed books to read during these *unpropitious* times—despite John's disapproval, he thought using the flowery adjective was a nice touch and might tickle Mrs. Applegate's reading bone), Selena moved her head in front of John's soft eyes and said, "If you're not going to do it, then I will. . . "

"Fine," he said and ran back to the store and tossed the note through the hole in the door.

APPARENTLY, the name "Machine" was Milo's nickname, Selena learned while reading the book about Milo's life as a professional soccer player: a name, according to author Ralfe Lagilio, who followed her around for a year before she retired from the League, given to her by Bailey Davis, her teammate on the 2007 World Cup team. The name was inspired by Milo's speedy return to the team after having only given birth the year before. The chapter on Milo's death called "Who or *What* Killed Milo?" was the most shocking to Selena. The "What" part was still unclear and startling to Ralfe, even though the autopsy showed traces of the inorganic compound sodium hydroxide, also known as "lye," in the toxicity report, which might've been the main contributor to her death. Whether ingested accidentally or voluntarily or according to Ralfe's suggestion, maliciously, Kurtivon Harburschmit, the coroner who performed the autopsy, concluded that Ms. Milota Rose died from cardiac arrest. The only suspect was Wayne Cornell, a professional basketball player whom Milo had been seeing off and on, not only after her second marriage, but also, based on tabloids, not in Milo's own words, rumored to be seeing during her marriage and possibly the main reason why Milo filed for divorce. According to Ralfe, these were all false accusations, which only put a strain on Milo's career as one of the most talented professional athletes of her time. Cornell was never charged with any crime.

As for the next read, *When The Sun Stopped Rising*, Selena put it aside for the morning and drifted to sleep next to John, who rifled through Selena's notes underneath a lantern.

That night, while spending the night at John's, Selena didn't have any strange dreams.

Instead, she fell heavily into Milo's story, recounting it through her own imagination, pointing out and highlighting certain chapters, words, or "clues" that stood out the most, as she began a slow process of digesting everything that she recently absorbed. It wasn't until the next morning when Selena woke up after a heavy, dreamless sleep and squeezed in the first few chapters of the next novel, *When The Sun Stopped Rising*, which primarily focused on the Rose family, their firmly planted roots in Pennsylvania, mainly Nikola's father, Victor Cashel Rose, "Cashel," Selena realizing, the name given to Milo's son. As far as Victor's side of the family, he came from a family of doctors. A few members of Hilda's side, her family being the Dulíks, originally from Czechoslovakia before the country became independent, were also doctors. Strangely, Hilda and Victor, Selena concluded, was a good place to start, in essence, her first "clue."

One of those clues being a name—

"*Patrick Britten*," Selena said, as she brought the news to John, who was outside on the back porch cooking eggs over the charcoal grill.

"Good morning to you," John said, not giving the name any of his attention.

"Morning," Selena said shortly.

With a spatula, John removed two of the three eggs from the pan and placed them on paper plates. One of the eggs was for his father, cooked "sunny side up." The other egg was "busted," just the way John preferred to eat it with a slice of white bread, which he also toasted with butter over hot coals. Finally, the third egg, for Selena, which he whipped in a bowl, then as soon as he poured the egg onto the hot pan, flipped it once before he folded it in half, like a "naked omelet."

Selena instructed him to make sure he didn't overcook it, only a few seconds on each side.

John removed the egg from the pan and placed it on Selena's plate.

"Sorry," he said, almost mockingly. "Don't have any steaks on hand. This is the best that I can do—"

"No," she said, smiling. "It's perfect. Thanks."

"You're welcome."

"So, where'd you get the eggs?"

"Mrs. Johnson brought them by this morning," he said. "Came straight from her chickens."

"It sure would be nice to have my own chicken coop."

"Well, I guess that's the difference between my neck of the woods," he bragged, "where you can have chicken coops and do all sorts of fun stuff, and *your* neck of the woods where you have HOA fascists breathing down your neck."

Selena rolled her eyes.

"You woke up in a peculiar mood," said Selena.

"Last night had me thinking—"

"Give it a rest," she said, annoyed by what she thought was John being paranoid. "Sheriff Atlas isn't going to throw you in jail for *borrowing* a couple of books."

"I'm over that," John said, waving off Selena's remark. "I mean Milo Rose, her story, how the sports world completely turned against her; yet, besides gossip, there wasn't one single shred of evidence that proved she was taking enhancements."

Selena said casually, "You know how gossip is the new truth."

"But it's not the truth."

"Doesn't matter."

"And also, she didn't mention anything about the inspiration behind the tattoo?"

Selena looked at John with a suspicious look.

"Did you have a bot read the book while I was asleep?"

"No," he said. "I read through your notes. I didn't see anything about this symbol you keep talking about. . . "

With a rigid brow, Selena gave John a look.

"Besides," he said, defensively, "I didn't want to wake you. You were pretty out of it."

"Thanks," she said, glad. "I needed the sleep."

John took his father's plate inside and called out to his father, who was in his workshop. For Selena, one of the perks about chilling at John's house: it was as quiet as a church due to a rather sparse household, unlike her "place" where she had a clash of three different generations fighting over space. Ever since John's mother passed away when he was a sophomore in high school, it was only John and his father living under one roof and yet, despite her passing, her presence still remained through the various antiques that they kept throughout the house.

John returned to the porch and together, he and Selena made their way back inside the house where they took their breakfast to the kitchen table. John pulled out the chair for Selena, making enough room for the bulky brace worn on Selena's leg. Then, after making the accommodations for Selena, he helped her to her seat.

"So, who's this Patrick guy—"

"*Britten*," she exclaimed. "Patrick Britten. I think he's the first person we talk to."

John paused right before he sat down in the chair at the head of the table.

"We?"

"Yes," she said. "We. I can't drive, not until my leg completely heals."

"About that," John said. "How's your pain?"

Selena shrugged.

"It comes in waves," she said and took a bite from the egg. "Back to Britten, the art dealer, his name is mentioned a lot in the book."

"I assume this art dealer, Patrick Britten, was buying—or selling—Hilda's art, right?"

"More like sleeping with Hilda behind Victor's back."

"For real?"

Selena nodded.

"It mentions that in the book?"

"Briefly, believe it or not," Selena said, "in fact, Victor was the one who introduced Hilda to Patrick. Apparently, Patrick's father knew Victor from work."

"Kind of inappropriate, you think?" John said and made himself comfortable at the kitchen table. "Makes you wonder about the author's true intentions."

"It'd be nice to reach out to Jaub—"

"Who lives in London," John reiterated, as though he was finishing Selena's thought for her, "and the planes all across the country are grounded. Remember, Selena?"

A tension developed around John's eyes, bringing more color to the upper part of his cheeks.

"What about email?" asked Selena.

"You can try," John said, "but I doubt he'll respond to you."

"The worst part about it was that Britten had the affair with Hilda three months after Nikola was killed."

John asked Selena, "Did it say anything about what Nikola's parents' relationship was like before their daughter's death?"

"No," she said. "Not yet. Well, I've only read the first few chapters. But if anybody knows anything about these symbols, it'd be Britten."

John asked, "And what makes you so sure that he's still alive?"

"I don't," Selena said.

"Okay," John said and asked about Selena's brother, how he was handling the blackout.

Selena gave him a shrug of "I dunno."

"Haven't heard from him in a minute."

John, who followed Bret on Streamerz, not because he was the brother of his girlfriend, but because, in John's own words, he made "good content worthy enough for a sub," was concerned after watching Bret's last post right before the blackout, and how he didn't look too well. Bret's face was paler than its usual shade with dark bags underneath his eyes, which John thought was unusual coming from a kid who was cleaner than most his age. Bret didn't smoke or drink.

Selena mentioned that he had been acting standoffish ever since Ashleigh Reap was reported missing but when asked, said that he wasn't close to her, except for passing her in the hallway at Del Soaka Falls.

John referred to Ashleigh in the past tense.

Was?

"You're starting to sound more like Bret," Selena said, recalling the last name she called her brother: "Morbid." She said over the pause, "Why so grim?"

John didn't have a good answer for Selena, but she thought it had a lot to do with him going to their vigil last night.

On the contrary, he didn't apologize for his usage of tense. Instead, he looked Selena in the eyes and said, "I'm just being realistic."

"Of course, you are."

"Selena—"

"Nothing in the report says that they've found any bodies," Selena said to John. "For all you know, all four of them could've ghosted Padadock. I would, if I didn't break my leg."

"But would you have returned back home if you didn't break your leg?"

Selena ignored the question and said, "You're right, to some degree, about something happening to them, but I fear this town isn't fit to handle whatever did happen."

"The whole thing is just strange, don't you think?"

After her recent experiences with the strange dreams, as well as the strange connections to a family that she had never even met, Selena said, "Lately, strange has become the new normal."

LATER that same morning, after using a weakened wi-fi signal at Knife and Fork, John managed to track down Patrick Britten, who, according to a search site, lived close by. He brought the information back to Selena, who was finishing up some reading at a nearby park.

Over her shoulder, Selena heard John behind her.

"Landfalls," he was saying from the edge of the parking lot.

Selena pulled her eyes from the novel *When The Sun Stopped Rising* and found John rushing over to her.

"What about it?" she asked.

He slowed down his gait and walked composedly toward the picnic table where Selena was sitting and said, "That's where your lover boy, Britten, lives."

"Landfalls, huh? That's no more than an hour away. Have enough gas to get there?"

"Full tank," he said, his face glowing.

"How'd you manage that?" asked Selena.

"Dean hooked me up with his gas guy."

The surprise rippled throughout Selena's face: her eyes wide, mouth open.

"My Dean?"

With a grin on his face, John nodded.

"What'd you say to him?" Selena asked.

John stepped closer to Selena.

"I told him the truth," he said bluntly.

"About. . . "

"About you," John said. "About these visions you've been having. . . ."

"John," Selena said, the anger rising up inside her, "what did you tell him that—"

"He understood, Selena," John said, trying to calm Selena.

John's words were like buttons pressing pause on Selena's anger.

With her face less intense, she said in a higher tone, "He did?"

"He doesn't think you're crazy."

Unsure whether or not to believe John, she turned to the lake where a late morning fog was hovering over the serene water.

"Maybe I am going crazy," she said, staring at the blanket of fog.

Before Selena could ask the question, John asked, "You sure you wanna do this?"

"You're sure it's the right Britten?"

"Patrick Britten moved from a suburb outside Philadelphia to Chesterville four months after Nikola's death. He only lived in Chesterville for a year before he moved to New York. Lived in Madrid for a while. Then Paris a few years before, eventually, he settled in Landfalls. The story makes sense. He moved to Chesterville, which is only a short drive away from Bluefield, while he was *allegedly* having an affair with Hilda."

"I dunno," Selena said, thinking. "I hate to show up unannounced."

"I'm sure he won't mind."

"How'd you know?" asked Selena. "What if we get there, waste all that gas, and he doesn't want to talk to us?"

"I'm ready whenever you are," John said, as he remained persistent on visiting Patrick Britten. "Not like I have anything else going on today."

Selena answered John's invitation in the form of a smile.

Excited, she grabbed her things, tossed them in her bag, and flung the bag over her shoulder.

Using the crutches for support, she skipped her way toward John's car.

DURING the car ride from Padadock to Landfalls, Selena brought up yet another name from *When The Sun Stopped Rising*: "Sturgeon 'Sturgis' Reap," she said, as she forgot to mention the name earlier to John. "Ashleigh's grandfather."

"Does Jaub suspect he might've been involved in Nikola's death?" asked John.

"No," she said. "But he does bring up Sturgeon's criminal past. He was sixteen when Nikola was murdered. He was questioned by authorities after a witness came forward claiming that he saw Sturgeon leaving the woods the day before Nikola's body was discovered—"

"No shit!"

"*However. . .*" Selena said over John, as her tone punched a hole in his excitement and left him somewhat deflated, ". . . the investigators working the case, couldn't find any evidence that linked Sturgeon to Nikola's death. Here comes the interesting part: A year later, he was charged for sexual assault, was underage, and since they couldn't charge him as an adult, he was sent to juvenile hall. Get this: Three years after that, he was charged and convicted for assault against a young woman, almost killed her, spent several years behind bars, was in and out of prison for the next ten years or so."

Once more, the excitement rose back up inside John.

Thinking out loud, he said with a tamed and restrained emotion, "I see why Conner decided to turn his life around. I'm sure that he didn't have to look too far for inspiration or potentially, where his life could wind up, if he didn't get straight."

"It kind of now all makes sense as to why he was always getting in trouble. . . "

"You remember what he did to Thurman last year?"

"How could I forget?"

"When I talked to him the other day, he said he did it because he was sticking up for his sister."

"Well. . . if I found out someone was picking on Bret. . . " she trailed off before she decided that it was best to leave the thought alone, ". . . I don't know what I'd do."

John said, "Maybe Britten could fill in the gaps for you."

"One could only hope," Selena said and drew her attention back to the road ahead.

GIVEN Patrick Britten's age—according to his wife, Marilee, he'll turn eighty-seven next July—the trip to Landfalls was more stimulating than productive for John and Selena, except for a couple of important findings that they learned during a brief conversation with Patrick and Marilee, who were both in the same predicament as those of Padadock, before the gracious couple began to pack for what Patrick called their "final vacation."

With the fireplace warming the living room, which was filled with various family photos of grandchildren and past relatives, Marilee, who was a decade younger than her husband and still as witty and bubbly as the day she met Patrick after he moved from Paris to Landfalls following the sudden passing of his mother, Clementine, helped filled in the blanks for her husband regarding his past travels, which were partly but not entirely contributed by the heavily publicized and controversial release of Henry Jaub's *When The Sun Stopped Rising*, and the scrappy journalists and pseudo-reporters, who harassed him after the book's original publication.

As a former nurse, Marilee took care of Patrick's mother after she broke her hip from a devastating fall down a flight of stairs, which happened roughly one year before her death. From all the stories that she had gathered from Clementine about her son during her recovery in the hospital, Marilee learned that Patrick was a tender man who carried many regrets about past relationships, especially one involving the grieving wife of his father's past colleague.

Knowing full well of Patrick's hesitation about expressing his past relationship with Hilda, let's just say Marilee was particularly careful about what words she used when Patrick struggled to find the right words.

After falling in love with Marilee, Patrick told Selena and John that he sought employment at an arts and crafts store where he later specialized in putting together picture frames. Despite the touching story about how Patrick and his wife, Marilee, met and how they lived happily ever after, Selena wasn't at all interested in warm hugs and kisses. When she brought up more questions surrounding Nikola's story, Selena's reasons being that she wanted to learn more about the town's history, *her* hometown, which was a white lie, Patrick struggled to remember the events after the young girl's death, as well as the symbol from Hilda's artwork, which he believed came from Hilda's dreams.

If anything, the takeaway from the conversation came from the black and white photograph that once belonged to Patrick's father, Russell, who used to work with Victor at a mental institution, The Cooper Institute, which, apparently, was where Nikola's father began a career in medicine before becoming a renown doctor in Philadelphia.

The photo of "THE COOPER INSTITUTE STAFF OF 1972" included Russell Britten, an orderly, Victor Rose (a twenty-eight year old intern at the time), and then finally, a familiar-looking man, "Dr. Melvin Hawks," whose face Selena had seen before, in particular, the upper part of his face, especially those thirsty eyes.

When Selena further questioned Patrick about Melvin Hawks, he became somewhat disconcerted about her interest in the doctor.

Both Selena and John picked up on Patrick's reluctance about sharing any knowledge on the doctor.

With Patrick's permission, Selena used her phone to snap her own digital copy of the photograph, which she stated was for personal use, as specified, a "collage she was creating," and "afterwards, she was going to frame it and mount it on a wall." The latter part, obviously, she came up with off the cuff, given Patrick's past craft.

AFTER they left the Britten's residence in Landfalls, John pulled the car onto the shoulder of the road and came up with a suggestion: "Why not just go straight to the source?" asked John.

Selena said, "You're talking about Hilda, aren't you?"

"She'll have the answers you're looking for."

"I dunno," she said more discouragingly. "Maybe this is all in my head. You saw the way Britten's wife was looking at me."

"They're old," John said plainly.

Selena rolled her eyes at John's comment.

"I'll tell you what," John said, squaring his body to a deflated Selena. "We'll visit Hilda and if she doesn't have the answers you're looking for, we'll keep looking—"

"It's not that, John," Selena said with a pouty face. "I just don't want to drag you along with me into the abyss."

"You're not," he said, more seriously. "In fact, I find all of this pretty fascinating."

Selena hit John on the arm.

"Well," she said with frisky anger, "I'm glad I amuse you."

"Selena—"

"A'ight then," she said over John. "So, how in the hell are we going to find Hilda?"

John paused, as Selena waited for a response.

"I already did," he said with a guilty look on his face.

* * *

WHEN John tracked down Britten, he also managed to track down Hilda Rose, who was currently residing in a nursing home called Forest Hills outside Bluefield.

As the two arrived at Forest Hills, which, from the outside, looked like an upscale apartment complex with a large overhang covering a driveway that wrapped around the front entranceway, similar to a fancy hotel, a strange feeling came over Selena, as if she had been here before.

After parking the car in the back of the parking lot, John turned to Selena, clearly nervous as she remained quiet or became more fidgety with her mannerisms. He observed Selena routinely wiping her sweaty palms along the sides of her loose navy blue sweatpants, as well as the black wool overcoat.

Before exiting the car, John leaned over the steering wheel and glanced upward at the dark clouds above.

"Looks like it's about to—"

As he was about to finish his sentence, the clouds opened up.

The downpour covered the entire parking lot, forcing the two to reconsider their options.

"We can wait till it passes," Selena said over a *tapping* sound of heavy raindrops hitting the windshield.

John reached along his seat and pulled out a black umbrella.

"No need."

Selena grinned.

"You're just full of surprises today."

Before getting out of the car, Selena said from a trance-like state, "Can you feel that?"

Everything about the moment felt incredibly familiar. The scene before Selena. The heavy rain outside. Each word used. Each movement they made or didn't make.

Concerned, John studied Selena's frozen face.

He asked, "Feel what? You okay?"

"I dunno," Selena said emotionlessly and without any expression on her face, turned to John. "It's weird. It feels like we're supposed to be."

John looked over Selena before he rushed out of the car and opened the door for Selena and together, the two made their way to the nursing home.

* * *

ONCE John and Selena made it to the overhang, John removed the umbrella from Selena's head and dried off the umbrella by giving it a shake. Together, the two entered Forest Hills where, in the dimly lit lobby, several residences and guests were sitting by a fireplace to keep warm. The receptionist, who greeted John and Selena by the front check-in desk, told them they were trying to conserve power. What the receptionist didn't tell John and Selena, even though both John and Selena could see the distress on their faces, was that the backup generator only had enough fuel to last them another day or two. John took the first cue and told the receptionist that they were here to see "Ana Dulík," which caused Selena to do a double take on John, who, in return, shot a glance at Selena, and without the two even uttering a word to one another, they had a sort of unspoken realization about Hilda's name. When the receptionist asked the two to state their relationship with Ms. Dulík, Selena chimed in, stating that both she and John were admirers of her work and that they were working on a college essay about famous artists of the twentieth century and how their work prevailed in a time without use of social media. The receptionist didn't have a single clue what Selena or John were talking about, nor did she have any idea that one of their residents was once a "famous artist."

Suspicious of Selena and John, the receptionist carefully eyed the two before she finally instructed them to sign their names in the visitor's log.

Relieved, Selena and John signed the log; and shortly after waiting inside the lobby, the two were greeted by a short and stout orderly with cloudy red cheeks. With an insincere smile on her round face, the orderly escorted them to Ms. Dulík's room.

Once the three reached Ms. Dulík's room, the orderly, using a loud and somewhat patronizing tone, told Ms. Dulík, who was sitting in a wheelchair by the window, that she had visitors.

Selena and John entered the room while the orderly waited outside.

The ninety-four year old Ana Dulík was incredibly lucid and well aware of the orderly Greta and the tone she used with her and without Greta listening, told both Selena and John in secret how much she couldn't stand that "fart-sniffing troll," then lectured the two on how arrogant it was to smell one's own farts.

Selena glanced over at John with a strange look before she introduced herself to Ana, who immediately corrected Selena by giving her preferred name: "Hilda." The sound alone of Hilda stating her own name forced Selena to shoot yet another glance at John, who wanted to say it, in fact, scream it through the smelly hallways, "I told you so!" John was next to introduce himself as "John" first, then when asked by Hilda, confirmed with slight modification "Selena's *friend.*" He never did like the word *boyfriend*, especially that boy part in it, given he was at the cusp of adulthood. John once wondered: Was there even such a term as manfriend?

After introducing themselves, Selena stated the reasons for the visit and fine-tuned John's lie by telling Hilda that she was doing a paper on "Famous People From Bluefield," which stimulated a response from Hilda, first prompting a hiccup of a laugh, then a wisecrack of her own.

"Good luck with that one," she said loathingly.

Hilda referenced the author Gustav Ludow, whose novel on the collapse of the steel industry won him several awards and several others whom neither Selena nor John had heard of but never felt the least compelled to further inquire about these notable names of Bluefield.

Selena waited for Hilda to finish before saying: "I was thinking more like. . . an underrated artist who took surrealism to a whole other level."

"Twice now in the past month I've received visitors who were interested in my artwork."

"Who was your previous visitor, if you don't mind me asking?" asked Selena.

"He visited me after one of your so-called elections," Hilda said dejectedly. "He said that he was a doctor, said his name was Vincent Something—I forget—if you ask me, I got the feeling he wasn't being completely forthright with me."

John asked, "What did he want?"

"What do they all want?" asked Hilda, her tone sharper and slightly bitter despite maintaining a calm demeanor. Then, Hilda answered for the two: "The pain of my past."

Selena turned to John and said, "We should go—"

"No," Hilda interjected, as she waved the two closer. "Please. Stay."

Hilda then asked them if they'd like a cookie.

Selena refused and said she wasn't hungry but made sure to thank Hilda for the kind gesture; whereas, John, less polite, jumped at the opportunity and grabbed a handful of ginger snaps from the box sitting on the TV stand next to Hilda.

John stuffed a couple of ginger snaps into his mouth and as he began to chew, he glanced at Selena, who was giving him a wide-eyed glare as though inaudibly telling him to behave.

He shrugged.

"What?" he mumbled innocently with a mouthful of cookies.

Hilda said, "A hungry boy's gotta eat."

After the introduction, which also included the "where-you-from" part—Selena being from the nearby town of Padadock and John, originally, from Oregon, before he moved to Pennsylvania after his biological parents both died when he was at the age of four to live with his uncle and aunt, who'd later fill the roles of "Mother" and "Father," Hilda asked why they *really* were there.

"Certainly not because you're trying to kill time by pestering a poor old woman who hasn't picked up a paintbrush in I can't remember when," she said jokingly.

Before Selena could answer truthfully what she and John were doing at Forest Hills, Hilda asked Selena about the brace on her leg.

"Broke it during a track-and-field event," she said, as she eyed the patch of scars from third-degree burns along the side of Hilda's neck.

"What sport?"

"Pole vaulting," Selena said, refocusing her eyes.

"You're a brave girl."

"Well. . . " Selena said and forced a smile on her face, ". . . Ms. Rose—"

"I don't use that name anymore."

"Sorry."

"Don't be."

"Ms. Dulík, to be completely honest, the reasons why we're here—"

"Hilda," she corrected Selena. "Call me Hilda."

"Of course," she said apologetically, "the real reasons why we're here today, Hilda, is that John and I wanted to ask you about the symbols in your artwork."

Hilda's face turned blank, almost timid by the comment.

Selena pulled out the folded-up piece of paper that she ripped out of her notebook from her coat's pocket, unfolded it, and then showed it to Hilda.

"These symbols," Selena said.

Hilda only glanced for not even a second at the symbols for she already knew them.

More intrigued, Hilda asked Selena, "Have you been seeing these symbols?"

Hesitant, Selena answered, "Yes. I have."

Hilda sighed.

"Unfortunately, I'm afraid you've wasted your time coming out here," she said and pointed at the notebook paper. "For years, people in the art world have been asking me about those symbols, why I painted them, where they came from, was it my own little signature, and every time I told them the same exact thing: 'I don't know.'"

"There must be some reason why you painted them—"

"No," Hilda said, her tone harsher. "I don't."

For a moment, she drifted off into a momentary reflection before she drew her watery eyes back to Selena.

"I was probably a few years older than you when I had my first child, Milota. I'm sure you know all about her. . . ."

"Yes," Selena said and turned to John, motioning for him to agree. "From what *we've* read, she was not only an amazing person, but also an amazing athlete."

"She was indeed," she said reminiscently.

Once more, Selena turned to John as though she was speaking for the both of them: "We can leave, if now's not a good time."

"No," Hilda said. "Stay."

"We heard about the recent loss of your grandson."

"Sometimes I forget how fast information gets around these days." From the corner of her mouth, she said, "People and all of their devices. If you get a speeding ticket, the Internet's first to find out about it."

"Not always a good thing, I suppose," John said, as though taking a verbal stance in his position against phones.

"Cashel knew the risks of being a police officer," Hilda said, not surprised by his death. "I can't tell you how many nights I waited for the phone to ring, telling me the bad news. But. . ." she sighed, ". . . it was his choice and his alone, and there was nothing I could say or do to make him pursue another career. Cashel certainly wasn't going to become a doctor. He was too much like his mother." She paused once more in a state of reminiscence. "I remember she'd go everywhere with that soccer ball. After a while it sort of became a part of her like an extra appendage. I'll admit it, though, there were times when it got a little out of hand, with her kicking that doggone ball around the house every minute of the day. When most people walked, you could hear the sound of their footsteps. *But* when my Milota walked, she didn't sound like most people. She came to be Milota plus Ball. The dribbling or the *thudding* of the ball hitting against the side of the house or banging around the inside of the garage as if she was treating the garage as her own makeshift goal: these were the sounds that she adopted into the woman whom she'd later become. But at the end of the day, despite how aggravating her interests could be at times, it was her outlet, and no matter what, I could never, *never* take that away from her."

With her mind engrossed about Milo's "outlet," Selena cleared her throat and said to Hilda, "Because of what happened to your second daughter?"

Hilda carefully eyed Selena before she caught her breath.

"Yes," she said, her breathing labored. "I suppose."

"Sorry for your losses."

Hilda gave Selena a closed-lip smile. Even though Hilda had never met Selena prior to today, Selena's words not only gave Hilda hope in younger generations, specifically, Selena's generation, but also proved that there were still decent ones, like Selena and John, ones who showed their elders respect, and seeing first-hand that not all of the kids were as cold, heartless, and self-absorbed as they were made out to be, helped put her at ease.

Hilda showed Selena and John the bed and asked them to have a seat, if they'd like.

After Hilda insisted, Selena and John sat on the bed across from Hilda.

"Three years before Milota was born, I was involved in a life-altering automobile accident," Hilda said.

Pointing, Selena asked, "Is that how you got those scars?"

"These?"

Hilda touched her collar.

Selena nodded.

"Yes."

With reflection, Hilda said, "A truck pulled out in front of my husband, causing him to swerve off the highway. When my husband, Victor, attempted to drive back onto the road, he made the mistake of overcorrecting. He lost control of the car. The car flipped several times before it settled in a ditch where it caught fire. Victor, who—believe it or not—didn't have a single broken bone in the crash, pulled my body from the wreckage. As for my condition," Hilda let out a cute laugh despite the seriousness of the story, "well, how do I say?" She briefly looked over the two as if she was once more confirming their age. "I was, as we used to say back in the day, screwed. My hip took most, if not all the damage. The doctors said it was completely shattered, like someone took a glass plate and flung it against the wall. They were worried I might never recover, let alone walk again."

The story was new to Selena's ears and hearing it come straight from Hilda's mouth, caused her to perk up and listen more intently.

"Before I went into surgery, I feared this was it," Hilda said, the memory flooding over her, "this was the last time I'd see Victor. At the time we were so in love. We married two years before. I was nineteen years old. Victor was much older than me and it was fair to say my parents, especially my father, weren't so adamant about giving me away. They came around, eventually. I don't remember much after the surgery. I remember the pain for sure. Weeks passed, months. Doctors were shocked by how fast I recovered." A glimpse of excitement flashed over her face. "I could even do the Twist."

"What's the Twist?" asked John.

Hilda waved off John's innocence, causing Selena to elbow him in the ribs.

"They said it was a miracle," Hilda said. "However, I remember I started to have these reoccurring dreams. . . "

Selena listened closer.

"The symbols," she said.

"I honestly don't know where they came from," Hilda said, "if somehow I hit my head during the crash. The doctors said my head was fine. I started to see more and more of the symbols everywhere until. . . "

Both Selena and John waited at the edge of the bed.

"I didn't," Hilda said.

Selena asked, "You mean they just. . . went away?"

"Yes," Hilda said. "After Nikola was murdered, the symbols returned. I think it had a lot to do with the trauma of losing a daughter." Then, Hilda turned the attention back on Selena. "So, why are you so interested in these symbols?"

Unsure whether or not to tell Hilda the truth, Selena summoned the confidence to say more candidly, "I'm seeing them as well."

"Is that so?"

"Yes," Selena said to Hilda, as she felt an unusual comfort from her presence. "Like you, I started to see them after *my* accident."

"With your leg?"

"Yes."

Hilda cracked open her mouth as though ready to speak.

"You think they're connected?" Selena asked, as she handed the piece of paper to Hilda.

"I don't know, Selena," Hilda said, looking over the sketches of circular symbols.

"Hilda," John said, chiming into the conversation, "I'm curious: What did Mr. Britten think about these symbols?"

Graciously, Hilda smiled, handed back the sketches, and said, "I take it you read the book by that parasite Henry Jaub."

John glanced over at Selena, then back to Hilda: "We did." John paused. "Is it true?"

"Is what true?"

He felt Selena's hand on his leg, since resorting to elbowing didn't work out. She made sure to tighten her grip as though telling John to use his next words carefully.

"The facts surrounding Nikola's death."

"That," she said, "and my relationship with Patrick, right?"

John was unsure whether or not to answer.

"What John is trying to say," Selena said more assertively. "'Is the book accurate? Or is it just some author's desperate attempt at making money from your tragedy?'"

"The book's true," she said. "Most of it anyway. And to answer your first question, Patrick was just as baffled by the symbols as I was. But what the book got wrong was that I didn't stop loving Victor, even though I might've blamed him for reasons that I couldn't explain." She studied Selena and John and observed the way the two interacted while in each other's company. "I can tell you two are close or forgive me by saying, in love," she nodded her head at John in particular, "especially you. . . "

"Well. . . ah. . . " John said bashfully, as he turned to Selena.

"It's okay to admit you're in love," she said. "I was in love with Victor and till this day, I'll always be in love with Victor. I was attracted to Patrick, his looks, his charm, but. . . I wasn't in love with Patrick. He found me at the right time at the right moment in my life when I needed someone the most and I'm afraid Victor wasn't there. What happened to Nikola. . . it destroyed him, as it almost did me. If it wasn't for painting, I probably wouldn't be here."

Hilda talked more about painting, as well as the inception behind several notable pieces that gathered an underground cult-like following among the art world, one of which was *"John Smith 2.0,"* a juxtapose of man and robot, the others *"Culling Cats,"* as well as *"The Garden of Eden,"* which Hilda described as a surrealistic painting of a desktop computer with the keyboard, as well as the mouse perched on the trunk of a toppled Joshua tree in the middle of a barren desert. The monitor appeared feministic in nature, curvy, seductive (said to be "Eve"); as for the keyboard, utilitarian by design, similar to a tool shed where each tool came in the form of a letter or number on a clunky-looking key ("Adam"); and last but not least, the mouse, serpent-like, feeding from the monitor, a reptilian creature with the tail of a white desert mouse sticking out of its mouth ("The Devil"). Hilda spent years, decades, talking about these pieces to art critics and collectors alike, explaining the details, as well as the symbolism behind each painting; and it was clear that, while recounting these previous topics, the conversation was starting to take its toll on Hilda.

Aware of Hilda's deteriorating state, Selena and John decided that they had already taken up enough of the poor old woman's time.

Before leaving, Hilda stood up from the wheelchair without any help and walked Selena and John toward the hallway where Greta was reading a pink-colored romance novel with a shirtless hunky-looking dude on the front cover of the glossy paperback. Selena was only able to catch a word *"China"* in the title, then an author's name, *"Valentine."*

Ignoring the sullen expression of Greta's face, Selena shook Hilda's hand and expressed her gratitude for allowing Hilda to share her story.

In return, Hilda, with a sharp-eyed and studious look on her face, told Selena how much she reminded her of an old friend whom she once knew.

"Well," Selena said, using crutches for support, "we better get going. We wouldn't want our folks back at home thinking we're missing, especially given the recent news."

"News?" asked Hilda, her brow furrowed into a wrinkled and papery letter v.

"The disappearances of four girls from Padadock," Selena said. "There may even be a fifth girl. It's a strange time for everybody—"

"Who's missing?"

John asked, "You haven't heard?"

"If you hadn't noticed," she said and once more, made a subtle jab at Greta, "we have limited means of information around here. For all we know, the world out there could've been wiped off the face of the earth, and we'd still have a hard time learning what happened."

"As far as we know, four girls are currently missing," Selena informed Hilda, "one you may know: Ashleigh Reap. Her grandfather went to the same school as Milota."

"Sturgeon?"

"Yes," Selena said, captivated by Hilda's startling interest in the case.

"You know him?" asked John.

"I knew him all right," she said. "I chased him away a few times after I caught him hanging out with Milota—"

The expression "hanging out" immediately grabbed Selena's attention for it had become incredibly offensive over the past decade and for those who threw the expression around freely and without repercussion were often scolded for its usage, in particular, the "hanging" part.

Despite what seemed necessary of Selena or her peers to call out the expression wherever it deemed inappropriate, Selena deliberated the context of the profane expression, as well as its usage in Hilda's sentence, and even though the thought climbed up inside of her, decided to give Hilda a free pass for Selena felt no obligation to correct Hilda due to whatever was currently acceptable or unacceptable, given that, back then, during Hilda's time, the expression was nothing short of innocent, an expression younger generations referred to as relaxing together or spending time in each other's company and not once did the expression require the least amount of scrutiny for such acts were merely the bidding of bored people with even more boring gripes.

"He was much older than Milota," Hilda clarified.

"When did you see him last?" asked John.

Thinking, Hilda said, "The last time I saw Sturgeon. . . right. . . " she tried to remember even though details were hazy, considering how long ago it was, ". . . last I saw of him was when Milota came home for winter break from Cornerbrook, about a month or so before she dropped out. I saw him with Milota. She looked. . . happy. Yet, she wasn't, if that makes a bit of sense."

"I read that she had issues with some of the players at Cornerbrook."

"I think so," Hilda said vaguely. "She was going through a lot. At the time, she was probably a little older than you two when we had a fight. She said some things that she'd later regret. I said things as well." Hilda said depressingly, "Terrible things. I think she was still upset at me for what I did to her father. It happened so many years ago and yet, she carried around my mistake with her throughout adolescence. Milota had every right to be upset at me. But when you're that age, it's harder to shake off something that is completely out of your control, and it's easy to get mixed up with the wrong crowd. It's like you're prone to carry around someone else's baggage. After our fight, I didn't see her for over two years or so. When she returned, well. . . she was no longer a child. That's for sure. She told me she got back into soccer. She had this drive inside her, this look similar to the one she had after Nikola died. It's like she was ready to conquer the world."

"Sturgeon's granddaughter, Ashleigh, is missing," John said, also watching Hilda, her face, as well as her gestures.

"What a shame," Hilda said, trailing off.

"Is something wrong?"

"No," she said and forced a smile on her face. "The man's been through a lot. He was basically run out of Bluefield. Despite my grievances with Sturgeon, I did feel for him though."

"From what we've read, Sturgeon was arrested multiple times."

"A lot of people, at the beginning of the investigation into Nikola's death, thought maybe he was responsible. He was questioned by investigators. Sure, that Reap boy was nothing but trouble, but he wasn't a killer. *But. . .* " Hilda lost her train of thought, ". . . I've made my peace."

Neither Selena nor John pressed Hilda.

Instead, the two once more thanked Hilda for her time and said their goodbyes, even though a part of Selena wanted to stay.

* * *

ON the quiet car road home from Forest Hills, Selena stared at the Cooper Institute staff photo on her phone and tried to remember where she had seen the doctor's face before.

It wasn't until John dropped her off back at her home and told her he'd text her later that she developed a strange and unsettling sensation inside her, which left her feeling sick and unable to eat or drink. She had, in fact, seen Hawks's face before but couldn't exactly pinpoint where she had seen his face.

Over the sound of the beating rain outside, she overheard Bret and another kid arguing outside.

Selena cracked open the guestroom window and eavesdropped over the argument.

Due to the constant beating of the rain, she couldn't catch what they were arguing about but from what she saw, the two appeared visibly upset with one another.

As the rain drowned out their argument, Selena caught the words, which were yelled out by Bret's friend, whom she later identify as Massacre: "*Forget about 'em! They're dead!*"

JOHN wasn't at all satisfied with the conversation with Hilda, in fact, if anything, talking with her made him more driven to find out what happened in Bluefield so many years ago. As a boy, who was raised only several miles from the small town, he heard about all the legends, the myths, the absurd claims about Nikola's death, one of them being that Nikola's father, Victor, was considered a suspect during the early stages of the investigation. Given his own history with his parents, whom he hardly knew, he had always been drawn to the tragedy surrounding Bluefield and its fallout after Nikola's bizarre death. Now knowing Victor Rose's background, it didn't seem like a far stretch to spend more time, not only focusing on Victor, but rather people around him, like, for instance, his coworkers.

Then, there was Ashleigh's grandfather, Sturgeon, whom John mentioned to Selena during the ride home but was immediately shot down and told to give it a rest for Selena wasn't in the mood for any of his conspiracies, especially ones linking Nikola's case to what was happening in Padadock, with the four Del Soaka Falls High girls still unaccounted for and considering the time frame since they were first reported missing, in particular Blaire Tudor, presumably dead.

John drove back to Knife and Fork to use the diner's wi-fi. He barely managed to get a signal, and the townspeople were giving Tom an earful about it.

As soon as he settled into a booth in the back of the diner, he picked up on a common mood, not a sense of fear or hopelessness, as John had seen every now and then on locals' faces, given their current situation, but rather a wrongness around their dark and cloudy eyes, which could've easily been misread as desperation. Each and every local was on edge, their demeanor more aggressive, their tempers short fused.

While passing one of the crowded tables, the once well-mannered Ronny, or "Ron-Ron," a contractor who recently ran out of gasoline to power up his generator, which, in return, powered up the tools he needed to work, snapped at the waitress over a petty inconvenience: the waitress, Annie, informed Ronny that he was only allowed so much salt to season his eggs, since the diner was forced to ration its salt due to the shortage, as well as an unforeseeable timeframe of the next food delivery. Nobody wanted to speak it—some threw it out there ambiguously for public consumption, blaming growing blackouts on certain entities such as "the government" or "the elites" who were using "us," the locals, like pawns—but it was on everybody's mind: *What if the power does* not *come back on?*

Given the current climate, John decided to sit in the back of the diner, near an exit door, just in case things escalated. After accessing Knife and Fork's wi-fi, he first began his research with "The Cooper Institute," scrolling through countless pages until winding up on an old news article from a once prestigious newspaper in New York before it was discredited.

In the archive, his eyes caught a headline: "CI DOCTOR ACCUSED OF EXPERIMENTING ON PATIENTS."

The doctor was the same man from the staff photograph, Dr. Melvin Hawks, the one Selena had been obsessing over ever since they spoke with Patrick Britten.

John read through the article, which, in it, the family member, the mother of one of Hawks's patients, Stuart "Stu" Berkley, accused "Hawks of malpractice after her thirty-five year old son, Stu, died while in his care."

Prior to Stuart Berkley admission into Cooper Institute, as ordered by the judge who ruled Mr. Berkley insane and concluded that he was best suited to serve his sentence in a mental institution where he would be monitored by a health professional, he was evaluated by multiple doctors, who diagnosed him with "schizophrenia."

The article didn't go into specifics about Berkley's claims.

John, however, found more information on another site, a forum which linked him to a post regarding Berkley's claims, several taken from excerpts in the novel *Lights, Camera, Arrest!*

After reading through the post, John couldn't determined whether the material in the novel was actually true or, as he first felt about Jaub's book on Nikola Rose, the mental droppings of a writer trying to sell books through shock and awe.

According to an excerpt in *Lights, Camera, Arrest!*, before Stuart Berkley attempted to murder his girlfriend, he was convinced that she was a Russian spy sent by the Soviet Union to steal his work—his work being writing. Berkley was a novelist, as well as a screenplay writer whose claim to fame was a science fiction novel, *They'll Never Know You Exist*, which he later adopted into a screenplay under the working title *"The Spectacle"*: about a scrappy blue-collared journalist who uncovered a secret plot by AI (artificial intelligence) that was impersonating the writers and editors of a local newspaper in a malicious attempt to turn the townspeople on each other by spreading "inflammatory misinformation," thus leading to the fall of a small town. The screenplay was picked up by a well-known producer, who bought the rights from Berkley's publisher, although the screenplay was never developed into a picture. The narrative around Soviets wasn't unusual, considering the paranoia spawned by the Cold War.

In Stuart Berkley's case, according to the site that covered "Strange Phenomenon," it wasn't the Soviet Union that everyone was talking about, either on the news or among social gatherings. Berkley's so-called "Soviet Union" consisted of a ruthless federation of "anthropomorphic tarantulas," more specifically, *"Atypus"* or "purseweb spiders," based out of Romania, originated from the southern part of the Carpathian Mountains. These *other* Soviets weren't people of the human kind, but rather surrogates, alternates for Berkley's Soviets, the insect kind, who wore the artificial flesh of humans but underneath, they were, in fact, arachnid, "infiltrating the Soviet Union."

The claims, whether true or not or simply Internet gossip, failed to provide any clear justification as to *why* Stuart Berkley attempted to murder his girlfriend before turning the gun on himself, botching his own suicide.

More confused and forced to refocus, John pulled up more articles on the controversial doctor, one being from outside the courtroom where he finished pleading his case about "Stuart Barkley" and "how traditional medicine failed to provide the results he (Hawks) was looking for."

Below the article was a grainy black and white photograph of Hawks and another man, who were making their way through a horde of reporters following the trial.

John scrolled to the bottom of the photo and read the fine print: *Melvin Hawks* (on the left) *and Kurtivon Harburschmit* (on the right), *who performed the autopsy on Stuart Berkley after he died from an aneurism two weeks following an experimental surgery.*

The coroner "Harburschmit" caused John to think twice about where he heard the name.

He texted Selena, who was currently resting from the recent trip, and asked her if she could do him a favor and look up the coroner's name from the book *MACHINE: The Life and Death of Milo Rose.* She confirmed to John that the coroner who performed the autopsy on Nikola's older sister, Milo: Kurtivon Harburschmit.

A year before Berkley's death, according to another article, Hawks lost another patient in his care: the patient was Anthony "The Hit Whisperer" Florentine, who died from an apparent drug overdose.

While researching the name "Anthony Florentine," John found tons of articles on the former record producer. During the Sixties, Florentine produced seven records for bands whose singles made it to the top 100 in the *Billboard* charts, earning him the nickname "The Hit Whisperer." Florentine's name was all over magazines, newspapers, and television programs. For a stretch of six years, he had become the face behind many one hit wonders, the wizard behind the curtains, until the summer of 1968, when Florentine's strung-out face was plastered all over the news after eight people were gunned down inside a San Francisco nightclub called The Pink Bowl. Seven of the eight people murdered were members of the relatively unknown band Johan Rhapsody and The Clones, who were in town performing a show at a nearby venue from the *Swirly-Eyes Tour* where they were opening up for Bobby Seagull. The wife of the lead singer (real name Terrance White), supermodel "Zenith," was also among the eight victims who were shot and killed during what was later known as "The Massacre at Pink Bowl." The shooting happened two months after the release Johan Rhapsody and The Clones' debut record *Forestland*, which failed to make a splash on the *Billboard* charts until The Massacre at Pink Bowl, which helped catapult their single, "Toad Licker Sticker Flicker," to the top 10 where the hit song sat the number three spot for one week before falling off the chart. Besides several rumors here and there that the lead guitarist, Clone B-71892 (Philip Hughes) was sleeping with Johan's wife, Zenith, there was no turmoil within the band, although many speculated that Florentine, who started to experiment with drugs, primarily delving heavily into cocaine, following the trip to Nepal, was experiencing a bad trip. According to details of the trial, Anthony Florentine was examined by medical professions, who declared him insane, stating he was hearing voices and these so-called "voices" instructed him to murder Rhapsody, Rhapsody's wife, and the rest of the band.

Out of curiosity, John researched the band Johan Rhapsody and The Clones and while looking over the artwork for their debut record *Forestland*, noticed a startling familiarity on the vinyl. He pulled up some of Hilda's artwork, mainly one piece with the symbol that Selena claimed she was seeing in her dreams, and compared it to the symbol on the vinyl.

Shocked by the discovery, John pulled the phone away from his face and contemplated calling Selena to tell her about what he believed to be a profound connection.

Perhaps Selena is right.

As John left Knife and Fork, he ran into Ashleigh's older brother, Conner, who, when asked about his sister, told him the search party was unsuccessful after Frank's bloodhound lost Ashleigh's scent around North Tryon (Conner was thinking about getting a bloodhound himself from the Pound, which he heard were basically giving dogs away, and it was only a matter of days before the dogs were scheduled to be euthanized).

With a similar look as the Knife and Fork patrons, Conner said to John, "Sometimes you just gotta do things yourself, right?"

John couldn't agree more with Conner and before parting ways, stopped and thought about asking Conner about his grandfather, Sturgeon.

Given Conner's state, John thought it'd be best to ask him some another time.

THE BROTHER'S SECRET
DECEMBER 3, 2048
PADADOCK, PENNSYLVANIA

SELENA woke the next morning to the sound of rain.

Considering they were out of eggs and all of the grocery stores in Padadock were closed due to shortage, the food was limited and all they had to eat for breakfast was canned beans, bananas, and freshly squeezed orange juice, which Lacey thought were disappearing from the pantry and was quick to turn the blame on anyone, except herself.

Based on Bret's odd behavior over these past couple of days, all fingers pointed at Bret, who Selena saw the other day walking from the pantry with a bookbag.

Throughout most of the morning, Bret had been acting suspicious and much quieter than his usual self.

In the back of Selena's mind, she suspected her brother was in trouble and yet, whenever she tried to make small talk with him, he was in no mood for conversations.

AFTER breakfast, Selena tried to send a text to John, asking him what his plans were for today.

John never received the text due to the poor reception, which was deteriorating by the hour. John could sense it in the air, the networks, the backup power, all of it shutting down, like everything that they experienced over these past two weeks were like preludes to the real blackout— the big one Bret had been warning him about over the past month. The one that would make the 2046 blackouts seem like a minor inconvenience.

Without informing Selena—after all, if there was the perfect candidate to accompany him, it was Selena—John decided to pay a visit to Britten's house by himself.

When he arrived at Britten's, he picked up on an eerie vibe. He knocked on the front door a couple of times but neither Patrick nor his wife answered the door. He walked around to the side of the house and when he peeked inside the bedroom window, saw what he worst feared.

He only caught their feet on the edge of the bed for the curtain covered the rest of their bodies. Somehow, after talking with Patrick the day before, he picked up on the vibe that he wasn't being forthright—at least, not entirely. He walked back to the front door and after he twisted on the doorknob, the door opened. The unlocked door was the second of three clues confirming his suspicions when Patrick told them that he and Marilee were going on their "final" vacation. The third one being the unpleasant odor coming from the bedroom.

John called out to Mr. Britten but received no answer.

When he arrived at their bedroom, he witnessed both Patrick and Marilee lying in bed, both holding hands, eyes closed, unresponsive.

"Mr. Britten?" said John.

As John approached the bed, he noticed the powder blue box of Equanimity, or "Queue," on the nightstand. He heard about the drug before, which some his age referred to as a "death pill" or "Reaper's medicine"—a friend of his, Lindsey, whose mother had terminal brain cancer, was prescribed the drug but never ingested it—however, he had never seen the drug in person before.

John found the two empty slots inside the blister pack, each one of the two death pills, from what John assumed based on a half-full glass of water on the nightstand, ingested by both Patrick and Marilee.

Strangely, John wasn't disturbed by their bodies; in fact, he felt quite the opposite. The two looked at peace and appeared as if they were taking a long nap.

After leaving Patrick and Marilee, John walked past a walk-in closet where he found dozens of old paintings, all framed, perched and filed against the wall. He snooped around the bedroom, then, after leaving the bedroom, continued his search inside a living room cabinet where Patrick kept the photo albums.

On a whim, he rifled through the albums, starting with the one containing the staff photo of Cooper Institute. He found more photos of Patrick's father, Russell, as well as another man who worked with him at the Institute. His name was Eugene Wallace, as stated on the staff photo. In at least twenty photos, Eugene was seen with Russell: outside work, spending time together at a family barbeque or at the pool or at the park. Apparently, their wives were also close.

Before closing the photo album, he pocketed a photo of Russell and Eugene, as well as their wives standing side by side on a beach, big smiles on their faces, dressed in summer attire, except for Eugene's wife, Carmine, who was wearing a loose floral-patterned dress to cover up the baby bump, Russell's arm wrapped around Eugene's shoulder, as Eugene held up the peace sign with his two fingers. Sitting next to the four was a boy (Patrick?), probably no older than five or six years old, his body somewhat out of focus in the background as he built a sand castle with a blue bucket. John came across yet another photo, in the very back of the album, one of Eugene's newly born, "Gene," in the hospital, the baby wrapped up in a blanket like a burrito in Carmine's arms. The three, Eugene, little Gene, and Carmine, huddled together like one body. The year on the back of the photo read "*October 20, 1971.*"

John pulled out the other photo from his pocket, flipped it over, and read the date "*Summer of '66.*" After searching through the rest of the albums, he couldn't find any other photographs with any other child, except the ones of Gene who was born five years later.

Lastly, before leaving the house, John snooped around the kitchen. While rifling through a drawer, he managed to find an address book that belonged to Patrick. In it, he flipped straight to the "W's" and found the name Wallace. Underneath, he found the name "Gene" with an address and a phone number below the name.

What do you know?

Gene had the same area code as John.

Assuming it was the same Gene from the photographs, he pulled out his phone and snapped a photo of the page.

As soon as John left Britten's, he tried to text Selena about his recent discovery about Gene, the son of Eugene Wallace, a close friend and based on the photos of weekend outings together, he'd go so far to say Russell Britten's best friend who also worked at The Cooper Institute. He waited for the text to go through, but it failed to send.

Selena, who was away from her phone, carefully watched Bret sneak downstairs.

Without nobody looking, except for Selena, who was peeking past the guestroom doorway, Bret stopped by the pantry and filled his bookbag with a couple of canned beans and fruit before he exited the house.

As fast as her leg would take her, Selena hurried to the window and through the guestroom window, watched Bret rush to his bike parked along the edge of the garage. Then, after he gingerly secured a bulky backpack over his shoulders, Bret peddled off through the downpour.

As soon as her brother rode away, Selena hurried to her nana's scooter, which was parked in the garage. The scooter's battery wasn't fully charged. The gauge showed about a half of a battery; however, due to the layer of dust covering the seat, the scooter looked as if it hadn't been driven in years despite Eleanor's so-called wild "misadventures" through Padadock.

After manually opening the garage, Selena hopped into the seat, she placed the crutches over the basket but the crutches were too long to hold in place. She decided to toss the crutches aside. Without wasting anymore time, Selena drove away.

ONCE Selena exited the neighborhood, she picked up Bret crossing Hoover Road.

Despite having gained distance from her, she managed to keep pace with her brother as she held the throttle to its fastest "rabbit" speed.

It wasn't until they reached the main highway, once a busy road where early-morning commuters traveled from Padadock to the nearest most populated city, Jonesy Town, that Bret took a shortcut through the woods. Unable to follow Bret for she ran the risk of crashing and possibly ruining the scooter, Selena kept to the highway, which was, not a surprise, desolate, considering a shortage of gasoline, every gas station in Dovership County, as well as the neighboring counties, including Mote, depleted, and mentally mapped out a trail through the woods. Selena even drove past many cars that were left abandoned on the side of the highway.

After safely following the highway to a side road, which would take her to the other side of the woods, she made yet another turn onto another street that led her downtown.

As soon as she reached 2nd Street, she picked up Bret yet again. Due to the lack of visibility from the heavy rain, it was hard to see him, as he vanished in and out of the gray wall of rain. As she tried to keep up with her brother, she thought she caught the tail end of him riding through old Downtown Padadock. She hadn't seen the area since before she left for Brighton, and within only that short span of three months, it appeared worse than the last time she saw it. Most of the area was still rundown; all of the businesses were closed. The trash added an extra layer over the streets and sidewalks. The rain, which acted like adhesive, soaked the trash; and yet, despite all of the waste scattered as far as the eye could see, she couldn't find a soul in sight.

By the time Selena reached Main Street, which, during her nana's youth, was once a thriving place full of artisans, bakers, and craftsmen, each business on either side of her gutted, boarded up, abandoned, she lost Bret on Tryon Street until she spotted his bike perched along the side of the bank, Samson's Trusts and Loans, which closed back in 2030, a couple of years after the second outbreak of coronavirus that left millions unemployed.

With the rain coming down harder, Selena had no other choice than to investigate the bank.

Before she entered the bank, a transformer on a wooden post across the street suddenly exploded from a power surge. A cloud of dark smoke emitted into a thick gray sky. The top of the street post caught fire, the heavy rain acting like an extinguisher to help bring down the flames.

Shaking off the minor scare, she peeled back the bottom part of a board of plywood covering the front entranceway and managed to drive the scooter inside the derelict bank. The windows below the ceiling provided enough light for Selena to navigate through the bank. She searched the main lobby area, as well as the teller booths, but couldn't locate Bret.

Lastly, she stopped at a staircase, which spiraled into darkness.

The rusty sign on the wall read: "VAULT" with an arrow pointing downward.

After hearing a rustling commotion behind the wall, she decided to abandon the scooter and use the railing to help her walk down each stair, using her good leg for support.

When she reached the bottom of the staircase, she saw Bret placing black garbage bags over his shoes and pulling the bags up to his legs and then securing the bags with duct tape around his thighs. While doing so, he was holding a flashlight inside his mouth and trying to keep the light steady on his handiwork.

"Bret?"

With his eyes wide and face long and slack, Bret suddenly looked up toward Selena's voice.

The flashlight slipped from his slobbery mouth, forcing him to grab the flashlight before it rolled down the grimy stairs and into the three feet of water that flooded the basement floor.

As he moved the flashlight back toward Selena, she saw his bookbag on one of the steps and next to it a kit for an oxyacetylene torch.

Protruding from the backpack was an oxygen tank.

The sight of the tank made sense, Selena concluded, as she recalled why her brother was riding so carefully on his bike, and she'd be lying if the thought of Bret carrying a fragile object in his bookbag didn't cross her mind.

"What are you doing?" asked Selena.

Bret didn't answer for he was too shocked by Selena's presence.

"Bret," Selena said, louder, "what are you doing?"

"Did you follow me?" Bret asked, his voice trembling.

"Why does it matter if I followed you?" asked Selena. "What are you doing with an oxygen tank?"

"You can't tell Mom. . . "

With her voice rising to a near-shout, Selena said, "Bret, what did you do?"

Right before her brother could answer, Selena heard the sound of girls screaming out from a distance. Three of them, she could tell. All three of their voices echoed through the damp darkness inside the basement.

"Who the heck is that, Bret?" asked Selena.

"They're safe, I promise," Bret said.

Using the railing, Selena hopped her way down the staircase.

"You shouldn't be here, Selena."

"Bret," she said, losing her patience, "goddamn it, what the hell did you do?"

"It's not my fault," he said in a whining tone. "They're just stuck. That's all."

"Who's stuck?"

"Kourtney," he said, "Billie, Ashleigh. . . "

"They're alive?"

Bret nodded.

"You're serious?"

Selena peered into the dark basement.

Bret redirected the flashing toward the flooded basement.

In the back of the basement was the bank vault.

On the top of the closed vault was a hole from what looked like a botched attempt at a robbery. The hole was about twice the size of a football. From the obvious drag lines running from the right side of the hole, it appeared as if Bret had been cutting through the heavy metal with the oxyacetylene torch before the tank ran out of oxygen.

Perched against the vault and partially submerged in water, a ladder was secured to the side of the vault by a piece of rope that held the ladder in place.

Below the vault, the surface of the murky water, which was about three to four feet deep and rising by the hour due to heavy rain, was covered in debris from a previous flood.

On the wall was a dark and moldy line running across the basement, indicating how high the water had risen during the flood.

Selena spotted a hollowed out crack pipe, as well as the several beer cans among the debris, which began to pile up along the bottom corner of the staircase. Among other debris, Selena saw aluminum cans of what used to be canned pineapples and baked beans. She recognized the cans for they were the same exact brand that Dean bought in bulk at the Savings Mart before Thanksgiving. The sight of the cans forced Selena to ask herself: *How long has Bret been coming down here?*

Selena searched through the basement but couldn't find the three girls anywhere in sight.

As she pulled her eyes back to the vault, she said, "They're stuck inside the bank vault?"

Bret didn't answer. Yet, he looked at his sister with a mix of fear and guilt.

"Serious?"

"Billie was supposed to have the combination," he said. "We've tried everything, but nothing is working. Kourtney thinks it has to do with the blackout."

Selena said, "Bret, we have to go to the police! Now!"

"There's no time, Selena!" Bret pleaded with Selena. "I'm almost there. If I can cut a hole wide enough, they can climb through it—"

One of the girls—Billie—screamed out to Bret, telling him that the vault was starting to fill with water.

"The police station's about a twenty-minute walk from here."

"We can't," Bret cried.

The beam from the flashlight highlighted the desperation on his face.

"Why not?"

Bret, who was on the verge of crying, turned to the vault while struggling to make eye contact with Selena.

"We just can't," he said, his eyes watery and bloodshot.

After leaning forward and witnessing the story in Bret's eyes, a story that would eventually emerge given the right timing, she trusted Bret and told him to do whatever it was that he needed to do in order to free the girls, even though every fiber of her being was screaming at her to find help.

Bret replaced the oxygen tank with a full one.

Selena asked, "How do you know how to use one of those things?"

"I watched DIY videos before the Internet crashed." He pulled out a pair of cup style welding goggles from his backpack. As he placed the goggles around his neck, he said to Selena, "If anything happens—"

"What do you mean?" asked Selena.

Bret handed Selena the flashlight.

"Forget it," Bret said and told her to shine the light on him, as he carried the portable trolley with the two tanks, one of oxygen and the other, acetylene, as well as the torch through several feet of water.

"Please be careful, Bret," Selena said from behind, as she waited helplessly at the base of the partially flooded staircase.

Once he reached the vault, he climbed up the ladder and secured the portable kit over a hook attached to the top of the ladder. Next, he secured the welding goggles over his eyes, protecting his vision from the bright flame of the torch. He called out, first to the girls inside, "Cover your eyes!" Then, he turned to Selena and yelled out, "Don't look at the light!"

Before he opened the valves, Kourtney shouted out from inside, "I don't care anymore what my parents will do to me, Bret! I don't care if I never see the light of day! You need to tell them that I acted out of self—"

"Cover your eyes," Bret said over Kourtney and ignited the flame.

While partially covering her eyes, Selena kept the flashlight on Bret as he began to cut away through the corroded metal, continuing where he last left before running out of oxygen.

Selena's patience started to wear thin, as the rain came down harder.

The rain gradually changed sound and among the rain, sleet hit the glass panes above, causing more concern.

Streams of icy rainwater raced down the staircase, running by Selena's feet. She tried her best to avoid touching the frigid water.

She peered closer at the interior structure of the bank, the dilapidated walls, which spoke in *pops* and *cracks*, as well as the wooden steps below her, which were soft and sunken in. She felt as if the entire bank had turned into a gigantic sponge and soon that sponge was going to freeze over and shatter into a million pieces.

While blotting out the torch, Selena pulled her eyes upward to the ceiling and noticed several areas, which were darker than other areas on the ceiling, and strangely, appeared somewhat swollen, like a bloated belly ready to burst through a belt buckle.

As Bret continued to burn away at the hole, Selena called out to Bret, "How much longer?"

Bret didn't answer for he was too busy cutting through the hole with the torch.

More *pops* and *cracks* could be heard throughout the bank.

"Bret," Selena called out once more, "get down from there. . ."

As soon as Bret pulled the torch away and checked on Selena, he heard a *creaking* noise directly above him.

Before Bret had a chance to react, the ceiling above him suddenly caved in!

Bret was knocked from the ladder. He dropped the handle of the torch and as he fell into the water, a waterfall of icy water poured on top of him.

Selena shouted out, "Bret!"

She couldn't tell if Bret was injured or even alive for that matter due to the amount of water pouring into the basement.

Considering the recent surgery, she felt as if she was in absolutely no condition to be swimming through what she knew to be contaminated water that hosted the kind of bacteria that could eat away the flesh of her leg, which, despite a speedy healing, was still vulnerable to infection.

Bret still didn't surface, and Selena feared that he was knocked unconscious.

"Goddamn it, Bret," she seethed, weighing her options.

She only had two: Risk developing infection, or worse, possibly lose a leg by jumping into harmful water to rescue her brother or the other, the cowardly option, don't do anything, and not only let Bret drown, but also let the three girls die with him.

Without giving the second option any thought, she looped the flashlight's string around her wrist and braved the unknown by taking a step into the water. Once she reached the very bottom of the staircase, the water came up to her waist but was rising slowly by the breath. Even the feel of water pressed against her skin was foreign and left her in a state of great trepidation.

By the time Selena reached the vault, the water was already up to her chest. She shined the flashlight into the water and as a figure of a body came forward, reached out and grabbed hold of the body. The body was different, though, larger, the clothes more raggedy, and the smell, which caused Selena to gag.

As Selena turned the lifeless body over on its front, she was suddenly startled by the grayish gaunt face of a bearded homeless man.

Selena recoiled in horror.

The stench of death overwhelmed her, forcing her to doggie-paddle away.

To the right of the massive hole where part of the ceiling collapsed Bret finally surfaced. He was bleeding from the top of his head but, according to Bret's ability to stay afloat, wasn't badly injured.

From inside the vault, Selena heard the three girls crying out for help. She swam over to the hole and peeked inside and saw the three girls staying afloat by stepping onto open deposit boxes that lined the interior walls.

The three clung to the wall and using the deposit boxes as footing, inched their way closer to the hole.

The first girl, Billie, made it to the hole, tried to squeeze her body through but could only fit both her arms for the hole was still too small to escape.

Once the realization of death set in, the girls started to cry, pleading and begging to Bret and his sister to help them.

The torch was floating in the water, the bottom part of the both tanks completely submerged underwater.

"Can you use the torch?" Selena asked Bret, as he swam closer to the hole.

As the water continued to pour inside the basement, they only had about three feet of space left before the basement was completely flooded.

Before the vault was nearly submerged in water, one of the girls, Billie, stuck her head from the hole and cried, "I don't wanna die! Please!"

As Billie desperately tried to pull back on a piece of metal, Selena noticed part of what Bret recently cut slightly bending backward.

While treading through water, Selena said before the water reached her mouth: "Get back!"

Selena handed Bret the flashlight, who, in return, shined the light on Selena as she dove into the water and forcibly removed the brace from her leg. The cool sting of water against the flesh of her leg sent a feverish chill throughout her body.

Once Selena's leg was free from the brace, she began to kick at the sides of the hole, more specifically, a piece of metal, which was obstructing the hole and preventing the three girls from escaping, until she managed to loosen it with a thunderous stomp against the metal. The force of the impact rippled throughout Selena's body and yet, she didn't experience any shooting pain in her leg, only a tightening sensation against her bones, and any pain that manifested was immediately shelved, for the safety of those three girls was the only task at foot. She kicked some more until the piece of metal chipped off from the hole. She kicked and kicked and each kick further widened the hole and then, on one last crunching drive with the heel of her foot, she kicked open the hole wide enough for the each one of the girls to escape.

Billie, as well as the two other girls, Kourtney and Ashleigh, squeezed through the hole and when they surfaced, only had a few inches left of space before the basement was submerged.

All three girls, as well as Bret and Selena, swam through the water until the water eventually filled up the entire basement, leaving them with no other option than to dive underwater. Right before the water reached the ceiling, each one took in deep breaths before diving into the water. Underwater, they swam toward the staircase, Bret using that flashlight to guide all four of them through the murky water.

Once they reached the staircase, Billie, Kourtney, and Selena surfaced.

Selena looked for Ashleigh but she was unaccounted for, which prompted Bret to swim back for her.

"Bret! Wait!" Selena shouted, as the ceiling directly above the bottom of the staircase suddenly collapsed, blocking the basement and preventing her from swimming after her brother.

As Selena and the other two waited on the steps, catching their breaths, two figures emerged at the top landing of the staircase.

Bret and Ashleigh, both shivering cold.

Apparently, Bret found Ashleigh, whose shirt snagged on a lightning fixture, and then, once Bret loosened her shirt, the two swam back to the hole in the ceiling and managed to exit through the floor above.

As the three reunited with Bret, Selena sat back and checked her injuries, primarily her leg.

Strangely, as the excitement was over, Selena felt no pain in her right leg; in fact, her leg felt normal, like it did before the surgeries—perhaps the adrenaline had numbed the leg. Either way, Selena embraced the moment, as she watched the three girls tightly hug Bret. The three couldn't thank him enough for saving their lives.

WHILE the five of them sought shelter inside the dusty office of what used to be a law firm across the street from Samson's Trusts and Loans, they took a moment to brainstorm a lie to tell their parents. Billie came up with the idea that the three had been trapped inside the abandoned Bakerwood Mine. The story went as follows: She, Kourtney, and Ashleigh snuck into the mine, out of curiosity, when, all of sudden, they fell into a mine shaft. She heard about this story last year when two kids from Plymouth fell into the mine and died. Then, Bret, while being Bret, heard the three inside the mine, fetched his sister, Selena. Together the two, Bret and Selena, brought rope to the mine. And if they questioned why Bret or Selena didn't tell their parents, they'd just say that, knowing their parents, they'd tell Kourtney's parents, who'd then ground Kourtney for eternity.

As though with incredible ease, Selena poked holes through Billie's story, saying that they'd need someone to go to the mine and then stage a fall, as well as the rescue, and that it'd be much easier to tell the truth.

She faced Kourtney and said, "You killed him out of self-defense, right?"

Before Kourtney could respond, Bret said, "She didn't kill him. I did."

Selena recalled the knife that she found in Bret's bedroom. Yet, somehow, she struggled to believe her brother.

"Is this true, Kourtney?" Selena asked Kourtney.

Kourtney glanced at Bret, then back at Selena, then bobbed her head.

"He was going to rape me," Billie said, backing Kourtney. "If it wasn't for Bret, then we'd probably be dead."

"Ashleigh?" Selena said to Ashleigh, who remained silent throughout the whole ordeal. Her face was pale white. "Is this true?"

After Selena asked once more, Kourtney repeated Selena's words, forcing Ashleigh to nod her head in agreement.

"It's true," she said finally while turning her eyes toward Bret.

Selena could see right through the guilt on her face.

The guilt was like a contagious disease, and she could see it spreading.

"Okay," Selena said quietly and acknowledged her brother. "We need to tell someone."

WHILE Selena and the three missing girls waited for Bret to return with Sheriff Atlas, Billie and Kourtney tried to explain the prank to Selena as best as they could, as she sat on the couch inside the office and rested her leg. Their words sounded rehearsed, and their body movements almost choreographed. The two confessed that they used, or better yet, took advantage of a gullible Bret and talked him into luring Ashleigh, who claimed she had a crush on Bret, inside the bank vault under the presumption that the two were both going to drop "lo-ro" from a batch of Teddy Bears that their dealer Styx recently obtained from his pharma-supplier, which might've potentially led to "other things." They told Selena to use her imagination. The notion of Bret doing "things," which she thought was worse than gross, repulsed her. The possibilities of two individuals bursting at the seams with hormones, not only that, floating off lo-ro, were endless and worthy of secretly documenting, which would make for hella likes on The Feed. But the two never planned to take it that far.

As stated by Kourtney and then reaffirmed by Billie, her brother, for the record, was *not* involved with the prank.

When he and Ashleigh were inside the vault, he heard a noise coming from outside. When he checked out the noise, Kourtney crept from the shadows and closed the vault while Bret was distracted, locking their main target, Ashleigh, inside.

Alone.

When Selena asked why Bret didn't tell anyone about Ashleigh's disappearance, Billie said that he had a "thing" for Kourtney. Clearly, Selena could pick up on the vibe between Kourtney and her brother when the two were together; however, it was clear to her that the feelings weren't mutual, Bret liking Kourtney way more than Kourtney liked him. She'd even go so far to think, even say out loud that Kourtney was not at all interested in Bret.

Then, as stated by Billie, the next day, after Selena's brother, Bret, demanded that she open the vault or else he'd tell someone (an adult) what they (Billie and Kourtney) did to Ashleigh, who was known to be bullied by other girls in her grade, the three of them (Bret, Kourtney, and Billie) went back to Samson's Trusts and Loans to free Ashleigh, using a combination to unlock the vault door (Selena asked where Billie obtained the combination and she told Selena she acquired the combination from a friend, who got the combination from a friend of a friend's grandfather, who once served time with a bank robber). Before she dialed in the combination, the three were attacked by a homeless man. While Bret fought with the homeless man who tried to rape Billie, Kourtney used the combination, which Billie kept on her smartphone. Kourtney managed to pull Billie away from the homeless man and lock both herself and Billie inside the vault in order to stay safe (when questioned how the two were going to free themselves from the outside, Billie mentioned that one particular hole, which Bret used to communicate with the three girls, and how she'd used the hole to relay the phone to him (According to rumors, the hole was created by bank robbers who once attempted to crack open the vault with explosives, one rumor being that robbers used sticks of dynamite on the vault). To Selena, parts of Billie and Kourtney's story sounded made up, coordinated. *How did they know the combination was going to work? Why didn't they see the homeless man before they arrived at the vault? Were they aware of the hole prior to being attacked by the homeless man? Was this their first rodeo and had they tried this prank on other "weaker" girls, who were prone to bullies?*

These questions ran cycles through Selena's head.

The most important one: "After my brother killed this homeless man, why didn't he use the combination you had to open the door?"

"The phone," Kourtney said over Billie before she could answer, "it got wet. It didn't work. Billie must've dropped the phone in a puddle when we were attacked from behind. Afterwards, I climbed up on one of those deposit boxes and tossed the phone through the hole."

"The phone would've worked after it was dried off."

"It didn't," Billie said. "Your brother said he put it in a box of rice. When he turned it back on, the combination was erased."

"And you didn't remember the combination?"

Annoyed by Selena's question, Billie said, "No, well, parts. It was a lot of numbers."

Selena turned to Ashleigh, who quietly sat in the corner of the office.

"And what were you doing when all of this was going on?"

Ashleigh shrugged.

"Just watching," she said expressionlessly.

"You didn't try to escape when Kourtney opened the door?"

Ashleigh once more shrugged.

She looked as if she was still in shock.

Instead of judging the girls, especially Billie and Kourtney, or telling the two that their actions, as reckless as they were, could've resulted in people dying, Selena told them that the only thing that mattered was that they were alive.

Ashleigh asked about Selena's leg, if she was okay, said she noticed the limp.

"Don't worry about me," Selena said.

DRESSED in plain clothes, Sheriff Atlas arrived at the scene with Bret, who was riding in the passenger seat of the sheriff's car.

Shortly after the sheriff discovered the three missing girls, as well as Selena inside the abandoned office, where they were seeking shelter from the storm, he contacted his deputies who, in return, notified the parents of the missing girls.

Through a walkie-talkie, the sheriff also contacted the paramedics. Besides severe dehydration and a likely possibility of being exposed to harmful bacteria, the most obvious injury: Kourtney's hand. She claimed that she cut it when she was squeezing through the hole.

Not too long after an ambulance arrived on the scene, both Billie's and Kourtney's parents showed up, reunited with their daughters, and then followed the ambulance to the hospital where Selena finally confronted her brother about the girls' story and the one gaping "*hole*" in it.

"The cut on the bottom part of Kourtney's hand."

Selena said she saw her hand before she escaped the vault.

"The bandage on Kourtney's hand," she emphasized.

Realizing that his sister had sniffed out the lie, Bret let out a sigh.

"*The story works*," Bret said while sitting next to his sister on the bench outside the hospital. The left side of his face glowing red from the EMERGENCY sign, one of the few lights powered by the hospital's backup generator. "And from what I can tell, they bought it."

"Mom and Dad didn't raise you to be a liar, Bret."

"Everybody lies."

"When did you always act like this?" asked Selena. "Why do you justify your actions based off what other people do?"

Selena waited in silence for an answer.

"I miss him. . . you know?"

Selena already knew the "him" Bret was talking about for the words that left his lips carried the weight of losing a loved one.

"So do I," Selena said, more softly.

"If he was still here, I never would've turned out this way."

"Besides your latest antics, you seem pretty normal to me." She looked into Bret's eyes and said, "Face it, Bret. You're just like Dad."

Selena paused, shook her head with mild disgust.

"If Mom ever finds out. . . "

"She won't," he said with certainty. Then depressingly lowered his head. "It's not like she cares about me anyway."

"Don't say that," Selena said, squaring herself to Bret.

"It's true," Bret said, internally seething. "Don't you hear the way her and Dean talk to me? Like I'm dirt!" His voice rose to a near shout for he could no longer hold in the emotion that had been building up inside him. "I don't matter to them. I don't matter to anyone. . . "

Selena scooted her body closer to Bret, whom she often referred to as her little baby brother, the adjectives in front of *brother* perfectly exemplifying his recent self-loathing; nonetheless, he was her brother, her family, her blood, which bound them together like some sort of cosmic glue.

"You matter to me, Bret," she said. "And so what if people don't care about you! Who the hell cares what they think? Despite whatever people say about you—cuz they will when you finally step out into the real world, trust me—just know that *I* care about you. *I* will always care about you. . . " she half-smirked, ". . . even if you make up lies to protect a girl you like." With a straight face, Selena said more seriously, "But you're getting older. You're growing. And soon, I won't be able to protect you. And if Kourtney doesn't feel the same way as you feel about her, the hell with her." Selena paused again. "My opinion: You can do much, *much* better. If I were you, I'd have nothing to do with her. But I'm not you, Bret. And I can't tell you what to do with your life or whom you want in it. You have to make those decisions for yourself."

"She's actually a good person," Bret said, referring to Kourtney.

"Good enough to risk going to jail?"

"It was self-defense!"

"Bret, she basically told me that she killed that man."

"She did?" said Bret, his eyes wide and curled with a glimmer of hope.

She didn't, but, like her nana, she was good at reading people, their expressions, their mannerisms, as well as the lies that slithered from their lips, especially the ones coming from the particular type of female whom she had dealt with many times in the past, with her spending most of her adolescence in the sports world and standing among other athletes, shoulder-to-shoulder, ego-to-ego, each one as competitive as a pride of lionesses fighting over a kill—it was fair to say Selena ran into her own share of Kourtneys, probably dozens of Kourtneys or Kourtney wannabes or Kourtney look-alikes or Kourtneys who appeared as if they were plucked off the assembly line, each one similar, if not the same as the other, their appearance, their vocabulary, their *labels*, both distributed and self-marketed, but of all the labels, one of them was forbidden to label along the perfect forehead of a Kourtney: self-centered narcissistic plotter who'd stab you in the shoulder blade with an ice pick, if it meant gaining more status in a branded society where products held more value than people and traits like strength, virtue, and dignity was a cardboard box filled with foam peanuts that would easily cave in under the slightest amount of pressure.

Selena nodded yes and put together the rest of the story in her head, in essence, filled in the gaps: Coming across a bloody toboggan and knife inside Bret's desk drawer, then remembering stepping on uncooked grains of rice, which her brother spilled on the carpet in his bedroom, then, Dean biting down on a shard of hard plastic—which she figured came from Billie's phone when Bret attempted to dry it out—when he was eating *Easy Rice* with tuna, then later that night, Dean complaining about how he had the runs so bad that he could water the shrubs, prompting Lacey to sing a childish tune, *"If you're fantasizing about running on the new fancy treadmill that Mrs. Clause bought you for Christmas but doesn't work worth a darn cuz we ain't got no* power *and then, all of a sudden, you smell something* sour, *diarrhea. . . diarrhea. . .* " thus, forcing Selena to chime in and tweak her mother's lame crack at a joke by dramatically shortening it, first keeping "treadmill," then adding "hearing something spill," which she thought had a better ring to it.

"*Less is more,*" she'd say.

Lastly, how could she forget the black dirt she saw underneath Bret's nails, especially coming from a boy who often shared similar traits as an indoor cat?

Then, Lacey barking orders at Bret to wash his hands before dinner.

Then, of course, Bret falling back into a bad habit of cracking his jaw, which Selena thought was a nervous tick and if Bret didn't retire the bad habit, then he'd wind up with "arthritis of the mouth."

She wondered if what recently happened at the bank vault triggered the habit, considering he started cracking his jaw right after Thanksgiving.

"Seems like the only true part in your story is Billie's phone," Selena said to Bret.

Bret confessed, "When Kourtney stopped responding to my texts the day after they said they were going to free Ashleigh, I knew something was wrong. I was able to text other people," Bret said, "but for some reason, whenever I texted her, the texts weren't going through. . . "

"Probably because she wasn't getting any service inside the vault."

"I guess," he said.

"Why didn't you go with them?" Selena asked, more suspicious about her brother.

"I told Massacre about what happened," he said. "He talked me out of not going back there, but I couldn't live with myself, knowing that maybe something had happened to them."

"Did Massacre go with you?" asked Selena.

Bret was hesitant to shake his head no.

"When I went back," he said, "I found the body lying outside the vault. I never saw what he did or tried to do to them. But they said he was going to kill them. Somehow, Billie knocked the knife from his hand when he was on top of her. Kourtney picked up the knife. . . "

Since Selena discovered the dead homeless man *outside* the bank vault, the one question that was still weighing heavily in her thoughts: "Then, how'd Billie and Kourtney wind up *inside* the vault?"

AFTER Selena and Bret were cleared to leave the hospital, Lacey handed off Selena's crutches to Dean and embraced her daughter before the rest of the family headed back home. While pulling herself away from her mother, Selena gave her brother, who was riding in the backseat of Dean's car, a friendly nod, reassuring Bret that his secret was as secured as a safe with her—at least the parts in their story that would incriminate, not only Bret, but also those three girls who lied to the sheriff.

John offered Selena a hand. Selena thanked John but told him that she could manage as she made her way to John's car.

The car ride from the hospital to Selena's house was quiet and spent mostly in a comfortable silence; and regardless of the lack of words spoken, the ride gave the two enough time to reflect about the recent turn of events, especially for Selena, who still tried to wrap her head around her brother's story, mainly the part where Billie and Kourtney were "pushed" into the vault by whom they assumed was a friend of the homeless man. According to Billie, who told Bret that she was waiting by the vault door while Kourtney stepped inside to fetch a traumatized Ashleigh cowering in the corner of the vault, she heard someone creeping behind her and before she could turn her shoulder, she was lying facedown on the ground with a shadowy figure closing the vault behind her. The last noises they heard before they were left alone in the dark was a pitter-patter of footsteps fading away, as the pusher left the bank. Although, Ashleigh didn't make so much as a peep about their "story," and somehow, deep inside her gut, Selena knew that she was hiding the truth about what really happened inside that empty, filthy shell of what used to be a bank.

As John parked the car in the driveway, he turned to Selena, who remained in a state of reflection.

Selena couldn't help but notice the fuel gauge being half-full.

As though baiting John into a quarrel, Selena said, "I talked with Dean earlier and asked him about your talk with him. He didn't know what I was talking about. . . "

As John embraced for Selena's soon-to-be wrath, he said carefully, "I didn't know any other way to convince you."

There was a tense silence between the two.

With everything that she had recently been through, she wasn't as upset as John anticipated.

John said over the tense silence, "Aren't you going to ask how I got the gas?"

"Honestly," Selena said, more carefree. "I don't wanna know."

With a puppy-dog-eyed look, John leaned forward and stared at Selena, whose scowl finally broke. John's look alone forced Selena to release the tension from her face in form of a laugh.

Sighing, she said, "How can I be mad at you?"

"How can anyone be mad at me?" John asked, nourishing a gleeful look on his face. "What can I say? It's like a gift. . . "

"Or a curse," Selena teased.

In a less tense silence, John cracked the driver side window and listened.

"You hear that?" asked John.

Selena cracked the passenger side window, letting the chilly air in and listened.

"What am I supposed to be listening to?" Selena asked, turning to John.

"Nothing," he said softly. "It's. . . it's so quiet."

"Yeah," Selena agreed.

"Usually," John said, "you can hear the cars on the highway, the engines, or an airplane flying above or muffled sounds of TVs or a hum of air conditioning units or generators. The ambience of man's creations. Now. . . nothing. But only the sounds of nature."

Selena listened closer and heard the sounds of nature: an owl *whooing*, the *rustling* of a creature—perhaps a fox or opossum walking through the woods behind Selena's house—callings of coyotes.

Listening closer, Selena said, "It's like someone turned down the volume of all the bullshit, and while doing so, other things— *real* things—got turned back up. It's amazing and at the same time, scary. Surprisingly, I'm kind of getting used to it. You?"

In the wake of Selena's response, John was torn apart by the revelation of *his* recent story, in particular, a story passed down to him by Eugene Wallace's son, Gene; and as John had Selena's ear, he contemplated whether or not to share the story with Selena for he knew the ramifications of what it might have on her.

The story, which the sprightly double-barrel shotgun-totting seventy-something year old retired audio engineer, Eugene

"Gene" Wallace II (The Second), called his pop's "deer story," was animatedly told in striking detail to John, who first misread Gene's exuberance as inebriation—John wondering: What was Gene's poison? Beer? Hard liquor? At first, Gene struck John as a whiskey man. Turns out Gene didn't have a poison, John later realized, wasn't even a drinker, if you could believe that, and Gene's odd behavior, as well as his don't-give-a-shit attitude was the doings of a world that didn't bat an eyelash when labeling him a "nut." Basically, what John saw before him was a man who developed a personality disorder over many years of abuse and rejection. Call it fate or just plain stupid luck, John approached Gene at a right moment in time when Gene was desperate to pass the story along to a person, in this case, John, who would finally listen to him without any judgment.

As Selena waited for a response from John, he contemplated whether or not to tell her about the strange artifact that Hawks carried around in his pocket like a totem (Gene's pop first thought it might've been a good luck charm) after he pulled it from Anthony "The Hit Whisperer" Florentine's brain while performing a risky surgical operation, allegedly curing Mr. Florentine of his illness. The same artifact that Hawks dropped, or so he claimed, "crawled" from his pocket after he accidentally struck a deer with his car while driving home from Cooper Institute in the middle of the night. The following words that Gene spoke to John were beyond reasoning or comprehension, which made the story even more susceptible for ridicule or worse, the slinging of labels, one including the smoke of a madman whose lungs were as black and charred as a chimney.

According to Gene, Hawks stood off to the side of the road and in disbelief, watched the artifact, or "shard," walk all on its own to the recently struck deer, which was lying motionlessly in a puddle of blood. The shard then proceeded to walk onto the deer's leg, which was broken, its bone protruding from the flesh. The shard then attached itself to the deer's broken bones where it injected a needle into its legs and Gene said his pop told him that the shard was drawn to the deer's wound, mainly "its blood." As the shard reconnected the deer's broken leg back together, the deer suddenly woke up from its deathly slumber and frolicked into the woods where, later the next day, Hawks, who hadn't slept at all the night before, tracked down the deer. With a hunting rifle, Hawks shot the deer dead and hauled the deer's corpse back to his house where he cut open the deer and removed the shard from its leg. The shard was still intact; in fact, it had grown significantly in size, from its original arrowhead-size to roughly the size of a fist; and as he'd later study in his research into the artifact, it was alive, not robotic or as he first postulated, a type of mechanism, and its only means of survival were similar to that of a parasite feeding off its host, in this certain case, a deer. Hawks stated to those within in his circle that it was "unlike any organism known to man," and this extraordinary creature needed to feed.

Under the guise of what Hawks claimed to be a medical breakthrough, the doctor tested his theory on animal subjects, primarily rats, replicating the damage that he accidentally inflicted on the deer before introducing the subject to the artifact. Regardless of Hawks's inhumane research, because as Gene stated to John, *"From the way my pop talked about Hawks, the doctor was just as insane as the very people he treated,"* the testing showed that this strange creature carried "regenerative qualities," not only on the tissue of the test subject, but also its bones.

As the internal debate waged inside John's mind, an argument between two different sides, one fueled by an unusual yet captivating story that oddly connected the dots to other stories, including Hilda's and dare he'd say, Selena's, and another being what John might've thought was simply hearsay, a rumor that began in one ear, only to come out distorted through another one's mouth, then another and so on and so on, he contemplated whether or not Selena should hear, in his own words, about a deer that was run over by a car, only to be resurrected by a metallic shard that was pulled from the brain of a mass murderer who claimed he was hearing voices.

Pushing aside the deer story, John asked, not Selena, but rather himself, "Am I getting used to all of this?"

He let out a visible exhale, a prologue to a laugh. He turned to Selena and grabbed her hand.

"Honestly," he said to her, "I don't even know how to answer that question."

"These past couple of days have been. . . "

Selena searched for the right word.

John filled in the blank: "Strange."

"I think we've unearthed a new definition of strange, don't you think?"

He pulled Selena's hand to his lips and kissed the top of it.

"I don't wanna lose you, Selena," he said.

Selena furrowed her brow, slightly pulled her head away.

"Speaking of strange. . . " she said, her words suspending over the two. "You're acting like something bad is about to happen."

The awkward pause caused Selena to turn her eyes outside the car where it began to snow.

Standing behind Dean's office window on the first floor was a slouched-over person, whom Selena thought was Eleanor. The lantern that she was holding partially lit up the bottom part of her wrinkled face.

John followed Selena's eyes.

"Who is that?" he asked.

"My nana," she said, peering closer. "She's just making sure I'm home."

"By the way," John asked, "how's Bret?"

"Bret's Bret," she said, as she watched the lantern fade into the darkness of the office.

John asked, "Where'd he find a torch?"

Selena said that he borrowed the torch from Bobby Tyrell, who ran an illegal chop shop.

In other words, he stole it.

"I know Bobby's little brother," John said to Selena. "His family's not exactly the forgiving type. If you want, I can talk to them. . . "

"Sure Bobby Tyrell has other more important issues to deal with, if you know what I mean."

John nodded, smiled.

"I know what you mean."

Selena said with a deadpan expression, "I don't recognize him anymore."

"Bret's going through changes. I went through them myself."

"You've been the same person ever since I've known you."

John shrugged.

"Yeah," he said, surrendering to Selena. "Maybe you're right."

"Of course, I'm right."

John focused on Selena and said more directly, "How are you?"

The smile faded from her face.

"Fine," she said shortly, as she struggled to make eye contact with John.

"Your mom said that, if it wasn't for you, then Bret and those other girls would've died."

Selena didn't respond to John's comment.

"Did Bret ever say what he was doing downtown?"

"Apparently, over the past couple of years, the bank has become haunted," she said.

In reflection, John said, "Of all the people from Del Soaka Falls to dupe your brother into a prank. . . Kourtney McCormick?"

Bret being involved in Billie and Kourtney's prank was the only piece of the made-up story that Sheriff Atlas managed to extract from them, which, the more Selena thought about it, made her wonder if it was all a part of the crafty story, as though it was thought out over the course of the three girls' disappearances and meant to show a minor yet deliberate hiccup to their story, the hiccup being essential to their story.

"He has a crush on her," Selena said.

"Crush, huh?" John paused in thought. "She doesn't seem like his type."

"What type is that?"

"Not saying your brother's a nerd or anything—"

"What are you talking about?" said Selena. "He's a total geek."

"You may be right, but she just seems like the type to date a gym rat."

"Amazing how boys would do anything to impress a girl they like," she said, facing John.

"I wonder what they'll do now," John said. "Last I heard all the networks are down—"

With a peculiar look on her face, Selena asked John, "Would you ever kill another person?"

"Me?" Surprised by the question, John recoiled. "To be honest, I don't think it's in my nature. Why do you ask? You think they killed that homeless man on purpose?"

Like John before, Selena thought about whether or not to tell John the truth about Bret and how he was taking the blame for Kourtney.

"You didn't answer the question," she said, dodging John's question.

"Would I kill someone?"

Selena nodded and waited for a response.

John sighed and like Selena before, found himself struggling to answer a simple yet complex question.

Selena made it easier for him.

"Say, someone did something to me, something unforgivable, would you kill this person out of retaliation?"

"Yes," John said without missing a beat. "I would. Absolutely."

"Because you love me?"

"I've loved you ever since I passed you in the hallway after leaving Mrs. Dilworth's class," John said, holding Selena's hand with both his hands. "For years, I thought I was invisible. But you saw me. And I saw you and I knew, right then and there, that I had a chance to be the person I've always dreamt of being."

As the tears flooded Selena's eyes, the two embraced one another.

Closely, Selena said, "Why don't you come inside?"

"I dunno," he said unsurely, "seems kind of crowded in there."

"Then, let's go somewhere."

"Really? After everything you've been through today?"

Selena shrugged and said, "I'm way too wired to go to bed."

John suggested: "I know of a party not too far away."

"What about the curfew?" Selena asked.

With a smirk curling along the side of his face, John said, "When has that ever stopped us?"

JOHN drove Selena to the "End of the World" party, which was being held at an open field in the countryside along the outskirts of Padadock. There were at least fifty or so people who showed up, mostly former graduates of Del Soaka Falls who came back home after the devastating blackouts forced closures at a majority of colleges and universities along the East Coast. In the center of the field was a massive bonfire, which could be seen from at least a half-mile away. Several of the partygoers had loaded up the back of their trucks with toss-out furniture and whatever they could get their hands on, most of the stuff picked from a nearby landfill called the Fox Hole.

John grabbed himself and Selena a red cup of beer that he poured from one of the five kegs. The two took their lukewarm beers to the bonfire where they talked to folks whom they used to chill with at The Soak Machine before grabbing a seat on a wool sofa that was soon going to be chucked into the fire.

Through the beating flames, Selena spotted, of all people whom she least expected to see at the party, Ashleigh's brother, Conner. He was sitting on a log like a slumped over catcher on the other side of the bonfire.

"Is that Conner?" asked Selena.

"Think so," John said after following Selena's eyes. Then, more certain, "Yeah. It's kind of weird seeing him here, you think, especially with what recently happened with his sister? You'd think he'd be home with her."

"They're probably saying the same about me," Selena said carelessly.

Before John could reassure Selena, she touched him on the arm.

"Give a minute, will you?" Selena said over John and excused herself.

"Sure," he said and glanced down at the nearly empty cup. "Want another beer?"

"I'm good," she said. "Thanks."

Using the one crutch that she brought with her, Selena limped her way toward Conner, who was sitting by himself smoking a vintage cigarette.

"Sup, Conner," Selena said.

"If it isn't our knight in shining armor," he said drunkenly.

She pointed to the empty spot next to him.

"You mind?"

Conner, who appeared intoxicated from, not only a slur in his voice, but also his movements, which were loose and heavy, held out his hand and in a rather exaggerated, flamboyant fashion, motioned to Selena to sit down on the log.

"How's Ashleigh doing?" asked Selena.

"She's just fine and dandy," he drawled and took a drag from the cigarette and blew out the smoke through talking. "I reckon you came by here to see me cuz I owe you a thank you, huh?"

"I just wanted to check up on you," she said. "See how you were doing. How'r you holding up?"

"How does it look like I'm doing?"

His cheeks flushed over with red-hot rage.

"What's going on with you?" asked Selena.

"So, when all of a sudden, do you give a flying shit about me?"

"You're right," Selena said bluntly. "I don't give a shit. I'm just trying to be nice."

Conner glanced over at Selena and let out a short laugh, as though he was impressed by Selena's bluntness—or dry sense of humor, he couldn't tell which.

What Conner couldn't deny, though, of all the people he rubbed shoulders with at Del Soaka Falls (most of the rubbing being the wrong way), Selena was nice to him, despite whether or not she was sincere or, in fact, "just trying to be nice."

"I see you're still with Johnny Boy," he said, drunkenly nodding at a blurry, wavy John.

Selena looked past the fire and shot a glance toward the row of kegs where John was talking to an old high school buddy, who was trying to dare John into doing a keg stand.

"Yep," she said. "You? You got a girlfriend?"

"You know me," he said laidback. "I can't shake 'em off quick enough."

"You never did go steady," she said. "You had too many distractions."

"What can I say?" Conner gave Selena a wicked grin. "My Achilles heel."

"I heard Ashleigh is fond of my brother."

Conner let out a noise from his mouth.

"She's just working your brother to get to that punk he hangs out with."

"Mayhem?"

He looked at Selena funny and said, "You mean Trip."

"Bleached blonde hair? Big gamer?"

"Yeah," he said. "That's Trip. I dunno what she sees in that kid. It's funny how girls tend to gravitate toward boys who scare the shit out of them. Speaking from personal experiences—"

"A case of 'Bad-Boy Syndrome,' I guess," she said and let out a sigh as she started to stand up. "Well, I'm glad your sister's okay."

Conner took another drag, angrier this time.

He said before Selena stood up, "She ain't really my sister, you know that right?"

Selena said, "What do you mean?"

"She's my cousin," he said, hanging his head. Then, he corrected, "*Half*-cousin."

"I didn't know that," Selena said flatly.

Before Selena could question why everybody, at least everybody she knew, thought Conner was Ashleigh's brother, Conner said to Selena, "We practically grew up together, which, sort of, I guess, makes us brother and sister."

"Makes sense," she said.

Conner looked at Selena similar to the expression on the face of a dumb dog.

"John's uncle—"

He asked before Selena could finish her sentence, "Makes sense? What the fuck's that supposed to mean?"

Selena waved off the comment.

"I'm teasing."

The reasons for Conner's rather emotional state were the results of a fight with his mother, Aileen, whose behavior toward, as he confessed, his "*half*-cousin" hit a rather sore spot, triggering a mountainous range of hostility, mostly stemming from the lack of a male figure in his life, more specifically, a father who was never in the picture. He only saw the man's face once when he was a boy, and if he passed him on the street, he wouldn't even recognize him, only a similarity in his chin.

He explained to Selena how Aileen acted when his half-cousin was around, all the coddling, the smothering and whatnot, the around-the-clock attention, and yet, despite her mawkish ways, Aileen often treated him as if he wasn't blood. And there was a saying among the Reaps: "*Blood was thicker than the chemicals in the water.*"

While mentally tracing up Conner's family tree, Selena said with question, "You two share the same grandparent?"

Selena paused, the name coming back to her.

With a dawning recollection, she said, "Grandfather?"

Conner nodded "yeah," and then, over his drunken beat, said to Selena, "Aileen took her in when she was around eight after my granddaddy was killed."

"What happened to Ashleigh's parents?" asked Selena.

"They divorced when she was a baby," Conner said. "Her momma took care of her until she got sick. Then, her granddaddy took care of her after her momma passed."

"When was this?" Selena asked, as she became more intrigued by Conner's *half*-family.

"Years ago, I dunno," he said, shrugging. "Ashleigh was like four I think when her momma passed."

"That's young," she said. "How'd Ashleigh's mother die?"

"Pills," he said.

"How old was she?"

Conner paused in thought.

"I dunno," he said. "Like her mid-thirties."

More quietly, Selena said, "Sorry."

"Don't be," he said. "Not like I knew the woman."

"But you knew her dad, Sturgis. Right?"

"How do you know my granddaddy's name?"

"You told me before," Selena lied.

"I did?"

"Last year."

Conner made another noise with his mouth.

"I don't remember."

"Well, you did."

"I don't remember much about him, memory-wise," he said. "I was around ten I think when he was killed." He furrowed his brow in confusion. "But I do know his story."

"Killed how?"

"Shot," Conner said. "I guess his past came back to haunt him. Besides, why you so interested in my granddaddy?"

Selena shrugged.

"I've just heard stories about him. I'm sure you've heard them as well—"

"Yeah," Conner said, as a flash of anger rushed into his face. "And not one of them is true."

Selena shot a glance over at John, who was still talking to an old friend.

"I do remember, though, how this town turned on him," he said, pointing to his eyes. "You can still see it in their eyeballs whenever they stare at me like somehow I'm to blame for a crime that only happened in their imaginations. He was never charged with the murder of that girl, and yet, the people in this town already made up their minds about him. What all these people don't know and I think *never* will know is that he turned his life around after he had Grace—"

"Ashleigh's mother?"

Conner nodded.

"A few years after she was born, he was involved in a DUI accident," he said, "ran his truck off the road, totaled it, was hospitalized, nearly died. The state wanted to take Grace away from him, but he did what every decent man would do and fought for her. From that point forward, he never touched a drink. He was given multiple chances at life, and shit, I guess it's fair to say that the accident was his final wake-up call."

"How about Grace's mother?" asked Selena. "Where was she?"

Conner turned his bloodshot eyes toward Selena.

Before he could answer the question, John showed up.

John and Conner talked for a minute, the conversation centered on his "sister" Ashleigh. He didn't correct John, which made Selena wonder why Conner opened up to her about Ashleigh, as well as his relationship with her. The two practically knew each other from birth, and if Conner never told her about his mother taking Ashleigh in to live with them at such a young age—when she "eight" years old, he said—then, to any person who didn't know their backstory, it'd seem as if the two were siblings or at least, partially related.

Given his current inebriated state, she turned the attention toward Conner and couldn't help but ask, "And how about you, Conner? Are you okay to drive?"

"I walked here," he said and relit the cigarette. "But I appreciate your concern."

"It's kind of a long walk, especially in the snow." She insisted, "John and I can give you a ride home."

"It's fine."

Selena turned to John, motioning for him to back up her request.

"Let us give you a ride home, Conner," John said and waited for Conner's response.

THE next morning, after John dropped off Selena at her parents' house, she saw Sheriff Atlas and Deputy Kohler's cars parked outside. John asked if he should stay and talk with the sheriff, but Selena insisted that she'd be fine and that she could handle any questions that the sheriff wanted to ask her, especially ones he considered inappropriate to ask her at the hospital.

When Selena walked inside the house, Sheriff Atlas was sitting with Bret, Lacey, and Dean at the kitchen table. Deputy Kohler was standing by the kitchen counter, observing.

"Speak of the devil," Sheriff Atlas said and stood up from his seat. He turned to Lacey and Dean and asked them if it was okay if he chatted with Selena alone.

As Deputy Kohler exited the house, Selena noticed the evidence bag in his hand, as well as the knife inside it. The same one Selena discovered in Bret's bedroom.

Before Lacey could follow the sheriff from the kitchen, Selena told Lacey to give her a minute while she talked to the sheriff. Bret was sitting at the end of the kitchen table with a pale and lifeless expression on his face. The expression alone caught her eye, forcing her to contemplate the pact and whether or not it was time to break it.

Sheriff Atlas guided Selena to the front porch while Deputy Kohler waited by his car.

"I talked with a gentleman who knew the deceased," he said. "According to this gentleman, Larry Rohon—also homeless— knew Walter Herby," Sheriff Atlas said to Selena. "Before Mr. Herby attacked Billie, as Bret and the three girls claimed in their statements, Mr. Rohon said Mr. Herby was given a hundred dollars to scare Billie and Kourtney."

"I don't understand," Selena said, thinking.

"Frankly," the sheriff said, "I don't either. Mr. Rohon wasn't making much sense."

"Why are you telling me this, Sheriff?"

"Before you arrived at Samson's, did you see anyone?"

"No," she said without thinking much about the question.

"You sure?"

"Yes."

"You didn't see a boy, around Bret's age, with dyed blonde hair?"

"Blonde hair?" Selena thought for a second. Then said, "No." She questioned Sheriff Atlas, "Did you find any money on Mr. Herby?"

"No," he said, sighing. "We did not. But we found plenty of lo-ro on him, enough to kill an elephant. I spoke to Trip Saber—"

"Trip Saber?"

The name struck a cord inside Selena, causing her eyes to light up.

"Apparently, he and your brother are friends," the sheriff said.

"Correct," she said with hesitation, "I've seen him over at the house before."

"Did Trip mention anything about the incident at Samson's? Maybe you overheard him and your brother talking about the three girls?"

"No. . ." Selena connected the sheriff's dots, ". . . Because of the dyed hair, right?"

Sheriff Atlas held up his hands.

"I'm just tying up loose ends, Selena," he said more patiently.

"Lots of people have dyed blonde hair in Padadock."

The sheriff said finally before taking off, "If there's anything you want to tell me, Selena—maybe something that you want to talk to me about after you speak to your brother—feel free to contact me." He said simply, "Tell you what: Why don't you take the weekend to think things over and get back to me on Monday. Sound good—"

Selena asked, "What about the bank? Are you going to talk to Mayor Benkins into possibly demolishing the building? It's unsafe."

"No need," he said. "Looks like nature beat us to the punch. The roof of the building caved in last night. Good thing there weren't any people inside. Someone was looking after you—"

"It should've been demolished years ago."

"You're preaching to the choir, Selena," the sheriff said, placing one hand over his hips.

"So," Selena said, "what'd Trip say?"

"He said he had no involvement," Sheriff Atlas said, shifting his weight.

An awkward pause formed over the conversation, the sheriff using the moment to study Selena's face.

"Well, then," the sheriff said with a closed smile and a slight squint in his eyes, "I better get going. Get some rest. And please contact me, if you anything else comes to mind. All right?"

The two made eye contact and strangely, had an unspoken agreement.

"Will do, Sheriff," Selena said.

The sheriff stopped at the bottom of the steps and before Selena walked back into the house, said from behind, "And Selena. . . thank you."

"For what?"

"If case you haven't heard," he said, "you're a hero."

"I'm no hero," she said, standing at the doorway. "I liked to believe anyone would've done the same thing, if they were in my shoes."

"Well, you did a noble act for the commonwealth, and we're all in your debt."

Selena shyly waved off the sheriff's compliment.

"During these trying times, you gave the town something that it desperately needed. . . "

"What's that?" Selena asked.

"Hope," the sheriff said and walked back to his car and waved at Mr. Toto, who was shoveling the snow from his driveway.

Before stepping into the car, he said to Selena, "By the way, did you hear the good news?"

"No," Selena said, stepping to the edge of the porch.

"The Tudors tracked down their daughter, Blaire," said Sheriff Atlas, who recently returned from Blaire's bereaved parents' house.

"The ninth grader?"

"Apparently," he said, "she ran away from home."

"I don't blame her," she said, more casually.

The sheriff made a noise with his mouth.

"Stay safe, Selena," he said, more dour. "And if you can, stay close to home."

"Why's that?" asked Selena.

"Just a gut feeling I have."

"About what?"

"Well. . . " he paused, then smiled a closed, insecure smile, but never finished his thought. "Just take care of yourself and those around you."

The sheriff got back into his car and drove away.

As the day dragged on, Selena spent the quiet time in her room mulling over the recent conversation she had with Conner last night, mainly what he said about his half-cousin, Ashleigh.

While Selena ran through the math in her head (*Ashleigh being seventeen years old, meaning she was born in 2031, her mother, Grace, according to Ashleigh's half-cousin, Conner, died from an overdose of "pills" while she was in her mid-thirties, let's say, when she was thirty-five, her daughter, Ashleigh, being four years old at the time of her mother's passing, meaning Sturgis and the Mother Mystery would've had their daughter, Grace, between 2000-2001*), a thorny sensation crawled up Selena's skin.

As Selena pulled out her yearbook from her senior year at Del Soaka Falls, she couldn't take her mind off the conversation that she had with Hilda at Forest Hills and how her daughter, Milo, dropped out of college in 2000 at the age of twenty-two, and the real kicker: Sturgis, Ashleigh's grandfather, according to Hilda, who alluded to a potential relationship with her eldest daughter, was interested in Milo. Sturgis would've been around twenty-eight, six years older than Milo. It was fair to say Sturgis was a complicated man with uncomplicated issues but, according to Conner, eventually cleaned up his act after a near-fatal car accident. But, Selena thought, *what if* the main reason for Hilda and Milo's fallout wasn't because Milo found out about her mother's extramarital affairs with Patrick Britten, but rather she was too ashamed to tell her mother the truth about her relationship with Sturgis? According to Hilda, Milo didn't talk to her for two years.

Selena flipped to the sophomore class and found Ashleigh Reap's photograph.

While keeping her finger on the photo, she pulled out the book *MACHINE* where she found a photo of Milota Rose.

She compared the two photographs, first placing them side-by-side, then with her hand, covering the bottom part of Ashleigh's face.

She had her eyes.

And the more she looked at Ashleigh's face, she saw Milo in it.

A few rows down from Ashleigh's photo was Trip Saber's photo.

In the photograph, Trip had brunette hair, not dyed blonde hair.

The more she stared at Trip's photo, the more she started to weigh-in on Mr. Rohon's words. Why would a homeless man lie to Sheriff Atlas about Mr. Herby, who, according to Lacey, was a veteran who once fought in the war in Afghanistan?

All of a sudden, the power came back on!

The TV's, the air conditioner, the desktop computer, all of it sounded with *clicks* and *chirps*, startling Selena.

So much noise!

Next were the sounds of voices: Lacey shouting out "Thank God!" while Dean, who, for the past couple of days, had been wound up like a happy meal toy, laughing away the frustration.

As Selena limped into the living room without the support of a crutch, Bret crept downstairs from his bedroom and made eye contact with Selena before he made a U-turn and marched back upstairs and entered his bedroom, closing the door behind him.

THE next day, when things were returning back to normal, Massacre (Trip) stopped by the house to play video games with Bret.

Selena snuck upstairs while the two gamers were distracted by killing the undead and without the two aware of her presence, watched the two of them interact, more specifically, how Trip was treating her brother, mainly talking down to him and insulting him.

After she had observed enough of the two interacting, she waited around the house until Trip left.

Selena pulled Bret aside and asked him if he'd care to join her outside.

As if the two had a mutual understanding, Bret finished updating his smartphone before following his sister into the garage. When mentioning the update, Bret said that the phone wouldn't work properly, most of the features on the phone couldn't be accessed unless he check-marked a box in an AGREEMENT FORM, which was, in Bret's own words, a gazillion pages long and filled with slick lawyer lingo that he couldn't understand and frankly, he told Selena, didn't have time to understand.

He assumed that the update must've been from the blackout.

Selena wasn't at all interested in the phone stuff; in fact, she hadn't turned on her phone ever since the power was restored and didn't plan on using it anytime soon.

Expecting an unpleasant response from her brother, Selena said straightforwardly, "I'm going to tell Sheriff Atlas what really happened. Now, before you get upset—"

"I'm not upset," he said, kicking at a foot of snow covering the edge of the driveway.

"You're not?"

"Massacre followed Kourtney and Billie the day they said they were going to open the vault for Ashleigh. I know he paid that homeless guy to scare Kourtney and Billie while he stood at a distance, filmed it, and posted it on The Feed. The two girls overreacted, grabbed the knife from the homeless guy's hand, and killed him."

"Did he ever post this video?" asked Selena.

Bret shook his head no.

"He told you this?"

"No," Bret said, shaking his head once more, "but I figured it out. Plus, Billie said it herself: There was someone else with them that day when they went back to the vault. Billie never got a good look at the person's face after she was shoved from behind. But I know it was him. After Kourtney stopped responding to my texts the next day, I noticed he was wearing different shoes. He hated those shoes. When I asked him about the shoes, he said his other pair got dirty."

"Why do you think he locked those girls inside the vault?" asked Selena.

"He knew how much attention I was giving Kourtney," Bret uttered, his voice trailing off. "Who knows? Who cares. . . "

"And the knife that Sheriff Atlas took with him?"

"Massacre asked me to hold onto it," he said, unaware that his sister knew he was hiding the knife along with a bloody toboggan, which might've belonged to Walter Herby, inside a drawer in his desk.

"You didn't question him why?"

Bret shrugged, struggling to look his sister in the eyes.

"Not at the time he gave it to me," he said. "I figured the blood on it was his." With both of his hands held behind his back as he leaned against the side of the house, he drifted deeper into thought. His glossy eyes were pinned on the snow along the driveway. "After I saw the sheriff outside the house, I started to think more about Massacre: 'Why was he so adamant about trying to convince me not to go back to the bank?'"

"You think he had anything to do with Billie's phone not working?"

"Maybe."

Over another silence, Selena asked, "Where'd he get the knife?"

Agitated by Selena's gazillion questions, he said after his first "I dunno" wasn't satisfactory, "He bought it from a pawnshop, I think."

"And you believe him?"

Bret looked up at Selena.

Again: "I dunno."

"So," Selena said, "what are you going to do?"

Visibly upset, Bret said, "You don't know what Trip is capable of? He'll kill me if he finds out I went to Sheriff Atlas and told him what he did. Which, by the way, he'll just deny."

"But you have proof?"

"What proof?" asked Bret. "It's all hearsay."

"If he bought the knife at a pawnshop, then I'm sure they'll have video of him buying it."

"I'm not even convinced he bought it at a pawnshop," Bret said.

"You really want to stick to this story?" she asked, as she stepped closer to her brother. "All for what, Bret? For some girl who doesn't even like you? For some friend who, from what I've seen, doesn't come across as a friend? The time is now, Bret, for you to put your foot down and take a stand for truth's sake."

"Who's going to believe me?" Bret asked.

"Maybe nobody will." Selena said more mindfully, "But if we, if *you*, stand by your truth, the truth about what happened will eventually come forward and when that happens, I assure you that you will remember this very moment, and the fear and the anxiety and all of the doubts you might have right now, they will be nothing more than ghosts to remind you: That you don't need them, that you're better off without them, and that, that you do *not* serve them anymore because, wherever you go in life, they'll always be there to lie, to trick, to serve you. Their sole purpose in life is to devour you. . . " Selena held out her hand and patiently waited for Bret's answer. "If there's something they can never take away from you, Bret, it's *your* truth."

THE following day was a Sunday.

The date: "December 6, 2048," marking the second and a half day with the return of power after the nationwide blackout, which, except for the Monday before Thanksgiving, lasted for two weeks. Considering what Selena learned from Dean and other members of her family, especially Bret, who reverted back to his usual conspiratorial self whenever he wasn't messing around with his Streamerz channel, not everybody throughout the country lost power and those who did end up losing power, especially up and down the East Coast, didn't lose it for the entirety of the two weeks. According to Dean, everybody was talking about the controversy surrounding the release of documents known as the "Loch Ness Files" and in the files were explosive allegations into the cause of the blackouts, including the near-catastrophic ones two years ago.

Like many, Selena was still out of sorts after having adjusted her life without power and for better or worse, missed the #powerfree lifestyle. She spent most of the day relaxing in her room. She managed to finish her book *Raven The Wise* and was ready to delve into the next book (currently she had several books waiting to be read, the first one, an ebook for a science fiction novel written by Stuart Berkley called *They'll Never Know You Exist*, and the other one, a non-fictional hardback about the controversy surrounding the Atlanta Hellhounds organization and what was publicly known as "Hellgate").

After resting her eyes for a moment, Selena decided to wash a load of laundry. Lacey spent nearly the entire Saturday using the washer and now that it was no longer in use, she figured that she might as well take advantage of the opportunity.

Once the clothes were in the wash, Selena stepped outside on the screened-in porch to escape Dean and his rants about the recent allegations about Lockhart and found her nana reading from a book herself.

Eleanor placed the book aside and greeted her granddaughter.

"New book, I see," Selena said.

Eleanor glanced at the cover.

"What are you reading?" asked Selena.

"*Song of Summer*," she said, "by Stanley Pruitt."

"Never heard of him," Selena said. "What's it about?"

Eleanor said while skimming over the synopsis, "It's about this guy who goes after a corrupt pharmaceutical company responsible for releasing a cancer drug on the market that wasn't FDA approved. The wife ends up dying after taking the cancer drug."

Selena, who couldn't help but think of her own story, looked at her nana in amazement.

"Sounds interesting. *And* thanks for spoiling it for me, Nana," she said with a spurious and well-performed outrage.

"Well, it all happens at the beginning of the novel," Eleanor said. "Most of the book, from what I've read so far, is the aftermath of the wife's death."

"How'd you find it?" asked Selena.

"Lacey found the book when she was going through a box filled with some of my old stuff that she found in the attic," she said. "I never did get around to reading it."

Eleanor handed Selena the book; and in return, Selena glanced over the front wrinkled cover where a slouched over man was standing on a beach somewhere along the Gulf of Mexico.

"That's weird," she said, looking over the book. Then, she turned to her nana. "It's just. . . I can't help but notice the similarities in our stories."

"*Your* story?" asked Eleanor.

While struggling to look her nana in the eyes, Selena said, "Forget about it. It's nothing."

"Do you want to read it?" asked Eleanor.

Selena handed the book back to her nana.

"No," she said. "I'm sure they'll make a movie from it one day—"

"That reminds me," Eleanor said abruptly, "I forgot to mention that your mother found some photos of me when I was younger while she was going through my old stuff. She was planning on putting the photos in the albums. Would you like to see the photos?"

"Sure," Selena said gladly.

Eleanor left the book behind on the cushion of the wicker couch and walked back inside the house. Before following her nana inside, Selena was drawn to the paperback on the couch.

Since she hadn't gotten around to updating her phone yet, she pulled out Lacey's phone that she borrowed while her mother was cleaning the bathroom and entered the author's name in the search engine and scrolled through other novels that Stanley Pruitt had written. Among his bibliography was a series called *The Blackout*, which left Selena in a state of awe.

As Selena read more about Pruitt and his background, as well as *The Blackout* series, which made him famous, the glass door slid further open, making a whooshing sound that startled her.

"Do you want to see them or not?" Eleanor asked, poking her head from the doorway.

"Of course," Selena said and by accident, suddenly dropped the phone from her hand.

She reached down and picked up the phone from the ground.

Expecting to find a crack stretching across the screen of the phone, Selena found nothing for Lacey's purple protective case preventing any damage.

"Did you break it?" asked Eleanor.

Selena waved off her nana's concern and said, "Don't think so."

As Selena pocketed the phone and made her nana promise that she wouldn't tell Lacey about the latest oopsy moment, she followed Eleanor back inside the house.

Based on Selena's recent interest in Bluefield, as well as an unsolved murder case that left a small town tied in knots, eventually, crippling it, there was one particular photo that Eleanor was excited to show her granddaughter. For Eleanor, it was a special moment in time captured between two colleagues, who were a little over a decade a part in age, whose friendship would soon warrant further explanation. As for Selena, it was the final piece of her puzzle.

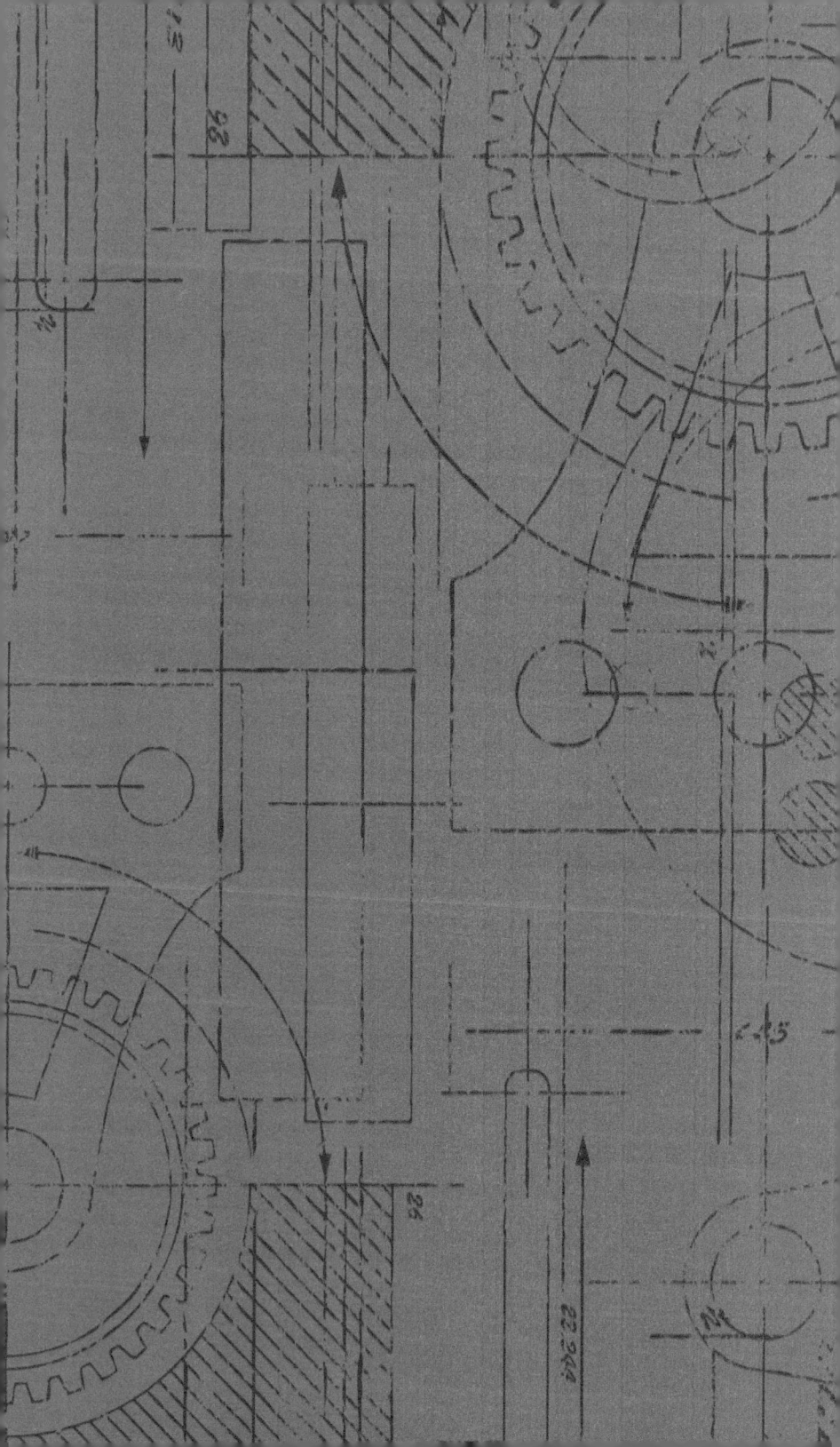

universal_computer

****

Login

☑ Remember me   Forgot password?
Create Account

Gum shoe mail

Recapitulation (Gist, Jazz, or Biological Folklore)
Groupchat created by universal_computer

_____

COMPOSE

Stupid, *Darwin!*

What were you thinking, *estúpido?*

"Should've saved *my bullets*," Darwin thought aloud, as the chaos intensified outside the store.

While cowering underneath the circular clothing rack inside the clothing store Threads, Darwin listened closer to the rioters continue the seemingly well-mobilized campaign of destruction on the streets, which would come in waves of fire and death.

Kingsport had fallen—or was in the middle of falling.

Every now and then, he'd hear the blast of a gunshot followed by a person screaming.

He could never tell if the person was a man or a woman for the screams all sounded alike.

Each scream braided with horror.

Sometimes, he'd hear a horde of them screaming, the weak and the innocent and the wild, an original soundtrack of various screams, either riddled with sheer terror or a deranged, disruptive, diabolic excitement which were the deliberate doings of a more malignant entity, a curator of the most egregious content. It was a trend orchestrated by a gnarly algorithm, which accessed, manipulated, and then managed the one area of the human brain where every primitive impulse was locked in a secured cage, the key safely guarded by the very hands who wrote a civil contract for a sustainable society. That contract was gone now, torn to shreds. And the cages were unlocked, the doors swung open, the hinges broken and beyond repair. Rage was the new sex. And like the old saying: "Sex sales!"

Once, Darwin heard a person, possibly a woman based on the pitch of her voice but he had been wrong many times before, screaming over another person, possibly a man who was hysterically laughing. Soon after those harsh, wrenching screams penetrated Darwin's ears, the blast of gun *rang* out and squashed the screams to a death-gurgle that faded into a fiery tide of madness.

But, Darwin specifically remembered, the laughing continued.

That awful laughing.

A demonic laugh cultivated from the bottom of a compromised brain stem.

The laugh of a man—or a puppet—possessed by his digital over-lords; nevertheless, an apparatus of Something Wicked.

Once Darwin felt it was safe to crawl from the hiding spot under-neath the clothing rack, he heard yet another mob of rioters, this one being louder than the previous ones hours ago, and more violent and armed with metallic instruments and weapons.

During their primal passing, which only lasted several minutes or so, but to Darwin felt like hours, a small pack of vandals *banged* and made disorienting beats along the secured metal gate guarding the storefront.

They found me.

A frightened yet curious Darwin summoned the courage to peek through the Hawaiian shirts hanging from the rack where, between the narrow crack, he traced the guttural noises to the front door. Under-neath the doorway he witnessed gauntly shadows drunkenly dancing behind a beating firelight of an overturned vehicle, which was engulfed in flames. Darwin knew once the fires burned out throughout Kingsport and the temperature started to drop, clothes would be at the top of their list, right below destruction.

Of all places to hide, he eventually figured out that he chose the worst place—and right now, Cashel was probably shaking his head and telling himself, *"Damn it, D, of all places to hide, you picked a gold mine."*

Darwin poked his head from the other end of the rack and came up with an exit strategy for it was only a matter of minutes before the fire monsters tore their way through sheets of plywood that covered the windows and found a way inside (the storeowners, two brothers, for-mer skaters turned to the male equivalent of fashionistas, must've an-ticipated or even foresaw the upcoming chaos, given the minor upris-ing during the first wave of blackouts) and yet, even though the store was locked up good and tight and after the vandals made several un-successful attempts at prying open the locked gate with crowbars or using baseball bats to beat the gate from its track, Darwin desperately searched for a way out.

As he frantically surveyed the store, he ruled out the air vent, which he used to sneak inside Threads (He knew that, if he couldn't find any other way out, he'd have to confront his claustrophobia once more after suffering from a severe panic attack the first go-around). He spotted the outline of the letters E-X-I-T above the backdoor. The door was locked from the outside, he remembered prior to sneaking inside Threads, and even if the alarm sounded (with the power being out, he thought it was highly unlikely), it'd be drowned out by all of the chaos on the streets.

The looters moved to the furniture store next door where, according to the distant sounds of glass shattering, they had better luck.

After the successful entry, the looters overpowered the other rioters and vandals, who were more interested in destruction rather than their own survival, and stormed inside, grabbing whatever they could get their hands on: chairs, sofas, cushions, rugs, even lamps, which, despite their uselessness during an energy-depleted time when an electric socket was as useless as an asshole on an elbow, might come in handy as a weapon. Soon, the clamor closed in to the wall that separated the two stores.

His racing heart pounded against his chest.

First, he heard a booming *thud*, which he thought was a looter moving around a heavy piece of furniture.

Then, he heard more *thuds*, which sent tremors throughout the inside of Threads.

As the thunderous noises intensified on the wall to the point where the wall began to shake, Darwin made a move.

While crawling out of the clothing rack, he heard the wall cracking followed by tiny pieces of paint chips and dry wall raining down onto the floor.

The trembling of the store caused the "*FINAL DAYS* **OF SUMMER SALE**" banner to fall from the ceiling.

Again, he thought, *they found me*.

As the chaos started to beat its way through the wall, he darted toward the exit door; and as soon as he opened the door, one of the vandals punched a hole in the wall.

Darwin was left in a frozen state, as a hyper fiery-eyed vandal poked his head inside and looked around in a state of madness before pulling his head from the hole.

Screams suddenly erupted from inside the furniture store next door, as vandals used the sofa as a battering ram to force their way inside the clothing store.

As the mob flooded inside the clothing store, Darwin made a run for it.

Once he left the alleyway behind the store building, he found himself back on the street.

It was much worse than he imagined.

Dozens of cars were overturned and set ablaze.

The streets were covered in puddles of blood.

Trails of blood led to dead bodies, which led to more dead bodies.

Dozens of dead bodies lying on the street, either shot, stabbed, or trampled to death.

To the right of him, he witnessed a man rushing past him.

Another man was chasing after him, forcing Darwin to take cover behind a street post.

As the two made their way past Darwin, the chase ended with the gunman shooting the fleeing man in the back right shoulder, knocking the man to the sidewalk where the gunman casually walked up to the man, who was lying facedown on the ground, and aimed the gun to the back of the man's head. The injured man rose up on his hands and knees and attempted to crawl away. As the gunman was about to shoot the man, execution-style, he holstered the handgun under his waistband, dragged the man's body to the burning car next to the curb, picked the man up by his collar and belt, and then hoisted his body into the shattered window in the back of the car. While the man was burning alive and screaming out in agony, the gunman stood frozenly and reveled in watching the man's tormented death. Not a single person in the vicinity assisted the man or even attempted to help. Yet, they continued to loot or participate in the destruction of Kingsport while the burning man fading into the background as though he was part of a backdrop. Several other people—three, Darwin counted, perhaps friends or associates of the gunman based on the camaraderie—emerged from the shadows along the alleyways and pulled out their phones and filmed the man for their overlords while the man was being burned alive. One bystander appeared as if he was laughing at the dying man.

From the look of the other two, they didn't appear to be Chupacabra or K-Town.

Darwin thought that they looked like everyday citizens.

Traumatized, he ran away in the other direction. He managed to find yet another hiding spot under an overpass on Easton Avenue located on the southeastern side of the business district, the spot, untouched by firelight, being quieter and more secluded. He sought shelter inside a rundown restroom where he used a lighter to locate a vanity where he washed up, starting with his face, where he cleaned the dark blotches of dirt that he collected from the air vent.

While resting in the back corner of the restroom, the first rays of dawn crept inside the small enclosure and forced him to wake and check out the aftermath of last night, like one scooping out the damage left behind a violent storm.

Darwin stepped outside the restroom where he was greeted by a purple-pinkish sunlight underneath the highway above. The light highlighted the horrors of last night: Based off the plumes of smoke, the riots spread throughout nearly the entire city of Kingsport, even reaching the Art District, which once seemed untouchable based on the outside draw which helped fueled businesses in the revitalized area, as well as its charity to a community that had been through hell and back.

He saw more dead bodies scattered on the street like debris after a storm.

Nearby apartments and condos ransacked.

Every now and then, a gunshot would ring out from a distance.

Darwin was so acquainted with the noises of death that they no longer fazed him.

Not too far away from Darwin—in fact, just a block away—a fatal automobile accident that left the two drivers dead. Among the smoky twisted metal, one of the drivers was hanging from the window of the electric car, which had been flipped on its side. The flaming battery giving off a smell in the air that burned Darwin's eyes, as well as the back of Darwin's throat. He heard the squeaky sound of brakes to his left. He turned toward the sound; and at the intersection, he saw a familiar face sticking out the driver's side window of a white van. He saw that face just hours ago, when he and Cashel were grabbing a bite.

Sue?

Beside the van was a gutter punk, probably no older than Darwin, talking to whom he confirmed as Sue. He inched closer for a better look at the kid on the street corner.

"Low-Key?"

Before Darwin could call out, Low-Key stepped inside the van after Sue offered him a ride.

Sitting in the passenger seat was a sickly boy who looked like Sue's son, whom Darwin had seen at the café a couple of times but didn't know him well enough to speak to him if they passed each other on the street.

As Sue started to drive away, Darwin chased after the van.

He managed to keep up with the van for at least two blocks; and once he saw the van make a left onto Caughlins Street, he took a shortcut through an alleyway in hopes of cutting off Sue before she turned onto the highway (Based off the luggage in the backseat, it was evident Sue and her son were leaving Kingsport and out of generosity, giving Low-Key a ride out of the city).

As soon as Darwin exited the alleyway, he found himself face-to-face with armed troops of the National Guard. The street was completely blocked, which forced Darwin to turn around and run the other way. He cut through a park and took yet another road to the highway. By the time he finally reached the highway, Sue was nowhere to be found. With his spirits deflated, Darwin walked to the edge of the railing where he had a better and broader look of the city.

Dampened by the thick smoke, the perfectly round and hot pink sun climbed over the tops of the skyscrapers, briefly lighting up the hellish cityscape before the smoke blotted out the sun.

With everything that Cashel had done for him, he couldn't leave him behind.

Determined to find Cashel, Darwin ventured back into hell.

When he made it back to the exact location where he last split up with Cashel, he found the cruiser in front of the ammunition store off Wilmore Avenue, where Cashel was responding to a "looting" in progress. There was hardly anything left of the store but a smoldering black shell of a building. From what he could tell, the inside of the store had been gutted. The sidewalk and road were covered in bullet casings. The store must've been set ablaze after the looting. Darwin couldn't help but wonder if Cashel was somewhere inside the building, either dead or dying. He imagined his body like a charred piece of nuked meat. More than likely, the store had been burning throughout the night, and knowing Cashel, his unwavering tenacity, he gave the looters a run for their money.

With the street clear of any rioters, he inspected the cruiser, which was riddled with at least a hundred bullet holes. The windows were shattered. The interior gutted and badly damaged.

He tried the radio, but it was smashed. Wires stuck out of the interface like rogue strands of curly hair.

Panic suddenly crept into Darwin's thoughts like a dark presence hovering over him, and he thought the worse while replaying the recent events in his head: *Cashel arriving at an ammunition store on Wilmore Avenue, only to be greeted by a barrage of gunfire from all angles; then as the bullets bounced off the cruiser like pellets of hail, several striking the windshield, Cashel, after forcing Darwin to the floor of the cruiser, kept driving until he reached the street over, out of harm's way, where he stopped in front of a closed salon, and then, grabbed a "service" pistol from the back of the trunk, handed it to Darwin, and then, smashed the door and broke inside—Cashel claimed he knew the owner of the salon and she'd be cool with what he was doing—and then,* Darwin remembered, *Cashel specifically told him to hide inside the restroom in the back of the salon and lock the door behind him, and that, once it was safe, he'd come back for him; however, he stressed to Darwin that, no matter what he heard outside,* "do not leave this room."

And that was the last time Darwin saw his friend: his dark, yellowish face, those glossy wide yet calming eyes, horizontally panning close as Cashel shut the door behind him.

With Cashel gone, Darwin was left with one more place, an establishment where he did everything in his power to avoid.

When Darwin arrived at the police station, the National Guard was assisting KPD establish a secure barrier around the building in order to prevent further destruction. The front entranceway appeared partially destroyed and set ablaze from Molotov cocktails.

Darwin sought out a friendly face that he had seen before at the station. The face belonged to Officer Gibbons, who, when asked about Cashel, said he hadn't seen or heard from him since he last spoke to him before the blackouts. Darwin, who was upset at Gibbons for not helping out Cashel after he radioed for backup, explained to Darwin that he was tied up in a foot chase with a perp after responding to a "187" and was unable to render backup to Officer Rose. But he made sure that he'd tell Officer Rose to contact Darwin as soon as he got in touch with him.

For the rest of the day, Darwin took shelter at Judy's place. Judy, who hadn't seen or heard from Cashel as well, said she was going to wait out the blackout.

The next day, with the power still being out, Darwin walked to the police station where Officer Gibbons gave him the bad news about his friend.

"I'm sorry, D-Win," he said. "A cleanup crew found his body yesterday."

The news didn't at all surprise Darwin, since for the entire night before he thought about all the ways his friend had died, if he was shot or stabbed or worse. He tried to block out the one image of that man burning alive. Several people standing around him, watching but not helping. Like a sick form of entertainment.

"Can I see him?" asked Darwin.

Officer Gibbons looked into Darwin's eyes and saw the balled-up anger nestled inside them, ready to explode.

Having patrolled territories off Highland Park ran by Chupacabras who marked their streets with fanged eyeball graffiti and capital C's similar to a big cat pissing, Officer Gibbons, knowing the look on Darwin's face, in fact, over seven years on the Force training his eye for such a look that served as a prelude to violence, acknowledged and granted Darwin's request.

Considering how close the two were (it wasn't rare for cops to pull soon-to-be gangsters off the streets and take them under their wing—Cashel's relationship with Darwin was more fatherly than brotherly, although, for Gibbons, sometimes it was difficult to distinguish the difference), the officer said over a tense pause, "Sure, kid."

After Darwin sat in the waiting room while Officer Gibbons finished up in the office, they rode over to the City Morgue, which was located a few blocks away.

Inside the morgue, which unlike the other buildings in the city was running off the power of a generator, Officer Gibbons escorted Darwin toward Cashel's body where he introduced Darwin to the coroner, Robert Henningway.

Once more, the officer asked Darwin if he still wanted to see Cashel and told him that there was no shame in backing out.

"Surely. . . " he said, ". . . this isn't the last image of him you want to remember?"

Darwin was determined to see Cashel's face, or what was left of it.

Officer Gibbons prepared Darwin about what he was about to witness right before the coroner pulled back the upper part of the white sheet covering Cashel's body.

Darwin, who had seen more dead bodies as a fourteen year old than any person should experience in an entire lifetime, which, for the average lifespan of a Chupacabra, was around twenty-three years old, stood strong and braced himself while holding onto the good images of Cashel.

Henningway went over each wound, starting with the gunshot wound.

"Executed," Henningway, who had been given a blueprint of the crime scene by the two detectives who were working the case, said to Darwin. "However," he paused, as he pointed at the marks and cuts all over Cashel's face and neck, "he was treated like a punching bag prior to the kill shot. Your friend here was one tough son of a gun."

Before the coroner could cover up Cashel's body, Darwin noticed the strange bulge coming from the lower right side of Cash.

"What's that?" he asked and pointed at what would be Cashel's hand.

Officer Gibbons said to the coroner, who was hesitant about showing Cashel's hand to Darwin, "Show him, Bob."

Henningway pulled back on the side of the sheet, revealing Cashel's hand, which had been split in two halves.

"The bones in his hand," according to Henningway, "crushed."

"Who did this to him?" asked Darwin.

He suggested: "K-Town Mafia?"

Admiring the boy's iron stomach, Officer Gibbons told Darwin about the five perps with K-Town Mafia brand tattooed across their bellies, four of them dead, one found last night.

"Barely alive," the officer said. "He's currently being treated at Macy Memorial."

"Treated?"

"He can't tell us what happened if he's dead, Darwin."

"That fuckin' animal kills a cop, and you treat him like he's human!"

"Darwin," Officer Gibbons said, trying to calm Darwin, "right now investigators aren't convinced that the deaths are related."

"What'd you mean?" asked Darwin.

Officer Gibbons turned to the coroner, who, in return, made it clear to Darwin.

Henningway said bluntly to Darwin, "One of the victims' spines was ripped from his body. Another victim's head sustained significant damage. His skull was crushed like glass. In all my years of examining the dead, I've never seen anything like it. You know any human that is capable of doing such things?" The coroner answered the question for Darwin: "'Cuz I don't."

"We'll get down to the bottom of this, Darwin," Officer said, reassuring Darwin.

Unsure whether or not to believe the coroner, Darwin looked around the morgue and in the back, saw four other tables that were covered with white sheets. He pulled his eyes back down at Cashel's right hand and looked closer at the perfect incision between his middle and ring finger and as he stared at the hand, started to realize that maybe the coroner was right.

Before leaving the morgue, Darwin told Officer Gibbons that he had to use the restroom.

The officer asked Darwin to hold it until they got back to the station, but Darwin convinced the officer that he really needed to go and that if he didn't go soon, then he was going to shit all over his pants and he explained to Gibbons that the last thing he wanted to smell on the ride back was the smell of shit—"You can air your car out all you want! You ain't getting rid of that smell from your car!"

Officer Gibbons agreed and told Darwin to use the restroom and emphasized that he "make it quick."

As soon as Darwin entered the restroom, he grabbed several squares of toilet paper; then he waited to hear footsteps in the hallway before poking his head from the door. Once he saw Gibbons walking back to the morgue to chat with Henningway, Darwin darted to the back exit door, pushed down on the handle, and opened the door. While holding open the door, Darwin placed a balled-up piece of toilet paper inside the strike plate and jammed it between the latch bolt, which prevented the door from closing all the way.

Later, Officer Gibbons dropped Darwin off at Judy's place.

Darwin snuck out as soon as Judy dozed off and braved the city, which was still left in near blackness. After walking hours through Kingsport, he finally arrived at the morgue. The backup lights were still on. Several workers were still there and from the sight of activity in the front of the building, appeared as if it was completely locked up. He checked the back of the morgue and to his surprise, the backdoor opened. Once inside, he snuck into the morgue and waited for one of the coroners, not Henningway, but an older woman, who was examining one of the members of K-Town Mafia, to step away. An hour or so passed before the coroner left the morgue to take a snack break. Darwin seized the moment and hurried into the morgue where he checked out the three other K-Town thugs, who were waiting to be examined. Henningway was, in fact, right, he concluded. One of the K-Town thugs had a gaping hole inside his chest. Despite his age, he had seen his fair share of gunshot wounds and the hole in the Klown's chest wasn't from a gunshot.

With the coroner grabbing a snack from the vending machine, he checked another body, like the one Henningway previously described, with his head crushed. He peeled back the lower part of the corpse's shirt and confirmed, based on the gang tattoo on his stomach, that he was, in fact, "K-Town Mafia." One of the leaders, based off his branding.

Lastly, he checked the wristwatch on the corpse's hand.

Immediately, Darwin was drawn to the gold watch and specifically recalled the conversation he had with Cashel about what he'd do after retirement and where he'd spend his money. Cashel joked about his pension and more cynically, how there'd be nothing left in it after Lockhart finished his first term and then, finally, what he said about a "gold watch" he'd receive as a retirement gift and how it was given to those who laid their lives on the line for very little pay, only to remind retirees of the little time he or she had left.

Cop humor, he'd say.

Noticing the unlikely swag that a member of the K-Town Mafia would wear, Darwin slid it from the corpse's wrist and turned it over and read the initials "F.S.G." on the back of the watch.

Distracted by a sudden noise coming from the hallway, Darwin pocketed the watch and left the morgue before the coroner returned.

After Darwin crept back into Judy's and spent a sleepless night trying to identify the owner of the gold wristwatch, the two detectives, who were in charge of a high-profiled investigation into the murder of Officer Cashel Rose, paid an early morning visit to Macy Memorial's ICU where Shaman, the lone survivor of the massacre, was being treated under heavy surveillance.

Shaman, a member of K-Town Mafia, was conscious and able to respond to questions and what would be an upcoming grilling by detectives, who were carrying the weight of the public on their shoulders. Since Shaman's jaw was shattered and wired shut and was unable to verbally communicate, he was given a pen, as well as a notepad; however, before Shaman was handed the two items, he was warned by the detectives that if should try anything, he was going to be spending the rest of his days flailing around in a whirlpool of pain.

First, the two detectives wanted to know what happened to Officer Rose, if Shaman was involved in Officer Rose's death.

Straight to the point, the first question: "Who pulled the trigger? Who shot Officer Rose?"

According to the coroner's follow-up report, she found traces of gunpowder residue on the hand of one of the victims, even though the crime scene painted a different story, indicating *multiple* shooters based off the trajectory of gunfire, which was mapped out and detailed in a ballistics report by forensics.

With the results of a recent report in mind, the detectives held onto the information by fudging their statement: a standard tactic used by detectives. In other words: play dumb and show the suspect that you know very little about the case. Some minor acting also involved.

Shaman didn't waste any time writing down the name of the gun-man:

Rimes

Which matched the name that the two detectives already ruled as the shooter, based off their recent intel.

However, considering the condition in which Rimes's body was found and how unlikely that it was Cashel who burst his head like a watermelon, the detective yet again pressed Shaman, who was certain about his answer.

Then, when asked to clarify who killed Rimes, Shaman wrote:

No. Man

"Noman?" asked the detective. "Who's Noman?"

Shaman showed the detective the notepad once more, the words *No Man*. Shaman stressed his point by underlining the two words:

No. Man

"If it wasn't a man, then *what* was it?" Stumped by the answer, the detective turned to his partner and picked up a similar confusion. "You saying it was an animal of some kind?"

Shaman wrote in the notepad:

SCORPEEUN

"A scorpion did this to your buddies?" Both detectives were wearing various levels of confusion on their faces, ranging from subtle to severe. "This guy for real?" Then the detective asked the shaky nurse, who was standing by the doorway, chewing on the inner part of her lip as if it was a popular trend: "What the hell did you give this guy?"

The nurse spastically shook her head and told him just a saline solution in the IV to treat his dehydration. Other than the intravenous fluid: "Nothing." She reiterated: "No drugs."

Once more, the detective asked Shaman about the scorpion. Shaman responded by holding up the notepad and circling what he previously written: "*No Man.*"

For the detectives, it was going to be a long night.

The nurse went to the break room and brewed a fresh pot of coffee for them.

SEND

DEEP FREEZE
RICKIE TRACE

PART ONE
PROXIMITY
TO
POWER

BOOK THREE

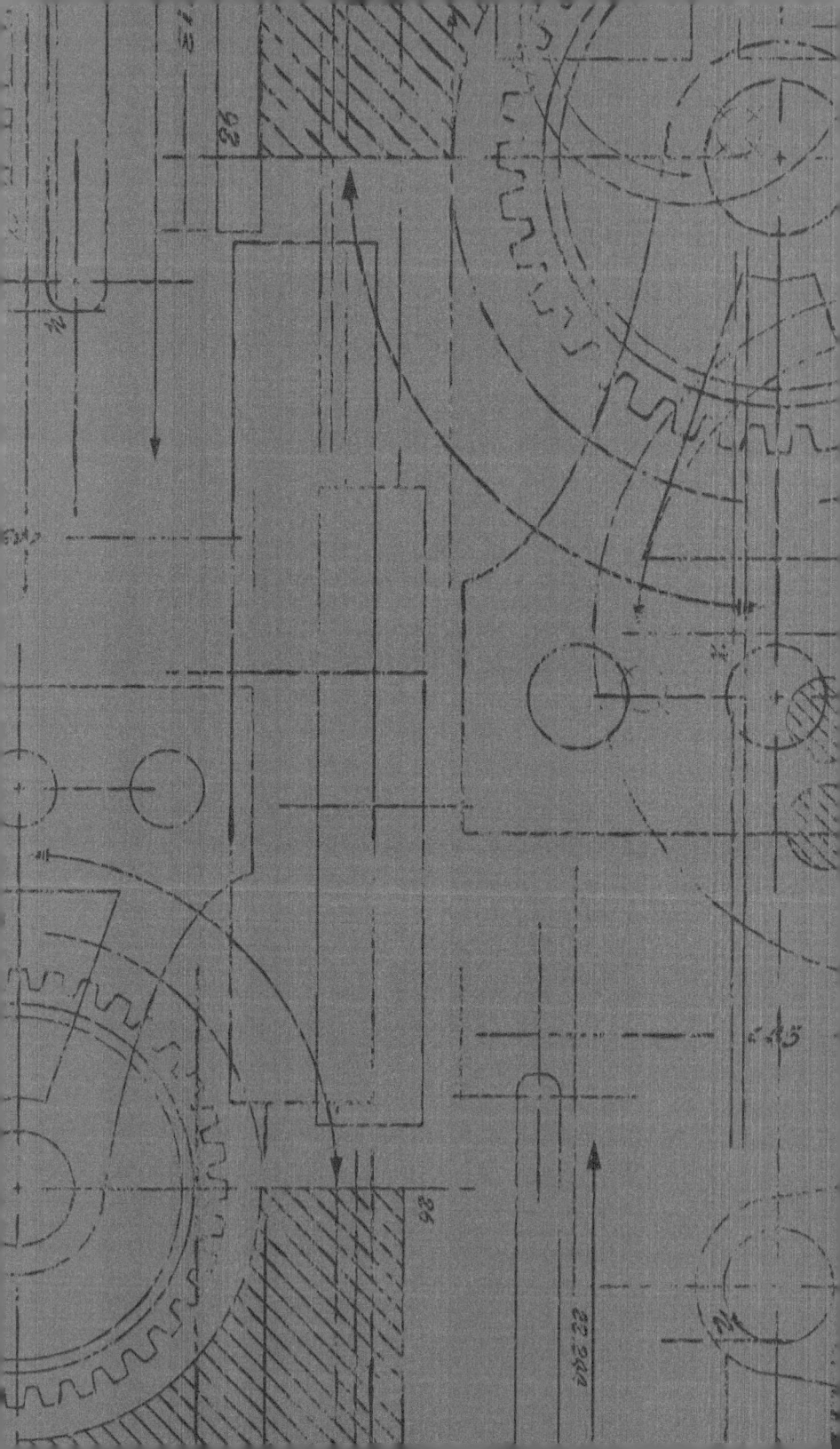

9/8/48
SEPTEMBER 8, 2048
ELVIRA, CALIFORNIA

AT 3:33 PM President Lockhart's motorcade pulls into the parking lot next to the USS Montana Museum, a retired battleship berthed in the Port of Loganson along Elvira Bay, while the shooter sets up his perch behind the thirteenth floor window of an abandoned hotel, which is located approximately 4.9 miles from the harbor.

Southwest of the target is Trac Island, where terminals reside, most of which are depleted, as well as a dilapidated shipyard that can easily be mistaken for a junkyard, further south a chemical processing plant.

To the shooter's northwest: the Greater part of Elvira, an orangish hazy blanket of smog and dangerous particles hovering over deserted beachfront properties, apartment buildings, drug hotels, low-income housing, a black market as well as illegal "pop-up" businesses.

Directly west of the hotel, the shooter's targets: 5.3 miles away, dead straight over a bridge along Presley Freeway, past stacked freight and cargo containers, through the cranes that tower over a shipping plant like the rusty prosthetics of a multi-armed giant, and finally, across a heavily polluted channel where the breeze off the Pacific shares the same characteristics as a chameleon evading a predator.

In other words: it's an impossible shot—that is, without the aide of E'Raknish.

Right before the shooter takes aim, he pulls out the burner.

His finger hovers over the last message on his voicemail in his inbox.

The name of the caller in the voicemail:

1 ⊠ Genie Beanie

The date of the message:

11: 49 PM AUGUST 30, 2048

As his finger starts to tremble, he contemplates whether or not to play the message.

The sound of her voice will be the end of him.

But every beginning has an ending.

THE GOLDEN GOOSE
AUGUST 30, 2048 (9 DAYS AGO)
EDMONDS PARK, MARYLAND

AFTER pacing around the hotel room, Genie, who was strung out and coming down from a bad trip of laced lo-ro, suddenly heard a squeaky car door opening outside.

She checked the window, only to find several of Bingo's men.

Three of them, she counted.

Are they real? Or, *am I still rolling logs?*

Next to step from the car was the greasy greaseball himself, Bingo, who was still recovering after being stabbed five times in the dick by Genie. In a subtle gesture, Bingo adjusted his perforated junk as if he was tending to precious cargo (rumor had it Bingo had to sit on the toilet while he pissed for the piss sprayed out like one of those portable sprinklers you'd find in the lawn of a blue-collared neighborhood). Genie grinned at the image of Bingo going number one.

But her amusement was only short-lived for the very thought of what they were going to do to her wrung the breath from her lungs.

As Bingo told his three men to spread out and search for her—"her," Genie assumed as she peeked through the narrow opening between the curtains, being her, the nineteen-year-old hooker who stole fifty thousand dollars from a pimp named Bingo who had as many holes in his dick as a trendy pair of blue jeans right before traveling to Mexico, or what might've looked like to her pimp as fleeing to Mexico, where she spent nearly half of all that hard-earned cheddar with a disturbed yet incredibly misunderstood young man who was head over hills for her, nonetheless, the one and only person on this giant floating rock who saw her, the real her—Genie rushed over to the cell phone on the table and decided to call the lover boy.

After the third call went straight to his voicemail, the panic cornered her like a blade held to her throat, leaving her no other choice than to leave a message: *"D,"* Genie said frantically, *"if it isn't my main man, it's me, your Genie Beanie, your savior, your* Diosa Dorada, *who's here to stick the wedge in that revolving door of yours. It's time to stop spinning in circles. A path has been written. A world awaits you on the other side of that glass. Can you read the signs? You see them, don't you? They're everywhere for I ignored them for so many years. Now the fog has been lifted. The signs, they speak. Listen closely. Can you hear the angels singing? They sing for us. They sing for you, D! These are the tools we have been given, you see? It's not too late to turn back. You see the door, don't you? It stands on its own, waiting to be opened. So, what are you waiting on, D? Open it. Walk inside. The path, our path—I've seen it—it's been forged by the cosmos, and now, I'm afraid my time here has come to an end and you're going to have to walk through that door alone. I'm tired, D. I'm tired of catering to these demons. No regrets, right? Don't think I wanted this to happen. My journey, it always ended here, but yours, it's just beginning. You rubbed me, D, you set me free, you brought me back to life, and it's time for me to return the favor before I'm summoned back to the darkness where I rightfully belong. Burn out or fade away, right?"*

A sweaty, jittery Genie paused, her eyes wide and messy. Once more, she checked the hotel room window where she saw the three lanky shadows forming over the sidewalk.

She calmed her breathing, then her voice.

"It is said that the mayfly only lives up to twenty-four hours after it moults from a nymph to an adult. Twenty-four hours. Think about all the things you'd want to do in one lifetime and try to squeeze it all in one day. In the span of twenty-four hours the mayfly's sole purpose is to mate and reproduce before it dies. The hotter the flame, the quicker the burn, but this flame, D, burned very slow and very bright and you've given me something more than I could ever accomplish in one lifetime: You gave me the idea of what it'd be like to birth a child, to raise that child, an entire life of millions of moments wrapped up into one single thought, a thought that the demons cannot touch."

Outside the hotel room, Genie heard whispers and footsteps.

"*They're closing in.*" She continued to pace around the room. Her thoughts were spinning out of control. "*I can feel it on my skin, D. Their darkness expelling from their fingertips, like fumes laced with microscopic spiders drenched in manmade chemicals, their potent irritants burrowing into the spores upon my flesh. It's all around us, and it's spreading. It's in the air we breathe. It attaches itself to everything. But you are protected, D. You can feel it shedding from your skin. Can't you, D? It wants to pull us back into the abyss and steal what's inside of us. It wants to infiltrate all that is good, strip it away, and make us do all of these horrible things. I know it wasn't you, D. It was these demons. They killed those people, not you. And they want you to finish the job. But you can't let them, D, otherwise you'll be right back on that merry-go-round, spinning round and round, one kill leads to another, following that crimson red string of yarn on your* Pyramid of Shit, *one mounted face connecting to another, then another, and sooner or later, once you've x'ed off each face, there won't be a single soul left on this earth, D, not one pneuma, not one spirit, not one phantom, for you have become exactly what their darkness has forged you to be: Death.*

The ambassador of the Underworld.

Death—

Genie's dilated eyes snapped toward the brass handle of the hotel room door slightly turning in a counter-clockwise movement.

"*Don't tell me you didn't feel something when we were together in* Sierra Madre del Sur, *D. I saw it in your eye. We should've stayed. NO REGRETS!*"

After the outburst, Genie started to sob, her body shaking.

"*I don't wanna die, D!*"

The hotel room door was suddenly kicked open, revealing three silhouettes standing behind the doorway.

With his face wrapped in shadows, Bingo stepped between his goons and entered the room.

Through Genie's eyes, she saw him, Bingo.

The red-eyed demon.

3:37 PM

PRESIDENT Lockhart steps out of the armored SUV and greets a jazzed crowd of supporters, not only amped to hear Lockhart's speech about his plan to create new tech jobs after the Congress-approved, controversial Jeremy's Act, which prevents discrimination against humans in a majority AI-run workforce, but also excited to watch Lockhart fly away into the sunset in the state-of-the-art Fuchs F1-Hella Chopper.

3:39 PM

THE shooter adjusts the scope of the modified rifle.

The E'Raknish is attached along his index finger—the "trigger finger"— and runs along the inner part of his thumb, where it links to the rifle's chamber.

The bullet inside, also E'Raknish.

Both the shooter's hand, as well as the rifle married in the power of a supernatural template of armor forged by the hot lava of Mount D'onwake.

On his left hand along the meaty area between the knuckles of the index finger and thumb is a tattoo of an armadillo, balled up in its protective shell and then another tattoo—or tattoos—the letters G-E-N-I-E between the two joints along each finger of his hand.

In the background, the burner continues playing the rest of Genie Beanie's message: "*Whatever happens to me, D, don't go through with it! It's not you, remember? It's these fucking demons!*"

An angry man's voice fills the background: "*Hand over the phone, Bitch!*"

There was a brief scuffle, which sounds like a garbage disposal chewing through silverware. The shooter traces back to the first images of Genie Beanie. His first memory.

The night he first met her: *Bitter from a recent dust up with her pimp, Genie flicks her head at him as she tends to a bloody scrape along her knee next to a broken vending machine outside the motel lobby. Annoyed by his presence, she said in what he'd later learn was her natural tone, "I don't need some gutter punk simping over me. You got it? Now, scram, you creep?"*

The shooter didn't scram; in fact, he stayed.

And he wouldn't take back a single moment that he shared with Genie Beanie.

3:42 PM

AFTER shaking the hands of supporters, the president, in what is made to look like an impromptu greeting, stops by the front row where he embraces his wife, First Lady Persephone A. Lockhart, who's wearing a black asymmetrical dress with a slanted hemline featuring a one-shoulder bodice to match the elbow-length satin opera gloves. The president kisses the first lady on the cheek before he makes his way onto the beastly USS Montana, a once superior ship of her class, its belt armor impenetrable by cruise missiles.

3:44 PM

WHILE adjusting the scope of the rifle, Lockhart, accompanied by his Secret Service, walks past a massive turret and anti-aircraft guns where his handler escorts him to the stage on the deck.

3:45 PM

PRESIDENT Lockhart waves at the crowd of Vets and Cabinet members before walking to the podium. Standing to the President's left is former mayor of Elvira, the President's lawyer and longtime friend, Bembe Pérez.

The banner above the two reads:

"ROLLING UP AMERICA'S SLEEVES!"

3:46 PM

WITH a live stream of Lockhart's upcoming speech airing on the untraceable phone with Internet access, the shooter places a photograph of María on the windowsill.

"Can you see it now, D?"

Genie's voice is much calmer.

"The light, it's so bright—" she says before the message ends abruptly.

The shooter focuses on his targets.

Two birds, one stone.

Lockhart only gets out three words before the shooter makes history.

3:47 PM

EXACTLY fifty-four seconds after the shot left the barrel, the bullet returns *back* to the side of the rifle and reattaches itself to E'Raknish worn on the shooter's hand.

As the shooter sets the bolt-action rifle on the floor, he removes his hands from the weapon, and E'Raknish leaves the chamber as well and couples to the shooter's thumb and index finger.

3:50 PM

THE President's motorcade rushes a badly wounded Lockhart to a nearest hospital: Saint Lucida Medical Center, which resides south of Pearl Beach.

The body of the former mayor is transported into the back of another armored vehicle.

Those in the rally believe Pérez didn't survive for the top part of his scalp was blown open like a cellar door, resulting in pieces of brain matter scattering all over the stage.

3:52 PM

AS the shooter exits through the rear entrance of Bayside Hotel, he's spotted by an eyewitness, Roberto Calle, who heard a gunshot from his patio roughly twenty-seventy seconds before President Lockhart and Pérez were shot.

Once the shooter notices Calle staring at him from the edge of the alleyway, he runs away in the other direction.

3:53 PM

NEWS of the shooting at the USS Montana floods The Feed, as well as every channel on TV.

Each headline about the assassination, starting with YNN:

"THE PRESIDENT HAS BEEN SHOT"

Then, The PC:

"MX. PRESIDENT SERIOUSLY WOUNDED"

CBC:

"WILLIAM LOCKHART RUSHED TO HOSPITAL"

Live News:

"US PRESIDENT DEAD?"

Century:

"PÉREZ DEAD, LOCKHART HOSPITALIZED"

ABS:

"WHO SHOT LOCKHART?"

News Today:

"ANOTHER SAD DAY FOR AMERICA"

YN4U:

"VEEP BRAWN PLANS TO BE SWORN IN AS ACTING PRESIDENT"

Right Hour:

"PRESIDENT LOCKHART ASSASSINATED"

3:57 PM

ALIVE, President Lockhart arrives at Saint Lucida where he is immediately taken into surgery to stop the bleeding before removing the bone fragments, including teeth, from his sinus and nasal cavities. A blood transfusion is administered. Also, a priest is ushered into the room to read the President the last rites, just in case.

4:11 PM

BEFORE the images of the shooting are blurred out moments later, multiple angles of the shooting are aired on television with a "GRAPHIC CONTENT" warning label.

In the videos, there appears to be multiple shooters, considering the direction of the bullet or bullets entry points.

One bullet appears to enter through the left side of Pérez's head, along his temple (the shot coming from due east), and then, another bullet strikes Lockhart along his right cheek before his mouth balloons outward, his teeth and pieces of his mandible shattering like glass (the shot, this time, coming from the west).

The videos make their way to The Feed, where the conspiracy begins.

Millions of voices expressing doubt and disbelief.

One of the most obvious conspiracies circulates on The Feed: Based on the angle that Lockhart was shot, the shooter must've taken the shot from a boat somewhere in the Pacific.

Yet, based on all the data that is gathered so far, only one shot was heard.

4:34 PM

AFTER hearing a commotion coming from a side alleyway, followed by a *screech* of tires, neighborhood punk and recent high school dropout, Alx Coal, comes across two empty water bottles on the ground.

Each bottle squeezed in, flattened.

Alx picks up one bottle and holds it close to his face.

The odor inside stings the back of his throat.

As he turns the bottle upside down, a droplet of a strange yellowish-green substance dribbles from the opening. When held up to a beam of hazy sunlight, the gel-like substances glistens like glitter.

He can't tell if it's hand sanitizer or bleach.

Either way, Alx knows that it ain't water.

5:01 PM

NEWS Channel 5 gives an "exclusive" update on the shooting.

The headline reads:

"WITNESS HEARS GUNSHOT 5 MILES AWAY."

In the report, Mr. Roberto Calle, a longtime resident of Elvira, saw a young Hispanic man with a shaved head exiting from the back of Bayside Hotel.

He claimed that the young man was "acting suspicious."

6:23 PM

THE person of interest is discovered outside a cantina, The Macho Taco, two miles from the USS Montana.

An eyewitness named Manny Cordova comes forward, stating for a local news reporter that he claimed he saw Flack only a few blocks away from the harbor earlier that afternoon.

He says that he was "acting suspicious."

Mr. Cordova specifically tells the reporter, "(Flack) was carrying a *long* case."

6:29 PM

FEDERAL agents locate the same rifle used to shoot Lockhart and Pérez lying below the thirteenth floor window of Room 137 inside Bayside Hotel.

Part of the rifle, mainly the chamber, as well as the trigger, the trigger plate, as well as the scope, heavily damaged.

The rifle, according to the agents, appears inoperable.

6:38 PM

PRESIDENT Lockhart is out of surgery, said to be in stable condition.

His entire jaw is "wired shut," says Dr. Ling, whose name has become synonymous with the words *rock star* after the news spreads to reporters.

Members of the media fawn over the doctor's handiwork.

In the plainest explanation, Dr. Ling states in a press meeting that the shooting was no different than a bomb going off inside the president's mouth.

He says that there's a possibility that Mr. President may never be able to speak again.

But the good news: President Lockhart is, in fact, alive.

6:50 PM

THE person of interest, twenty-four year old Jared Flack, is hauled into the Elvira Police Station where he is interrogated by Federal agents.

Jared claims that he's innocent and says he's never stepped foot inside PRINT USA, which is located three blocks away from The Macho Taco.

Surveillance footage shows the arrest outside The Macho Taco, as well as a street cam footage taken of Jared—according to facial recognition—walking from a construction site in front of PRINT USA hours before the arrest, precisely seven minutes after Lockhart and Pérez were both shot.

7:00 PM

BREAKING News across all news channels, as well as The Feed: "The weapon used in the shooting has been recovered." The reporter calls it a "semi-automatic rifle" commonly used in the US military.

According to reports, the rifle was found by Federal agents on the fourth floor of the PRINT USA building, which is temporarily closed due to renovations.

Reports also back up the claims of the shot coming directly from the "east," not west.

An animated simulation video of the assassination attempt shows a schematic representation of the south side of PRINT USA building, as well as the street, and a diagonal angle the shooter takes when firing the single shot, or what analysts call a "near-perfect" shot, one only taken by a highly trained sniper.

After safe playback, weapon analysts determine that the sound of the rifle being fired near a channel is the result of a single shot, not "two," as first suspected, and the doubling or "delayed" sound is the reverberation of gunfire echoing off nearby buildings, causing reflections.

Analysts also conclude that the bullet struck Lockhart on the left side of his face, *not* right.

7:23 PM

AFTER an Elvira police officer leaks the person of interest's name to the press, Jared Flack's face is plastered all over every news channel.

Jared Flack's background, which isn't hard to find on the Internet, paints the story of an extremist who got involved in politics after Lockhart won the presidential election four years ago. One post Flack made back in 2046 categorizes him as an "Election Denier," his post stating that Lockhart cheated and didn't fairly win a rightful seat in the oval office.

To sell the idea that Flack may be, in fact, the shooter: Flack is a former Marine, dishonorably discharged from the Marines after refusing his mandatory vaccines, including several controversial ones, thus labeling him as an "anti-vaxxer," said to be one "*helluva shot who could shoot the wings off a bat from three miles away.*"

7:26 PM

ON the TV screens inside every bar in Elvira, photos of Jared Flack surface on the air.

Some taken several years ago.

Patrons vigilantly watch from below the monitors.

Their eyes held upward and glued to each TV screen as if they're listening to a sermon.

One photo of Jared marching at anti-Lockhart protests, one of them being an anti vax protest in Washington, D.C., where hundreds of thousands of protesters who lost their jobs after refusing to get the jab marched down Pennsylvania Avenue.

Another one showing Jared, along with several other animal activists, being arrested after he chucked a milkshake filled with wet concrete mixture at a security guard during a protest outside a research laboratory, which was experimenting on innocent ducks.

7:56 PM

ACCOMPANIED by Elvira Police, Federal agents escort Jared Flack, drunken with rage, seen wearing a white veil worn over his head, from the front of the police station to an armored vehicle.

A mob of reporters and spectators wait outside the station, demanding Flack respond to allegations of being the shooter who attempted to assassinate the President of the United States.

Shear chaos erupts, as Federal agents readjust their grips around a wild Jared and manhandle him through a narrow passage in the mob.

The accused shooter's actions stir the frenetic tempers of the crowd, causing those in the vicinity to become more aggressive as well.

The *clicks* of cameras sound like a million ticking time bombs.

From behind the white covering, Jared maintains his innocence, screaming to a bloodthirsty mob, *"Conspiracy*! It's all a fucking conspiracy! I'm innocent!"

One of the spectators flings a dead jellyfish at Jared, which hits him along his waistside and then falls to the ground, making a heavy *splat*!

As Jared continues to scream his innocence, two Federal agents place him inside the back of a government vehicle and drive him away from the police station.

8:58 PM

ROBERTO Calle, the witness, who saw whom he believed to be the shooter leaving Bayside Hotel, is found inside his garage after one of his neighbors, Cecil Smithen, pries open the garage door.

With the end of a water hose duct tapped inside his mouth, Roberto is bound to the chair of a riding lawnmower. Every piece of gas-powered lawn equipment, including the lawnmower, is running and making quite a racket. Multiple water hoses are attached to the exhaust of each engine: all water hoses funneling into one connecting hose, which is routed to Roberto's mouth.

Mortified by the discovery, Cecil rips off the water hose from Roberto's face and calls 911 and as he remains on the phone with the dispatcher, comes across a pile of nude photographs of Illegal immigrants scattered on his work desk.

Even more mortified by the pornographic images, so much that Cecil can barely bring himself to look at the photographs for some of the Illegal immigrants appear underage, he utters with disgust first and then a deep-seated anger, "What the fuck, Roberto. . . "

8:59 PM

AFTER a group of men wearing suits and sunglasses show up at the small Local 5 studio, the previous headline "WITNESS HEARS GUNSHOTS 5 MILES AWAY" is deleted from their website. The link to the article, which previously mentioned Mr. Calle's account after he phoned in a report to Channel 5 and told a reporter about the gunshot, reads as follows:

"PAGE NOT FOUND."

THE GRANDSON'S BURDEN
SEPTEMBER 9, 2048
ELVIRA, CALIFORNIA

AT 3:25 AM, Vernon "Hawks," a prosthetist who ran a successful business in Boston where he specialized in prosthetics, as well as provided services, including physical rehabilitation to veterans who were wounded while in combat, arrived at the hospital after taking a red-eye from Boston to Los Angeles followed by hopping a rideshare to Saint Lucida.

He met up with Assistant Director of the FBI, Jin Forsake, who had recently spoken with the acting Director Clive Leonard, about the latest update regarding Lockhart's condition.

"He's stable," said Assistant Director Forsake. With a more personal touch, he asked, "How was your flight?"

"Adequate," Vernon said eagerly. "I caught the tail end of the press conference right before my flight. Has your team recovered the bullet yet?"

Hesitant to respond, Forsake said to Vernon, "Not yet. But given the ample manpower we've got working on the case, we will. Our main concern at this juncture is Lockhart and making sure he doesn't die."

"Right," Vernon said, thinking about the important election around the corner and how, without William Lockhart, the party was doomed. "Of course. That's why I'm here."

Assistant Director Forsake escorted Vernon past the Trauma Room to the ICU unit where outside Lockhart's room several members of his Cabinet, as well as General Booker, were gathered. First Lady, Persephone, was also present. Her black dress was caked with her husband's blood.

Despite all of the theatre around him and most importantly, the legacy of his eccentric grandfather that followed him around like a sour odor, a looming presence, an uncanny vibe that prompted the contemptuous *rolling* of one's eyes, Vernon remained exceptionally calm.

These people who stood tall were merely children playing dress up.

Vernon had work to do.

And he'd be lying if he said it *wasn't* going to take a little bit of luck to create, what could be, one of his greatest pieces to date.

COLD (REDUX): STILL LIFE
JUNE 2, 2049 - JUNE 5, 2049
PADADOCK, PA

SIX months after all-hell froze over, Selena paid a visit to Bret, Lacey, Dean, and her nana, Eleanor, before making the trip to the Reap's place to check on Ashleigh, who seemed different after the celebration of her eighteenth birthday.

Grabbing hold of her swollen belly while stepping into the garage, Selena partially lifted the bottom part of the loose floral patterned silk dress worn under a beige cardigan that she recently "obtained" from the Bashars, their neighbors who lived in a cul de sac, the dress more than likely belonging to Mrs. Bashar, who was baking a Granny Smith apple pie moments before everything turned to hell.

Turns out Mrs. Bashar was quite the fashionista who owned all sorts of dresses and various articles of clothing that she collected during her international travels, including a loose plaid Moroccan burnoose that Selena wore out of style during a brutal winter.

As Selena stepped into the garage, she walked over to her loved ones, who were bunched up next to the lawnmower, and removed the dusty bed sheets from the statues.

Each statue varied in expression: Dean, who was pacing in his office, checking emails on his phone, when the Freeze happened (Apparently, based off the scowl on Dean's face, he was reading an email that was quite upsetting, shards of crushed phone in one stone hand, his other hand curled into a chipped fist and held in an upward motion, as though he was ready to punch a hole in the wall); Lacey, also standing during the Freeze, was posed in a jogging-like motion (Selena discovered her mother's body on the side of a street not too far from the house, both of her arms had broken off during the fall, pieces of a white ear bud still lodged in her ear, Selena and John spent the winter scrounging up enough glue to piece the arms back to the statue); and as for Selena's poor nana, Eleanor, she was sitting in the wicker couch on the porch, doing puzzles on her eTablet when the flickering images beyond the screen had turned her flesh into stone.

Eleanor was wearing a thin smile on her face, as if the Freeze brought her comfort, dare Selena say, peace.

Lastly, as her younger brother, Bret, his statue was also left in a sitting position. She found Bret in front of his computer in his bedroom. One hand holding up the trendy three-digit trinity sign that used to be a modern-day peace symbol back when the Internet was a place where people retreated to be their most authentic self—while the other one extending a web cam at an angle, taking what looked like a personal selfie. He had a silly, lazy-eyed expression stilled on his face like a messed-up doodle that was drawn by a cross-eyed sketch artist. She didn't hate Bret, but she hated the look of the statue; in fact, Selena struggled to look at it. A part of her wanted to smash it to bits and pieces in a heap of rage. A part of her, truthfully, wanted to burst out laughing for the Freeze had found her brother in his most intimate moment.

After covering the statues back up with the clothed sheet, except one, her stepfather, Dean, Selena called out to John, who was re-fortifying the front door from potential marauders rumored to be seen in the area.

"I think I found a solution to our chicken problem," said Selena, as John stepped inside the garage and acknowledged Selena's potential solution.

"You know what. . . " John said with a smirk on his face, ". . . that actually might work."

Moments later, after John used a dolly to lug the heavy statue to the backyard next to their chicken coop where a wild animal tried to chew through the wire, Selena put a raggedy cowboy hat on the top of Dean's head.

"All you need now is some straw and you got yourself a scarecrow," John teased.

Selena didn't react to the joke. Instead, she stared at Dean and then, with a pensive look on her face, asked John, "You think they can see us?"

John paused in thought.

Then, with a straight face, he said bluntly, "No, Selena. They're dead."

Deflated by the comment, Selena walked back into the house and finished putting together a floral arrangement for Ashleigh, which mostly consisted of annuals, as well as wild flowers that she had gathered from her backyard and other areas throughout the neighborhood.

When Selena asked John if he wanted to join her in walking over to Ashleigh's place, he declined and said that he'd better finish securing the door. But, he said while struggling to look her in the eyes, "Send my best."

After the Freeze, Ashleigh, who was the only survivor of her family, moved into what used to be Mr. Toto's house across the street. Mr. Toto and his wife died just a few months after the Freeze. When Selena went to check up on them, she found the two in their backyard, lying in the lawn with an empty box of Equanimity next to them. Selena and John buried their bodies next to one another in the backyard.

While carrying the arrangement in Lacey's green vase, which included dwarf blue cornflowers, black-eyed Susans, and scarlet flax, Selena walked past Mr. Abrams, whose statue next door was sitting on the rocking chair on the front porch. Like many of who were turned into stone, his head was held downward at the smartphone in his hand.

Selena waved at Mr. Abrams, said hello, and then chirped a common line that she overused, but not once did it ever get old: "Keep your *head* up!"

Mr. Abrams wasn't exactly nice to Selena. He didn't talk much to her, except for when he told her to turn down the music whenever she was washing her car. He also gave Selena rather surly looks whenever he saw her hanging out with John.

Selena arrived at Ashleigh's. She knocked on the door. Eventually, after Selena knocked a third time, Ashleigh was slow to answer the door.

"Thought these might cheer you up," Selena said and handed Ashleigh the vase of flowers.

"Thanks," Ashleigh said quietly.

All of a sudden, Selena felt a kick in her lower abdomen.

In a state of awe, she pulled back on the dress until it was tight against her skin, revealing a small baby bump. She felt yet another kick from the fetus inside, prompting her to grab hold of Ashleigh's hand.

"Feel," she said, as she rested Ashleigh's hand on her belly.

"I can feel it," Ashleigh said, as a smile curled along the side of her face.

For Selena, it felt like months since she had seen such a look on Ashleigh's face.

And the sight of the look made her smile.

Later that night, John made a fire in the fireplace using the remaining firewood that he gathered during last winter. Both Selena and John sat by the fire.

Selena told John about their baby and how she felt it kick when she visited Ashleigh.

"You think it's a boy or girl?" asked John.

"Girl," she said with a blank expression.

"You sound pretty sure of yourself." He leaned over Selena's shoulder and asked, "Care to make a bet?"

Subdued by the beating firelight, Selena said with an undertone of resentment, "What are we betting on? We practically share everything anyway."

"Okay," John said, trailing off. "Fair point."

The two sat together in silence and watched the fire before them.

In a deep reflection, Selena said with lines furrowing between her two brows, "You remember before I broke my leg last year I had a strange feeling that something bad was going to happen?"

"I remember you had doubts about competing."

Selena shook her head.

"These were more than just doubts, John."

"You talking about premonitions?"

"Sort of," she said hesitantly. "Before the blackouts, I had a similar feeling. Remember?"

"Vaguely." John tilted his head to the side, trying to get a better and closer look at Selena's face. "Why'r you telling me this?"

"I dunno," Selena said, more quietly. "I have that feeling again. When I was visiting Ashleigh earlier today, she started talking about Connor and how much she misses him and that she's having these thoughts—"

"What kind of thoughts?"

"The kind you keep to yourself."

"Should I be concerned?"

Selena shrugged.

"Did she mention anything about, you know. . . "

"Harming yourself?"

"Yeah."

"No," Selena said. "She's just having a hard time adjusting to all of this. It's been over six months, and I'm still not adjusting. I don't think we'll ever adjust. I came *this* close," she said, pinching both her thumb and index finger together, emphasizing the tiny length of space, "to telling her about Milota. All of a sudden, that feeling, the one I felt last year, came out of nowhere."

"You're just scared," John said, rubbing both of Selena's shoulders. "That's all. To tell you the truth, Selena: I'm terrified."

Selena gave John a thin but reassuring smile, as she looked him in the eyes: "Why?"

"The baby," he said with his head down and removed his hands from Selena. "Bringing it in this *new* world. You really think it stands a chance here?"

"No," Selena said honestly. "But we have to try, right?"

John didn't answer.

"Right?"

"Yeah," he said, looking up at Selena. "Of course."

Two days later, while Selena and Ashleigh were doing their weekly exercises, which mostly consisted of mild yoga and certain stretches that would help with the pregnancy, along the bank of a remote lake roughly a half of a mile from the neighborhood, Selena only made it ten minutes into the workout before the headaches returned.

"Are you okay?" asked Ashleigh.

"It's just a headache," Selena said, holding the side of her head in her palm.

"Again?" Ashleigh asked, "Can you take something for it?"

"I'm afraid to take anything," she said and held her head downward and rested her eyes.

"What about some aspirin?" Ashleigh asked. "I think I got a bottle back at the house."

As Selena cracked open her eyes, she found herself staring at the floor of the lake where she witnessed the ghostly face of what looked like a fisherman. She recognized the statue's face for she had seen it several times in town. Selena didn't know the man's name nor did she know anything about him, only that he used to shop the outdoors store along Padadock Square. She would remember his face, however, his new face, frozen in an excruciating expression as the phone that he once held in his hand turned him into a scarecrow, a lawn ornament, a decoration, a reminder, a moment, or worse, a disposable item.

Despite taking a low-dose of aspirin from Ashleigh, the headaches worsened throughout the morning, forcing Selena to rest in bed.

The next day, with the headache still nagging at her, Selena began to experience a dull pain in the right side of her stomach-area, which sharpened throughout the day.

By the late afternoon, she started to experience shortness of breath.

As Selena's symptoms persisted throughout the rest of the day, John sought out advice from one of the neighbors, Janet, who used to be a nurse. Janet was living by herself off Meadow End Street. Her husband, Tom, was victim of the Freeze. He was turned into a statue while playing solitaire on the computer. She didn't take Tom's death well; in fact, she botched a suicide. Even went through the trouble to make a noose from an electrical cord, which she tied around the rusty rim of an old basketball goal that broke off three seconds while she was left dangling. She didn't want to live, but it was at the very moment, when she was hanging from a noose for three whole seconds, that she desperately *wanted* to live.

When John brought Janet over to the house, Janet went over Selena's symptoms and immediately concluded that Selena needed an ultrasound in order to take a look at the fetus.

"The hospital isn't safe," John stated, as he dismissed Janet's advice.

"That was months ago, John," Janet said.

"What makes you so sure that the hospital will have what you need?" asked John.

"I don't," Janet said more impatiently. "But it's better than just sitting here, waiting. . . "

"Waiting for what?"

"Waiting for Selena's condition to worsen."

Janet mentioned a condition known as "preeclampsia," which could lead to complications—maybe severe—if left untreated.

Either way, as Janet put it, they simply couldn't ignore Selena's symptoms for the sake of "safety."

John pulled Ashleigh aside and asked her to stay behind and watch over the house and while the two interacted, Selena picked up on a vibe between them, an awkwardness displaying an act, like John and Ashleigh were hiding a secret from Selena, only reinforced by Ashleigh's interest in John's whereabouts during the workout earlier that day; however, considering a possibility of going into labor much sooner than she had anticipated, John's affairs, whether true or not—she leaned toward the "not" part, but Selena's emotional side, who, as of lately, bore multiple faces, was dying for a good fight—were the least of her concerns. The voice inside Selena screamed at her to forget such triviality for flesh was only flesh and the swapping of flesh was merely an outlet to cope with what she assumed to be The Apocalypse.

"Consider the times," a wise man once told her.

With very options to choose from, John decided to follow Janet's sound advice. He used the remainder of gasoline to drive Selena to the nearest hospital, which was raided just days after the Freeze. Those who survived the Freeze grabbed everything that they could from Padadock Hospital, leaving very little supplies to treat the surviving patients. He didn't have the exact number of people who survived the Freeze in Padadock, but if he had to guess, he'd estimate somewhere in the ballpark of a third of Padadock. It wasn't quite an extinction of the human race (John, Selena, Ashleigh, Janet, and a handful of others were still here, most of them on the opposite spectrum of age, either survivors were very young, babies and toddlers, or very old, the elderly), but he'd claim it was damn near close to one while others, like Janet, would often say that they were in the "early stages" of extinction, as if they were dinosaurs staring up at the sky, watching the great comet descend through the upper atmosphere—what often troubled John the most and at times, made John rather hesitant to reach out to Janet was that she didn't mind having "lesser" folks around town. She once said that she "enjoyed the silence." It was this particular mindset from Janet that caused once-sociable creatures, like John, to develop eyes in the back of his head.

When Selena, John, and Janet arrived at the hospital, the outside of the building appeared as if a violent storm had swept through the area. The front windows of the EMERGENCY room were shattered. Bricks and street signs used to breach the once-fortified hospital were littered all over the parking lot. Bullet-size pieces of glass everywhere. Some of the statues were left un-touched while others had toppled over either during or following the Freeze. Some shattered into a thousand pieces while others had broken off a limb, finger, toe, nose or ear. Others, simple broke.

After the Freeze, it wasn't out of the ordinary for a survivor to stumble upon a body part that had been turned to stone. Selena once thought it might've had something to do with their diet—why some shattered and others chipped or cracked.

The cold hard truth: Nobody really knew and some, unlike Selena, couldn't afford the luxury of knowing or at least, making an attempt to find clarity in a world where the leaders were no more. John once told Selena there was a reason why you'd find the word *ass* in assumption because those who assumed that they knew the answers as to why those with smartphones—or any device connected to the Internet for that matter—turned to stone while those without these certain electronic devices didn't were talking straight from their ass.

The three moved through a maze of cars in front of the hospital. Each car in the parking lot, as with everything that had been left out in the open, raided. Fuel siphoned from the cars. The tiny doors to the tanks left open as though stating to gas-seekers that the car had been drained of fuel, which over these past six months, had become more precious than water.

When they made it to the ER, they managed to squeeze under a piece of plywood, which had been screwed into the frame.

John held out his hand for Selena, who, despite her reluctance, grabbed his hand.

After carefully guiding Selena into the hospital, John followed Janet's lead to the birth center, a wing where the labor rooms were located, as well as what would be Selena's OB-GYN, if the hospital was still operational.

The interior of Padadock Hospital, like the outside, was completely trashed. Selena counted at least two-dozen people in the waiting room: each one turned to stone; their heads held downward; electronic devices in their hands, some crushed from the weight of their stony grips.

"Just ignore them," John said and reminded Selena to keep her eyes on him.

When they reached the labor wing, Janet found the sonogram, still intact, as well as a transducer, while snooping through rooms.

Despite being portable, since the device was way too heavy, as well as bulky to lug back to their home, Janet told Selena that she had to perform the ultrasound here. The battery was low, down to only one bar, and flashing bright red, but Janet was able to get it running. As for the conductive medium, which was required for a proper reading, and being that sound waves didn't travel well through air, Janet needed some gel to apply to Selena's skin.

Thinking, John pulled out a bottle of hand sanitizer, which he kept on his person at all times, and asked Janet, "Will this do?"

Janet paused in thought.

"Yes," she said. "I think so. Not exactly recommended. Can you find anything else? Any type of gel around the room?"

They searched the entire room for the proper gel but couldn't find anything.

Janet was left with only hand sanitizer.

"Isn't that your last bottle?" asked Selena.

John said hesitantly, "I have a secret stash back home."

"Holding out, are we?"

"I like my hand sanitizer."

John's comment forced Selena to recall the recent visit to Ashleigh's and the moment when she excused herself to the restroom where she found a "stash" of hand sanitizer in the closet.

She connected the dots, or in this case, the hand sanitizer.

Right then and there, she knew.

Yet, surprisingly, Selena didn't care about John and his secret relationship with Ashleigh for the child that she bore was far more important.

After he handed over the bottle, Janet applied hand sanitizer to Selena's abdominal area and gently ran the ultrasound probe over Selena's skin.

As Janet started to pick up a reading on the sonogram monitor, John heard two thuds of what sounded like car doors.

"You hear that?" said John.

Janet's hand froze on Selena's belly to listen.

More sounds, human sounds, this time clearer.

John rushed to the window and peeked through the blinds and saw two raggedy dressed men walking through the parking lot. One carrying a rifle. The other, a shotgun.

"We have company," he said to the others.

"How many?" asked Janet.

"Two. . . " John counted, as he watched the two men locate their truck.

"What's happening, John?" asked Selena.

John watched one of the men walk toward the truck.

"John?"

The armed man placed his hand over the warm hood of the truck, then whistled and flicked his head in a nod at the other man, who removed the rifle from over his shoulder and readied it in his hands.

"Shit," John said, "they know we're here. . . "

As Janet proceeded to look at the sonogram, a reading of Selena's fetus started to appear on the monitor.

"Shit!" As one of the men stood guard by the truck, the other one started to siphon the gasoline from the truck.

"Enough with the shits, John," Selena said, more upset. "What's happening? Talk to me!"

Janet placed her hand on Selena's shoulder and told her to relax.

"They're stealing our gas," he said.

"Maybe they were following us," Selena suggested.

As a reading suddenly appeared on the screen, Janet's eyes widened in both wonder and horror as the image before her wasn't exactly the image of a traditional fetus.

For a second, Janet thought maybe the hand sanitizer had screwed up the reading.

Intrigued, she stared even closer at the monitor.

Selena turned her attention toward Janet and acknowledged the strange reaction on her face.

Before Selena could rotate around toward the monitor, the battery's icon flashed in the corner of the screen right before the battery died. The screen suddenly went blank.

"What did you see, Janet?" asked Selena. "Is my baby okay?"

Janet shook away the shock; and while trying to recollect her thoughts, John cried out over the two, "We have to leave! They're taking everything. . . "

"Janet?"

"I couldn't get a good reading," Janet said, trailing off.

"But you saw something?"

"No," Janet said shortly. "I didn't."

Frustrated with Janet, Selena wiped away the leftover hand sanitizer that hadn't completely dried on her belly and stood up and checked the window.

The two marauders were filling their bags with everything that could find inside the truck.

Once they grabbed whatever they could find, they hurried back to their car and sped away.

"Let's get out of here before more come back," Selena said.

Brushing off the recent scare, John asked, "Did you get a look at the baby?"

"No," Selena said, holding Janet in the corner of her eye.

"Did the device not work, Janet?" John asked, glancing over at Janet, who removed the battery from the back of the device.

"It's dead," she said, struggling to meet John's eye.

"Great," John said in defeat. "So, what now?"

Before Selena could respond, she heard the sound of a metal tray crashing to the floor outside the room! The tray rattled along the floor before eventually falling silence. Selena's eyes widened, same with John's, as their eyes were pinned on one another's. In a dramatic fashion, both of their heads mechanically turned to the hallway.

"We're not alone," whispered Janet.

After John told the others to stay behind, he decided to check out the noise.

Along the way, he reached down and picked up a piece of stone, which appeared like part of a forearm that had broken off a nurse, who shattered into hundreds of pieces on the floor.

With the piece of stone in hand, he located the tray, which was overturned on the floor. He searched the room but couldn't track down anything that might've knocked over the tray. Perhaps a squirrel or even a raccoon, which he had been seeing more of during daytime hours. Ever since the Freeze, there had been more animals roaming around throughout the daytime. Animals like raccoons, foxes, or coyotes that you'd mostly see at night.

As John started to leave the room, he sensed a presence.

The smell was first to raise his alert: a metallic odor of blood that wafted throughout the air.

As he stepped back into the room, he saw the top part of a backpack behind the leather chair in the corner of the room.

"Show yourself," he said, as his heart began to race.

With the stone gripped tighter in hand, John gave the hider one last opportunity before it was Clobber Town.

Skittishly emerging from behind the chair was a frightened young man whose left hand was wrapped in a bloody T-shirt. He looked a few years younger than John; however, it was hard to tell his age for the Freeze had expedited the process of growth—at least for those who were left to survive on his or her own.

"I was just looking for some bandages," he said, his voice crumbling with fear.

"Are you alone?" asked John.

With a grimace on his face, the young man nodded.

"Be honest," John warned, as he lifted the stone in his hand.

"Swear," he said. "It's just me."

John noticed the young man's injury.

"Looks bad."

The young man moved from the corner of the room.

While lowering the stone, John introduced himself to the young man: "Name's John."

"M.J.," he said.

"Where you from, M.J.?" asked John.

M.J. answered, "Nowhere."

STAG/N/ANT
SEPTEMBER 10. 2048
BLACK SITE. CUBA

THE US Intelligent Agency's go-to interrogator named "Bamby," short for bamboo shoot, which was what he was known to use to extract or better yet, pry out vital intel from terrorists and militants over the past two decades than any data collector, asked the shooter "one last time" what he planned to achieve by taking out Lockhart.

With his frail, sweaty body curled in a fetal position in the shadowy corner of the dirty, rat-infested cell, the shooter said with a narrow beam of light cutting across his dark, bloodshot eyes, "Fuck you, *hijo de puta!*"

Bamby reached toward the side of his face and pulled out the bamboo shoot resting along a crease at the top of his ear and held it in the beam of hazy light cast from the doorway.

"Please," he said more tenderly, his eyes soft and filled with sympathy, "I don't want to do this, kid. But you're giving me no other choice. . . "

As Bamby stepped forward, the shooter said, his voice shivering, "Go ahead. Do what you have to do." The shooter held up his hand, revealing a missing thumb and index finger: "But just remember, you only have eight of 'em to work with."

Bamby stepped closer.

As he braced himself for Bamby's shoot, the shooter said, "Whatever pain you inflict on me won't even compare to the pain your boss had caused me. . . So, go ahead. . . Bring it. . . "

Bamby stopped for a moment, looked over the tenacious sixteen-year-old waiting in the dark shadows of the cell, and kneeled down toward the shooter's level.

With all sincerity, he said to the shooter, "I'm truly sorry, kid. This is going to hurt. . . "

Then, as he was about to do what he did best, the shooter made it easy for Bamby.

And he held up his left hand, as though offering it up on a silver platter.

LOCKHART'S FATE
SEPTEMBER 12, 2048
ELVIRA, CALIFORNIA

AFTER Vernon checked on Lockhart, who was still recovering from the recent surgery, Assistant Director Forsake stopped by the hospital room for a quick word.

The two stepped into the hallway where Vernon was first to mention Lockhart's condition.

"He's one helluva fighter for sure," Vernon said, amazed by Lockhart's resiliency.

"Will he live?" asked the Assistant Director of the FBI.

"He'll live," Vernon said with confidence, "although, to say he has a long road ahead of him would be an understatement. I've treated soldiers with similar injuries like Lockhart's. Before I began Extremity™ I was a combat medic on the frontlines of Taiayi—"

"—I've read," Forsake said, folding his arms across his chest. "Quite impressive."

Acknowledging the comment, Vernon said, "Once, I treated a troop from the ROC after he was hit by a diffusion round directly to the face. He was young, not even twenty years old, just a baby. The lower part of his face had more holes in it than a mesh lining. His mandible jaw was barely intact and was only hanging on by muscle and ligament. The troop," he paused, trying to put a name to the face, "his name was Lee, I remember, didn't have much longer to live." Lee's face was covered in blood. Frothy blood bubbled along the corners of his mouth. "His injuries were too great for a little ole combat medic. But I had to work with what I had, which, to say, was very little. Lee's grabbing me by the arms while diffusion rounds are *whizzing* right over my head, one caught me in the ear," Vernon pointed to the top of his right ear, which was fully intact, a faint crooked line visible from where artificial flesh was jelled to the missing dime-sized cartilage. "I looked straight into Lee's eyes and in that moment, *time froze* and we both knew that Death was present. I liked to believe He was hovering over my shoulder, waiting to wrap both of His bony arms around Lee, but then something. . . *human* happened. Lee's eyes sharpened with intensity. He redirected his eyes toward my utility belt where I was carrying a piece of med-wrap. I followed his eyes and knew exactly what he was trying to tell me. As the second wave of combatants closed in, I wrapped up Lee's jaw and dragged him back to the med-tent. The whole time he's looking at me with those same eyes, holding onto me like a blade, as though we both had an unspoken agreement on the battlefield. He didn't want to die, a part of him, I believe, knew he wasn't going to die as long as I did my job, even if the job caused him a great deal of pain."

Forsake said, "And did Lee survive?"

"Yes," said Vernon. "When faced with the presence of death, humans and their resiliency to live by any means necessary can often be mistaken for superpowers. And Lockhart, despite what the American People may think of him, is as human as they get."

Appreciative of the story, Assistant Director said to Vernon, "The FBI is thankful for all that you're doing."

"Forgive me for being so forthright, Mr. Forsake: You could've chosen from dozens of doctors in this particular field to operate on the President. Does my grandfather have anything to do with why the United States government chose me?"

"What gives you that impression?" asked Forsake.

"Lockhart's injuries weren't caused by what I'd call a traditional bullet," Vernon said, as he waited for a response from Assistant Director Forsake.

CASTIN' INTO THE DARK
SEPTEMBER 13, 2048
SOUND CITY, TENNESSEE

DRIP-*drop, drip-drop, oh, how the minute hand weighs so heavily over the clock!*

In a nutshell, the exuberant Century personality ran through the brief synopsis of the latest current events: *Five days after the assassination which, not only resulted in the tragic demise of former Elvireño mayor, Bembe Pérez, whose funeral was scheduled for the upcoming Monday*—may Science rest his atoms—*but also left the President of the United States*—your steely-eyed Dragon—*severely wounded, Jared Flack,* whom the Finger Soldiers, nuttier than your momma's peanut butter, are calling "Mr. P" for Patsy, *had been identified as the shooter who used a rifle, which was legally purchased at a Gun Show last month, to fire what those Hounds of Hell, those robotic corporate shills in the MEDIA, were calling "two shots," not one, but a big fat "number two," despite hundreds of conflicting statements taken on September 8th, as well as the following days stating that people in attendance of the Rolley Poley hearing only "one shot," not two, the first one, BANG, according to sources, missing the target, the bullet ricocheting off the searchlight on the retired battleship and striking one of the attendees, Howard Pines, a freelance photographer, his precious CaMMDoc snapping away when all of a sudden "The Spear of Death" in the left side*—For Science's sake, please tell me your CaMMDoc wasn't damaged, young Sir! Strike me anywhere but leave my CaMMDoc alone!—*the shot causing Pines to fall backward, making a soft landing to the deck*—Pines, not exactly, Mr. Fit, if you get my drift, a fella who couldn't quite keep his claws off snookies, but those pillowy soft love handles came in handy—*the CaMMDoc, not a scratch, the bullet, however, lodged two inches below the ribcage on his left upper abdominal, a nasty itch, then, the second bullet, BANG, hitting the first target, Pérez, five foot eight, in the left temple before exiting the upper right part of Pérez's head and striking the second target, the six foot Dragon himself, directly in the left cheek*—what the Docs at Saint Lucida were calling a "through-and-through," however, what the quacks failed to mention to the American People was that when Ole Bully was nudg-

ing by those Pearly Whites he was making a goddamn mess of the place like a Bull in a China Shop, the damage inflicted to Lockhart's mouth more exten-sive than initial reports, but this Dragon wasn't slain, my dawgs, in fact, it was nothing more than a little recon *couldn't fix* (reconstructive facial surgery), *squeegee peasy, the rest is easy, no big deal, right? Ask your fav celeb in Hollyweird.*

And don't get me started on this so-called "magic" bullet!

You've seen the footage, probably replayed it over and over and over again. Our good pals over at Raw Feed— *I'm referring to my lovely lady Maver-ick—put together one helluva montage that would make your head spin! Don't say you did it out of* dis-*respect for your Prez cuz I know you did. Yes you did,* Georgie Boy. *And right now you're probably thinking the same thing as every George out there: How in the world can a bullet zigzag through a crowd and hit its target, then hit the brakes, circle back around in the most diabolical U-turn known to man, and strike its target from the op-posite direction. You heard the final report: A second shooter was ruled out, debunking that a second shot came from the West, right?* <u>WRONG</u>! *Dead wrong! Look at the footage. Lockhart's head moves down and to the left. Now, together: Down and to the Left. Sing with me: Down and to the Left. Down and to the Left. Down and to the Left. Which indicates that—*you hit the nail on the head*—a shot was fired from the West. But how could that be? When was the last time you looked at a map? West is the Pacific and if there was a second shooter camped out somewhere along that pretty blue horizon, why haven't we heard a name? The Coast Guard combed those waters and couldn't find anything. Which begs the question: What is the United States government hiding from us? Was the President about to give a speech about jobs or was he about to recite his own eulogy? I must say: I lean toward the latter. Why? I don't know why. Take the first lady, for an ex-ample, who was dressed as if she was attending a funeral. One may ask: Did she predict what was going to happen? Or, was she simply bringing* black *back in style?* Once you go black, you throw the competition out of whack. *Am I right? Perhaps your pal from Missouri was part of an experimental drug trial that he could later push on the American People: They say 'Death Sales.' What about immortality? It wouldn't seem so* out-of-the-blue, *especially coming from a snake oil's salesman who got filthy rich from pharmaceutical companies! One thing is for sure: If Lockhart pulls off an upset, then his political career is far from dead; in fact, the Dragon himself, Pruitt's biggest fan, Mr. Bookworm-in-Chief whose past <u>Summer Reading Lists</u> would only sow the seeds of the chaos to come, has transitioned into a Phoenix rising from the ashes of a First-Term failure!*

Roll up your sleeves, my dawgs! Let's get down to the bottom of this!

As for Flack, so-called "Mr. P," his motives still remained unclear but the growing narrative on the screw tube last Thursday: Flack, "Mr. PP," the extra P inspired by the 1979 flick Pusher Prophet, about a delusional, highly paranoid vigilante and former drug user who decides to hunt down corrupt priests responsible for operating underage sex rings below the churches through-out the city, was obsessed with Lockhart and blamed Lockhart for all the drugs that were pouring through the border, destroying our youth like an incurable cancer, and not standing up to Mexican cartels. Flack "Mr. PP" was transported to "Lockland," a federal prison located in southern California where he was said to be kept in a secured wing of the prison and moni-tored around the clock.

Now, you may ask yourself: *What was Flack doing in the area? Was he there to watch the President flex the muscles of his military might? According to the latest report, Flack was visiting an ex-girlfriend, Lori Simon, former pro who's put more wieners in her mouth than any contestant in a hot dog eating competition* (Apparently, the hit duo, Simon and Gagfuckel, cleaned up their act and joined a vegan cult that wor-ships the oh-so Holy Kale). *Many are speculating*—an emphasis on *speculating*—*Simon was compromised or as the loggers on the lube would say, 'burned,' and to avoid facing jail time, was working with the F-B-I-don't give a shit as part of a deal they made after Simon was caught with possession of three pounds of lo-ro. Yikes!*

The over-the-top personality continued his Sunday night spat-tering, following Flack's arrest with a photo, as well as a contro-versial cell phone video, which was circulating on the Internet.

As you may know, there have been videos and photos making rounds on your Drip Feeds, you glutinous deviants, two in particular: One, a photo of Flack's reflection in a billboard sign across from the PRINT USA building, rifle in hand, taken what the timestamp suggests, only minutes before Rat-a-tat-tat. Some believe that the photo was doctored using AI technology. What are your thoughts, my dawgs, my devoted tree huggers? *As for the video, let's talk about the video, which was taken by a man named Alonzo Franco, who was with his twelve year old daughter visiting family in the area, Flack, clearly visible in the background, appeared to be exiting from a side door of PRINT USA, which was connected to an alleyway.*

Once the clip surfaced in that endless pantry fully stocked with jars of peanut butter you call the Internet, the clip went viral, spreading from one jar to another. Let the contamination begin! Yellow showers here we come! Rain, baby, rain! The fly in the ointment, the pube stuck between teeth: The original video taken by Franco magically disappeared *from his phone.*

What are the chances that the original video is the same as the video that was released to the masses? So, off you go, peanuts! Now, you are free! Don't be afraid to get "too *deep*," if you know what I mean all of you non-*fakers* out there? But you know who's not fake? *Franco.* Alon-zo, you are not off the hook, my man! *Why, Franco? Why? Alonzo Franco, who's not a fan of storing photos on the cloud*—a smart fella, but I'd say he has a blind spot when it comes to preserving a piece of historical evidence that could crack open the oculus like a bottle top, spilling all of her gooey secrets—*when asked to explain the reasons why he didn't save the photo, he said he didn't trust the cloud.* And do you trust what these shills are peddling? *In an interview, Franco specifically stated that he didn't recall deleting the video. It wasn't unusual for photos or videos, especially older ones, to disappear, as he assumed it was only the phone's way of freeing up space or memory*—he guessed it was one of the downfalls that he ran into by not using the cloud.

"*Is it too late for me to take back what I said about Franco?*"

But bullshit aside, let me throw the bone back to you, my righteous dawgs: If the Feds were in possession of credible intelligence that proved Lockhart's life was, in fact, at risk, then why in the hell would his campaign still hold a presidential rally?

ORANGE PILL
SEPTEMBER 13, 2048
DEATH VALLEY, CALIFORNIA

ONE-by-one the passing faces disappeared all around Agent Barney Rotten.

Each and every facial feature receded into flesh.

Eyes.

Noses.

Lips.

The recently hired thirty-year-old stud-cataloger fumbled for the bottle of pills in his pocket.

Rotten's trigger was the fountain in the main lobby where a massive "ɹ ᴄ" logo dizzily spun within itself on an endless loop. The "ɹ" randomly rotated inside the "ᴄ" while the "ᴄ" rotated along its axis, causing the "J" to appear in sync with the "ᴄ" every three seconds.

For three seconds, Rotten killed himself a thousand times in his head.

The last series of extremely unpleasant thoughts, or what Dr. Wilcox referred to as "confronting one's own mortality," happened last week, after returning home to his apartment.

The feeling suddenly crept up inside him like a drinking glass filling with water, starting from his belly and rising upward through his chest, his head being the brim. Pressure of accepting the stressful position as "chief" cataloger was upon Rotten and pressing down on him like an oppressive thumb. His mind was racing and yet, each thought felt as if it was running in slow motion. The challenges that presented themselves were not only pressing, but also gargantuan.

Certifiably, Rotten was a walking, talking data-collector. He was all of the little things that a phone couldn't pick up, even if a phone had eyes: the sweat along the brow, a beat, a pause, the pitch of one's voice, the certain body movements. He was it. The asker and the observer. All of his biases pushed down to the pit of his belly, where instinct dwelled like a dark, mythical creature among the acidic bile of reason. He knew that if he stuck to the script he'd be in the clear: read the subject, read gestures, analyze each and every response, proceed with appropriate questions as it best suited the agenda, be patient, rinse and repeat.

Doom and gloom clouded over his thoughts when he was standing in the kitchen, all of that grayness smothering him.

As he reached for a knife, his eyes caught the tiny scar-like mark below the cuff of his sleeve.

A friendly reminder.

Or, a warning.

While confronting his own mortality by leaping into the fat logo, his body being grounded up like sirloin, Rotten pulled out the unmarked bottle, popped open the lid, slammed the triangular-shaped light orange pill into the back of his throat, and then swallowed it down with a mouthful of saliva before those violent thoughts turned to action.

One thousand one.

As his mind began to calm, his hands less shaky, Agent Motley approached him from behind.

"Good morning. . ." the agent said with a playful wince, ". . . you must be the new chief cataloger I've heard so much about."

"Yes," he said after acknowledging the agent. "Barney Rotten."

Her face, once featureless, no eyes, no mouth, no nose, only flesh, suddenly appeared after the blink of an eye.

A sort of on-off switch.

His little three-headed orange friend working its magic.

At first, he was unaware of her reaction when she laid eyes on his face.

By the time the expression faded, she was left gawking at him.

"Barney?"

He tried to connect the dots, but her face, her name, all of it was drifting further away.

"It's me," she said, "*Laura.*"

The name, as well as the way she smelled, brought forth a stream of memories, most of them focused around being inside Laura, both physically and emotionally.

He had forgotten how much he loved the way she smelled.

Six years since he embraced not only her smell, but also her touch.

It had been six long years since she rescued him from the depths of hell.

Only to be cast into the tragedy that devoured him.

Nothing changed and yet, everything had changed.

"Laura," he said, "of course."

Based on the sudden rise in his voice, he was still attracted to Agent Motley, despite the years on her face.

She still carried the same charge that pulled him into her.

He asked himself many times before: *Why didn't it work out between us?*

We clicked, didn't we?

Knowing the change in his tone, he remembered his training.

"Good morning. . . " he said, less excited.

"Laura," she said, smirking.

"Right, Laura," he said, more awkwardly.

Surprised by Rotten's youthful glow, she said, "You haven't aged a day."

"It's nice to see you again," he said.

"Well," she said with a light chuckle, "we're going to be seeing a lot of each other."

"I look forward to it," he said, as he scraped the bottom of his thoughts for a quick follow-up before the awkward silence set in. "I didn't know you worked here. I take it you left your job as a bartender. . . "

She looked around the main lobby.

"Obviously, *cataloger*," she teased. "Bartending was a side-hustle. So, have you been seeing anyone since we last saw each other?"

"Here and there," he lied.

Laura grinned at the remark.

Still a ladies man, she remembered. But still sad, only this time it was pushed further down in his dark and heavy eyes.

The truth, and Rotten would never admit it: Laura was his only rebound after the divorce.

"Surely, there's some lucky lady."

Pushing aside Motley's curiosity, Rotten asked, "How about you?"

"Work," she said, her voice like a chirp.

"Busy day?"

"Always," she said. "How 'bout you—" she paused before finishing her question, "—It completely slip my mind. You're going to be talking with Subject *B*-37 again," she emphasized the letter B. "I heard he's a handful. . . "

"I've dealt with worse," Rotten said.

Motley understood the comment as soon as it left Rotten's lips. She recalled the tragedy that followed him around like a shadow and if she didn't know any better at the time when they were seeing each other, it was a tragedy that could easily define him and eventually, destroy him.

"So," he said and released the tension in his chest with a sigh, "any advice?"

"Good luck," she said, smirking once more.

She wasn't just being friendly.

According to Rotten's analysis, Agent Motley was still attracted to him and possibly still had feelings for him based on, not only a subtle change of color in her face, but also the way her eyes danced around his face, mainly his lips.

Being able to read people was one of the perks of a cataloger.

And one of the many downsides.

After arriving on his floor, Rotten walked past the security guard, who was watching the critically acclaimed hit show *Barking*

Up The Wrong Tree with the controversial social commentator Jake Barker on the Century channel.

The security guard flipped the channel back to JeneCorp's network, J C C, which was airing an informational video on clean and renewable energy, including wind and solar energy, as soon as he saw in the corner of his eye the human lie detector approaching the post.

Rotten extended the JENECORP clearance tag clipped onto the breast pocket of his navy blue bulletproof jacket and held it against the scanner.

The light above the scanner switched from red to green, green meaning enter, red stop.

The gates opened, and Rotten threw a subtle nod at the guard, who said in return, "He hasn't made a peep all day."

"By the time I get through with him, he won't shut up," Rotten said, walking toward Cell B-37.

Under his breath, the security guard muttered, "Arrogant prick."

Rotten arrived at Cell B-37 where the shooter was revealed sitting on the edge of the bed.

His look changed dramatically ever since he was set on a warpath following the death of his close friend and mentor, Cashel Rose. Unlike the long, greasy, shoulder-length black hair with a dyed green streak that he sported during his scorched earth days, his head was "shaved," as identified by Roberto Calle, the eyewitness from Elvira. Given the subject's violent history, the security detail felt it was mandatory to keep his head shaved for even a single strand of hair could be used as a weapon.

The security guard remotely opened the door for the cataloger, who, before stepping inside the cell, placed the JENECORP clearance tag into his breast pocket.

"Can I get you anything, Mr. Acosta?" asked Rotten.

The shooter said sharply, "How about some decent food? I'm getting pretty sick and tired of eating that cardboard shit you call food—"

"So, I see you're finally ready to talk, Mr. Acosta."

"Do I look like a Mister to you, Company Man?"

"What do you want me to call you?" asked Rotten.

The shooter fell back into his old ways.

Frustrated by the shooter's silence, Rotten asked again, "What are you going by these days? Darwin?" He noticed the tattoo on the shooter's hand. "Armadillo?" Finally, "D-Win. . . "

The sound of the name, D-Win, caused him to clench his teeth as his jaw tightened.

"D," he said, biting down the bottled anger.

"Fair enough, Mr. Acosta—I mean, D," the cataloger corrected, as though the minor mistake was a deliberate attempt at rousing a response from the subject, D. "Let's forget about yesterday and start over from the very beginning. My name is Barney."

"I know who you are, you fuckin' chameleon."

"I'm here just to talk. . . What do you say?"

D couldn't help but notice the watch the cataloger was wearing.

"The watch," he said, nodding at the cataloger's wrist, "where you'd get that?"

"I'll tell you what," Rotten said. "Let's make a deal. First, you have to tell me all about that device you were wearing and in return, I'll tell you all about my watch. Deal?"

"What are you going to do with that gringo?" asked D.

"Jared Flack?" asked Rotten, who already knew the identity of the shooter, who was pinned for the shooting. "And where did you hear about that name?"

"That amigo of yours told me about him when he was jamming bamboo shoots underneath my fingernails."

"I'm afraid I can't speak for the United States government," he said. "I assure you, D, there will be no torturing here. Only words. I ask questions. You answer them. Fair enough?"

"Whatever."

"The reason for my visit today, D. . . " Rotten said, sitting down in the chair across from the bed.

D backed away a little, remained on guard.

Rotten held up both his hands, displaying to D that he wasn't a threat.

"I need you to tell me everything you know about this device and if you fail to provide me with any relevant information, i.e. where you found it, i.e. how does it work, i.e. why does it appear different from its original state, I'm afraid you are no use to us, which means you are wasting my valuable time, which means you are wasting the Company's valuable time, and those who stand in our way, i.e. you, Darwin Acosta, a former gang member of the

Chupacabras, will be properly discarded. It's pretty simple, D. You either tell me what you know or you don't and if you don't, then it's *adios muchacho* for you. I'm just following orders. *Comprendido?*"

With an unspoken agreement, D said more seriously, "Are you going to kill him?"

Rotten said, "It's not up for me to decide."

"They're going to kill him, aren't they?"

"No," he said. "But we did exchange a lot of important property to obtain you."

"What kind of property?" asked D.

Rotten was hesitant to answer.

"Let's just say the kind that's going to change the world. Now," he said, reaffirming their previous understanding, "back to the questions: the device, when did you first make contact with it? And be specific. . . "

D glanced down at the silver-ish wristwatch on the cataloger's hand and then slowly moved his eyes back to his steely eyes.

"Fisher's Neck," he said.

"Do you remember the date?"

"Three weeks ago," he said. "Saturday night. It happened after *Escape from Kingsport.*"

Rotten, who was wearing an earpiece, listened to a voice on the other end while, at the same time, he acknowledged the recent information provided by D.

"Escape from Kingsport?" Rotten asked, even though he already knew the answer.

"Some art gallery where elites rub their noses in each other's *culos.*"

The voice confirmed D's date.

"The event took place on August 22," Rotten said. "Does that sound about right?"

D flicked his head in a nod, which was directed at the side of the cataloger's head.

"I dunno," he said. "Is that what your handler is telling you?"

"At the time, were you still with Ms. Jeanne Daul?" Rotten asked, ignoring the question.

"Genie and I went our separate ways after we returned to America."

"Now that we have established an accurate timeline," Rotten said, again ignoring D's previous comment, "can you explain to us what you were doing at this art gallery?"

"The trail stopped in Fisher's Neck, with the former police commissioner's wife," he said.

"Shaolin Gunna was your last breadcrumb?"

D nodded.

"One of them," he said. "*Sí.* Originally, I was there for Shaolin, and if the opportunity presented itself, then I was going to do what was necessary."

"Why kill Mrs. Gunna?"

"To send a message to her husband."

"But you didn't."

"Too many people around. Plus, moments later after the event ended, I was given a gift."

"A gift?"

"I like to think that I found it, but, in a strange way," D said, thinking back at the events that transpired in an alleyway next to the art gallery, that strange object glistening in the darkness, "it *found* me. Like, somehow, it knew everything about me and when it jumped up and grabbed me by the hand," he glanced down at his disfigured hand, his missing thumb and index finger, which were both bandaged up, "I could see and feel each and every person that it touched before me. It was like all these people had something in common. They were nothing alike and yet, this one thing, it bound them together."

More intently, Rotten said, "And what was that, D?"

"Pain," he said, holding tears in his eyes. "The pain of injustice. The pain of not belonging. The pain of betrayal. The pain of rejection." D found himself reflecting inward, toward his *own* pain. "The pain of losing a loved one."

"Why did you avenge Cashel?" asked Rotten.

"Like some people say, 'Everyone has a breaking point,' and some people, I guess, experience it sooner than others. For some, I guess, it comes in different forms. Some people may go an entire lifetime and not experience this break at all. It doesn't make them any less human."

Leaning in closer, Rotten asked once more: "But why Officer Rose?"

With the tears falling from his eyes, D thought about his *amigo.*

"He was the only friend I had."

"If you will, D, describe how you felt when you killed Mrs. Gunna after you first discovered this gift—"

D said abruptly, "It's not just a gift, you know? It's not a device either."

The cataloger appeared more surprised than confused, not by the response, but, more or less, the accuracy of D's confession.

Studying D closer, Rotten asked, "What makes you so sure, D?"

"It spoke to me."

"Spoke to you?" Rotten readjusted himself. "And what did it say?"

D inhaled through his nose and held in the breath before letting it out through his mouth.

"It thanked me. "

In that very moment, D thought about Shaolin's final moments. The memory was still fresh in his mind. The images striking: *While D towered over the bloody corpse of Shaolin Gunna, the letter opener held in his right hand, which was wearing the E'Raknish template, he snapped his attention toward a shadowy-faced* Cashel *looming in the corner of the sunroom. His dead face was soaked in moonlight while the corners, the grooves, as well as the eye sockets remained as dark as the night. His moonlight eyes glistened. He didn't exactly utter those words to D. But in his own way, as he lowered his head in a nod, his presence alone, although as brief and subtle as a phantom, was reason enough for D to carry out his campaign of street justice*—or revenge, to D, there was absolutely no difference between the two.

From that moment forward, after he witnessed what appeared to be his past friend, D often questioned himself whether it was, in fact, the ghost of Cashel or simply, a figment of his imagination, which, ever since he coupled with E'Raknish in Fisher's Neck, felt splintered right down the middle of his own skull, a deep and winding valley separating his own thoughts from the unlikely metallic passenger who was hitching a ride.

Rotten asked D, "And how exactly were you able to lift the fingerprints off a man as untouchable as fashion designer Pip Godard?"

"I didn't," D said.

"Then, how did his fingerprints wind up on the letter opener used to kill Mrs. Gunna?"

"Don't know," D said.

Rotten glanced down at his wristwatch and held D in his penetrating stare.

"Tick tock, D."

"Maybe, now that I think about it," he said, backtracking his previous statement, "I touched something that he touched whenever he wasn't fucking Franklin's wife: the same doorknob Pip touched when he entered Shaolin's crib, the same handle on the fridge that Pip touched when he grabbed himself a cerveza, or the same marbled kitchen countertop that he used to fuck Shaolin."

"You mean the device you were wearing came in contact with Godard's fingerprints?"

"*Sí*," he said. "I think so."

"You think so?"

"I know so."

"And the bullet used to kill Franklin Gunna during a supposed B and E gone wrong? Somehow, this device managed to replicate Godard's fingerprints?"

"I don't know exactly how it does it," D said honestly. "I don't have an answer for you, but I think it goes back to what I was saying earlier: When it touches something, a person, an *object*, whatever, somehow, it leaves behind a signature, right? Take Gunna, for example, whose pockets got so deep you'd think he had holes in them—How the fuck does someone in a position like that manage to buy separate mansions, one for the wifey and the others for weekend excursions? You'd think with all of that money he'd buy that bitch security? So, where did he get all of that cheddar? I'll tell you, *Barney*. Gunna got stupid rich from gangs, like K-Town, by being bribed with a cut of profits as long as he made sure to turn a blind eye on their criminal activity while, at the same time, providing those *cabrones* with immunity. I don't know how I didn't pick up on it sooner. Maybe I was too distracted. I don't know. But sooner or later, everybody on the streets knew K-Town was just another long arm of the government and Gunna's retirement prize was a middle-finger to gangs like the Chupacabras or the Black Squids that K-Town was protected."

"Pretty smart for a sixteen year old. How you know these things?"

"The fuck if I know," he said. "I read about it on The Feed. Local perp breaks into Gunna's house days after his estranged wife gets perforated by her 'headline lover' and shoots him dead. Forensics match the bullet with the perp's gun, which, from the fucking get, I know in my bones ain't true. I didn't plant that boy toy's fingerprints on that knife. I didn't use a different bullet to shoot that dirty police commissioner. It was this. . . creature that did all those things for me."

"Quite an accomplice, if you ask me," Rotten said. "So, are you saying it wasn't you who stabbed Shaolin Gunna sixty-eight times or shot her husband between the eyes or. . . " he leaned in closer, ". . . attempted to assassinate the President of the United States?"

"No," D said expressionlessly. "I did all those things. But I had no control over what happened afterwards."

"You sound pretty confident that you knew this so-called 'creature' was capable of replicating fingerprints or altering rounds."

"That's where you're wrong, Barney," D said. "I didn't know what it was capable of doing. But one thing I do know for certain: This is where I belong. . . " he pointed at the floor, ". . . right here. Being poked and prodded." D leaned away from the cataloger, his back rested against the impenetrable frosty glass wall. "You ever stop to think that maybe it deliberately disguised me all the way up to this point? Maybe this is all part of its plan. Maybe," D said, "you should just ask it what it wants?"

"And prior to Fisher's Neck: each and every member of K-Town Mafia, gunned down in the span of one year."

"Nah," he said, his voice cool and mellow. "That was *all* me." A smirk flashed on the corner of his face. "You'd be amazed what can be accomplished in one year when you got the KPD behind you. I mean, if there was one thing Franklin Gunna did right, it was allowing his former boys in blue to take a step back and leave it to the streets to sort out justice."

Frustrated, Rotten asked D, "I know I'm sounding like a broken record here, but why Lockhart? A part of me gets why you went after K-Town, especially after what they did to Rose, but again, why a temporary political figure who has no control over what individuals do to other individuals? Regardless of his politics, Lockhart didn't directly kill Officer Cashel Rose—"

"How can you say that with a straight face?" D asked, as the blood filled his face and eyes. "Rimes, K-Town, Gunna, Neuvak Pharmaceuticals: What do these names all have in common?"

Rotten shrugged his shoulders and said, "You tell me, D."

"William Lockhart," D said. "These are all puppets, and William Lockhart is the puppeteer whose strings needed to be severed?"

D motioned his two fingers, index and middle, like a pair of scissors.

"Sure you don't have it the other way around?"

"Lockhart had a chance to deliver what he promised to voters and how he was going to clean up all the corruption in Washington, but once he was elected into office, he showed his true colors."

"You're starting to sound righteous, D," Rotten said. "According to your rap sheet—"

"I ain't no saint," D said over Rotten. "Never said I was."

"So you did all of this stuff for yourself? Killing all those people isn't going to bring your loved ones back. How would your madre feel about what you did—"

"She doesn't feel a fucking thing!" D shouted. "She's gone!"

Rotten held up his hands, trying to calm D.

All of the emotion that emitted from D was so hot that Rotten could sense the warmth in the air.

Outside the cell a security guard appeared, shock stick in hand.

"We're fine," the cataloger to the security guard, then to D, "aren't we, D?"

"Fine," he snapped.

The security guard left.

"She doesn't feel anything anymore, but you do, D," he said. "You feel *everything*, and that means you're still human, right?"

In a calm and more rational thought, D told himself over and over moments before he started to plan out the assassination: *Maybe before that serpiente went into politics his intentions were decent. The same goes for his amigo, Franklin Gunna.* Two lawyers, one from Missouri and the other from Maryland, one a bookworm, the other rough around the edges, both of whom *went to a prestigious law school in New York, trying to suppress the burden of their padres.*

Can't blame them for trying.

Once more, Rotten attempted to extract D's real motive.

"Let's try this again, D: Why Lockhart?"

D thought about the day that he returned from Sierra Madre del Sur after he and Genie visited with his madre, seeing several Ads for the antipsychotic drug, Serophren, on The Feed. The drug, in fact, had been advertised everywhere: on billboards, on TV, on signs.

It wasn't until he read what was in the drug that he put two and two together.

The active ingredient called halozine, the same chemical that he found in the drug, Coreqcil, which his madre had been taking.

There was a connection, a link between the two drugs, and everything started to make sense.

"He had a chance to stop companies like Neuvak, to prevent them from spreading their poison to people, like my madre. Instead, he did nothing. Who knows how much money they gave him? I'm sure once he got a sample of power and how, obtaining a role of power, where his actions could have ripple effects on the lives of people he served, something that started out, like 'doing good,' became nothing more than a bumper sticker. It doesn't mean anything. Not anymore. It's to reassure people that he's 'rolling up his sleeves' and putting in the long hours and giving speeches from the goodness of his heart—or what heart he has left. But on the contrary, it's all for show like a bumper sticker, easy to pull off but leaves behind a sticky residue that tarnishes the surface of what was once good. The only people William Lockhart serves is the monster staring back in the mirror and companies like Neuvak, all they do is make sure the monsters like Lockhart remain in power—"

"Isn't that what you're doing?" asked Rotten. "By seeking vengeance against those people who wronged the ones you loved, you are ultimately trying to obtain power?"

"I did what I thought was right."

"Lockhart didn't force your mother to pop halos like Sourpunks."

"Maybe not," D said, forcing himself to remain calm, "but maybe she reached a point where her doctor gave her no other choice."

He thought about the last images of his madre, the harmful side effects of taking the drug, Coreqcil, and how it completely destroyed her mind.

Why didn't he see the signs during the trip?

Graphic visions of his *hermana*, Carolina, ghostly pale and dripping wet with water from the Rio Grande, silent yet her presence warning him to turn around, to stay far away in order to spare him from the pain of seeing the current state of his madre, who was prescribed the antipsychotic after an outburst at work.

One of the villagers explained to D that, prior to her outburst, his madre had been depressed for weeks, hardly left her home, spent all day and night glued to the tube, watching the news—D imagined his madre's eyes spinning in circles from hours of absorbing all that conflicting information and *dis*information, all of it meant to confuse and disrupt signals in her brain, like she was punishing herself through her own self-manufactured interrogation.

She stopped eating. She stopped talking; and in a way, she stopped living.

Her mind was completely gone, shattered like fine white china.

Eventually, she lost her eyesight: one of the side effects of halozine.

His madre couldn't even recognize D when he visited her.

When he returned from Mexico and saw those Ads, he did the research.

His madre wasn't the only one.

There were more like her.

Zombified by halozine.

Their minds, robbed.

"Like Gunna, Lockhart doesn't give a shit about the many lives that were destroyed by that poison, as long as his pockets remain full."

"Why not go after the pharmaceutical companies?" asked the agent.

"Do you go after the hustler or the hustler's supplier? Or, why not go after the person who's responsible for keeping the supplier in business?"

"If what you're saying is true, then why wouldn't these companies just put someone else in power? Another candidate? What if Lockhart is disposable? Someone else is surely to take his place, right? So, D, why go after Lockhart because you and I know it isn't about your mother or K-Town Mafia or F.S.G. or that dead bimbo. . . "

D furrowed his brow in confusion.

Rotten asked, "Where do you think you are right now?"

"The hell if I know."

"Guess."

D looked around the strange cell.

"Looks like a prison. But if I had guess, based on the heavy security: somewhere private."

"Close."

Rotten reached toward his breast pocket and pulled out the JENECORP clearance tag, which was tucked inside.

D read the name of the company on the tag.

"Now you know what's at stake here. So, tell me, D, who exactly am I talking to right now: Is it Darwin or is it E'Raknish?"

In all seriousness, D held up his injured hand and said, "My hand's fucking killing me."

"I'll ask the doc if he can give you something for the pain."

After Rotten concluded the session with Darwin Acosta, which would be continued at a later and more appropriate time when the subject was ready to explain why he held so much interest in the cataloger's wristwatch, he paid a visit to the Research and Development level where scientists from around the globe, including technician Lance Carmichael, were trying to understand the ins and outs of the template—or what subject B-37 referred to as a "creature"—which was being kept behind glass, along with remnants of the rifle used to shoot President Lockhart, also kept in a separated secured container.

Once Carmichael acknowledged the cataloger's presence, he excused himself from the scientists and other technicians and engineers, who were running schematics, as well as diagnostics on a ball-shaped E'Raknish via scanner, and returned the vial of blood to a shelf labeled "GWEN" inside the freezers.

Carmichael shook Rotten's hand; and before he shut the freezers, Rotten caught a glimpse of yet another vial in the rack. The vial was labeled "LOCKHART." He did a double take at the vial, as if his mind had tricked him during the first passing. His eyes caught the tail end of the name, "LOCK," as the freezer doors closed.

Acknowledging Rotten's interest in the vial, Carmichael said to Rotten as he touched him on the shoulder, "You can never be *too* safe."

The technician's comment went over Rotten's head, for any follow-up to the comment would require more than a line or two from Carmichael.

Keeping a tight-lip on the reasons why JeneCorp was in possession of the President's blood, Carmichael introduced him to the Head of the BioTech Division.

"This here is Niles Baldwin," he said.

Rotten shook the seventy-four-year-old's hand.

"Nice to meet you, Mr. Baldwin."

"Please," he said, "Niles."

"Nice to meet you, Nile."

"*Nilesss. . .*" he corrected by extending the last part of his name with a hiss, ". . . with an s."

"Forgive me," he said. "*Nilesss.*"

"This is chief cataloger, Barney Rotten," Carmichael introduced Rotten for Niles. "He's the one cataloging the subject, B-37, in hopes of acquiring a better understanding on the side-effects of E'Raknish."

"Your work is appreciated, Barney."

Rotten's gut suddenly sunk for he was struck by a momentary ambivalence as he stared into Niles's eyes. He dropped all of his training. At that moment, Rotten was no longer a cataloger, but rather the remnants of a lost man who found a glimpse of resolve in Niles's eyes, which sat behind a familiar yet youthful face. The seventy-four-year-old appeared much younger than his age, and yet, he carried his age in those flat and murky eyes, which were the color of floodwater.

"Have we met before?" asked Rotten.

"I don't think so," Niles said with a subtle squint of his right eye.

Carmichael said to Rotten, "Niles here was recently pulled from one of our side projects to give us a hand. If it wasn't for Niles's expertise, then we'd be miles behind in our research—"

"More like demoted," Niles teased, drawing a laugh from Carmichael.

"You may know Niles by his other name, Osiris."

"*The* Osiris?" asked Rotten. "The one who created Splinter?"

"Correct," Niles said humbly.

"I've heard a lot about you."

"Hopefully," he said with a glint in his eye, "not too much."

"Only the good parts," Rotten said like a fanboy, as Niles excused himself after a technician needed his assistance.

While Rotten watched Niles walk away, he caught several other strange men, who were present in the labs. Carmichael informed him that they were representatives from Neuvak.

One of them being Phoenix, who was shadowing several of Niles's technicians.

When Rotten asked Carmichael about the suits, he stated that they were visiting JeneCorp for the dime-tour and never gave any other information about them other than the classic roll of his eyes, a gesture indicating to Rotten that he wasn't interested by their presence but was in no position to state his feelings about Neuvak.

Carmichael escorted Rotten to the weapon that was used to shoot Lockhart. He pointed out dozens of symbols running along the handle, the scope, as well as the chamber of the damaged rifle, which manifested after one of his assistants held a black light to the modified weapon.

"After we slightly increased the temperature inside the container, these symbols appeared."

"Why heat?" asked the agent.

"Forgive me, Rotty, but I couldn't help but overhear your recent conversation with the subject," Carmichael said, "but if he's correct about the template and how it's some kind of creature, then I can only assume that it's no different than any organism that needs a host to survive."

"You're talking about a parasite?"

"Precisely."

"How do you explain these spiral-looking symbols?"

"Not sure yet," he said. "Could be a brand that it leaves behind after it attaches itself to the user, or if the kid's correct, a host. Or, there is one theory that's been weighing on my mind for quite some time. . . "

"What's that, Carmichael?"

"What if it's a fingerprint?"

The cataloger turned toward E'Raknish, which was hovering inside the container.

Rotten couldn't help but notice the change in its current state and how, strangely, it shared a similar appearance as an armadillo.

Later that night, the air was heavy inside Subject B-37's cell.

While trying to catch some shuteye in his cell, D tossed and turned throughout the night, his feverish body covered in sweat, the sheets scattered along the stiff bed drenched and wadded up.

Images flashed inside his mind, ones showing him the moment he was captured after he left Bayside Hotel.

He desperately held onto these images as he tried to make sense of them.

FBI agent, Lesley Frye, who chased after D on the street; the resident who spotted D leaving Bayside Hotel; the car that nearly turned D into roadkill; the bottle of bleach that the FBI agent squirted all over the

E'Raknish: all of these images flooded D's mind like a fever dream.

He rewound back to the very beginning, moments after he pulled the trigger; and from there, he pieced each image back together and placed them in correct order:

He watches the time change on the marquee, going from "3:59 PM" to "4:00 PM."

Fourteen minutes going on fifteen have passed since the world froze.

The faces on the street appear like background actors in a movie.

Darwin can't quite put a word to it, but they look neither normal nor natural.

In a way, he feels as though everything around seems choreographed.

As he cuts through an alleyway, the thought suddenly dawns on him.

Why didn't I see the signs sooner?

Genie Beanie, I love you, you're the best thing that's ever happened to me, but why the fuck couldn't you just keep your mouth shut.

What if that hood rat Venus told someone about me, my plan?

It's no longer a matter of *if* she did. I know she did.

Venus is a girl scout, despite her profession.

What if she opened her mouth about me?

Venus gets around, knows a lot of people.

She's quite a storyteller who's known to gossip.

She probably narked on me.

I know she did!

Of all people to talk to about me, why Venus?

What if she tipped off the Feds?

If so, then they're onto me.

On the sidewalk, Darwin walks by a skater kid on the street. The skater eyes him down.

Couldn't be?

The kid's working with the Feds.

Has to be, right?

Who the fuck wears high-tops while trying land kick flips?

Paranoid, Darwin searches for an alternate escape route.

I'm walking straight into a trap.

After cutting through another alleyway, a white painter's van with the words "Port Palette" underneath a logo of a painter's palette suddenly speeds up behind him and blocks the entrance to the alleyway. Two undercover agents, dressed like painters, in blue jumpsuits speckled with white paint, pour out of the side of the van. Darwin makes a run for it. Yet, another van, same façade, speeds up to the other end of the alleyway, which forces Darwin to cut through a building via an "EMPLOYEES ONLY" door.

The chase doesn't last long.

Once Darwin makes it back to the street after taking a shortcut through a scrap yard, one of the undercover agents, Frye, he remembered, *who's as persistent as a famished lion, leaps from behind a bush along a narrow back alleyway in a lower income neighborhood and knocks Darwin to the ground. He pulls out a bottle filled with bleach from his back pocket and squeezes the bottle, emptying the bottle, the stingy bleach from inside shooting at Darwin like a projectile. Darwin dodges the bleach.*

After the two scuffle on the ground—surprisingly, the E'Raknish tightening along Darwin's hand and fingers, not making an attempt to kill the agent (it could, easily, tear him into shreds)—*the agent pulls out yet another bottle filled with bleach and as he's about to squirt bleach onto E'Raknish, E'Raknish suddenly chews off Darwin's thumb and index finger, causing* him to cry out in agony. *Darwin grabs hold of his bloody hand and tries to stop the bleeding. Frye squirts bleach over E'Raknish, causing the template to lock up, the bleach temporarily dazing and then, eventually, disabling it.*

The agent removes the bandana from around his neck, whips it open from its twisted knot, and throws the bandana over E'Raknish, smothering it.

With E'Raknish tucked between his arms, Agent Frye walks up to Darwin and kicks him directly in the face, knocking him unconscious.

Moments later, other agents track down Frye. *One of the agents places a white clothed bag over Darwin's head; and with the help of another agent, they carry his body to the van and toss him inside.*

Drifting in and out of sleep, D rewound through the images, stopping at the very moment the agent pulled out the water bottle and dowsed E'Raknish with water.

But it wasn't water, D realized, as he focused on the memory.

Agent Frye squirts a yellowish-green substance onto E'Raknish.

How did the agent know to use bleach on *E'Raknish?*

Somewhere, while drifting in and out of consciousness, he heard Frye talking on the phone. He overheard the agent refer to the voice on the other end as "Rouse."

D opened his eyes and sat up in bed and thought about the substance that caused E'Raknish to freeze up.

He looked down at his three fingers and removed the bandage along the two missing ones.

Along the surface of the perfectly severed fingers, both his thumb and index, glistened particles leftover from E'Raknish in a pale light cast from the outside hallway.

They couldn't see it, D told himself.

Not with the naked eye.

But D could.

He could see E'Raknish, and it spoke to him and told him that the plan wasn't over.

Getting caught is part of the plan.

NIGHT (REDUX): STRAY IN A STRAY LAND
JULY 24, 2046 - JUNE 5, 2049
CLIFFSBURG, MD - PADADOCK, PA

VERY few words were exchanged during the drive from the fallen city of Kingsport, for Sue and her son, Jack, were left traumatized by the unrest, which had escalated in a matter of hours.

Every now and then, they'd run into a messy cluster of stranded cars on the highway, as well as wrecked vehicles, which had been cleared from the road. Despite a few manmade detours that forced them to drive through a ditch or along dirt roads before passing roadblocks, the highways were relatively calm and open. Like the city, the countryside provided them with its fair share of difficulties, like, for one: the limited supply of resources, including food, water, and gas, which Sue had plenty of, stocked her van full before their departure; however, driving around in a van stocked with supplies meant they were a target for opportunists, and the fact that Sue knew these things made the drive tenser than she'd like it to be, especially in the presence of her son, who, at any moment, could have one of his fits.

As for their passenger, Low-Key, it was the first time he had ridden inside an automobile in over two years—the last ride the boy remembered was being transported with other strays from a detention center to a public library where he was dropped off like a postal package. He had forgotten what it felt like to place his life in the hands of another person. The hands belonging to a woman whom hours ago he witnessed shoot a pusher dead. Despite Muty's grift, he wasn't any ordinary stray like Low-Key. As Muty put it in his owns, he was from another world where such a valuable necessity like time had been shattered and didn't hold any bearings in Low-Key's reality. Low-Key, who was aware of Sue's choice to take the law into her own hands, still didn't know whether to treat her as a friend or an enemy. But he told himself that the world was a dark place and even darker after the blackouts, and during these times of great darkness, it was good to know people who carried a torch in the form of a gun blast.

The Blackout in Kingsport was only the very beginning for the lack of power and electricity stretched miles outside the city, spreading from one spit of a town to another like cancer that had metastasized throughout the country.

With only a half-full tank left of fuel, Sue reached the point in the drive where she felt comfortable about parting ways with the stray whom she had picked up in Kingsport.

She parked the van in front of a church in Cliffsburg, a town in the valley with the population of roughly twenty thousand residents located along the edge of the Maryland-West Virginia border, and opened the side door for Low-Key: "This is as far as I can take you."

Not expecting a change of heart in a woman who seemed somewhat at ease with herself after gunning down a stray just hours ago, he said teasingly, "Can't talk you into letting me tag along with you?"

"I'm afraid not," Sue said.

Either she was one helluva actor or she was the real deal.

Low-Key leaned toward the latter. Her resilience was rather impressive.

With a frown creeping onto his face, he said, "I had to ask."

"You'll be fine here."

"You sure?"

"Beats Kingsport, right?"

Low-Key scanned the area.

"It's quieter," he said, as he was hesitant to leave.

"You'll be fine, M.J."

Low-Key paused.

"What is it?" asked Sue.

"It's just. . . n'nobody has called me that name in. . . well, I can't remember when."

"It was the name you were given by the two people who brought you into this world. Don't be ashamed of it. And don't be ashamed of them."

While taking in the comment, Low-Key looked over Sue.

"Thanks for the ride, Sue," he said and then nodded at Jack, who was sitting in the passenger seat. "Take care of your mother, Jack."

He gave Low-Key a closed, tight-lip smile before turning his attention back to the crossword puzzles that he had been working on throughout the trip.

Low-Key leaned over the seat, pointed at the crossword puzzle, and said, "*Mortgage*."

Jack looked at Low-Key with utter bafflement.

"Twelve across," he said, putting at the number on the crossword, "From Old French, meaning '*dead pledge*.'"

Jack wrote in the word M-O-R-T-G-A-G-E. The letter "R" in *mortgage* connecting to O-R-P-H-A-N, nine down and the letter "E" connecting to G-A-D-G-E-T, seven down. Jack checked the words and then the other letters, which matched.

"Thanks," he said.

Low-Key shot a glance over at Sue, who remained stern and confident in her decision, then parted ways with the mother and her son.

After watching Sue drive away, Low-Key walked on a paved walkway to the church, Arms of Grace, where, on the front lawn, he saw the sign showing two arms with a heart wrapped with thorns in the center of two open palms.

Below the sign read the passage:

He saves the needy from the sword in their mouth;
  he saves them from the clutches of the powerful.
So the poor have hope,
  and injustice shuts its mouth.

Contemplating whether or not to enter the church, he drew his attention back to the passage before him and lost himself in those words. Both his parents, he remembered, were churchgoers, who often referenced the Bible and the characters in it, posted publicly to their friends on social media, especially his mother, about how those in power were trying to strip away their religious rights, often played the victim in a toxic culture where victimhood went through as many cycles as the moon, and felt as though society was persecuting them for their beliefs.

Low-Key had never actually stepped inside a church before.

His parents, despite their intolerance for those who shared a different opinion as them, never demanded Low-Key to join them in Sunday Service. Even though they always asked Low-Key whether or not he wanted to join them in service and even though Low-Key always refused each time they asked, he felt as though they already knew his answer to their question.

He pulled his eyes away from the sign.

To his left, two people were laughing, one of the laughs crackled with phlegm, the laugh of a heavy smoker.

Along the side of the church, he witnessed several other strays helping load cardboard boxes into the back of an unmarked van.

Before continuing forward, he suddenly turned the other way around and made his way into town where he wandered around the streets, snacking off leftover food inside packed dumpsters, and staying close to the one place, which brought him the most comfort over these past couple of years. Except for the mad and often times, disorderly rushes to grocery stores, as well as gas and charging stations, most of the residents of Cliffsburg went about their business, which was a polar opposite of what went down in Kingsport, with the riots, as well as the violence and destruction. For the most part, the locals were somewhat peaceful to one another ("*Love thy neighbor*" was a common verse he heard his mother say before she lost her job, whereas, afterwards, it became a verse designated for only certain individuals who didn't fall under the category of "them" or "they" or "those things"), and yet, despite a dust-up here and there, the notion alone that other towns could be generally safe, like Cliffsburg, left him feeling more at ease.

After spending the day in Cliffsburg, Low-Key decided to follow Sue's lead and head West. Cliffsburg was nice and all, nice scenery, cleaner air, which was refreshing and a shock to Low-Key's system after cutting his teeth in a smoggy concrete jungle where the lions were shapeshifters and frequently took form as a bureaucrat dressed in a suit and tie, but it was a small town that was increasing in population, not quite overcrowded but reaching its capacity; and from what he gathered while walking through a town plagued with construction sites and powered down, graffiti-tagged robots, which were vandalized and stripped for parts, unfinished buildings and developments, half-tarred streets extending from two lanes to four, all of which had been put on halt due to the blackouts, the locals didn't look favorably upon outsiders, both the human and robotic kind, especially those who were limited in funds. Low-Key felt it in their eyes, the resentment, a similar shade he saw in both his parents' eyes, watching them behind those glazy windshields as locals drove by, the eyes that immediately turned away after first glance. The eyes didn't lie, and they were telling Low-Key to get the hell out of here or else.

Staying within a throwing distance from the traffic ambience, as minimal as it was, he didn't wander too far from the main highway; however, he made sure to keep a safe distance from the highway in fear of crossing paths with trigger-happy locals, who were known to shoot what they deemed a potential threat on site, or worse, desperate travelers, who were escaping major cities, which, according to a stray named "Mango," like the pop singer, whom Low-Key ran into before leaving Cliffsburg, collapsed following the blackouts. *"Just find a steep hill and look to the horizon,"* he said. *"The plumes of smoke act like beacons, warning the living to eff off."*

Following Mango's advice, Low-Key stayed away from major cities, first stopping in a town called Huckley, West Virginia, where he managed to grab a hot meal at a soup kitchen. There, he met an older man, a local artist and sculptor named Copy with a number 0 (zero), spelled Cøpy. The two talked for hours, Copy sharing his stories about how he was once a millionaire and how he rubbed shoulders with the very elites whom the residents of Huckley despised. Unlike many struggling artists who desperately tried to break through into the mainstream, Copy happened to know a cat, who knew a cat who knew the founder of MyCircle. One thing led to another, and in the matter of weeks, Copy's work ended up on the office walls inside MyCircle. From that point forward endless doors were opened up for Copy: galleries, exhibitions for celebrities, TV shows, documentaries. And yet, after all of that fame and fortune, Copy wound up in Nowhereley, West Virginia, breaking bread with strays like Low-Key over a plate of lasagna that tasted as though it was scrapped off the street after spending a day's hardwork painting a mural of the snake-riddled hairy bush around Medusa's Vadge along an abandoned coal breaker, the rust-covered plant acting as his new canvas in a project he called "The Modern Day Messiah."

Low-Key only stayed in Huckley for two days.

After Huckley, he kept trekking west through the hilly countryside, grabbing whatever food he could find at his disposal. By the time he reached the town of Kent, a sleepy town that emitted what could be perceived as the stench of death, Low-Key resorted to killing a dog (he didn't know what kind of breed it was, for it was small and weasel-like, but he was so famished after a long and exhausted trek that he had no other choice). He found a large boulder in the woods and made a camp where he cut the dog's matted hair with a pocketknife before skinning it, and then, while using a honed tree branch as a skewer, cooking the dog's flesh over a flame.

After Kent, he came across Hopper, yet another ex-coal town a few deaths away from being a ghost town. It was in Hopper where he ran into one of those trigger-happy locals, whom Low-Key had been warned about during his travels. Low-Key managed to escape the gunfire after he wandered onto a stretch of land that he thought was public property but ended up being the property of a toothless, swirly-eyed man who had as much firepower as a battalion.

After Hopper, Low-Key, who was still shaken up from dodging bullets, one of which grazed his shoulder, decided to take his chances on the main highway. It was there, just miles outside a town called Bratt where he found an abandoned electric bicycle in a wet ditch alongside the road. Low-Key claimed the bike as his own and rode through two other towns, Mount Jefferson and Klernersville, before the front wheel popped a gear, causing him to crash and wreck the bike.

In the next town, Monroe, Low-Key was able to treat his wounds, mainly a severe case of road rash, which left him with two red palms that had been flayed like the peel of an apple, after locating a first-aid kit behind a checkout counter of a convenient store, which, like most convenient stores he came across during his travels, had been raided. Most of the items inside the store, including sodas or snacks or "wild" and "wonderful" mountaineer memorabilia, were either stolen or trampled upon and trashed. He used the collar of his shirt to mask the putrid stench of the clerk's body behind the counter. The clerk had been shot three times in the chest and left for the crows, which had picked most of the flesh from his face.

After Monroe, Low-Key wound up in a ghost town, Loganson, where he mistook the howling of gusty wind as tormented banshees wailing inside ruined houses along the haunted hollers. Despite the apocalyptic-like eeriness of Loganson, Low-Key, with his sore bones and bandaged hand, was overwhelmed by a great sense of purpose, a feeling that he could best describe as déjà vu or better yet, a feeling similar to déjà vu. Low-Key told himself over and over that he was on the correct path and that soon he'd find what he was looking for—but what exactly was he looking for? He didn't have the faintest idea. But soon, he told himself, he would.

After two weeks of living on his own, backpacking from one dead or dying town to another, Low-Key wound up in Grace, Kentucky, a lively town that hugged the winding Scholar's River, which flowed from Ohio to Tennessee, cutting its way through the heady part of Kentucky like a serpent. Right before he arrived in Grace, he witnessed something that he hadn't seen since before he left Kingsport: a light working, this one being from a floodlight along a two-lane road. First, he heard the clicking noise of a light flickering above him; and then, as Low-Key drew his eyes upward, the amber light switched on. One light led to another in a domino-like effect and it was as though the lights were guiding Low-Key to the town.

By the time he reached the town, the shades of dawn covered the sky. The lights were lit up across Main Street: street signs and lamps, small businesses, marquees, including the one above the Twin Theatre, which, before the blackouts, was screening two movies: the schlock horror cult classic, *Man-Creature* (this one being the 2045 version, making the movie the seventh remake since the original version, which was released in 1982), then the political thriller, *Eye-Eye Captain Eye*.

The next morning, it was declared that the blackouts were unofficially over, so the locals of Grace claimed. The electricity inside each household was properly working. Except for a few traffic lights that were still flashing yellow, most of the power throughout Grace returned; however, fuel was still in short supply—most of the residents relying on electric cars, scooters, bikes, and skates to zip around town. A bouncy public servant named Joanne found Low-Key sleeping on a park bench. Both his hands were badly infected. Joanne persuaded Low-Key to get treatment at the nearest hospital, which was one of the few buildings in Grace that had been using a backup generator throughout the duration of the blackouts.

After a nurse named Robin treated the infected cuts and abrasions on his hand with local antibiotics and fresh gauze, Low-Key spotted a familiar-looking face while he was leaving the ER.

He looked twice, then thrice, before he stopped at the doors leading to the waiting room and walked back to the room where he saw Sue, the woman who helped him escape Kingsport, lying in a hospital bed.

The side of Sue's face was badly swollen, cuts covered with black blood peppered over her face, her right arm bandaged up; and after convincing Robin that he knew the woman, Low-Key was determined to learn more about how she fell into a coma.

The doctor believed that Sue was struck by a car and left for dead. Her body was discovered by a local named Frank along the side of Dauber Road about two klicks from the old water park, which, when Low-Key asked Robin to elaborate for he wasn't fond of *klicks* or old water parks, was just over a mile from "Splash City," an abandoned amusement park that was shut down ten years ago following a fungus outbreak and all that remained of the once fun and lively park was overgrowth.

Traumatized by the discovery, Low-Key could hardly recognize Sue due to her injuries, but he was most definitely certain that the woman lying in the bed was Sue. Immediately, Low-Key thought about Sue's son, Jack—he believed—and when Low-Key asked if there was a boy with her, Robin explained to him that Frank found Sue six days ago and soon after he found her, he brought her straight to the hospital.

According to Local Frank, who owned a sporting goods store up the road, there was nobody else with Sue.

When Frank, who had much more important issues on his mind, like paying the bills after two weeks of being left in the dark or trying to get his business back in order, bluntly asked why Low-Key was so interested in finding out what happened to the woman in the comatose state, he told him that he was in her debt.

More empathetic to the stranger's concerns, Frank drove Low-Key to the exact spot where he found Sue's body; and from there, Low-Key thanked Frank for all of his help and searched for the boy, Jack.

After two days of searching for Jack, Low-Key decided to check out the water park, Splash City.

When Low-Key made it Splash City, he was left in awe and couldn't help but imagine what it looked like without all of the overgrowth. In his mind, he tried to remove those vines climbing up the massive spiraling water slides or the weeds that choked empty swimming pools and lazy rivers. As hard as he tried to visualize a place that was once filled with life, laughter, and joy, he could only see the lush green life before him, thriving in its own way, growing each day, spreading over everything it touched. He once heard of places like Splash City, where people gathered and played and shared the same spaces, but he had never seen them before, only the aftermath of what came before. If anything, the sight of Splash City left Low-Key feeling hopeless, not only for himself, but also humanity and what was left of it.

After nearly giving up on his search, Low-Key finally located Jack after tracking a pungent odor to the restrooms where perched against the side of the building was the corpse of a boy. He couldn't tell whether or not Jack died peacefully for his body was as stiff as a board. His fingers were curled inward in a stiff and frozen clench. The fingernails dug deep into the flesh. From what Low-Key could tell, Jack had been dead for at least a few days, perhaps longer than six—as Robin stated the amount of days Sue had been hospitalized. Feeling more hopeless, Low-Key's mind started to run, filling with questions, the most important one: *Why would Sue leave behind her own child?* The answer to Low-Key's question, although unproven, was abundantly clear to him after he returned to Grace with Jack's belongings, including the book of crossword puzzles and a stuffed three-horned Jackson's chameleon, and informed Robin the devastating news about Sue's son, Jack.

She left her shift and accompanied by Low-Key, drove to Splash City where he showed her the boy's corpse, confirming Low-Key's story.

After contacting the sheriff's office, the sheriff of Grace, Sheriff Charles Brooke, arrived on scene where shortly after examining the body he called in the coroner, who drove out to the site and transported the corpse back to a morgue. Low-Key gave Sheriff Brooke his statement and in it, he stated his relationship with Jack and how Jack's mother helped him escape from Kingsport and when asked to elaborate his business in Grace, Low-Key stated the most obvious: He was a stray who was "passing through." Compliantly, Low-Key rode back with the sheriff to the office where he further elaborated on his "stray"-ness, and explained as best as he could how winding up in the same town as the same woman who helped him escape a dire situation was merely coincidence or dare he'd call it, "fate."

After Sheriff Brooke released Low-Key, he caught up with Robin back at the hospital. Still skeptical about his presence in Grace, Robin, after careful deliberation, decided to share one particular item that she discovered in Sue's possession when Frank brought in Sue: an empty medicine bottle, the prescription made out to someone other than Sue or her son.

When asked about the prescription, she told Low-Key that the drug was meant to treat seizures.

Eventually, after spending weeks in the hospital, Sue managed to wake from the coma.

By then, her son's body had already been buried, since it could no longer stay in the morgue. Other than several nurses and Sue's doctor, the first face Sue saw while she was recovering was Low-Key's face.

Surprised by Low-Key's presence, she was able to explain the reasons why she left her son. The memories surrounding the accident were hazy and fragmented, especially the moments before and after a vehicle struck her from behind, which were blank, like a moment in time that had been blacked out and redacted from her mind. Prior to her awakening, Low-Key already pieced together the dots, including the main reason why she and her son, Jack, were heading west, most of it centered around the weather, he recalled, in particular, the humidity, which she believed was contributing to Jack's seizures and causing him to have more of them, and Sue felt as though the change in the climate, more importantly, a drier one would be a possible solution (then factor in stress, which more than likely played a key role in triggering the seizure), and yet, regardless of Sue's reasons as to why she left Jack, he knew she was only trying to save him.

While frequently paying visits to Sue at the hospital, one day Low-Key met a young, heavy-browed woman, Liza Avallone, her last name, according to Liza, was Italian, her father raised in the small village of Sarliari, known for being one of the many locations throughout the countryside where the legendary Calitori shot his Spaghetti Westerns, Calitori's most popular one being *Draw of the Gringo*, her father having grown up only a spitting distance away from where Ringo Gringo shot the outlaw Black Hat dead during a draw. Her father being a hundred percent Italian meant she was fifty percent Italian, whereas the other half was Lewisburg, Pennsylvania. Liza, having first caught Low-Key's eye, then his ear, wasn't the least bit reserved about bringing up her heritage, mostly Liza's Italian half, even though she had never been to Italy before but said she was planning on one day visiting the birthplace of her father. She was only a couple of years older than Low-Key, whom, if he had to guess his own age, he'd say that he was seventeen and even that age was spoken with a moderate hesitation followed by a wince, the facial expression alone adding three extra question marks behind the word *teen*. With age aside, Liza commented on Low-Key's raggedy attire, his look, mainly the one in his eyes (she'd say she could see it, that badness), and when Liza was asked to explain herself, she'd say she had "an eye for it."

Being drawn to baddies, like Low-Key, who spent the last two years hanging out with other baddies, who'd make him look like Saint Maurice, Liza snuck out of the psychiatric wing during visiting hours and sought out Low-Key when he stopped by the hospital to check on Sue and her progress. When he bumped into Liza a third time, this one being after she spilled the History of the Avallones to him while he was grabbing what he'd call a pot-luck dinner from a vending machine, he asked her about the reddish mark around her neck. Liza was upfront with Low-Key by first acknowledging how she looked, the raw abrasion being her own scarlet letter O, then plainly stating that she was a survivor of an attempted suicide.

Two weeks ago, before the blackouts, Liza did something awful that, even till this day, she said that she regretted, *but*, at the same time, didn't regret for the act itself had proven to her that life was not only as precious as a flower, but also definitely worth living, despite whatever hardships she endured. During the quiet parts of the day, Liza, however, often told herself: What if the *rope didn't snap?* The thought alone killed Liza, knowing that she came only threads away from being deleted from this world. After a local kid found her body underneath the Charlotte's Bridge, her only injuries, besides the damage to her windpipe, leaving her with a raspy smoker's voice, was a sprained ankle and a knot about the size of a golf ball on the side of her noggin after she bumped it on a rock during the fall. When Liza finally regained consciousness and saw that strange, gangling kid looming over her body, his face appeared almost angelic. Each breath was like a beautiful hymn and her body was an instrument among the orchestra of the undying, a cell to be copied, the knowledge passed down from the next cell, then the next, and a soon-to-be scar that she'd wear around her neck was nothing more than a tarnished ring, not only an un-adorned reminder of the preciousness of the ongoing song in which she embraced with a glad heart whenever she found herself staring in a mirror, but also a mar left behind from the battles fought and victoriously won.

When Low-Key asked why she did it—if she didn't mind tell-ing—she told him that the reasons why she tried to kill herself was because she was bullied on The Feed and after a while, after absorbing all those names and labels, she felt as though death was the only escape.

After hearing Liza's story, Low-Key told her that he was glad the rope broke. The two liked each other, that was clear, and not once did they ever have to share their feelings about one another for their immediate bond was as tight as any social contract.

Having unburdened herself to Low-Key, Liza asked Low-Key about his name and where a guy would come up with such a name like "Low" + "Key." Hesitant about sharing his street name—which was, more or less, given to him—Low-Key rallied enough courage after Liza shared with him a part of herself that was in-credibly raw; and honestly, it made him like her even more.

According to Low-Key, the name was given to him by a drug dealer named Muty who came up with the name after observing him in action.

The short version: Muty branded Low-Key with the nickname after the stray helped him out of a jam.

The long version: Muty was being hunted down by a notorious gang of self-proclaimed fascists in Kingsport called "The Stone-masons," who, according to Muty, didn't like Muty based on not who, but *what* he was (When Liza slightly prodded with a follow-up question, Low-Key explained the "what" part, the what, ac-cording to Low-Key, being what his drug buddy referred to as being a half "cuttlemusk," a mutant species that once resided in a seaside village of raw sewage known as D' Oce Pac—Low-Key told Liza with a straight face not to look for the village on a map because, fact, it didn't exist—at least, not in their world). After Low-Key tried his best to explain Muty and his background with-out losing Liza's trust (she'd be lying if the thought about whether Muty actually existed or was a character conjured inside Low-Key's imagination didn't cross her mind), Low-Key made sure to state the obvious: The Stonemasons didn't like cuttlemusks, despite Muty only being "half cuttlemusk." Apparently, his mother had a thing for tentacles. He'd even go so far to say those fascist pigs wanted to cleanse the country of cuttlemusks, which prompted Liza to roll her eyes, signaling Low-Key to wrap up the story.

While being pursued by Stonemasons, Muty sought refuge inside an abandoned house where Low-Key was squatting in the attic. Unaware of the stray or strays inside, Muty locked the door behind him and hid behind the wall. One of the Stonemasons caught a glimpse of Muty, hollered out to the others, who surrounded the house. Meanwhile, Low-Key peeked through a hole in the side of the house and saw the gang brandishing all kinds of firepower. Fearful of his own safety, Low-Key rushed downstairs, grabbed Muty, whispered in his ear to stay "low," then guided him to the hiding place behind a brick wall in the basement while bullets flew overhead. Scurrying as low as a frightened feline, Low-Key made it to the basement door where he used his fingernail on his index finger, which was shaped like a "key," to open the door. There, the two hid. Inside the basement were other strays, like Low-Key, squatting in their own designated junk piles.

By the time the Stonemasons unloaded their steel, there was hardly anything left of the house for it had been lit up like the Fourth of July.

Afterwards, Low-Key introduced himself as Maurice Joseph, but the other strays called him "M.J." Muty didn't care much for the name, so he gave the kid a new one.

A month passed, and Low-Key and Liza became close to one another. He continued to hang around Grace and not once did he think about moving on, except for when he brought up the idea of heading west to Sue, who heard from one of the nurses, who heard from a friend who lived in California, that parts of the West were in shambles, most of the cities burned down to the ground, like ruined relics of the Old World. "West is Death," she specifically said.

The nurse, Robin, who was born in Blankinton, which was about an hour drive from Grace, clarified the rumors after receiving word from her mother who heard on the news that it wasn't safe to travel to the West Coast.

Sue recovered from her injuries and was released from Grace Memorial and told Low-Key when he was checking up on her that she no longer had plans to travel west and that she was going to stay put for the time being. Autumn was approaching fast and all of the leaves throughout the town were starting to change colors. As Jack's legal guardian, Sue had Jack's body exhumed and spent the money that she saved from working at a diner in Kingsport to cremate the body and store his ashes in an urn, which she kept within arm's reach. For the time being, Sue stayed at a hotel until she was well enough to work again. Sue ended up finding a waitressing job at the local diner, Snibby's; whereas, Liza, who, after kindling a close relationship with Low-Key, decided to return back to society, landed a job at a catering company. She put in a word for Low-Key and eventually, convinced her boss to hire her friend but only under one condition: he'd take a drug test every two weeks. Since Low-Key wasn't a drug user, by default, as a majority of the strays were (except for the one time he popped the purple-colored lo-ro pill and experienced one helluva nasty trip that landed him in the ER after spending a night running away from tarantulas the size of elephants, he never touched a drug before in his life), he found no issue with the tests. After Liza and Low-Key earned enough money to pay rent, Liza moved back into her old apartment with her roommate, Fawn. As with her boss at the catering job, Liza managed to talk Fawn into providing Low-Key with a place to stay.

After spending a couple of months in Grace, Low-Key felt as though it was time to move on.
The days were getting colder, and from what he was told, the weather forecasters were predicting a brutally cold winter. The notion of potential blackouts were in the back of their minds, especially Fawn's. After overhearing a conversation between Low-Key and Liza about the government and catching wind of their grievances with the current administration, Fawn informed both of her roomies about a so-called community in Pennsylvania leading a charge in "personal sovereignty." Members of the community were against the current administration's agenda, as well as the blatant lies coming out of the White House in the press secretary's response to the certain allegations, some of them "unfounded," according to Fact Checkers, and refuted after controversial articles dripped onto The Feed, an unpopular one being a conspiracy centered around culling Americans, comparing citizens to deer, and how the blackouts were deliberately carried out, orchestrated by the President himself in order to, not only create economic collapse, where everyday callused-hand Americans

would be forced to give up their dignity and rely on the aide of the government assistance program (G.A.P.), but also reduce the size of the population, helping release the strain on the nation's electrical grid, which was struggling to keep America's lights on. The article spawned from back alleys and festered on the digital public squares after an old photo was released onto The Feed. The photo showed Lockhart, before his term as the star governor of Missouri, holding a worn paperback *The Blackout*, written by the author Stanley Pruitt. Many on The Feed believed Lockhart came up with the idea from the fictional series of novels, which revolved around nationwide blackouts.

An independent report conducted by a watchdog group, which the media, in an attempt to bury the report, discredited the group and hid the findings from the public, showed the number of Americans who died during the blackouts—*non*-fictional ones— that lasted over the span of two weeks. The numbers were staggering and said to be somewhere in a ballpark of eight digits.

The community, or organization or what Liza told Fawn sounded like a "summer camp for anarchists," was known as "Reborne," spelled with a backward e, a self-sufficient, self-relying group of individuals who strived to be free from the shackles of government and maintain an energy independence, residing on a twenty-three acre autonomous stretch of land.

During the final week in November, Low-Key and Liza and Fawn decided to give Reborne a chance.

Fawn heard about Reborne through a friend, who informed her that the only way to pinpoint the exact location of the organization was via one of those back alleys in a public square.

She chose to carry out a vigorous investigation on Gumshoe's latest social media site, Pop!

All she had to do was search for a backward letter "e," and then, from there, follow each of the breadcrumbs, which led her to a set of precise latitude and longitude numbers, directing her to a GPS where, on a Gumshoe map, Fawn pinpointed Temper Ridge, a small town twelve miles from Roil, Pennsylvania.

Before their departure, Fawn ended up getting cold feet and decided to stay in Grace and wait out any potential blackouts, since she had survived the last one and planned on surviving the others, if they should occur. Both Low-Key and Liza were set on Reborne. Low-Key brought the news to Sue the night before their planned departure. He asked if Sue wanted to join them, but she had already gotten comfortable in Grace; and yet, Low-Key felt as though Sue wasn't being completely honest with him. His suspicions came true the next day, when he went to say his final goodbyes to Sue and most importantly, to thank her for saving his life. When he arrived at Sue's new apartment, she was nowhere to be found. Low-Key, who was worried after speaking to Sue the day before, asked several of Sue's tenants if they had seen her. According to one neighbor, she spotted Sue leaving her apartment earlier that morning, which wasn't unusual; however, she made note of Sue's behavior. And she was also carrying her boy's urn in her arms. She told Low-Key it was none of her business to question a grieving mother.

After Low-Key left Sue's, he recalled a conversation with Sue a week ago and how she had been spending a lot of her time by Lake Ballpoint. Low-Key rode an electric bike to Lake Ballpoint where he first found Sue's van in the parking lot, then moments later, Sue herself lying on the shore of the lake, unresponsive, no pulse, not a single mark that Low-Key could find on her body. Beside her was an empty urn. Jack's ashes floated along the surface of the water. Before he left Sue, he came across an empty baggie with a slight powdery residue inside.

Following Sue's death, Low-Key and Liza didn't waste any more time in Grace. Instead the two stuck to their original plan and bought a bus ticket to the city of Roil, Pennsylvania.

Once their arrival in Roil, Low-Key and Liza backpacked through the hilly Courtly County countryside until they finally made it to their destination:

REBORN∃

Their motto engraved on the sign above the wooden gate when Low-Key and Liza were first greeted by two bohemian ladies: "*Carry anew.*"

Upon their arrival, Low-Key started using his old name again: Maurice Joseph "M.J." Ravel. Despite the first-day-of-school like nerves, it didn't take long for M.J. and Liza to settle into their new homes at Reborne, who provided the two with their own separate cottage, as well as a daily task of their choosing. M.J. chose janitorial work, whereas Liza, since she already had a couple of years of experience in catering, chose cooking; however, most of her mornings involved skinning rabbits and other animals, a chore, nonetheless, in which she detested and often did with her eyes partially closed and an overemphasized grimace on her face. M.J. and Liza, who had been knighted as official "newbies" a part of a diverse community where everyone was a newbie with no special privileges or advantages, lived at the Reborne community for roughly two years, give or take, before the organic veil of a clean and old lifestyle lifted, exposing Reborne's three leaders, Sarah, Mike, and Eddie, for what the organization truly was behind the scenes: a pent-up cult of passive-aggressive extremists with enough firepower to blast any invader, foreign or domestic, to smithereens; and such a motto like "*carry anew*" was code for returning to the old, tribal ways where a "*If you aren't with us, then you're against us*" type of mentality was spelled out in a language that neither M.J. nor Liza picked up at first. It wasn't until Liza stumbled on a vast stockpile of weapons inside a locked barn that she started to see the subtle signs throughout the compound, as well as subtle hand gestures that certain newbies made, one being the subtle wave with only a pinkie finger held upward. She'd spot that hand gesture several times throughout the day, whenever a newbie walked past another newbie, the two only acknowledging one another with a flick of a pinkie finger. After Liza found enough evidence to confirm her suspicions, she immediately brought her findings to M.J.'s attention, as well as a potential danger the two faced if they continued to reside in Reborne; however, it was more than evident that the longer they stayed in Reborne, the harder it was to leave. Three days after Liza poisoned and eventually killed a fellow newbie, Zach, who broke into her cottage and raped her in the middle of night (as evidence, Liza had the cuts and bruises to show M.J.), M.J. discovered Liza's body in the kitchen after she failed to return to her cottage the night before. After the investigation into Liza's death, the Reborne board, which consisted of twelve members known as "Oldies," unanimously ruled Liza's death a "suicide," but M.J. suspected it was Zach's brother, Christian, whose reasons as to why he allegedly murdered Liza and framed her death as a suicide were abundantly transparent; and considering M.J. was the only person who was aware of the heinous act Zach committed against Liza, even though he never witnessed the rape with his own two eyes (Before Liza went behind M.J.'s back and decided to take matters into her own hands, M.J. devised a plan on how he was going to "handle" Zach, and it certainly didn't involve obscenities, although a plentiful amount of obscenities and profanities and all sorts of foul language would most definitely be used while he mentally listed ways to "handle" Zach, one of the ways involved plunging a spear through his chest and blaming it on a toss gone awry during an impromptu javelin contest on a windy day), there was no mistake that M.J., the quiet young man who moped floors every night, had a target on his head.

On December 4, 2048, during a snowstorm that left a majority of Pennsylvania with at least a foot of snow by the next morning, M.J. snuck out of Reborne in the dead of night.

In fear of further retaliation from Christian, he stole a gun from the stockpile before his sudden departure. M.J. didn't expect any newbies to come after him, but like the ole saying: *"It was better to have a gun and not need one, than to need a gun and not have one."*

While still pushing aside his grief following the tragic loss of Liza, whom M.J. had bonded with over the past two years, especially after the miscarriage of their baby, M.J. used the survival skills that he acquired while at Reborne and sought shelter underneath a bridge until the snowstorm passed.

By the time the storm cleared, he spent the next three days trekking through the wilderness until he reached a small town, Orange Leaf. He could hardly recognize the world for, according to a grief-stricken local who recently lost all three of his children, every single electronic device (phones, computers, tablets, televisions, etc.) connected to The Feed had somehow turned people into stone.

M.J. couldn't believe his eyes and for a while, wondered if he was a part of a malicious joke or prank. He walked around Orange Leaf, where, every now and then, he'd run into the statue of a person. He knocked on the statue, which was made of stone, tap on it, flick it, wave at it, and yell at it, demand response from it. The common theme: each and every statue was holding onto one of those electronic devices that the local previously mentioned, either cracked or broken or crushed, each statues' gray, hardened eyes fixated on what was left of the devices.

When M.J. sought out the local who recently lost his children, he asked him to explain what happened. The local told M.J. that those who survived, about a quarter of the town, he guessed, were calling it the "End of Days," another local, a spastic man who interrupted him and told M.J. it was the "Great Reboot," screaming about how his predications came true and how nobody listened to him while the town lost power over two weeks ago before returning just three days ago, right before M.J.'s arrival, but rather pegged him as a whacko who was a sucker for conspiracy theories, and as M.J. parted ways before the exchange between locals turned heated, he warned M.J. that if he so much as dared to look at the screen of any electronic device, it would be the last thing he'd ever see before he wound up as a courtyard statue.

Very seldom did M.J. come across any animals that were turned into stone and whenever he did, for instance, a miniature poodle on the front porch steps of a house, he couldn't tell whether it was real or fake. A yappy pet or a lawn ornament?

While wandering through the town, he noticed more animals than humans. Mostly dogs and cats. The local mentioned that survivors were trying to roundup as many as they could find for it was clear, based the local grocery store, which had been gutted, and most of the stores looted and ransacked, that the animals, especially the dogs, weren't man's best friend anymore, but rather an enemy.

After only spending a day in Orange Leaf, M.J. decided to push forward. M.J.'s destination: Lewisburg, which was Liza's hometown. Prior to Liza's death, she told him all about Lewisburg and how one day she'd like to go back, possibly start a new chapter with M.J. The last she heard both her parents were still in Lewisburg. Even though Liza rarely talked to her parents, she was still close to her father. M.J. made it his mission to track down Liza's folks and inform them that their daughter, Liza, was dead.

When he finally made it to Lewisburg, which, given the devastating situation with, not only what the survivors were calling the End of Days, but also a brutally cold winter, was a week trek across Pennsylvania opposed to what it'd normally take, which was about a half-day or so, M.J. located Liza's old house. There, M.J. was greeted by Liza's father, Santino, "Tino," for short, a restaurateur turned shotgun-totting gunslinger; however, Liza's mother wasn't so fortunate.

After earning Tino's trust with a childhood story about his daughter chipping her front tooth off a mechanical horse, M.J. informed him about his daughter's death and as reaffirmation of his trust, gave Liza's father a totem of a clay wolf. Liza, who was fond of the animal as a child, the wolf being an unofficial animal of Italy, crafted the totem while they were at Reborne.

M.J. spent the afternoon with Tino, talking about his daughter, her life and her death, while Liza's mother's statue remained seated at the kitchen table. He was aware of the suicide attempt; and after his daughter's fallout with his wife, he lost all forms of contact from Liza.

According to Tino, Liza never survived the suicide, and the person whom M.J. had gotten to know afterward was a copy of his daughter, more or less, a ghost.

After the conversation was cut short, M.J. said what he needed to say and then he moved on. He spent the next couple of months, moving from one house to another, doing what he once did best, which was squatting. Some of the houses had already been cleared out by marauders, while others, like the one he discovered in Bluefield, were gold mines. There was a three-story house in an upper white collared neighborhood, once owned by a former CEO of a Ready-Meals depot turned investor, family of four, all turned into decorative coat hangers, which had a stockpile of enough food and water to last M.J. for the next ten years.

By late spring, after M.J. returned to the house following a successful fishing trip where he caught a largemouth bass for dinner, he saw two trucks parked in the driveway. A band of armed men were emptying out the house, all of that food M.J. was sitting on, bottled water and medical supplies, all of it loaded into the back of the trucks. M.J. was no match for the marauders, and he had no choice than to wait until they left, grab as much items as he could fit in his backpack before they returned, and then move on to the next house.

On June 5, 2049, after seven months of living on his own, M.J. was spotted by a newbie of Reborne, who was rolling with a band of territorial marauders. Normally, the heavily armed marauders would pay no mind to M.J. for he was a waste of bullets and carrying nothing more than measly scraps in his backpack and enough ammunition to use on himself, if it came down pressing that red fuck-all button. Most marauders were after much larger finds, stockpiles like the one at Mr. Ready-Meals' house, and often times, in order to access these stockpiles, it required much firepower and in a world where ammunition was hard to come by, each bullet counted, including the one.

The ex-Reborne newbie, Jupiter, "Jupe," was what most at Reborne called him, didn't know M.J., personally, despite what he was told after M.J. ran away. M.J. had only crossed paths with Jupe several times during the two years at Reborne, but when Jupe saw M.J. alongside a highway covered with vines and lush overgrowth he immediately recognized M.J.'s face, and M.J. recognized the rage for it blended in with the heavy foliage that surrounding his dark eyes.

Since the highway was barely passable, their pursuit turned into a foot chase, which forced M.J. to seek shelter inside an abandoned warehouse until the band of marauders gave up on the search; however, during the pursuit, M.J. injured his hand while he was climbing over a wrought iron fence where his right hand slipped and the sharp tip of the iron post ended up penetrating the center of his palm. When M.J. yanked his hand away, he was left with a hole the size of a silver dollar in the center of his palm. Eventually, after combing ransacked neighborhoods for medical supplies but coming up empty, he stumbled upon a local hospital in the town of Padadock where he met three individuals— friendlys, he'd later learn—one of the individuals being a young man named John, who, after introducing M.J. to the other two, Selena and Jane, said in a joking manner as he described M.J. when he first laid eyes on him.

In John's own words, he compared M.J. to "a deer in headlights."

NIGHT FRUIT
SEPTEMBER 15, 2048
DEATH VALLEY, CALIFORNIA

CARMICHAEL buzzed Rotten into his office.

"You wanted a word?" asked Rotten, as he stepped into the nearly pitch-black room.

"After listening to your last session with subject B-37, I couldn't help but notice the change in his mannerisms when you brought up the author Pruitt."

Rotten said, "You know I don't like you spying on our conversations."

Carmichael shrugged.

"Well," he said, "get use to it, Rotty. Comes with the territory."

Rotten pushed aside the frustration with Carmichael and said clearly, "The subject was tired. As you've noticed, he's been having trouble sleeping."

"Who hasn't?" Carmichael said arrogantly. "You want to hear my theory?"

"More theories?"

"Yes," he said. "It'll only take a minute."

Rotten's lack of response signaled Carmichael to spill out his so-called "theory."

"You're aware of the game dominoes?"

"I haven't played it before, but, yes, I'm aware of it."

"I believe E'Raknish is similar to the game in that each and every person who comes in contact with the template becomes, in a way, connected to it."

"What's the connection, Lance?" asked Rotten.

"*Memories*," he said. "Subject B-37 has memories of people whom he has never met before. It's the one thing they all have in common: Each and every one of these people has come in contact with the template. Stanley Pruitt, Rowan Oxley, Misty Boole, to list a few. . . Your subject has never met them before and yet, he knows everything about them."

Carmichael picked up a squared jar containing a shard of E'Raknish, which was the size of a pencil tip, submerged in a gel-like substance—"secure," as he reassured Rotten.

"This shard here was collected from a crime scene by a seasoned detective of the KDP," Carmichael said, admiring the tiny shard of E'Raknish. "Detective Dat Kneemo, former partner and mentor to none other than Cashel Rose, was investigating the death of Toni Kibbler, who died by the hands of—"

"TKO," Rotten interrupted. "I've read all about him."

"But what you haven't read, Rotty, is that Kneemo went against protocol and instead of archiving the shard as evidence, he brought it to a specialist in New York City after he witnessed the shard attach itself to a smartphone—*attached*," he emphasized, "as if the shard was drawn to the phone."

"How do you know all this?" asked Rotten.

"That specialist was James Loli and he was a very good friend of mine," Carmichael said after a pause. The sound of James's name rolling from his tongue caused his tear-logged eyes to soften and drift further into the shard. "When James couldn't determine what the shard was. . . " he held the jar up in the air, ". . . he brought it to me."

"Or, after realizing what the shard was capable of, you kindly *borrowed* it from him and forgot to return it," Rotten said while reading Carmichael's gestures.

"And I thought you were off the clock."

"Don't you know, Lance? I'm *always* on the clock." A sudden thought occurred to Rotten as Carmichael attempted to defend his name and his honor. "After all of these years, you still don't know what it is?" said Rotten, amused by Carmichael's story.

"I don't know what it is, but I do know what it can do. . . what it *will* do. . . "

Rotten waited for a response.

Carmichael placed the jar back on the desk and walked closer to Rotten.

Looking him squarely in the eyes, he said with confidence, "It will help protect the one piece of property in JeneCorp's possession that cannot by replicated—for now, that is. Some call it a wrench in the system. Others call it a weapon."

With his flick of his head, Rotten asked more directly, "And what do you call it?"

"I call it God," Carmichael said.

INK βLΛKT
SEPTEMBER 16, 2048
PLEW, VIRGINIA

RECENTLY canned reporter for the Channel 5 News in Elvira, California, Stella Nilsson made her way across the raised walkway before arriving at the fifth floor of the eerily quiet parking deck.

While fumbling for her car keys, she heard a masculine voice call out her name from behind a concrete pillar.

She pulled the portable shock stick from her purse, and as she switched on the weapon, said to the shadowy figure standing between two parked cars.

"Who's there?" Stella said, brandishing the shock stick that had enough charge in it to set a creep's hair on fire.

"I assure you, Ms. Nilsson, I mean you no harm," said the voice.

"How do you know my name?" asked Stella, as she readjusted her grip around the weapon.

She made eye contact with a dark manly figure looming in the shadows.

Being a stickler for details, she first acknowledged his description, despite having very little, only a body of blackness: Both his arms held down by his side, his left arm being slightly shorter than his right, maybe an inch or two shorter, which she assumed was caused by a break or fracture at a younger age, the bone not properly growing as the one on his right.

"I know a lot about you, Ms. Nilsson," he said. "I know you were recently let go from your job based off false accusations, the consequences for poking your head into a story that you had no business reporting."

"No offense," Stella said, taking a step closer to her car, "but if you're from Raw Feed, then you can fuck off." She trailed off, "*I don't have time for this shit. . .* "

"I don't work for the press. But I do know the truth about what happened in Elvira."

"Who are you?" asked Stella.

"Who I am is irrelevant at this point. All that matters is what happened in Elvira."

"You're talking about the death of Roberto Calle?" said Stella.

"Bingo."

"And?"

"I know Mr. Calle didn't kill himself."

"And what about all of those illegal photos he had in his possession?"

"Typical frame job."

Stella asked again, this time more amused by the creeper, "Who are you, really?"

"Did you ever stop to ask yourself: How does a family man and former Border Patrol agent with an impeccable record for over thirty years turn into a sadist overnight?"

"One could only speculate that Calle wasn't hiding a double-life."

"You're not in the profession of speculation, Ms. Nilsson."

"Then what do the facts tell you?"

Stella squared herself to the shadows.

"What the fuck do you want from me?" asked Stella.

"I need you to expose a monster," the shadowy man said. "A person of your persistence. A person with a heart of steel. With your determination, you can help me drag the monster out into the light for the entire world to see."

Curious, Stella asked, "What kind of monster?"

"The multi-armed beast that is JeneCorp."

Stella furrowed her brow.

"What the hell does an ogee company have to do with Calle's death?"

"They have *everything* to do with Calle's death," he said. "I'm afraid there are many more, like Calle, who poked their head into the lion's den, and tragically, were dealt with. . . "

"What about my protection?"

"I can't guarantee your protection, Ms. Nilsson," he said. "All I can offer you is a door, and it's up to you whether or not you want to step through that door."

"What's on the other side?" asked Stella.

"One of many steppingstones that will help you rise to where you need to be—"

"Which is?"

The strange shadowy man paused.

"It's only when you're on the monster's level you have a fighting chance; otherwise, what's the point, right? Who would believe you? I will provide you with an ample amount of resources to assist you in building your tour de force. All you have to do is do what you do best, Ms. Nilsson."

Stella contemplated the offer.

"I can't leave my mother."

"Your mother will be taken care of. Her bills. Her treatment. It's done—once you agree to the job. But," he said before she could answer, "I will warn you: What I'm asking of you is considered to be a long shot. It's incredibly risky and many others before you have failed and if you're not careful, the consequences could be dire for you—"

"Then, why me? Why not find someone else?" Stella said, her breath labored from a sudden increase in her heart rate. "There are hundreds of other reporters out there who'd gladly help you with your story. And not to mention, reporters who still have their jobs. . . "

"They'll never see you coming," he said, first off. "*And* we both know not having a stooge to report to wouldn't stop a person of your caliber. I've read about your work in the Clean Water Project and how you alone exposed the nonprofit for dumping toxic waste into the city's drinking water. Someone like that should've won a Pulitzer. But, of course, OW Media demoted you and stuck you with the late night fluff, and ever since then, you've been trying to claw your way back to the top."

Stella couldn't forget such a story, which nearly killed her. Even the thought of writing the exposé brought on the near panic attack that she had been battling ever since it was published six years ago.

"I assure you, though, if you keep your nose to the ground, you will be responsible for saving the lives of millions." He paused once more as though his silence dangled the anticipation in the air and then said with an unexpected charm, "No pressure."

"I don't know even know who you are," Stella said, more upset.

"For now," he said, "you can call me Blot."

"Blot?"

"What do you say, Ms. Nilsson? Do you want to be on the right side of history?"

Stella weighed her options and thought about the grind and busting her tail to pay off all the mounting hospital bills, considering no news organization would hire Ms. Grabby Hands.

But if she had a story, one that would earn her back into the good graces of society, what she was accused of doing would blow over people's heads. Lately, the public had come down with a severe case of amnesia, especially after one of its fellow citizens had something—in her particular case, a story that might open the lid to a world of scandal and corruption—which would benefit its general interest. Although shallow and nuanced, it was a slogan for modern day civilization: The Oppressor versus The Oppressed. Stella, given her past exposés and often, radical investigative journalism, was a champion for The Oppressed, who constantly pumped their blood, sweat, and tears into the machine, which methodically rewarded The Oppressor.

Stella's lack of response was the response.

Before Blot vanished back into the shadows, he said to Stella, "Inside your car, you will find the first bread crumb. I wish you the best of luck, Ms. Nilsson."

Stella called out to Blot, but he was nowhere in sight.

Confused, she checked the rest of the parking deck, but couldn't locate him.

As she cautiously made her way back to the car, she saw a folder on the passenger seat.

Carefully, she opened the car door and sat inside the car and closed the door behind her.

Inside the dark green folder were macabre photographs taken from a crime scene. Photos of a middle-aged man, his face barely recognizable due to the cavernous gunshot wound, as well as the middle-aged man's two dogs, a white English Cocker Spaniel and a miniature poodle, both of whom were shot dead in what displayed clear-cut indications of a murder-suicide.

According to the coroner's description, the deceased, Nicholas Eugene Fincher, was shot in the face on Sunday, October 26, 2014. The report stated: Mr. Fincher died from a "self-inflicted gunshot" to the head.

Another photo, taken by a spectator showed two deadly serious-looking men wearing "FBI" jackets, both standing among a small crowd of deputies from the local sheriff's office behind yellow caution tape wrapped around the front lawn of "Leatherby Manor," the location of yet another more brutal crime scene in Whisperfront, Maine, unrelated and yet very much related to the death of Nicky and his two dogs.

Lastly, the three photos: first one showing a deputy of Beaux County Sheriff's Department, Lance Horton, inside an alleyway behind the sheriff's office, shot to death in an execution-style, highly-professional; then another photo of a massacre inside the sheriff's office, each and every person inside the sheriff's office shot in similar fashion as Deputy Horton; a third and final photograph of the supposed shooter, Que Phit, who, prior to the massacre inside the sheriff's office, escaped from a mental hospital in Cedarside.

In a ballistics report, a forensic investigator concluded that the handgun Nicky Fincher used on himself, the "Beretta 92FS," was the same exact weapon used in the massacre at the sheriff's office.

Lastly, wedged in the crevasse of the passenger seat was a white ear bud that must've fallen out once Stella opened the folder. The ear bud, Stella inspected, was a digibuddi and located on the side of the bud was a play/stop button. She inserted the digibuddi inside her ear and pressed the play button. Following *pops* and *clicks* and *snap* and *crackle* sounds of old tape hiss was the voice of a FBI agent, Agent Schuster.

In the recording on the digibuddi, Schuster, along with the agent's partner, Agent Porter, the two FBI agents were speaking to a bewildered deputy from Beaux County Sheriff's Department, Levy Wallace.

"How many times do I need to spell it out for you, Agent. . ."

"Schuster."

"Karp and McClintock, those were the names they told me," the deputy said with frustration in his voice. *"As for their badges, they looked exactly like the ones in your pockets. Trust me. I have seen ones you can buy off the Internet and these certainly weren't them. These looked like the real deal. So, if you're telling these two yahoos weren't with the Federal Bureau of Investigation, then who in the hell were they working for?"*

TWO OF A KIND
SEPTEMBER 17, 2048
DEATH VALLEY, CALIFORNIA

ON the other side of the country, the leg of E'Raknish suddenly twitched as soon as it picked up on the faintest whiff of menstrual blood over thousands of miles away.

The sleepy-eyed technician, who was inspecting E'Raknish on the worktable, pulled himself away from the magnifying glass and closely examined the template without the aide of a special lens or a black light. First, he made sure E'Raknish still remained in its dormant state by tapping it with a probe. E'Raknish didn't budge when poked and prodded.

Lastly, he double-checked the restraints fastened around each extremity, which seemed secure.

As soon as the technician switched the black light back on and returned to his inspection before Carmichael returned from his meeting, he was a hundred-percent certain he saw E'Raknish move yet again, this time its other leg—or was it an arm? The technician didn't know which for he was kept in the dark about the background of E'Raknish, who or *what* it was. He was nothing more than a Yes Man. "Inspect the device for more symbols." Yes, Sir. No questions asked. A final note before he proceeded with work: "And whatever happens, don't remove the restraints." Again: *Yes, Sir.* Only this time, the technician paused before speaking those words and when he finally spoke them, there was a deflation in his voice as the words fizzled out like obstructed air.

The technician picked up the probe from the table, this time his hand trembling.

As he was about to give E'Raknish a poke, the lights inside the lab suddenly cut off!

Fumbling around in the pitch black, the technician said to the virtual assistant, "*Mark*, lights on!"

The assistant, Mark, switched on the lights for the technician.

As the technician drew his eyes back to the worktable, E'Raknish was missing, its restraints still fastened, untouched.

More frantic, the technician looked around the lab but couldn't find E'Raknish.

"Mark. . . "

Before he could utter the rest of what he was trying to tell the virtual assistant, the technician felt something crawling on his back.

The notion of death suddenly gripped him, causing him to freeze in a paralyzed state of fear.

As he rotated his head around, E'Raknish was climbing over his shoulder.

Left in a semi-unresponsive state, he moved his eyes toward the table where he saw a shock stick. He mustered enough courage to reach for the shock stick as E'Raknish made its way onto the side of the technician's neck. The feel alone of the template's legs—or arms—were like the edges of knives after being held under hot flames. He could feel each extremity digging into his flesh, leaving behind a bloody trail of pinpoint-like prints. The technician managed to get a finger on the handle of the shock stick, then eventually a hand. Once he grabbed the shock stick, he slowly lifted it toward E'Raknish.

Once E'Raknish became aware of the technician's next move, it climbed directly onto the technician's face, leaving him more hesitant about using the shock stick. The technician's hand was still gripped on the shock stick, ready, despite running an elevated risk of shocking himself. All of a sudden, the internal workings of E'Raknish opened up before the technician's eyes, exposing the hundreds and thousands of tiny razors churning like grinders.

Before the technician could make an attempt to shock punch E'Raknish from his face, it was already too late. E'Raknish tore the technician's face to shreds, one of the blades precisely penetrating the back of the frontal lobe, instantly causing paralysis in the technician's face, as well as both his arms and legs.

Once the technician was no longer deemed a threat, E'Raknish scanned the technician's key card and used a copy of it to escape from the lab.

While scurrying along the side of the wall like a mouse, E'Raknish ran into a hail of gunfire when it reached the 5th Floor.

A team of security guards, altogether six of them, attempted to cripple E'Raknish, but were outmatched once E'Raknish evaded their explosive rounds. E'Raknish cut its way through each guard, severing limbs and slicing specific arteries.

Motley arrived on the scene shortly after E'Raknish had its way with the guards and forced the template into hiding after laying down heavy gunfire.

Not too far away was Rotten, who recently finished having a conversation with Darwin. He checked out the commotion and once he arrived on the scene, was filled in on the current situation.

After accessing the situation, he told Motley to take cover while he switched on the sprinkler system, forcing E'Raknish to seek cover inside the head of a dead security guard.

Subtly, Rotten pulled down the sleeve over his wrist, covering his watch.

Thinking that maybe E'Raknish was hiding underneath a body, he checked underneath each guard, Rotten's search leading him to one guard in particular. The guard had been decapitated; his head, however, was nowhere to be found. He listened closer over the hissing sound of water raining down all around him until he heard a *pitter-patter* tapping behind him. He turned around, only to find E'Raknish using the security guard's head as a cover from the water, like a crab hiding in a shell. The only parts exposed were the legs, which protruding from the base of the head, where normally a neck would reside. Rotten shot a couple of rounds at the head, trying to shoot the fleshy poncho off E'Raknish.

As E'Raknish dodged more gunfire, it suddenly leaped up at Rotten, causing Rotten to stumble backward. Poking her body from the cover behind the wall, Motley fired a couple of shots at E'Raknish, but the gunshots had no effect on it. Rotten suddenly tripped over one of the guard's bodies and fell to the floor, thus making himself vulnerable for attack.

E'Raknish pounced on top of the cataloger.

Motley aimed at E'Raknish, readied herself; and at the last second, Motley held her gunfire in fear of hitting her partner.

As Rotten shielded himself from the razor-laced mouth of E'Raknish, he revealed part of the wristwatch underneath his sleeve.

The many razors inside E'Raknish stopped spinning, and the two were left at a standstill.

After recognizing the wristwatch Rotten was wearing, E'Raknish scurried toward a fire exit and managed to escape the facility.

Motley rushed over to Rotten's aide.

"Why didn't it kill you?" asked Motley.

"I dunno," Rotten lied, as Motley helped him to his feet. "Must be my lucky day."

COUGH DROPS
SEPTEMBER 18, 2048
WASHINGTON, D.C.

THE day was long and drawn out, and Vernon exhausted most of the day speaking to politicians, from both aisles, including several members of Lockhart's Cabinet, one of them being the Secretary of Energy from the Department of Energy Carol Rapp, who sent a chill down Vernon's spine when she shook his hand. The tightness of Rapp's grip, those bones digging into his bones, the glare, as sharp as a pinprick, was an indicator of the world that rested upon his shoulders. Handshakes and beady-eyed glares and scripted platitudes aside, Vernon reassured each and every one of them that Lockhart was going to recover and resume his role as the Commander in Chief, despite only ten days ago a shooter nearly blew off the bottom part of his face.

After Vernon called it quits for the day and left Walter Reed, Vernon bumped into the Assistant Director of the FBI, who, when asked about the sniffle, said he was battling a cold. The reasons were a change in the seasons or better yet, the temperature, with last week being somewhere around ninety-plus degrees, only to drop in the lower fifties in two days.

Vernon gave Forsake an update on Lockhart's condition.

Forsake, who, every now and then, sniffled up loose phlegm that, in return, would drain into the back of his throat, told Vernon the story about his great grandfather, Byakuya, a *Nisei*, meaning "second generation," (the name later passed down to his son, Forsake's grandfather, then his grandfather's son, Forsake's father) who served as a Japanese translator for Military Intelligence during World War II. During the time, the country looked at Byakuya and those who looked like Byakuya as the enemy after the attack on Pearl Harbor, which led to the country's involvement in the war. In 1942, months after the attack, Japanese Americans, including Byakuya's parents, immigrants who were *Issei*, or "first generation," were forced to relocate and were sent to detention camps, particularly those who lived along the West Coast, in Byakuya's case, San Francisco. The main reason why Forsake was telling Vernon the story of his great grandfather and how, despite Byakuya's hard-working parents being placed in a detention camp for no particular rhyme or reason other than the condemnation of their own heritage, Byakuya remained loyal to the very country that he served, which, for Vernon, was hard to comprehend, given the unfair treatment.

To put Forsake at ease, Vernon reaffirmed his loyalty, not to the President, but to the country.

Following a strangely tense conversation with the Assistant Director, Vernon's escort, who had been monitoring Vernon's every move ever since he stepped foot in Washington, drove him to the five-star hotel where he was currently staying until Lockhart showed signs of improvement.

When Vernon returned to his room, it was past eleven o'clock and he was looking forward to sleeping in his bed after spending the previous night catching about an hour's worth of rest on a sofa in his temporary office at Walter Reed.

As soon as he stepped foot into the room, he picked up a fragrance in the air.

He reached for a light switch on the wall and as he was about to turn on a light, the lamp on his desk lit up, revealing a strange man standing by the window.

Vernon made an attempt toward the door until he heard a resonant voice, which was coming from a shadowy figure sitting in the corner of the living room.

"Have a seat, Vernon," said the voice.

With his hand gripping the doorknob, Vernon, who was tempted to open the door and make a run for the elevators, peered into the room where two silhouettes patiently waited.

One of them was a tall, physically fit, scar-faced man wearing a black glass eye in his right eye socket, as well as a black lightweight trench coat, which concealed, not only a weapon worn in a shoulder holster, but also the extensive augmentation along the right side of his body; while the other one, a dark-skinned man seated in the leather chair closest to the sparse book shelf.

"Please," the voice said again, "I'm not going to say it twice, Vernon."

Vernon eased back into the room.

As he walked past the kitchen, the strange man in the chair said, "The folder on the counter. Pick it up."

Vernon turned his shoulder and in the dim lighting, noticed an old, discolored manila folder lying on the kitchen countertop. The edges of the folder, curled and frayed, aged.

"What is this?" asked Vernon, feeling more unease in a space, which he currently referred to as "home." "Who are you people?"

"Why you, right?" the seated man said. "This is the question you've asked those in power, but the answer you've received hasn't been as satisfactory as you had hoped. Am I right?"

Vernon didn't answer.

"We could've chosen from countless individuals to repair Lockhart, right?"

"I've never even met the man before in my life, if that's where you're getting at, Mister. . . "

"Rouse," he said for Vernon, "Tahr Rouse."

"Prove it," Vernon said, his breath more laborious.

The seated man leaned forward into the hazy beam of light and *briefly* revealed himself.

Tahr Rouse, as stated, the CEO of JeneCorp.

But *what the hell does he want with me?*

The messy beard on his thin face concealed his sunken in cheeks. He wore these dark rings underneath both eyes, as if he hadn't slept in years. His appearance was gaunt and sickly, and he wore several layers to hide his weight loss. Yet, his hearty voice carried the resonance of a man who had reached his prime.

Tahr sat back in the chair and said more comfortably, "Your presence, Vernon."

Confused by Tahr's vagueness, Vernon said, "What about it?"

"You're going to ask what we want with you," Tahr said with superiority. "*Your* presence." He shot a glance over at the darkly dressed man with the robotic arm who hadn't moved an inch ever since he reached for the lamp to turn it on. "It's that simple, Vernon. We want the certified Hawks name."

"And what makes you sure that I will follow in my grandfather's footsteps?"

"Regardless of the outcome, you pick up that folder, Vernon, not because I say so, but because it's how you've been wired."

Again, Vernon didn't respond for he was unaware of Tahr's point.

"Our good friend, Mark, ran a thorough analysis on your timeline, Vernon, and it concluded, through your behavioral patterns, your posts, as well as your interests, that you will leave Hawkthetics™ after you review the contents inside that folder, and it's only then, after spending sleepless nights tossing in your bed, that one morning you finally decide to resume where *he* left off. Mark is all over the place when it comes to identifying specific dates or times. But you will pick up that folder; and once you do, whether tonight, tomorrow, or next month, you are set on an incessant path that will define humanity's next steps into the future."

"And *what if* I decide to destroy what's inside that folder?" asked Vernon. "Does your Predictor Engine factor in free will?"

"You won't destroy the folder, Vernon. Do you know why?"

"Why's that?"

"*Curiosity*, Vernon." He placed his hands together, all ten of his smooth fingertips touching one another, the hands formed into the shape of a diamond. Without missing a beat, Tahr asked Vernon, "Tell me, Vernon: why prosthetics? Based on quite an impressive background in medicine, which I'm sure makes for one helluva pick-up line for the ladies—"

"I'm already taken," said Vernon. "But you already knew that, right?"

Tahr smiled off Vernon's attitude.

"You could've chosen from any particular branch of medicine: Cardiology, neurology, orthopedics. . ." he stopped before listing the last and more appropriate branch, which would come in handy while treating the seemingly irreparable damage to Lockhart's mouth, ". . . dentistry."

Behind his closed mouth, Vernon clenched his teeth together.

"Before you answer," Tahr said superiorly, as Vernon cracked open his tightly pressed lips, "I'll tell you why: You didn't want to be anything like him, but whether you like it or not you are very much like him. Legs, feet, toes, arms, hands, fingers. . ." Tahr held up one hand, moved his fingers, ". . . what do they all have in common?" Tahr tapped the side of his temple. "Based on *your* human nature, Vernon, one day you will find yourself reflecting on your own life and while doing so, you will trace back to where this obsession began and in your search, you will eventually come across *his* work, the very same work you've written off, pegged it as pseudo-science. In that folder before you, you will find nothing but truth, truth that has been hidden from the public, from you, in particular, a patient of his grandfather's, a disturbed man whom your grandfather cured with a life form not of this earth, rather look at it as a gift from another world. Once you realize the endless possibilities of what could be accomplished with this gift, this new element, the way I see it, a game changer in how we view science, energy, medicine, and technology, you *will* finish what your grandfather started."

Vernon witnessed Tahr's pearly whites in the darkness.

Tahr said with a grin, "All things stem back to the beginning."

"All of that," Vernon said doubtfully, as he pointed at the folder, "that's in there?"

"And more."

"How about the people who died under my grandfather's care? Are they in there?"

"Open the folder and find out yourself. . . "

On a whim, Vernon suddenly picked up the folder from the countertop and grabbed a lighter from the drawer of hot plates and set the folder on fire.

As flames crawled up the folder, starting from the bottom-up and spreading toward his hand, Vernon tossed it in the sink and said to Tahr, "So, did Mark predict that scenario?"

"In fact. . . " Tahr said, as he reached over toward the desk and grabbed yet another similar-looking folder and held it in the air, ". . . it was the first scenario that Mark predicted. There was an eighty-seven percent probability that you would destroy the folder once I hinted at what was inside the folder."

Vernon turned on the faucet and ran cold water over the rising flames, causing the blackened folder to smoke. While waving away the smoke, he noticed several of the loose papers that were untouched by the fire. The pages were blank.

"Very cute," he said to Tahr. "So, is that the *real* one?"

"I don't know," Tahr said teasingly, "is it?"

"What the fuck do you want?" said Vernon, as he began to lose patience with his two guests.

"We want Lockhart to be ready by October," Tahr said.

"Ready for what?"

"The election, of course."

"That's impossible."

"How so?"

"He'll be lucky if he ever speaks a word again," Vernon said, his tone loud and harsh. "He's looking at months, even years, of speech therapy."

"Maybe so, Vernon," Tahr said and once more, held up the folder. "*But* we have an alternative method. Controversial, of course, but highly effective."

"Effective?" Vernon questioned. "Sounds like you're using Lockhart as a guinea pig."

Tahr shrugged and reiterated his claim by waving the folder in the air.

"All in the folder, Vernon," he said. "Whether you like it or not, Lockhart is going to be our October Surprise and with the help of your grandfather's *pseudo*-science, you're going to make it possible."

"Why are you so desperate to have Lockhart on the ticket?" asked Vernon.

"Something *big* is about to happen, something, in my opinion, that should've been addressed sooner by my old man during his tenure at JeneCorp," Tahr said to Vernon. "And we need folks whom we can count on, folks like you and Lockhart to get us where we need to be. . . "

Frightened by the answer, Vernon asked anyway: "And where's that?"

"The New World," Tahr said after a pause.

"What about Forsake?" asked Vernon.

"What about him?"

"What's his role in all of this?"

"Forsake is nothing more than a Yes-Man."

Yes-Man, right?

"So you need puppets?" Vernon said, more tensely. "People to nod their heads and go along with whatever you demand?"

"Exactly," Tahr said and once more, grinned. "I mean, if you think about it, just a minute ago I told you, in a very discreet way, to burn that folder before you, and guess what? You did."

Vernon took a moment to think about Tahr's proposal or better yet, demands. Right now, he couldn't distinguish the two from one another.

"What will happen to Lockhart after he's reelected?" asked Vernon.

"That all depends on Lockhart and whether or not he retains his. . . his loyalty to us."

"So, he's expendable?"

"What world are you living in, Vernon?" Tahr asked but didn't expect an answer from him. "Everybody is expendable, including myself."

Vernon peered closer at Tahr and began questioning his motives, most importantly, his reach for power and how far it extended.

"I help out with Lockhart and then I'm out. . . for good."

"You're in no position to making deals, Vernon," Tahr said. "We could find another candidate who would gladly fill your shoes, but we'd prefer to keep this a family affair—"

"*What if* I say no?"

"We're not asking you, Mr. Hawks," he said and shot a glance at the villainous-looking man with the black glass eye. "My friend, Agent Noble here, would make a United States Intelligent Agency's interrogator look like a four-star rated nail stylist. Let's just say he can be very persuasive. And he has very little patience for bullshit."

Vernon, who wasn't a strong man, could barely bench press his own weight, moved his eyes toward the still one-eyed agent and could feel the strength projected from his silence alone.

"Once Lockhart secures a second term in office your role with JeneCorp will be reevaluated. You have my word that we will take your input into consideration. Until we cross that bridge, I highly recommend that you save yourself the trouble and comply with us—"

"You make it sound like I have no other choice."

"You certainly do have a choice, Vernon. Two of them. Lockhart or Noble here?"

Once more, Vernon moved his eyes toward Agent Noble and focused in on his robotic arm and tried to imagine what he could do with it when given the opportunity.

"Lockhart," Vernon said in defeat.

"Excellent choice," Tahr said and stood from the chair.

Adjusting his sports coat, he walked from the room and placed the folder on the countertop.

"I expect you to do your homework over the weekend," Tahr said and tapped on the folder. "We start on Monday. And Vernon. . ." he said, before walking away, ". . . one last thing: Some of my people will be present to help guide you through the operation. A word of advice: Please, don't be the elephant in the room."

Following Tahr's departure was Agent Noble, whom Vernon thought looked older than what the shadows suggested, a trick of the lighting.

"If you change your mind," Agent Noble said and eyed the folder below, "you know what to do. . . "

After Agent Noble and Tahr left his room, Vernon walked to the window where he peeked outside and witnessed the two step inside a vehicle parked along the curb and then watched them ride away. The escort from earlier remained parked on the street, watching Vernon. Never had a choice weighed so heavily upon Vernon's shoulders. The weight—at least some of it—was soon lifted as he walked back into the kitchen and cracked open the folder.

#GRAYSCORPION
SEPTEMBER 19, 2048
DILBERT, NEBRASKA

CEYLON Talley, a truck driver for Cresto Transports, stirred from the strange noise coming from the back of the convenient store while he was trying to catch big titties bouncing up and down on a trampoline. Both his eyes bolted open, as he remained in a rested yet incredibly attentive state. The blood from his raging hard-on pressed against the zipper of his blue jeans like the pitch of a tent escaped to his other extremities, forcing him to readjust himself.

Being the type of person who slept through hurricanes or hails of gunfire—like the Highway Massacre in Melmosa, Colorado, last spring, when he was asked to give his statement to a police officer but could only give recount only one person of interest, the pole dancer "Valeria," a beautiful blonde who, when he closed his eyes, transformed into a human billiards table—Ceylon was left flabbergasted by the low-pitch noise for it was unlike anything he had ever heard. The noise also made his skin crawl. He rolled out of the coffin-like cot, poked his head from the passenger window of the cab, and scanned the parking lot. One observation caught his eye: A robin's egg blue smartcar parked behind the store, Tidbitties.

The driver side window was smashed. Pebble-sized pieces of glass were scattered along the concrete below. There was movement coming from inside the car, but it was too dark to see and the car was parked several feet outside a floodlight to witness what was going on inside the car.

First, Ceylon grabbed his smartphone and then his baseball bat from underneath his seat and exited the truck.

With baseball bat in hand, Ceylon inched his way toward the back of the store where inside the smartcar he discovered a strange metallic creature drinking the blood from a gaping slit in the driver's throat. The blood was dribbling from the cut, lots of it, slowly but steady, like the water from a hose with a slight kink. He peered closer at a straw-like apparatus, which extended from the inside of the creature. The apparatus was held directly underneath the continuous stream of blood, which was being funneled into what Ceylon perceived as a mouth. He once more heard a familiar low-pitch hum that he reckoned was coming from the creature, but he wasn't a hundred-percent positive.

Cautiously, he stepped closer to the vehicle.

"Can't be. . . " Ceylon said and called over a fellow trucker, who was making his way back to his eighteen-wheeler after grabbing himself a bag of Sourpunks from Tidbitties. "Hey, man," he said, waving the trucker over, "look here. Is that the fucking Gray Scorpion?"

"Gray Scorpion?"

"You know, Gray Scorpion, Gray Scorpion. . . "

The trucker looked closer at what Ceylon was pointing his finger at inside the car.

Startled by the blood, he shouted out, "Fuck me sideways. Looks like a big ass spider."

Ceylon holstered the bat underneath his armpit and pulled out his smartphone from his back pocket and filmed a fifteen-second video clip of the creature, which would later be identified by JeneCorp's Recovery Unit as E'Raknish while monitoring The Feed, but to many of those, like for instance, Ceylon, who followed latest trends on The Feed, knew it as #GrayScorpion.

"Post this shit on The Feed," Ceylon said, labeling the video with the popular hashtag.

The trucker asked Ceylon, "You gonna call someone?"

Ceylon waved his hand.

"Fucker's dead anyway."

After posting the video of E'Raknish, Ceylon left the scene while the other trucker eventually left and didn't bother calling the police.

Ceylon walked back to his truck, returned the bat to its rightful position under the seat, and, then, while fighting off the burden of the night, decided to fill up his thermos with coffee before hitting the road. While exiting Tidbitties with a full thermos of burnt coffee, Ceylon walked past the smartcar, only to realize that the Gray Scorpion was gone. He picked up his pace and as his walk turned to a slow jog, he heard the roar of an engine behind him! A silver Lycanrager model XS sped directly at him, forcing him to roll out of the way. The thermos, which was closed, fell from his grip and *clanked* and then rattled over the concrete.

"Watch where you're going you fucking inbreed!" Ceylon screamed out.

After brushing off the dirt from his clothes, he stood to his feet and picked up the scratched-up thermos from the ground; and as he began to walk back to his truck, he couldn't help but notice that Lycanrager speeding away into the night and how it was swerving back and forth, crossing the median or at times, running off the side of the highway, its tire kicking up clouds of dust.

Following a near-death experience, Ceylon safely made it to his truck where he checked his latest post of The Feed, refreshing for likes, then scrolling to other #GrayScorpion, several of the posts winding up on The Feed days ago, one of them showing a video of #GrayScorpion darting across a fairway on the ninth hole of a golf course right outside Las Vegas on a sunny afternoon, chasing after what looked like a white-tailed jackrabbit, and then another post showing an out-of-focus video of #GrayScorpion eating the entrails of a dead chihuahua right outside the bedroom window of a tween in a white-collared neighborhood, then, later that same night, several posts on the Strip, one of them showing #Gray-Scorpion darting under a crowd of tourists and then another one, not too far, #GrayScorpion draining the blood from a dead prostitute lying on the dark corner of the rundown street, and then the next day, a #GrayScorpion sighting in Utah, the startling post showing #GrayScorpion leaving the body of a gutted coyote on the side of highway, then, yet another photograph taken by a passenger while waiting at a stoplight in a small town in Colorado, #GrayScorpion attached to the hub cap of a nearby car, then, lastly, a newer one that Ceylon hadn't seen before, the photograph taken by some kid in the back of a van while riding with his family to Mount Rushmore, the van shown riding alongside a truck, more specifically, Ceylon's truck, #GrayScorpion, like a raised font blending with the letter "e" from the word *Cresto* in the faded logo on the side of the truck.

Freaked out by the image, Ceylon refreshed The Feed once more and before he could wrap his head around #GrayScorpion, his recent post had already gone viral. In a matter of minutes, his couple hundred of views turned into thousands; and then after yet another refresh of the page, the post had billions of views. As soon as glorified tabloids disguised under the banner of news sites picked up on Ceylon's post, the video was like a wild fire that could no longer be contained.

THE BARN SCENE
SEPTEMBER 20, 2048
FULLER - MERCY, IOWA

JUST after two o'clock in the morning, while refueling two Fuchs UH-60 Shadow Falcons, or "F-Cons," for short, on the state-run, government funded farm called the Greenway Stewardship Association, which specialized in harvesting corn, one of the two pilots who was in charge of transporting JeneCorp's elite Recovery Unit, heard a *ping* sound coming from one of the Company's go-to trackers, Man Pullman, who developed a surveillance device from a particle of E'Raknish extracted from Darwin's blood in order to help pinpoint the missing E'Raknish. The device gave off a *"ping"*-like sound whenever it picked up the whereabouts of E'Raknish and on the screen, displayed "hot" and "cold" signals, hot being the magnetic-like pull toward connecting templates was the strongest, cold being the weakest.

Roughly the size of an eTablet, the radar-like device pinged whenever E'Raknish exited—or "decoupled"—from its host, which E'Raknish used to mask its signal, wearing the flesh of other life forms as a protective suit. Until then, the teams were left following the trail of dead bodies.

Standing outside, the other F-Con Agent Prescott, who was keeping tabs on #GrayScorpion, as well as monitoring and running background checks on each user who posted the hashtag, discovered Ceylon's video post showing E'Raknish feeding off the blood of a traveler. In a matter of several clicks, he was able to pull up countless feeds around the gas station, one showing the video of the driver of a silver Lycanrager XS coming inches away from striking Ceylon.

He managed to identify six of the seven letters, as well as numbers on the license plate—the last remaining digit, the number "7" filled in after running the rest of the plate into the database on his eTablet where he found a ninety-nine percent match to a Lycanrager XS.

The driver, Dillon Hogg, lived in Fulton, which was the next town.

According to the video, Hogg was headed east.

"Got a winner here," Prescott said.

Ecstatic, Pullman picked up a blip on his surveillance device, which matched the coordinates on the Lycanrager's GPS, coming from a small town called Mercy just south of Cedar Rapids.

Within only minutes after E'Raknish popped up on the radar, a local field office of Telepine, a subsidiary of JeneCorp, who was aiding with the retrieval of the recently runaway E'Raknish, intercepted a 911 phone call from a mortified woman named Helene Schroeder.

In the call, Helene reported an automobile accident on their property, and when her husband (Wes) went outside to check on the driver's condition, he was killed by something that she could not explain. The so-called "dispatcher" reassured the frightened caller that police were on the way and would be there as soon as possible.

Unfortunately for Helene, nobody was coming to help her.

Once the word was relayed to Agent Faraday, he brought the information to Agent Noble, who was geared up for a fight. One of the most notable differences in his appearance: the black eye patch that he wore over his right eye socket.

"Call just came through," Faraday said to Noble. "Sounds like our target."

Pullman confirmed the address of the recent phone call.

"Not useless after all," Agent Noble said arrogantly, referring to Telepine.

He motioned his team to ready up.

The two teams entered the helicopters, and one after another, the helicopters flew away.

During the flight, Carmichael watched the snippet of the latest #GrayScorpion video, which, after it was removed from The Feed, was sent to him through as an attachment via text message.

The video showed E'Raknish replenishing itself.

Using the headset, Rotten, whom the others thought was a fifth wheel and had absolutely no business being a part of their mission, caught a glimpse of the video on Carmichael's phone and asked, "Why blood?"

Carmichael replied, as Rotten read the technician's gestures, "Think of blood as a main fuel supply for E'Raknish. The human body constantly makes millions of new red blood cells every second of the day. It's quite a remarkable system when you break it all down, and for E'Raknish blood is no different than what us humans look at it as food."

"A blood parasite."

Agent Prescott teased Pullman, "Forget a squirt gun. Should've brought a wooden stake."

The others laughed at Agent Prescott's comment.

Carmichael emphasized, as he used the heel of his boot to tap on the black cooler by his feet, "Firepower will slow it down, sure, but my special concoction here will temporarily cripple it."

Remaining stern, Agent Noble asked Carmichael, "And what happens if you cut off its food supply?"

"I reckon it will go into a dormant state or worse, stop living."

"Worse? Isn't that the whole point?"

"Not for our employer, Agent," Carmichael said directly to Prescott, who turned quiet.

Fully aware of a small window they had to locate E'Raknish before it found, as Carmichael earlier put it, a potential "new host" that would essentially cause E'Raknish to disappear from the radar, Noble asked the pilot, "How much time until we arrive?"

"ETA three minutes," the pilot said.

Then, Noble: "You heard it, boys. . . " he eyed Motley, ". . . and girls. Game faces."

Three minutes later, JeneCorp's Recovery Unit arrived at their drop point a half-mile away from the address of the latest 911 call.

Noble helped Carmichael carry the heavy-duty water cooler from F-Con, which they secured to a four-wheeled battery powered transporter.

While Rotten exited from the F-Con, he accidentally bumped into the cooler, which caused the transporter to tilt and nearly turn over on its side.

"Heads up, *Rotty*," Noble said with resentment in his voice.

Motley noticed Rotten's discomfort around the other agents, in particular, Agent Noble.

"You good?" she asked Rotten.

"I just wanna get this over with," he said with a sense of desperation in his voice.

Rotten checked the time on his wristwatch, which read: "2:23."

"We'll find it, Barney," Motley reassured Rotten. "Don't you worry."

Pullman read the device, which displayed a satellite view of the address where a hot red dot was flashing on the screen. The red dot moved from the front of the barn to the rear; then it suddenly disappeared.

"We have to move," Pullman said. "We've been ghosted."

Motley teased: "From what I've heard, it's not the first time you've been ghosted."

"You have to give it to ole Moochie," Pullman said, more playfully. "She's much smarter than she appears to be."

Motley flashed a grin.

She asked, "How you know it's a she?"

"How'd I know?" Pullman repeated. "Because she's got all kinds of tricks up her sleeve—"

"Must've heard the helicopters."

Noble ordered his team: "Move!"

With Noble leading the recovery mission, the remaining JeneCorp agents, as well as the lone cataloger, all of whom were heavily armed, followed by splitting up into two teams.

After quickly moving through the open field under the cover of night, the two teams arrived at a small embankment along the edge of the Schroeder's property. Using night-vision goggles, the agents from both teams surveyed and accessed the situation. The gravel driveway led up to a ranch-style house in the middle of an open field. The kitchen and living room lights were turned on, but there was no activity coming from the house. Roughly fifty feet behind the house was a barn where the heat signature was the brightest and strongest.

Through a synched-up comms link, Pullman said while reading the device: "The signal was last seen coming from the barn. It's in there. Trust me."

"Last time we were told to trust you and that little toy of yours we wound up hunting down a rusty tractor."

The same Lycanrager XS from earlier, which sped through a wooden fence that surrounded the Schroeder's property and crashed into the side of the barn, was still smoking. The driver of the sports car, partially thrown from the driver's seat, was hanging from a punctured windshield, his bloody corpse lying across the damaged hood.

With the night-vision goggles, Noble spotted the owner of the house, Wes Schroeder, lying on the ground not too far from the wrecked car. He appeared motionless.

Using the infrared of a special thermal camera, Agent Knox picked up the visibly warm human body coming from the kitchen inside the house. The shaky, illuminated body was standing by the window, waiting for police to arrive.

"Possible witness inside the house," Knox said. "Alive."

"Handle it," Noble ordered.

"Be more specific."

"Neutralize the witness, Knox."

Frustrated by Noble's order, Knox grabbed two agents, Faraday and Slayer, and proceeded to the house while the remaining agents, Offspring, Motley, and Bowie, and the cataloger Rotten, followed Noble and the rest of the JeneCorp Recovery Unit toward the barn.

Faraday temporarily shut off his comms and whispered to Knox, as they made their way to the Schroeder house: "Knox, what the fuck?"

"Just follow my lead."

When the three agents arrived at the backdoor closest to the kitchen, Knox asked Faraday for the canister of knockout gas.

"Hand over the nightie-night."

Faraday hesitantly handed Knox the canister of knockout gas and grabbed a water hose from the side of the house. He cut the hose in half and placed one end to the canister, and then slipped the other end underneath the door. He opened the valve and released the gas into the kitchen.

"She'll live," Knox reassured the two agents. "In a couple of hours, she'll wake up with one helluva hangover."

Within only a few seconds, the agents heard a couple of *thuds*, as well as a high-pitch *clank* of a butcher's knife falling to the kitchen floor.

Knox peeked through the window and verified that Ms. Schroeder was unconscious.

"Witness neutralized," Knox said over comms.

Back to Noble: After confirmation from Knox, the agent, with the muzzle of the assault rifle positioned in a high-ready position while the stock pressed firmly against firing side arm, said to the team, "Weapons free."

Rotten switched off the safety of his gun, as he shot a glance over at Pullman and a faint blip on the device.

"Eyes peeled, brother," Pullman said, as he eyed Rotten.

Pullman strangely held his gaze on Rotten, who, despite catching a glimpse of the techie at JeneCorp every now and then during walks toward Catalog, wasn't quite sure whether or not to trust him.

The team arrived at the barn.

Accompanied by a former jarhead, Agent Offspring, Noble cracked open the partly damaged barn door and stepped inside. The floodlight provided enough light for the agents to momentarily switch off the night-vision.

Inside the dusty barn were over a dozen of mooing cows, which remained inside their stalls. The random *mooing* of cows made it harder to listen for E'Raknish. Offspring was next to enter. Following Offspring was Agent Bowie, a highly trained marksman who could literally shoot the wings off a butterfly. Behind Bowie, Motley and Rotten, who ordered Knox and Faraday inside while Slayer covered at the main exits: there were two of them, the barn door, as well as the second floor window of the upstairs loft.

Standing at a safe distance outside the barn were Prescott and Carmichael, the brains of the operation, who monitored a video that was linked to each body cam worn by the team members.

"We're walking straight into a trap," Offspring said, his voice shaking.

"Our own little kill box."

As the agents checked each stall, Bowie came across a dark and empty stall.

After Bowie opened the door, he realized the stall wasn't empty. On the ground lay a dead cow on its side, its guts spilled from its belly.

"Dead cow," Bowie said over comms.

All of a sudden, the blip appeared on Pullman's device.

The blip stronger than before, hot and bright and flashing red.

"Step away from the cow, Bowie," Pullman warned.

Ignoring Pullman, he shined the rifle's flashlight on the dead cow and in that dusty beam of light, saw the glare of a metallic object inside the blood and guts. The object started to move, the guts swirling and churning inside the cow.

"Guys. . ."

As the agent stepped closer for a better look, E'Raknish suddenly leaped out of the cow and latched onto his throat, slicing open his jugular.

With his finger pressed against the trigger, the agent wildly fired off one round after another, not coming close to hitting the target.

E'Raknish fled from Bowie's neck as soon as the other agents arrived at the stall.

The cut to the agent's neck was so deep that it nearly decapitated him.

Either way, he was dead within the matter of seconds.

Taking lead, Noble confirmed Bowie's death as Pullman tracked E'Raknish's whereabouts.

"East wall," he said, "twenty paces."

Once the team arrived at the back of the barn the agents shined their lights on a wall covered with all sorts of farming, as well as gardening tools, from shovels to axes to chippers to saws to hooks to knives to toppers to pitchforks to spears to trowels to rakes to wrenches, each and every piece made from various metals, including cast iron.

Noble called out, "Pullman? Where now?"

With the blip flashing red on the screen, Pullman said, "It's right here. . ."

Ready to unload on the entire wall, Offspring cried out, "Where goddamn'it?"

Noble said to Carmichael, who was paying close attention to Noble's video, "What exactly are we looking for, Lance?"

"Look for one that appears new," Carmichael said, as he noticed the age of each rusty, dull-looking tool hanging on the wall. "Unlike the others, it'll give off a glare when you hold a light to it."

"You heard the man," Noble said.

The rest of the agents switched on their flashlights and shined them on the tools.

Offspring shined the light on one particular tool.

"The scythe," he said, nodding at what looked like a relatively newer tool. "Look, , , "

As Offspring inched closer to the scythe, Noble and the others flanked the tool and readied their weapons.

With the muzzle of his rifle, Offspring poked at the scythe.

All of a sudden, the scythe dropped from the hook and fell to the workbench below, causing the agents take aim, including Faraday, who opened fire on the scythe.

"Cease fire!" shouted Noble, as he glared at the trigger-happy agent.

Faraday stopped firing.

"Faraday, you jumpy twig head," Offspring said, both frustrated by Faraday and startled by the gunfire. "You're gonna get us killed—"

"Twig head?"

"Noble. . . " Carmichael said over comms, as he suggested cutting off the lights and instead, using thermal-vision to track E'Raknish.

"Switching to thermal," Noble said and switched off the lights. The others followed suit.

As soon as Noble returned to his goggles, he picked up the warm, rectangular-shaped object on the wall of tools. He switched off thermal-vision and then switched on a flashlight, revealing a blood-caked axe, its surface disguised by dried blood. He switched off the light, and then, yet again, switched on thermal.

With his voice lowered, Noble said, "The axe. . . "

Agents directed their attention to the bloody axe.

"Smart bastard," Offspring said, taking aim.

As the agents closed in, E'Raknish slowly uncurled and unfolded itself, exposing its limbs.

Over the tense silence, Noble switched off the thermal vision and said, "It's go time. . . "

Noble was first to fire, then the rest joined in.

As predicted, the gunfire managed to slow down E'Raknish but didn't stop E'Raknish, especially from attacking yet another agent, this one being Offspring.

As bullets ricocheted off E'Raknish, it quickly leaped onto Offspring's head, forcing agents to cease-fire. With a stinger-like blade roughly eight inches long, E'Raknish stabbed Offspring directly in his right eye, penetrating his brain, mainly the region that sent electrical signals to all four of his extremities, in particular, his arms and legs.

Unable to control himself, Offspring drunkenly turned the hot weapon on the other agents as though E'Raknish was operating him—or better yet, controlling him like a puppet.

His limbs were as loose as a doll, swinging back and forth with each movement.

During the wild shooting, he shot Knox directly in the head, killing him. One of the bullets clipped Pullman in the arm and forced him to take cover inside a stall. Others riddled the wall of the barn, striking a large gas tank outside. Fuel shot out from the bullet hole and began to puddle underneath the tank.

"Light 'em up!" Noble ordered.

Together, the agents open-fired on both Offspring and E'Raknish.

Offspring flailed around until Motley stepped forward and struck E'Raknish with two direct shots from a twelve-gauge semi-automatic shotgun. E'Raknish fell from Offspring's perforated head; and as soon as the stinger-like blade was released, Offspring was a goner.

Once E'Raknish was on the ground, Rotten said to Noble, "We need to box it in a corner."

Both Noble and Rotten flanked E'Raknish; other agents filled up the semi-circle and fired at E'Raknish, sending it into a corner.

All of a sudden, not one but *two* blips appeared on Pullman's device, each one within inches from one another.

In a state of perpetual shock, each surviving member of the team watched the template split into two halves, straight down the middle, and then regenerated the four razor-sharp limbs that it lost during the separation.

"Guys. . . " Pullman said over comms, ". . . I'm picking up two readings."

"Tell us something we don't know," Noble said and returned to firing. In between gunshots, Noble said to Carmichael, "Are you seeing this, Lance? How's this even possible?"

"Your guess is as good as mine," Carmichael said, as he watched a real-time coverage from each of the agent's body cams.

Once E'Raknish split in two halves, one of the halves scurried underneath their feet and ran toward the door, leaving behind a trail of straw dust.

"Coming your way Slayer," Rotten said to Slayer. Then, he nodded at Motley and before he could utter it, Motley touched Rotten on the shoulder and told him, "I'm on it. . . ."

Realizing Slayer was completely outmatched, Motley chased after the second E'Raknish.

While Noble, Rotten, and Faraday backed the other template into the corner of the barn with heavy gunfire, Slayer struggled to keep the other E'Raknish from escaping.

Motley darted through the barn doors when E'Raknish was only several feet away from the agent, whose bullets bounced E'Raknish and failed to stop it in its tracks.

With her shotgun, Motley fired two direct shots at E'Raknish, causing it to stagger and then stumble backward. Together, while using the hail of gunfire to their advantage, both Motley and Slayer managed to guide E'Raknish toward the transporter, which was carrying the cooler.

Before the two reached the cooler, the transporter automatically drove into the barn.

"Rotten. . . " Motley said over comms, ". . . come in. We have the target pinned in."

"Hold it off until we've bagged the other one."

"Rotty," Motley said, as she was forced to reload the shotgun, "we're running out of ammo."

During the reload, E'Raknish managed to push back against Slayer's gunfire.

With his comms off, Agent Prescott, who had plenty of ammunition, said to Carmichael, "I should lend 'em a hand—"

"No," Carmichael said coldly. "They know what they signed up for."

"They're going to die, if we don't step in—"

"So be it."

"What about the other half?"

"We only need one."

With Motley's safety on his mind, Rotten stopped firing at E'Raknish.

The transporter finally arrived at Noble's location.

After kicking open the lid of the heavy-duty cooler, which was filled with a translucent gel-like lubricant, Noble ordered Rotten to keep firing.

Rotten fired at E'Raknish, the bullets backing it up into a corner.

The continual gunfire from Rotten and Faraday provided Noble with enough time to pull out an expandable picker from his utility belt. On the end of the picker was a claw-like grip.

As he approached E'Raknish with the picker, Motley cried out, "Barney, help. . . "

Unable to reload the shotgun in time, Motley was forced to pull out a handgun as E'Raknish trudged its way toward the two agents.

"Leave her, Rotten," Noble ordered, as he was about to grab E'Raknish with the picker.

Rotten disobeyed Noble's orders and darted outside the barn.

Without Rotten's gunfire from pushing it back, E'Raknish suddenly leaped up at Noble.

Before E'Raknish could strike at his throat, Noble snatched E'Raknish with the picker.

"I got you now, you motherfucka," Noble said madly.

Relieved, Faraday hollered out in victory.

Agent Prescott stepped in right as E'Raknish was bearing down on Motley and Slayer and laid down heavy gunfire, which gave Motley enough time to reload her shotgun.

Shortly after, Rotten made it outside and helped push E'Raknish back.

As Noble struggled to get a handle around the picker for E'Raknish kept squirming, he was forced away from the cooler. The violent kicking and thrashing from E'Raknish began to weigh on him, as he began to lose his grip.

All of a sudden, Noble backpedaled and tripped over Offspring's body.

His grip loosened around the picker's handle, freeing E'Raknish.

After scurrying underneath a loose piece of siding on the side of the barn E'Raknish rejoined the other half.

By the time E'Raknish was fully integrated with its other half, Motley, who had taken lead, managed to push it back with the blasts of the shotgun.

Rotten stopped firing and smelled gasoline.

Then, he pinpointed the odor coming from the puddle of gasoline spreading further and further from the leaking tank, completely saturating the ground.

And Motley was headed straight toward the puddle!

"Laura, get back. . ."

Ignoring Rotten, Motley continued to fire at E'Raknish.

"How do you like that?" she shouted out, as the emotions overcame her. "Feel good? Now, suck my fuckin—"

The shot ricocheted off E'Raknish, causing sparks the fly.

All it took was one spark; and before Motley could pick up the odor and trace it to the fuel tank in the corner of her eye, a massive explosion erupted from the tank!

The others took cover and shielded themselves from the debris of scolding hot metal.

Pieces of flaming debris, including scraps of metal and even Motley herself, rained down on the side of the barn, catching part of it on fire, including the roof, which part of it collapsed from the debris.

Once the smoke cleared, Noble located E'Raknish. It was slightly twitching on the ground. Except for part of its wounded limb, the tip being chipped off, the missing piece roughly the size of a bolt, there wasn't a single scratch on E'Raknish.

With his boot, he stepped on E'Raknish before it could recover, grabbed it with the picker's claw, and carried it to the gel-like lubricant inside the cooler. E'Raknish immediately froze up, not dead, but more or less, as Carmichael suggested what would happen to E'Raknish if its food was cut off, left in a dormant state as soon as it was submerged in the lubricant. Noble closed the lid. Mission accomplished.

After an intense search, Rotten found the remainder of Motley's body inside the barn.

Several of the cows fled from busted stalls, some lying on their sides, either dead or dazed.

Rotten was still left staggering from the explosion, ears ringing, mind buzzing, legs like wet pasta.

So far, he counted six casualties altogether, including Agent Motley, as well as Wes Schroeder and Dillon Hogg.

As Rotten gripped Motley's lifeless hand, he heard the *crunching* sound of a steel-toed boot stepping onto a batch of wheat straw behind him.

Noble raised his right arm in the air; and before Rotten could rotate around toward the sound behind him, Noble suddenly struck downward, pistol-whipping Rotten in the back of the head, instantly rendering him unconscious.

Prescott entered the barn and before he could condemn Noble, was tossed the same gun used to knock out Rotten.

"He's flying back with you," Noble said sternly.

The top lighting of the flames along a partially collapsed rooftop darkened Noble's left eye and displayed the face of a man who was without soul, only darkness.

As Prescott and another agent carried Rotten's body to the helicopter, the leftover piece of E'Raknish, roughly the size of a bolt, slinked its way from the debris and attached itself to a field mouse.

#LESISMORE
SEPTEMBER 20, 2048
DILBERT, NEBRASKA

AT precisely 6:53 AM, Special Agent Frye and his partner, Agent Laredo, pulled into the gas station, JCGAS, the double-sided S-shaped ogee arched over "JC," the old school symbol representing oil, gas, energy, and electricity.

A majority of the parking lot was marked off with crime scene tape.

Dozens of cruisers from Dilbert PD surrounded the nearby convenient store, Tidbitties.

A white tent had been set up behind Tidbitties where local detectives were investigating the deceased victim inside the smart-car.

After taking charge of the crime scene, Frye was able to obtain several statements from police officers, one of them being from the clerk and co-owner of the convenient store, Titus, who, according to his statement given to the officer, witnessed the Lycan-rager speeding away from the gas station several minutes before eyewitnesses saw the body.

He showed Frye the surveillance footage of the Lycanrager nearly hitting one of the patrons, the trucker, Ceylon, who also gave his statement to police officers. While watching the footage, Frye caught a glimpse of the driver, whose head was cocked backward at a ninety-degree angle, his mouth gaping open, stretched cartoonishly far, with a metallic spider-like thing hanging from it. The fluorescent light above the gas pumps glistened off the thing inside the driver's mouth.

If it ain't our boy, *E'Rak-ah-tak-tak*.

Frye thanked Titus for his cooperation and escorted the clerk to his partner, who had a couple of questions for him.

While Titus talked with Laredo, Frye made a phone call to Telepine.

DEEP CUT
SEPTEMBER 20, 2048
MOJAVE DESERT, CALIFORNIA

WITH an IV attached to his right arm—the head nurse was specifically instructed by her superiors to avoid his left— Rotten woke up in a hospital bed inside a stale white room.

As he sat upright, he felt a heavy, stabbing pain rush through his head.

He grabbed the knot on the backside of his head, which was incredibly sore.

A scraggly-bearded man dressed in oversized black clothes, whose face was all but a dark, blurry smudge, entered the room.

Rotten couldn't recognize the strange man's face for it remained featureless.

"Take it easy, Barney," the strange man said, as he placed a city hand on Rotten's shoulder.

As Rotten eased back into bed, the strange man, after acknowledging the bewilderment riddled upon Rotten's face, summoned one of the nurses who arrived with a syringe.

On the other side of the bed, the nurse inserted the needle directly into Rotten's IV, pumping an orangish-peach colored substance into his veins.

"Whaa..." Rotten said, panicked, "...what'r you giving me?"

The strange man held both hands in the air, both tips of his index fingers and thumb pressed together, forming the shape of a triangle.

Within only seconds after the orange stuff entered his veins, the strange man's face materialized.

"Tahr," Rotten said, recognizing the man standing by his bed-side, "what the hell happened?"

First off, Tahr apologized for Noble's behavior, in particular, his short temper, which he had been instructed to control.

"Even after all these years, he still flies off the handle."

"Thought JeneCorp hired the best of the best—"

"He was upset," Tahr said. "I assure you. He won't lay a fin-ger on you ever again."

"Thought you were looking after me, Tahr."

"I take full responsibility for Noble's actions," he said.

"Maybe it's time to educate Mr. Noble and maybe, once he finds out the truth about what I'm really doing here, next time he'll think twice before fucking with me."

"If Noble and anyone for that matter knew *what* you were, Barney, then it'd compromise my agreement to your boss. I should've listened to you, Barney. You had no business being on that team, and for that, I apologize—"

"Will he be punished?" asked Rotten.

"Noble has been with the Company longer than you've been alive, Barney. He's loyal, and these days, loyalty is hard to find. So, no, he will *not* be punished."

Rotten looked around the room, partly retro and yet, at the same time, modern.

"Where am I?"

"You're currently in the South Wing," Tahr said. "Accessed through an underground tunnel, which will take you to the main facility. The project broke ground back in 2020; and after a few hiccups with a shortage of building supplies and whatnot, the fa-cility was finished two years ago. Still has that new building smell to it, doesn't it?"

Rotten didn't answer for he was too sore in the head to think straight.

"Anyway, how are you feeling?"

"Other than my head feeling like it's about to explode," he said, "fine. What about the template?"

"Back where it belongs," Tahr said, "in fact, as we speak, Carmichael is prepping a sample to take to Washington. Don't worry. . . " he acknowledged the change in Rotten's color, ". . . it's in good hands—"

"How about the witness at the barn?" asked Rotten.

"She's taken care of," Tahr said. "The narrative has already been framed. A drunk driving accident caused the explosion. Owner of the property died in the accident. His wife was under the influence of lo-ro at the time of the explosion. Even if she talks, nobody will believe a word she says. She's lost all credibility. So, there's nothing to worry about. We're solid—"

"And the video on The Feed?"

"We're going to let the story run its course and leave it up to the public to use its imagination. We'll squash it only when it's time to squash it. For now, let 'em make up whatever bullshit they want, if it gives 'em the illusion of power."

"It's evolving," said Rotten.

Perking up from the comment, Tahr asked, "What makes you say that?"

"I saw it do things that I've never seen it do before," he said, "the way it blended in with its surroundings. The way it sensed us coming from miles away. It's becoming more like us. . . "

"Isn't that the reason why you're here, Barney?" asked Tahr. "To study it? Learn from it? If E'Raknish is what you and your boss say it is and what it has a potential to be, then incidents like the one in Mercy only help us understand it and as you say, its evolution."

"People died, Tahr," Rotten said, swallowing a bubble of anger rising up his throat.

"Listen, Barney," Tahr said, as he acknowledged the anger hiding behind the cloudy corners of Rotten's eyes. His resonant voice was surprisingly softer when he said to Rotten, "I'm sorry to hear about Agent Motley. Why didn't you tell me about your *history* with her?"

"What history?" Rotten said grimly, as he pushed down the anger.

Tahr patted Rotten on the shoulder. His eyes ran down Rotten's left arm, mainly a massive slit running down his entire forearm, not a scar, but, more or less, an old wound that hadn't properly healed: between the narrow, hairline-like opening, the two flaps of skin pressed against each other, like a belly button.

"Right," he said with a faint flick of a smile. "Don't forget, Barney: You're *still* human, despite what that devil put inside you."

The anger melted from Rotten's face. The pupils in his eyes widened, as his skin started to perspire. The fear gripped him like an invisible hand, first squeezing his chest, his ribcage, and then his throat. Tahr's reminder was enough evidence to cause alarm and at the same time, relief for Rotten couldn't help but wonder whether or not he was still JeneCorp's fail-safe, that was if it wasn't recovered, the template. But the missing E'Raknish was, in fact, recovered, which he put him in the clear. Underneath the blanket, he crossed his fingers.

"Does it still make me expendable?" he asked, his voice somewhat shaky.

Tahr shot another glance at Rotten's left arm and tapped him on the shoulder.

"You're off the hook, my friend," Tahr said and then made his way toward the exit. "So, the next time you see Agent Noble. . . you might want to thank him."

"YOU CAN'T KILL *US*"
SEPTEMBER 23, 2048 - ?
WASHINGTON, D.C.

THE surgery on the President's mouth was a success.

After thirty-six hours of being under the knife, former President William Lockhart woke up from his drug-induced sleep.

Carmichael and Vernon were standing by Lockhart's bedside.

Vernon was still left in a state of awe by the capabilities of E'Raknish and how, with further study, it had the potential to revitalize and *reshape* modern medicine.

His grandfather, he realized, was correct about E'Raknish.

Carmichael held a mirror to Lockhart's face and showed him the new appliances inside his mouth.

The top and bottom gums, as well as his teeth and the roof his mouth were a hundred percent E'Raknish.

Altogether, twelve of his teeth, including the molars, premolars, and one canine of the bottom right side of his mouth appeared like glorified crowns—"bling," as Carmichael teased.

Security Service allowed several photographers inside the hospital room to take photographs of Lockhart while he was in good spirits. Also included in the photograph were the doctors and nurses responsible for the successful operation. The acting President, Lockhart's vice president, Mallory Brawn, as well as two members from JeneCorp, one of them being Lance Carmichael, who headed up the surgical operation, and one member from Neuvak, were in the historical photograph.

Not to his surprise, Vernon Hawks, "The Specialist From Boston," who, throughout the duration of the radical procedure, felt as though he was playing the part of a background actor, was asked to *not* be included in the photo, which, in the beginning, didn't sit well with him, considering the long man-hours he had spent helping the former President return to his JeneCorp-funded seat in the oval office.

Lockhart was asked to speak a few words to the press, which his staff advised him to avoid, considering nobody knew exactly what was going to come out of the former President's mouth.

Ignoring the advice, Lockhart had ten words: *"They can shoot at US, but they can't kill US."*

And once those ten words were published and spread all across The Feed, the line ended up becoming a national slogan written across tee shirts and hats, as well as the theme, which would later be used on the upcoming campaign trail.

The video of Lockhart later leaning from the hospital window and waving toward a crowd of supporters below projected a sense of strength, as well as resiliency, and gave a gift that the country had been longing for, which was hope. The gift of hope was a prize that every American could rally behind and support, unabashedly and unequivocally. For once in what felt like decades, the hope for a better and brighter tomorrow was as tangible as apple pie.

To the political pundits, it was no surprise that Lockhart's popularity shot up in the polls; in fact, skyrocketed faster than any President in the past three generations.

In a matter of days, William Lockhart, once one of the most divisive Presidents in the history of the United States, whose adversaries once referred to him as "Lock-up-Hart," due to all of the corruption that followed him around like an unshakable odor that lingered underneath an air freshener, or "Lock, Stock, and Barrel," due to the overwhelming government spending and the pile of debt that he created in only one term while in office, or a most popular one, "Shady," a nickname that he had been branded with after the blackouts, became one of the beloved figures in modern day politics.

Everybody was calling it a "phenomenon."

And rightfully so.

BLAKT OUT THE SUN
SEPTEMBER 25, 2048
DEATH VALLEY, CALIFORNIA

AFTER watching a more detailed news report on the drunk driver who ran his brand new Lycanrager into a fuel tank on a stretch of private property in Mercy, Iowa, Rotten decided to brave the heavy downpour and take a break, stating to the security guard at the main entranceway in front of JeneCorp that he was stepping out to grab himself a drink.

He drove the eCar to a hyperloop station, which he soon discovered was temporarily closed due to the rainfall. From there, Rotten drove to the nearest town where JeneCorp agents and employees were known to unwind after a hard day's work: a small desert town, Eden. Considering the GPS built inside his car was tracking his every move, he figured, after a second thought, that it was best to stay close in order to avoid drawing any red flags.

Rotten drove to a local favorite, Mirage, and grabbed the secured contents from the glove compartment.

Fortunately, after he entered the bar, he didn't see anyone from JeneCorp.

Regardless of the clientele, Rotten kept his head down and went straight to the bathroom in the back of the bar and locked the door behind him. The inside of the bathroom was grungy and decorated with graffiti of the local gangs and tribes and doodles depicting disturbing criminal acts, some involving violence toward the outsiders, mainly workers of JeneCorp, and a variety of slurs against AI written all over phlegm-blood-cum-piss-stained tile walls. Stuck to the top corner of a cracked mirror was a used condom, the load inside like clumpy glue holding it in place.

Rotten placed the baggie on the edge of the vanity. He zipped out the baggie and pulled out a syringe from inside. Next, he rolled up his left sleeve, revealing the slit running down his forearm. The end of the slit was covered with the timepiece of the watch, which was unconventionally worn on the underside of his wrist in what many called "upside down." The hour and minute hand along his wristwatch folded inward, allowing Rotten to remove the frame; however, the two hands, both the hour and the minute hand, remained intact along the end of the slit, shrinking and sliding underneath a tiny opening along his skin. He pulled back on the two flaps, revealing two hands of what used to be a watch. Both the minute and hour hands connected to one another and formed into a slide along a zipper that Rotten used to peel open his forearm. Inside his arm was a more intricate and ornate version of E'Raknish, which replaced the ligaments and tendons and the carpus, as well as part of Rotten's ulna and radius bones. Everything else was good ole fashion human: flesh, blood, muscles, veins, all of which intertwined around the latticework of E'Raknish.

With time running out, he pulled out the vial of cloned blood, which he stole from the freezers inside JeneCorp's labs, and inserted the vial into the syringe and after locating a plump vein on his other forearm, injected the blood into his body.

The reaction to the cloned blood was instantaneous, causing a seizure-like effect with every muscle in his body tightening. For a second, his eyes rolled into the back of his head. He never lost consciousness; yet, once the violent spell passed, his body became less tense. His eyes eventually returned to normal. He collected himself, zipped close his forearm, and decided to pocket his wristwatch for he wasn't quite finished with his night scheme.

One of the drunks was pounding on the bathroom door while, at the same time, jiggling the door handle.

Rotten opened the door, only to find himself face-to-face with a squinty-eyed drunk who had his fist raised high in the air, ready to pound on the outsider's face.

Startled, the drunk shouldered his way into the bathroom, pushing Rotten aside.

He ignored the drunk, even though the disturbing thought of making that silly, startled expression permanent on the drunk's face crept up inside him. *Nobody would take a man seriously with that kind of look*, he thought. The laughs he'd receive. It might even be the death of him.

Still feeling the effects of the venomous gori racing like fire ants through his veins, he stole one of the patron's smartphones from the table while the patron was busy copping tail in a dark, dingy-looking booth, and exited via the backdoor of Mirage. He grabbed a raggedy blanket covered in sticky liquid from a dumpster in the back alleyway.

From the shadows, a small figure scurried behind Rotten, causing him to flinch and worse of all, react. That minor reaction, that sudden flick of a head, that swelling of his milky-white eyes, left the rat in suspension.

As Rotten sharpened his gaze, the rat began to turn into stone, starting from its beady black eyes and spreading outward to each limb until the entire rat had turned into a garden ornament.

As soon as Rotten realized what he had done, he holstered the gaze by shaking it away like a floater in his eye and then reminded himself to keep his head and eyes down to the ground, don't flinch, don't react—reacting could mean the death of an innocent.

With the blanket worn over his head like a hood, he avoided the surveillance camera in front of Mirage and played the part of a cloaked drunk stumbling his drunken self through the street.

Once he was clear from the cameras, which were unable to use facial recognition to identify him, Rotten removed the blanket from his head and used E'Raknish as a lock pick to break into a solar power box on a street post, which was connected to the satellite linking system. The end of the two tiny clock hands protruding from a prick-size opening at the end of the closed slit along his wrist reshaped into a connector. He bent his left hand backward in a sixty-degree angle toward the top of his wrist, the joints as flexible as rubber, and then inserted the connector into the interface. The streetlight above dimmed and flickered before returning to full power.

While E'Raknish was jacked into the system, he pulled out the stolen smartphone and used the gaze by deep-diving into the phone's camera.

Over two thousand and five hundred miles across the other side of the country, inside FBI's headquarters located in **Washington, D.C.**, a smartphone lying on a cherry oak desk suddenly made a *pinging* sound, which, despite its high pitch, reverberated like a hum throughout the Assistant Director Jin Forsake's office.

A ghost call.

The screen of the smartphone suddenly flashed white, drawing the dark eyes of Forsake.

The ping was sudden, quick, and short lived, creating a broad and untraceable reading.

Forsake cautiously picked up the phone from the desk and stared into the dark screen.

His eyes suddenly glazed over.

Left in a trance, he moved his eyes toward the dark bathroom on the other side of the office and witnessed two lit eyes in pitch-blackness.

Still left in a trance-like state, he walked toward the dark bathroom and as soon as he entered the bathroom, he vanished into the pitch-blackness.

Over the beat of heavy rain, Rotten caught a glimpse of a moving figure in the corner of his eye. He turned toward the curtain of rain that ran down the side of the bridge like an infinity fall. He scanned the streets; and once he saw nobody in sight, he walked down a slope that led toward the bridge. Rotten arrived at the wall of rain below the overhang of the bridge. The rain was so thick that he could hardly see on the other side. He took a deep breath before stepping through the waterfall. Once Rotten was through, he searched underneath the bridge; and it was only when Rotten focused on the shadows that he realized he wasn't alone.

As Rotten stared at the shadows on the other end of the bridge, the shadows suddenly came alive and out stepped a shadowy figure.

"I thought we had an agreement about contacting me—"

"There's a mole in the FBI," Rotten said to Blot.

"What makes you so sure?" asked Blot, as he stayed in the shadows.

"The explosion in Mercy wasn't caused by a drunk driver," Rotten said.

Blot pulled out an eCig from his pocket and took a small drag, causing his face to temporary light up with a bluish pale glow, which revealed Assistant Director Jin Forsake.

"I take it you recovered the template without drawing too much attention."

"Yes, but someone in your agency is covering up JeneCorp's tracks. My guess: it stems all the way to Craley. He can't be trusted—"

"Craley is doing everything in his power to hold Lockhart's feet to the fire."

"From the public's perspective, it certainly doesn't look that way—"

"What am I really doing here, Barney?" asked Forsake.

"To warn you," he said.

"Is that what your little friend there told you?" Blot said, pointing the eCig toward Rotten's wrist.

"JeneCorp is working on a machine that's going to change the world forever," he said.

"What kind of machine?" asked Blot.

"As of now, I don't know exactly. But I think it involves Chloe—"

"If they find a way to unleash her powers onto the world, the world as we know it will be no more. That kind of technology is decades away—"

"How do you think I contacted you, Jin," Rotten said impatiently.

"You called me."

"The shadows don't lie. . . "

"But the ghost does—"

"How did I contact you, Jin," Rotten asked.

"I saw you from my desk. . . awaiting in the darkness. . . "

"No," Rotten said. "Before the shadowrun. . . "

Blot drifted off, recalling the past events before he used the shadows to travel to Eden.

In his recollection, he saw an image of a brilliant white flash.

The flash came from the phone on his desk.

Then, following the flash was a sound.

A resonant hum-like noise.

He picked up the phone.

And then, as he drew his eyes toward the screen, he lost himself inside the Void.

"You're using *her* power, aren't you?" asked Blot.

The gori?

"*Bingo*," Rotten said, mocking Blot. "Now, Mr. Blot, imagine this very power in the hands of people like Tahr Rouse. Just think about all of the destruction he will cause."

"Rouse doesn't have much longer to live," Blot said. "The man's sick. He's replaceable."

"And what makes you think whoever replaces Rouse will be any different?" Rotten stepped forward, closer to Blot. "Something is coming, Jin, and you have to ask yourself: What are you willing to sacrifice to bring down JeneCorp?"

"I have a dark horse who's building a story that will cripple JeneCorp," Blot said.

Rotten asked, "Who exactly is this dark horse?"

RE-LIABLE SOURCES
OCTOBER 26, 2048
ELVIRA, CALIFORNIA

GIG Tapé knew Roberto Calle like a brother, so he claimed to Stella, who agreed to meet the car mechanic in secret along the abandoned West Front Pier.

The two grew up in Elvira, so Mr. Tapé claimed. The two shared many memories together, mostly the kind of drunken memories, which had been chewed up and spat out in fragments due to the effects of alcohol. Even confirmed these claims by showing Stella photographs of the two together. Most recent one being the week before a shooter attempted to assassinate the President of the United States. Gig and Roberto hanging out at a cantina, The Prickly Cactus. In the photo Gig and Roberto were sitting at the bar, seated side-by-side, Roberto taking full advantage of his retirement from Border Patrol, throwing back a shot of Tequila while Gig raised his glass brimming with cerveza. If photos weren't enough to prove to the investigative journalist turned reporter turned hired pen, Mr. Tapé showed Stella the staple-sized scar along the upper part of his right brow from where Roberto accidentally kicked him with a chapped soccer ball when the two were kids. He claimed that if it weren't for his hermano, Roberto, who, being the quick thinker he was, used a string of floss, unscented, the cheap kind, and a clothespin to stitch the laceration close, then he would've bled out.

Stella knew a man couldn't bleed out from a cut to the head and Mr. Tapé was simply exaggerating, but she understood his point: Gig and Roberto were close, and the two stayed close all the way up till Roberto's death.

After talking exclusively with Mr. Tapé late into the night, Stella left the conversation feeling sick to her stomach. With a rare likelihood of seeking justice for Roberto's death, Mr. Tapé had trusted Stella enough to hand over a video snippet that he screen-captured on his phone before it was taken down from The Feed.

In the video post, Roberto was speaking directly to his handful of followers, informing these followers of a strange man looming outside his house. The video was posted just hours after he spoke with the reporter (Stella) from the Channel 5 News about witnessing the potential suspect in the shooting of President Lockhart.

As Roberto peeked outside the front living room window, he was able to capture a brief shot of the stranger outside. The only distinguishable features of the blurry man were the scars on the right side of his face, the unusual glare coming from only his right eye, which was perhaps wall-eyed based on its relation with his other eye, and then, finally, his left hand.

As soon as she found a clearer image of the stranger, she paused the video. He was standing between two dead shrubs and appeared to be making his way around the side of the house, toward the garage, the bottom part of his face, as well as his entire body concealed by black attire. Stella zoomed in on his black-gloved hand, and based off its limp and flattened state, one of his fingers, the pinkie finger, appeared to be missing.

Stella spent hours on end combing The Feed for a man who matched the description of the man seen outside Roberto's home but had no luck.

Roberto stated that the strange man planned to kill him.

What gave Roberto that impression?

The video didn't state.

However, the video highlighted the imminent danger.

According to Roberto's current paranoid state during the time of the filming, it was clear to Stella that he feared for his safety and that someone was, based off a tremble in his voice, out to end his life, "silence him for good," for what he witnessed earlier that day. And if anyone knew about being silenced, it was Stella.

Mr. Tapé made it abundantly clear to Stella that he hadn't shown the video to anyone.

But Stella needed more proof.

Later that night, it was handed to her on a silver platter; or in Stella's case, a cocktail napkin with the word *cassava* written in a dried-out blue pen. The back half of the word was written in a faded blue etching.

Stella moved her eyes upward toward the bartender, who shot a glance at the familiar-faced man sitting at the end of the bar.

"Julian?"

After the initial surprise wore off, Stella grabbed the cocktail napkin, stood up from the bar, and followed her former boss, Julian Waters, to a dimly lit booth in the back of the restaurant.

"What's going on?" asked Stella.

"Have a seat," Julian said, paranoid.

Stella held up the napkin.

"What is this?"

Julian pointed to the seat across from him, insisting that she take a seat.

While carefully looking over Julian, Stella decided to sit down.

Before the two caught up on old times, Julian asked, "Are you ghost?"

Stella pulled out her phone, which was turned off, and placed it on the table.

"Who do you think you're talking to?" asked Stella.

"Apologies," he said. "I just wanted to be sure." He looked over Stella, as though he hadn't seen her in ages when, in fact, it had only been just under two months since she was fired. "It's been a minute, has it not?"

"Julian, what's going—"

"Listen, Stella, before I fill you in, I just want to tell you how sorry I am for the way things ended between us. No hard feelings?"

"What goes around comes around," Stella said with resentment.

Julian sighed again, as he had been doing throughout their reunion.

"If I had to do it over again, Stella, I would've stood up to Corporate and told them not to let the door hit their ass on the way out. But the truth is I'm not you, Stella. I don't have the stomach like you."

"Heard they dropped the hammer on you pretty hard. What was it? Prostitutes?"

An awkward pause developed over the conversation.

"Jules," Stella said, leaning closer, "Is it true?"

"Sadly, yes," he said. "But those photos were taken ages ago. A few years back, they resurfaced. Some hacker got his hands on them and tried to blackmail me through a ransomware—"

"You're not talking about what happened in '40 with the lay-offs, are you?"

"The fucker was going to destroy us."

"You mean destroy *you*. How could you, Julian? Think about what happened to Eddy—"

"Don't you dare bring up that man's name," Julian said, his voice laced with anger. "He had his demons and I take no responsibility for his actions."

Studying Julian's face and the redness in his eyes, Stella dropped the subject.

"I assume Shelby didn't take it lightly."

Julian downed the rest of his drink.

"She's already filed for a divorce."

"And what about Jack and Harriet?"

"They're staying with Shelby until we can work something out."

"Sorry."

"Are you?"

Stella shook her head in disgust, threw up her hands, and attempted to leave the booth.

"Please, Stella," Julian said and reached out, "forgive me. Just hear what I have to say. . . ."

Stella gave Julian one more chance, and she told herself, if he copped an attitude with her, she was out.

"There's no other way of putting it," he said, his voice much calmer. "It was a smear campaign—"

"And it's all my fault?"

"I didn't say it was."

"Sure as hell sounds like it."

"Listen, Stella," Julian said patiently, "you were just doing your job."

Stella slid the napkin across the table.

"Cassa—"

Julian suddenly held up his hand, indicating Stella to lower her tone.

He said more quietly, "The moment I first saw you at the bar I realized you weren't back in town to catch up on old times. You working on a story, aren't you? *The* story?"

Before Stella could answer, Julian waved his hand.

"Forget that I asked," he said. "I can't tell you how many times I've seen that look on your face and I know when I see that look, as I'm seeing it right now, it's best that I step out of your way." He leaned in closer to Stella, "From what I can tell, it's big. Isn't it?"

Stella cracked a smile.

"You can read me like a book."

"And that's why we made a good team. There was a balance between us."

"Listen, Jules—"

"I think I might have what you're looking for," Julian said over Stella.

Stella glanced down at the napkin.

With her emotions restrained, Stella asked quietly, "Does it involve Roberto Calle?"

"Mr. Calle is only the tip of the iceberg."

Stella asked, "Your source?"

"I can get you someone who's spoken with a former employee of JeneCorp," Julian said to Stella. "His name is Vinny Pronto, people call him 'Rags.' Pronto served time with Ian Dever, a Vet who's currently serving a ten-year sentence at Ashburton Penitentiary after he put some guy in the hospital. And based on his age, it's likely that he dies in prison, which is, in all probability, why JeneCorp isn't too concerned about Dever spilling all their secrets. Although, I should warn you, Stella, before you go any further: You must know if Pronto's story about Dever gets out, JeneCorp will try to destroy you again and this time, they may succeed."

"When has a story ever prevented me from doing my job?" asked Stella.

"That's what worries me about this one in particular, Stella. These are dangerous people."

"So," she ignored Julian's concern, "what'd you got for me?"

Julian looked around the restaurant before leaving his seat. He told Stella to scoot over and he sat next to her.

"According to Pronto, who was released last year after doing a stretch for armed robbery, he said that Dever told him JeneCorp was involved in the 2046 Blackouts. Apparently before Dever was arrested, Dever briefly worked as a security guard for JeneCorp but was let go by JeneCorp some time ago after getting caught playing 'Who's Your Daddy?' with one of his coworkers. He still kept in contact with some of the guards at JeneCorp, who, after a night out of partying with Dever, revealed some damaging information that could bring down JeneCorp. According to Dever's pals, the blackouts were deliberate—'staged,' he said. You first create a narrative that highlights a problem when, in fact, there's no problem—in this case, the energy crisis—and then, you rely on the government to fix the problem. All of it was a front to keep their man in office. Lockhart swoops down like the Man of Steel, shows the public his resolve by applying pressure to JeneCorp and all of a sudden, the lights are turned back on. It was all in coordination to help him win back voters who had lost confidence in him."

"But shortly after the blackouts, his poll numbers hit rock bottom."

"Polls are like the stock market," Julian said, causing Stella to roll her eyes at the poor analogy. "And where are the polls now?"

Stella said under her breath, "I take it the assassination attempt helped out Lockhart in those regards. Plus," she added, "how he handled the cell phone tower attack in Lawson County—"

"America loves a man who can take a bullet, but you know what Americans despise?"

Stella didn't answer.

"A man whose packed tightly inside the pocket of a multinational empire that has its thumb on the country's light switch, and I reckon JeneCorp will do anything to keep him in office, even if it means silencing those who attempt to take away their power. It's a blatant power grab."

Shaking her head, Stella said, "It's circumstantial. In some way or another, everybody suspected Lockhart had a hand in the blackouts. That narrative is already out there—"

"Maybe you're right, Stella, in some way or another," he said, holding down his head, "and that's what scares the hell out of me."

"What? That some people are finally waking up?"

"*Some* people, not everybody."

"People need to know what's going on."

"Do you honestly think people care about what's really going on?"

Stella leaned forward, peeking into Julian's range of vision.

"What proof does this Pronto guy have?"

Julian tapped his finger on the napkin.

Stella looked down at the *word* handwritten on the napkin. She asked, "What's it mean?"

Julian nodded at Stella's phone on the table.

"See for yourself."

"You sure?"

Julian nodded.

Cautiously, Stella turned on the phone while Julian told her, as though in code, about a floral store in the area, which had a variety of lovely flowers that might interest Stella. The store was known to make some of the most beautiful bouquets—one would be perfect for Stella's mother, who was still recovering back in Virginia.

Without speaking it, Stella picked up on what Julian was trying to convey to her. She typed in the word *cassava* into The Feed. As the results popped up, Julian motioned his index finger up three times, signaling for Stella to scroll up the page. As soon as she arrived at the post that Julian wanted her to see, he balled his hand into a fist, indicating for Stella to stop scrolling. The post: A photo of *Cassava* Floral Arrangements on Rath Street, which was taken by a tourist from Wisconsin, who was visiting the Elvira area.

Another post revealed that the tourist was in town for Lockhart's speech.

Back to the photo, which was taken outside Cassava: The photo showed the front store window of the store, as well as a showy sign above.

Stella researched the tourist's background: His name Rocco Bolivia, a graphic designer who was a former soldier in the United States Army. Bolivia fought in the Iraq War; and apparently, based on his other posts, after he returned home from what would be his final tour, Bolivia found a niche for fonts and typefaces, especially ones used in store façades, billboard signs, and advertisements. She scrolled through over a dozen photographs of signs of local businesses: *"Mama's Deli," "Shane Shank Shack," "Coral's Wreaths," "Painter's Paradise," "Shock-A-Rock."* However, of all these photographs, there was something odd about *"Cassava."*

"I heard pink roses are popular around this time," Julian hinted to Stella. "They may make for a nice gift for your mother."

Carefully, Julian motioned his fingers at Stella by pinching both his thumb and index finger together, then spreading them outward. Stella, following Julian's instructions, zoomed in on the photo and while doing so, caught the reflection in the store window, in front of a display case of "pink roses."

In the reflection a man, out of frame, was seen walking toward Rocco. His face positioned exactly where the pink roses were located. The words *pink* and *roses* drawing Stella's eyes away from the man's left hand, which appeared distorted.

While solely focusing on the left side of the man's face, which matched the same face from the still in Mr. Tapé's video, Stella pinched her fingers over the screen, thus zooming out.

"Have you seen this man before?" asked Julian.

Stella immediately captured a screen grab of the photo before the post was more than likely taken off The Feed.

Dumbfounded, Stella turned to Julian, who, after acknowledging the fascination on her face, told her that her phone was dying when, in fact, she had over half-a-charge left on the battery.

Stella turned off the phone, back to ghost.

"How'd you find that photo?" asked Stella.

"His face doesn't ring a bell, does it?"

Unsure whether or not to confess, she said to Julian, "Maybe. So, how'd you find it?"

"You wouldn't believe if I told me."

"At this point," Stella said, "I'll believe anything."

"Her name was Airy, short for Arielle."

"And was she one of your regulars. . . "

"No," Julian said but quickly corrected himself, "I mean yes, but like I said, ages ago. But it doesn't matter. The day after the assassination attempt I get this message from Airy, saying how she misses me and that she wants to hang out sometime. She says she has a birthday coming up and she sends me a link to Cassava's website, hinting that she wants me to buy her some flowers. 'Pink roses,' she emphasizes. Ever since I've known Airy, she's hated flowers."

"All women love flowers."

"Not Airy. She hated the smell or whatever," Julian said and trailed off. "So, immediately I know she's either messing with me or throwing me a bone. Sure enough, the next day, I find the photo while searching The Feed. I find the pink roses. I find the face. *His* face. Given the blurriness of the photo, more than likely, it's undetectable by any facial recognition software. Probably why it hasn't been taken down yet."

"What's the connection?" asked Stella.

"He was the same man who showed up at the studio—"

"FBI?"

Stella recalled the moments when she returned from the studio after talking with Mr. Calle: all those men in suits, ordering the News Team to shut down the story. She didn't recall seeing a man who looked like the one in the reflection of the floral store window or the face in Calle's video; however, she recalled the feeling that she felt when those suits barged into the studio. Never had she been so frightened in her life. The fear had a way of blurring important details.

Julian's laughs pulled Stella from her thoughts.

He asked comically, *"Did they look like FBI to you?"*

"No," Stella, who could spot a phony badge when she saw one, said to Julian.

"The following week a witness, Mary Flores, who read about your report before it was taken down, contacted the studio and asked to speak with you. I had already let you go, so I decided to pay a visit to Mrs. Flores. She said she saw a man prowling around Mr. Calle's house the night he killed himself. I showed Bolivia's photo to Mrs. Flores and sure enough, she matched the two faces. The face from the window reflection and the face she saw outside Mr. Calle's. The next day, Mrs. Flores died from a heart attack. 'Natural causes,' her daughter told me."

"What about Airy?" asked Stella. "Did you ask her how she found the photo?"

"I would, if I could."

"How do you mean?"

Julian said, "Airy died four months ago. Overdose, from what I read."

"If Airy didn't lead you to the photo, then who in the hell did?"

Julian was equally as dumbfounded as Stella.

Studying Stella's face, he said carefully, "I take it you've already talked with Gig Tapé."

Stella asked, "How the hell do you know about Tapé?"

"Please," he said innocently. "Who do you think you're talking to here?"

"He has this video showing what looks like the same guy from the flower photo. Have you seen it? The video?"

"No," he said abruptly and pulled his eyes from Stella's. "And I don't want to."

"You showed me yours," Stella said playfully, as she leaned in closer to Julian. "Now I can show you mine. Only fair."

"I trust your judgment."

"Tapé told me I was the only person who's seen the video."

"Understandable, considering the people who are after it. . . "

"If not the FBI, then who? JeneCorp?"

"Stella," Julian said closely, "if Calle was right about what he saw, then we're sitting on one of the most elaborate cover-ups in American history."

"We?"

"We could partner up, like we did back in the day."

Confused, Stella furrowed her brow.

"How'd you know about Tapé?" she asked, suspiciously looking over Julian.

"How do I know about him?" Julian repeated, as his voice was lowered to a soft whisper. "I know about him because you're Stella Nilsson, and I know your ass wouldn't be back in Elvira if you didn't have a lead and the way I see it, the only leads are the ones close to Roberto Calle and as you've said, the video Calle took before he was *murdered*, in my opinion, that's your smoking gun."

Not exactly the answer Stella wanted, but she'd take it.

Stella asked, "How do you know what's on the video?"

"If you say the man in that video is the same man from Bolivia's photo, then I believe you." More thoughtfully, Julian said over the heavy silence, "Although, there's one more thing, and it revolves around the mystery men who visited the studio. That one man in particular."

Furrowing her brow, Stella said, "You know who he is, don't you?"

"All I have is a name," Julian said. "Noble. While you were away—"

"You fired me, Jules!"

Julian held up his hand, telling Stella to lower her voice.

"After speaking with Pronto I paid a visit to the parents of Manny Quinn, a marine who died in combat while doing his second tour in Iraq. They were generous enough to show me a photo of their son and his unit. Ian Dever was part of the unit. The two, according to Manny's parents, were close and apparently, Dever kept in contact with them. I also saw another face in the photo, and as soon as I laid my eyes on that face, I immediately recognized him. Manny's parents said that they didn't know much about Noble, only that he served with their son when he was dishonorably discharged before the US withdrew from Iraq. I did my research on Noble and found out that he was suffering from mental illness."

"Is he working alone?" asked Stella.

"I highly doubt it."

"By any chance, you wouldn't have a photo of this Noble fellow. Would you?"

Julian said to Stella, "Follow me."

Stella ended up following Julian back to his two-bedroom apartment where he was currently staying while he finalized the divorce with his soon-to-be ex-wife, Shelby. He reached inside the empty battery case of a flashlight located on the top shelf of the kitchen cabinet and pulled out a USB flash drive, prompting a comment from Stella, saying how she hadn't seen one of those (the flash drive) in ages. He brought the flash drive to what looked like a relic of a desktop computer, which was twenty-five old years to be exact. Most of the newer models didn't have USB ports, and, in a way, it made Julian's computer a rarity, which he adored. He inserted the drive into the port in the back of the computer and using the mouse, ran the cursor over a folder labeled "POPEYE."

Stella leaned over Julian's shoulder and read the name of the folder.

"*Popeye?*" said Stella, her voice curved like a question mark.

Julian waved off the name.

"Inside joke," he said and double-clicked on the folder.

Inside were photos that Julian had taken of Manny's unit, after the former marine's mother granted him permission. One of the photos in particular was a close-up shot of the marine, Lance Corporal Noble with no scars. He said Noble was twenty years old during the time of the photo, which was taken in 2008.

Stella asked Julian, "How'd he get the scars?"

Julian said, "Beats me. It definitely wasn't from the War in Iraq, though."

Intrigued, Stella asked, "What makes you so sure?"

"I found a photo of him after he returned home," Julian said plainly. "No scars."

"Is he married? Does he have any kids? How about relatives?"

All in correct order, Julian answered, "No, no (?), and no. However, he dated a girl named Loli who lived in Dellarango. She had a child back in 2012. She said she didn't know who the father was."

"Sounds like you did a lot of the legwork for me," she said, surprised. Then, asked, "Why?"

"Reputation, Stella," he said. "You've worked in this industry long enough to know reputation is everything. And it's time to restore my reputation. Both of ours."

Appreciative of Julian and everything he had done for her, despite what he was forced to do after the Robert Calle report, Stella asked Julian, "Why didn't you tell me all of this sooner?"

Julian thought briefly and said, "I was worried about your safety."

"Bullshit," Stella snapped.

Julian removed the flash drive from the back of the computer, squared himself to Stella, and said bluntly, "If you continued to pursue Calle, these people. . . well, do I need to spell it out for you, Stella? You saw what happened to Calle. . . "

"Then, why pursue Noble?" asked Stella.

"You win," Julian said in defeat. "I can try talking you out this till I'm blue in the face, but I know your stubborn ass too well. *But* please, if you would indulge me, Stella. Is the story worth risking your life?"

"If it means telling the people about what really happened," Stella said carefully, "then yes. It most certainly is—"

"You could be in Virginia right now—"

"But I'm not, am I?"

"Taking care of your mother."

Stella sharpened her eyes.

"Leave her out of this."

Julian held up his hands in surrender.

"All I ask is why?"

Hesitant about whether or not to speak his name to Julian, she said, "I have a contact on the inside. He's turned out to be a credible source."

"Who?"

"I don't exactly know his name, but he calls himself *Blot.*"

Julian chuckled at the nickname.

"Your contact is from some guy who got his name from a 1998 porno film?" Julian smirked at Stella and said, "Fitting."

"So, about Vinny Pronto, can you set me up with him?"

Julian looked Stella over and said, "I think I can arrange a meeting."

"Don't think," she said and poked her finger into Julian's gut, causing him to squirm. "Do."

"Who's the boss?"

"Clearly," she said, smirking. "Not you. Not anymore."

"Is that so?"

"Curious," Stella said. "What does Pronto get out of all of this?"

"He said he saw in the news about what they did to me. He claims JeneCorp was behind the smear campaign, wanted to get back at them."

"So, it's personal?"

"Absolutely."

Stella asked, "How about his protection?"

"He's currently staying in a motel under a disguised face and name. He's safe," Julian said with a shrug, "at least, for now."

After the conversation with Julian, Stella left his apartment feeling more uneasy about pursuing JeneCorp. While making her way to her car, she kept a close eye on her surroundings, including her six o'clock, where most of her attention was directed; however, she failed to take the shadows into account.

As soon as she faced forward after sneaking a glance over her shoulder, Blot was standing in the shadows on the other side of her car!

Grabbing her chest, Stella gasped from his dark presence.

Startled, she said to the silhouette, "Can you stop doing that please?!?"

"Do you trust him?" asked Blot.

"Julian?" Stella said but didn't get a response from Blot. "Sure. We've worked together for years."

"He could be leading you into a trap," Blot said.

"Maybe," she said. "Or, maybe Pronto's recount about Dever is a gift and inside is a bombshell. If you think I'm not gonna chase down a good lead, then you don't know shit about me."

"Your friend is right about one thing. These people are dangerous."

"Dangerous, no doubt, but they're not ghosts," Stella said convincingly. "They exist, which means they can be held accountable. Bring 'em out into the light, remember?"

"Well, just make sure you don't find yourself on the wrong side of a séance."

"Are you saying I'm going to wind up like Renny Jacobson or Deputy Horton or those other people in Whisperfront? What the hell have you gotten me into—"

"All I'm saying is just be careful on this one," Blot said, stepping closer to the beam of light cast the floodlight. "Mr. Waters may be compromised."

Stella reached for her car keys.

"I appreciate your concern," she said and opened the car door.

"And Stella. . . "

Stella looked up at Blot, whose dark and beady eyes were pinned on her like a blade.

". . . Don't ever mention my name to anyone else again," Blot said grimly. "Otherwise, it'll be the very last words you'll ever speak."

Surprisingly, despite the previous back and forth, Stella believed every single word in Blot's threats.

And the notion alone caused her blood to run cold.

"Got it," Stella said unsteadily and entered the car.

Right before driving away, she glanced in the rear view mirror, only to see Blot himself sitting in the backseat, his dark silhouette cutting through her eyes.

Startled by his morbid presence, Stella suddenly switched on the overhead light, resulting in his silhouette to vanish into thin air.

She kept the light on for the remainder of the drive home.

FRENCH FRYE
OCTOBER 27, 2048
WASHINGTON, D.C.

INSIDE the FBI headquarters, the Office of Professional Reassessment held an emergency hearing with Special Agent Frye and Special Agent Laredo following Attorney General Richard Craley's demands for accountability in wake of what officials referred to as an "intentional attack" against a cell phone tower in Lawson County, which resulted in a widespread outage among the twenty-plus thousand residents.

Both Frye and Laredo, who were seated in the hot seat in front of the panel where among the six members was Assistant

Director Forsake, believed Wayne Curtis didn't carry out the attack all by himself.

Frye was first to state for the record that Curtis had help in destroying the cell phone tower, which led to the outage.

Leading the hearing was Director and Chief Counsel, Willow Sikes, who specifically asked Special Agent Frye, "You're referring to these boogeymen of yours? *Reborne?*"

"Correct, Director," Frye said hesitantly, as he glanced at Laredo.

"Here we go again," one of the members on the panel said under his breath.

Already left on-edge by the reassessment, Frye asked Sikes, "Permission to speak freely, Director?"

Below the table, Laredo kicked Frye in the shin, warning him to swallow his personal vendetta against Reborne.

Director Sikes allowed Frye the floor.

"How many times does one have to tell a lie in order to believe it as truth?" he asked, quoting an excerpt from *The Shepherd's Gambit*, book one from the series *The Crook and The Knife* by science-fiction author Timothee Chu.

Of all people on the OPR panel, Here-We-Go-Again, who despised Frye's misguided views, was about to respond to the question when Frye suddenly interjected: *"One,"* he said boldly. *"It only takes one time."*

Frustrated by Special Agent Frye's bravado, Director Sikes said superiorly, "Are you here to lecture, Special Agent? Or, are here to provide us with facts, *not* fantasy? Please, if you would, get to the point?"

"Based on the intel that we've recently gathered from an informant working on the inside at their main compound, Special Agent Laredo and I are positive that Reborne is planning another attack."

"What makes you so sure that Mr. Curtis was part of Reborne?" asked the Director. "Given a rather *spotless* background and a transparent social media presence, Mr. Curtis shows the hallmarks of a lone wolf and not one shred of evidence indicates him of 'tribing' up, as you call it."

"With all due respect, Director," said Frye, "maybe you don't understand what this domestic terrorist organization is capable of."

"And you do?"

"They are a *threat* to our national security—"

"There has been no sufficient evidence to suggest that Reborne is linked to any terrorist activity. From what I've gathered, they're a bunch of green hippie survivalists inspired by the anti-technology revolution that emerged from central Africa nearly two decades ago."

The Director's comment, whether true or not, provoked a tamed reaction from several members of the OPR panel, prompting Here-Wo-Go-Again to follow up carelessly: "And I'm sure, at the time, the complacent leaders of the DRC were saying the same exact thing about those Swag Cultists before all hell was unleashed, sparking one of the most violent coup d'états in history."

Forsake interrupted before Sikes and the others could further grill Frye, "I think you're failing to grasp the bigger picture here, Special Agent Frye. If you're right about Reborne, then it's in FBI's best interest that we continue to monitor their movements and so do vigilantly until we have confirmation that their intentions are malicious. We're not in a profession of hearsay, Special Agent Frye."

"According to this informant of yours. . . " Sikes said, reading from Frye's statement before glancing at the agent over the top of here bold black-rimmed glasses, ". . . Reborne's recruitment has substantially increased over the past month. Is that correct?"

"Based on my intel," he said, "yes. That's correct."

"And was Wayne Curtis among these recruits?" asked Sikes.

Frye said despairingly, "No, Director."

Laredo chimed in, "Mr. Curtis recently contacted Zachary Malldough, who is what Reborne referred to as an 'oldie' of the group, meaning one of their original founders, who, based on his past posts on The Feed, has not only shared anti-government sentiment, but has also shown the classic behaviors of a domestic terrorist."

"I appreciate your concern, Special Agent Laredo, but at this juncture in time, the Attorney General wants to make an example out of Mr. Curtis to prevent any further attacks from happening in the future—"

Frye then chimed in, "Reborne is planning a strategic attack against JeneCorp power substations in a coordinated effort to interfere with the next presidential election."

"Is this what your informant has relayed to you, Special Agent?"

Hesitating, Frye lied, "My informant made it abundantly clear that an attack was. . . "

Frye drifted off, as though his actions were rehearsed.

Sikes removed the glasses from her face.

"Special Agent?"

"Imminent," Frye said confidently.

Mindfully, Sikes said to the agent, "Can you give us a moment, Special Agent Frye?"

As Sikes turned to her other colleagues on either side of her, Frye opened a manila folder on the table and grabbed a photograph that he recently obtained from his so-called "informant."

He brought the photograph to Sikes and placed it in front of her.

"This photo was taken in early July by my informant," Frye said to Sikes, who lifted up the glasses back to her face "Two months before Elvira."

Sikes studied the photograph before passing it around the other members on the OPR.

In the grainy photograph, which was taken at a distance from a tree line surrounding the Reborne compound, Jared Flack was skinning rabbits with members of the Reborne community.

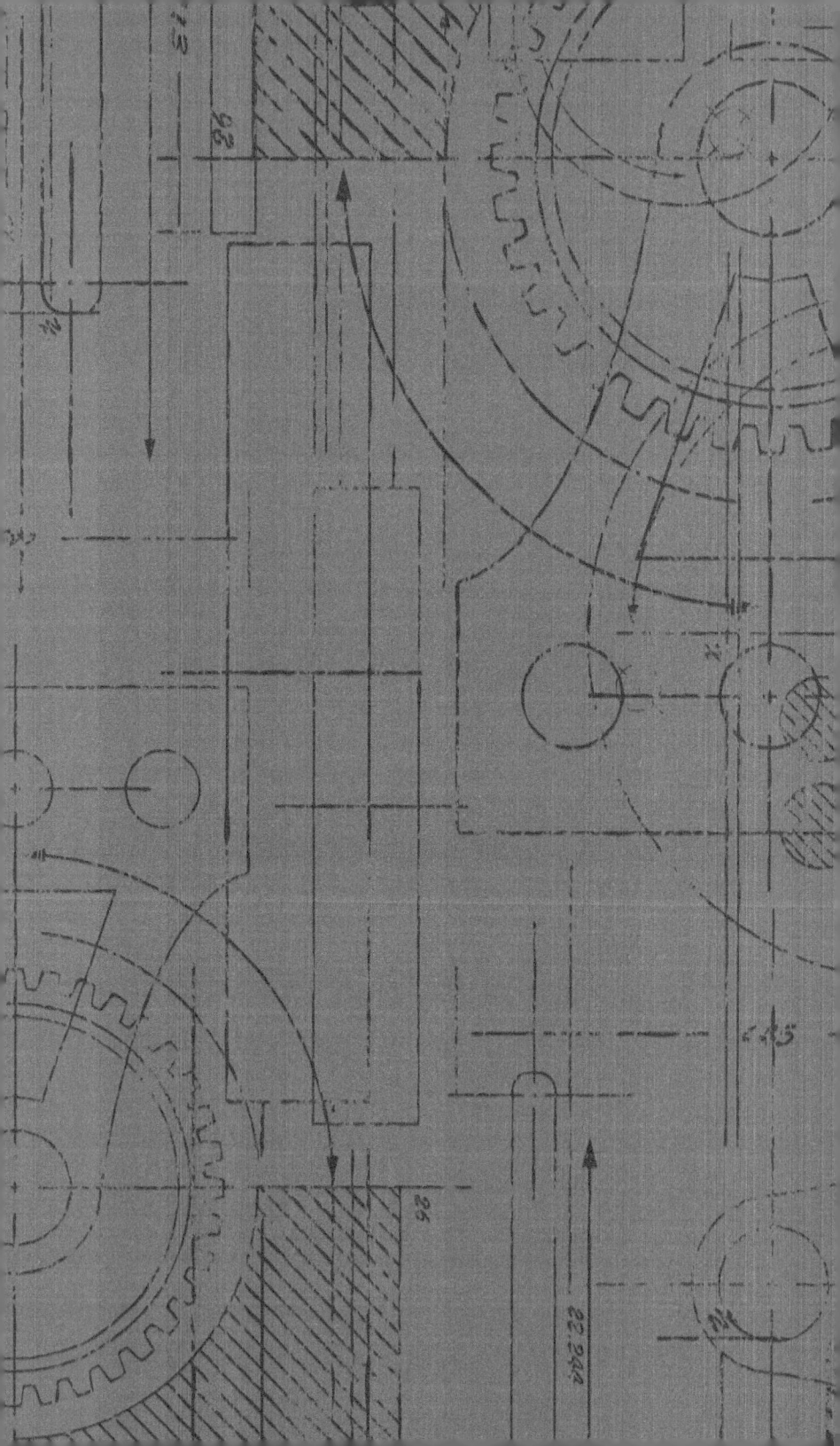

TEST SUBJECT #12

NOVEMBER 4, 2019
TOKYO, JAPAN

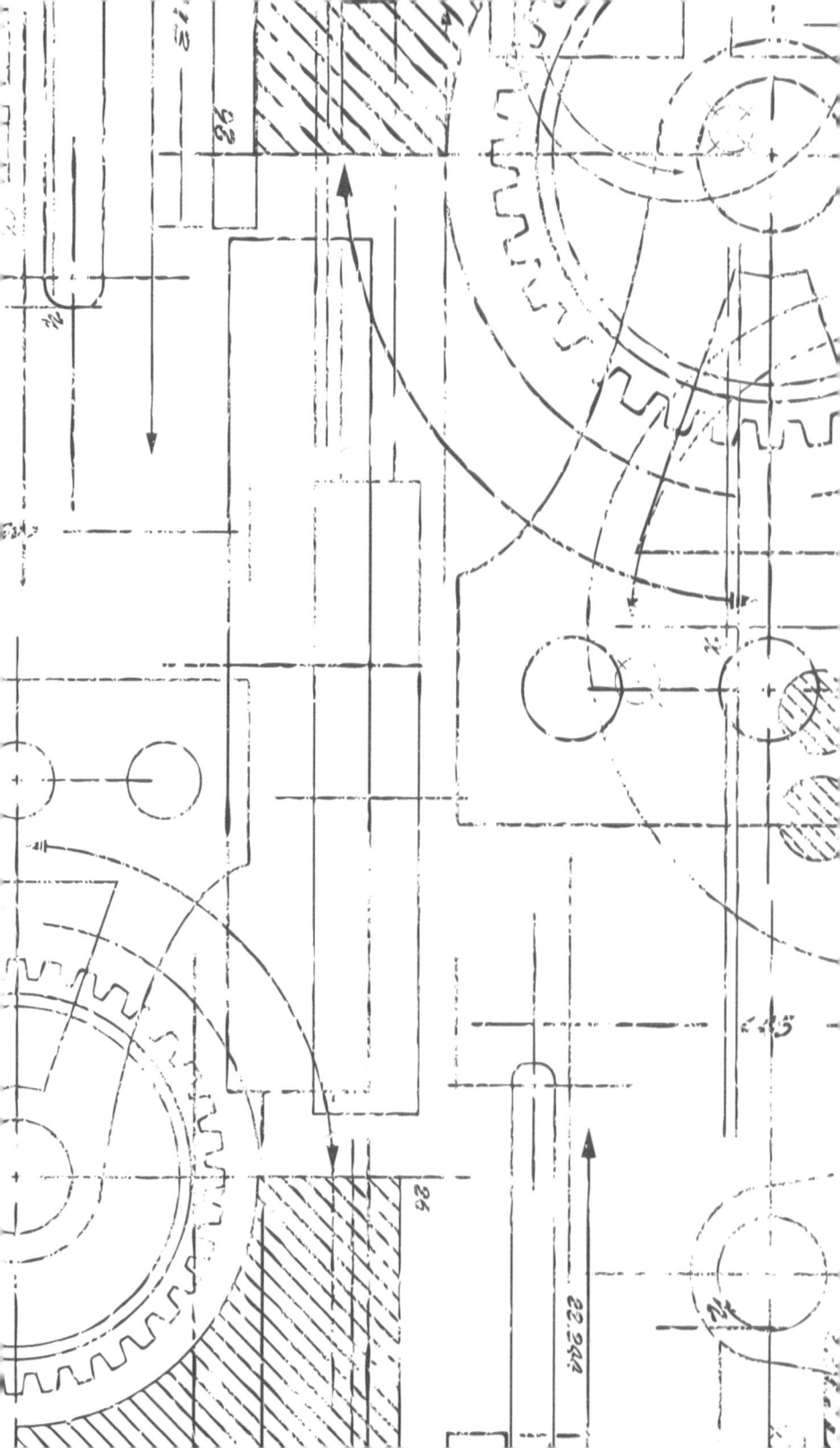

ONCE Reece properly fitted the final subject of the twelve test subjects with the temporary brain-computer interface, Ari received a firm and confident "thumbs up" from his partner.

"If you would," Ari said to the test subject, "blink your eyes twice to make sure the eye contacts are properly secured."

As Ari paid close attention to her eyes, the test subject blinked twice.

"Very good," he said.

Ari released the bundled-up nerves with a heavy sigh right before speaking into the camera, which was recording the twelfth trial run.

The door opened behind Ari, causing him to turn to Niles, who, after wrapping up a conversation with a couple of bigwigs from Neuvak, joined the rest of the team.

The sight of Niles talking to a bunch of suits behind his back stirred a mixture of emotions inside Ari and forced him to refocus on the task at hand.

Ari held up an index card for the camera:

Subject #12 – Georgina Brass

"Okay," Ari said, his voice trembling, "today's date is. . . "

The camera panned slightly toward the calendar:

NOVEMBER 4, 2019

After the shot of the date, the camera panned back toward Georgina.

"This is test subject #12, forty-nine year old, Georgina Brass, from Lakeview, Michigan," he said, shooting a glance at the monitor to his immediate right.

Displayed on the screen was Georgina's face, which was out of focus. He motioned to Yamato, who, following Ari's orders, zoomed out and carefully adjusted the lens of the camera until the blurry image appeared clearer. This time, Ari reciprocated with a "thumbs up."

"Ms. Georgina Brass, diagnosed with an early onset of glaucoma back in 2007, lost her eyesight nine years ago after receiving an experimental vaccine at the height of the influenza pandemic. Ms. Brass's case is incredibly unique in nature, considering the rarity of adverse reaction from the vaccine, and she has. . ." Ari grabbed a piece of paper from the desk and held it up for the camera, making sure to angle the bottom part of the paper for a clear, accurate shot of the test subject's *signature*, ". . . voluntarily signed the waiver form, which states that Neuvak or none of Neuvak's associates are liable if any injury should result from today's trial run. *But* I assure you, Ms. Brass," Ari placed his hand on top of Georgina's hand and reassured Georgina, who, in return, tightly squeezed his hand, redirecting and funneling all of that pent-up anger from living the past decade in darkness into her mighty grip, "you're in good hands. Now with that said. . ." Ari said, wincing as he struggled to release his hand from Georgina's death grip. Once he managed to release his hand, Ari touched Georgina on the shoulder. "Please relax, Georgina," he said in a more agitated tone. "You'll be fine—"

"Cap is plugged in," Reece said impatiently.

Ari said to Georgina, "Remember: Today's trial will determine whether or not you'll be approved as a candidate for the neural implant. If it makes you feel more at ease, think of the trial as test-driving a brand new car."

"Does it come with power steering?" Georgina asked, the sassiness acting as a shield to conceal her nervousness.

"Not exactly." Ari cracked a thin smile. "But our good pal Max here might be out of job."

He reached down and petted the chin of the Golden retriever, a service animal named Max, who was sitting by Georgina's side.

"Max may not approve."

Georgina's voice, like her brow, was slightly slanted.

"Sorry, Max," Ari said to the dog and leaned closer to Georgina. "Are you ready?"

Eventually, Georgina found the strength to nod her head in agreement.

"Ready," she said and took in a deep breath through her nose and out through her mouth.

After shooting Niles a glance across the room, Ari gave Reece the go-ahead to switch on the brain-computer interface, the first phase of a two-part phase, known as a temporary Splinter cap, which was covered in dozens of tiny LED lights. Four lights in the back of the cap switched on, glowing a pale blue color.

While standing at a distance, Niles grabbed hold of the canine of a coyote that he wore on a necklace and nervously massaged it as though it was good luck charm.

"You're going to feel a slight tingling sensation in the very back of your head," Ari said and guided Georgina through the process. "It's completely normal."

Another monitor showed a visual mapping of Georgina's brain.

As a set of four more lights in the back of the cap switched on, the primary visual cortex of Georgina's brain started to light up orange on another monitor, indicating "activity."

"We are now bypassing the damaged optic nerves and sending electric signals into the visual cortex, which will speak directly to the special smart contact lenses that you were wearing," Ari explained to Georgina.

All of a sudden, Georgina saw these flashes of light, as well as dark shapes outlined by colors in her range of vision, which caused her to let out a gasp.

The images alone nearly robbed the breath from her lungs.

"What was that?" cried Georgina.

"Did you see something?" asked Ari.

"Flashing lights—" she said, "—Figures. I can see figures. . ."

Ari touched Georgina on the shoulder, reassuring her that the flashing lights meant Splinter was working and established a line of communication from the cap to the contact lenses.

As Reece increased the stimulation of the areas around the primary visual cortex, Georgina's sight slowly began to restore, first tracing shapes and patterns and then, eventually, once the reflections dissipated, objects bloomed from the darkness and appeared before her.

The first object: A red cube that Ari held before Georgina's eyes.

"What am I holding up, Georgina?" asked Ari.

All traces of darkness completely faded from her vision.

The blur cleared, revealing a dark-skinned man holding up an object.

"A block," she said, struggling to control her emotions.

"Remember try not to cry, otherwise it may cloud your vision."

"Sorry," she said, sniffling.

"That's all right," Ari said, as he too tried to hold back the emotion. "Now, what color is the block?" he asked.

Georgina said, "Red. It's red. . . "

She could no longer control her emotions as Ari held up more objects, photographs, as well as a mirror. Georgina named each one with great elation until she arrived at the mirror.

The sight of Georgina staring back at her own reflection in the mirror caused her to breakdown in tears.

Ari said, "It worked—"

"I can't believe it," Yamato said.

"You did it," Reece said, laughing.

"No," Ari said. "We did it."

"Well done, my friend," Niles said with a blank expression before he exited the room.

After the breakthrough with Georgina Brass, Ari and the rest of his team were ready, in fact, days away from proceeding with the next phase in the trial, which was the surgical operation of a neural implant. In the meantime, they took the rest of the day off to celebrate the recent success, especially after the mounting setbacks over the past three weeks, including the failure to restore full mobility in test subject #10, the paraplegic Dan Mazanelli, who was involved in a skiing accident in Aspen last year, which left him paralyzed from the waist-down. The stakes were particularly high for Ari and company, given Mazanelli's long-standing history with Neuvak Pharmaceuticals, as well as his more than charitable contributions to a handful of Top 10 tech companies in Silicon Valley. Somehow, Niles, who, despite his software and coding skills, handled more of the business side of Ari's creation, managed to smooth talk his way into the good graces of Neuvak.

The only person missing from the celebration was none other than the smooth talker himself, Niles Baldwin.

Later that night, as the celebrations dwindled through the dim corridors of the office, which overlooked a neon-washed Tokyo, Ari stayed behind and put away all of the gear while the rest of the team decided to call it a night.

Yamato, who, besides Ari, was last to exit, crept up behind Ari. His presence alone startled the former game developer-turned-miracle-man, causing him to flinch.

Pulled from his deep thoughts, most of them centered around Niles and his strange behavior as of lately, Ari said, "Can I help you, Yamato?"

Yamato asked, "How does it feel knowing that you potentially saved millions of lives?"

"Don't get so ahead of yourself, Yamato," said Ari. "This is just one of many steps—"

"But it is a remarkable achievement," he said. "How are you feeling?"

Ari sighed.

"Well," he said hesitantly, "to be honest, for a split second, I felt like I was seventeen years old again."

"Beats algorithms and augmentation, huh?"

"Damn straight."

"I can't even remember what I was doing at seventeen years old—"

"Why are you still here, Yamato? Isn't it past your bedtime?"

"I should be asking you the same thing, Ari."

The air in his throat clogged, leaving behind a trail of despair behind his words.

Ari could almost read Yamato's mind.

He said softly, "You saw them as well, didn't you?"

"What's that?"

"The vultures swirling overhead."

"You don't trust them, do you?"

"Do you trust sleeping with a cobra in your bed?" asked Ari.

"Sounds like I wasn't the only one," Yamato said. "Reece brought up their names while he was getting shit-faced. I swear he'll open up like a book from the faintest whiff of alcohol." His brows curled with both curiosity and confusion. "What do you think they wanted?"

Ari asked, "What did Reece say about them?"

"He thinks they're going to pull the plug on the project."

"What gives him that idea?"

"If I had to guess. . . " Yamato said and briefly paused in thought, ". . . Phoenix's presence. What would a former member of NGHT ('Night') be doing with the heads of Neuvak?" His lips curled into a half-grin. "Reece says Phoenix's old man is friends with one of the heads. Got him a spot on Neuvak after NGHT was disbanded."

"Reece doesn't know what the hell he's talking about."

"I suppose it's the alcohol talking."

"Perhaps."

"Then, what?"

"It's pretty obvious, Yamato," Ari said. "They want full control over U.C."

"What do they want with Splinter?" asked Yamato.

"I don't know," Ari said, trailing off.

Ari was, in fact, aware of the many outcomes if U.C. should wind up in the wrong hands—or at least, speculated what could be accomplished, none of them promising for the greater good of humanity, if Neuvak seized control over the project, his baby, universal_computer (U.C.).

Shrugging off all of the potential disasters from his own creation, he finished his thought by clearly speaking it to Yamato: "And that's what keeps me up at night. . . "

"Well," Yamato said and gathered the rest of his belongings, "*not* tonight. Try to get some sleep." Then, he teased, "All geniuses need their beauty sleep. I read that Albert Einstein was a fan of sleep. I read that he caught at least ten hours every night."

"Ten hours, huh?"

Yamato innocently shrugged.

"That's what I read."

"I'd kill for ten minutes of sleep," Ari said.

Yamato pointed his finger at Ari as though he was ready to wag it.

"Go to bed, Ari Bhatt," he demanded.

"As you wish, *Doctor*," Ari teased back and watched Yamato exit from the building.

In a state of reflection, Ari walked to his desk, opened the bottom drawer, and pulled out the original pair of goggles that he used during his universal_computer experiments. Clunky, boxy shaped goggles similar to a VR headset, which were used to trick the user's perception of reality.

Ari decided to take up Yamato's advice and called it a night. On the way back to his apartment, Ari caught the glowing bar sign in the corner of his eye. He walked down a seedy alley as tight and narrow as a dorm hallway until he arrived at the bar, Niles's go-to bar, Third Street Ale House.

Only a few patrons were seated at the bar.

No surprise, Ari found the one person who had been absent, both mentally and physically, throughout the day.

"Niles. . . " Ari said and pointed at the empty stool next to Niles, ". . . may I?"

With a slur in his voice, Niles said, "Be my guest. . . "

His eyes were bloodshot red.

Ari couldn't tell how long he had been drinking, but he knew Niles was beyond his limit.

Despite the surprise appearance, Niles could care less about Ari's presence for his eyes playfully shot back and forth across the bar and engaged in a game of eye-tag with an attractive Japanese woman in her late twenties seated alone in a dark booth.

Ari followed Niles's red, cloudy eyes toward the booth.

"Friend of yours?" asked Ari.

"Nah," he drawled. "Just soaking up the exotic wild life—"

"I knew I'd find you in here," Ari said and ordered a gin and tonic from the bartender. "So," his voice was serious, "who died?"

Niles obnoxiously laughed off Ari's question.

"Hilarious," he said, shooting a sideways glare at Ari. "You never pegged me as the comedic type."

"You good, Niles?" asked Ari, more concerned. Mindful to use his words wisely, he studied Niles's disheveled state, as well as the whiskey drink in his hand, and said carefully, "Shouldn't you go easy with that stuff, especially after what happened a couple of weeks ago?"

With the slur cut with a mild bark, he said defensively, "Don't tell me how to live my life, and I won't tell you how to live yours. Got it?"

"Yeah, sure," Ari said, holding his hands up in surrender. "I definitely got it—"

"Besides, how many times do I have to tell you people? There's not a goddamn thing wrong with me. The doctor said so himself. And if a doctor says I'm *good*, then I'm *good*. Got it?"

"Fair enough," Ari said in defeat and sipped from his gin and tonic.

He was in no mood to argue with Niles and his health issues, the recent one being the health scare, which resulted in Niles being hospitalized. The classic symptoms of a heart attack: tightness in his chest, shortness of breath, overwhelming feelings of an impeding doom. These, however, were also the symptoms of an anxiety attack, which was what cardiologist, Dr. Tanaka, said to be one of the best cardiologists in Tokyo, believed to be Niles's diagnosis after he performed a cardiac catheterization. In fact, Dr. Tanaka stated that Niles's heart was strong, best he'd seen in any of his patients—"no blockage," despite what a young, inexperienced ER doctor claimed after misreading Niles's EKG after he was wheeled in on the slab.

In the tense silence, Niles observed the concern on Ari's face, as ripened as a fruit.

The high that he experienced earlier in the day had nowhere else to go but straight down.

The faster you rise, the harder you fall.

"Did I tell you they gave me three days to live?" said Niles.

His voice was mellowed.

"No." Ari raised his head from its hung position. "You didn't. But they were wrong."

Niles made a noise with his mouth.

He threw back the rest of the drink and ordered another one.

Ari said, "Can't imagine what was going through that beautiful head of yours."

Niles cracked a smile, as brief as a blink.

"I thought about all the shit I've missed out in life," he said in reflection. "Thought about all the shit I was going to do after I was released. An entire bucket list that stretched from here," he said, nodding at the bar and then flicking his eyes toward the mysterious svelte Japanese woman seated in the booth, "to Ms. Maneater over there. Only moments after the Heart Doc said I was all good and that I was good to go, all those thoughts, that list, it all just disappeared."

"Curious," Ari said, intrigued, "what were some of things on the list?"

Making yet another airy noise with his mouth, Niles waved off Ari's question.

"Come on," Ari said, verbally prodding at Niles, "name just one."

"One?"

"Just one." Niles named the first "thing" on his list that came to mind: "Antarctica," he said. "I've always wanted to see the glaciers, but—"

"But Vicky isn't the traveling type?"

"That's for the damn sure," he said. "Woman hates leaving the house."

"Not a social bug?"

"More like a house cat," Niles said. "But don't tell her I said that."

"Of course," Ari said over the more comfortable silence.

Niles's previous story, not the bucket list, but the events surrounding another more disturbing story, weighed on Ari's mind. The opportunity suddenly presented itself.

"Listen, Niles. . . " Ari said, preparing himself for Niles's response, ". . . it's not my place to ask, but given your recent health scare, I think I deserve the right to know—"

With a drunken expression drooping over his face like loose deli meat, Niles said bluntly, "I wasn't abducted by aliens, you bonehead."

Yamato Tomato, Ari thought.

Now, bonehead.

Why all of a sudden the nicknames?

Ari brushed off the insult and asked Niles, "How long have we known each other?"

"Shit," Niles slurred. "I dunno. A'least ten years—"

"Thirteen to be exact."

The bartender arrived with Niles's drink. He didn't waste anytime sipping from the drink.

"Why'd you ask if you already knew?" asked Niles.

"You've shared everything about yourself with me, Niles," Ari then said from the corner of his mouth, "maybe too much, like, for instance, with Vicky and her rather poor taste in music." He whispered in Niles's ear, *"Don't tell her I said that."*

"She'd have your balls in a pickle jar if she found out you were dissin' her tunes."

"We've known each other now for thirteen years, and you haven't shared any details whatsoever about what happened to you last year, other than '*you got lost.*' It was a bad time. . . for *all* of us, Niles. Nobody knew if U.C. was going to survive, especially during a time when the average attention span for a user had shrunken so dramatically that it was nearly impossible to maintain a viable model that would carry us into the fourth quarter. Indulge me, please, Niles: What did you and Phoenix talk about earlier today?"

"Believe it or not, Phoenix and I go way back," Niles said with a touch of drunken arrogance in his voice. "Well before NGHT. Even before I met the one they called 'Oh!(*sigh*)Rez.'" Niles flicked his eyes toward Ari, who didn't appreciate the tone in his partner's voice when he spoke about his alternate ego, or what he called at times, his "nom de guerre," his *war name.* "We both worked at Tailorsoft for a while, before I joined eClipse. I was helping them with the launch of their first OS, which ended up being a shit-show. So, no offense, Ari my man, whatever Phoenix and I talked about isn't any of your business—"

"Niles, you were missing for thirty-three days."

"Wow, Ari," Niles said sarcastically, "thanks for reminding me." He squinted both his eyes in thought. He directly asked Ari, "Why do I feel like you're interrogating me?"

"Whatever happened to you is between you and Vicky and your shrink, but I'm your friend, right?"

"Sure, man."

"Friends don't keep secrets."

"What in the hell makes you think I got secrets—"

"What happened in Cordoba Valley?"

"I'd tell you if I remembered, Ari."

"Come on, Niles. . . "

"You really what to know what happened?"

"I think I deserve a right to know," he said.

Niles pulled out his necklace. He massaged the canine tooth between his fingertips and held it up for Ari to see.

He asked Ari, "Did I ever tell you the story behind this tooth?"

"No," Ari said casually. "Just thought it belonged to your dead dog. You kept it as sort of a souvenir or a reminder or something sentimental. I don't know. Where I come from it's considered rude to talk about the dead."

"You're from California."

"I mean, my ancestors—"

"I don't have a dog."

"You don't?"

"No," he said, furrowing his brow. "I thought you knew this."

"Do now."

Niles stared at the tooth, Ari's eyes following Niles's in a hypnotic-like state.

"I never lied about what happened," Niles said, his eyes never leaving the tooth. "I was lost, *but*. . . not the kind of lost that you or everybody else thought. Believe me when I tell you this," he said, looking Ari directly in the eyes, "I don't remember much about what happened, only bits and pieces. The truth: After we were dropped by NGHT, I needed a reset—"

"We all needed a reset, Niles."

"You fell back into your work," he said, not missing a beat. "As for me, I wanted to get lost, go off the grid, unplug. I found this holistics-specialist through a close friend of mine who claimed she got rid of his PTSD. Some even called her a witch doctor."

"Serious?" said Ari, who still unsure and slightly hesitant about how to react to Niles's reasons for going MIA. "What was her name?"

Niles, who was also reluctant to share, said with climbing anticipation, "*Zagazig.*"

"What the hell kind of name is Zagazig?" asked Ari.

"Don't even try looking her up because her services are what I call 'word-of-mouth,'" Niles said, as he vapidly dropped air quotes, "not for the general public, if you get my drift. Besides, you can't even find her on GPS. She's basically a ghost—"

"But you found her, right?"

"I had to specifically follow handwritten directions, but yeah, I found her."

"And what happened?"

"That's the thing," Niles said. "I can hardly remember anything from the moment I left Q2 West Tech Conference to the moment. . . " the triggers were the words itself, ". . . I found myself wandering down Mulholland Drive. . . "

While speaking about the conference that took place in San Diego, shades of the past event, once soaked in grainy darkness as though the memory itself was stylized by black and white film noir, started to fill with color and vividness. He saw a face—he remembered a face. Narrow and glowing. High cheekbones. The facial structure of an actor. Dark and sinister eyes. Suave. He specifically remembered now passing that face while making his rounds through the convention center. He swore the guy could pass as Ted Bundy's twin. He remembered the guy's eyes were everywhere, mainly tracking down the female kind. The slight throbbing of his nostrils while he picked up their scent. He remembered watching the guy, who was acting suspect, as he scanned the crowds in the main floor before sneaking backstage.

Ari observed a stillness of Niles's face, as well as the thoughts churning behind his eyes.

Pulling Niles from the fleeing images, he first asked, "Is something wrong?"

"No," Niles answered, his tone was short and sober.

He messed with the teleprompter, thought Niles.

Colored images filled his head: With the spotlights glaring down on him, Niles was standing on stage in front of an audience full of techies from all across the world, reading from the scroll of the teleprompter when, all of a sudden, he came across a typo. He stopped himself from reading the typo and squinted his eyes and reread the last part of the sentence first to himself and then when he started to read the line out loud, he stopped yet again and fell into a state of panic as the color of embarrassment crept into his glossy flushed face. When he saw the typo appear a third time on the teleprompter, he swallowed the dry lump down his throat and powered through the words, "*E'vo Remo'das.*" These words meant nothing to him and when he spoke them, it felt as though he was uttering the disjointed word, "*Evolution,*" while addressing the recently new source-code editor, Visage++, which allowed him to reconstruct arbitrary data by editing on the fly.

After observing the life returning to Niles's face, Ari asked, "So, does being covered in coyote's blood have anything to do with this Zagazig lady, who, by the way, sounds made up?"

"I don't know what to believe anymore."

He was there, Niles thought, standing among *the crowd.*

Niles peered through the bright spotlights and saw the man whom he had earlier passed on the main floor standing with Zagazig in the audience.

There was only one of them, *not two.*

Only the Bundy look-alike.

Not Zagazig.

Did she even exist?

Or, was he conjuring the old hag in his mind like a film projector?

"Everybody thought you were dead," Ari said, his voice pulling Niles away from the memory. "If people ever found out that you intentionally went missin—"

"They're not going to find out," he said over Ari, his voice more serious. "Right?"

"Right," Ari said, easing away from his friend. "Of course. Our secret. What if this woman gave you something? Some kind of substance that screwed with your head?"

"I don't recall taking any substances—maybe I did—but I specifically remember him giving me this after my awakening. . . "

"Him?"

Niles saw him, not her, standing at the doorway.

His silhouette looming in the hazy light.

Those eyes, he saw, dark and sinister.

"Niles?"

He snapped from his trance.

"Him?"

"I said that?"

"You remembered him giving you something."

Niles showed Ari the coyote tooth.

"*She* gave me this," he corrected. "She said it'd protect me."

"Protect you from what?"

"Evil spirits maybe."

"Evil spirits?" Ari tried to hold in his laughter. "How much did you have to drink?"

Niles didn't respond.

Yet, he sat there, silent and somber, soaking in the radiance of the past.

Ari asked, "Did you ever stop to think that maybe you got swindled by a con artist?"

"I've seen plenty of these types before," Niles said. "But this bitch, she was on a whole new level."

Ari said, "Well, does it work?"

"The hell if I know," Niles said and sipped from his drink.

"Well," Ari said, staring at the tooth, "it is unusual to say the least."

"Strange how you bring this up, of all times, when I've been thinking a lot about what happened last year," he said amusingly.

"Your recent health scare might have something to do with it. A trigger perhaps."

"Possibly or. . . " Niles moved his eyes forward and fell into a deep state of reflection, ". . . I brought something back from Cordoba Valley and now, it's reaching out to me. Again."

"How many drinks have you had?"

"I've been seeing things, Ari."

More concerned, Ari asked, "What things?"

"Details surrounding Cordoba Valley," Niles said. "I can't tell if it's my mind playing tricks on me or if the memories are starting to return. Like the memories have always been there, hiding underneath all of the bullshit. All I know is that something happened to me before I left San Diego. Something strange. . . " he suddenly perked up and pulled himself from the thought alone of being trapped in a dark, dusty room in the middle of nowhere, ". . . have you ever been blackout drunk before?"

Ari shrugged.

"Once or twice, maybe." Thrice, Ari concluded, the last time as fresh as a daisy. "You remember that night after I released *Dagger Eye*?"

"How could I forget? That's the night you fooled What's-His-Name into shaving the eyebrows from his face."

"George," Ari said.

"Oh yeah," Niles drawled. "*Curious* George. So, you know what I'm talking about?"

"But you didn't have any traces of alcohol in your system."

"And there lies the mystery," he said. "The entire month I felt like I was blackout drunk."

"To be honest, Niles, it just sounds like you were having a mental breakdown, a mid-life crisis, which is totally normal. I mean. . . " Ari said, his thoughts stumbling around as he searched for the most appropriate words to use without drawing any unwanted reaction from Niles, ". . . I don't know why you hid this from me. You could've told me this sooner. You needed a break. We *all* needed a break, especially after NGHT pulled the rug from underneath our feet."

"Considering what went down at Four Lakes," Niles said with a grave tone, his manner cool yet devilish, "it's understandable why you delved so hard into your work. Clearly, you wanted to put Four Lakes in the back of your mind—"

"How many times do I have to tell you, Niles?" Ari asked. "I had no involvement with Doctor Sonnenberg's mad scientists experiments. You can relay that to your boy, Phoenix."

"But you did know him through Ahmad?" asked Niles.

"Briefly," Ari said.

"Which is why you fail to see the bigger picture, Ari, my boy," Niles said, mockingly.

"What bigger picture?"

Niles asked, "*What if we could* go beyond just curing The Blind?"

"I'd say then we're no longer following the science," Ari said, swallowing the lump of anger down his throat. "That, my friend, is man trying to play God."

Niles finished his drink and paid the bartender while Ari stayed behind at the bar and marinated in his thoughts regarding Niles's question. "Never underestimate the power of *what if*," he was once told after he left behind the video game industry to pursue a project that would change the way people perceived reality.

"I suppose it's the alcohol talking," Yamato said to Ari moments before he met up with the one person who had the connections to open doors for Ari. If it weren't for Niles, Ari knew, then universal_computer would've been a pipe dream.

While Ari stewed in his thoughts, Niles stumbled his way through a narrow alleyway where he tripped over a full trash bag on the ground.

He staggered to his feet and brushed off the wet grime from his clothes and inspected the dark object on the ground.

His palm was covered in blood.

The smell in the air was incredibly foul.

Below him was not a trash bag, but rather a dead dog.

Niles pulled out his phone and using the flashlight, shined a light on the black and tan Shiba Inu.

The cause of its death, Niles determined, was unknown; however, it was lying in a puddle of blood and Niles, despite possessing the liquid courage, was too freaked out to roll the dog over to inspect its wounds.

As Niles moved the light to the dog's face, he saw, not the face of a Shiba Inu, but rather the face of a coyote, which was missing a canine.

He was struck by more of those visions—or memories—from his time in Cordoba Valley.

Trapped inside a claustrophobically small, sour-smelling, empty bedroom with the windows boarded up by plywood, Niles, who was naked and trembling in a fetal position, flinched from the sight of a petite woman cracking open the rickety door. A beam of light speared through the darkness, highlighting his panicked, wigged-out state, as well as the bowl of coyote's blood lying on the gritty, beetle-infested floor.

Moments later—memories later—a police officer from the Los Angeles Police Department was wrapping a blanket around Niles's shoulder after he was involved in a near-fatal car accident on Mulholland Drive. The smoking car was overturned in a ditch alongside the road. The driver of the car was pale and left in a state of shock, for he couldn't formulate the words to the officer in question as to how Niles managed to survive after being struck while he driving at least fifty miles per hour. The driver claimed that he hit a "coyote," its body went flying in the air, sent at least 20 yards across the road. The car's headlights spotlighted the horror lying on the road. The images alone of the bones in Niles's arms, as well as his legs, each one shattered or broken or protruding from the skin or even twisted ninety-degrees in the opposite direction, only to mysteriously snap back into their proper place, left the driver utterly speechless after he stepped out of the vehicle to check on the "coyote," and whenever he tried to explain it to the police officers, the story only made the situation worse. After listening to the driver's story, the police officers made the driver blow into a breathalyzer machine in order to measure the amount of alcohol he had to drink that night. The results didn't show any traces of alcohol. The officers then conducted a DUI test on the driver. He passed that test too. Yet, despite these results that cleared the driver of any impairment, he still wasn't making a lick of sense.

Niles snapped from the memory.

Below him was a dog, a Shiba Inu, *not* a coyote.

As Niles collected his thoughts, he received a phone call from Phoenix, who had unfortunate news about one of Niles's test subject.

Of all places, he thought he'd never wind up back at that hell.

He pushed aside his grievances and hailed a cab.

When Niles arrived at the hospital, Phoenix caught Niles in the waiting room where he informed him about his test subject,

#12, Georgina Brass, who recently suffered a major stroke and had been hospitalized.

He was still somewhat buzzed, despite the initial blow of being punched by reality.

Overcome with emotion, Niles demanded to see Georgina. Before Phoenix could further explain what happened to Georgina and fill in Niles on the severity of Georgina's condition, Niles attempted to wave down a nurse.

Phoenix grabbed at Niles's arm and tried to restrain him, but Niles demanded answers from a hospital worker. He found one, another nurse, who confirmed Georgina's condition.

"*Konsui*," said the nurse.

Which Niles misinterpreted as dead or the "dead sleep."

"What?"

"A coma," Phoenix translated, as he tried to calm Niles. "She fell into a coma."

More panicked, Niles said, "When?"

"About an hour ago," Phoenix explained.

"But I thought you guys were monitoring her."

"We were," Phoenix said.

"Then, how did this happen?" asked Niles.

"I don't know, Niles," Phoenix said more directly. "You tell me. . . "

As the shock wore off and the guilt settled in, Niles was left speechless.

All he could think about was Georgina and those around her.

Like all the test subjects, she had no one.

No family.

No friends.

Except for Max and an older sister, who was nothing more than a ghost to her, she had not a single person to stand up and speak for her.

A part of Niles felt torn inside for specifically choosing subjects who had very little, if not, no people in their lives and believed the trials he and Ari conducted were immoral and unethical.

"*These are the sacrifices we have to take*," he said to Ari, who was skeptical about the trials.

Ari's limited vision was why Phoenix brought Niles a "revisal" in the contract.

In other words: "Ari is on his way out."

In essence: Ari was finished.

"He's not the right fit for our future plans."

The rage washed over Niles like a flood.

"But if it wasn't for Ari," he seethed, trying to avoid any unwanted attention from the hospital staff, "then none of these breakthroughs would've happened."

"Tell that to Ms. Brass," Phoenix said, his demeanor as cold as a machine. "Niles, you said it yourself. It's time we start thinking bigger. And I quote, 'Ari's thinking too small.' Why stop at curing The Blind or The Paralyzed?"

"I was just speaking out of my ass, Phoenix," Niles said.

"Neuvak doesn't see it that way," he said. "So, if you had to guess, how long will it take to accomplish this grandiose idea of yours? And bear in mind, you'll been given carte blanche over the entire project."

For Niles, it sounded too good to be true.

But he told himself that he and Phoenix went way back.

Finally, Niles said, "We're talking years down the road."

"Estimate?"

"Given if there aren't any setbacks, which there will be, I'd say ten years, maybe less." Before he parted ways with Phoenix, he asked, "What about Ari?"

"He'll stay on for as long as we need him to—legality of course—until then, we want you to take his replacement under your wing. Show him the ropes. He's flying in tomorrow."

Niles asked, "Does this replacement have a name?"

"Carmichael," Phoenix said. "Lance Carmichael."

Phoenix ordered Niles to get some rest.

According to Phoenix, tomorrow was going to be a long day.

Niles went against Phoenix's orders and without anyone looking, managed to sneak into the ICU where he found a woman, as the nurse said, in a coma.

She was hooked to a breathing tube.

Niles confirmed that it was, in fact, Georgina lying in the hospital bed.

He left before the nurses caught him in the room and exited via the staircase.

Outside the emergency room, he hailed a cab.

As soon as he stepped into the cab, the other passenger door opened.

A strange, darkly dressed dyed blonde-haired woman sat next to him in the backseat; and as soon as she locked eyes with him,

Niles recognized the same Japanese woman, who was checking him out at the Ale House earlier in the night.

Lady Loner who ended up winning the game of eye-tag.

"Can I help you?" asked Niles.

"The fare's on me," she said first to the driver, then Niles.

"Listen, lady, it's not about money—"

"Then," she said, her gaze cutting right through Niles, "how about the company?"

With his face long and slack, Niles said flippantly, "Whatever."

The Japanese woman closed the door.

After snapping from his dazed state, Niles was next to close the other door.

Together, the two rode off in the taxicab.

Their destination, Niles stated for the driver, his apartment; however, the Japanese woman in the passenger seat wasn't at all interested in spending the night with Niles.

"So," Niles said, "what's this all about?"

"You and your creation," she said. "It sounds interesting—"

"Who are you?" asked Niles. "Did Phoenix send you to sweeten the deal?"

"I just wanted to get a closer look at you. . . "

Niles was exhausted, but he managed to slip out a laugh.

"Let me guess," he said. "Ari put you up to this—"

"Ari is just a pawn like you, Mr. Baldwin," she said rudely and then leaned closer. "I want to speak to the other Niles."

Shifting his weight, Niles began to lose his cool with the passenger.

He asked, "Who do you work for?"

"I don't work for anyone," she said innocently. "You can think of me as a messenger or just a curious observer pointing out the glaring target on your back."

Baffled by the passenger's tenacity, Niles said, "Are you threatening me?"

"Have your ever heard of a company, JeneCorp?"

"Of course," Niles said, losing himself in the passenger's seductive eyes. "Who hasn't?"

"For the past five years, JeneCorp has been hunting me down in order to extract a weapon I carry inside me—"

"What kind of weapon?"

The passenger said, "The very weapon I'm using on you right this moment."

Niles's face suddenly darkened to a near shadow, even as the ceiling light inside the cab began to brighten from the surge of energy.

"*Clever*," he said, his bafflement fading into a cool confidence.

His mannerisms, everything about Niles, changed for he turned into a personification of the ultimate traveler, a death walker.

"I'm speaking directly to you, *Stranger*," she said, gazing into the voids of the shadow cowering behind Niles's crimson eyes, "I don't know what your plans are with Mr. Baldwin, but just know that one day he will sacrifice himself for the greater good of *your* kind. And when the time comes, he'll give humanity a tool to fight—"

"*What exactly are they fighting*," the Stranger inside Niles said, "*except for themselves?*"

His voice was deeper and darker, throaty.

"Me," the passenger said clearly. "And in time, your future employers."

The ceiling light above suddenly flickered and burned out.

Niles shook off the temporary dizzy spell and asked again, "What weapon?"

The passenger pulled out a Kave lighter with a serpent engraved along its side.

She opened it and flicked the wheel, igniting a flame.

"Just be careful how you use it," she said. "It has a tendency to spread."

She closed the lid of the Kave, snuffing out the fire.

As she handed the Kave to Niles, the taxi arrived at the front of Niles's apartment.

"Sleep tight, Mr. Baldwin," she said to Niles as he exited the cab.

Speechless by the latest interaction, he walked back to his building while the passenger remained in the backseat.

She told the driver to take her to the airport for she made a promise to an old friend.

The driver looked into the rear view mirror where he witnessed the Japanese woman sitting in the backseat.

"As you wish," he said and drove to the airport.

In the reflection of the cab's passenger window was Chloe, who watched the Tokyo nightlife pass before her heavy eyes.

If she stopped, she told herself countless times, then they'd find her.

Moving was living.

Living was killing.

And Chloe's eyes were growing oh-so tired.

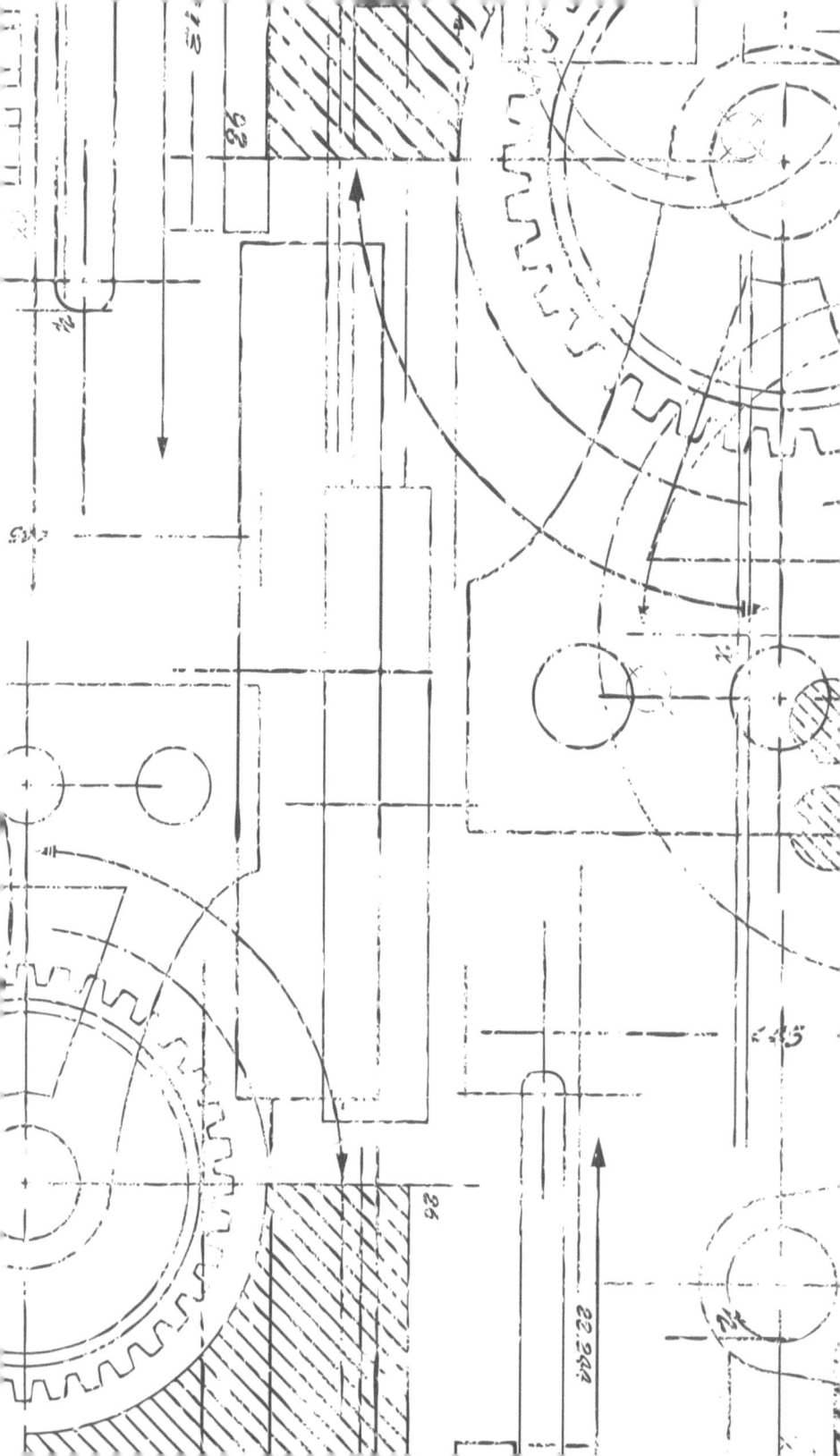

DEEP
FREEZE
DALIVIA
PLAUT

PART TWO
CROWDED
SEAT

BOOK THREE

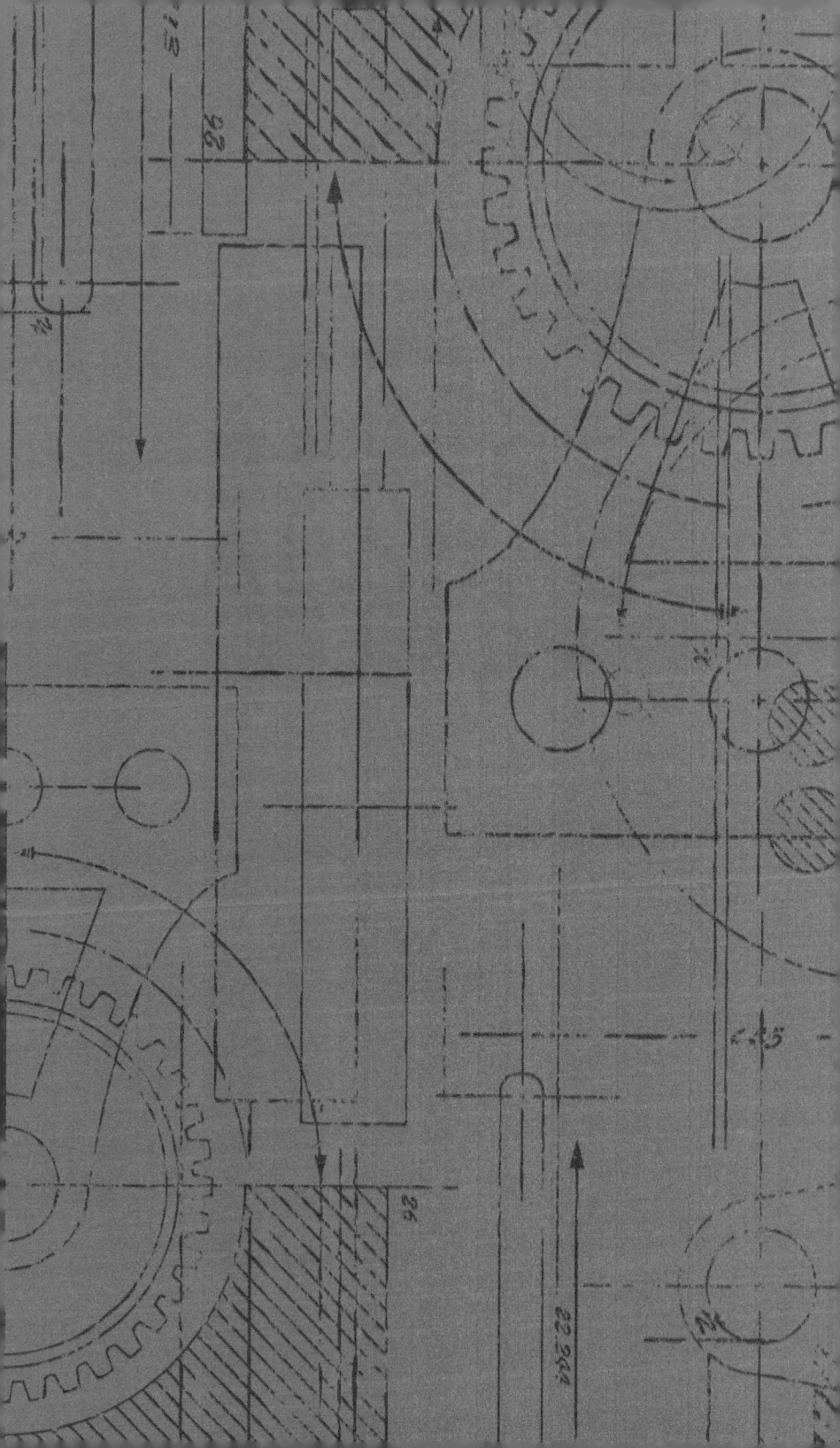

AT exactly 9 PM, right on schedule, every single drip on The Feed called the winner of the 2048 Presidential Election: the incumbent President, William Lockhart, and his running mate, Mallory Brawn, the congresswoman from Texas, declared victory over their opponents, Senator Jeremiah Shaw, the son of the late President Robert Shaw, whom pundits believed to be too inexperienced, especially in regards to foreign affairs, and flip-flopped on too many of the key issues—like, for example, the eradication of artificial intelligence—and would one day make a fine president, and Shaw's scrappy and yet controversial pick, Lavra Shevchenko.

The election wasn't even close, according to the numbers.

Lockhart won by a landslide, despite an eleventh hour attempt by Shaw's camp to divert its opponent's momentum and thwart its inevitable victory with the release of the shocking headline surrounding JeneCorp, who funded Lockhart's campaign.

Political pundits brought up the other controversy while viewers waited to hear Lockhart's victory speech.

The controversy erupted two days ago with the suicide of Stella Nilsson, a former Channel 5 News reporter from Elvira, California.

Part of Stella's story, which she had been working on for months, was leaked onto The Feed. The main focal point of the story was centered on an apparent suicide of Roberto Calle, a retired Border Patrol agent, who, based on the conditions in which Calle's body was discovered, as well as the photographs in his possession, was disgraced by his former colleagues, claimed to witness another shooter other than Jared Flack, and how Stella had evidence that linked Calle's death to an agent who worked for JeneCorp.

Within hours of its release, a fake bot account picked up an error in a photograph, which had been included in Stella's story. The photo being the same one taken outside the floral shop, Cassava, by Rocco Bolivia, the graphic designer; and in it, the bot highlighted Noble's left hand, which was off, as well as the shadows around the agent, which didn't match the precise direction of the sun. However, the agent's hand was a red flag. His hand had four fingers, including a thumb, which was accurate. Agent Noble didn't have a pinkie, only a small stump, and if one asked, he'd say he lost it while overseas. The photo, however, did **NOT** show Agent Noble's stump. Instead, shown in the photo was a narrower, alien-like hand in which a pinkie finger didn't exist, thus labeling it a "fake," or in this case, according to professional photographers, "altered." The day before the election, after the altered photo spread across The Feed like a virus, the owner of the most sought after photo came forward with the original. As on-the-fence voters suspected, Agent Noble was **NOT** in the original photo provided by Bolivia, who was compelled—conspiracy theorists may say persuaded or even pressured—to release the photo after a visit from those in Lockhart's circle. In the photo, there was nobody in the reflection of the store's window. Experts claimed that AI technology, despite all of its ambiguity in advancement, as well as the many breakthroughs in the ability to self-correct, still struggled to *re*-create what enthusiasts called the testament of the warm-blooded artist: "the human hands." Not too long after the original photo surfaced, Shaw's campaign released a written public statement, denying any involvement in the release of the altered photo and stated that they had no affiliation with second-rate reporter, Stella Nilsson, who failed to investigate her own sources. By then, in a way, voters had already made up their minds.

The misleading photograph was what many believed why Stella ended her life.

A once well-respected journalist-turned reporter, whose name was dragged through mud following a retracted article, only to be later torn to shreds after a month and a half of "nose-to-the-ground" hard work discredited, the blight of a once radical yet formidable term like renegade had downgraded into a mere two-dimensional cutout of a false idol who was deemed defective.

The night before Stella's body washed up along the polluted shore of Pearl Beach, a surveillance camera picked up Stella Nilsson on the bridge. Facial recognition confirmed Stella's identity. In the fifteen-second footage Stella was seen stepping onto a railing along the edge of the bridge and then jumping from the bridge, ultimately plummeting to her demise.

Before he could give the command, Vernon received a Vid-Chat from his girlfriend, Sammie, whom he had been dating for three years and was planning to ask her hand in marriage as soon as he finished assisting JeneCorp.

She asked him if he wanted to chill.

She didn't follow politics and could care less about politicians, whom Sammie thought were all the same. Sammie didn't care at all for elections either, hadn't voted in one since she graduated from high school (Her aging parents begged her to vote for "*their guy*," even went so far to bribe her a hundred bucks to vote for "their guy," which, at that age, was a lot of money, despite Sammie hating "*their guy*" with a glorious passion, not his policies—she didn't entirely disagree on some of the polices he pushed—but his mannerisms, his total in-your-face arrogance, his maniacal behavior, and she often wondered why her parents adored him so much and she had a hard time believing it was based on him being what they referred to as a "*businessman*" who, in their mind, could bring the country out of a crippling recession left behind by an incompetent administration whose greatest tool in the bag was not a pen, but rather a sword stained with the blood of their allies and their political adversaries).

Knowing Sammie's stance on politics, Vernon thought it was odd timing that she vidchatted him as soon as Lockhart declared victory.

She said that she caught a glimpse of the results, being that Vernon had taken part in Lockhart's recovery and all, and in a way, Vernon was part of history even though he didn't take any of the credit.

She told Vernon that she was about to open a bottle of Pinot and order a pizza.

What a great combination?

Pizza and Pinot!

Vernon wasn't in the mood, and he said he was going to call it a night.

Before ending the VidChat, he made sure to tell Sammie how much he loved her.

"Love you more," she said and ended the call.

Vernon's eyes shot toward the screen.

With the scar covered up with heavy makeup, President Lockhart, who was accompanied by Vice President Brawn, walked onto the stage in Philadelphia.

Frustrated by the sight of Lockhart, Vernon commanded the smart TV to turn off and threw back yet another shot of aged Webster's Tennessee Whiskey.

With a grimace etching through his face like a joker's smile, he slammed the shot glass onto his grandfather's notes, which were strewed over the coffee table, and sat back in the couch and closed his eyes for a minute and embraced the burn of whiskey sliding down his esophagus and eventually, settling into his stomach.

Buzzing from the whiskey, Vernon cracked open one eye, the other one still tightly shut.

His eye immediately found the shot glass as though Webster's special concoction had given him laser-eyed focus.

The bottom of the glass magnified a face in the black and white photograph on the table.

Vernon sat upright, the rush of blood causing him to take a beat to catch his consciousness before it slipped away into the grayness. Once the dizzy spell passed, he removed the shot glass, which left behind a brown whiskey ring circling a familiar face in the photograph. With a facial recognition app on his smartphone, he scanned the face, who belonged to Victor Cashel Rose—according to the app, Rose was twenty-five years old at the time the photo was taken.

As his grandfather, Dr. Melvin Hawks, was performing brain surgery on Anthony "The Hit Whisperer" Florentine, Rose was standing in the back of the operation room with other interns. Vernon had seen the face before in more personal photographs of his grandfather: old, faded, and crinkled ones left to Vernon's father, who kept all of his father's belongings in a storage unit on the other side of town, mostly dusty boxes of moth-riddled clothes and medical awards and those rare photographs that young and joyous Vernon once riffled through as a boy before his father decided to empty out the unit, which, to Vernon, seemed like a choir that his father kept putting off each year. He shared many memories of his father and the summer he and his father emptied out that unit was definitely one he remembered. The thrill of discovery. The secrets left to fester in the dusty darkness. One minute, he held them in his hands, those secrets; and then, the next, it was like they never existed, like a dream. Even till this day, Vernon didn't know what his father had done with all of those belongings, if he had dropped them at a Goodie store or pawned them off for cash or worse, dumped them in the bay. Considering Vernon's father never spoke a word about his old man and most of what Vernon learned about his grandpa was marred by the misdoings of a madman, he leaned toward the latter.

As Vernon gumshoed the name "Victor Cashel Rose" in the search bar and scrolled through the results, the top one being an obituary from Bluefield, Pennsylvania, he clicked on a medical site and right before the page opened, the Internet access shutdown. He tried once more, only to receive a "SERVER DOWN" message. He checked wi-fi; and strangely, it was down at the moment and not receiving a signal.

All of a sudden, the lights to his condo turned off, leaving Vernon in total blackness.

Vernon sensed he wasn't alone.

Someone or something was inside the condo with him.

He searched the darkness, trying to pick up any movements.

In a scan across the kitchen, he caught what looked like the figure of a body standing behind the countertop, watching him with glossy marbled eyes.

As he blindly fumbled for his phone on the coffee table, he felt a warm draft along his neck and as he rotated around, the power turned back on.

More frantically, he searched the condo but saw nobody in sight, including the figure that he thought he witnessed in the dark, which turned out to be a clothing rack on the other side of the kitchen.

The only difference that he found: a business card on the edge of the coffee table.

As his eyes bolted back up, he searched the condo once more.

Unless it slipped out of the folder when he was scattering around the contents, files and photographs, he didn't know any other reason as to how the card wound up on the coffee table.

He picked up the card for a state-of-the-art indoor golf training facility called 12 Holes. The graphic on the business card showed the time-lapse image of a golfer swinging a golf club, each frame of the swing appeared twelve times, each one fading into another, the golf club appearing like the hour hands of a clock. It wasn't until he flipped the card around when he started to feel uneasy.

On the back was a handwritten address: *"Topeka Center Drive Chaff, MA 02780."*

The hairs on the back of his neck suddenly stood up, forcing him to grab a baseball bat from the mantle and thoroughly check each room of the condo, as well as the closets, and every single nook and cranny. Although Vernon couldn't find anyone, he thought a presence was still inside his condo.

Somewhat rattled by the sight of the card, which appeared out of nowhere, Vernon stopped by his neighbor's condo and asked to use his wi-fi for a minute.

No questions asked, his neighbor handed Vernon an eTablet.

Vernon first gumshoed the address on the back of the business card, which was the location of a storage warehouse next to an abandoned industrial park. Based on a hunch, he looked up the golfing facility, 12 Holes—he remembered not too long ago one of his assistants mentioning the place—and sure enough, he was right.

After Cooper Institute shut down many decades ago, the building was gutted and renovated and turned into an indoor golfing facility.

Vernon pulled out the business card and once more, looked over the address. He went back to his condo and pocketed the photograph of Victor Rose; and right before leaving the condo, he peeked through the blinds, only to spot the same vehicle that had been following him every since he returned to Boston. He saw the two campers inside. More than likely, they were either Secret Service or *JeneCorp*. Given recent knowledge on the smart metal, E'Raknish, which was installed inside President-Elect's mouth, Vernon was ninety-nine percent positive it was Tahr's goons who were parked across the street, waiting and watching as if Vernon was a liability.

He felt as though he was back in high school, sneaking out behind his mother's back.

The thought alone tickled him and yet, at the same time, brought on great anxiety.

After coming up with an impromptu night mission, Vernon commanded his virtual assistant, Orchid's Bella, to cut off the lights. He left the condo via back door and walked through a dark alleyway until reaching the main street where he rented a self-driving transportation pod from the secure locker. Once inside, Vernon punched in the GPS coordinates of the address. The runtime of the drive was roughly under an hour, directly south of Boston. He arrived at his destination on time. The storage warehouse was unlit and the only light came from a couple of floodlights in a cracked parking lot. He disabled the pod and while scanning the eerie night, made his way to the front door of the warehouse. A rusty chain was interlaced with the door handles of the front door and secured by a padlock. He picked up a rock from the ground and used the rock to smash the padlock.

"You can never go wrong with old tech," he said to himself.

He removed the broken padlock and pulled the chain from the door.

Using the flashlight on his phone, he walked down a dark hallway until he reached the main storage room where he located the light switch and flipped on the lights. One after another, the overhead fluorescent lights flickered on, revealing a room with a low ceiling that stretched as far as his eye could see. Before Vernon were the many aisles of metal shelves filled with boxes and each one was labeled with a letter and a number. He thought about how it'd take several months, perhaps even years, to comb through all of these boxes.

Overwhelmed by the amount of storage, he walked down the first aisle that he came across, only to feel that similar presence, like the one he felt back in his condo, following him. He heard a noise coming from two aisles over. He decided to check out the noise, only to find a bolt from one of the shelves on the floor. He picked up the bolt and as he stood upright, Assistant Director Forsake was standing directly behind Vernon.

"I apologize for the discretion," Forsake said, startling Vernon.

"Jin," Vernon said, his heart racing, "what the fuck—"

"I had no other way to contact you," he said. "I hate to be the bearer of bad news, but your place is bugged."

"Yeah," Vernon drawled. "I was starting to get that feeling. It's JeneCorp, isn't it?"

"They're tracking everything you do or say."

Thinking about the business card that magically appeared on the coffee table, Vernon trailed off, "How did. . . ."

Forsake, who already knew what Vernon was going to ask, said to Vernon, "Doesn't matter. What's important is that you're safe in here."

"That was you messing with my connection, wasn't it?"

"It was the only way I could lure you here."

Vernon looked around.

"And where is here?"

Forsake nodded at the box on the shelf behind Vernon.

"Take a look for yourself," he said.

Cautiously, Vernon, while keeping a close eye on Forsake, grabbed the box from the shelf. The front of the read "EMPLOY-EES R-W." He placed the box on the floor and pulled out a folder containing the R's. He went straight to the name: ROSE, VICTOR. He held up the file.

"Victor Rose," Forsake clarified. "He's the guy in the photo-graph."

Vernon pulled out the photograph from his pocket and briefly studied Victor's face.

"Why does he look so familiar?" asked Vernon.

"He was a friend of your grandfather's," Forsake said coolly. "And he's the one responsible for letting mankind's savior and ultimately, its destroyer out of the cage."

"E'Raknish," Vernon said clearly. "But how?"

"Victor's wife Hilda was severely injured in a car accident. Shattered hip," Forsake said, as Vernon listened closely. "Chances of Hilda walking again were slim to none. So, Victor had no other choice than to turn to a friend for help. *Your* grand-father, Melvin. At the time, E'Raknish, despite its medical break-throughs, was still unpredictable. Melvin was working with the United States government to develop an implant to control peo-ple's thoughts—"

Vernon balked at the very idea of his grandfather's past work.

"I know, right?" Forsake said cynically while reading Vernon's gestures. "The project was called Operation Yellow Brick Road. After the accident, your grandfather was forced to make a decision: either abandon the project or help out his friend. Victor was desperate and believed E'Raknish was the only way forward in his wife's recovery. Following setbacks at Cooper Institute, some of which included accusations of Melvin experimenting on his patients, Melvin, capitalizing on the opportunity to study E'Raknish on a human subject, decided to help out Victor's wife. Over time, Melvin became obsessive and wanted to tell Hilda about E'Raknish. But Victor knew if people found out that she had a piece of government property inside her, they'd pick her apart like a lab rat. So in order to protect his wife, Victor buried the truth. When he confronted Melvin, it was said that the two got in a heated argument. Melvin accidentally tripped and hit the back of his head on a table—"

"I was told he died during a robbery. . . Police never caught a suspect. . . "

"You were told a lie, Vernon," Forsake said, his tone softer. "I'm sorry you weren't told the truth about your grandfather."

In a state of eureka, Vernon said mindfully and humbly, "It all makes sense."

Forsake looked at Vernon strangely.

"My father was a child when his father died," Vernon said, as he was lost in thought. "I always wondered why he chose to become a lawyer. Of all the professions, he chose one where he had a target on the back of his head. Now, hearing what you've said about my grandfather, it all makes sense. In a way, I always knew. He was searching for the man who murdered his father. Turns out he might as well been searching for a ghost."

"It's amazing how the things we experience throughout our lives shape us into the people we are today. Then," Forsake said, "there are the people in our inner circles who give us certain taps to mold us into place."

"If what you're saying is true, then my father was molded by a lie."

"How did you feel after your father was gunned down by Lapp's brother?" asked Forsake.

"In the beginning, angry, like I could take my anger and wipe out humanity with it," he said. "I remember feeling like it was so easy to turn toward vengeance, like it was the only solution to avenge my father. I soon realized the greatest revenge in life is living your best life, helping others, doing good."

"Believe it or not, Melvin was same way, and I believe Rouse sees Melvin in you, which brings me to the subject of Victor and Hilda's daughter, Nikola." He braced himself for the story by taking in a deep breath. "After E'Raknish successfully coupled with Hilda, she gave birth to her first child, Milota. However, when Hilda became pregnant with her second child, Nikola, the template started to. . . evolve. . . "

"Evolve how?"

"Some believe it started with Florentine—"

"The psycho who killed all those people at a San Francisco nightclub?"

"That's right," Forsake said. "But if you trace back to the very beginning, the moment that first domino fell, it all starts with Victor's wife, Hilda, and the child she birthed."

Vernon asked, "What was wrong with her?"

"In 1988, when Nikola was seven years old, something extraordinary happened. . . " Forsake said to Vernon, who was still left in disbelief, ". . . a new, highly advanced version of E'Raknish happened. Many believed Nikola was murdered when, in fact, she was reborn."

Vernon asked, his voice trailing away, "Reborn into what. . . "

"Years, decades of evolution," Forsake said, "forged by the very blood that keeps it alive."

"You're talking about an entirely new life form."

"Doesn't mention that in those notes of yours, does it?"

More intrigued, Vernon asked, "What happened to Victor Rose?"

"Not too long after Nikola's rebirth, Victor was found dead inside his house. According to the autopsy, he swallowed a handful of painkillers and washed them down with alcohol."

"If Hilda's child was so important, then how come it doesn't mention anything about her in Tahr's file?" asked Vernon.

Forsake asked, "You honestly think Hilda would be alive if JeneCorp knew about her?"

"How the hell would I know?"

"If JeneCorp ever found out Hilda was still alive, then they'd scour the edge of the earth to find her."

"That is, if she's still alive," Vernon said, thinking. "She must be how many years old—"

"Old enough to know the difference between a person and a piece of valuable property and if JeneCorp gets their hands on her, she'll no longer get a say in whom or *what* she wants to be."

Forsake said closer to Vernon, "How exactly do you think the American People would react if they found out the truth about Lockhart's brand new appliances? Why do you think JeneCorp is keeping such a close eye on you, Vernon?"

Vernon mulled over Forsake's question.

Then, after taking a beat, he asked Forsake, "And Hilda's child? Nikola?"

"Do I need spell out for you, Vernon?" said Forsake. "The template *is the child*."

Vernon remained in a state of awe by the recent discovery.

To further emphasize the template's existence, Forsake explained an incident that took place over a month ago—September 20th—when the template claimed the lives of six individuals, four of those individuals being JeneCorp agents, the other two being salt-of-the-earth Americans, who found themselves in the wrong place at the wrong time. Their names were Wes Schroeder and Dillon Hogg. Following the accident, Schroeder's wife was later admitted into a hospital after suffering a mental breakdown.

The news that followed the incident, which garnered the most attention: the snowballing of a trend that had taken on a whole new life after Ceylon's post, #GrayScorpion.

After the trendy hashtags were taken down and eventually contained, a series of new posts—bearing the same #GrayScorpion—began to emerge by fake accounts where chat bots shifted the "gray-scorpion" narrative to a "rogue robot" that "escaped from a man's basement." There were even interviews with the man, a morose inventor named Bobby Chain, who was a deep fake generated by AI, all of it deliberately carried out to appear on the surface as a hoax, a way to mislead the American People from the real truth. Sure enough, these actions by tech companies had created more conspiracies that revolved around Dillon Hogg, the supposed drunk driver, who theorists claimed was a paid actor. There was another Dillon Hogg, *not* the same Dillon Hogg who crashed into Schroeder's property, but another one who died from a self-inflicted gunshot wound to the head a week after news broke of the drunk driving accident. Hogg's death only fueled the imaginations of those who were clinging to the realizations of their own prophecies in which the abundance of easily accessed information made connecting dots as common as coincidence.

"Whether you like it or not," Forsake said to Vernon, "you're in deep, and if JeneCorp ever finds out about this conversation, I'm afraid you may share the same fate as Stella Nilsson."

"The reporter?"

"Don't believe everything you see, Vernon."

"The Feed showed her death—"

"And do you believe a person who's about to expose one of the largest companies in the entire world decides to go for a night swim in the middle of the night? It's what they do, Vernon. They find people whom you care about, in Stella's case, her former boss, Julian Waters, and they turn them against you by threatening to kill the people you love. In Waters' case, his two children." Forsake asked Vernon, who was still at a loss from all of the information that was being dumped on him, "Are you aware of the paradigm shift?"

"Paradigm," Vernon said, thinking. "You're talking about patterns?"

"I'm talking about a fundamental change in assumption and what we approach as basic science. In the past, AI was considered knowledge-based. As we further change from the assumption that artificial intelligence is based on knowledge, the shift shows us AI is not knowledge, but rather driven by data. AI is nothing more than a great harvester of data, a master, and what you may assume is Ms. Nilsson in that video is only a construct in your mind, Vernon. For example, take Ludwig Wittgenstein's drawing the rabbit-duck illusion. One may perceive the drawing as a rabbit, while another may perceive a duck. The same goes for the deep fake. One may assume there is a real-life person in that video, based on the accurate characteristics, while another may see a composite of data compiled into what JeneCorp wants you to believe is a real-life person—"

"How the hell do you know all of this?" asked Vernon.

Forsake sighed and at first, struggled to find the words.

"I know this because Stella Nilsson was working with me," he said, his tone more somber.

Shocked by Forsake's confession, Vernon said, "Why?"

"If you knew exactly how your life was going to pan out, each step, each decision, the outcome of each event, would you do anything differently or would leave it all up to fate."

"I don't like the notion of not being in control over my life."

"But how do you know if you're actually in control of your life or you're being manipulated into *thinking* you have control?"

"I don't," Vernon said simply.

"And that's exactly why JeneCorp has to stop," Forsake said. "They have become too powerful, and if we don't stop them, then I'm afraid no one will."

With his voice shaking, he said, "We?"

Forsake sharpened his eyes on Vernon.

"Our last shot at exposing JeneCorp—"

Hung up on Stella's death, Vernon blurted out, "But there's video of Nilsson jumping off the bridge!"

"Videos can be manipulated, Vernon," Forsake said, "same goes for photographs. JeneCorp possesses the kind of technology that can make the *unreal* real and adjust the levels of realness. You honestly think some random bot account found Bolivia's photo on The Feed? They found a random photo, manipulated it, then passed it off as key evidence linking an agent of JeneCorp to a crime, then, finally, strategically exploited the inauthentic nature of the photo in order to make Stella look like a hack journalist who was building her exposé based around a photo manipulated by AI. JeneCorp practically admitted that they killed Roberto Calle in order to prevent him from speaking out about Acosta; and yet, the only person who was trying to prove it is now dead. The whole thing was a setup, and Stella. . . she took the fucking bait!"

"And what makes you think I'll be successful?" asked Vernon.

"You already have the keys to the castle," Forsake said. "I have a guy who's working on the inside. You have a scheduled trip to Death Valley this upcoming Friday."

"I don't appreciate you spying on me—"

"The FBI monitoring your keystrokes is the least of your concerns," Forsake said, ignoring Vernon's frustration. "Once you've arrived at JeneCorp, I need you to find my guy and together, you two must prevent the launch in Tokyo."

"How much do you know about what's happening in Tokyo?"

"Enough. And you?"

"All Rouse said is that Carmichael needs my help in running a dummy program on Splinter. Several eleventh hour-tests need to be conducted before the final launch in December."

"Do you even know *what* JeneCorp is launching?" Forsake asked, his tone sharper and more serious.

Vernon hesitated.

"From the impression I was given, it's a new OS update. A 'game changer,' is what they're calling it."

Forsake snickered at Vernon's ignorance.

"They're not just going to change the game, Vernon. They're going to prevent anyone from playing it ever again. We're looking at total annihilation. The powers that be flipping a final *off* switch on humanity. The entire world left in the dark. No question about it: Millions of people will die. You thought the blackouts two years ago were disastrous? What JeneCorp is planning is going to be *ten times* worse."

"You think it has something to do with E'Raknish?" asked Vernon.

"It has everything to do with E'Raknish," Forsake said. "Here," he said, pulling out a small vial that contained the Prussian blue substance, which he called a highly aggressive "preemptive agent." The agent would corrupt E'Raknish with a single drop.

"This won't be enough. JeneCorp has miles and miles of cable that have been modified with E'Raknish—"

"One drop is all you need," Forsake emphasized. "Once the agent touches E'Raknish, it will spread through its body like a cancer, first incapacitating it until its entire system shuts down, and eventually, destroying it for good. The tricky part: You must locate each piece of the template in JeneCorp's possession, including the one in Carmichael's office. Apply the agent to each piece."

"My keycard restricts me from entering certain areas."

"That's where my guy comes in," Forsake said. "He will open doors for you."

"Won't they know E'Raknish has been infected before I leave to Tokyo?"

"The agent will go undetected for four to six hours, which should buy you enough time before your flight. For the time being, I need you to carefully watch Carmichael. Study his every move."

"Four hours?" Vernon said sarcastically. "Not two? Or, three? How about three hours and fifteen minutes—"

"*Six hours*, tops, which means *only* apply the preemptive agent the day of your flight," Forsake said impatiently. "And remember, Vernon: Our main priority is Tokyo. If you can't gain access to Carmichael's E'Raknish, then it's not the end of the world."

"But JeneCorp will just reproduce more E'Raknish, and we'll be back to square one."

"We'll cross that bridge when we get to it."

"If this agent destroys E'Raknish, will it destroy Chloe?"

"Only if the agent is applied after she is amalgamated with E'Raknish. So, just make sure it doesn't come down to that. But if for some reason you find yourself in a jam and it comes down to destroying Chloe to save millions of lives, then so be it. . . ."

"It's a lot to take in," Vernon said, surprisingly relaxed by carrying the weight of the entire world on his shoulders. He asked as he grabbed hold of the small vial and looked it over, "What is it?"

"It's extracted from a *qaab root* plant, which contains cyanogenic-like compounds, unstable in water, highly toxic to E'Raknish, exclusively grown in the volcanic soil of Mount D'onwake."

Vernon smirked at the name.

"Mount D'onwake is a fairy tale."

"If you read the file on Anthony Florentine, Vernon, then you'd know that line between fiction and reality is only drawn by those who tend to look at this existence from a broader, transactional perception."

He asked mockingly, "Is that what the shift tells you?"

"It's simple, Vernon: Locate each template. Place a drop of qaab root extract onto the template. Then, last but certainly not least: Get the hell outta there."

Running through Forsake's plan in his head, Vernon said, "You're missing one crucial part of your plan." He was somewhat frightened to utter his next words: "How the hell am I going to get past Agent Noble?"

NATURE OF THE BEAST (OVERLAP): SOURCE ROCK
NOVEMBER 13, 2048 - NOVEMBER 21, 2048
SAN CRISTÓ, CALIFORNIA

IT was a Friday, and despite the superstitions that surrounded the day, the sight of the date on his eCalendar didn't phase the seasoned detective, Wyllie Finnegan, for the coroner's recent report, which ruled Stella Nilsson's death as a "suicide," thus closing the case, left behind a thorny ache in the pit of his stomach and any rising whims of the supernatural and the silly were purely viewed as the impetuous inventions of past generations that took one of the most important commodities for granted.

Detective Roselle Rupert walked past her partner's desk and noticed the evidence bag with a kidney bean-sized piece of rock in his hand. On the rock were two engraved lines, which the detective believed to be the lowercase letter "L."

Next to catch Rupert's eyes was the case file on Stella Nilsson and then, lastly, the eTablet, which contained a gallery of photographs surrounding Stella's death. One in particular: a photograph of Stella's body washed up on shore. Part of a wiry plastic soda can holder was tangled in her wet sandy hair. A close-up of the photo showed a massive crater in the center of Stella's bluish-purple face, her nose completely smashed and caved in. The coroner stated that Ms. Nilsson must've struck the bottom of the Lanada River during the fall, his theory, being that it was a low tide during the time of the video, which showed Stella plummeting to her demise.

And, of course, Rupert didn't have to point out the obvious: the facial recognition software, which matched Stella's face seconds before she "jumped" off the bridge. Considering the harsh condition of Stella's face when her body was discovered, the facial recognition software would **NOT** be able pick up a clear reading *if* her face were damaged before she jumped.

As Rupert stood at Finnegan's desk with a squinty-eyed glare on her face, she made sure to restate that the case was officially closed.

"If the lieutenant finds out you're still obsessing over the Nilsson case, you're ass is going to be out of a job, Wyllie."

"It doesn't make any sense," he said, looking over the piece of evidence in his hand.

As Finnegan returned to Stella Nilsson's file on his eTablet, he scrolled through photographs of Stella's house, both the exterior and interior of the house. The one key piece of evidence that the two detectives first acknowledged: "the lights," Finnegan said, as he showed Rupert the photos of Stella's house.

"So what?" Rupert said, shrugging. "We went over this. Her house was up for sale."

"Who the fuck leaves on all the lights?" asked Finnegan, as he sorted through each photo of Stella's house. "Every single light, even the exterior lights. Lit up like Christmas."

"Maybe she was planning on having a house showing?"

"At night?" Finnegan said, leaving Rupert without a response. "If she wanted to *off* herself, why would she take a self-drive back home after leaving Coyote Lounge? You saw the video of how drunk she was before getting into the car. She couldn't even find her own two feet; and yet, two hours later, she's walking straight lines?" He sighed loudly, which was followed by a groan: "Doesn't make sense, Roselle."

According to the toxicology report, Finnegan reminded Rupert, Stella's BAC (blood alcohol content) was doubled the legal limit. Not to mention, dangerous levels of Chlorodionysus in her system.

Rupert leaned closer, the volume of her voice lowered: "You're saying the facial recognition got it all wrong?"

"I'm saying there are too many unanswered questions."

"Here's a thought: Stop asking them." She whispered in his ear, "Want my advice? Lay off the *shabki.*"

Rupert gave Finnegan a look before walking away.

When Finnegan returned back to his crummy apartment where his neighbor next door was making a racket with the VR game *Hate Train* version_8_0, he put on the vinyl record of Johann Sebastian Bach's *Air on the G String* (Orchestral Suite No. 3) and pulled up the interior photos of Stella Nilsson's house on projector-gram. Despite Stella's recent death, the house was still on the market.

While combing through the photos on the public listing and comparing them to the ones on his eTablet, which were taken by forensics after the discovery of Stella's body, he picked out one discrepancy in the photo of Stella's master bathroom.

In one particular photo (the one which was on the market), there was a small decorative rock perched next to a eucalyptus-scented candle on the bathtub; however, in the photo on his eTablet (the one taken after Stella's death), the decorative rock was nowhere to be found on the bathtub.

Finnegan called his partner via VidChat.

After several pulses, Rupert finally answered the call.

From her ruffled, sleepy-eyed state, Finnegan woke her up.

"What is it, Wyllie?" asked Rupert, her face pale and glowing from the running sleep machine. She checked the time. "It's two o'clock in the morning—"

"Sorry to call at this hour, but I've been looking over Stella's file—"

"Again with this shit?"

"Hear me out—"

"Wyllie, give it a rest."

"Was there anything taken from her residence?"

Rupert thought for a second.

"No," she said. "Not that I'm aware of. Why?"

"If you ask me, it's a strange time to put your house on the market, especially while working on an exposé against JeneCorp. Seems like the last thing on her mind would be selling a house."

"Or maybe she saw something that scared her and she wanted to get the hell outta there," his partner said, again, as though she was doing everything in her power to avoid reopening a closed case. "Why are you really calling me, Wyllie—"

"Sorry to bother you, Roselle," Finnegan said shortly and ended the call.

He scoured The Feed until he located the same decorative rock with the engraved message "*Words Will Never Hurt Me*" on a discount store.

Below was the label: "ADD TO SHOPPING CART."

The detective paid for the order.

One week later, while sitting in his dark apartment and smoking from a bowl of crushed *sitoshahki* scales that he recently acquired from the black market in Chinatown, he received a *ding* on his phone, indicating that the drone had dropped off his package.

With the moon full in the night sky, he stepped out of the apartment and picked up the delivery from a secure locker and carried the package back to his apartment. He brought the secured box to his desk, opened it, and then, after pulling out the rock from the evidence baggie, matched the newly purchased decorative rock with the smaller piece, which the coroner extracted from Stella Nilsson's skull. The two letter L's on the rock matched the word "*Will*" in the message "*Words Will Never Hurt Me*."

"I knew it," Finnegan said to himself. "I fucking knew it. . . "

Given light of the new matching rocks, Finnegan, who after contemplating whether or not to call Rupert, decided to drive over to Stella's house.

As soon as he reached her neighborhood, he couldn't help but notice the power outage. Like his apartment, the entire block was left in pitch-black darkness. He thought about the intersection that he drove past before arriving at the neighborhood, those streetlights flashing yellow, and began to wonder if the whole South Pointe area lost power. If anything, the outage would make it easier to sneak inside her house.

He checked his phone upon exiting the car. He didn't have any bars. No signal. Which the detective thought was unusual, considering his phone was never affected during past outages, or what he worst feared, blackouts, at least in his neck of the woods.

Once he made it to her house, he used the passcode that he obtained from the realtor to enter the pitch-black house. He closed the front door behind him and while using the flashlight on his phone, went straight to the master bathroom where, after inspecting the bathtub, he came across a fine gray dust-like powder along the caulking on the tile floor. He ran his fingers across the gray powder and held it up to the light. The color of the powder matched the same color as the decorative rock. As he sat in the darkness, he visually mapped out the crime: Stella Nilsson arriving home after leaving Coyote Lounge, making herself a warm bath, and then, while doing so, being attacked from behind, the attacker attempting to drown Stella but Stella put up a fight but the attacker overpowered her and snatched the rock from her hand and used it on her, then, lastly, after the attacker rendered Stella unconscious, Stella's body was dumped in the Lanada River, since it was hard to make what happened right here look like a suicide when, more than likely, it wasn't the attacker's intention, so the attacker moved straight to a backup place: hack a vulnerable technology and make it look as though Stella Nilsson killed herself after the latest smear campaign against her name and her work.

While he reached for his phone to call Rupert but soon realized he didn't have any reception, he heard a *creak* coming from the hallway just outside the bathroom. He slowly moved his eyes upward, only to witness two bright flashes of light in the darkness followed by a sudden *pop pop* of gunfire coming from the black silhouette of a man standing behind the doorway.

The wind was knocked out of Finnegan, forcing him to look down at the bullet holes in his chest and the blood soaking his shirt.

Before he could spot the shooter, he fell backward. His body rolled and fell into the bathtub where he took his final breaths.

Stepping into the glow of the phone's light was the cyclops himself, Agent Noble, who was sporting a fresh scar on the top of his forehead.

After confirming Finnegan's death by feeling the pulse on the side of his neck, he tossed the junk gun under the vanity before peeling away translucent ID theft stickers from his fingertips.

The stickers, which were created with E'Raknish replication, left behind a set of fingerprints on the gun handle, as well as the trigger.

He walked back to his car, which was parked across the street, and lugged a large duffle bag into the house where he scattered trash, as well as a collapsible piece of cardboard, shit-stained drawers, and stinky laundry over the living room floor. The items belonged to a known squatter and scourge to San Cristó, Chad Fickle, who was recently tagged and released from jail after attacking an elderly lady with a fishing rod.

Twelve hours later, after Detective Finnegan's body was discovered inside Stella Nilsson's house earlier that morning, it didn't take the San Cristó Police Department long to match the fingerprints on the junk gun to Chad Fickle.

By sundown, the police had already made an arrest.

FINAL HOURS
NOVEMBER 22, 2048
DEATH VALLEY, CALIFORNIA

ROTTEN was nearing the end of the session, and D, despite the monotony of questions he was asking, didn't want the charming cataloger to leave. After months of cataloging, D bonded with Rotten and the two built what Rotten considered a friendly relationship, which was, more or less, manufactured and for the most part, one-sided, but, nonetheless, a relationship that D was forced to recognize as a way to better acknowledge and understand—or at least try to understand—the purpose of his existence during these final days. D reached a point in the session where he could speak more freely, especially a name which hadn't touched his lips ever since his first few sessions.

"*Genie*," he said, the name bringing warmth to his face, "'Genie Beanie' is what I called her, she was *mi roca* whose pneuma made each breath in my lungs worth savoring—"

One word immediately caught Rotten's ear.

"Pneuma?" said Rotten. "Where did you hear about that term?"

"Genie," he said. "I remember she first used it when she was talking about her experiences after she almost OD'd." He held up his fingers, both his index and thumb, pinched the two together, nearly touching one another as a way of showing Rotten the space between life and death. "She came this close to dying, you know?"

"What did she take?" asked Rotten.

"Lo-ro," said D. "Must've gotten a bad batch. Probably counterfeit. When Genie lost consciousness, she fell into this dark place, like 'hell,' she described it, but much worse, where time didn't exist. She told me she was trapped there for days, even though when she finally came to it, had only been minutes since she lost consciousness. She met this one cat with horns and said that she wasn't alive or dead, but somewhere in the middle. Her pneuma, her spirit, was all that remained, in its purest form, while the flesh from the world of the living was this vessel—if you ask me," D said from the corner of his mouth, "I thought Genie was making it all up in her head. But I told her that I believed her—"

"Why?" Rotten asked, reading D's gestures.

D shrugged.

"Who am I to tell her otherwise?" he said. "If she believed it was true, then it was true."

"Tell me more about Genie," Rotten said after reading the relief in D's face.

"She was three years older than me," he said. "Yet, she seemed so. . . so grown up. A lot of people she chilled with said she was out of her mind. *Loco*. I never saw her that way. To me, she was everything. And even if she came forward about the sex ring and testified against FSG and Lockhart, I knew nobody would've believed a word that came out of her mouth—"

"But you did?" asked Rotten, as he carefully listened.

"I believed every word she said to me," D said pensively. "The only truth that matters is the truth of the one you love. She could tell me anything, and anyone who told me any different was the liar."

Rotten braced for the worse.

"Even up to the end?" he asked.

The thought of what happened to Genie sent a ripple of raw emotion through D, a combination of rage and sorrow so heavy that it pulled him down into his last memory of Genie.

"Two weeks before Elvira, she was rolling a lot—"

"Chlorodionysus?"

"Lo-ro," he said, nodding. "Yeah. You'd think after her first OD she'd break the habit, but somehow, it had a hold over her."

"Why was she using again?"

"Why?" D repeated, replaying the trigger that sent his Genie Beanie into a downward spiral. "Why wouldn't she get back into lo-ro, especially after what happened in México? Of all people, B, you should know what happened was completely out of my control."

"Of course," Rotten said, siding with D. "*But* how about what happened in Edmonds Park? You could've protected Genie—"

"No," he snapped, cutting off Rotten before he could finish his thought. "There was nothing I could do."

"You said it yourself: *Bingo put a price on her head.*"

"As you know, B, *mi amigo*, once you enter that line of work, there's no escaping it."

"Knowing how risky it was to get involved with a girl like Genie, why did you fall for her?"

With tears filling his eyes, D said, "When I saw the story on The Feed while I was scoping out Elvira. . . " he held back the emotion, ". . . many times I wanted to stop what I was doing and track down Bingo and his crew and make them pay for what they did to Genie."

"Why didn't you?" asked Rotten.

"Doubt," he said. "There were doubts."

"That doesn't sound like you," Rotten said, studying D. "To do what you did takes motivation and extreme discipline."

"And a little bit of help," D said, referring to E'Raknish.

"Agreed." Rotten then asked, "So, why did you have doubts?"

"I didn't have doubts," D said more clearly. "I wanted to kill every single person who laid a finger on Genie. I wanted to burn down entire cities and breathe in the smoke of my enemies. I wanted to stand in the ashes of those who stole the one good thing keeping my ass in check, *but* it wouldn't let me. Whenever I attempted to leave, my body. . . "

Rotten studied D's face and clung to each one of his words as they hovered in suspension.

"My body locked up," D said after a short moment of clarity. "Somehow, it put up this invisible barrier, like a wall preventing from leaving Elvira. It was. . . I dunno. . . it was restraining me from giving into these urges. It was *reminding* me—"

"Reminding you of what?" asked Rotten.

"Time," D said. "All of these questions I kept asking myself, 'Was it selfish of me to stay in Elvira? Was it selfish of me to seek revenge in Genie's name? Would Genie want me to avenge her?' was me trying to convince E'Raknish for more time."

"Time for what?"

More upset, D asked Rotten, "Did you not see the story? They didn't even try to cover it up or make it look like a random attack."

"If that's the case, then are you saying Genie's death was part of the plan?"

D thought over Rotten's question.

"Yes," he finally answered, as the tears fell from his eyes. "If Genie was never killed, especially in the manner she was killed, I don't think I would've had the *cojones* to pull the trigger."

Rotten tried to push aside his own feelings for D, as he thought about Stella Nilsson and her death and how his own colleagues, one in particular, discarded the former reporter like trash.

After wiping the tears from his face, D asked Rotten, "What are they gonna do with me once you're through with your cataloging sessions?"

"Honestly," Rotten said, "I don't know, D. But whatever they have in store for you, I assure you there won't be any pain. I'll see to it that they take care of you. You have my word, D."

"Thanks," D said quietly, his red, tender eyes smiling at Rotten.

As the two sat in a comforting silence, there was a commotion outside the cell.

Rotten stood up and walked to the door and peeked through the window and saw several security guards and agents surrounding one of the subjects in the hallway. Among the agents was one of his colleagues, Noble, who was trying to restrain a hysterical woman. Inside the cell were four security guards, each one lying on the floor, not moving, unconscious, maybe dead.

The subject, Rotten soon realized as he stepped foot from the cell, was much older than what he was told through word of mouth around JeneCorp. She was one of the most dangerous people in the world—"one helluva witch," Motley once teased.

The alpha and the omega.

As Noble and another guard helped the badly wounded subject to her feet, one of the security guards, who woke from his unconscious state, stood up in a wobbly state while he grabbed hold of the backside of his head. As soon as he saw the subject being escorted to a medical bay, he picked up the wand from the floor and charged at the subject, tempting to shock her.

"You fucking bitch!" the guard shouted out, as he reared back the wand.

Noble released the subject, causing her to fall to the floor.

Before the guard could retaliate against the subject, Noble threw a swift karate-like chop, the blow landing directly to the guard's windpipe, immediately crushing it. In a choking manner, the guard dropped the wand as he fell backward and grabbed his throat, which had a massive dent in it.

While two guards rushed to the incapacitated guard's aide and began to work on him, Rotten stepped farther into the hallway. Behind him, D crept closer to the doorway for a better look at the subject on the floor. D witnessed the chaos inside the white room across the hallway. Bodies scattered everywhere, as well as what looked like a robot missing its head. A cleanup crew was standing around it, using extinguishers to put out the fire.

Bruised and bloody, the subject turned her eyes toward D and in that moment, the two made eye contact. He felt gripped by the sight of those frosty aged eyes, as if each one was a hand extending outward and grabbing hold of not only his body, but also his soul—his "pneuma."

While losing himself in her eyes, D was left slack-jawed and frozen in a trance-like state.

One after another, apocalyptic images started to fill his head.

Death and destruction.

The collapse of civilization.

In the gray ruins emerged an endless cycle of images depicting renewal; and before D could embrace them, all of these images streaming through his mind, he suddenly heard Rotten calling out his name.

"*Darwin?*"

Rotten snapped his fingers in front of D's face, pulling him from the trance.

As D tried to make sense of what just happened, Rotten turned to Noble, who was escorting the beaten subject to the medical bay.

While walking past the two, Noble eyed Rotten and said hostilely, "Mind your fuckin' business, Cataloger."

Lastly, the agent glanced at D and once he witnessed the confusion on D's face, he turned to Rotten once more and looked at him with disappointment.

Every agent and guard in the hallway knew D had been compromised after having made eye contact with the subject.

And so did Rotten.

Later that night, after D spent the rest of the day in a fog, he drifted off to the sound of Carolina's voice.

Her voice grew louder and clearer over a climbing sound of footsteps in the hallway outside the cell.

As the footsteps approached D's cell, his sister held his hand and guided him from the cell. As the group of shadowy figures approached from behind, Carolina walked D to the rear exit of the JeneCorp facility and once she opened the exit door, a brilliant sunlight shot into the darkness of the hallway. D stepped from JeneCorp and found himself back in Mexico.

He lost Carolina as he was trekking up a steep slope, avoiding snagging the JeneCorp getup on cacti and thorny bushes.

At the top of the hill was his childhood home, a place where his madre once resided, and as soon as he scanned his surroundings, he realized he was back in Sierra Madre del Sur.

Savory smells consumed the air, enticing him to approach the house; however, he feared entering for the final ghastly images of his ill madre left him severely scarred.

As he found the courage to enter the house, he found a familiar-looking woman standing in the kitchen. In front of her was a large cast iron pot where she was cooking a stew.

"I hope you brought your appetite," she said, as she used the wooden spoon to stir together the ingredients.

D stood at the doorway, hesitant about entering.

"Don't by shy, Darwin," she said.

"How'd you know my name?" asked D.

"I know a lot about you, Darwin," she said, patiently stirring the simmering stew. "I know you get rather testy when you're hungry. But then again, who doesn't? Am I right?"

With his stomach growling, D decided to enter the house.

He closed the door behind him; and as he approached the kitchen, he recognized the woman.

"You?" he said, referring to the older woman from earlier in the hallway outside his cell.

"Me," she said.

"I thought they killed you."

"Soon, they'll get their chance. But for now, why don't you join me for supper?"

"What are you making?" asked D.

"Rabbit stew," she said. "I remember when I was a young girl my father used to make it for me whenever I was feeling under the weather. I don't remember much of my childhood, but the one thing I'll never forget is my father's famous rabbit stew."

"Smells good."

"Thank you," she said and smiled at D.

"So, who are you?" asked D.

She set the wooden spoon on the countertop and said, "My name is Chloe."

"Nice to meet you, Chloe."

With a softer smile on her face, Chloe said, "It's nice to meet you, Darwin."

"So, how do you know about me?" asked D.

"Barney, 'B,' as you like to call him, he told me about you," she corrected, "well, he told me *indirectly*. You see Barney and that bag of bolts work in the same department; and moments before our little scuffle, I managed to gain access to the last person it came in contact with: another cataloger named Lonnie Hamlin. It's all a bit technical, Darwin, but Lonnie left behind a sort of digital fingerprint, if you will, temporarily imprinted on Mark's optical input. JeneCorp installed deflectors inside the droid's optics, making it nearly impossible for me to peek inside the mere flawless creation; however, what those boneheads at JeneCorp failed to take into account was ole Marky Boy's latest receptor responders, which were automatically disabled once it concluded a session in order to save power. What I'm getting at, Darwin," she said, acknowledging Darwin's utter bafflement, "apparently, Lonnie and Barney shared frequent chats in the break room before your sessions; and once I was able to access Lonnie, I was then able to access Barney and all of the conversations he had with you. A lot, huh?"

"Access? You mean his thoughts?"

"You're a fast learner, Darwin," Chloe said and returned to the stew.

"You can read minds?"

Chloe shrugged first, then nodded.

"If that's one way of looking at—"

"What other way can you look at it?" asked D. "Are you reading my mind right now?"

"Does it feel like I'm reading your mind?"

D thought for a second.

"No."

"Then, I'm not."

D looked around the kitchen.

"Is this a dream?"

"Does it feel like a dream?"

D shook his head.

"No," he said. "Strangely, it doesn't."

'Well, then, Darwin, it's not a dream; in fact, it's whatever you make it to be."

"What does JeneCorp want from you?" asked D.

"What every company wants. . . " she started, as she made her way into the garden outside. While plucking away several leaves of basil, she snatched a black snake slithering past her. She held up the snake to her face and said, not only to D, but also the snake, "*Power.*"

After she released the snake back into the garden, she grabbed a handful of rosemary from a shrub and brought it into the kitchen where she placed both the basil leaves, as well as the rosemary into the stew and stirred them in. She leaned forward and smelled the stew.

"Almost ready," she said and returned to D's question. "I know things may look dire, but do not fret, Darwin, things will get better and in the long run, they will return to normal."

"I don't even know what normal looks like anymore—"

"You and me both, but. . . " Chloe said and held her eyes in thought, ". . . I can only assume it looks like a world where people come together. Take the stew here: It takes time and most importantly, *patience* for all these wonderful flavors to naturally come together. But, of course, one may ask: 'Am I forcing flavors to come together?' Some may argue that 'yes; in fact, by merely introducing a new flavor to the mix, I am trying to change the original recipe.' Some may prefer to eat a rabbit bland and without any seasoning. To be honest, I'd say it's a small minority and wherever there's a minority, there's always a majority, and the pendulum will more certainly always swing both ways, and it's not my position to question one's preference," she said, stirring, "but rather suggest and offer flavors that will elevate the dish to its fullest potential and once the ingredients come together," Chloe tilted her head from the very idea, "it makes for one helluva dish, don't you think?"

She spooned out the stew and with her hand held underneath the spoon in order to catch any drippings, carried it over to D's mouth, asking him to sample the stew.

D obediently opened his mouth and tasted the stew.

"It's really good," he said. "One suggestion: I think it needs a little more salt."

Chloe then tasted the stew and said in agreement, "I think you're right."

She added a dash of salt to the stew and after she lowered the flame on the stove, she told D that she was all out of polenta. She asked if D would care to make a dish of his own.

"*Arroz con lima*," D said, as it was the first thing that entered his mind. "It'd be perfect with the stew."

"A worthy alternative, I'd say." She held out her arms. "The kitchen is all yours?"

"Really?"

Chloe waved D farther into the kitchen.

"Come," she said. "Just tell me what you need."

After shyly stepping forward, D listed all of the ingredients: Butter, rice, chicken broth, lemons, garlic, and last but not least, cilantro.

Chloe fetched each and every ingredient for D, including a bottle of chicken bouillon by the brand Neuvak.

As instructed, she stepped aside and gave D the floor.

D made the Arroz con lima the same way his madre used to make it, first by adding the stick of butter to the pot and letting it melt over the heat before adding the rice. From there, D added the rest of the ingredients, including the juice, as well as the zest of a lemon.

Once the meal was prepped and ready to be served, there was a knock on the door.

Chloe answered the door and to D's surprise, his madre was first to greet Chloe.

Next to enter the house was Carolina.

After Carolina was Miguel, Cashel, Gibbons, Judy, Sue and her son, Jack.

Then, after Jack, it was the head of The Chupacabras and the head of K-Town, both standing side-by-side, their differences put aside.

Lastly, Genie stepped inside the house.

D's eyes widened from the sight of his Genie Beanie.

The two embraced one another as though they hadn't seen each other in ages; and afterward, D escorted Genie to the chair closest to Chloe in the middle of the table. In a chivalrous manner, he held the chair out for Genie, who thanked him. D sat next to Genie and held her hand. Chloe asked D to say grace. The guests bowed their heads and held each other's hand while D thanked Chloe for the delicious meal.

After grace was spoken, Chloe dished out rabbit stew alongside D's Arroz con lima to each one of the guests. Together, everyone ate, shared stories, cried, and laughed.

Once supper was over, Chloe walked back to the kitchen where she grabbed a pill from the drawer. She brought the powder blue pill, which labeled "Q-13" back to the table and handed it to Genie, who said she'd do the honors.

"Will it hurt?" asked D.

Chloe said, "Of course not. Think of it as taking a short afternoon nap, then once you wake up, your friends and family will be here, waiting for you."

Genie grabbed D by the hand and told him to join her in a walk outside.

D said his "temporary" goodbyes to the guests and exited the house with Genie.

The two walked toward the sunset.

Genie found a rock on the side of the hill where the two had a postcard-like view of the valley and the sun setting just below the mountains. She instructed D to open his mouth. As D held open his mouth, Genie placed the pill on his tongue. D closed his mouth and swallowed the pill.

"How long will it take?" asked D.

"Not long," Genie said and held D's hand as he started to drift off.

D's final words: *"Te amo mi* Genie Beanie."

As D closed his eyes, Genie embraced him.

D fell to sleep in Genie's arms and somewhere, before a pink sunset the faint sound of a flatline could be heard running across the great valley.

BETWEEN THE DEVIL AND THE DEEP BLUE SEA
NOVEMBER 23, 2048
DEATH VALLEY, CALIFORNIA

WHEN Rotten returned to his living quarters, which were unaffected by recent blackouts, he was still left with a feeling of utter disgust by Tahr's latest decision to abruptly terminate the cataloging sessions with Darwin Acosta, also known as "Subject B-37," which was not only supported, but also heavily encouraged by Agent Noble, and Rotten was convinced that, if it wasn't for the short-tempered agent, he'd still be cataloging vital information for JeneCorp. But that time had passed, and Rotten's clearance tag no longer permitted him from gaining access to Subject B-37's cell, which was currently whited out.

Even though Rotten was properly trained and mentally prepared for moments such as these, the subject, like most subjects, being expendable, stepping aside from a job wasn't as easy as he anticipated and he'd be lying to himself if he said that he never shared any brotherly feelings toward Subject B-37. However, with recent revelations about Vernon's girlfriend, Sammie, whose body was discovered along a greenway last week after she was stabbed to death by a hired knife during an early morning jog, as well as the company that he built from scratch—his other baby, Hawkthetics™—which was burned to the ground by the same company ApexImplants, Vernon's rival and main competitor, that funded Sammie's death, Barney Rotten needed to reach out and touch someone.

And that someone was the cold shoulder of Death itself.

His own personal tour guide who'd escort him to the one person whom he was forbidden to contact during the duration of his mission.

As the disgust spiraled into a deep-seated anger racing through his veins, Rotten closed the door behind him and pressed his back against the door. He rolled back the cuff of his sleeve and looked down at the wristwatch, the minute hand positioned directly to the left of the hour hand in which sat below the number 12.

With keen focus and intensity, he stared at the hands of E'Raknish, the minute hand slightly trembling as though he was doing everything in his power to prevent it from moving.

All of a sudden, the minute hand ticked closer to midnight.

Three minutes till minute.

The sight of the minute hand left Rotten breathless, forcing him to reach down for a breath.

Rotten hurried to the bathroom, opened the medicine cabinet, and grabbed the bottle of Prosopagtamine™, and as he was about to pop a triangular orange pill, he became lightheaded. He dropped the bottle into the sink. The pills scattered and danced all around the vanity, most of the pills falling down into the drain. He left the bathroom and went straight to his bedroom where he grabbed an emergency bottle of Equanimity, as well as a needle, and filled the syringe to a lethal dose.

Next, he rushed to the closet and grabbed two cooling blankets, as well as the AED device and a sheath from the back of the closet, then grabbed a fifth of vodka from the kitchen, and then brought the items into the living room. He cleared away all the items from the coffee table until it was free of debris. He placed the two defibrillation pads on the proper areas on his chest, one above his right nipple and the other below his left nipple.

With the pads secured, Rotten pulled out the lava blade from the sheath. He switched on the blade, which starting to radiant like fire.

As the blade was heating up, he temporarily removed the casing from his wristwatch, revealing the slide of a zipper. He unzipped his left forearm and with the scolding hot blade, cut off a piece of E'Raknish, which was about the size of grain of rice. He carefully placed the piece of E'Raknish under the cooling blanket and closed his arm; and once the piece had cooled down, he poured vodka over E'Raknish, completely dousing it in order to mask its whereabouts. Once the piece was soaked with vodka, he inserted it into his right ear. Eight tiny legs extended outward from E'Raknish like a drunken spider. Once it found its footing, E'Raknish crawled deeper inside the canal and embedded itself into Rotten's eardrum.

Lastly, he wrapped his body with cooling blankets and lowered his core body temperature.

Once his body reached the ideal temperature, he injected himself with the drug, Equanimity, which would stop his heart within a matter of seconds.

Lastly, he set the timer of the AED to five minutes and waited for the hand of Death to grab hold of him.

He closed his eyes for a second and the moment he opened his eyes, a red light washed over the entire apartment. The night sky forever stuck in a bloody dawn. As he rose from the coffee table, the cooling blankets fell off his body. He peeled away the defibrillation pads and walked to the window where the red light was pouring into the apartment.

From a distance was Mount D'onwake, the tallest mountain along the range, and in its looming shadow sat the small town of N'ighku.

Rotten glanced down at his left wrist, which had been modified into a more fitting watch. A round gauge filled with his blood encapsulated by a glass vial no larger than an eyeball emerged from the underside of his wrist.

"The blood watch," Rotten said and carefully watched the blood empty from the gauge.

Five minutes in his world felt like an eternity in this cruel, dark one.

He told himself that he had a lot of ground to cover.

Without wasting time, he left the apartment and trekked through the red washed desert until he reached N'ighku, which, from the outside, looked like a ghost town. Each building was worn down by deadly dust storms, the exterior, including the shutters, in shambles. The dust-covered glass windows partially shattered while others remained carelessly boarded up. The inside of the buildings breathed the phlegmy, guttural sounds of a dying beast reaching out its gnarly, Stygian hand, except for one particular place: a local bar, the V Tavern, which was humming a repetitive tune. The words intensifying, clarifying: *Whesh'a, wahsh'a, umm, whesh'u, wahsh'u, numm.*

The sound of the low-pitched chant caused Rotten's head to spin.

As he stepped onto the front porch of the bar, he glanced up at the glowing letter "V" in the word *tavern,* which appeared much larger and bolder in the sign.

Locals referred to the place simply as "The V."

All of a sudden, Rotten was struck by a dizzy spell, forcing him to check the blood watch.

The gauge was significantly lower and nearly half-full and for a moment, he wondered how long had he been in the desert—hours, days, or even weeks?

Two worlds clashed like two magnetic forces repelling against one another; and one of those worlds, Rotten's world, made a desperate attempt to pull back one of its own.

Rotten fought against the pull and as his eyes crossed a puddle on the ground, he fell witness to the rippling letter V in the sign above, flipped upside down, appearing like the letter X.

With a slap to the face, Rotten recovered and managed to push aside the dizzy spell.

Before entering the lively bar, he glanced at himself in the reflection of a broken mirror. His skin was pale and the closer the gauge fell to empty, the paler and grayer his appearance.

He gathered the confidence and opened the front door. Those strangely spoken chants were suddenly replaced with a commonplace chatter of a bar: mostly sports talk, pussy talk, and a dash of grievances surrounding the toxicity of modern day politics.

Following the braking conversations, the long-faced patrons turned their heads toward Rotten, who stood awkwardly by the front entrance.

The bartender, Clay, was first to speak: "*If it ain't our good pal Barney,*" he hollered out.

Clay's words acted as a cue for the rest of the patrons to carry on with their business.

Surprised by Rotten's presence, Clay waved Rotten over to the bar.

Rotten shouldered his way through the crowded dining area where patrons were wearing bling on various parts of their body and sat at a stool at the end of the bar. Three serious-looking patrons, who looked as if they didn't belong in the jovial atmosphere, stood out like a raised scab.

Hanging on the walls were the silver framed paintings of the exploits of Annexus, one being a ritualistic hunt with Annexus using E'Raknish to hunt down vamps, as well as a painting called "The Skinny," which depicted a great battle at the base of Mount D'onwake, where the Annexus tribe fought off hordes of zombies caused by a ripple effect of The Black Plague outbreak. Many Annexus died during the great battle.

Clay threw a bloodstained towel over his shoulder and leaned up against the backside of the bar.

"What brings you to this neck of the woods?" asked Clay.

"Listen, Clypt'O," Rotten said bluntly over the chatter, the sound of Clay's *other* name causing the patrons to stop talking and turn toward the bar as if the air had been sucked out of the bar, "I appreciate the kind gesture here," Rotten said, referring to the inviting atmosphere, "but I have urgent intel that you need to hear. . ." he nervously glanced around at the patrons, ". . . without any distractions."

"I see," Clay said with disappointment.

The once intoxicating camaraderie melted away from Clay, who acknowledged the urgency in Rotten's voice.

Business-like, he headed straight toward a light switch next to the wall of liquor and flipped off the lights, revealing the real nature of the tavern. The jukebox music, the televised *Feast* on the overhead screens, the chatter, all of it came to a blaring silence. The interior of the building was no longer festive or decorated with historical paintings or Vamp products, swag, and memorabilia, but rather a much colder one. The walls, as well as the tables in the dining area and the bar, which piled before Rotten, were burnt and covered with soot. The ceiling near what used to be the restrooms was partly collapsed and the acid rain from the dark red sky above dribbled inside like a leaky faucet.

Rotten rotated around and over his shoulder, he witnessed those three members of Annexus, sporting E'Raknish on various parts of their body, lurching in the darkness. All of those patrons were gone, nowhere to be found, as though they were merely connected to the light.

A hot filter.

"Clypt'O," Rotten said cautiously, "tell 'em to back off. I mean no harm."

As though controlled by Rotten's mind, the blood watch rotated in a clockwise-like motion along Rotten's wrist, freeing E'Raknish. The two tiny hands of E'Raknish extended outward and formed into a handheld knife.

Revealing himself as Clypt'O, Clay lifted up his worn blue baseball cap from his head and ran his gnarly, clawed hand through her greasy long hair and faced forward, revealing E'Raknish in the dim light, which was normally as tiny as a pea, but given the circumstances, was roughly the size of a grape, which was attached to the center of his forehead. Like his hand,

Clypt'O's appearance was much different as well: his pneuma grayer and wrinkled and coarser. His eyes, or the illusion of eyes, were as black as a raven's.

The vibe inside the ruined building was tense, like two animals ready to square off.

As the three Annexus members crept closer to Rotten, who was willing to defend himself at all costs, Clypt'O nodded at the three.

"*Uk'sha*," Clypt'O hollered out.

The three stepped closer into the dim lighting and partly revealed their faces, which were similar to Clypt'O's.

Once more, Clypt'O hollered out, "*Uk'sha. R'pikna.*"

Eventually, the members of the tribe backpedaled into the shadows.

E'Raknish was inserted back into Rotten's wrist. The blood watch moved back to its proper place.

Glancing around the shabby, soot-covered interior of the building, Rotten said to Clypt'O, "I almost forgot about the extent of the damage from the last eruption. They're getting worse and more frequent, aren't they?"

"We make do with what we have—"

"By creating illusions?"

"If it brings peace to those left in N'ighku," Clypt'O said, his feet crunching through all the rubble, "then so be it. Despite all of our advancements, we are still at the mercy of D'onwake." Before Rotten attempted to respond, Clypt'O said more forthright, "You're breaking your cover for being here, and I know you didn't travel all this way to hear about our minor inconveniencies. So, *pleh. . .* " the words suddenly stuck like adhesive to a slick surface and Clypt'O made an "eh"-ing sound followed by a stuttering buzz that trailed off and then unified into a tightened recovery response, ". . . if you would excuse me for a moment."

While grabbing a knot ballooning along the center of his forehead, in particular, E'Raknish, which had overpowered his pineal gland, Clypt'O grabbed a syringe, as well as the dirty jar half-full of the creamy secretion, melas'jus, from a top shelf above the bar. He pulled out a key from around his neck and unlocked the lid of the jar, which was secured with a rusty padlock. Using the syringe, he inserted the needle into his swollen pineal gland coupled with E'Raknish, and after pulling back on the plunger, extracted the buildup of secretion inside his forehead.

"You good?" asked Rotten, as he watched Clypt'O release the secretion into the jar.

"The downfall, I suppose, of being linked to E'Raknish," Clypt'O said, recovering from the sudden buildup of secretion in his head, which, in relevant terms, he once compared to Rotten as hawking up a loogie. "Annexus's greatest strength and yet, our greatest weakness. At the end of day, it always comes down to balance, and lately, B'aus, let's just say he's been overexerting himself. I'm sure you can understand. But then again, you're not a hundred percent Annexus."

Rotten scowled at the remark before scouring the rest of the bar.

"I didn't see him around here," Rotten said over his shoulder. He asked Clypt'O, "Where is that sneaky *twin* bastard of yours hiding?"

"B'aus is no concern of yours."

"The instability of N'ighku is making your condition worse, isn't it?"

"It's not entirely to blame, *but*. . . " Clypt'O said, referring to the melas'jus and why he was producing more of the special hormone as of lately, ". . . I'm sure it doesn't help either."

Rotten couldn't help but notice a radiating mark left behind the needle on Clypt'O forehead.

"Must hurt," he said, nodding at Clypt'O's head.

"I don't feel pain, Barney." He pointed at the pea-sized E'Raknish on his head. "I'd say it's an ability that falls into the category of strength."

"Or weakness—"

"Please, Barney," Clypt'O said more clearly, "enlighten me. Why are you here?"

Mindful of his words, Rotten said carefully, "JeneCorp's planning an event that will lead the people of *my world* toward their extinction. The fate of E'Raknish is in peril, its main source of energy hangs in the balance, and if JeneCorp continues down this path, E'Raknish will be nothing more than a relic, Clypt'O."

"You were instructed to closely monitor and study the evolution of E'Raknish in your world, *not* interfere. You took an oath before D'onwake; and if you fail to delivery with your promise, Barney, there will be severe consequences."

"If it means saving E'Raknish from its ultimate demise, then I'm ready to accept these consequences. After JeneCorp has its way with E'Raknish, there won't be anything left to study."

"Do I need to explain the consequences for you, Barney—"

"You wrong about E'Raknish," Rotten said bluntly. Behind him, he heard a noise, which he thought sounded like a growl coming from one of the Annexus members. "Why do the old ways of Annexus often get confused with these misguided new ways?"

"And what exactly do you know about the old ways of Annexus, half-breed?"

"I know Annexus wouldn't stand for mass genocide," he said, referring to a preserved painting of The Skinny mounted crookedly on the wall, "because, if JeneCorp has its way, that's what's coming."

"And what? E'Raknish is trying to warn us?"

"Yes."

"Warn us how?"

"*The blackouts*," Rotten said confidently. "How do you prevent what's about to come next? You make people less dependent on the one vessel that will ultimately destroy them."

"Technology," Clypt'O said. "Humans greatest strength, yet their greatest weakness."

"If what you've said about B'aus is true, it's clear that he's become too comfortable in my world and he's starting to corrupt E'Raknish, which means. . . "

He's starting to corrupt you.

Rotten was terrified to utter those very words for the things Clypt'O was capable of left him catching the words before they left his mouth.

"What did Rouse promise you?" asked Rotten.

"The two most important things in your world, safety and security," Clypt'O said, "then, last but not least, part of the security end of the package, a share of the Company. In other worlds, he promised Annexus a sit at the table."

"It's all a setup, Clypt'O," Rotten pleaded. "Can't you see? All JeneCorp wants from Annexus is E'Raknish."

Clypt'O mulled over Rotten's predicament.

Walking closer into the dusty, dim light, he said to Rotten, "When I first found you, Barney, I hadn't met anyone like you before. You might've been a lost young man back in your world, an outcast, bound by flesh, who spent his formative years hiding behind a mask, surrounding by fear and paranoia, which led to a near-debilitating disease, but here, you had purpose, potential. You weren't one of us—not entirely and the truth is, Barney, you'll *never* be one of us—but you displayed the one characteristic that is sown into the fabric of Annexus: *Resiliency*. The fortitude to hold one's palm over a flame and not bat one single eyelash. You are molded by the holy fire, Barney, whereas otherworlders, like Raquel—"

"*Don't*," Rotten warned, his razor-sharp eyes aimed on Clypt'O black eyes.

Clypt'O held up his hand in surrender.

"Fair enough," he said. "My point is most otherworlders would've submitted themselves to the Void after being bit by a doppel-mängler, a misunderstood creature whom many back in your world fail to grasp its sole purpose, which is to recruit otherworlders, like yourself, Barney, who one day will bridge the gap between your world and mine—"

"Last I've heard is that those parasites have gone extinct," Rotten said, referring to the flying toad-like creature whose bite bound him to what he often mistook as hell. "So," he said, nodding at jar of melas'jus, "if I were you, I'd conserve that nightmare fuel of yours."

"Not all parasites are meant to be treated or worse, eradicated, but rather embraced, which is a rudimentary concept that your world still doesn't comprehend. Or another way of looking at it, the people of your world very much understand this concept and share the similar characteristics of those in the High Order, and glaht'tuhn'ee has poisoned their flesh and grah'yee'd has blinded their vision to see beyond the veil of ke'ah'nah'ti, obstructing any progress to be made—"

"What are you talking about?" asked Rotten, more suspicious.

"Ever since Sheik disappeared from the skies, our world has become completely unstable," Clypt'O said, referring to the great serpent. "Each moment without Sheik to protect D'onwake, the Eventide spreads farther and farther, stretching from Leatherwood to the Sacred Sands, swallowing everything in its path. The aftermath of Black Death has caused vamps to run scarce and even the vamps who have abided by our agreement are contaminated. And there's only so much resiliency one can endure before having to make an ultimate sacrifice: Either join the Eventide or carry on elsewhere."

Rotten said, "You're talking about leaving?"

"Enlighten me, Barney: If the people of your world found out who you were—the bond you share with Annexus—do you think they would embrace you? Do you think they would embrace us?"

"Hard to say," he said. "Eventually, they would, I guess, but I've been wrong before. What are you trying to say, Clypt'O?"

Clypt'O looked at Rotten with a strange look on his face.

"We're not all boo'shyees here," he said, holding up the key attached to the necklace hanging along his chest. "We do get out, some I'd say more than others. For example, take Mor'tah, that horny devil over there. . . " Clypt'O nodded at one of the Annexus members, who was concealing himself in the tricky shadows behind Rotten, a beam of dim light faintly glistening over a saber-like E'Raknish erected from his crotch, ". . . after Mor'tah got those slippery hands of his on the melas'jus, he traveled to your world and to put it mildly, misbehaved. Made Bundy look like a Mr. Rogers. Mor'tah's the reason why I was forced to lock up the melas'jus."

Repulsed but not at all surprised by Clypt'O's comment, Rotten grew a third eye in the back of his head, making sure to keep Mor'tah within his peripheral vision.

"You look like you've seen a ghost," Clypt'O said, pointing out the slow-change of color on Rotten's face, becoming more and more grayer, a sure-indicator that his body in the other world, the one he called home, was fading and would soon be food for worms.

Rotten turned toward his left where he witnessed through a shattered window the ominous-looking clouds darkening the red sky above.

"Tick tock, B," Clypt'O said with a glint in his eye, as though he was imitating Rotten's own words.

Rotten glared toward the shadows behind him.

He said to Clypt'O, "You think someone like Mor'tah will be able to survive in my world?"

"Eventually, Mor'tah will have to learn how to adapt to your customs; otherwise, he will be handled." Clypt'O said amusingly, "Knowing how much your people find Mor'tah's type fascinating, he might just make it after all. Hell! He might even turn into a celebrity—"

"How many times do I have to tell you—"

"Speaking of time, Barney," Clypt'O said, acknowledging the approaching storm on the horizon, "your time is almost up, and that brings me to your new mission: The doctor you've been following, Vernon Hawks, is scheduled to board a plane to Tokyo in ten days your time. I need you, Barney, to make sure that flight doesn't reach its destination."

Rotten asked, "I thought you said I wasn't supposed to interfere?"

"If you didn't come here, I would've found someone else for the job," he said, "but now that you're here, it might as well be you. After all, you wouldn't be here if it weren't for us. So, in a way, you owe us one."

Anticipating the first shock, Rotten said while eyeing the approaching storm, "What do you want me to do?"

"All you have to do is bring down the plane while it's over water."

"Why not just take out Hawks before he boards the plane?" asked Rotten.

"It needs to be done this way, and this way only. Understood?"

"But what about the other people on board?"

"They're expendable, Barney," said Clypt'O, "and anyone who's expendable is replaceable. Sorry. That's the deal—"

"Vernon Hawks is secondary," Rotten said, trying to weasel his way out of his new mission. "Why not go after someone more important like Lance Carmichael?"

Clypt'O said, "Hawks is JeneCorp's rising star, and Rouse knows Hawks may be compromised, which is why he had his highly-trained assassins frame the destruction of Hawks's company, as well as his girlfriend's death on Hawks's competitor, ApexImplants, thus, in return, setting off a string of unlikely events that'd force the disgruntled doctor to create an alliance with JeneCorp. Rouse and his state-of-art AI might've been wrong on several things, but after it ran a diagnostics, it came up with a revised prognosis on Hawks's future and results showed a 99.9% guarantee that Hawks would partner up with JeneCorp, and the untimely demise of Ms. Whitsett would serve as his tipping point. However, there's still the 0.01% chance that Hawks will carry out his little scheme to sabotage E'Raknish. Despite these overwhelming odds, he's *still* human. Which makes him too unpredictable."

"You don't have to worry about Hawks anymore," Rotten said, trying to convince Clypt'O to reconsider the next course of action. "I've obtained enough data to study E'Raknish for ages, data stemming all the way back to when E'Raknish was first put on the map." The very idea of how E'Raknish wound up in his world caused him to crack a laugh. "It all started from an accident, a goddamn shipping error, Clypt'O! One of your Annexus stooges mishandling an export of vamp blood," Rotten said with a frantic excitement. "A shard of E'Raknish chipped off during processing and somehow, wound up in the vamp blood. . . ."

One of the Annexus members didn't take Rotten's comments lightly, as he stepped from the shadows, E'Raknish drawn out into two fangs.

"*R'pikna!*" Clypt'O ordered.

Ignoring the threat looming behind him, Rotten said, "Clypt'O, there has to be another way to handle Vernon. Let me talk to him—"

"This is the *only* way."

Rotten heard distant rumbles of thunder. He glanced down at the blood watch on his wrist, which was nearly empty.

With the same strange look on his face from before, Clypt'O said, "Did you forget, Barney? In here, time is a broken clock. It can move forwards *or* backwards. So, what makes you certain E'Raknish accidentally entered your world? Did you ever stop to think Barney that maybe some *things* happen for a reason?"

Shocked by Clypt'O veiled admission, Rotten demanded him to elaborate.

The bolt of lightning suddenly cut through the black sky and caused Rotten to flinch.

"Don't worry, Barney," Clypt'O said with a mischievous smirk. "All you need to know is that 'Where E'Raknish is going, there won't be a short supply of food—'"

As Rotten embraced the energy growing heavier around him, he thought about the blood, the gori that JeneCorp was storing in the labs. Rotten once heard it was the type of blood that would deem humans irrelevant, obsolete. Having sampled the gori, Rotten knew firsthand of its effects, and E'Raknish was the only thing durable enough to handle its power.

Another bolt of lightning, this time much closer.

"Don't forget," Clypt'O said, as he drifted back into the shadows behind the bar, "if you fail to deliver your mission, I won't hesitate to rip E'Raknish from the one thing you hold most dear. And mark my words, Barney, it'll be like no pain you've ever experienced—"

Yet another bolt of a lightning, this time penetrating the ceiling above and striking Rotten!

Gasping for air, Rotten bolted upright and found himself back in his apartment.

The cooling blankets fell to the floor.

Violently shivering, Rotten caught his breath.

Every muscle in his body was tight and convulsing so badly that he nearly broke a rib.

He stood to his feet and tried to move the blood back into his extremities. He stumbled into his bedroom and grabbed a couple of blankets and tried to warm himself. Finally, after the shivering lessened, he walked to the bathroom where he looked at himself in the mirror.

He had no face.

Panicked, he ran his cold hand over his eyes, nose, mouth.

Not a single facial feature could be seen or felt, only his flesh.

One giant blur of a face.

He found an orange pill lying on the vanity and swallowed it and by the time he splashed his face with warm water, the drug had already worked its magic.

Once more, he looked in the mirror and relief washed over him.

DEEP SHIT
DECEMBER 2, 2048
CLOVERSON, TEXAS

THIRTY miles south of Austin.

Located inside the heavily secured ranch-style house surrounded by a hundred acres of land was the home base of a one-woman operation.

Located at a safe distance outside the house, heavy-duty generators were warm and running at full speed, even though the lights inside the West Wing bedroom were switched off. One light remained on, and it came from the flickering glow of a computer screen.

Last night, the first dump—or segment—known as "Loch Ness Files #1," the debut of a collection of exposés from controversial and widely-criticized journalist Mavis "Mavs" Caste's new project <u>FLAMING SPEAR</u>, was a success just hours after it was unleashed on The Feed. Based on the overwhelming reception, the overall reaction being net-positive despite nearly half of the country was left in the dark due to recent blackouts, the first dump kept Mavs's diehard followers engaged, the name "Flaming Spear" spreading like a wild fire across The Feed, and that dangling carrot (". . . "), which Mavs left at the end of Loch Ness #1, had even her most vocal critics on their toes.

In Loch Ness #1, Mavs brought to light a more thorough and accurate timeline surrounding the death of disgraced reporter and fellow journalist, Stella Nilsson, who, according to the SCPD, plummeted from the Holmes Bridge into Lanada River, the current carrying her body to the Pacific where her body was washed ashore on Pearl Beach. Stella Nilsson's death was ruled a suicide based on circumstantial evidence, later proven as a false narrative concocted around Stella's September 8th report in order to make her death carry the "appearance of a suicide."

With permission from Stella's mother, Mavs hired a well-respected independent coroner to perform an autopsy after Stella's body was exhumed. According to the coroner, Stella didn't die from drowning or a fall from the Holmes Bridge; and based on a cascade of evidence to support Detective Finnegan's theory, Stella Nilsson was murdered. In the report, the coroner stated that Nilsson was "bludgeoned to death." The murder weapon wasn't like trying to find a needle in a haystack. Instead, it was right in front of everybody's nose—no pun intended.

After Detective Finnegan was shot to death while searching for missed evidence inside Nilsson's house (Mavs also released proof, showing that the surveillance monitor of convicted killer, Chad Fickle, was hacked the night Finnegan was killed), Mavs managed to uncover Finnegan's past purchases and one item in particular stood out the most and pointed Mavs directly to the killer's weapon of choice: a decorative rock, which wasn't like any ordinary knickknack. Through rigorous testing, the coroner concluded that the rock, based off raw forensics, matched the same weapon used to kill Stella Nilsson, thus Mavs turning her focus to the footage taken on the night Stella leaped to her death. Mavs and her motley crew of cyber jocks who used The Feed as their own battleground dissected the video, frame-by-frame, and determined, based on hard data, that it was, in fact, a deep fake, which lead into a continuation, Loch Ness #2.

Waiting behind the computer screen with the prompt on the window before her, Mavs finger hovered over the "ENTER" key.

She reread the message, asking her for permission to send "Loch Ness #2."

The cover-up of Stella Nilsson's death lead into the next dump—or segment—which played out like one of the gripping dramas on The Feed. In Loch Ness #2, Mavs shined a flashlight into the dark, seedy closet which was the September 8th Assassination Attempt of President Lockhart and directly aimed that light on the shooter, America's very own boogeyman, Jared Flack, who, according to her findings, including evidence to support the claim that Flack was wrongfully accused of firing the weapon that took the life of a former mayor of Elvira, Bembe Pérez, and left the President of the United States severely injured, shared a similar fate as Stella Nilsson: The video of Flack leaving PRINT USA was bogus, partly AI generated to make it appear as if Flack was the shooter fleeing from a location where the alleged shot was fired when, based on several eyewitness accounts, the real shooter on September 8th was sixteen-year-old Darwin Acosta, who was positioned inside Bayside Hotel.

Standing in the shadows in the corner of the office, Blot asked Mavs, "Once you hit that button, they will hunt you down; in fact, they're probably watching you right now, as we speak."

"I know," she said and turned to the body cam attached to the bulletproof vest. The 24-hour coverage of her daily life warranted enough concern for Blot to question whether or not she was fit for the job. For Mavs, her paranoia didn't have any limits when it came to releasing bite-size pieces of easily digestible information to the public (She was transparent, to say the least); however, for Blot, the many surveillance cameras mounted on Mavs's ranch property was enough to win him over. And the catch: Mavs knew she was bait. She said, "And I will be ready."

"What does Century think of your latest feat? Will they stand by your side or will they fold like a lawn chair?"

"I should ask you the same thing about your boy, Rotty," she said and readjusted the microphone above the desktop. "Last I saw him he looked like he was about to crack. . . ."

"It's not Rotten who I'm worried about," Blot said. "It's companies, like Century, who, for years, built up their brands as voices for the common American citizen, only to become the very entity that they stood against." The answer wasn't satisfactory enough for Mavs, clearly, as she rotated her head over her shoulder and glared at Blot with rancorous expression. Blot elaborated on his previous remark: "Barney Rotten has been thoroughly deepriefed about his undertaking. Tomorrow, JeneCorp will be rolling out the red carpets for all of its employees and making sure the lights are on and the runways are open, if you get my drift."

"As you wish," she said nonchalantly and faced forward, returning her thoughts to her partnership with the independent media company. "I trust Century to do the right thing. JeneCorp can't silence all of us, you know?"

"But they can, and it doesn't matter the slightest what kind of fancy gadgets you have," Blot said, referring to the anti-AI plug-in connected to the high-tech camera.

"If it brings me reassurance—"

"You saw what recently happened to Mr. Barker."

"Jake was, how do I say, a passionate hombre, and the body can only take so much passion."

"You and I both know he didn't die from natural causes."

"Speaking of Barker," Mavs said, "I could use an extra hand here. For reassurance."

"How about those cyber jocks of yours?"

"They're about as aloof as cats."

"I'll see what I can do," Blot said. "But no promises."

Mavs rotated around in her chair and glanced over her shoulder at the shadowy figure in the corner of the dimly lit office.

"I've been dark for too long, my friend, and my followers are going to start getting worried," she said and winked at Blot. "See you on the other side." A name suddenly popped into Mavs's head. The one she had filed away in her memory bank. "One more thing. . . ." Mavs said, before going live, ". . . does the name *Swagahgali* mean anything to you?"

"It's a mining city in the Democratic Republic of the Congo. Why do you—"

"I'm aware of that," Mavs said for she didn't appreciate when facts were recited back to her. "What I meant to say is. . . Why did Stella circle the name in her notes? From what I discovered on The Feed, there were rumors—conspiracies—about Swagahgali and a legend surrounding one of the abandoned mines, saying there's lost film of a metallic artifact discovered on the skeletal remains of a John Doe. To me, it sounds like it could be evidence of E'Raknish. . . "

"The film was destroyed in a mudslide after a severe thunderstorm," Blot said. "Tragically, the film crew, who was filming a documentary in Swagahgali, perished in the mudslide. And so did these remains."

"Loyal News, yeah? Based out of London?"

"You've done your homework."

"Is it a dead end?"

Again, her voice was curved like a question mark, as though she was waiting for a cue from Blot to further proceed with an investigation.

Blot asked, "Is that what you think?"

"*What if* there's a connection?"

"Maybe," Blot said suspiciously.

"That's it? *Maybe*? That's all you got for me?"

Full stop.

For the time being, Mavs put her theory to bed.

She shrugged and moved onto other business.

"A'ight," she said and removed the strip of black electrical tape from the lens of the camera positioned on the desk and hit the mute button ("◀") on the keyboard, which brought her back to the live stream, Raw Feed's *Giving It To You Raw*.

She said directly into the camera, which was recording a live stream of the upcoming dump, "Here it is, all you Raw Dawgs." She held her index finger over the enter key on the keyboard, teasing her followers. Then, slowly, she dropped her finger, as if it was a bomb. "Loch Ness #2 dropping in three, two, one. . . "

Mavs hit the enter button, sat back in her chair, and waited for the chaos to begin.

A ONE-WAY TICKET TO HELL
DECEMBER 3, 2048
LOS ANGELES, CALIFORNIA

FOLLOWING the recent "incident" with Mark, who was currently decommissioned for repairs and upgrades, Rotten managed to convince Tahr that his invaluable services would come in handy in Tokyo and would only help lessen the strain of the process, as well as smooth out any wrinkles, especially among his fellow JeneCorp employees who were feeling on edge about the upcoming Second Ascension.

With a seat secured, Rotten boarded JeneCorp's electric-powered airplane, Crane Aviation. He was already piss-drunk, his speech two drinks away from being slurred, and putting good use to his air legs after spending the two hours before boarding at a pub outside the terminal. Hammering away one shot after another of whatever hard liquor he could wrap his numb lips around. Not only building up his confidence, but also preparing his body for the horror that awaited him.

While Rotten strolled to his window seat, he waited until the flight attendant left her post; and as soon as the distraction was sprung, he pocketed a handful of airplane bottles from the bottom of the food cart. The passenger, a contractor hired by JeneCorp, was an engineer lending a hand in Tokyo. His name was Tom, but his name didn't matter at all to Rotten because he was merely a temporary puppet.

Just moments before boarding the plane, he planted a shard of E'Raknish, as thin and tiny as a strand of hair, on the back of Tom's neck. Its sole intention: Slip inside a pore on his skin and wreck havoc on his hair follicle, driving Tom madder than a hag with one of the worst cases of shingles. As though on cue, Tom left his carry-on bag in the overhead bin and all of a sudden, went to town on that flaming red neck of his at the exact moment Rotten crossed the food cart. He didn't entirely make a scene or delay the takeoff, but his minor inconvenience was enough to draw the flight attendant away from the food cart, leaving it vulnerable.

Before taking his seat, Rotten spotted Vernon, who, given the tense situation, appeared surprisingly calm, which gave Rotten the impression that he failed to follow through with his first task:

Taking out Carmichael's E'Raknish, or any of the remaining templates inside JeneCorp's facility in Death Valley. Upon seating, he eyed the hatch along the floor, which would take him directly to the front hold of the cargo compartment below the cabin where he planned to release E'Raknish, which, in return, would slip into the engine and shut it down.

The flight attendant stopped by each seat, instructing passengers to fasten their seatbelt.

Rotten lost track of time.

Before he could regain his bearings, the diversion was created.

The signals in which he communicated with E'Raknish were hindered due to the alcohol.

Once more, the strand-like piece of E'Raknish suddenly dug into Tom, who sprung up from his seat just moments before settling down.

The window was closing, Rotten knew.

He had to act fast; otherwise, he would miss the opportunity.

As several other flight attendants tended to Passenger Tom, leaving the hatch door exposed, Rotten made a move to the cockpit. Only a few steps in, he caught Vernon in the corner of his eye.

All he could think about was the number one.

A percentage: 0.01.

Such a small number.

Yet, it was still a number—at least a fraction of a number.

Which meant all he needed was a push.

Rotten suddenly rotated around and then headed toward Vernon's seat.

Right as he approached Vernon, he tripped over his own two feet, stumbled toward the floor, and during the fall, bumped shoulders with Vernon.

Rotten grabbed the back of Vernon's seat, preventing him from falling into Vernon.

Without Vernon realizing, Rotten dropped a photograph into Vernon's lap.

Then, after a swift apology, Rotten exited the plane.

As Vernon shook off the latest drunken encounter, he glanced down at the photo in his lap. He grabbed the photo; and as he was about to call out to Rotten, he noticed the face in the photo.

"Sammie?"

Shocked by the discovery, Vernon flipped over the photo and found what looked like a metallic earpiece taped to the back of the photo.

The tiny symbol on the bottom of the earpiece indicated E'Raknish.

But the face in the photo, Sammie—*how would he have gotten this photo?*

The photo was taken two years ago while Vernon and Sammie were at a ballgame.

Hesitant, Vernon turned his attention back to the earpiece.

As his thoughts started to spin, he specifically remembered Forsake's words: *"That's where my guy comes in,"* he said. *"He will open doors for you."*

Vernon inserted the earpiece into his ear.

On the earpiece was a loop of audio, a throaty voice saying: *"Hawks is JeneCorp's rising star, and Rouse knows Hawks may be compromised, which is why he had his highly-trained assassins frame the destruction of Hawks's company, as well as his girlfriend's death on Hawks's competitor, ApexImplants, thus, in return, setting off a string of unlikely events that'd force the disgruntled doctor to create an alliance with JeneCorp. . ."*

As Vernon allowed Clypt'O's confession to sink in, Rotten scrambled from the airport.

Two and a half minutes till midnight.

Feeling E'Raknish tightening against his left ulna, Rotten downed another airplane bottle of vodka, which helped ease the squeeze of Death.

But he knew it wasn't going to stop.

Clypt'O had already taken hold, and soon, he would rip his pneuma.

Apparently, Clypt'O, unsure about Rotten's commitment, already had a Plan B in order.

Plan B being a blonde-haired flight attendant, who was activated within minutes after takeoff.

She excused herself from the other flight attendant and when she found herself alone, regurgitated a ball of E'Raknish from the pit of her stomach. She pulled out E'Raknish, which was covered in saliva and vomit, from her mouth and released it below the cabin.

Two minutes till midnight.

Time was running out and there was only so much alcohol he could consume before he passed out, which would be the death of him.

Rotten downed yet another airplane bottle in an attempt to mask Clypt'O's pull.

After stumbling to his car, he sped to the nearest hotel outside LAX and made a phone call to Forsake.

"Contact me through ghost—"

"Don't have time, Jin," Rotten slurred, as he stumbled through the hotel parking lot.

"What I'd tell you about using a secure line?" Forsake whispered sharply, as though he was in the vicinity of unwanted ears.

"I don't give a shit about your fuckin' rules," Rotten snapped, as he flexed every muscle in his body and tried to keep E'Raknish from migrating up his arm. "I need your help, Jin! Now, god-damn it!"

"What's happened to you?"

"It's Clypt'O. . . " Rotten said while fighting off the pain that strummed each and every nerve in his body as if the nerves were strings on a guitar. "He's gonna tear me to fuckin' shreds, Jin." More weaker, he begged Jin, "Please, Jin, whatever it takes—"

"Hold tight," Forsake said. "I'm sending a guy your way. Where are you?"

Rotten wore the grimace on his face as if it were a mask.

"A hotel called the Lucky Horse right outside the airport. . . " he said, as he struggled to hold up his head, ". . . I'll send you co-ordinates."

From what Rotten could tell after a clumsy inspection, the hotel had power, and based on the half-full parking lot, as well as the full ice machines, hadn't lost any power anytime soon, which, in that brief moment, made Rotten wonder how long the hotel had power or if the hotel ever lost any power during the black-outs.

Rotten ended the call and while holding his left arm, stumbled into the Paris-themed lobby of the hotel where a sleepy, bearded front desk clerk dressed in a black and white stripe shirt with a black beret said in a forlorn monotone voice, not to the guest, but rather the sound of the *chirp* of the door opening, *"Bonjour,* wel-come to the Lucky Horse Hotel. . . " He moved his eyes upward from the *Stargazer* comic book to Rotten and perked up from the sight of the half-human, half-Annexus lurching before him, ". . . you a'ight, man? You having a heart attack or something?"

"Or something," Rotten said, grimacing.

Even speaking hurt.

"You sure you good?"

"I need a room," Rotten said, his body trembling.

"Listen, man, I can call someone if—"

He nodded at all of the various racehorses on the wall.

"How does this work?" asked Rotten.

"Well," the clerk rotated around toward the wall behind him, keeping Rotten in the corner of his eye, "you just place a bet on the room of your liking—"

He placed a bet on number 36.

"*Runs With Horns*," the clerk said. "Excellent choice."

The clerk grabbed the room's key from the wall and as he was about to hand it over to Rotten, he snatched it out of his hand, paid for the room, and left the lobby before the clerk could instruct him on the "rules" of the hotel.

Rotten stumbled from the lobby and grabbed a bag of ice from the cooler outside. He held the bag of ice against his left arm, which temporarily helped with the pain. He could hardly stand up straight. The sidewalk before his eyes was slithering like a serpent, the gravity starting to weigh down on him, an entire world moving down in elevator-fashion, collapsing and bringing forth yet another world, a deeper, darker one rising from the depths of the black asphalt.

Rotten stumbled past Room 35, a yellow door.

The sidewalk below started to spin.

He took three more wild and exaggerated steps.

One more step, and he was home.

Swaying back and forth, he finally arrived at Room 36.

The red door before him swelled and shrunk and pulsated.

The color of the door matched the gray horse's attire.

His eyes crossed the minute hand of his wristwatch.

One minute till midnight.

Creeping closer to twelve, the minute hand started to tremble.

Rotten suddenly heard Clypt'O's words crawling through his ears: "*Tick tock, B.*"

He saw Clypt'O standing to the left of him with a glint in his eye, wearing a peculiar look of his face that he once witnessed before.

Back at JeneCorp.

In the labs with Carmichael.

A similar look worn on the face of Niles Baldwin.

Rotten peered past the flesh and beyond the façade, he witnessed B'aus.

Looming in the darkness.

Hiding inside Niles.

Like a parasite.

Clypt'O leaned forward and whispered in Rotten's ear, "*Someone had to keep an eye on you.*"

As Rotten reached for the door handle, a bolt of pain shot up his left arm. His fingers curled inward. He tried to pull back his stiff, calcified fingers into their proper place, but the blood was thickening and every tendon was like trying to bend steel. His legs suddenly became heavy. He lost balance.

Unable to gain composure, he blacked out and fell to the ground.

In the blackness a face materialized above him.

Raquel.

Her nose ring glistened in the dying sunlight.

With a strange little smile on her face, she helped him to his feet.

He was sixteen again. A disturbed Goth kid who adored Raquel and looked up to her as if she was the only person who existed in the world.

She told him to remember the pact.

"By sundown," she said, "we leave together."

Rotten looked around the Emerald Park and found a spot next to the river.

"I was thinking the same thing," Raquel said, as she guided him toward the glowing meadow.

When they arrived, he pulled out a wadded napkin from his pocket and opened it, revealing at least five purple pills.

"How many will it take?" asked Raquel.

"Two should be enough," he said and placed two pills into her open palm.

Right before Raquel popped the pills, Rotten said abruptly, "Wait." With more clarity, Rotten looked around Emerald Park. All of a sudden, the once eerily quiet park sprung with life: parkgoers appeared, some setting up romantic picnics while others walking dogs or watching birds in the trees or simply, admiring and absorbing the natural life around them.

Rotten held Raquel's hand before she could raise the pills toward her mouth: "This isn't supposed to happen. We're about to make a terrible decision." More urgently, Rotten pleaded with Raquel, "Take a look around. We can make this world into whatever we want it to be. We don't get to let *them* decide anymore."

"It's too late, B," she said hopelessly. "This place is beyond saving. . ."

The atmosphere around them grew heavier, darker, and grimier, realistic.

The park was littered with trash and debris, including the artifacts of Raquel's version of humans: drugs, syringes, needles, used sex toys, condoms, vomit. A man was fucking a hooker behind the bushes. A snapping turtle was choking on a piece of bread laced with a razor blade. A group of teens were filming acts of random violence and savagery, mostly beatings. An elderly man was hanging himself by a noose over a walkway. Some kid with a VR headset was pushing passerbys in front of speeding cars.

Raquel popped the pills into her mouth.

As her eyes rolled into the back of her head, Rotten desperately tried to revive Raquel.

Her pulse weakened.

She was fading.

Rotten had no other choice than to follow her into the darkness.

A coarse hand slapped Rotten across the face, snapping him from his numb daze.

A leathery grayish face appeared before him.

"I sure as hell hope you're Barney Rotten," the stranger said.

As Rotten gathered his strength, he frantically looked around the bathroom, only to find himself in a bathtub filled with icy water. Despite not being able to feel his limbs, he made a desperate attempt to exit the bathtub, but the stranger who called himself "Willie," said that the water would help weaken E'Raknish.

"Who the fuck are you?" asked Rotten.

His tongue was swollen, and the words that dripped from his mouth were as thick as honey.

"Our mutual friend said you were in need of help. Well, I'm here to help."

"How'd I wind up in here?"

"I found you outside the hotel room, rambling on about some girl named Raquel—"

"How long have I been out?" asked Rotten.

"Well, I arrived here about ten minutes ago," he said, "I left as soon as I got the call from Jin. So I'd say roughly twenty minutes. Just curious. . . " he nodded at the watch that he attempted to remove from Rotten' wrist but failed, ". . . what happens at midnight?"

"I die," Rotten said bluntly.

Flabbergasted, Willie said in his creamy-thick Southern drawl, "A'ight. So then, I assume it's E'Raknish, right? So what da hell happens when I remove it from your arm?"

"I die," he said again. "But this time, like everybody else."

"And you're sure you want it removed?"

"It's the only way to rid Clypt'O's grip over me," Rotten said, his eyes swimming around the sockets of his skull.

"What the heck kind of name is Clypt'O?" Willie joked. "Must be a weird dude."

"You have no idea," Rotten said, weaker.

"Well," Willie said, sliding over a bag of surgical tools, "let's get this over with, shall we?" He pulled out an anesthetic first and then a bone saw. "From the elbow down, correct?"

The sight of the bone saw caused Rotten to pass out.

"I'll take that as a 'yes,'" Willie said comically, as he numbed the already numb area around Rotten's elbow.

When Rotten opened his eyes, he found himself lying next to a naked woman with the tattoo of a scorpion on her back right shoulder. His left arm was lying underneath the left side of her body. The arm was dead and all the blood had been cut off from the elbow-down, creating a sort pins and needles sensation as the naked woman rotated around and freed his arm.

As the blood moved back into his arm, the slender, athletic woman faced Rotten.

Laura, his rebound after his high school sweetheart, "Nisha," who showed him, if only briefly, what a normal life could look like after Raquel's death.

Who had given him a boy whom he couldn't even bring himself to mention.

The thought of his name, even when it dangled on the tip of his tongue.

The sound of his boy's name, as well as the thought, drove him mad.

But he told himself over and over again: "We could've given life another try."

If Nisha was his angel who saved him from venturing back into the abyss, then Laura was his devil who satisfied all his immediate yet temporary needs, as well as wants without the promise of stability.

A hungry-eyed devil, post-pill and pre-cut, a messy-haired lover before a well-respected colleague, who, every now and then, would rehash all of their past exploits. He loved Laura; yet, at the same time, he loathed her.

Two speed demons in a rush to find connection.

He told himself that it could've worked out with Laura, like it once did with Nisha before the death of their son, but he was only lying to himself.

They were too alike.

"Bad dream?" said Laura.

"Yeah," he said, pressing his body against Laura's. "But I'm much better now."

"What was your dream about?" Laura asked, as she ran her fingers along Rotten's left arm.

The scar was gone.

He looked into Laura's eyes, not Agent Motley's.

"Isn't it bad luck to share a dream before breakfast?"

"I've never heard that before," Laura said with a smirk on the corner of her face. "Is that like a 'Rotten' saying?"

"I dunno," he said. "I heard it once from someone. Can't remember who."

"You don't strike me as the type to fall for superstitions."

"You've only scratched the surface."

"Well," Laura said, sliding her hand below the damp bed sheets, "considering you're already had your breakfast, it looks like you're going to have to share."

"But I'm still hungry," Rotten said and kissed Laura on the lips.

Rotten woke up from surgery with a massive hard on.

The feeling of Laura running her fingers over his arm echoed through the empty space.

Willie couldn't help but notice Rotten pitching a tent underneath the covers.

"*Rise and shine*, Beauty Queen," he said and welcomed Rotten back to the land of the living.

He lowered the volume on the TV, which was airing a breaking news report about the recent disaster over the Pacific Ocean. Rotten caught only several sound bites before the volume was muted. He read a tail-end of the closed caption, the report stating "*Crane Aviation's Flight 357*" crashed after "one of the engines exploded," pieces of the "plane" scattered along turbulent "waters." "*No known survivors among the wreckage.*"

Rotten perked up a bit and told Willie to unmute the TV.

The ghost of an arm was the very least of his concerns.

Willie said while grabbing the remote, "They're saying the plane took off at LAX."

"Yeah," Rotten said. "I was on that flight."

"For reals?"

Willie shot an uneven glance at Rotten and turned up the volume to its max.

The report restated: "As of now, no known survivors among the wreckage. The cause of the explosion is still left unclear. According to the Coast Guard, rescue divers are currently searching for the black box."

"What exactly were you planning on doing in Tokyo?" asked Willie, who suddenly retracted the question. "Forget I asked. Let's talk about you. How you feeling?"

Groggy from a cocktail of drugs, Rotten noticed the blood-spotted bandages worn around the stump of his left elbow.

He even tried to wiggle his fingers, which Willie had placed inside a water cooler.

"Takes a while to get used to," Willie said, sitting down in a chair next to Rotten.

"Easy for you to say."

Willie rolled up the pant legs of his blue jeans and displayed to Rotten both prosthetics. Lastly, he pulled the sleeve over his left arm. Unlike the legs, which were both made from titanium, the arm appeared like any other arm; however, the skin, as he pointed out, was made out of silicon.

"Triple amputee," he said, rotating around toward the other queen sized bed behind him. On the bed was a spread of prosthetic left arms. Altogether, there were three arms, the first one was pretty basic with a hook for a hand; the second one, slightly more advanced than the one before with a pincer-like grip; and the third one had a hand with five fingers. "This here is a collection of my oldie goldies. They'll come in handy for the time being," he said, trying to muster a laugh from Rotten, who failed to find any humor in the pun. "I recommend the second one."

"Why that one?" asked Rotten.

Willie said with a wink, "Chicks dig a fella with a claw."

"You knew Vernon Hawks?"

"I sure did," he said, lifting one of his prosthetic legs. "He's the one who gave me these bad boys."

"Then you know he was on that flight, right?"

"Shut the fuck up," he said, shocked. "Serious?"

Rotten nodded.

"Yeah," he said, trailing off. "As serious as serious can get."

"Fuck," he said and momentarily drifted off in reflection. "You're one lucky son of a bitch."

"Right," Rotten said and decided to keep his story limited.

He couldn't yet get a good read on Willie.

"As for your arm, it was a clean cut," Willie said, turning to the large jar on the nightstand. "I managed to cut out E'Raknish. No problem."

Inside the jar was E'Raknish in the shape of a metal octopus with its many tentacles unraveled like a ball of wires floating around a gel-like liquid. What used to be an hour and minute hand of a clock were two antennas attached to its head.

In a state of disbelief, Rotten stared at a subdued E'Raknish. The sight of E'Raknish was like a weight lifted off Rotten's body. For so many years, he had lived and thrived with E'Raknish, using it like a tool and embracing the concept: Better to have one and not need it than not to have one and need it.

Without E'Raknish, he was frightened to death, yet oddly optimistic about the next chapter in his life.

PARADOXXED
DECEMBER 5, 2048
CLOVERSON, TEXAS

BACK at Jock's Ranch, Mavs's team was caught off guard and outgunned by JeneCorp's cleanup crew after the release of Loch Ness #5.

Leading the dynamic yet methodical crew past the security cameras, Agent Noble managed to cut the power to Mavs's property, as well as take out a backup generator, leaving the hacker-journalist scrambling through the darkness of the house.

Mindful of Blot, Agent Noble came prepared for he was armed with the one item that Mavs failed to foresee: Light.

Lots of it.

A stadium-like package of bright and inescapable light.

Over dozens of military-grade spotlights set up around Mavs's property, each one aimed directly at the house, leaving very little shadows for Blot to travel.

Dozens of drones hovering above, which were also armed with weaponized-light, aimed spotlights onto the house, adding more top lighting and casting dark shadows along Mavs's eyes.

After catching a bullet in the left side away from any major organs, Mavs, who sought cover behind a wall, kept her head down and avoided the heavy gunfire.

Despite being in the grip of winter, bullets of sweat streamed down the side of her face.

Staying as low as possible, she reached up to her desk and grabbed the singe kit from behind the monitor. She pulled out the singe stick and after connecting it to her hard drive, she cleaned away the blood from her thumb with a bottle of water and then dried the thumb with her T-shirt. Once her thumb was clean and dry, she burned the password to her Feed account into her thumbprint, preventing any jocks from accessing the "Loch Ness" files, which were stored on a backup server off site. For a couple of seconds, she felt a series of pinpricks along her thumb, creating a thorny yet tingly sensation. The certain pinpricks were the product of each character of a robust password being imprinted, or "singed" into the impression of whorls and lines of her unique fingerprint.

As soon as the message confirmed that the password successfully transferred via singe, she grabbed a uni-adapter, which she never left home without, and pressed the battery-powered igniter underneath the desk, which, in return, set fire to an entire workstation. She crawled over all of the dead bodies scattered on the floor. Cyber jocks whom she had known for years. The bond (even though she hadn't met most of them in person, yet only their avatars) was as robust as her password.

Trying not to get lost in the carnage all around her, she focused her eyes forward. Her hands and knees trudged and slid through blood puddles of both cyber jocks and Raw Feed colleagues, most importantly, close friends whom she considered family. All shot dead.

As JeneCorp agents closed in, she grabbed a shotgun from QR (pronounced "Cure"), one of the most talented jocks whom Mavs was lucky to acquire for her team. QR was dead. He took a bullet straight to the dome. Sniper-shot. Died instantly. The thought alone of QR, such a youthful spirit, a wild card who was as wild as his wild dyed green hair, who often freelanced for Raw Feed, forever silenced, forced Mavs to press on. She told herself, *"The memory of QR would live on forever."* And she was his curator who would keep his code alive.

With only two slugs in the chamber, Mavs managed to take out an agent, who was creeping around the living room window. Two buckshots at the agent, a face full of shattered glass blinding the agent. Mavs tossed aside the useless shottie for the dire sound of a pump action *chi-chu* carried no effect on the agents, especially Noble, who approached from the rear of the house.

As Agent Noble, who was strapped with a flashlight on his vest, cornered Mavs against the wall, Mavs spotted a hand reaching from a shadow behind an overturned sofa.

Blot?

She couldn't see Blot in his entirety, only his arm, which stretched from a roughly three foot by six foot long shadow.

Noble set his sights on Mavs.

"Give it up," he said. "You're surrounded—"

Mavs suddenly leaped toward the sofa.

The agent fired.

The bullet grazed her arm as she rolled behind the sofa.

As she reached for Blot's hand, Noble fired again, this time between their two hands, which forced Mavs to retract her hand away from the gunfire.

As the agent took aim at Mavs's head, Blot suddenly emerged from behind one of the spotlights outside the residence and drove an aluminum baseball bat through the bright light, shattering the bulb, thus creating more shadows inside the house.

Mavs rolled into one of those shadows along the floor where Blot was waiting with both his black arms open like a black umbrella.

As Agent Noble open fired on Mavs, Blot grabbed her and pulled her into the blackness.

A hail of gunfire rained down on the floor, one of the bullets penetrating the shadows.

Noble rushed over to the spot where Mavs disappeared and reached his hand to the floor, but the gateway had already closed.

The shadowrun happened so fast, like opening a door and walking into a dark room, only the transition from dark to light was slow and gradual, similar to a dimmer switch.

Eventually, the light returned to normal, a soft and warm fade-in, like the opening of the first scene, and Mavs found herself inside a strange room.

She was no longer in Texas.

She was in **Mason, Virginia**.

Following the *creak* of the hardwood floor, Forsake appeared next to the bathroom door.

"You're safe now," he said.

The shock wore off and all that was left was a disorder of thoughts and feelings.

Mavs didn't know how she had gotten here or what had happened and a part of her felt as if she had woken up from a vivid dream.

In a delirious state, Mavs looked around the inside of the rustic cabin.

Her eyes found a familiar face.

She said to Forsake, "Jin?"

"It's nice to see you again, Mavis."

"Where am I?"

"You're in a safe house in Virginia—"

"Virginia? But how?"

"If I told you," Forsake grinned, "then I'd have to kill you."

Mavs looked around the room, which was lit up by several lamps.

"You have power?"

"Never lost it," said Forsake. "Perks about living in the middle of nowhere. I can't say the same about those outside Mason."

"So, where's your so-called friend?"

Forsake's demeanor changed from laidback to serious.

"Around," Forsake said with darkness in his eyes.

Mavs asked, "They won't stop until I'm dead, will they?"

"No," Forsake said bluntly.

Grimacing, Mavs attempted to sit up.

"You're shot?"

She looked down at her side and gently pulled back her damp and sticky shirt as if she was peeling away a band-aid.

Just below her ribcage was a gunshot wound, one entry point, no exit.

Which meant the round was still inside her body.

"You need to get that looked at?" asked Forsake, as he examined Mavs's lower back.

"I'll manage," she said. "Besides, right now, a hospital is probably the last place I'd want to be."

Forsake grabbed a first aid kit, as well as a bottle of whiskey from a cabinet behind the bar.

"Don't be ridiculous," Forsake said and after slipping on a pair of surgical gloves, tended to Mavs's injuries.

As he poured whiskey on the wound to help numb the pain, she said with a hiss, "Despite all of the technological advancements, we still resort to folk remedies—"

Forsake grabbed a pair of tweezers and said, "There's a reason why our ancestors managed to survive for so long."

"Yeah?"

"They worked with whatever they had."

"Do you not have any anesthetics?"

Forsake held up the bottle of whiskey.

"What do you think this is?" he asked.

"I mean, like, like something you can give me."

"Here." He handed her the bottle. "Drink up, buttercup."

"I don't touch the stuff."

"It'll help with the pain."

Mavs gave it a try, swigged, then gagged.

"How did people ever drink this shit?"

"With their mouth," he said plainly. "Now, one more."

"No way."

"Don't make me force it down your throat."

Mavs took one more swig and made a face.

As the alcohol somewhat eased Mavs's pain, Forsake managed to remove the bullet.

"A souvenir."

As her head started to spin, Mavs said, "Now, I got street cred."

"I'd say the moment you released Loch Ness Files was the moment you became King of the Streets. People are talking, Mavis. Word is spreading about JeneCorp—"

She said loosely, "How you know?"

"I work for the FBI. I know everything."

With a loose smirk on her face, she uttered, "Not everything."

There was a moment of comfortable silence between the two.

In reflection, Mavs said to Forsake, "If The People ever find out what's going on behind the scenes, they'll turn on their own government. We're talking about an uprising. . . "

"Maybe."

"If you say that JeneCorp, one of the most powerful entities in the world, is working with all the tech companies to turn every single device against people in order to bring about this. . . new era. . . then isn't it the story itself that keeps the people tuned in and glued to the means in which they *receive* the story, which will ultimately destroy them?"

"What are you trying to say exactly, Mavis?" asked Forsake. "That we're no different than JeneCorp? That we're contributing to the destruction of civilization? Do I need to remind you what's at stake here?"

"Are we doing more harm than good?" she asked.

"Not if we warn them before it's too late," Forsake said. "That's why the last segment must be released prior to noon on Monday, otherwise. . . " he trailed off for he didn't have the strength to finish his sentence or, in this case, spell it out for Mavs.

"The last two are stored on a server off site, already queued up for midnight, one tonight and then, the final one, tomorrow night. But will it be enough time?"

Forsake sighed.

"I don't know," he said. "One could only hope."

Mavs let out an airy noise from her mouth, which sounded as if she didn't have the strength or energy to laugh.

"I spent my whole youth drowning in hope and you know what I've learned?" she asked but didn't expect Forsake to answer. "It's a lie. It's just another meaningless word. I think Chu was right. We're all living under the boot of self-denial and we use hope as a cloak to shield us from the truth."

More seriously, Forsake said, "But some words *do* matter. *Your* words matter, Mavis. Most importantly, *Stella's words* matter.

If any of those agents acquired any information that could be used against us, then it doesn't matter what we do."

"I wiped everything," she said, more confidently. "They got nothing." Amused by her own clever thinking, Mavs held up her thumb. "If they want what we have so badly, then they'll have to pry it from my cold dead hands."

A thought popped in Forsake's head.

"That reminds me," he said and removed the bloody gloves from his hands and pulled out a small box from his pocket. "I have something I want to give you—"

"Jinni Boy," Mavs said, grinning, "When you said you liked me, I thought you were only be nice. . . "

Forsake furrowed his brow.

"It's not like that," he said. "Think of it as a gift."

"What is it?"

"Open it," he said and handed it to her.

Mavs opened the box and inside was a white contact lens.

"You remember those ridiculous visors that the cops used to wear back in the day to deflect Leon's gaze?"

"How can I forget?" she said and looked over the glossy lens. "Are you saying what I think you're saying?"

"JeneCorp found a way to shrink down the screen to a contact lens. It beats walking around with one of those bulky helmets, right?"

"Where'd you get this?" Mavs said, intrigued.

"Doesn't matter," he said.

Mavs asked, "Why are you giving me this?"

He said thoughtfully, "Despite how you may feel, I believe you're our last *hope* in exposing JeneCorp, which means you have to stay alive."

"Like I've I said, the last two are queued up," she said carelessly. "By Monday afternoon, it doesn't matter if I live or die."

Disappointed but not at all surprised to hear the words coming from Mavs, Forsake grabbed her hand and stared into her heavy eyes as if it was the last time he'd ever look into them.

Mavs suddenly pulled away before she could get lost in Forsake's eyes.

"Any word from your guy, Willie?" asked Mavs.

"He was supposed to deliver E'Raknish to me yesterday and the fact that I haven't gotten it yet means—more than likely—JeneCorp intercepted it after Willie left Rotten."

"Without E'Raknish, Flaming Spear is pointless," said Mavs, upset. "We have no proof!"

"Sure we do," Forsake emphasized. "*Lockhart.* Lockhart is all the proof we need."

Mavs said exaggeratedly, "You try getting the leader of the free world to open up his mouth nice and wide and say 'Ah!' in front of millions of people."

"I won't have to," Forsake said, composed. "After the release of the Seventh Dump, he'll be pressured by the press to show voters what he's been hiding behind that silver tongue of his."

Mavs sighed.

"Good luck." She glanced over at Forsake, who once more appeared disappointed. "So, how's Rotten holding up?"

"Last I heard he was struggling with his transition. He'll live, though."

"That's good," Mavs said. "And Hawks?"

Forsake shook his head no.

It was all down to Mavs to hurl Flaming Spear into the heart of the dragon.

No pressure.

Shortly after Forsake left for Washington, the security detail arrived at the safe house and as instructed by Forsake, watched over Mavs while she made sure the last two dumps were released on schedule.

Feeling more anxious after waking up from a heavy alcohol-induced nap, Mavs found a generic brand of painkillers inside Forsake's medicine cabinet. She flipped the bottle upside down. The pills were past the expiration date but only by a few weeks. She downed two pills with a sip of water from her hand after holding it under the running faucet.

As far as her mobility, Mavs was still incredibly sore and whenever she made any twists or turns with her hips or as with moments before, leaning over the vanity for a sip of water from the faucet, a streak of pain bolted up her abdomen. Mavs avoided tasks which required such movements and shuffled her way through the cabin.

She was roughly an hour and half left until the next dump, Loch Ness #6, and the anticipation was killing her. She couldn't sit still, even though her body was screaming at her to rest before the shit hit the fan.

The sixth and second-to-last file dump, which, up until the previous five—the first two covering the events surrounding September 8th, including the investigation into the murder of Channel 5 reporter, Stella Nilsson, as well as the background of the real shooter behind the assassination attempt against President Lockhart, which forced the White House to publicly release statements, slamming Caste as an opportunistic journalist baiting for her own personal gain and interests and that there was no merit to "these allegations," then, the last three dumps covering Lockhart's disastrous first term as president, his shady deals with JeneCorp, billions of American dollars being pumped into the state-of-the-art facility in Tokyo, all of the bailouts and bribes, one of them being with pharmaceutical company, Neuvak, as well as Neuvak's sister company NGHT, and the top-secret "Medicate USA" project headed by former software developer, Niles Baldwin, before he was acquired by JeneCorp's BioTech Division, also, Lockhart using taxpayers' money to invest heavily in AI companies while rolling back restrictions from a previous administration, and in essence, allowing these reckless companies to reshape America's workforce, then, lastly, exploring a deep dive into the newly discovered element, E'Raknish, unlike copper or cobalt, not only the key conductor for Chloe's gori, but also durable enough to carry out the Second Ascension on a global scale, a worldwide purge of "corruption" that formerly operated under the working title, "Med-USA," which JeneCorp was preparing to rollout right before Christmas time, as well as highlighting revised statements framing E'Raknish as though it was a kind of gift to humanity that would usher in a new purer era, instead of Mavs's approach, which presented in detail, based on a series of illegally-obtained cataloging sessions conducted by JeneCorp, irreparable damages E'Raknish posed to democracy and The People it served (*After all, after Mavs and a ragtag team of cyber jocks managed to hack into JeneCorp's network, she provoked an illuminating question, when have you ever seen the President smile?*)—was perhaps one of the most vital and yet controversial pieces in Flaming Spear.

The massive hundred page file dump, which revealed the full extent of JeneCorp's corruption, included hundreds of documents, which were legally obtained by Mavs, linking JeneCorp to the "2046 Blackouts," incriminating evidence that showed the company taking part in fabricating two national headline stories, the first regarding JeneCorp's sister company, Hornet Energy, and the publicized "Meltdown" at one of their "Nuclear Power Plants," which was located off Ahnna River in Glint, Illinois, where the nuclear reactor was reported to have "overheated" for reasons "unknown," causing widespread panic and the evacuation of residents in the towns surrounding the plant; however, after an investigation was conducted by a private watchdog group, Lionable, it was concluded that "there was no evidence of a meltdown." Instead, Hornet Energy was retiring the forty-year old plant to build a brand new one. The second story, which gained more coverage and popularity due to the participants involved, regarded a near-catastrophic accident at a power plant run by JeneCorp's East Division at Shell Island off the coast of Georgia, forcing the Company to bury the reactor to prevent an environmental crisis. The story garnered nationwide attention, prompting viral campaigns against nuclear energy, massive boycotts from A-list actors and activists, "Lights Out" trends spreading into areas powered by nuclear. As with the story in Glint, the incident at Shell Island was bogus. The plant was over sixty years old, and JeneCorp was cutting ties with Georgia due to overwhelming incentives by the state, which was pushing for natural gas (over 60% of Georgia relied on natural gas, the remainder being hydroelectric and solar).

In a coordinated effort by the United States government, these stories were orchestrated by JeneCorp to make their own company look like the villain and wherever there was a villain, there was a good guy to keep the villain in check.

The last drop, a sort of cherry on the top after the release of Loch Ness #5, was the dozens of affidavits from former JeneCorp employees who claimed that the Company deliberately pushed power grids beyond their capacity to force critical policy issues, which were blamed on the failures and incompetence of the previous administration by altering the data, all of it carried out in order to build favorability for the good guy, the knight in shining armor, William Lockhart, riding in on his white horse, prepared to save America from the clutches of power-hungry witches, thus confirming most of The People's suspicions about the illegitimate President who'd resort to the most drastic measures to retain his seat in the oval office.

Altogether, Loch Ness #5, plus that anticlimactic end-credit scene of affidavits posted right before JeneCorp sent its demon dogs on Mavs and her crew, received enough public outrage that the Investigating Committee on Foresight subpoenaed the head of JeneCorp, Tahr Rouse, as well as representatives from Neuvak Corporation and Pharmaceuticals and CEOs from several multinational technology companies, including eClipse, Tailorsoft, Gumshoe, and Orchid.

As for Lockhart, Mavs knew the subpoenas were all for show, political theatre.

Even the congresswoman Susanna Lamp, the soccer mom turned lady maverick, JeneCorp's most vocal critic who was ready to slap regulations on JeneCorp so hard and fast that it'd make the Company's head spin, even if her devil-may-care attitude left her with a glaring target on the back of her head, was going to be licking her chops chapped and raw after she received the early Christmas present.

With the latest dump on her mind, Mavs used Forsake's dinosaur of the computer and inserted the uni-adapter into the USB port before logging into her Friction account via thumbprint.

There, Loch Ness #6 still remained on queue, one hour and fourteen minutes away from being posted onto The Feed.

Let the countdown begin.

While pacing around the kitchen, Mavs spotted one of the bodyguards messing around with his phone.

Forsake had given Mavs's bodyguards specific orders about staying off their phones.

Mavs approached the bodyguard and reminded him of the dangers of the device and how, in under forty-eight hours, that device was going to turn him into a modern day clothes hanger.

"I apologize, Ms. Caste," he said and lowered the phone.

As he was about to pocket the phone, Mavs caught a glimpse of the message on the screen—an "AGREEMENT" form asking for the user's permission to update the phone, otherwise the phone was able to work properly.

Mavs asked for the phone.

An eClipse, Version 8.3.

The bodyguard handed over the eClipse phone to Mavs.

Unsettled by the latest update, which she immediately saw as a red flag considering the previous dump that underlined eClipse's involvement with JeneCorp, she scrolled through fine print in the form.

Sections varied, each one providing pages and pages of slippery lawyer lingo: "SUSTAINABILITY," "AI ALLIANCE," "PHASE 2.0," "GEN-E-SIS TECHNOLOGY," "THE CLEAN INITIATIVE," "DRIP FEED," "PRINT (S)" "AKQUIRE," "*JEREMY'S ACT REVISED."

At the bottom of the form was a section "DATA HARVESTING," which, in a nutshell, read that, by the user agreeing to the form, "I" (the user) was allowing eClipse to collect data on all of "my" (the user) devices, i.e., Feed, social media, texts, emails, photos, videos, trash, search history, personal accounts and information, such as address, birth, social security; therefore, given a more stable and "sustainable" period in accordance with the Activation Clause the harvested data would be inserted, or "integrated," into an assigned vessel—a "PRINT"—delivered by an artificial womb under the provision of "GEN-E-SIS 3000™."

In a state of shock, Mavs looked up at the bodyguard.

"What the fuck is this shit?" she asked. "Is this a joke?"

"Looks like an update," he said.

"Did you read through it?" she asked, tension in her voice.

The bodyguard shrugged.

"Nobody ever reads that shit."

The point.

"This isn't a fucking update," she said, trailing off. "This is extinction. . . ."

After asking to borrow the guard's phone without "asking" the guard, Mavs left the kitchen and took the phone back to the computer. She plugged the phone into the uni-adapter; and as she waited for the latest "update" to appear on the monitor, she suddenly heard a noise coming from outside the window. She walked to the office window where a bodyguard should've been standing by the front porch. She couldn't find the heavily armed guard anywhere in sight. She leaned past the doorway and peeked into the living room. Relief washed over her as she spotted the tail end of another guard casually patrolling the foyer.

As Mavs walked back into the office, she accidentally kicked a metallic object on the floor. The small object, which was no longer than marble, skipped toward the rug where it came to rest along the loose threads of the fringe.

Mavs picked up the object from the floor and inspected it: a bullet, at least part of a bullet, which was cut diagonally by the closing of the gateway, a clean and surgical cut.

The agent, Mavs remembered, the gunfire.

What piqued her interest was the item inside the bullet.

Tiny circuitry.

Terrified by the discovery, Mavs rushed back into Forsake's bedroom where she found the same bullet that Forsake had pulled from her side inside a coin tray on top of the drawer.

Mavs's own "souvenir" that she carelessly tossed into a tray carrying thumbtacks and pocket change.

As a growing suspicion mounted, she carefully picked up the bullet and held it close to her face. There was a tiny flashing of a green light coming from inside the bullet.

She searched through Forsake's desk for a magnifying glass. All she could find was a pair of old glasses, which she held over the bullet.

The sight of the tracking device caused all of the blood to rush from her face, leaving it pale and ghostly.

She heard yet another noise, similar but this time closer.

Following the noise was a *thud* against the floor.

She crept from the office and spotted a shadow cutting across the kitchen.

"Jin," Mavs said, her voice trembling, "is that you?"

She heard a *creaking* noise behind her.

On edge, she rotated around, only to find yet another shadow moving along the front porch.

She checked the front of the house.

The bodyguards were gone; however, the shadows remained.

Two of them, one shadow darting underneath the floodlight above the driveway and another one creeping behind a shrub along the front lawn.

Mavs locked the front door and hurried back into the kitchen.

The guard was gone, the backdoor partially opened.

In a frantic state, Mavs grabbed a cast iron skillet from the drawer and placed it on the stovetop and cranked up the heat.

Sweaty and wide-eyed, she waited until the cast iron was hot. As she was about to place her thumb on the cast iron and burn the password from her print, she felt the barrel of a gun pressed against the back of her neck.

"Not so fast, buttercup," Agent Noble said from behind.

"It's too late," she said. "JeneCorp is finished—"

"We'll just see about that," he said and slid his other hand in front of Mavs. "Hand please."

"Go fuck—"

Before Mavs could finish her sentence, Noble pulled the trigger.

Mavs fell to the floor, dead.

With a knife, Noble cut off her thumb and tossed it to Agent Prescott, who entered via backdoor of the kitchen.

"Target acquired," Noble said. "Tag it and bag it."

Agent Prescott said with a grin on his face, "Cutting it close, aren't you?"

Noble didn't laugh at the joke. Instead, he directed his attention to Mavs and the blood puddle forming underneath her head. He carried a weight of sorrow in his eyes before he clenched his teeth. The sides of his jaw swelled in anger, the emotion directed, not at Mavs, but rather inward.

More grimly, he said to Prescott: "Ready the plane."

"Yes, sir," Prescott said and carefully place Mavs's severed thumb in a plastic baggie.

RAID
DECEMBER 6, 2048
TEMPER RIDGE, PENNSYLVANIA - PIERRE, PENNSYLVANIA

FOLLOWING Attorney General Richard Craley's resignation, Lukas Woodall, who, like Lockhart, also compromised by scandal and sensitive information and given the gatekeepers who possessed the one commodity more precious than currency, which was leverage, easily "handled" (the tech company, Tailorsoft, recently obtained spicy photos of the acting Attorney General partaking in extramarital affairs and the unaltered images were considered unflattering and lecherous enough to ruin his career—that is, if the photos were ever released to the public), gave the green light to take down the extremist organization.

Once the orders were funneled down by Director Sikes, who had very little knowledge about E'Raknish, only the conspiratorial ramblings on madmen on The Feed, and was, without a doubt, according to Rouse, so lost in the dark that she couldn't even find her own hand if it was right in front of her face, Special Agent Frye led a counter-terrorism unit to the hidden compound.

Accompanied by other agents, Frye met up with FBI informant, Jupe, who confirmed that all of the Reborne members were currently sound asleep, "out of it," he said, all thanks to a plethora of sleeping pills that he mixed into the food.

Jupe stood behind a tree and from the woods, watched flashes of gunfire flicker through the snowy night darkness.

The next morning, after the massacre in Temper Ridge, M.J. found himself trudging into the town of Pierre.

Cold, hungry, and exhausted, M.J. stopped by a gas station where a family of four had been turned into stone: The dad stood outside the passenger window, looking at a cracked smart phone in his wife's stony hand, while his two children, a boy and a girl, sat in the backseat of the minivan with tablets in both of their hands. M.J. closed his eyes as he reached inside the minivan and grabbed the headset from the boy's head. With the edge of his sleeve, he brushed off the dust of concrete for he still thought that maybe the paving or whatever was caused by a type of virus that originated from electronic devices, mainly smart phones, which seemed to be the trend.

He placed the cans, which he thought would make decent ear warmers, in his backpack.

From a distance, he heard the sounds of helicopters above. He hid behind an abandoned car along the side of the road and watched three helicopters fly overhead.

Based on previous findings in the town of Orange Leaf, he was left with a wrenching sensation inside his gut.

He didn't understand the world anymore or what had happened in a matter of twenty-four hours.

Was this all a nightmare? And if so, *I wish someone would wake me up.*

The only thing that gave M.J. strength to push forward was delivering his message to Liza's parents who lived in Lewisburg.

At this point in time, it was the very least he could do.

THAW
DECEMBER 10, 2048
JOSS ISLAND   NTARCTICA

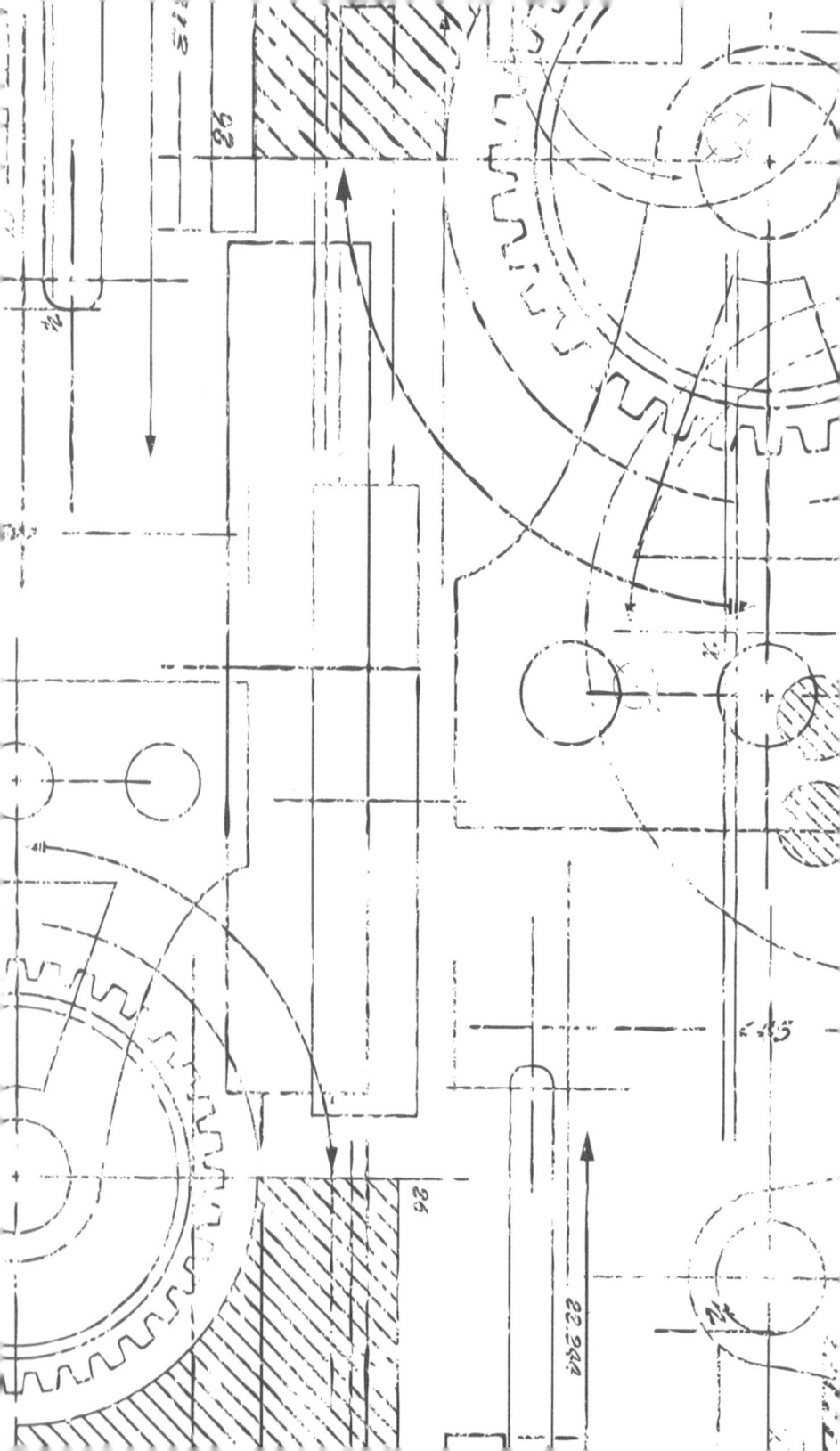

THREE days after the Freeze, Niles boarded a last-minute flight from the Holcomb's Springs Strip located in Southern California to Cheech, New Zealand. Upon his arrival in Cheech, Niles drove a short distance through the rugged countryside until he reached a guarded compound.

He drove past a rusty sign:

CHARON POST

The compound was home of a former military base used by the US in World War II during the Pacific War before it was abandoned after the war and later purchased by JeneCorp, making the installation a hub for flights coming in and out of Antarctica.

From Charon Post, Niles, along with a team of scientific researchers scheduled to relieve the Mice who had spent the past two years gathering research data at the Franklin Station, took a C-6 Bough cargo aircraft to Joss Island.

The researchers—the "Mice"—didn't speak to Niles throughout the duration of the flight; in fact, each and every December for the past fifteen years, Niles acted as if he was a fifth wheel, a piggybacker, more or less, who, at times, exhibited the impression of someone who was *not* present, or one might look at it, Niles's presence was intended to stay on the down-low, a hush-hush passenger who kept all to himself, rarely interacted with passengers, and not once did Niles ever state the reasons for his visit or exploration or what many perceived as yet another wealthy thrill seeker merely exploiting his company's resources to vacation at the ass end of earth.

After the C-6 Bough safely landed on the Echo Kilo airstrip on Joss Island, Niles, as well as the researchers, rode a Terra Bus Caterpillar to Franklin Station, which housed up to twelve hundred residents, where exhausted Mice were anxiously waiting for their replacements.

Departing from the team, Niles went his separate way and met up with Eiger, a city Mouse, who, despite the commonly used nickname throughout Joss Island, was as loyal as a house cat. Surprisingly excited to see Niles despite Niles's aloof behavior, Eiger helped Niles with his luggage, which he placed on a sled that was hitched to a snowmobile. Accompanied by Eiger, Niles rode his own snowmobile to Klarc Base, a much smaller base located two miles from Franklin Station on the far side of Waning Crescent Peninsula.

Being one of the main contributing benefactors of the scientific research that was conducted on Joss Island, JeneCorp provided Niles with his personalized hut along the edge of Klarc Base, away from other mice, the hut being equipped with blackout windows which prevented any sunlight from entering the hut (the windows came in handy during the summer months when the sun was out twenty-four hours a day), as well as fully stocked food. Nearby were amenities, including a spa and sauna and a billiards table, which were located within walking distance.

The day was tedious and drew out like a streak of light that never darkened or faded.

As Niles unpacked all of his belongings and eventually situated himself inside the hut, Eiger paid Niles a visit and asked him if there was anything he could provide to Niles to make his stay more pleasant.

Niles, who, as with the passengers, rarely interacted with the help, invited Eiger into his hut and made him a cup of warm lemon ginger tea.

Over strained silence, Eiger couldn't help but verbally prod at the annual visitor who was widely known to treat his privacy as sacred as scripture: "Fifteen years you've been visiting here, correct?"

"That long, huh?" said Niles.

"The mice have made bets that you're here searching for aliens."

"If there's one facet that doesn't fail the people of Joss Island, it's their imaginations."

Eiger asked, "Of all places to spend your time, why this White Hell?"

"I'm here to undo a wrong."

"And what do you expect to find here?"

" A worthy connection," Niles said, his cold, chapped hands massaging the hot mug.

"But not with the humans, I suppose," Eiger teased.

"You think you've seen the entire world until you visit Joss Island, and then, you soon realize, once you've stepped foot here, you haven't even scratched the surface of what this place has to offer—"

"The Ice has a way of putting more important things into perspective."

"Tell me about it," Niles said, drifting more inward. "During my travels, it's fair to say I've grown tired of being around people, as you might've pointed out. I wouldn't necessarily call it a disliking, but, more or less, a bad case of déjà vu that repeats itself over and over—"

"And I thought you liked coming here to see us mice," Eiger joked, provoking a thin smile on Niles's face.

Niles asked more directly, "Wanna know the one truth that I've learned about people?"

Niles paused, as though he waited for Eiger to answer.

"They're boring," Eiger said.

He laughed a phlegmy, raspy laugh sanded down by over thirty years of smoking.

"Boring, yes, greedy, and self-absorbed," Niles listed, as he struggled to find amusement in Eiger's answer, "but most importantly, they're easy to manipulate."

"Tell that to my wife," Eiger teased again, drawing more laugher at his own remark.

Niles could barely bring himself to laugh at Eiger.

There was a pull on his face, a weight.

Possibly too tired to laugh.

"And predictable," he said.

"Predictable, huh?" Eiger sipped from the tea, pulled out a chair from underneath the table, and sat down across from Niles, who appeared weighed down by regret. "I don't think anyone could predict what your employer managed to pull off. What JeneCorp accomplished will forever change the course of humanity. Pretty damn gutsy, if you ask me."

Respectfully disagreeing with Eiger, Niles said, "All we did was expedite our own demise."

Eiger held out his hands as though to showcase himself.

"We're still here, aren't we?"

When Niles didn't respond to his comment, Eiger picked up the strange sense that his presence wasn't wanted anymore.

Before leaving, he said to Niles, "If you're looking for God, then I'm sorry, mate, you came to the wrong place."

Eiger thanked Niles for the tea and went back to his hut.

The morning rolled into the next day.

Expecting to be greeted by the early morning darkness, Niles was greeted by the sunlight.

Every December when he vacationed on Joss Island, he felt as if he was a teenager again, at least, during for the first few days of his readjustment to time: reliving his past weekends, which consisted of drinking beers and coding throughout the wee hours of the night and then oversleeping and waking up well into the afternoon when the sun was not only so high in the sky, but also everybody seem so alien based on their lively, awakened states.

With his gear packed on the back of his snowmobile, Niles walked back to his hut where he came across a worn Kave lighter with the engraving of a serpent in the bottom of his luggage. He discovered the Kave two days after the Freeze.

Considering that JeneCorp was taking an "all-hands-on-deck" approach during the days surrounding the Freeze and needed its Head of the BioTech Division close by just in case there were any hiccups in the days following the launch, Niles originally canceled the vacation.

Protected by the protective contact lenses, he stumbled upon the aftermath of the loop when he stepped out of JeneCorp for a breather. Only one day had passed since the launch of the stream, which was running on every electronic device throughout the world, and everybody at JeneCorp was on edge. Niles wanted to hear the empty sounds cast from the streets of Tokyo. He wanted to know what it sounded like after all hell had frozen over.

In the dim night, while basking in the deadly silence, he heard the whimpering of a lost dog coming from the end of an alleyway, which ran along the side of JeneCorp's facility.

Curious, Niles decided to check out the noise and what he discovered left him horrified.

With a crushed phone in hand, the owner of the dog was standing still in front of his apartment door. The flickering overhead light brought his pain in and out of the night darkness, displaying glimpses of the horror that was unleashed onto the world. His rocky gestures displayed the face of a man who died an excruciating death. When Niles reached out his hand to touch the statue, it fell over on its side and shattered into pieces, leaving behind not a single trace of blood.

Mortified, Niles rushed back to his house and as he contemplated packing his bags, he came across the Kave in the very back of a drawer.

Pushing aside the memory, Niles pocketed the Kave and left the hut.

Along the way to Mount Nyx, an inactive volcano which Niles had been drawn to ever since a trip to Joss Island two years ago, he rode past the wind farm that helped power both of the two bases. Niles drove the snowmobile over the Overview Hill; and once he made it to the clearing, he removed the scarf from the bottom part of his face and embraced the sighting of Mount Nyx, which sat like a dark tumorous growth along the surface of the endless glaring white horizon.

Through his binoculars, he spotted tracks around the hill, which lead him to what looked like an abandoned snow cat. The driver's side door was open; however, Niles couldn't find the operator of the vehicle in sight. Niles rode the snowmobile toward the snow cat; and as he earlier confirmed, the vehicle was abandoned. He found a set of footprints in the snow heading directly toward Mount Nyx. He left behind the snowmobile; and by foot, he followed the prints. About twenty paces in, the prints changed pattern and appeared messy, each print wandering aimlessly in circles, some dragged along the snow as though there might've been a struggle.

As Niles closely inspected the prints, he heard a sudden bone-crushing *crack* below his feet. The sound was as explosive as a hand grenade and forced Niles to leap toward safer ground. The upper part of his body bounced off the side of the hole as the snow beneath his feet gave out. He fell into a fissure in the earth. The sides of his body smacked and slid across jagged walls, which surrounded the fissure. He fell at least five stories through the narrow crack before both his feet finally struck earth. His right ankle broke in the fall, causing Niles to scream out in agony.

Once the initial shock wore off, he peered upward through the fissure. The surface roughly five stories above and yet, the opening of light appeared as though it was miles away.

Soon, the pain set in, centered around his ankle and radiating throughout his body. In a frantic state, he felt around his hard and rough surroundings, first the rough and coarse ground under his body. The Kave immediately came to mind. He reached into his pocket and sure enough, he pulled out the Kave lighter. He gave the Kave a shake before opening the lid. After all of these years, the lighter still worked. The flame was dim and fading; nonetheless, it provided enough light for Niles to recognize the interior of the small cave.

Niles grabbed hold of the side of the fissure and using the wall for support, stood to his feet. Guided by the light of the lighter, he found an opening in the cave, which led him toward yet another cave, this time a cavern that stretched as far as his eye could see.

The flame slightly flickered from a draft coming from the other end of the cave. The atmosphere was warmer and more humid than above the surface. He limped his way through the cavern until he reached a glowing light coming from a chamber. The closer he approached the light the more he felt pulled into the light. He entered the chamber, which was about the size of a bedroom dimly lit by a reflective light cast from the beams of sunlight pouring into the side vent of Mount Nyx. Below was a small kiddy pool of black ooze. Niles held his hand over the bubbling pool of ooze and immediately recoiled from the stinging heat. He held the dying flame close to the pool and witnessed the warped reflection of the parasitic passenger who had stolen not only his face, but also, he soon realized once the pain in his ankle strangely diminished, his body.

Before he could recognize B'aus staring back at him in the reflection, a black hand emerged from the simmering hot pool and grabbed Niles by the ankle.

More black hands emerged.

Niles fought off each one, but he was soon overpowered.

Dozens upon dozens of hands tugged and grabbed at him until each hand had a handle over him. The hands violently dragged into the black pool. . .

Somewhere in **Swagahgali**, a young man named Musa suddenly gasped for air!

His eyes bolted up as he pulled himself from the strange images of a man drowning.

The rain intensified outside.

They were about to be in the thick of the storm.

Lightning struck and briefly lit up a misty darkness and shortly after sudden claps of thunder cut across the sky, startling the other villagers.

As Musa rose from the floor he heard distant voices underneath the beating of rain, which he thought was strange considering the voices were softly spoken and yet, he wondered how such a voice could be heard over the heavy rain.

He stepped from the hut where he peered through the wall of heavy rain and noticed a light coming from the church.

Two shadows appeared along the walls inside the church.

With the thunder rumbling through the dark, stormy night sky above, Musa cautiously approached the church where inside he witnessed two men—foreigners—speaking to one another in the middle of the nave.

Drenching wet from the rain, he cracked open the doors and found Tahr Rouse and the now Head of JeneCorp's BioTech Division, Lance Carmichael, inside the church.

Carmichael said to Rouse, "What do you think happened to Baldwin?"

More images flooded Musa's mind.

Among those images was Niles being pulled into a void by Seekers.

"Don't know," Rouse said, tormented by the disappearance of JeneCorp's most valuable assets. "But whatever he was searching for down there, it sounds like he found it."

The wood floor suddenly creaked below Musa's feet, causing Carmichael and Rouse to turn their attention toward Musa.

A familiar voice from behind: *"Qu'est-ce que tu fais?"*

Following the question a wet hand touched Musa on the shoulder, causing him to flinch.

Musa rotated around and found a dumbfounded Jean standing at the doorway.

Not too far away, a bolt of lightning streaked through the dark sky, bringing out the village behind Jean.

Musa spun back around and pointed at the two strange men inside the church.

Both Carmichael and Rouse were gone, as though they never were present.

In French, Jean asked Musa if he was well.

Shaking off the recent images, Musa said, "It was just a bad dream, I suppose—"

"You're bleeding," Jean said abruptly and pointed to Musa's forehead.

A trail of blood trickled from a dark round spot, similar to a popped zit but much deeper, on the center of his forehead.

With the damp sleeve of his shirt, Musa wiped away the blood.

Using the stretched-out collars of their T-shirts as umbrellas, Jean escorted Musa back to his hut as the thunderstorm intensified.

DEEP FREEZE ELLIS KROSS

PART THREE

"A PRELUDE TO SOMETHING WICKED"/ THESE GLOSSY MAGS AREN'T FOR WHOLESALE

BOOK THREE

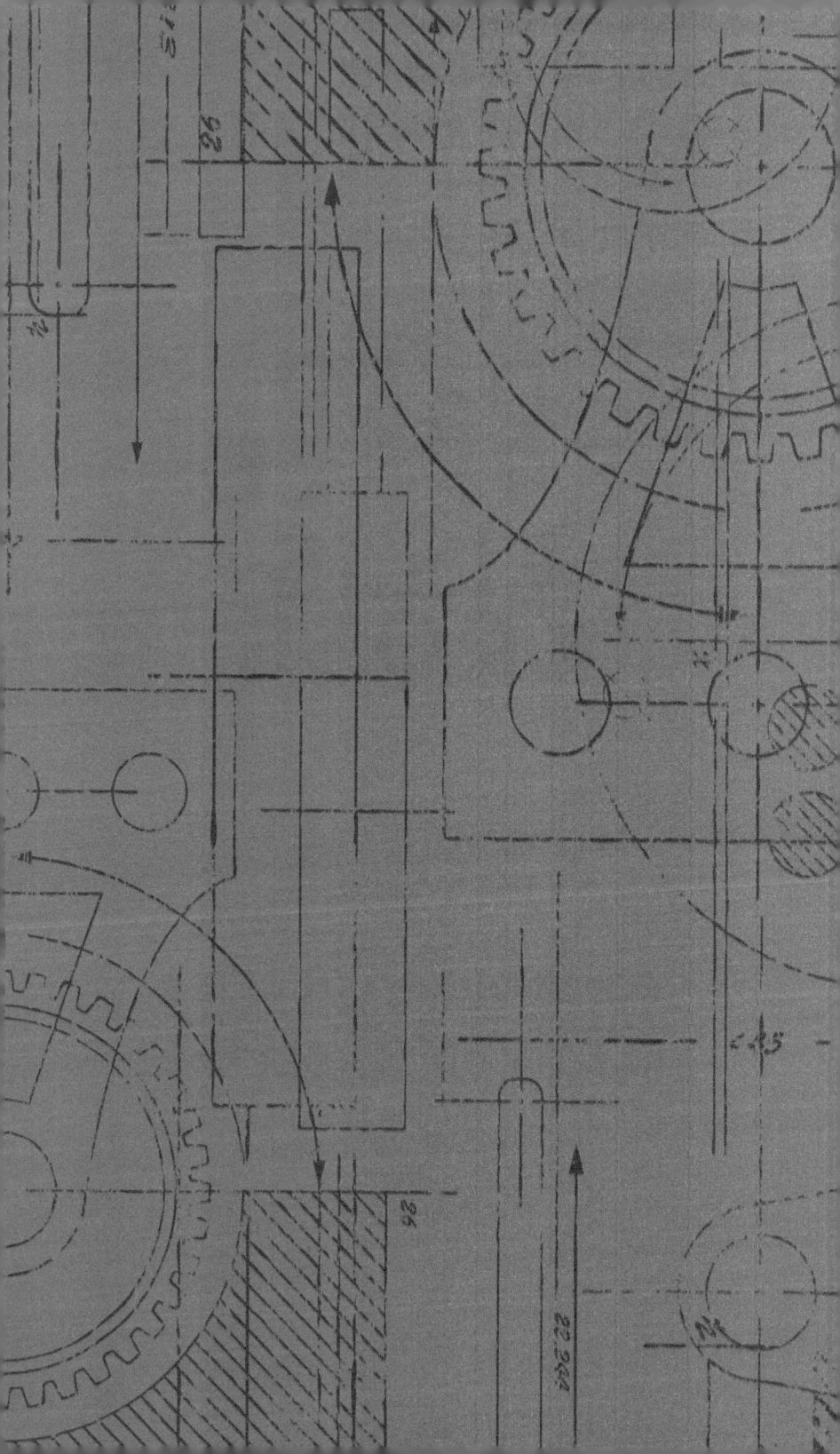

HANDLING NATURE (REDUX): PRECIOUS BLOOD
AUGUST 7, 2053
PADADOCK, PA

WHILE Brett was playing on the playground, he caught his left arm on a sharp piece of metal protruding from the slide. It wasn't until Brett made it to the bottom of the slide that the cut began to gush blood. The sight of strings of red blood running from the cut caused the four-year-old to suddenly wail, his cries forcing John to rush over and check on his son. It was his very first injury, a deep cut, a real gusher of a cut that covered Brett's arm, hand, and fingers in deep red.

In order to stop the bleeding, John had no other choice than to remove his T- shirt and firmly press it against the laceration.

As Brett's cries intensified throughout the neighborhood streets, John carried his son to Ashleigh's house where M.J. opened the door to greet John and little BB.

"What's going on?" asked M.J., as he stepped aside and let John inside.

"Brett cut himself," he said, out of breath.

Ashleigh, who was in the middle of shucking ears of corn, put aside the leftover husks and rushed from the kitchen to the main foyer.

Freaked out by the sight of the blood, Ashleigh asked, "Are you okay, Brett?"

Brett was too shocked to answer her, even though the sight of Ashleigh brought him a sense of comfort.

M.J. grabbed the first aid kit from the bathroom and by the time he brought it over to Brett, his cries eased down to phlegmy sobs and a runny nose.

John placed Brett on the sofa and carefully removed the T-shirt from Brett's arm.

He searched for the cut, but the cut was nowhere on his arm.

"Weird," he trailed off, as he frantically inspected Brett's fore-arm.

No cut.

Nothing but only dried blood caked on his wrist and hand.

"Where'd all that blood come from?" asked M.J.

"Good question," John said.

More panicked, he grabbed a rag from the kitchen and soaked it with water and then hurried back into the living room and cleaned away the blood.

Again, no cut.

"I saw it with my own two eyes," John pleaded. "Brett cut his arm on the playground." He looked up at M.J. and Ashleigh. "You believe me, don't you?"

"Of course," M.J. said.

Ashleigh leaned in closer to Brett and smiled at him.

The sight of Ashleigh's wide smile caused Brett to smile.

In a silly voice, she said to Brett, "Looks like little man here is a fast healer, aren't you BB?"

Brett cackled.

John wasn't laughing, though.

He was left speechless by what he believed was his son's gift.

THE WHITE H@ HACKER
AUGUST 8, 2053
TOKYO, JAPAN

ONE of the main computers suddenly received a *beeping* alert as one of his technicians was using a special soldering iron to repair partially damaged E'Raknish wire on the back of the computer.

"What I hit?" said the technician, as he lifted his head from the smoking solder.

"You didn't hit anything," Carmichael said, as he stormed into the computer room.

"Sure?"

"It's *not* you," he said and read the latest spike job.

As the technician removed the protective plastic googles from his head, he walked around to the front of the monitor where a red flag was flashing on the screen.

"Then what is it?" the technician asked Carmichael.

"Not what," he said. "Who?"

"You're serious," the technician said and found himself strangely admiring the hacker's persistence, as well as tenacity.

"He's becoming a real nuisance, this one is."

"I thought E'Raknish was put in place to protect Chloe from any cyber attacks."

"It's fair to say it's only an attack when you steal something."

"No data was stolen?"

"Nope," Carmichael said and through a prompt, pulled up a detailed summary.

"Then what the fuck does he want?"

"My guess. . . " Carmichael said, as he skimmed through the gibberish of code before securing the firewall, ". . . it's probably just some kid in his mother's basement screwing with us."

Once the firewall was enabled, the alert shut off.

"Why?" asked the technician.

"He's testing our vulnerabilities," Carmichael guessed. "Who knows?"

Carmichael couldn't help but laugh as a message slipped past the firewall.

"Looks like he left his calling card."

On the screen a pictogram of a gold *fish* appeared one pixel at a time.

THE BLIP—*NO,* NOT THAT KIND
AUGUST 9, 2053
WHISPERFRONT, ME

ROUGHLY five hundred and thirty miles north of Paddock sat a three-story beach house along the rugged coastline of the Atlantic Ocean.

Seated at his desk inside the sleek office, which, like most of the rooms, had the large panes of indestructible glass covering the rear of the house, making for one helluva view of the ocean, was

JeneCorp's former Recovery Unit tracker Man Pullman, who began to pull out the hair from his head.

In the past forty-eight hours, he'd hear the sound every now and then while trying to finish the final draft of his novel. Written under a penname, Derrick Nam, the working title was *Jane, or The Modern Medusa*—a nod to Mary Shelley's *Frankenstein*—which followed a deeply disturbed scientist who constructed an artificial body around his young love interest's head after she was executed in a guillotine during the late 18th Century.

The novel was loosely based around Chloe, and yet, despite its fictional storyline, the novel was Pullman's way of trying to make sense of the past four years.

Numerous times while drafting the story, Pullman asked himself whether or not it was considered "too soon" to write about a tragedy that still plagued not only the country, but also a majority of the world.

But then again, the human experience gave him reassurance.

When did art ever give a shit about timing?

He heard the familiar *blip* once more while working on the closing line of the novel.

He pulled out more hair until he noticed the gray strands along the top of his shoulders from where he mindlessly ran fingers through hair. The sight of his fallen soldiers was a reminder to put an end to his new unhealthy habit.

With Pullman's head spinning with words (he compared writing to putting together a puzzle with extras pieces), he stopped writing from the vintage typewriter that he borrowed from Al the gold digger whose very last moments before the Freeze consisted of him taking a phone-break in his workshop while digging out a stringy booger from the corner of his nose.

With the soothing repetitive sounds of waves crashing outside, Pullman tilted his head to the side, his right ear arched upward like a cat.

The sound was coming from the walls.

A flash of rage ran through his body.

His muscles tightened.

"Goddamn it!" he shouted out, as he stood from the desk.

Tempted to smash the typewriter to millions of pieces of the floor, he scampered around the house, checking each room or closet or nook or cranny before finally locating the sound underneath a stack of boxes in the back of a hallway closet. He pulled out the surveillance device that he hadn't used since days before the Freeze.

On the device was a reading coming from Pennsylvania, but more specifically a town called Padadock.

Confused by the blip, Pullman brought the device to the kitchen table and took a moment to take in all of his surroundings: the typewriter, the unfinished manuscript on the desk, the fog, the ocean, as well as the heavy grayness that sat over the shore. Then, lastly, the two owners of the house, both turned to statues in the living room, more or less, a stark yet daily reminder to Pullman of the dangers that he faced as soon as he stepped foot outside the house. The wife lounged on a white leather sofa while she watched what used to be a flat screen television before Pullman blindly beat it with the fireplace poker and removed it from the house and tossed the remains into the Atlantic Ocean. The husband, as tense as a snare drum, was plumped on the stool behind the bar, his index finger forever frozen in a flicking position as he scrolled through what used to be a smartphone, which shared a similar fate as the flat screen television, as well as every single electronic device inside the house; however, the dark clouds that hovered over the two statues, especially the husband, still lingered well past their showy graves.

What the hell am I doing here?

He often told himself whenever he wasn't toiling away with his masterpiece: "This may be a house, but it's not a home."

More like a glass prison.

A square snow globe.

Maybe once love shook this house.

Once, maybe, life fell from the ceiling like confetti.

But not anymore.

He moved his eyes back to the typewriter and asked himself: *Am I any different from them?*

After another ten minutes of contemplation, he grabbed a bottle of Dailies from the medicine cabinet in the bathroom. Ever since the Freeze, he thought he'd never use the eye drops, even in the face of emergency, considering one of the active ingredients was halozine.

Without the eye drops, Pullman knew that the results of staring at the loop of Chloe on electronic devices—in his case, a phone—would be disastrous. Even so much as glancing at the loop or forming a thought around the loop whenever the loop accidentally found its way into his range of vision would lead to serious health issues and side effects, some being irreparable. In essence, after the acquisition of Neuvak Pharmaceuticals, JeneCorp, a Trinity of Power (Big Energy, Big Tech, Big Pharma) had, not only Pullman by the balls, but also every survivor of the Freeze.

Or, as the locals called those who hadn't turned to stone, the "Selected" ones part of a "trial run."

With a pen, Pullman jotted down a list of specific instructions to follow just in case he experienced negative side-effects from the eye drops: "*Drive to the Base Station; Reach out to Blot ASAP; Mention The Blip; Check GPS Coordinates; Pass along message to Barney; Emphasize the Urgency!!!. . .*"

After psyching himself up, he took a breath before using the Dailies, one drop for each eye. Only several minutes after he let the Dailies set in, he began to feel a great sense of grogginess as though he was too exhausted to properly think, as though his brain was stuck on autopilot and the autopilot was faulty. He grabbed the handwritten note and remembered his next steps, despite every inch of him yearning to sit back and take a beat or two and relax, maybe even grab a snack. Snacks were good, in fact, encouraged when taking halozine.

Pullman broke into the neighbor's house next door and grabbed the first phone he could find inside the house—a smartphone clung to the stoned hand of a man sitting on the toilet, mid-wipe. Displayed on the neighbor's phone, which, when awakened with the touch of a finger, played the same loop of Chloe, her glitchy voice scrambled, every other syllable minced. Pullman was able to make out several words, the same ones that streamed throughout the world, about being "*stung by Medusa's gaze.*"

With the phone in hand, Pullman was able to look into the flickering ghostly images on the screen without being turned to stone, which meant the Dailies were working; however, the sight of Chloe's milky white eyes left him with a dull headache, as well as a temporary negative afterimage of Chloe's eyes, similar to a dark and ball-shaped area left behind after staring at the sun. Worse, if he stared too long, meaning a second or two, he was struck by a dizzy spell that forced him to sit until it passed. Either way, he thought it was best to avoid eye contact from the screen, even though the temptation to look nagged at him.

Before Pullman left the house, he noticed in the corner of his eye two more statues, this time in a bedroom. He peeked inside the room and found two children lying on the shag carpet, each one wearing VR headsets. From the position of their hands grabbing at the air, they appeared as if they were in the middle of playing a game when the Freeze took place. The sight of the children's laughing faces left in frozen states stirred a mixture of emotion inside Pullman, again, reminding him what was at stake.

Since there was no working phone service at his location, he wandered back to his house and dressed and armed himself with a loaded handgun. Every now and then—if it was from moving from one side of the room to the other or making sure he locked up the house before leaving—he would get these waves of lethargy, tempting him to put off the list.

I shouldn't have taken halozine on an empty stomach.

He told himself that he should *grab a snack.*

After a couple of slaps to his face to help arouse a sense of motivation, he placed the surveillance device in his satchel; and using a gas-powered truck, which Pullman seldom used to gather resources, like food or water, located within a walking distance, he drove to an eClipse base station located in Gull Cove and after yet another quick pep talk, hooked the phone up to the transceiver. Chloe's face pixilated and crumbled and eventually, vanished into the black screen. Following a soft reboot, the smartphone returned to its factory settings. Pullman accessed the Wi-Fi through a satellite Internet constellation, which had been streaming Chloe's loop, and contacted Forsake via FaceNet by entering his email address.

Roughly eight hundred miles south of Whisperfront, Maine, Forsake, who, for the past three and a half years, had been growing out a beard, was tracking a whitetail near Rag's Mountain in **Mason, Virginia**, when all of a sudden his digital wristwatch let out a *ping* followed by a flash of a bright white light. Forsake's eyes glazed over from not only the sound of the ping, but also the sight of the flash. He stopped following the deer, lowered the rifle, and drew his eyes toward the dark cave located within the opening of the forest. Trance-like, Forsake casually strolled to the cave, using the butt of his rifle to push past the heavy foliage. He stepped foot into the darkness.

At the eClipse base station in **Gull Cove**, the screen on Pull-man's phone cut to a deep black.

Terror rushed through his body, as he anticipated Blot's arrival.

He frantically sought out shadows, the ones stretching from the tower above or the ones behind the shelter housing, casting enough darkness for Blot.

"Show yourself," Pullman said while nervously looking all around him.

All of a sudden, the door to the shelter cracked open.

With the handgun tucked under his belt, he crept toward the shelter. As he cracked open the door, he moved his hand toward the handle of the handgun. A narrow beam of light cut through the window at the upper wall of the shelter, casting enough light inside to witness the dark figure standing in the corner of the room.

"Blot?" said Pullman.

"Long time no see," Blot said, as he remained deadly still among the angled shadows. "I see you've been taking good care of yourself."

Lightheaded from the Dailies, Pullman braced himself against the doorway.

Blot said, "Come closer. I won't bite—"

"I wouldn't have contacted you, if it wasn't an emergency."

"Well, for your sake, this better be good then."

"Oh," Pullman said, releasing the nervous tension with a laugh, "it's more than good. It's a gift from the gods—"

"What did you find, Man?" asked Blot.

For a moment, Pullman had a relapse in memory and was forced to check the list.

Mention The Blip.

"I picked up a blip on my SD, strongest signal yet coming from a town in Pennsylvania."

"How sure are you that it's not another anomaly, like the one in Kingsport?"

"Nobody ever proved me wrong about Kingsport, did they?"

"Yes, but it wouldn't be the first time that toy of yours picked up a false reading—"

"Several months before the Freeze, I monitored the last blip coming out of Mercy, days after the extraction. The blip ended right here, in this exact same spot on my SD?"

"Padadock?"

"Correct," Pullman said. "Whatever brought it to Padadock, I'd say it was important enough to travel over nine hundred miles and risk being spotted by the local wild life—"

"Thus," Blot finished, "creating conspiracy theories all across The Feed and in return, pressuring those opportunistic snakes at JeneCorp to take full advantage of their bot farms to formulate a new narrative. Curious, Man, why didn't you inform JeneCorp about the last blip?"

"The signal was faint, surfaced sporadically on the monitor, way too inconsistent to report, which meant, more than likely, if *it* was ole Moochie, *it* was piggybacking from one host to another in order to disguise *itself*," he said and made a face. "Clever, I'd say, since the technology wasn't able to pick up ole Moochie after the coupling process. Or," he shrugged, "the blips were just misreadings. But I will tell you: *Not* this blip. This is much different than the ones before. This mooch is a kicker and if it has coupled with a host, then how am I able to pick up a reading? Or, if it hasn't coupled with a host. . . yet. . . then, all I can ask myself is. . . 'Why?' There are way too many questions here, Blot."

"JeneCorp recovered most, if not all of E'Raknish after the Freeze," Blot said. "It could be a trap set by the Company in order to flesh out any remaining disrupters—"

"Or, it could be exactly what we need to put a halt to this goddamn catastrophe," Pullman said and once more glanced down at the list. The word *Urgency* seized his dwindling attention. "I need you to contact Barney—"

"Rotten's too far gone."

"But he's the only one who's handled ole Mooch."

"He's still wanted by Annexus," Blot said. "If he so much as breathes on E'Raknish, they'll sniff him out. I'd like to think they would be sympathetic toward his plights, but I lean more toward the idea of Annexus tearing him to shreds after he failed to complete his mission."

"I'm sure, if it came down to it, he'd be glad to take one for the team."

"Even if there is still E'Raknish out there, hiding among us, what makes you so sure that it will undo what had already been done?"

"I don't know," Pullman said, drifting off. "*But* it has to, right?"

"It's too late, Man," Blot said. "They've already won. All we can do now is cling on for as long as we can before succumbing to the next chapter in human evolution."

"There's *nothing* human that comes next, Blot."

"Maybe so, but it's the future we've paved for ourselves."

"I didn't ask for any of this shit," Pullman said. "Would you rather sit on your hands and do nothing?" He pulled out the "ACTIVE" surveillance device (SD) and held it up for Blot to see. "You're probably right. This is probably a trap. But if it's not, Blot, if we had the chance to find JeneCorp's most valuable resource before the Company got its scaly hands on it and use it as a weapon against them, I don't think I could live with myself, knowing that we had a shot to make things normal again."

"Whether you like it or not, Man, this is the new normal: *To drop or not to drop.*"

"Hell nah, not me," Pullman said, emotionally shaking his head. "You call dropping poison into your eye every day in order to prevent from turning into a headstone normal? I won't accept that." He said to Blot after catching his labored breath, "Now, you know where I stand. Either contact Barney or don't. It doesn't matter to me." He held up the surveillance device again and pointed at the flashing red dot on the screen. "You know where to find me."

SPOILED ROTTEN
AUGUST 10, 2053
SINCLAIR LEPRIEUR, LA

A quarter after midnight.

Of all the places in the country, given a limited use of updated technology, which, in return, forced a majority of residents to revert to the days pre-smartphone, many areas in the Deep South were getting by without relying on Dailies to survive, in fact, many spots in Texas, Mississippi, Alabama, Georgia, as well as Louisiana, despite limited resources that required moderation (except for alcohol, which there was plenty of), embodied a sense of normalcy, those pre-Lockhart days, especially in one particular area where the way of life seemed frozen in a different time where the only Feed was the kind you fed to cage-free chickens or other farm animals.

After spending the past four hours throwing back one shot of moonshine after another, Rotten was shitfaced and could hardly stand on his own two feet. The air was thick and soupy and it didn't take long to sweat.

One of the locals, a frequent at Gator Hole, approached from Rotten's right side and leaning over the slippery bar, told him that he looked like snatch in heat and with a concealed laugh hiding behind his sweaty, lippy grin, asked him if he needed a hand.

The local, Gums, who, every now and then helped out Rotten at the shop, burst out laughing, displaying the very item that earned him such a name.

"As a matter of fact, Gummy," Rotten slurred, "I'm doing just fine and dandy with this here bad boy."

Rotten attempted to thrown back another shot.

His clunky left arm fell off from the stump of his elbow like a widow-maker, the prosthetic clanked heavily against the bar before hitting the floor. The sight of Rotten's flimsy arm caused several other patrons in the bar to laugh.

As Rotten reached down to pick up the arm, the legs of the stool slid away from him, causing him to fall forward and bust his chin.

More laughter, all of it directed at the man of the hour: Barney "Shitfaced" Rotten.

Gums helped Rotten to his feet and picked up the prosthetic from the floor.

Rotten snatched the arm from Gums's grip.

"Hands off the merch, Gummy Boy," he snapped.

"Maybe you should just call it a night," Gums said patiently. "What'd you say, Barney?"

Once Rotten positioned himself back upright, he threw back yet another shot of moonshine.

Pointing at the nearly empty bottle of moonshine in front of Rotten, Gums said more closely, "You drink 'nuff of that stuff you're fittin' to wind up as blind as those rads up in N'Orleans."

"Do I look like the type to gouge out my own eyes?" Rotten asked, as his body swayed back and forth.

Gums elbowed him in the side, preventing Rotten from tipping over.

"No," he said. "But I'm serious, Barney. That stuff will make your ass blind."

"How does one's ass go blind, Gummy?"

"You know what I mean?"

"You sayin' I got an eye for an asshole? What are tryin' to say, Gummy Bear?"

"Easy, Barney," Gums warned. "Don't go sayin' something you might later regret. . . "

Rotten's eyes crossed the two beautiful black ladies standing by the billiard tables.

One of them, he realized, Krystal, who was wearing a sexy getup, including a crop top and a dangerously tight leather skirt that eroticized her godly booty.

More straight-faced, Rotten trailed off, "I have enough regrets as it is. . . "

As his most primal impulses took over, the blood raced through his veins.

Rotten couldn't stop shooting glances over at the two ladies on the other side of the bar.

Gums followed Rotten's eyes toward the two ladies, one in particular, who managed to lasso Rotten's eye like a baby calf.

The one, Krystal, he knew, had seen her many times before with Rotten, had warned Rotten many times about her and the heartless bodies that she left in her wake. She was one of Rotten's regulars, he'd say, who, despite being out of Rotten's league, had sunk her claws into Rotten.

She was incredibly wealthy; and Rotten, who wasn't a type to kiss and tell, often told him in the shop that she was too ashamed of him to invite him to her elite gatherings.

The other one, shorter than Krystal in height and could pass as a younger sister, he had seen several times before at the Hole, didn't know her name or her background, but he heard that she owned a brothel.

Displaying more confidence, Rotten wiped off the greasy stains from the flimsy prosthetic, securely reattached it back to his stump, and walked over to the two, Krystal first acknowledging him with a bright smile, then her dyed-blonde haired guest, who gave Rotten a once-over.

In a flirty way, Rotten asked, "What brings you out tonight, Ms. Bawl?"

"Well, after a long day's work, a lady's got to play—"

"That is, if you call role-playing-as-a-corporate-shill-peddling-daily-downers work."

"Unlike you, Grease Monkey, I got quotas."

"As you can tell business has been slow lately," he said. "It's like all of a sudden everybody turned into a Do-It-Yourselfer."

"Excuses, excuses, monkey boy."

"Not an excuse," he said. "Just an observation."

"Well, you do tend to overprice for your services." She paused. "*But* not everybody likes to get their hands dirty."

"You got plenty of dirt on your hands from hanging 'round all them fat cats."

"Those dirty paws write large checks."

Rotten moved in closer to Krystal

"You didn't stop by," he said, more sober and direct.

"I did earlier," she said. "You weren't there." Her yellow-contact eyes narrowed. She said more sharply, "Obviously."

Rotten asked, "Who's your friend here?"

Krystal introduced her friend, who was also dressed in a provocative manner.

"This is Maya."

"Oh-my-Gaia," he said, admiring Krystal's friend, "if it ain't my new best friend, Maya."

She giggled at Rotten's drunken rhyme.

"Hi-ya," she said in a frisky manner. "Just so you know, my favorite fruit happens to be papaya."

"Good to know," said Rotten, more excited. "I'm a big, big, *big* fan of papaya. I'd even go so far to say that I love papaya so much that I couldn't live without it."

"Comfort food, huh?"

"More like a necessary food."

As Rotten shook Maya's hand, he kissed the top of her hand.

Maya shot a glance over at Krystal and said to her, "He's cute. So, is he the one who's been stealing you away from me?"

Krystal couldn't help but shake her head in disapproval at Rotten's inebriated state.

With a sigh, Krystal said to Rotten, "He's the one all right. So. . . " she turned to Maya, who was rather smitten by Rotten's drunken charm, ". . . what are we going to do with him?"

Maya's eyes traced Rotten's body, her thorough inspection ending with his right hand. She held up his hand and looked over the oil and grime underneath his fingernails.

"Just make sure he washes his hands first," she said to Krystal.

For some, like Maya, sex was work.

For others, like Rotten, it was medicine, quick and instant yet short-lived.

And every time he found himself in the presence of a beautiful woman, he OD'd.

He died.

Then, he was reborn.

After the three extinguished the midnight flames back at Rotten's love shack situated along the bayou, the first pink shades of dawn painted over the dark sky.

While Rotten lay sprawled out in a messy, sweaty bed, Krystal thanked him for a good time and then kissed him on the forehead.

Fully dressed, she exited the bedroom.

Maya, who was last to leave, stood by the lit doorway of the bedroom.

With his eyes half-opened, Rotten watched Maya's dark silhouette blow him a kiss.

"Goodnight, Lover Boy," she said and vanished into the night darkness like a femme fatale.

As Rotten dosed off, he suddenly heard a *creak* coming from the other side of the bedroom.

He bolted upright and scanned the darkness of the room.

"Hello?"

Nobody answered.

"Krystal?"

Krystal was gone, had left a few minutes ago.

He heard yet another *creak* coming from another side of the bedroom.

Over Rotten's shoulder, a dark figure appeared in the doorway; and before Rotten could turn and face it, the figure was gone.

He rolled out of bed, threw on a pair of boxers, grabbed a cigarette, and brought it outside on the back porch, which overlooked the bayou.

As the pastel colors of dawn spread across the reflective surface of the calm water, he drifted off into the growing light. He only took one drag from the cigarette before passing out.

He shut both of his eyelids; and as the lit cigarette inched closer toward the bench, gradually but surely, the tiny amber starting to heat up the wood, a bucket of ice-cold water was suddenly tossed at his face.

Startled, Rotten violently woke up and flailed around the wet bench.

With his bloodshot eyes wide open, he searched the porch but couldn't find anyone in sight.

To his right, he heard the sound of a bucket dropping to the ground.

He followed the sound and found Blot towering in the shadows in the corner of the porch.

"You son of a bitch," Rotten seethed and charged at Blot.

Rotten attempted to tackle Blot but ended up crashing into the galvanized trashcans, knocking them over. He brushed himself off and stood to his feet. Blot opened the back door and like a matador, lured Rotten to tackle him.

Enraged, Rotten charged at Blot, who was standing in the shadows of the living room.

As soon as his body shot through the doorway, the door suddenly closed behind Rotten.

The entire living room fell to blackness, and Rotten found himself falling into the blackness.

When Rotten finally landed, he barreled into a body of murky water. The entry was like an icy punch, sending a shock throughout his body.

Flailing underwater, Rotten collected himself and swam up to the veiled light of dawn above him.

Once Rotten surfaced from the water, he struck the top of his head against the underside of a wooden dock.

More shock ran through his body, this time rushing from his head.

At first, he panicked.

Only a narrow space of air between the water and the dock.

He felt trapped; and while frantically trying to escape, he started to hyperventilate.

To his right, he found an opening.

Trying not to hit his head again, he swam underneath the dock.

Once he made it to the clearing, he looked around the lake.

He was no longer in Sinclair Leprieur.

Instead, he found himself at Forsake's home in **Mason**.

Dazed by the foreign surroundings, Rotten managed to climb his way up to the dock.

As he pulled his body from the water more bubbles surfaced from below in what he believed was gas exiting his body. The side effects of shine, he told himself. He ignored the stirring below and lay on the dock where he took a minute to catch his breath. The sound of moving water lulled him into a sleepy state, and he knew, if he closed his eyes, he'd have a difficult time opening them for he was too drunk and exhausted and weak to properly function.

Over the sound of his heavy breathing, he heard footsteps from behind.

He rolled his head to the side, briefly scanned his surroundings.

Behind him was a cabin, Forsake's cabin. The floodlights turned off.

Then, closer, standing at the other end of the weathered dock, was Forsake himself. His face no longer bearded, but rather cleanly shaved, revealing a thinner look from years of surviving off a natural, unprocessed diet.

Startled, Rotten sat up.

With a dry towel worn over his shoulder, Forsake strolled along the dock and offered Rotten a hand.

"What the fuck is this?" asked Rotten.

"Dry off before you come inside," Forsake said, as he tossed the towel to Rotten, who didn't react or make any attempt to catch the towel. Acknowledging his confusion, he stepped closer to Rotten: "It takes a few minutes to get used to a run. Some compare the experience to the feeling you get after regaining consciousness, unsure about the moments before winding up in a foreign environment, wondering whether you're in a dream—"

"Or a nightmare," Rotten finished, as he looked around the eerie foggy lake.

"Exactly," he said. "But rest assured, Barney, you're very much awake."

Rotten grabbed the towel from the dock and asked Forsake, this time demanding an answer, "Where am I?"

"Doesn't matter," he said. "All that matters is that you sober up before your next mission."

Rotten drunkenly laughed at Forsake's comment.

"Where the fuck have you been for the past four years?" he asked but didn't expect to hear an answer from Forsake. "You vanish off the face of the earth, and now, you're giving orders—thanks but no thanks."

"A former colleague of yours Tracker Man Pullman picked up a blip yesterday. He told me that he could use your expertise."

"Expertise?" Rotten, still drunk despite the rude awakening, laughed. "Is he serious?"

"He seems pretty certain that whatever popped up on his radar is worth looking into—"

"Ever stop to think that it's probably a trap?"

"I've considered that, but what if it's not?"

"I don't give a fuck what it is, *Blot*, or whatever the fuck you're calling yourself these days," Rotten snapped. "You can tell that tracker I'll be no use to him. You tell him I'm out."

"Out, huh?"

Frustrated, Forsake asked Rotten to follow him back to the cabin.

Rotten didn't budge.

"I can tell you've already given up on life," Forsake said, as Rotten sat up and dried off his face and then his stump.

"What life?"

He showcased the serene lake around Rotten, as well as the natural wildlife, which, despite the current state of the country, still flourished.

"This life. . . right here. . . " he said, approaching Rotten, ". . . and I'll tell you, Barney. No matter what they did to it, no matter the extent of their destruction, it's still worth protecting."

Rotten pulled his eyes away from Forsake and once more, absorbed the view around him.

"You've been here this whole time?" asked Rotten.

"Yes," he said and sat down next to Rotten. "You blame yourself for what happened, don't you?"

Rotten sat there, silent and stewing.

In his hot silence, he looked below the dock, only to witness the ripple of water.

Then the shadow of his passenger, waiting for the right opportunity.

"Well, I'm here to tell you, Barney, that it's not your fault. Whatever happened, happened. And there wasn't a goddamn thing *we* could've done in order to prevent what was coming. We tried, but at the end of the day, they were one step ahead us. The sooner you can accept that, the sooner we can move on."

Rotten asked, "How do we move on when we are ultimately doomed to fail?"

"And what kind of people would we be if we stood back and did nothing—"

"I'd say the kind who knows a thing or two about not wasting other people's time."

Forsake pulled out a revolver from his back pocket and slammed it on the dock before Rotten.

He stood up and said over Rotten, "If you're in such a rush to die, then do yourself a favor and pick up that gun and point it to your head and blow your fucking brains out!"

Forsake stormed away from Rotten.

As he reached the end of the dock, a gunshot suddenly rang out!

Forsake flinched and then froze in shock.

Behind him, Rotten's arm lowered from the sky as he hung his head downward.

Rotten sat motionlessly, his body limp and lifeless.

As Forsake began to walk away from Rotten and not once turning around to check on his old friend, he heard yet another gunshot ring out from behind!

The sound of a person falling onto the dock followed by the *clinking* sound of a knife striking the dock forced Forsake to rotate around, only to find Maya, dripping wet, clutching her midsection. Below her was a knife in the shape of a crescent moon, each side deadly sharp, a versatile weapon most commonly used for slitting throats. While sitting on her knees, Maya removed her bloody hands from her chest, revealing the gunshot wound, a direct shot straight to her heart.

Her death was quick and painless.

As the rest of Maya's body flopped forward onto the deck, Forsake eyed Rotten, who was standing upright. He lowered the revolver to his side.

"Looks like people want you dead."

"She must've slipped through during the run," Forsake said, as he noticed the circular bloodstains along the dock.

He followed the blood trail to Maya's right foot, which had been severed directly below the ankle. A clean and perfect cut from the closing of Blot's gateway. The red circular dots on the dock emphasized where Maya had applied pressure to the severed limb and hobbled her way toward him like a peg-legged pirate.

"Did you know her?" asked Rotten.

"No," said Forsake. "But she must work for the Company."

"Or the Company must've somehow gotten to her," Rotten said, checking on Maya. "You'd be surprised what a person would do for resources."

Again, Rotten found himself looking back at Maya's right ankle, the shadow cut.

"What'd you think they promised her?"

"Food, water—who the hell knows?"

Rotten asked Forsake, "So, what now?"

"If JeneCorp used you to get to me, then, more than likely, they know about the blip, which means they haven't found it yet."

"Or, they have and it's a trap."

"There's that—

"So, why's a lifer like Pullman helping you out?" asked Rotten. "You trust him?"

"I've been keeping a close eye on Pullman for some time," Forsake said. "And I take it he's been keeping an eye on you as well."

Rotten drifted off, thinking about the days after Agent Noble knocked him unconscious following the mission in Mercy: Rotten sneaking off to Mirage to contact Blot; and then afterwards, Rotten heading back to the bar, spotting Pullman inside Mirage, Pullman buying Rotten a drink; then, Rotten forgetting to return the phone that he stole from a patron; the customer making quite a fuss; Rotten purposefully picking up the phone "off the floor," and handing it to the bitchy patron; Rotten telling the patron he must've dropped his phone right as he was about to return it.

Seated at the bar during the incident, Pullman noticed the phone was not cracked.

In fact, there wasn't even a mark on the phone.

Pullman turned to Rotten and made a face, as if Pullman didn't just wind up in Mirage out of the blue to grab a drink.

Forsake said, pulling Rotten from his trance: "I never told you about Pullman because I still couldn't get a good read on him or his allegiance."

Rotten asked, "What makes you so sure his allegiance is with you?"

"Well, for starters, he's already on the way to track down the blip. . . " he said and checked the time on his analog wristwatch, ". . . he should be there any minute now."

"And where is there?" asked Rotten.

"Small town in Pennsylvania," he said. "Padadock."

Rotten nodded at Maya and asked Forsake, "And how do you know Pullman's not working with the Company?"

"I don't," Forsake said, reaching out his right hand. "But that's the risk we're going to have to take. I mean, what else are you going to do? Spend the rest of your final days repairing old cars that won't mean shit in a couple of years? Hiding from those who stripped everything away you—"

"There's nothing more dangerous than a man who has nothing to lose."

"And that's precisely why I need you, Barney. . . "

Rotten handed the revolver back to Forsake, who grabbed the pistol with his left hand while his right hand remained extended.

Forsake said, "What do you say?"

Rotten made his answer by shaking Forsake's hand.

Forsake walked Rotten back to the cabin where Rotten dried off and dressed into a new pair of clothes that Forsake let him borrow.

Next, Forsake pulled out a medicine bottle from a drawer and offered him a generic version of Prosopagtamine™.

Rotten eyed the triangular-shaped pill in Forsake's palm.

The temporary "three-in-one" remedy engineered to treat three different illnesses, except for the one disorder that Rotten had been experiencing ever since the Freeze: compulsive behavior.

"That won't help me now," he said. "Can't remember the last time I've taken one—"

"I need you sharp, Barney," Forsake said, holding out his palm. "Please, Barney, you know what you're capable of doing to yourself. I need the old Barney. . . "

Rotten grabbed the pill and downed it with a cup of coffee.

"I almost forgot," Forsake said and grabbed yet another bottle, this time from his office. "I managed to get my hands on the 'other' version of Dailies, the drops not intended for public consumption, or what you call part of the Company's complimentary gifts given to the United States government in exchange for Mr. Acosta."

He showed Rotten the bottle of eye drops.

Rotten asked, "What is this?"

Forsake handed the eye drops to Rotten, who looked over the bottle, which appeared similar to Dailies but instead had a "+" symbol next to the brand.

"Just in case things get hairy up there," Forsake said. "It'll temporarily give you the power of the gaze without the drowsiness of halozine. One drop in each eye. Use *only* when needed."

Rotten looked over the ingredients and unlike the Dailies, it didn't have halozine.

More intrigued, Rotten asked Forsake, "How come you didn't mention these before?"

"I wasn't aware of them until after the Freeze," he said. "By then, it was already too late."

Rotten once more looked over the bottle and the power he possessed in his palm.

Curious, he confirmed, "Just one drop in each eye?"

Forsake nodded.

"Remember: *Only* if you need it," he said.

"How will I know when I need to use it?"

"We may be outnumbered, Barney, but this. . ." Forsake said, pointing at the drops, ". . . it will level the playing field. Plus, if we can get our hands on E'Raknish, then we may just have a shot at putting an end to this madness—"

Rotten asked, "Where are you going to be?"

Forsake said, "I'll be around."

"Of course," Rotten said, disappointed in Forsake's vagueness.

"One last thing," Forsake said, nodding to the far side of the room.

Rotten redirected his attention to the upgraded prosthetic on a table.

"You thought I was just going to send you into harm's way with your dick in your hand?" he joked, as he walked Rotten over to the prosthetic.

"Beats your last one," he said, as Rotten tried on the prosthetic, which was more flexible and easier to use than that junky P.O.S. that never stayed on half the time.

Inspecting the prosthetic, Rotten said, "Thanks."

Shortly after Rotten was given his new swag, Forsake received a flashing white ping on his phone.

His eyes darkened, as he stared at the darkening screen on his phone.

More seriously, he said to Rotten, "Pullman has arrived in Padadock. You ready?"

"Yeah," Rotten said. "Ready."

Forsake walked to the hallway closet, opened the door, and stepped inside.

Holding out his hand, Forsake said from the darkness of the closet, "Right this way."

Hesitant, Rotten walked up to the closet.

"What do I have to do?" asked Rotten.

"Just grab my hand," Forsake said and as he stepped farther into the closet, his body drifted off into the shadows.

As Rotten stepped past the doorway of the closet, he watched Forsake's hand vanish into the shadows.

Then, he reached out and grabbed his hand.

NOBLE SON
JULY 31, 2053 - AUGUST 7, 2053
WILBUR, NC - JONESY TOWN, PA

EVERYBODY in the stands was cheering for the racehorses, which were making the stretch turn.

A majority of the audience was rooting for the dark horse, #8 "Flying Cloud," who started to catch up to the stud, Hornet's Stinger, who was currently positioned in first place.

As Noble was perched along a small hill next to Pine Lake Racetrack, he adjusted the scope of his sniper on one particular spectator, who was jumping up and down with excitement. A few feet over the spectator's shoulder there was another spectator, who looked as if it had no earthly business being at the race. It wore a black fedora, which covered up its scaly face. As the horses reached the finish line, Hornet's Stinger breaking away from the group, the mysterious spectator removed the hat from its hairy, scaly head, then shed the rest of its attire, revealing the werewolf snake, who was ready to pounce on its prey while the rest of the audience was too focused on the race.

While its fangs were extending from its gaping mouth, Flying Cloud was slowly catching up to Hornet's Stinger.

The crowd went wild, anticipation built, one layer after another, the suspense heightened—nearly tangible—for the energy filled the air.

As the two horses crossed the finished line, Flying Cloud winning the race by the length of a nose, the werewolf snake uncoiled its body and towered over the innocent spectator and just as it was about to strike at the spectator, Noble took the shot, hitting the werewolf snake directly between the eyes.

The head of the stone figure, which was wearing a Halloween mask that Noble recently acquired at a costume store nearby, shattered to pieces. Clouds of gray dust shot up into the air followed by fist-sized chunks of stone falling to the bleachers. Despite the destruction, the headless figure remained upright. Its right arm was held high and angled over what used to be its head as it posed in what looked like a selfie.

As crowds erupted in jubilation, Noble spotted more creatures lurking past spectators.

Second to reveal itself was a Culexx, both its wings stretching outward from its holey jacket, ready to bite the neck of a spectator.

Noble focused his aim and shot the Culexx twice, the first shot clipping its wing and another shot striking the top part of its head. The bullet ended up breaking off part of the shoulder of the stone figure while its head remained intact. The silicone mask was still attached to the head, despite a massive bullet hole, which ripped open and peeled back the silicone.

More creatures emerged.

More monsters.

Rat King.

Blood Demons, or "Drifters."

The tree demon.

Vamps.

Black Plague.

Even one of the Five Fistfuls, who was dressed in a red cloak.

All of them ready or in the middle of attacking spectators.

Noble picked off each one.

After the carnage, Noble removed his eye from the scope, revealing yet another story.

The spectators were already dead, all of them, had died from the Freeze, including the spectators that Noble dressed up or decorated like monsters.

After Noble left his position and walked up to the stands to survey the so-called "casualties," except for one wayward shot,

which ended up striking the arm of a non-mask-wearing spectator, he gave himself a self-analysis and concluded that he hadn't
completely lost his shot.   Not completely.   Although he was
somewhat rusty, he knew there was room for improvement.

While Noble gathered the rest of the salvageable Halloween
masks throughout the stands, the timer on his wristwatch *beeped*,
alerting him that it was time to leave and that he had more pressing issues to address.

The track was eight miles away from home, and altogether, the
walk was roughly two hours and forty minutes, which would give
Noble plenty of time to make it back home before lunch.

Before heading back home, he stopped to check on one of his
many crab traps, which he had scattered along the pier.   He
checked the first one tied to the pier.   The trap was his most durable one and despite the unpredictable season, he had a lot of
luck catching crab with the trap.

As he pulled the trap from the water, he noticed part of it was
damaged.

Noble's catch: the small plush toy of a rubber duck.   The bill
of the duck was snagged on the wire.   He pulled the dirty toy
from the trap and inspected it.   The sight of the toy reminded
Noble of the world before the Freeze and the little things and the
most trivial ones that people took for granted.   He tossed the toy
duck back into the ocean.

Following a thorough inspection, Noble suspected that a
clever opportunist tampered with the trap while he was off killing
imaginary monsters.   He combed the pier for clues.   He found a
set of footprints leaving the scene.   He checked his watch.

The grumpy old bastard can wait, Noble thought.

Pressed for time, he decided to follow the tracks, which led
him to a marsh along the inland waterway.   The tracks led him to
a bank where he found more impressions.   Soil and overgrowth
was matted down from what appeared to be from a boat.   He
gave up on his pursuit and walked back home located along the
shore, which covered Main Street.

Before entering, his eye crossed a faded bloodstain on the
porch, as well as the faded blood splatter along the side of the
doorway.   Despite how many times he cleaned that stain, he could
still see it, still faded and foreign, and each and every time he laid
his good eye upon it, he felt an unexplainable emptiness inside
him, wondering how it got there.

As his thoughts churned, like clockwork, he was greeted by the groans of his ailing ninety-one-year-old father, but this time, unlike the other ones, he was complaining about a severe pain in his abdomen, which Noble first waved off as typical hungry pains.

Noble was only lying to himself.

His father, Kaolin, was a man of grit and valor, a man who had quite an enormous appetite, and to watch him carry on about pain, Noble knew it was serious.

Noble's father, a highly decorated admiral who once served as Chief of Naval Operations of the United States Navy during the China Conflict, didn't have much longer to live—Noble, who had watched many good men die in the field, knew Death was close by. Ole Boney was perhaps waiting outside on the front porch, taking a smoke break before he knocked on the door.

Well aware of his father's time and what little he had left, Noble wanted to desperately fast-forward to the end.

Where was a universal remote control when you needed one?

The sight alone of him withering away in bed was excruciating to watch.

Despite being absent throughout most of his childhood, Kaolin wasn't the type of father who received the "Father of the Year" award to add to his medals. However, he never mistreated his son. In fact, the short amount of time the father and son did spend together wasn't wasted. Yet, Kaolin filled the time with stories and insights about the world, especially the good people who occupied it. Not once did he ever strike his son whenever he misbehaved. He never spoiled him. It was fair to say that there weren't any hard feelings between the two.

Noble reassured his father that he'd feel better after he ate.

In a state of agony, Kaolin eyed the sniper that his son rested against the doorway.

His complaints about pain were redirected toward the sniper and how it was time for his son to move on and make peace with the world.

Noble gave his best explanation: "If you don't use it, then you lose it."

With contempt, Kaolin waved off the comment.

Since they didn't have any crab to eat for lunch and the grouper, which Noble caught yesterday, had gone bad after the fridge lost power due to a faulty solar panel, the two were stuck with canned beans and an expired granola bar that tasted like petrified dog shit.

Two days later, after Noble found a box of "Q" while ransacking an abandoned beach house, which was one broken stilt away from collapsing into the Atlantic, Noble decided to say goodbye to his father.

During Kaolin's last supper, a Salisbury steak TV dinner laced with Equanimity, he brought up the conversation of legacy with his son.

Noble wasn't at all interested in *legacy* and scorned any use of the word.

There were many women whom he intimately encountered during his lifetime and more than likely several of them had bore his child. Considering Noble's line of work, he was a hard man to contact and the job required lots of traveling. The thought of bringing children into the world or the possibility of having his own blood out there, in the wilderness, was at the very back of his mind. He'd even go so far to say he never thought about it.

By the end of the supper, Kaolin was ready to go back home: Little Springs, Arkansas.

Noble prepared his father for bed and then handed him a photo of home.

In the photo was Kaolin and his wife, Noble's mother, Landa, Noble's brother, and lastly, Noble himself. Noble was only eight years old at the time, his brother two years older. All four of them were standing along a cliff overlooking a valley in the Ozarks. Kaolin held the photo in his hands and drifted off to the thought of home.

One week later after Noble first lost track of the Crab Thief, he spotted a young girl messing around with the traps during a heavy rainstorm.

Every muscle in his body tightened with rage.

For the past five days, he had been camping inside a concealed area inside a gutted bait shop with a perfect view of the pier and waited to catch the Crab Thief red-handed. During long hours of waiting, he imagined what he'd do to the Crab Thief whenever he caught him—or her—if he would kill him or her quickly or slowly and if slowly, Noble imagined how he'd do it. Fishing hooks came to mind, each one hooked to the flesh of the Crab Thief. Hundreds of fishing hooks attached to wire used to suspend the Crab Thief like a grotesque public display, sending a warning message to those who dared lay a finger on his traps.

As he prepared himself to sneak up on the girl, he suddenly slipped on a slick spot along the patch of grass, resulting in him dropping the sniper to the ground.

The noise exposed Noble's position and forced the girl to run away with a bagful of crab.

Who would've thought a young girl being the Crab Thief?

He chased after the Crab Thief and took a short cut through the pines. Along the way, his foot caught a tree root, causing him to trip. His face planted against the sandy ground, leaving behind several scratches and abrasions along his cheek; and when he managed to stumble back to his feet, his right hand touched a piece of wood, roughly six inches in length, protruding from his lower right side. He wiggled the loose piece of wood in his side but couldn't feel it or even the coarseness of the wood when he pulled out the debris. He felt absolutely nothing. The stain, he remembered. *Faded* but not so *foreign*. The blast of a handgun, which woke him from his deep slumber, sounded closer and closer, *familiar*. In order to stop the bleeding he tore off the bottom half of his shirt, wadded it up into a ball, pressed it tightly against the wound, then used his belt to secure the shirt against the wound.

Once the pressured was applied to the wound, Noble still managed to cut off the Crab Thief before she reached her boat.

Noble was able to get a better look at the Crab Thief.

She was missing her left arm entirely. The left side of her face was frozen in a droopy state, as if the Freeze had caused her to have a massive stroke. The sight of, not the girl's face, but the missing arm triggered a memory: Three months back, when the temperature started to warm, he stumbled upon an alligator chewing on part of a severed arm, which looked as if it had been cut off by a hacksaw. As soon as Noble made his presence known, the gator scurried like a zigzag back into the wetlands, leaving behind the arm. Half of the arm, the top part, he inspected, including the bicep, elbow, and part of the forearm, was flesh and bone. The flesh appeared as if it was in the first stages of decay. The bottom half, however, wrist and hand, were stone. Pieces of a phone were embedded into the stony palm.

Noble forced his drifting eye toward the girl, who, after making eye contact with Noble, ran to the boat and rowed away using two oars, which she jerry-rigged for one hand.

Impressed by the girl's audacity, Noble never chased after her.

Later that afternoon, as the rain lessened to a drizzle, Noble was paid a visit by an artificial raven as he was sipping from a flat and skunky beer underneath a canopy on the front porch.

Tempted to snipe it down, he recognized the "⅃⊏" logo on the side of the raven's wing as it landed on the front steps of the porch. The raven opened its beak and out from its mouth popped an omni-projector, which displayed Rouse's hologram.

Rouse took a seat next to Noble on the porch.

"What part of 'I'm finished' didn't you understand, Tahr?" Noble asked while sipping from the beer.

"I sincerely apologize for the disturbance, Noble, but a delicate matter has been brought to my attention and the Company needs someone of your expertise."

"Delicate matter?"

Noble attempted to laugh, but the laugh came out like a snort.

"An hour ago a surveillance team picked up on a signal in Pennsylvania. They're one hundred percent certain it's E'Raknish."

Noble attempted to respond but could only make it through a couple of words before Rouse interrupted.

"Before you say no, I'm going to throw it out there: Stefan is going to lead the mission."

"Prescott's still inexperienced," said Noble. "He'll get your entire team killed—"

"And that's why I need the best of the best," Rouse said. "I need the Noble Son."

A silence built over both human and hologram.

Noble slurped from his beer.

"I gave you my answer four years ago."

Rouse glanced up at the faded bloodstain on the side of the porch.

"Very well," Rouse said and walked from the front porch. Before he vanished back into the artificial raven, he turned his shoulder and asked Noble, "By the way, how's the retirement?"

"Swell," Noble said with a grin on his face.

Liar.

Rouse pointed at the wound on Noble's side and said, "Take care of that, Agent Noble."

"I'm not an agent anymore."

"Sure you are," Rouse said, cracking a smile. "You'll always be an agent."

In a flash, Rouse's hologram vanished.

The projector lowered back into the raven's beak.

The raven cawed at Noble before it flew away.

Noble looked over the beach, which was littered with the remnants of beachfront properties.

Soon, he knew, the erosion would spread closer, the ocean swallowing his home, resulting in Noble to move once again.

Later that same night, while lounging around the house, Noble's wandering, bloodshot eye landed on the yellow rubber duck that he found in his front lawn the day after he tossed it back in the ocean. Based on the unusual Michigan-shaped oil stain on the duck's side, Noble could tell it was the same duck as the one he discovered in the crab trap. Before his father's death, he gave it to him as an inside joke about "lame ducks."

Enraged by the sight of the duck, he pulled out a secure VidLine from storage where he kept all of his guns and ammunition, safely connected the bulky device to the eClipse transceiver, and made a video call to Tahr Rouse.

Rouse picked up the call and was first to speak: "That was fast," he said.

"Are you still interested in tracking down that blip?" asked Noble.

"Recons have already scoured the area. They're holding a deeprief session as we speak," he informed Noble. "Agent Prescott said his team will be ready to depart at zero dark thirty."

"Tell 'em to save me a seat."

"That's the spirit," Rouse said. "I'll have a chopper pick you up."

Noble ended the call and removed the bandage from his side. Surprisingly, the wound had stopped bleeding and didn't need any further attention from Noble, other than super glue to prevent the wound from reopening. Once the wound was sealed, he pulled out a special black case from the drawer: a going-away present from JeneCorp, which was part of his retirement. Inside the case was an electronic smarteye that connected to a portable drone.

Shortly after Noble talked with Rouse, a helicopter arrived at Noble's coordinates in Wilbur. After refueling, the helicopter flew Noble roughly five hundred miles north to the closest major city to Padadock, which was Jonesy Town, where Noble met up with his team to plot their next course of action.

UNNATURAL SELECTION
AUGUST 10, 2053
PADADOCK, PA

ROTTEN smelled smoke.

An orange fiery light grew below the doorway, gradually lighting the inside of a closet.

The line of light intensified and brought forth a shelf of cleaning chemicals, as well as a mop bucket.

Prior to the shadowrun, Rotten vaguely remembered Forsake's words *"Just grab my hand."* But even the hazy memory of those words felt like they came from the lost echoes of a dream.

Following those words the deafening blackness opened its mouth and swallowed him whole.

As the smoke poured underneath the door, he exited the janitor's closet, only to find himself in the back of a rundown convenient store, which had been ransacked.

He crept through the smoky, dimly lit aisles until he reached the front of the store. The windows were partly boarded up. Several windows were shattered, revealing an apocalyptic orange-washed sky outside. The sun was blotted out by the dense cloud of smoke that sat over the entire town like a bloated smoky beast whose burdensome breath brought disease and death.

As Rotten was about to exit the store, he witnessed two agents carrying rifles patrolling the street.

Trying to conceal his cough with the crook of his elbow, he ducked back inside the store.

As he backpedaled toward the checkout desk, he heard a boot stepping over a shard of glass, resulting in a *crunching* noise.

Before Rotten started to rotate around toward the noise, a smooth city hand slipped over his shoulder and firmly pressed against his mouth, preventing him from uttering a sound.

Rotten's eyes moved toward the far corner of his vision where he caught a glimpse of a man in an oxygen mask.

"Eyes peeled, brother," Pullman said in a muffled whisper.

With his hand still pressed against Rotten's mouth, Pullman allowed Rotten to face him.

Once he laid eyes on Pullman underneath the oxygen mask, Rotten breathed a sigh of relief.

With his other hand, Pullman held his index finger in the vicinity of his lips, signaling Rotten to be quiet.

Pullman slowly removed his hand from Rotten's mouth.

"Long time, no see," Rotten whispered. All of a sudden, he was forced to cover a cough, as the smoke was irritating his air passages, including the back of his throat, which started to sting. He nodded at Pullman's oxygen mask and said, "I see you came prepared."

"Before I left for Padadock I noticed the AQ around the blip was off the fucking charts, near hazardous levels. From the Company's perspective, if you were trying to set a trap, it wouldn't make much sense to create a deterrent."

Rotten noticed how quickly the fire was spreading and voiced it to Pullman.

"Makes sense," he added.

"Given the recent drought in the area, it won't take long before the entire town is engulfed in flames."

"By any chance," Rotten said, nodding once more at Pullman's oxygen mask, "do you have an extra one of those?"

Pullman reached in his bag and pulled out yet another oxygen mask.

"Thought you'd never ask," he said with his voice lowered to a near whisper.

Rotten put on the mask.

"Thanks."

"Didn't think you show," Pullman said.

"Save the reunion for a later time," Rotten said, looking around. "What the fuck is going on here?"

"It's Noble," Pullman informed. "He's burning down the entire town."

"Why?"

"He's trying to flush out E'Raknish."

"With heat?" Rotten repeated. "Good luck."

"Yeah, but who's not a fan of fire?"

"Fire's number one fan: Us."

"That's right," Pullman said. "Humans."

"You're thinking E'Raknish has already coupled with a new host?"

"Seems that way."

Rotten nodded at the SD worn like a purse over Pullman's shoulder.

"Getting any readings?"

"I lost ole Moochie once I arrived in Padadock earlier this morning. The reading came from the laundry room of a house located just off 2nd Street. From what I could tell there was a family occupying the house. Whoever they were, it looked like they left in a hurry."

"A laundry room?"

"A laundry basket to be precise," he said. "Last readings were off the charts. Nothing like I have seen from what I'm used to seeing with E'Raknish."

"How so?"

"E'Raknish doesn't leave behind any traces."

"But this one did?"

"Hey," Pullman said, shrugging, "that's what the device read—"

After the two agents' survey, Noble's drone *whizzed* overhead, causing only Rotten to duck for cover.

"Don't worry, Barney Trouble," Pullman said jokingly. "I hacked his surveillance drone so that it can't read our heat signatures. Who do you think built their tracking systems?"

Impressed, Rotten said, "Nice work, Tracker."

"Just keep in mind, though," Pullman warned, "JeneCorp's got all sorts of eyes on us, including the eyes of the furry four-legged kind. Given the time crunch, there are way too many to hack."

"You're talking about artificials?"

"Yep," he said. "So, just be aware."

"Don't worry," Rotten said. "Not much of an animal lover anyway. So, what's next?"

"We find E'Raknish before Noble."

Rotten asked, "Any ideas?"

Another heavily geared agent strolled by the convenient store, setting ablaze businesses with a flamethrower, thus pushing the fire closer and closer into the downtown area.

"I spotted one of the locals entering through the back of the town's church," Pullman said.

"Yeah," Rotten said. "So?"

"So, the drone hasn't picked up any readings coming from the church, which means there is something inside the church that is masking their heat signatures."

"Maybe it's worth checking out. . . " Rotten said and nodded at Pullman, ". . . You lead the way. . . "

Once the area was clear to exit, he followed Pullman from the convenient store.

Altogether, Noble was leading a team of six agents, two of them with flamethrowers and the other two heavily armed and combing through each home or building in Padadock. Each one of the agents were wearing Company-issued oxygen masks, more condensed than Pullman's, fitted over each nostril like an artificial nose, leaving no room for leakage, the oxygen tubes stretching over the ears like a bang of hair and connecting to a portable oxygen tank worn on a belt buckle.

Finally, Agent Noble and Agent Prescott, also geared with oxygen masks, stood at an intersection along Main Street with their captive, John, who was tied to a streetlight post.

Secured around John's wrists was an indestructible zip-tie that held his arms behind the post, preventing him from wiggling himself free. One of his wrists—his right one—was wrapped in a hardened lime-green cast with various signatures, messages like "Get Well Soon", silly doodles, and smiley faces from the townspeople of Padadock. One of those doodles was drawn by M.J., who used a permanent marker to sully the cast with a doodle of a rocket-shaped penis and a lopsided pair of testicles, which John attempted to hide by using a black marker to sketch a butterfly over the offensive doodle.

The drone disconnected into two drones that broadcasted Noble's filtered voice: "*You have nowhere else to run. You are completely surrounded. Make it easier on yourself and come out from where you're hiding. If you give yourself up now, I can assure you that we will not harm you. But. . .*" his voice grew with frustration, "*. . . if it makes it more difficult for us to do our job, then I can't guarantee your safety.*"

Agent Prescott whistled at Noble, redirecting his attention toward the massive dark creature approaching through the dense smoke.

Noble pulled out a child's green and white turtle-patterned sock from his back left pocket of his pants and held the sock up toward the creature's phlegmy snout.

As Noble's voice continued to shout out dire warnings from the smoky skies above, Rotten and Pullman stayed low, ducking behind parked cars and posts in order to avoid being spotted by the agents on patrol.

Once the area was clear, the two cut through several businesses before spotting House of the Lord, a Carpenter Gothic-style church, which was located a few blocks away.

As Rotten and Pullman waited behind the corner of an alleyway, the drone hovered directly above the two, forcing Rotten to question whether or not Pullman's hack worked.

Noble's filtered voice rained down from above: "*Can you smell the smoke? If so, then that means your time is dwindling by the second. So give it up!*"

As the drone proceeded with its scan of the town, Rotten and Pullman breathed a sigh of relief and continued forward from the edge of the alleyway to the back of an abandoned vehicle parked along the curb of the street.

Pullman was first to dart across the street where he sought cover behind the car.

As Rotten attempted to flee, an agent snuck up behind him.

Blot suddenly leaped from the shadows of the alleyway and grabbed hold of the agent before the agent could apprehend Rotten.

Startled, Rotten rotated around, only to find Blot pulling the agent into the shadows.

The agent's arms and legs were flung outward, as he was yanked from his feet and swallowed by the shadows. Blot closed the gate of the shadowrun, severing both the agent's arms, as well as his legs. The limbs suspended in midair before falling to the ground.

Blot emerged from a shadow behind a dumpster on the opposite side of the alleyway.

"Thanks," Rotten said, facing Blot.

With his body concealed by the shadows, Blot said, "Next time watch your six."

Pullman ran back toward the alleyway and noticed the four severed limbs on the ground.

"Nice to have friends in dark places," he said and patted Rotten on the back.

Rotten nodded at the dumpster nearby.

"Open the dumpster," he said to Pullman, who, in return, was rather hesitant to follow Rotten's lead.

After Rotten picked up both the agent's arms, Pullman opened the dumpster for Rotten, and Rotten tossed each one inside. Lastly, he threw the agent's legs inside.

"No traces," he said and more closely, ordered Pullman in a tight whisper, "Move!"

The two moved three blocks, untouched by the fires, until reaching House of the Lord.

Before entering the church, Rotten looked over his shoulder and gathered a wider and much broader view of the town. He could see several lights turned on inside the town, which ran off a two-part system of solar and hydropower, a nearby dam supplying most of Padadock's power—and yet, despite all of their recoveries from the blackouts, it still appeared vacant.

"Where is everybody?" he asked Pullman.

"Hiding, I assume."

"*No*," Rotten said, searching for the others. "What *don't* you see here?"

He thought over Rotten's question and spoke the first thing that came to mind: "Statues?"

"Where have they all gone?" asked Rotten.

"Don't know," Pullman said and found a newspaper, which was being held against the door of the church by a stiff breeze. He picked up the newspaper, *Popular Times*, and read the headline on the front page.

After skimming the newspaper, Pullman handed it to Rotten, who read the front headline out loud:

ON THE BRINK OF NUCLEAR WAR!

Pullman downplayed the shocking headline: "Nobody believes a word that Company rag has to say. It's all propaganda to keep the Selected trembling in their boots. But," he said, flashing a grin, "I will say this: 'It does make for great TP.'"

Rotten discarded the newspaper, and the two entered the church, Pullman leading the way.

The inside of the church was dark and densely quiet and firelight from outside was growing brighter as minutes passed, creating a pulsating glow through the stained glass windows.

Once it was safe to breathe, the two removed their oxygen masks.

While making his way through the nave, Rotten searched each pew.

"Not a soul in sight," he said to Pullman, who didn't answer for he was intrigued by a door behind the altar.

"Not a religious man. Are you, Barney Trouble?" asked Pullman, as he walked through the ambulatory and shot a glance up at the apse above where he witnessed a glass artwork of a dove soaring in front of a brilliant sun, the glass divided into twelve sections, each section representing the Twelve Apostles.

Not at all interested in sharing his religious views with Pullman, Rotten said with frustration, "You said you saw one of the locals come through here?"

Pullman cracked open the door, revealing yet another room.

"Have a little faith, brother," he said, nodding at Rotten to follow him.

Rotten followed Pullman into a dimly lit sacristy, which was filled with dusty furniture, including an armoire carrying vestments, including albs and other garment used for service. Piles of cardboard boxes packed with Holy Bibles were haphazardly stacked in the corner of the room, exposing yet another door.

Pullman made a *psst*-noise at Rotten, redirecting the flashlight to the mysterious door in the corner of the room.

After climbing over the boxes, Pullman opened the door and shined a light inside, revealing a spiraling stairwell made from stone that trailed off into the darkness.

"Could be what's masking their heat signature," Pullman suggested.

With a grin, Rotten said, "You first, Tracker."

Both Rotten and Pullman ventured at least three stories underneath the church.

Rotten shined the light on the walls, which, like the stairwell, were made from stone.

"This place must've been here for centuries," said Rotten.

"You're telling me," Pullman said with a slight tremor in his voice.

The two arrived at the bottom of the stairwell, which opened up to a wine cellar.

Rotten caught a dark figure darting across the beam of the flashlight.

"Hello?" Pullman said.

All of a sudden, a gunshot *rang* out in the dark, first the flash of a muzzle, then the blast, or vice versa, Pullman couldn't tell which came first, the light or the sound, for the initial shock left him dropping to the floor.

The shot grazed Pullman's arm, the bullet nicking the sleeve of his shirt.

"Friendly," Rotten shouted out, as he tended to Pullman.

He heard footsteps circling them.

Once more, he shouted, "We don't work for the Company! We're here to help!"

All of a sudden, another flash of light burst through the darkness of the cellar, this time the beam of a flashlight that shined directly on Rotten's face.

With his arm raised in surrender, Rotten shielded the light and saw more figures, dozens of them, mostly small and hunched over figures.

"You good?" Rotten asked Pullman.

"Yeah," he said, as Rotten helped him to his feet.

A younger voice shouted out from the other side of the cellar, "Stop right there!"

"We mean no harm," Rotten said, hands up, both real and prosthetic.

Another voice, this one much older and raspier: "State your business!"

Rotten nodded at Pullman, giving him the cue to explain himself.

"You're up," he said.

Pullman stepped forward and said to the strangers, who were seeking cover behind an overturned table used as a type of barricade.

"Less than twenty-four hours ago, I picked up a signal on my tracker." He paused, held his hands in surrender, and stated that he was unarmed before reaching into a bag and pulling out the SD. "On this device here," he said, "which is able to pick up readings on a highly-sought-after material called 'E'Raknish,' a smart metal, if you will, used to conduct the Freeze."

"Freeze?" a stranger whispered to another. "What the hell is he talking about?"

"I think he's talking about the curse."

"Not a curse," Pullman said over the strangers.

"Then what?"

"Think of it as a reckoning—"

"Who are you?"

Feeling the weight of their presence, Pullman said patiently, "My name is Man Pullman, and I am a former employee of JeneCorp—"

"Thought you said you didn't work for the Company."

"I used to," he said defensively, "But not anymore. During my time at JeneCorp, E'Raknish was known as a template, primarily used for augmentation and bodily enhancements, designed to give ordinary people extraordinary abilities. My *former* employer, JeneCorp, the same Company who sent those men up there. . . " Pullman said, pointing up at the low ceiling, ". . . found a way to convert these self-reproducing templates into conductors, which are able to withstand gori, an incredibly rare and renewable energy source, as powerful as the sun, exerted by a mutation, only found in the blood of those who carry the Medusa Strain. . . "

In the quiet darkness, an elderly man said to a young boy: "Did you catch a single word he just said?"

Another shot was suddenly fired at Pullman, the bullet zipping inches away from his head, nearly striking him dead.

Pullman was forced to seek cover.

The same old, raspy voice said from across the cellar: "You're not making sense, *Maaan.*"

Pullman cried out, "Enough with the goddamn shooting!"

"Put down the gun, son," the elderly man said to the shooter, who revealed himself as a six-year-old boy. Then, he asked Pullman, "What are you trying to say, Mr. Pullman?"

After he composed himself, Pullman said in layman's terms: "The people who are currently burning down your town as we speak are looking for a valuable item, far more conductive than any metal on earth, smarter than any smart metal, and this metal's main function is to power the loop that has been running on every single electronic device connected to The Feed for the past four years, *not a curse*, but rather, an extinction, and these people are convinced that one of you is in possession of this item. And trust me when I say this: They will do whatever's necessary to obtain this item, even if it means killing every single one of you."

One elderly man uttered from the corner of his mouth, "*I've heard that plot before.*"

Another elderly man asked, "How come your device doesn't have one of those loops on it?"

Pullman said, "I'm not connected to The Feed—"

Rotten chimed in, "To put it simply, what my friend here is trying to say: E'Raknish is one of the main reasons why your friends and loved ones are dead."

"And who are you?" an elderly woman asked Rotten.

"I'm a former employee of JeneCorp."

"And why don't you work for them anymore?"

Rotten thought carefully about his answer.

He stepped closer into the light and after looking the elderly woman in the eyes, said to her, "I chose to side with the living. The Company represents Death, and I couldn't take orders from an organization that chooses who should live and who should die."

More of the locals stepped forward from hiding and revealed themselves. Rotten counted at least thirty locals altogether, except for a few adults (from early twenties to late forties), each one ranging from one end to the other end of the spectrum (the very old being around their eighties or early nineties and the very young being no older than six or seven years old).

Looking around, Rotten asked, "Is this everybody?"

One of the locals, a stout elderly woman, said, "This is it."

Another local, Millie, similar grit, said in a sarcastic tone, "Your former *colleagues* took out at least six of us. There's still a handful out there. Probably dead. We managed to hide down here before they spotted us." She looked around in awe at the impressive wine collection, most of the bottles aged at least twenty years. "Looks like the pastor was holding out on us."

"And where is the pastor?"

"Pastor Paul," said the local. "Dead. He died last year from a heart attack—"

"Where are the others?" asked Rotten.

"Didn't you hear a word she just said?"

"Not them," Rotten clarified. "The ones who weren't selected."

"Those," the local said. "We don't talk about them—"

"After the Freeze, as you call it, we moved those who weren't claimed by loved ones to the coliseum," a younger local, Suzie, who was carrying a black cat in her arms, interrupted.

"Think of it like a mausoleum, a place to pay respect for those who didn't make it."

One local teased, "More like a museum."

Neither comment sat well with Suzie.

An older local said more realistically, "Suzie thinks all of those people who turned to stone aren't dead. She believes they're trapped inside the stone, kind of like that one movie—"

"Totally different situation," another local passionately argued with his elder. "You're talking about someone who's cryogenically frozen."

While cautiously eyeing the cat in Suzie's arms, Rotten said over the locals, "We don't have time for debate. Has anyone come into contact with E'Raknish in the past twenty-four hours?"

An elderly local, Frank, asked, "What the hell does this E'Raknish look like?"

"We're wasting time, Barney," Pullman said, as the frustration started to mount. More directly, he asked the locals as a collective, "Who lives in the blue house off Terrace Street? The one with the maple tree in the front yard?"

M.J. stepped forward and made his way to the front of the group: "That's where John lives."

"Who's John?"

Next to make a move was Ashleigh, who was holding the hand of John's son, Brett. Instead of stepping forward, the two stepped farther into the shadows.

Millie said, "He's also unaccounted for."

"By any chance," Pullman said, "is he wearing a cast on his arm?"

M.J. shot a glance over at the town's doctor, Charles, who was hesitant to nod at M.J.

"Yes," M.J. said. "Is he in danger?"

"I'm afraid the Company's agents captured him," Pullman said. "You know who else lives with John?"

Again, M.J. was hesitant to reveal more information.

"Ashleigh," said M.J, as he waved her closer. "It's okay. They're here to help."

Eventually, Ashleigh and Brett stepped forward.

"This is John's son," M.J. introduced Brett to Pullman and Rotten. "His name is Brett."

Rotten asked Ashleigh, "Are you his mother?"

Wary of the two strangers and their questions, she said in a sharp tone, "What does me being his mother pertain to you?"

M.J. held his hands up, trying to calm Ashleigh, who remained on edge by both Rotten and Pullman's presence.

"Easy, Ashleigh," he said. "They're not with them—"

"Then who are they with?"

"We're just here to help," Pullman said.

Once more, Rotten asked, "Are you the boy's mother?"

M.J. said more closely to Rotten, "We don't talk about her."

"Is she here?"

"She died during childbirth—"

"*Maurice!*" Ashleigh shouted out, her tone as sharp as a razor cutting through the dusty air.

In a more careful manner, Rotten pointed at Brett and asked M.J., "He wouldn't have happened to come across anything unusual in the past couple of days, would he?"

"Like?"

"A rock or a metallic toy or anything metal?"

"He plays with rocks all the time."

"Did he bring any home with him?"

M.J. asked Brett, who responded by shaking his head no.

"Is that a 'No'?"

Pullman interrupted, "The signal was last seen inside a laundry room. Did you recently fall into some dirt or mud? Maybe you accidentally picked up something on your clothes—"

M.J. asked Pullman, "How the hell is he going to remember that? Besides, John takes care of the laundry."

While M.J. and Pullman were arguing over the boy, Rotten drew his attention toward Brett's eyes and for a second, he watched his eyes change from blue to green.

Rotten immediately pulled aside M.J.

"Listen, kid," Rotten said closely, "I know you know something. Is there anything unusual about the child?"

"How do you explain unusual?"

"I dunno," he said and then listed, "unusual abilities, deformations, strange birth marks. . . "

M.J. thought over Rotten's remarks and one particular trait or feature on his list stood out the most.

"He does have a mark on his stomach," he said. "John says it's a birth mark, but, if you ask me, it looks more like a burn."

"Can he show us this mark?" asked Rotten.

M.J. thought again, this time looking over Rotten and deciding whether or not he was on his side based on his persistence in locating the so-called "E'Raknish," which, to M.J., sounded as if it was made-up.

Trusting his instincts, M.J. nodded at Ashleigh.

"Lift up his shirt," he said.

After making a face at M.J., Ashleigh eventually lifted up Brett's shirt, revealing the spiraling symbol of E'Raknish.

Both Rotten and Pullman stepped closer to Brett for a better look.

"Is that what I think it is?" asked Pullman.

"Looks like it," he said.

"But how?"

Suzie's cat, originally named Alley Alba after his favorite meal, albacore tuna, before given a shorter name like Stash, due to a tiny white mustache underneath his whiskers, was starting to make a fuss. She lowered Stash onto the floor, set him free, and said, "Hey, Brett, show 'em that thing you did yesterday."

With a long, slack face, Brett looked at Ashleigh and then M.J. as though he was waiting for their approval.

Finally, M.J. said, "Show 'em the trick, Brett." M.J. held up his fingers and wiggled them in the air. "The one with your fingers..." he said, "... after Stash scratched you the other day..."

The four-year-old carefully held up his right hand while the tips along each of his five fingers suddenly stretched outward, the flesh and fingernails formed and molded and hardened together like a wicked callus. The end of each finger was as sharp as a cat's claw.

Pullman, who was left gawking at the boy, turned to Rotten as if he was witnessing the same thing. He was; in fact, Rotten was also left with a slack expression on his face.

"Do you mind?" said Pullman, as he waited for Ashleigh's approval to inspect Brett.

Hesitant, she said to M.J., "We don't know these people, M.J."

"It's fine," he said.

Pullman inspected Brett's hand, those razor-sharp fingers.

He asked M.J., "How long has he been like this?"

"Every since he was born," M.J. admitted, "John said that there was something special about him."

Rotten asked, "Was the child injured recently?"

"Yes," M.J. said. "As a matter of fact, he was." He pointed to Brett's arm. "Massive cut on his arm. I didn't actually see the cut. But there was a lot of blood."

"Explains the laundry basket," Rotten said. "Blood must've gotten on his clothes."

Pullman asked M.J., "What do you mean you didn't see a cut?"

"John said the cut closed up before he had time to dress it," M.J. said.

In awe, Pullman said to Rotten, "It's inside him."

More leery about the two, M.J. asked, "What's inside him?"

"E'Raknish," Pullman said. Then he turned back around to Rotten: "Who knows what in the hell Rouse will do if he finds out about this child."

"Who's Rouse?" asked M.J.

"Head of JeneCorp," Rotten said. "He's also the reason for the Freeze."

"We have to get the child out of here—"

Rotten asked, "Can you hack one of those drones again?"

"I'm afraid that window has already closed, brother."

"We need a diversion to lure the agents away from the church."

"We can't bring them with us."

"We have to get all of these people to safety, Pullman," Rotten said, full stop. "I'm not going to leave them behind."

Pullman suggested: "How about our mutual friend? Can he get these people out of here?"

"Way too dangerous," Rotten said.

The others didn't have a clue about the "mutual friend" whom Pullman and Rotten were referencing; and frankly, neither Pullman nor Rotten had the time to explain Blot or the dangers of a shadowrun when overused and how, in all likelihood, if Blot were to exceed these limitations of the shadowrun, he would succumb to the Void.

As his eyes drifted in thought, Pullman said, "If the blood shows up on radar, then can't we use that to our advantage?"

Rotten eyed the cat rubbing his chin along the back of Suzie's leg.

More concerned, Ashleigh asked, "What about John?"

Pullman said, "There's nothing we can do. Sorry—"

"There is one way. . . " Rotten said to Pullman and nodded at Stash, ". . . but you're not going to like it. Is the cat real?"

M.J. parroted, "Real?"

"Is it artificial?"

"Didn't know that sort of technology existed yet," said M.J.

Pullman said, "It exists all right."

Acknowledging Rotten's interest in her cat, Suzie picked up Stash, causing the cat to let out a meow. Despite the cat's cries, Suzie held Stash in her arms and protected him with her life.

Pullman asked Rotten, "What do you have in mind?"

"You're thinking the boy's blood shows up on radar, correct?"

"In theory, yes."

"Can we test it out?"

"By doing so, we'll give away our position."

"What if we took a sample of the boy's blood—"

"His name is Brett," Ashleigh said, her tone stern and scornful.

"*What if* we took a sample of Brett's blood. . . " Rotten reassured Ashleigh, ". . . just a small sample, and then we took that blood sample and injected it into Stash here?"

"Once the blood is transferred into another host, the blip will disappear from radar."

"We cut Stash," Rotten said, this time reassuring Suzie, "just a nick. Then, we let it loose."

"Who's to say it won't just hang around the church like a timid scaredy cat and get our asses spotted?"

"From what I can tell, it's feral," Rotten said, more convincingly. He asked Suzie, "Am I right?"

"Yes," Suzie said hesitantly.

"It's a survivor. After all, it made it this far. It'll retreat from danger, and after I nick it, it'll get as far away as it can from me. Not only will it test out your theory, but it will also create a diversion. It's worth a try. . . "

Losing patience with Rotten, Pullman asked, "And is that *your* theory, cat whisperer?"

"Do you have any better suggestions?"

"For starters, where in the hell are we going to get a syringe?"

Doctor Charles raised his hand as if he was in class.

"I have a syringe back at the house," he said and stepped forward as if he was a shy student. "I can get it for you. It's not far from here."

"Once you step foot outside the church, the drones will pick you up."

"Then, I'll go," Rotten said.

"It's too risky—"

"It's the only way," Rotten said. He asked the doctor, "Where's your house?"

After Doctor Charles gave instructions to his house, which was only two blocks away from the church, Rotten didn't waste any time. He exited the church, only to witness the flames inching closer and closer. He put on his oxygen mask and made a run to the doctor's house as drones hovered above, Noble's voice laced with a harsher tone as he warned the locals that if they didn't surrender in the "*next ten minutes*," then he was going to "*execute*" one of their own (John).

These threats alone forced Rotten to move with urgency.

In a dark alleyway across the street, Noble's smarteye, which had been inserted into the eye socket of a black bear, twice, even triple, the size of an average black bear, honed in while scanning Rotten exiting the church. The glowing red smarteye connected to a feed on the other half of the drone, which Noble was holding in his hands.

Shortly after the artificial bear tracked Brett's scent to the church, it returned to Noble, who, in return, removed the smarteye from the bear and replaced it with the bear's other eye, and then inserted the smarteye back into his socket. He gave the order via comms; and afterwards, he petted the black bear on top of its head and gave it an "atta boy."

Once Rotten arrived at the doctor's house, he followed the doctor's instructions and grabbed the case with a syringe and rubberband from a medicine cabinet in the upstairs master bathroom.

After acquiring the syringe, Rotten made his way downstairs. He only made it down half of the staircase before a kitchen light switched on, forcing him to retreat back upstairs. He heard a *creak* of the hardwood floor below. Out from the beam of light stepped one of the agents, armed to the teeth. Next, a hallway light switched on. Then, the foyer light.

Rotten was forced to hide inside a dark bedroom where he pulled out the eye drops from his pocket. He followed Forsake's orders: "*One drop in each eye.*"

After using the eye drops, Rotten first felt a burning sensation running down the corners of his face. The burning sensation soon lessened into a cooling, almost thorny sensation, which felt like pins and needles along his eye sockets. The beam of the hallway light cut through the darkness of the bedroom, horizontally stripping the upper part of his face like a mask and revealing his eyes, glazed over and ghostly, as if he was wearing the eyes of the Death loop.

With the power of the gaze at his disposal, Rotten waited for the agent's shadow to move to the living room before making his way downstairs. By the time he reached downstairs, the agent had turned on all the lights on the first floor, preventing Blot from entering.

Mindful of Blot, the agent nearly stepped into a shadow along the living room floor.

He heard a creak in the floor, similar to the one he made earlier.

While creeping around a coffee table, the agent shouted out, "Is that you, Blot?"

Rotten snuck up behind the agent and concealed himself behind a wall. He poked his head from behind the corner and tracked the agent's course to the dining room.

With the agent's back turned, Rotten snuck up from behind; and as soon as the agent rotated around, Rotten used the gaze on him. Sure enough, the agent came prepared with a new type of contacts that he wore over his eyes.

Unlike the previous protective lenses, which were inserted over the eye and often resulted in corneal abrasions if worn for an extended amount of time, these eye shields were implanted into the back of the eyelid and accessed by merely blinking one's eye. With both of his eyes changing from green to a murky brownish white film that pulled over his eyes like a moist curtain, the shield acted like a translucent third eyelid, similar, in fact, inspired by nictitating membranes that were most commonly found in cats or other mammals. The gaze had absolutely no affect on the agent.

"Nice try, traitor," the agent said to Rotten.

Surprised by the agent's preparedness, Rotten knocked the assault rifle from his hands. He tackled the agent into a glass case filled with rare china and porcelain figurines of animals. The case, along with all of the contents inside, shattered into thousands of pieces.

The agent recovered from the fall and wrestled with Rotten, who managed to sneak in several blows, hitting notes of sweet chin music.

After dusting off the blows, the agent returned with a devastating blow to Rotten's face.

With his nose gushing blood, Rotten started to grab items throughout the house—plaques or various awards, as well as trophies, one being a two-foot tall softball trophy won by a team consisting of doctors throughout the county—and tossed each item at the agent, who shielded himself from the projectiles, except for one, a glass vase that shattered over the agent's head.

The agent pulled out a baton-like staff, which extended into a shield and blocked the projectiles.

As the agent closed in on a backpedaling Rotten, he lowered the shield from his body.

All of a sudden, the agent charged at Rotten and rammed him through the basement door.

Rotten crashed into the door, which flung open. He tripped over his feet and tumbled down a flight of stairs.

As the agent stood at the basement doorway, he switched on an overhead light. Rotten was nowhere to be found, and the only trace he left behind was his prosthetic, which lay on the basement floor.

The agent brandished a handgun from a concealed holster and walked into the basement.

When he reached the bottom of the staircase, he came across Rotten's prosthetic. He picked it up and looked it over.

"Got something that belongs to you," the agent said into the darkness of the basement.

Mindful of Blot, the agent made sure to stay close to the light. It wasn't until he scanned the entire basement and noticed the open window that he realized Rotten had already fled.

Or did he?

For a second, he saw the shadows moving throughout the basement.

Like a dark floater in the corner of his eye.

Was it his mind playing tricks on him?

Or was it Blot, waiting for the right opportunity to pounce and drag him into the shadows?

The agent heard the sound of a door opening upstairs; and despite the urgency, he welcomed the noise for it gave him a reason to leave the basement. *"Get out,"* a voice inside was screaming at him. *"Or, you'll be sorry. . ."*

Rotten, having escape through basement window, switched off the living room light.

As the agent made his way back upstairs, he spotted a small figure bouncing past his vision. He fired three shots at what he'd later find out was only a tennis ball. What the agent didn't realize—at least not until it was too late—was that the ball was a distraction created by Rotten, who had connected the outdoor water hose to the running faucet of an utility sink in the laundry room and then ran the hose through the living room where he waited for the agent to enter.

Rotten removed the kinked hose from his clenched teeth and held it tightly in his hand, his thumb inserted into the nozzle, plugging any water from escaping.

As the agent made his way back into the living room, he reached for the light switch.

Once the agent switched on the light, Rotten had the nozzle of the dripping hose pointed directly at the agent's face.

Before the agent could duck, Rotten released his thumb, thus resulting in a burst of water to hit the agent in the eyes, partially knocking out the protective eyelids. One of them, in fact, dangled from his left eye like a long and white booger.

Grabbing his eye, the agent blindly fired a couple shots at Rotten, who, in return, pushed the agent into a shelf behind him. Rotten slipped on a slick spot on the floor and fell into the agent. The handgun fell from the agent's grip during impact. More items on the shelf fell to the floor as well. One of the items was yet another vase, which shattered into pieces, one of those pieces being a shard in the shape of a blade. With one of his eyes opened, the other one, which was without a shield, tightly shut to prevent from feeling the wrath of Rotten's gaze, the agent reached for the shard of glass. His fingers inched toward the glass, as Rotten struggled with the agent. Eventually, the agent managed to grab hold of the shard and as soon as he reared back his arm, Rotten grabbed the agent by the testicles, each one held in his palm; and then, he squeezed.

The sudden rush of pain shot up the agent's groin and forced his other eye open!

In that very moment, Rotten gazed the agent, who, in return, attempted to stab Rotten in the neck before Death became him.

The shard came inches away from Rotten's neck before the agent suddenly turned to stone. Any closer, the tip of the shard would've penetrated Rotten's jugular.

Rotten rolled from the agent's stony body and gathered himself by taking a moment to catch his breath.

In a slumped-over posture, he witnessed two dark figures outside the house. He checked the front window and spotted an agent, the one carrying a flamethrower, approaching the house.

Rotten grabbed the dead agent's handgun from the floor, and then, before exiting the house via backdoor, grabbed the black John Lennon-sunglasses from a bronze tray on the countertop.

Another agent, who was prowling around the alley right before he was given word about the location of the child, came across blood splatter on the side of a building, as well as the ground. He followed a trail of blood to the dumpster where he found the other agent's limbs, cleanly severed, a sure sign of Blot's handiwork. These findings prompted him to contact Noble to inform Boss Man of the entity whom they were anticipating on showing up in Padadock.

Once word of Blot's presence was confirmed and relayed to Noble, Noble instructed the remainder of agents to be mindful of their unwanted guests who were about to crash the party.

By the time Rotten reached the church, Pullman was waiting for him outside the sacristy.

Noble's filtered voice, which could be heard from the drone passing overhead, was rougher and cut with impatience.

In his dire message, he was threatening to execute John if the locals didn't show themselves in the next "*three minutes*." Little did Rotten or the others know that Noble, based on the intel gathered by the artificial bear, already had a lock on their position.

Pullman whispered, "You get it?"

"Yeah," he said behind the shades. "But the gig is up. They know we're here."

From the urgency in Agent Noble's voice, Pullman had a feeling that time was no longer on their side.

Before Pullman could question Rotten, he studied the cuts and bruises all over Rotten's face, as well as the two obvious differences in his appearance, one being his missing left arm and then the other, the John Lennon shades.

"You good, Barney Trouble?"

"Yeah," he said with a grin. "Just ran into some trouble."

"What's up with the shades?" asked Pullman.

"I felt compelled to memorialize an agent."

"Should I be concerned?"

"Not yet," he said. "Just be careful not to look directly into my eyes."

Pullman patted Rotten on the back and together, the two rushed down the stairs to the cellar below.

When they returned to the cellar, M.J. and another local had Stash ready for the injection of Brett's blood. Ashleigh brought over Brett and raised the sleeve along his arm and told him that he would only feel a prick and that there was absolutely nothing to worry about.

"Are you sure you want to do this?" Pullman asked Rotten.

"Just make sure to closely monitor the radar," he said. "I want to know if that blip appears."

Pullman tended to the surveillance device and kept tabs on it while Rotten pulled out the syringe, as well as the rubberband from inside the case. He wrapped the rubberband around Brett's arm and waited for a vein to reveal itself.

Impressed by his ability to wrap that band around Brett's arm with only one hand, M.J. nodded at Rotten's left stump.

M.J. asked, "So, how'd you lose the arm?"

With his keen focus on Brett's arm, more specifically, a plump vein, he said, "Long story."

As a tense silence filled the room, Rotten glanced up, only to find the locals gathered around the two. Among the locals was Ashleigh, who remained suspicious of Rotten.

While M.J., as well as the locals waited in anticipation, Rotten decided to give them the cliff note version: "I was left with no other choice than to have my arm amputated in order to sever the cross-dimensional binds that kept me connected to an *unforgiving* Third-Eyed Parasitic Body Snatcher from a dark realm that would make this place seem like an amusement park."

Ashleigh asked in a flippant tone, "Cross-dimensional binds?"

Rotten looked up at Ashleigh and said while trying not to gaze her, "E'Raknish. Think of it as a bridge connecting two worlds."

One local uttered with a trace of sarcasm, "You mean this so-called *smart* metal?"

"Correct," Rotten said, holding up his ghost of a left arm. "I wore the template on my wrist, whereas, Brett here, he wears E'Raknish all over."

"You're talking about Hell," said M.J., "aren't you?"

"I've heard it called many names: Ne'i'th'r We'l't, Sheik's Domain, The Other Web, *Midnight World*, Marz, but never Hell, although I'm sure it can easily be mistaken for what most perceive as hell." Rotten nodded at M.J., then asked, "So, how do you know about it?"

"I knew someone from that world," he said. "A long time ago. He was. . . different."

"I'm sure he was."

"He spoke about legends, about Annexus, like they were fantasies—"

"I'm afraid they're not fantasies," Rotten said. "They're all true."

Pullman interrupted, "Rotten, we don't have time for chit-chat?"

After finding a vein, Rotten inserted the needle into Brett's arm.

Brett didn't make a peep from the needle; in fact, he remained surprisingly calm as Ashleigh stroked the backside of his neck, reassuring him that it'd soon be over.

As soon as Rotten pulled up on the piston and the bulb sucked blood into the tube, the blip—although faint—suddenly appeared on Pullman's device.

"Got something," Pullman said. "I think it's working. . . "

Once Rotten had enough of Brett's blood in the tube, he rushed over to Stash and picked up the cat. Stash struggled in Rotten's arm. Suzie stepped in and comforted Stash in her arms and reassured the cat. Rotten injected the blood into the cat's rear left leg. Surprisingly, Stash, except for letting out a deep, drawn out meow, didn't put up much a fight with Suzie. Once Rotten removed the needle from Stash, the blip then disappeared from the radar.

"I can't believe it," Pullman said in awe. "It actually worked."

Rotten grabbed Stash and with Pullman by his side, rushed the cat upstairs.

Suzie followed the two to the church's exit where Pullman opened the door for Rotten as he kneeled down with the cat cradled like a football between his right arm and armpit.

"Make the cut," Rotten said while holding down Stash.

"Sorry, buddy," Pullman said, as he pulled out a pocketknife and made a tiny incision in the cat's leg, drawing enough blood to show up on radar.

Stash hissed at Pullman and ended up scratching Rotten's arm before it clawed his way free and then scurried away into the smoky night darkness. Pullman returned to the surveillance device and watched the red dot on the monitor move away from their position.

Suzie called out to Stash, but Rotten held her back. She kicked and squirmed in his arm and attempted to chase after Stash. Rotten told her, in fact, promised her that Stash would be fine on its own and that there was nothing she could do right now, except leave Padadock for the sake of her own safety. But *was it a lie?* The question, along with many others, eddied up to the forefront like embers of doubts smoldering inside his cloudy mind. Despite what seemed like a false promise in order to temporary stifle and contain the girl's understandable outburst, he believed, in fact, provided foundation to his own promises about what he said to Suzie and marked them as truth by justifying a cat's willingness to return back to its guardian: *The scent,* Rotten told himself, Suzie's scent. Stash had her scent memorized—he didn't know if a cat was capable of carrying such memories, but he rightly convinced himself it to be true. The way it rubbed its body against her leg, he thought, it was Stash's way of claiming the girl as its own, Stash's own tracking device. Once the cat's excitement wore off after being cut, Rotten reassured himself that the cat would track down Suzie's scent. It had to. There was simply no other way.

On the other side of Main Street, Noble picked up on the blip from one of the drones, which was following Stash.

With his patience wearing thin, he ordered Agent Prescott to check out blip while he maintained his position next to John, watching the young man, waiting but not wanting to fulfill the very thing he had declared he was going to do if his demands were not met.

The gun hadn't felt heavier and burdensome along his side.

In a matter of several labored breaths, Noble's drones tracked the fleeing feline to, of all places, Suzie's house, which was a few blocks away from the church.

After informing the locals of their successful diversion, Pullman escorted them back upstairs while Rotten made sure nobody was still inside the wine cellar. One of the stragglers whom Rotten discovered, Mr. Bracket, formerly Professor Bracket who once taught at the university prior to the Freeze, was filling a bag with bottles of aged Pinot Noir; and as soon as he laid his beady, panicky eyes on Rotten, he sincerely apologized and hurried away with a bulky bag of wine bottles, which *clinked* and *clanked* as he sprinted from the cellar with a slight skip and hobble.

Once Rotten finished his inspection, he made his way to the stairwell.

Before leaving, he heard his name being whispered from a dark corner of the cellar.

The voice was as sharp and prickly as a cold breeze, leaving Rotten frozen in his tracks.

"Blot?"

No response.

While slowly easing the sunglasses along the slop of his nose, he glanced down at the three long scratches on his forearm, which were left by Stash, and a strange pulling sensation suddenly came over him, as if he had microscopic magnets in his blood, buzzing and vibrating and pulling to his polar opposite. He felt exposed as though the darkness itself was not only watching him, but also studying Rotten the same way a predator would keenly observe its prey and tracking his every movement, his every compulsion, his every gesture—as subtle as it was—his every everything.

Carefully, Rotten removed the sunglasses from his face and peered into the darkness, which began to pull him deeper and deeper into its gnarly and cancerous yet inviting mouth.

Before he lost himself in the darkness, Rotten climbed from his paralyzed state and hurried up the stairwell where he met up with Pullman in the nave.

Pullman pulled Rotten aside and more worried about Rotten's condition, asked, "You good, Barney? Look like you've seen a ghost."

"Good."

Pullman said, "I was told that there's a sewer system that will take everybody out of town."

"What about Brett's father?" asked Rotten.

With locals in the vicinity, Pullman leaned in closer to Rotten and said in a lowered voice, "Forget about him. Noble's got him. More than likely, he's going to kill him anyway. Besides, we didn't come here for them—"

"You get these people out of here," Rotten said. "I'll handle Noble."

"Barney—"

"It's done."

"You're going to take on Noble with one arm?" said Pullman. "You nuts?"

All of a sudden, the front doors of the church burst open!

At the doorway stood an agent, who was carrying a flamethrower.

Rotten brandished the handgun from his waistband and opened fire on the agent. One round struck the agent in the shoulder and spun him around, exposing the fuel tank inside his backpack. He aimed at the tank and fired a shot. All of a sudden, the tank exploded and threw fiery debris throughout the inside of the church. The front half of the church caught fire. The flames licked their way closer to Rotten, forcing Pullman to rush the locals from the other exit. Before exiting the church, Rotten told Pullman that he was going to rescue Brett's father.

M.J. overheard Rotten speaking with Pullman and told him that he was coming with him.

Rotten told M.J. to stay with Brett, to watch over, to protect him.

Lastly, as a way of reassuring M.J. similarly to reassuring Suzie, he handed M.J. the oxygen mask and looked M.J. squarely in the eyes and emphasized his words for the young man, *"Make sure Brett is safely evacuated from town."* M.J. nodded his head in agreement.

While Rotten went after John, Pullman and M.J. led each local from the church in an orderly fashion.

Using sleeves or articles of clothing to cover their noses and mouths, the locals closely tailed Pullman, who passed along his oxygen mask to those more fragile and weaker and struggled with the smoky air, especially the elderly.

As Pullman escorted the locals across the lawn, M.J. and Mr. Bracket were last to leave the church. Pullman only made it ten yards or so before being stopped by yet another agent carrying a flamethrower. The agent ordered the locals back against the side of the church. The front half of the church was completely engulfed in flames, and pellet-sized wood chips and shards of flaming debris rained down all around the locals.

With the locals, Pullman included, lined up next to the church as if they were facing a firing squad, the agent pointed the flamethrower toward the farthest end of the line; and right before he was about to torch the locals, one-by-one, a shadowy figure stepped into his peripheral.

A familiar shadow.

A deathly shadow.

More alert to his surroundings, the agent turned to the shadows dancing along the grass and mistook them for the beating firelight playing tricks on his mind.

Before he faced the locals, the agent witnessed more of those familiar shadows, as tall as a giant prowling around him, forcing him to track down each one. The shadows came together and appeared as one man or one beast, who was toying with the agent and causing him to spin round and round. Frustrated, the agent torched the shadowy presence but the flames hit nothing but air.

After giving up on Blot, the agent, who was overcome by a sort of "fuck-it" attitude, turned the torch back toward the locals; and as he pulled the trigger, M.J. grabbed one of Mr. Bracket's wine bottles, a vintage Pinot Noir, a bottle that the former professor was looking forward to enjoying, a lovely thing with notes of fruit so sweet that it'd make one's cheeks pucker. With the dusty wine bottle in hand, M.J snuck up behind the agent and struck the agent in the back of the his head. Surprisingly, the bottle never shattered. Instead, it made a dull *thud* against the agent's skull.

Dazed, the agent faced M.J., who, yet again, struck the agent in the head, this time shattering the bottle.

A complex yet fruity mixture of wine and blood with heavy notes of oak and smoke washed over the agent's face.

The agent appeared almost drunk as he stumbled backward, giving the locals an opportunity to pounce.

Three of them didn't miss a beat: One of the adults led the charge and then Ashleigh and Mr. Bracket followed suit and attacked the agent.

As they dogpiled the agent, M.J. wrestled the flamethrower from the agent's arms, removing straps from his backpack.

Once M.J. came into possession of the flamethrower, the other three backed off, giving M.J. room to torch the agent, who was slow to stand to his feet and too disorientated to fight back. He held out both of his hands in surrender and begged the young man to let him go.

In a sobbing, pleading voice, the agent tried to convince M.J. that he wouldn't pursue them.

"I swear it," he cried. "Please. . . show mercy. . . "

M.J. shot a glance at Brett, who was hiding behind the leg of Pullman.

Rotten's words rang in his ears: *"Protect the boy at all costs."*

With his eyes sharpening like blades, M.J. aimed the flamethrower at the agent.

He pulled the trigger.

As the agent screamed out in horror, he was baptized by fire.

While his body engulfed in flames, some of the locals couldn't watch for the agent's screams were too excruciating to bear.

Others watched on with steely miens and glittery, glossy eyes.

Whether they watched or they didn't watch, each surviving local of Padadock would remember this very moment for it was the moment where they took back their power.

The steeple suddenly collapsed as the fire chewed its way through the church. The roof was next to cave in, kicking up a cloud of sparks through the night darkness. The ash rained down on the locals. Once the flames overwhelmed the agent, Pullman led the locals to the sewers.

As the fire raged behind him, Rotten arrived at Main Street where he spotted Noble standing with Brett's father, John, who was tied to a post.

In his icy-glared scan, his eyes crossed Rotten, who, before being spotted, ducked behind a parked car along the curb.

Keeping as low to the ground, he crept toward the other side of the car's bumper and peeked around a rear window where he made eye contact with John. When he looked into John's eyes, he saw, not Brett's father, John, but Darwin Acosta, "D," who was tied to the post; and despite being unable to move for he was fixed in place by those restraints, he still managed to tremble with fear. The longer Rotten held his shielded gaze on John, not D, the quicker he was pulled into the vivid memory of his old friend: The moment Rotten first arrived at JeneCorp, Rotten getting acquainted with his new subject, B-37. Even though E'Raknish was no longer coupled with Darwin, Rotten could feel remnants of its presence, as if it had left behind a stain on D's very soul, a stain that couldn't be removed, as Lance Carmichael put it, a signature.

He shook away the thought before it could overtake him and focused on luring Noble away from Main Street. More than likely, he was wearing contacts and if he was wearing the ones that the other agent was wearing, those third eyelid thingamajigs, given Noble's strength and agility, it was going to be extremely difficult to remove them. Or, he thought as he glanced down at the handgun in his hand, there was the old-fashioned way.

As Rotten stared at the gun, his eyes fell upon the scratch on his arm.

Again, he found himself staring at the scratch.

Ever since he was scratched, he noticed a difference inside his body.

A feeling, incredibly familiar, one that he felt whenever he was in the presence of Clypt'O—it was that sort of pulling sensation, as though he was being pulled closer to his final destination, a place where he'd surely be torn to shreds. He returned to the scratch, the cat, Stash, its claws, his skin, the warm flesh, a mild fever, the blood, Brett's blood being transferred into Stash.

The anxiety grabbed hold of Rotten.

An invisible hand.

With no pills on hand, he fought through the sudden attack. His airways were tight and narrowing. The fiery world around him started to spin. The pulling sensation intensified. Millions of invisible ghostly hands rising from the street to pull him into the darkness. He focused on his breathing and felt the smoky air feel his lungs. He embraced the smoke, the tiny cancerous particles clinging to the tissue that made up his body. Yes, he said, my body. Flesh and tissue. Stay with me, he told himself. Don't venture into the darkness. Unlike before, after the amputation, when he felt himself being stretched apart, when there was no longer any glue, he could feel its return. That cross-dimensional glue. The E'Raknish template re-connecting to bones and tissue and blood.

While gaining control over his breath, Rotten calmed himself.

He suddenly heard the grit below the sole of a boot rubbing against the asphalt.

The harsh noise forced Rotten to look over his shoulder.

Below, he caught the shadow rising behind him.

Not Blot.

Something far worse.

Before he could spot the agent looming behind him, the barrel of a gun was pressed against the backside of his head.

The voice of Agent Prescott cut through his ears: *"Drop the gun."*

Rotten did as the agent demanded and dropped the gun to the ground, then stood to his feet.

As the agent escorted Rotten away from the back of the car, Rotten removed the sunglasses and found an opportunity to gaze Prescott when the two reached the side of the car.

Rotten's wide and menacing eyes, which were the color of the moon, found Prescott's in the reflection of the driver's side window.

With a crooked grin curling around the corner of his face, the agent pointed at his eye, referring to one of the protective lenses that he was wearing: "Never leave home without 'em."

Noble called out from the intersection: "Bring him over here!"

Prescott escorted Rotten to Noble's position.

Noble asked Prescott, "You track down the blip?"

"It was a cat," he said. "Must've been a false reading."

Noble nodded at Rotten.

"Is he alone?" he asked the agent.

"As far as I can tell. . . " Prescott said and jammed the barrel into the back of Rotten's head, ". . . are you alone, Barney?"

With both his hands help up in surrender, he said with a quiet shamefulness, "It's just me."

"Good."

Prescott asked, "What about the townspeople?"

From the post, John, who was squirming through his restraints, cried out, "Leave 'em alone, you Company trash!"

"Easy, Johnny Boy," Noble said, dismissing Prescott. "They're not going anywhere."

Rotten said to Noble, "Don't be so sure of yourself."

Once more, Noble nodded at Rotten: "Where've you been hiding for the past four years?"

"Sinclair Leprieur," said Rotten. "You?"

"After Little Springs, a small beach town off the Carolina Coast," Noble said to Rotten. "If I knew you were so close, I would've paid you a visit."

"So, why'd you leave home?"

"The place went tits up after it fell to Natties."

"I take it they weren't so convinced to take the drops—"

"Would you?" asked Noble. "Knowing what it does to people's minds?"

"Maybe you got a point."

Frustrated by the causal nature of the conversation, Prescott said over the two, "Don't mean to interrupt you two, but do I need to remind you, Noble, of this traitor's loyalty? Did you forget what this piece of shit did right before the Freeze?"

"Last I checked," Noble said, more suspiciously, "having *cold feet* ain't exactly considered a crime. It's just makes you a chickenshit. Ain't that right, Barney?"

"Or, I'm just lucky."

Noble laughed a booming laugh.

"Nobody's luck is *that* good."

The frustration boiled over Prescott, whose jaw tightened with rage.

Rotten acknowledged, not only the agent's sudden change in behavior, but also the familiarity in Noble's words and how he delivered each one.

"I see you've been working on your tan," Rotten said, pointing out Noble's darker skin tone. "Must be nice."

"Living near the ocean has its perks."

"Sounds pretty daunting, you'd think. . ." Rotten said, as he carefully watched Noble's gestures, ". . . being around all that water."

A serious expression weighed down Noble's face.

To Rotten, the reaction in Noble's expression was the giveaway.

"You get used to it," Noble said in a flat, expressionless tone.

"Is this coming from Agent Noble?" asked Rotten. "Or Clypt'O?"

Noble's face slackened in a deadpan expression.

"Who the fuck is Clypt'O?" asked Noble.

"You're not good at hiding," Rotten said and while holding up his stump, nodded at Noble's prosthetic arm. "What do you say we make this a fair fight, huh?"

With his teeth clenched, Agent Prescott stepped forward.

"Maybe *you* should've stayed hidden, traitor," the agent seethed and pulled the trigger.

The gunshot suddenly rang out throughout the fiery, smoky streets!

Rotten's head violently whipped to the side.

The shot left a crater in right side of his forehead.

Blood and pieces of brain matter sprayed from the wound as his body fell forward.

John watched in shock, as Rotten's lifeless body flopped to the ground.

Noble, who also shared a similar shock, although more restrained, watched on as well.

"What the fuck did you do?" John cried out, his face long and pale.

Prescott turned the gun to John, causing John to wince.

"You're next, if you don't shut your fuckin' mouth—"

"Holster your weapon, Agent Prescott," Noble ordered, as he brandished a gun and aimed it at Prescott.

After the standoff, the agent finally put away his weapon by slamming the barrel of the gun into the black leather mouth of the holster.

Noble walked up to Rotten, who was lying facedown on the street. The blood poured from a gaping hole in his head. There was a yawning sorrow filling up his watery eyes.

Under his scratchy breath, he uttered, "This wasn't supposed to happen. . ."

The orange glow of the firelight darkened into a red light, which washed over Rotten's face. As the red light intensified, Rotten cracked open both his eyelids. First, he saw a red light, which didn't give away the dreaded place that he dared not speak of for it carried a shade of doom similar to a town engulfed in flames. It was the sound, a doubling effect. Sounds within sounds and even those sounds sounded foreign yet familiar. Two sets of footsteps, each one out of synch. He focused on the set of footsteps closest to him, the sound of the footsteps walking along asphalt canceled out, revealing the *crunching* sound of a heavy step digging through rocky soil.

While grabbing the top of his throbbing head, which no longer bore a gaping hole, he rose to his feet.

Next to catch Rotten's eye was his left arm, including his left hand. He moved around each finger and embraced the feel of each one. How pleasant it felt to have ole lefties back, despite its unusual appearance.

He heard a voice before him: "*Please. I don't want to fight, Barney.*"

Rotten followed the voice and saw not Noble but rather that unforgiving and ruthless Third-Eyed Parasitic Body Snatcher approaching him.

Amazed by Rotten's good fortune, Clypt'O asked with a mirrored-shine charm, "What gave me away?"

Rotten acknowledged Clypt'O and said, "The eyes are windows to the soul, right? When I stared directly into Noble's eyes, I saw no soul—no pneuma—but rather an *uninvited guest* who had worn out his welcome."

"Well, it's getting a little crowded in there."

"Didn't think I'd ever see you again."

Clypt'O grinned at Rotten's subtle jab at him.

"Welcome back," Clypt'O said. "Nice to see you too."

"Did the AI predict this would happen?" asked Rotten.

"No," Clypt'O said. "It certainly did not. But sometimes, you just gotta go with the flow."

Rotten took a moment to absorb his surroundings. It didn't take him long to realize that he was standing in the belly of Mount D'onwake. To the left of him was a stream of hot lava, and yet, despite being immersed in so much heat, he managed to tolerate the environment.

"How am I here?" Rotten looked up into the smoky darkness of the central vent in the volcano. Then, to his right where pillars of rock formed into an entire cityscape, which stretched as far as the eye could see. "Shouldn't I be dead? Thought I removed E'Raknish and any link I had with this god-awful place. . . "

Nodding at Rotten's arm, Clypt'O said, "Technically, you are dead. But it looks like whatever scratched you made quite the impression."

Rotten glanced down at his arm, in particular, what used to be the scratch, which was crawling with E'Raknish. His skin was translucent and rubbery, and inside his arm were thousands of spider-like templates coursing through his veins.

Freaked, Rotten removed his eyes from both his hands and arms for the sight of E'Raknish was too much to handle.

With his hands held out in surrender, Clypt'O said to Rotten, "I assure you, Barney, I mean you no harm." Then, he pointed at the inside of the volcano. "It's the setting, isn't it?" He said bluntly, "To be honest with you, after Annexus abandoned Mount D'onwake, I don't care much to come back here." His eyes, all three of them, drifted off in reflection. "Too many memories." He pointed toward a door carved in the side of yet another vent. Above the door was a glowing green EXIT sign. "What do you say?"

Clypt'O walked to the clunky metal door and opened it, revealing a dark hallway.

Hesitant, Rotten followed Clypt'O through the narrow hallway, which led them to the center of a theme park where there were dozens of rides and rollercoasters, a live stage, various games, gift shops, restaurants, and concession stands.

As Rotten stepped from the exit of the rollercoaster ride *The Escape From Mount D'onwake*, he was left in a state of awe by Clypt'O's so-called "setting." Enjoying all of the park's festivities were hundreds of guests, each one had been turned to stone. Inside the palms of each statue were electronic devices, i.e. smartphones, tablets, watches. Some were still wearing VR headsets over their heads. On a massive jumbotron suspended along a high rise of another familiar sounding ride, this one called *Sheik's High Rise*, was the same loop of Chloe—the Death loop.

While taking in the once festive atmosphere, imagining what the park must've been like before the Freeze, Rotten asked Clypt'O, "Where are we?"

"Loganson, West Virginia," Clypt'O said. The words in his mouth became more scornful as he specified the location. "The name of the attractions doesn't ring a bell, Barney?"

Rotten caught the sign alongside a banner.

Midnight World.

"One day," Clypt'O said while giving Rotten a tour of the theme park, "a fella named Hank Abernathy decided to create this merry little park after a near-death experience. Abernathy had what doctors called a predisposition to gravity. In short, he was quite a heavy fella whose ticker stopped ticking one day. After being brought back to life, he claimed that he had these visions." Clypt'O pointed at the rides, showcasing each one. "Apparently, he got inspired." Clypt'O said under his voice, "*Never in a million moons did I ever think some bastard would profit off a place we once called home.* But. . . " he chirped, ". . . it was only a matter of time, I suppose."

Annoyed by Clypt'O's mind games, Rotten said, "Enough with the illusions, Clypt'O."

Clypt'O said more seriously, "As you wish, Barney."

Not only did the floodlights dim all around them, but also the night darkness, which fell to a near pitch-black. When the light eventually returned, Clypt'O revealed a more authentic appearance of the world that he once called home. The darkness brightened to a grayish, gloomy, overcast sky where, below, the veil of apocalypse covered the ruined landscape filled with debris and carnage from the wake of the latest volcanic eruption. In a distance was Mount D'onwake, which appeared faded due to the heavy cloak of clouds and smoke. Among the wasteland were hundreds of figures, each former inhabitant frozen in place, similar to the stoned bodies in a post-Freeze world, as though the figures remained in a wicked state of preservation.

In disbelief, Rotten turned to Clypt'O and said more tenderly, "I can see now why you cling to Noble. He's the only person keeping you bound to his world, isn't he?"

Clypt'O asked, "Would you want to stay here?"

"How about Annexus?" Rotten asked. "Did anyone survive?"

"Only a few who managed to escape before the Eruption, all thanks to my melas'jus."

As he kneeled down and ran his fingers through to the dark, bloodstained soil, Rotten asked, "Is Noble aware of your presence?"

Clypt'O towered over Rotten.

"To Noble, despite having destroyed part of his memories, it may seem like a distant vision, an altered memory, glimpses into another reality. Although Noble is no longer with us, pieces of him remain. Memories," said Clypt'O, "the ones left undamaged. The only problem: You stay in a person's body for too long, you start to get lost in it and all the dead they carry around with them. And Noble carries plenty of his dead."

Rotten asked, "When did Noble suspect he wasn't himself?"

Clypt'O said, "I suppose when we—" he stopped himself mid-sentence and corrected himself, "—I first arrived in Padadock."

After Noble arrived in Padadock, he witnessed a flash of a memory, so bright and quick that it was as sudden and short-lived as the flash of a muzzle after a gunshot. In the memory, he was sitting in a chair on the front porch with the sight of a rough, junky ocean before him. Before he snapped himself from the memory, he witnessed himself sticking the barrel of a handgun into his mouth and as the taste of ocean brine and steel filled his mouth, he squeezed his finger. The second unexplained event happened when the blip returned to radar—the blip coming from the furry black feline, Stash. Noble started to remember the truth about what happened, disturbing visions of his own grim demise, as well as his father's. The last several being a sequence of graphic images of his father's skeletal hand, Noble then placing an old family photo in between his father's boney fingers, then lastly, the grotesque human skeleton lying in a soiled bed. He blocked out all of these images and pushed them back to the farthest regions of his mind. To Noble, at least the part of Noble that was still clinging to existence, these weren't visions or truths or even memories, but rather intrusive thoughts invading his mind.

Rotten stood upright and faced Clypt'O.

With a straight face, he asked Clypt'O, "Why target Noble? You could've chosen someone closer to Rouse. Instead, you picked JeneCorp's favorite and most loyal agent. . . "

"Not *all* loyal," Clypt'O said, hinting at the agent's recent retirement following the Freeze. "Don't let looks fool you, Barney. He's got his fair share of skeletons." He returned to Rotten's question. "I suppose he was the right man at the right time." He then returned his focus toward the wasteland, showing Rotten the events following the Freeze, when Mount D'onwake erupted, Clypt'O scrambling to find a target, in this case, Noble being his most immediate host, then slipping his way into a rat, which was one of the easiest vessels to possess, then crawling through the ventilation system inside JeneCorp's Death Valley facility, then, using the tail of the rat to write the Melas-spell *"E'vo Remo'das"* from a puddle of Chloe's blood moments after the Second Ascension, and then, finally, Noble reciting those very words, *E'vo Remo'das*, after he stepped inside the cool operation room where Chloe's severed head was synched up to the death machine.

Rotten said to Clypt'O, "If I didn't know any better, it sounds like you have regrets—"

"You don't have to be stuck here, in this wasteland, for the rest of eternity," said Clypt'O, as he acknowledged the concern attached to Rotten's face. "There's still a way for you to return to your friends, but. . . " he paused and took a moment for Rotten to digest his reasons for choosing, of all people, a man who attracted death like flies to shit, ". . . you may not like it."

Anticipating Clypt'O proposition, Rotten said defensively, "If you think I'm going to let you inside my head, then spoiler alert, Clypt'O, it's not going to end well for you—" Rotten suddenly caught his own words, the breath nearly escaped his lungs in a soft gasp. He said with illuminating clarity, "You already know what happens, don't you?"

The E'Raknish templates moved faster and faster along Rotten's jellyfish-like arm, causing several templates to ball-up and clot, only to be redirected and reestablished into an entirely new streak of veins, which released pressure from the traffic jam. Clypt'O was right. All along, Rotten told himself, Clypt'O didn't need AI to predict the future. Most importantly, he didn't need a quasi-computer system to handle Vernon Hawks's Predicament.

What were the odds?

0.01%.

Where did Clypt'O come up with such a number?

Did he simply pull it out of his ass?

Or, did it dribble out of that tumorous knob along his forehead like pus?

0.01%.

Rotten cursed the number. He crumbled it up until it was reduced to zero, in fact, less than zero, and rid it from existence and reminded himself that the number after zero percent was only 0.02 percent and that half of 0.02 was zero or in his case, less than zero.

The predicament alone crippled Rotten, as such a small and insignificant number felt neither small nor insignificant but rather the opposite.

But why didn't Clypt'O tell Rotten sooner about his special ability, which could've come in handy prior to the death of his son? He could've saved him—*I could've* saved him.

The ability to foresee the future, the Freeze playing a major part in the future or lack thereof.

The answer suddenly struck him over the head, and Rotten realized right then and there that the reason for Clypt'O's reticence was based around the evolution of E'Raknish.

John's son.

The boy, Brett.

0.01% was the secret.

With his index finger, Clypt'O motioned toward the pea-sized E'Raknish on the very center of his forehead, which was attached to his pineal gland, or his "third eye," and said, "I see everything, Barney."

"But you didn't see Prescott pulling the trigger?"

"No," Clypt'O said hesitantly. "But eventually, you die, sooner than later. You have to ask yourself, Barney, each decision you've made up till this point: Was it voluntary or *involuntary*?"

Rotten thought about the black cat, Stash, who was as loyal to Suzie as a number to a percentage. He thought about how, if he hadn't picked up the cat, hadn't even suggested the idea of using the cat as diversion to lure the agents away from locals, more specifically, the special boy, Brett, more than likely the cat wouldn't have scratched him, which meant he would've never had this very conversation with Clypt'O after having his head blown open like a watermelon.

"Or," Clypt'O said over Rotten's spiraling thoughts, "were you simply following a charted path."

Without thinking of the catastrophic results of allowing Clypt'O inside his mind—the notion along killed him—Rotten pushed away each gloomy, doomed thought that sprang up inside him and said with intensity, "*Show me.*"

"If I show you everything that happens, it's possible you can change the course of the future; however, I can show you a sneak peek."

Rotten asked, "What do I have to do?"

"All you have to do is look into my eyes," Clypt'O said, as his eyes, including his third eye, started to fade and darken into a dull grayness.

Clenched by the heavy fist of Clypt'O's third eye, Rotten witnessed teasers or "sneak peeks" of the future, *his* future, each fluid sequence of images playing out in a stream of consciousness. The images appeared before his very eyes, as if he was experiencing them in real-time.

While Rotten remained in a stupefied daze, he listened to Clypt'O's narration: *"There's not an exact point in time when you turn corrupt, but it takes place sometime after the Freeze, when your transformation slowly takes over. When you return home from Padadock, you will be contacted by Rouse, who will make you an offer you cannot refuse. This is the beginning of a close relationship between you and Tahr Rouse. Eventually, you end up becoming Rouse's right hand man and together, the two of you elevate the Company to its fullest potential."*

In the images of their unlikely alliance, Rotten spotted the first of several words along a text message sent via ghost call: "*E'vo.*"

Rotten recited the word in his mind.

E'vo.

He suddenly pulled himself from the trance and uttered, "What about the child?"

While toying with Rotten's mind, Clypt'O said, "*His future is uncertain. But it doesn't look too promising for those closest to him.*"

Rotten saw images of John struggling with agents of JeneCorp, whose interests remained on one particular area of John's body, his injured hand, which they placed inside a more compacted guillotine-like device called *Remo'*.

Falling back into a trance, Rotten mentally read the word to himself.

Next was Brett's mother, Selena, whose body was exhumed by the Company.

Back in a laboratory, JeneCorp's finest scientists combed through Selena's bones, in particular, the femur and tibia bones.

There was an engraving on one of the bones.

Part of the word was unclear; however, three letters stood out the most: *das*.

As soon as Rotten saw these letters, Clypt'O was in. The text, the maker of a guillotine-like device, an engraving on the bone: these were all of the images Clypt'O needed to slither his way inside Rotten without him even being aware of his presence. Thinking was reading, and seeing was the ultimate curse that bound itself from one world to the next.

After Selena's fate was showed to Rotten, he saw Ashleigh, who, not too long after the fire in Padadock, died on her deathbed in a remote location, off the grid, in a dense wilderness. Over a pile of wood collected throughout the forest, her body was cremated by M.J., who, overcome by defeat, failed to protect her. The look on his face was primitive and the emotions that drove him gathered meaning, purpose. His face, as crinkled as an aged paperback, almost appeared to float behind the heat of the flames.

Lastly was an image of dozens of statues, all lined up and positioned together as if they had been left in storage. Each statue, Rotten realized, was hunched over or remained in a seated position. Each one was of an elderly person. There was one statue in particular of an elderly woman with a crater along her hip from the results of time and pressure. Lying next to the chisel and the mallet was the crinkled glossy paperback of a romance novel *China's Veil* from the CHINA ROSE series written by author Frenchie Valentine.

Two hands, which were protected by chain mail gloves, reached inside the crater, which was roughly six inches in diameter, and pulled out a template of E'Raknish.

"*One day, Rouse will send you on a job in Tokyo,*" Clypt'O said. "*There, you will be tasked to catalog a rogue print, a real nasty bitch who you will be the death of you, if you let her. While taking a break, you will be interrupted by an old friend before you complete your session.*"

A fleeting glimpse of a rogue print whom he was tasked to catalog appeared before Rotten.

The rebel journalist.

Mavs.

Another image of two similar sized hands, dried and unprotected, this time they were reaching inside a dirt hole to unearth an important hard drive buried by Mavs.

Another image, much closer to home: Behind a parked car along Main Street, Pullman witnessed Rotten being shot in the head. His body flopped toward the street. Blood and brain matter everywhere.

And then, moments later, Rotten rose from the dead.

The wound in his head closing up, then healed.

Disturbed by Rotten's immortality, Pullman later contacted the one person close to Rotten.

"He wouldn't," said Rotten.

"*Don't underestimate Forsake,*" Clypt'O said. "*Without Forsake we don't evolve into who we're meant to be.*"

"We?" said Rotten, as he Clypt'O crept further and further inside him.

Rotten tried to fight off Clypt'O's spell, but he was overwhelmed by his power.

A text, a maker, an engraving: all in that specific order.

A graphic imaged flashed before Rotten's eyes: After an epic battle through the jock-riddled streets of a neon Tokyo, Forsake managed to corner a wounded Rotten, as he attempted to crawl away. Towering over Rotten, Forsake sprayed a liquid nitrogen-like freezing agent over his head and then, once his head was frozen completely, he used the chisel to crack open his forehead, and with his protective gloves, pulled out E'Raknish and held the tiny ball between his fingers.

Afterwards, Forsake would hire a fishing crew to sink E'Raknish in a weighted capsule in the deepest, darkest depths of the great Mariana Trench located in the Pacific Ocean.

Clypt'O words, as well as his cosmic yet ill-defined thoughts filled Rotten's head, consuming each essence of his being. Among the sly takeover, Rotten witnessed a glimpse of their evolution: Following Rotten and Clypt'O's demise, Seekers of the Eventide sought out their warped, Siamese-soul; and instead of dragging the two-headed pneuma into the Void, the mob ripped the pneuma apart, leaving behind only a shapeless shadow.

Rotten confused the images for another, B'aus, who fell into a cave in Antarctica where he stumbled upon a black pool, a gateway to Mount D'onwake, only to be pulled in by Seekers who torn B'aus to shreds and spat out his vessel through yet another gateway.

From an unlit area in the back of the restaurant, Rotten witnessed Stella and her former boss, Julian Waters, joking about Stella's source.

"I don't exactly know his name, but he calls himself Blot."

Julian chuckled at the nickname.

"Your contact is from some guy who got his name from a 1998 porno film?" Julian smirked at Stella and said, "Fitting."

Coupled with Rotten, Clypt'O said to himself: *"It is here, among the Eventide, where we're given the ability to travel freely from one realm to another. But to say we easily adapted to our new abilities is an understatement."*

More images of a past timeline, memories, appeared before Rotten.

Bloodthirsty for revenge, the shadow entity traveled back to Rotten's world, only to find itself in the year 2003, a nation on the brink of war, an opportunity organically manifested, creating the last and final phase of Rotten's transformation. In the days ahead, decapitation strikes in the Middle East were deemed a success in combating the War on Terror, a veiled slogan to cover up an unknown virus that spread throughout a small village in Iraq.

"Remember the choices, Barney," Clypt'O reminded Rotten.

Fast-forward through the timeline, and Rotten recalled an image of himself getting scratched by a black cat named Stash.

"If I didn't pick up the cat, it never would've scratched me," Rotten thought. *"Which means none of this would've happened."*

"But it did happen."

Each and every moment, each decision you've made, each action that you've taken, voluntary or involuntary, *led you to this exact moment.*

Clypt'O showed Rotten the images in Iraq, and those who came in contact with the shadow virus dying within days, leaving the US military with no option than to activate the iso-agents of a seek and destroy unit, the resurrection of Reapers under a new and more accepted title, Reconnaissance, Evaluate, Inform, Neutralize, or "R.E.I.N.," the insignia being a white horse, not to be misinterpreted as moisture from the atmosphere, even though iso-agents were not only known to use the cloak of dark clouds as disguised right before they were deployed to a contaminated site, but also known to order bombings to areas which posed threats to humanity.

One of those iso-agents of REIN was Byakuya "Ken" Forsake, who, after assisting with the neutralization of a site in Iraq, unknowingly carried the shadow virus back home, where his four-year-old son, Jin, was infected. Days later after Ken's return home, he died from the virus; however, Jin was immune; and for the next fifty years of his life, he would learn how to live with the shadow entity, his dark alter ego, who'd later be known as—

Rotten cried out, "*Enough* already!"

The sound of the name was too much for Rotten to handle.

He convinced himself that Clypt'O was wrong. All along, Rotten told himself over and over that Clypt'O was wrong about everything and that he was messing with his head.

Clypt'O pulled himself from Rotten; yet, despite an image of Clypt'O appearing right before Rotten, Rotten still felt Clypt'O inside him, like a voice in his head, a creeping feeling or thought swirling around a pool of life and death.

Standing next to Clypt'O was a raggedy-dressed man, who was reflecting on a beach among a similar ruined landscape marred by nuclear fallout.

Clypt'O said to Rotten, "One day, in a not-so distant future, you will rescue this man in the eleventh hour. You cannot stop the Freeze from happening, but you can save him."

As he recalled passing a familiar young man back in JeneCorp right before the Freeze, Rotten asked, "Who is he?"

"Chloe's son," Clypt'O said. "Aaron."

"What's his role in all of this?" asked Rotten.

"He will once and for all destroy the Trinity of Power that is JeneCorp," Clypt'O said. "And you will save him, Rotten. *We* will save him."

Aaron stared out into the horizon along the Atlantic Ocean.

The skies were gray and overcast and low as it carried death and its stench lingered like dew along the calm surface of the water.

Behind Aaron, the debris protruded from the dunes like tumors.

"Without Aaron," Clypt'O said, "the fate of humanity hangs in the balance—"

A wave of energy suddenly rushed through Rotten's body.

His eyes bolted open.

The fire was more intense, closer.

The side of his face was pressed against a puddle of his own blood.

The eye drops he had taken earlier in the night had worn off, returning his eyes back to their normal shade and color, leaving him with a nagging headache. He thought he remembered Forsake telling him that headaches were one of the many side effects of using the eye drops. With a throb of pain behind his sore eyes, the blurry, alien figures before him materialized. He peeled away his face from the gummy street and as he blinked the blur from his eyes, he saw the agent, Prescott, snapping his fingers in front of Noble's slack-jawed face.

"Earth to Noble!" Prescott shouted out.

On the third *snap* of his fingers, the echoes of a gunshot rang out!

Noble's head whipped backward, as the blast of a gunshot left a crater in the backside of his head.

Mindful of a possible shooter in the area, Prescott ducked down and scanned the fiery streets but couldn't locate any shooter on site. There was no shooter, he realized, only the one who ate a bullet on the front porch of a beach house off the coast of Carolina.

Carefully, he walked over to Noble and kneeled down over his body and inspected the gunshot wound. The color of his flesh was much grayer, slimier, and based on its current state, appeared to be in the early stages of decomposition. Dead bodies don't do that, the agent told himself, at least not right after feeling the cold hand of death.

Considering the rapid decay, the sight of Noble's body left Prescott even more bewildered as he attempted to wrap his head around the concept of death and the science behind organic matter when it no longer provided the nutrients of life.

But *how?*

As Prescott tried to make sense of the condition of Noble's body and most importantly, how the back of his head exploded outward, the angle of the gaping hole indicating a gunshot came from his mouth, and then, all those pieces of brain like fecal matter scattered over the street, he turned his eyes toward a moving figure in the corner of his eye. There, the agent witnessed Rotten rising to his feet as if he was the walking dead.

In a calm manner, Rotten glanced down at his left arm, which began to grow like a flower in time-lapse-like speed. The arm, however, didn't properly grow back to its normal size. Yet, the arm was much shorter in length than his right, at least two to four inches shorter and much thinner as if he only did bicep curls with his right arm and not his left.

Rotten pulled himself from the images of his newly grown arm and stared at an empty space where an arm once bloomed in front of him, that ghost of an arm, and recognized his old stump. The only difference was the five small nodule-like bumps protruding along the dry, scaly skin of his stump. He wiggled the ghost fingers and each one of those small bumps started to move, almost like a twitch or a spasm.

With his right arm, he ran his other hand over his forehead.

The gunshot wound began to close, leaving only a string of dried blood caked along the side of his face.

Lastly was the scratch on his other arm, which began to heal.

"Impossible. . . " Prescott said in disbelief.

The agent grimaced from a sudden rush of pain between his ribs. Each and every line on his face was as deep as a trench. The pain shot up from the center of his body as the blade twisted.

While Rotten remained fascinated by the bumps along his stump, John eased Prescott's body to the street.

Without Rotten acknowledging what had happened, he cut off the piece of Prescott's black undershirt and wrapped the cloth around his right hand.

Rotten moved his eyes upward at John, who was rising to his feet. He acknowledged John's wrapped hand and then the cast on the ground, which he managed to remove while in restraints.

He approached John, who brandished Prescott's knife.

"How the fuck are you still alive?" asked John, as he held the knife in a defensive posture.

"I dunno," Rotten said.

He honestly didn't know how he survived the gunshot. He was equally as baffled as John.

"Don't take another step!" yelled John.

"But we have to get outta here," Rotten urged, as the flames spread to the building closest to them. "Once the Company learns about Noble, they will send more agents, and they won't stop until they find what they want: your son, Brett. . . "

Pullman arrived on the scene. He stepped in between Rotten and John; and without trying to draw much attention to himself, he timidly looked over Rotten. Pullman's look said it all, which forced Rotten to recall recent images in his head: *Pullman watching from a safe distance as Rotten rose from the dead after being shot in the head.*

"I see the gaze has worn off," Pullman stated, as he wore the face of a man who was trying to conceal his shock. He then asked, "You good, Barney Trouble?"

"Yeah," Rotten said. "Good as I'll ever be." He then asked, "Where is everybody?"

"They're safe," he said and nodded at John. "How about you? You good—"

"Where's my son?"

"Brett's fine," Pullman said. "He's with Ashleigh—"

"Who are you people?" John asked.

"We're nobody," Pullman said, as he held up both hands. "We're just here to make sure your son is safe from the Company."

John looked down at Prescott, who died from the stab wound in the back.

"What do they want from him?" he asked.

"To use what he has inside him as a weapon," Pullman guessed. "Who knows?"

John pointed the knife at Rotten.

"And who the fuck is this guy?" he asked, more so indirectly.

"He's with me," Pullman said and motioned at John to put down the knife. "We're on your side. Trust us."

A globe of crackling silence swallowed the scene, leaving the three in a tense standstill.

While holding his injured hand, John suspiciously eyed Rotten.

Pullman pointed at John's hand.

"I can take a look at your hand, if you like," he said.

"Nah," John said, protectively. "I'm *good.*"

"You sure? I have a first aid kit—"

"Yeah," he interrupted with a short and stubborn tone. "Sure."

John was more interested in Rotten and how he was able to look Death straight in His black eyeballs and defy Him; and strangely, Rotten was likewise interested in John, mostly his injured hand, which he seemed to be concealing from the others. Together, the two shared a sort of mutual understanding as if they, both John and Rotten, didn't know why they were so skeptical and yet, so interested in one another. They just knew without any explanation.

After John concluded that neither the tracker or the cataloger meant him any harm—he was still somewhat on the fence about Rotten and frankly, freaked out about, not only watching what looked like a fatal gunshot wound heal so quickly and inhumanly, but also watching him recover and clearly speak words after the direct gun blast to the dome—John followed Pullman to a man-hole where the three trekked through a sewer underneath Main Street until they reached the end of the tunnel along a river. There, the rest of the locals were gathered around a bank, drying off and collecting themselves from the recent horrors.

John reunited with Brett, M.J., and Ashleigh. Rotten had grown obsessed with the knife that John used to kill Prescott and questioned himself as to how there wasn't one single drop of blood on the blade. Did Agent Prescott have the knife on him before John freed himself? Or, did John remove the knife from Prescott's black leather sheath without Prescott's knowledge? And if so, did he wipe away the blood from the knife before he wrapped his hand in the cloth? He returned to the first and most likely scenario, which was the knife still being holstered inside the agent's sheath after John freed himself. If he didn't use a knife to kill Prescott, then what did he use?

Unable to find a sane answer, Rotten noticed the unusual in-teraction between John and Doctor Charles. As though in sync, the two displayed quiet and subtle head nods at each other, similar to John and Rotten moments before they exited Main Street; however, John and the doctor's mutual understanding was much more obvious and came off as, dare he'd say, a pact.

The girl, Suzie, suddenly hollered out, "Scratch!"

Her voice was filled with rapture and at the same time, great relief.

A part of Rotten, the good part, was relieved as well.

Pullman checked the surveillance device and couldn't find any reading.

"No blip," he said, acknowledging Rotten.

Rotten checked on the chatty cat in Suzie's arms. He shined a flashlight on the incision that he had made prior to releasing the cat into the wild. He couldn't find any cut on the cat. He ran his fingers over the vicinity where he had cut, pulled his hand away, and then rubbed his fingers together, only to find several crumb-like specks of congealed blood scattering from his fingertips like skittish bugs.

After the reunion, Suzie brought Stash over to other relieved locals, who huddled around the two, each one of the locals sneaking in friendly rubs along the cat's neck and chin area, as if the cat was a kind of good luck charm.

SPRING FEVER
AUGUST 11, 2053
CHATTAR ALAYASHI, BANGLADESH

WEAVING throughout the various stations that surrounded the assembly line inside the main factory floor of JeneCorp East One Division's state-of-the-art manufacturing plant, the Head of Operations, or what employees referred to him behind his back as the "Company Ho," Horace Leeward, was approached by one of the engineers, Asif.

Deeply flustered by the recent finding, Asif, who preferred the term "artisan" opposed to engineer, informed his manager, Horace, who was in charge of overseeing the progress of the Creative and Development team, that the he and his fellow arties hit a snag with the latest rollout.

"A minor hiccup," Asif referred to the snag in production.

Interrupted from making his rounds through the factory, Horace pulled Asif away from other so-called artisans, who were split up into different departments under the CD team based on their specific craft, which covered detailed aspects of the print's overall design and makeup, including physical and internal components: Hair, Nails, Skin, Dental, Hygiene, Speech, Organ Function, Motor Skills, and Eyes to name a few departments.

The last department and perhaps the most vital one of the process: the installment of a neural implant, *Springer*, which, in relation to architecture, a lowest *voussoir* of an arch, was a spin-off of Ari's stolen IP, a decade-long creation, his "baby," *Splinter*. Originally titled Q-ube right before its final completion but changed at the eleventh hour due to a slight modification, or tweaking to its design, which made the final product more of a hexagonal prism than a cube, was similar to a memory card; however, it was able to store up to a petabyte of data, which the researchers at JeneCorp concluded was sufficient storage to handle the human brain.

Asif's field of expertise was the step before the installation of Springer into the cerebral matter: the eyes, which branched off into three smaller departments, or subcats (subcategories).

The first subcat was Design (i.e., color, shape, appearance).

The second: Sight and Functionality.

The third: Mobility.

When asked to clarify the issue, Asif, who had been working in Sight and Functionality for a year before he was demoted to Mobility after he failed to properly inspect several prints who lost their vision midway through a performance test and mucked up a simple task of walking in a trial run earlier this month, which led to the damaging of several pieces of expensive equipment, gave his unauthorized input on what he believed to be the culprit of the "hiccup." Which was exactly that, a hiccup, and all of it stemmed from the artificial womb, but more specifically, as he noted, a structural issue, a sore or perhaps a tear in the cervical wall, resulting in the womb to produce these mysterious spasms, or "hiccups," as he called them, which were somehow interfering with one of the final stages of the printing process in which JeneCorp adopted from Doctor Harcourt's theory. Prior to Harcourt's untimely departure, the former doctor pointed out to the counsel that the womb, which had been streamlined after a rather unethical installation of electroshock probes that would help trigger an instant response from the womb, thus stimulating and ultimately, increasing production, was not only unstable, but also incredibly vulnerable and if they (those asspipes at JeneCorp) expedited so much as a single delivery, than there'd be severe consequences, despite Trinity's marketable appeal of a print being one hundred percent free from carbon emissions, corruption, or impurities.

Asif waved over his fellow colleague and close friend, Philipp with "Three P's," whose duty was to maintain the integrity of the artificial womb, which involved monitoring the womb, cleaning the womb, as well as making sure it remained free of any hardened secretions or natural deposits, including vascular tissue or waste run-off, and last but not least, nurturing the womb—in other words, speaking to the womb as though it was a human being.

Philipp, who was rather timid while in Horace's presence, said with a tremble in his voice, "I can have her running properly in twenty-four hours."

Horace asked, "Any sooner?"

"Afraid not," Philipp said while regaining his confidence. "But I assure you, in twenty-four hours, she'll be as good as new."

Horace warned, "You have twenty-four hours. Get it done."

The two artisans rushed back to work, as Horace then continued to make his rounds through the factory where he stumbled upon yet another hiccup, this one being less manageable and considering a newly established extended time frame, worthy of a closer inspection.

While passing the Wildlife Department, one of the artisans who was struggling with one particular product in the Family Ursidae, part of the Carnivora Order, informed Horace about an issue regarding modified inhibitors, which were built into the product's circuitry in order to restrict its hunger, and how the MIs weren't functioning properly. As stated by the artisan, the unspecified animal, whom he called "Jäger," was ravenous for blood, in particular "human blood," and it was making one helluva a racket as it growled and roared and bellowed while ramming its head into a secured gate, leaving behind swells in the metal cage door.

DÉJÀ VU
AUGUST 13, 2053
PADADOCK, PA

OVER the throb of his heart pounding against his chest, Rotten saw her face in the dead of night.

Second night in a row he saw an image of her.

A memory?

Or, a vision?

Nonetheless, an image of the boy's mother Selena, so vivid and frontal, sitting at a campfire. Her face, Rotten witnessed, lit up by a beating firelight of flames burning through the cool night darkness. As she looked at Rotten, her lips formed into a warm, timeless smile, and Rotten wondered why him—Why me? Her smile was so bright and beautiful that, for Rotten, it felt as if he was staring at the sun, and he had no other choice than to look away before the rays blinded him. He caught a reflection in a metal canteen lying on the ground where he saw himself wearing the face of another man.

That man was John.

And as he pointed out, Selena was only a few months pregnant.

This was a memory, Rotten told himself. Had to be.

As Rotten drifted off into the fire, a sudden shattering of glass penetrated his ears, transporting him to another location.

One blink he was losing himself in the smile of a young woman whom he had never met before, even though he knew everything about her, then the next blink he was standing in the middle of a downtown, watching yet another major city in America burn to the ground.

He couldn't tell which city for each one looked all the same after the Freeze.

A wasteland consumed by filth and lawlessness, leaving only the hollowed, disease-riddled bones of man's creation.

Armed to the teeth, the Selected packed the ruined streets in hopes of sending a dire message to those who still carried a single brain cell of independent thought.

Written in pale blue spray paint, one of the Selected, a raggedy, hooded man whose face remained cloaked by the shadows, posed the question on the storefront window of a pawnshop:

IF the BLACKOUTS were inspired by the BOOKS written by author Stanley Pruitt, who was under the influence of E.Raknish at the time he wrote the books, which were intended to PREVENT PEOPLE from becoming DEPENDENT on technology, i.e. SMART DEVICES, which would ultimately destroy them after staring into the DEATH Loop of Chloe's gaze, which was — and still is — coupled with E.Raknish, THEN WHY FOR FUCK'S SAKE would LOCKHART, also coupled with E.Raknish, also inspired by Pruitt's books that planted the seed of using BLACKOUTS to advanced his own political career, also SHOT by Acosta's E.Raknish bullet, sit back and allow the FREEZE to happen under his watch?

As Rotten stood back and watched a once prosperous city consume itself before him, like a shackled beast gnawing off its own leg in order to free itself, the answer couldn't have been any clearer to Rotten.

The boy was the answer, Rotten knew, and the answer was the secret.

With heavy eyes, he tracked down the boy in the chaotic crowd, walking among them, like a phantom.

If the world ever found out about Brett and what he carried inside him, a part of Rotten—the good part—believed that people would accept him and most importantly, protect him.

But another part of him leaned toward the most practical scenario.

Not too far away, he saw yet another message spray-painted on the front of a ransacked convenient store next to a JeneCorp gas station:

Liberty and E'Rekvish For ALL!

All of a sudden, one of the Selected picked up the severed head of a dead print, lit its hair on fire, and as he reared back his arms yet another Selected pulled out a pin and stuffed the live grenade inside the mouth of the print.

The Selected flung the flaming head through the window, shattering the glass.

The explosion suddenly transported Rotten from night to day.

Not a vision.

A memory, so close that he could touch it and hold it in his palms.

Using a razor blade to acquire the dead agent's protective eyelid, which wasn't destroyed by the gaze, he was able to gain access to a corrupted tablet with one shielded eye, the other one being tightly closed whenever he found himself inches away from the abyss. After the extensive search through JeneCorp's Archives, Rotten still couldn't stop thinking about her.

Brett's mother, Selena Barbary.

Since her brother, Bret, spelled with one "t," not two, was a well-known figure on The Feed, what some used to call "influencer" (exactly what kind of influence was still left unclear to Rotten), she wasn't too hard to find among the forbidden Archives.

He looked up surgeries in or around Padadock in the following days after that one important date: September 20, 2048.

The day a piece of the template went missing in Iowa.

The piece spawning the trendy hashtag: Gray Scorpion.

He narrowed down his search to September 26, 2048, when Selena had surgery on a broken leg following a track meet, which abruptly ended due to a horrific accident.

From that date forward, Rotten, like a protective-eyed detective, was able to put together the missing pieces to the puzzle of the lost E'Raknish. Since Selena didn't have a social media presence, he turned his focus to her brother, Bret, more specifically, a video that he posted right after the Blackout, the weekend right before the Freeze, Bret informing all of his loyal followers that he may be "going away" for a while—vacation or jail, he was rather vague in what sounded like a scripted statement—then he ends the post with an apology.

With one of his protected eyes glazing over from staring into the abyss, Rotten didn't waste any time pulling up an article written on "DECEMBER 5, 2048," the day after the remaining power returned, about three missing girls being discovered, alive but traumatized and slightly malnourished, as well as Selena and her brother, Bret, Selena being the one responsible for rescuing the three girls from a flooded bank vault, which was unusual, Rotten thought, considering the severity of Selena's break.

How could someone recover so quickly from such a horrific injury?

To Rotten, as he redirected the question inward, it couldn't have been more obvious.

After saying his goodbyes to locals, including M.J., as well as Ashleigh, whom, after learning more about Selena and her brother, he realized was another key player in the unraveling mystery (He didn't exactly know why but he could sense it, like she was somehow connected to Selena), then lastly, John, as well as his four-year-old son, Brett, all of whom sought out shelter in a large concrete corridor underneath a massive dam in Snake's Creek, a small town which was located roughly ten miles north of Padadock, Rotten ventured back into the wild under a false excuse of searching for food and supplies.

Pullman was the only one who sniffed out the lie.

As Rotten stepped foot from the exit, Pullman wedged his foot in between the doorway.

"We need to have a quick word," he said and followed Rotten outside.

"Sure," Rotten said.

Pullman closed the door behind him and in a lowered tone, said, "You staying outta trouble, Barney?"

Rotten asked bluntly, "What do you want, Man?"

"If they find you, they'll kill you." He said before Rotten could respond, "Let me tag along with you."

Rotten said, "I told you, 'You need to stay here.'"

"When they send more drones, which they will, I won't be able to disguise you."

"And?"

"They won't stop," Pullman said. "You know this, right? Noble is just the beginning."

With an empty sleeve hanging along his left side like a scarf, Rotten kept walking.

Unsure whether or not to tell Rotten about the momentary blip he received moments after he was shot in the head by Agent Prescott, Pullman swallowed the words that dangled along the tip of his tongue and told himself some other time. Instead, Pullman said with a buttery confidence, "Just watch your back, you hear?"

"Will do."

As Rotten proceeded to the dense forest that surrounded the dam, Pullman reminded Rotten while using a raised voice, "There's nothing back there! Our focus remains here with the boy!"

The sound of Pullman bringing up yet again the boy, Brett, caused Rotten to marinate in his own thoughts. He began to question Pullman and his growingly obsessive behavior toward Brett and his so-called "talents." He felt almost compelled to disarm Pullman's charged remarks with a joke about the "bubble-wrap"-like aerosol spray that Pullman referred to as "fire-retardant skin" which firefighters wore over their bodies before tending to a fire. In Pullman's defense, the film acted like a second skin, especially along exposed areas like the face, neck, arms, or legs, adding a protective layer over the skin in order to prevent any burns, or in the boy's case, cuts. One single drop of blood could expose them to the Company's radars.

With or without the fire-retardant film, the boy, Brett, Rotten knew, would be fine as long as he remained in the company of friends and family.

And Pullman, as far as Rotten knew, didn't fall in neither of those two categories.

As for the now indoor cat, Stash, there was also a joke among Pullman's remarks.

Instead, Rotten said shortly, "Got it."

He proceeded toward the forest and never looked back until he was provoked once more.

"Barney. . . " Pullman said with a long pause, which forced Rotten to acknowledge Pullman, ". . . if you do go back there, don't come back empty-handed."

Pullman relieved the tension by cracking a smile.

Rotten didn't smile, at least not on the outside.

During a roughly ten-mile trek south through the forest where even the furriest of furry creatures couldn't be trusted, Rotten skipped the nearest town to pick up supplies and made his way back into Padadock, where he had unfinished business.

Along the way, Rotten spotted a helicopter heading northbound away from Padadock, which forced him to seek cover behind a tree. Due to the heavy canopy overhead, he couldn't quite tell if it belonged to the Company. Either way, he was left with a nagging thought of whether or not the Company was headed toward Snake's Creek. According to Pullman, the dam helped masked their heat signature; and as far as Pullman could tell, there were no drones in the area.

Once the skies were clear, Rotten decided to push forward toward Padadock.

When he finally arrived, he surveyed the damage for the first time in daylight, which painted a more disturbing picture. Most of the town, especially the downtown area, was destroyed by the fires, except for a couple of streets lined with houses that were untouched by flames, one of those houses being John's, the blue one off Terrace Street, with the maple tree in the front yard.

Rotten headed straight to the blue house; and right before he stepped foot inside, he began to see more of those images, distant yet so close, like the ones of Selena by the campfire. The images would appear almost randomly, a sequence that flowingly played out inside his mind like a scene from a movie. In the images, John was there, and he was finishing with chores inside the house. He followed John into the kitchen.

The images directed Rotten to the kitchen sink where John used a faucet to wash the blood from his hands.

That dried blood, which was caked onto John's skin, belonged to Brett, who recently cut his arm on a slide at the playground.

Rotten mentally connected the scene in the wine cellar under the church with Suzie and M.J. mentioning the incident where Stash swiped its claws at him.

Next was another scene, which happened the day before when M.J. further explained to Rotten and Pullman how Brett cut his arm while playing on a slide.

Then, finally, another scene, another memory of the time Rotten discovered a cast lying on the street after he retrieved his prosthetic. He inspected the cast, John's cast, inspected all of the doodles and sketches first, and then the edges of the cut, which were clean, almost surgical, impossible from the shaky hand of a man who was bound by restraints.

Rotten turned his focus to the sink.

As John dried his hands with a hand towel, he noticed a glittery object inside the drain. He briefly switched on the garbage disposal, only to hear the *grating* sounds of metal being chewed up.

Rotten leaned over the sink and inspected the drain.

Empty.

John reached his hand down into the garbage disposal and pulled out a spoon.

As he placed the spoon in a silverware container inside the dish holder, the template, which had taken the shape of a fork, suddenly pounced on John's hand and sunk its tine-like claws into John's knuckles, leaving behind a trail of blood along the sink, as well as the countertop where the agents of the Company identified E'Raknish's signature through the special black light.

Shaking away the images, Rotten looked up at a window above the sink and saw a headstone in the backyard.

He remembered hearing Pullman say that two blips popped up on his SD, which he believed was a misreading. One of them coming from the laundry basket in a laundry room, which Rotten found was empty.

After leaving the laundry room, which was connected to the kitchen, Rotten walked through the back door and made his way to the headstone underneath an oak tree.

The ground below the headstone was covered with loose dirt. The grass surrounding the dirt was matted down as well. He lost track of how many footprints there were, but there was at least three people surrounding the grave.

He looked around the backyard and saw another image in his mind.

From the backyard, Rotten witnessed John carrying Brett in his arms as he rushed him into the house. The side of Brett's arm was bloody.

He rotated back around to the grave and in his mind, saw the template rising from the grass.

As recently stated, Brett's mother, Selena, died during childbirth.

Yet, the dirt appeared fresh, as if the grave below was recently dug up.

Rotten found a snow globe next to the unmarked headstone.

Another image in his mind: He was handing Selena, who was in a wheelchair, a gift.

A snow globe.

He pulled himself from the image and stared at the snow globe in his hands.

Inside the snow globe: Selena's "Dream House."

Driven to exhume her body, if the Company hadn't already, Rotten rushed back to the house and grabbed a shovel from the garage; and by the time he made his way through the kitchen, he suddenly encountered a familiar shadow in the corner of his eye. He stopped in his tracks moments before reaching for the door handle and turned to the shadow standing in the corner of the living room.

"You're wasting your time, Barney," said Blot. "You just missed them."

"The Company?"

"Who else would it be?"

Rotten asked Blot, "What in the hell's happening to me? Why does it feel like all of this has already happened?"

"You're starting to see the bigger picture."

"John didn't injure his hand by getting it jammed in the door, as he confessed. I take it Doctor Charles is the only person who knows about what really happened. Right?"

"I don't know," Blot said, staying close to the shadows. "You tell me."

With the recent conversation with Clypt'O coming to mind, Rotten finally decided to ask the one who referred to himself as Blot, "Who are you?"

"Right now," Blot said, "it doesn't matter who I am. All I can say is that the next few moments will be the most important ones of your life. My advice: *Listen* to your gut."

Rotten heard the sound of car door slamming shut outside.

As he turned toward the front window where a blurry, distorted figure appeared on the front porch, he shot a glance into the living room, only to find the shadow of a standing lamp along the corner of the wall. Two strings, two on-off switches, hung below the shade of the lamp. The left string was much shorter than the one on the right.

Rotten began to see the bigger picture.

Cautiously, Rotten set aside the shovel and opened the front door.

Walking up the front porch steps was none other than Tahr Rouse.

Rotten confirmed, "Alone?"

"But," Rouse said, as his eyes flicked upward, as though indicating that there was a drone up above who might or might not be disguised as the crow perched on a tree branch, "I'd be lying if I said we weren't being watched."

Rotten's eyes remained on Rouse, who hadn't aged a day since he last saw him.

Which would've been before the Freeze.

"I had a feeling you'd come back here," said Rouse, who patiently waited for Rotten to assume the role of host.

Rotten stepped aside and allowed Rouse inside the house.

While Rouse roamed freely through the foyer, Rotten asked, "Why are you here?"

"I have a job for you."

Rouse reaffirmed his proposal by declaring his unadulterated trust.

The word *trust*, especially coming from the mouth of a man who carried as much as trust as an endangered honey badger, sent a wave of anger through Rotten's body.

"Job? You're serious?"

"Before you get upset, Barney, you should know that whatever happened between us in the past is water under the bridge—"

"You have a lot of nerve showing your face around here. . . "

"It's Darwin," Rouse said before Rotten could lose his temper.

Rotten remained more attentive and willing to hear Rouse's proposal.

He said, "What about him?"

"He's dead," Rouse informed.

"When?"

"One of our agents found his body last month in El Cruz or what remained of it. . . " he said while letting the words soak in. In a softer tone, he said straightforwardly, "He was decapitated, Barney."

Rotten's immediate reaction was first rage, or at least, he displayed the appearance of a man who was enraged.

With a slight tremble of his lips, Rotten asked Rouse, "Who?"

"You may know him," said Rouse, as he maintained a cool and calm composure. "His name is Lesley Frye, former Special Agent Lesley Frye of the FBI. Our agents picked Frye up a week ago. Apparently, according to the former FBI agent, Darwin wasn't his first. He said there were many more. Dozens, Barney," Rouse emphasized. "After the Freeze he allegedly went on a killing spree, taking out those whom he deemed unworthy of breathing the same air he breathed," he said, studying Rotten's facial gestures. "Mostly criminals, the worse of the worst, those who escaped from prison after the Freeze—"

"More like released."

Rouse's eyes wandered away from Rotten's as though he was swallowed by a thought. Yet, as he peered closer into Rouse's eyes and the expressionless gawk that surrounded both eyes, he saw nothing inside Rouse. Before Rotten could get a better reading on his former boss, Rouse perked up and in a lively manner, looked into Rotten's eyes.

"I guess Frye had sort of soft spot for Lockhart. Surprised you haven't run into any of these types along your journey—"

"Types?"

"Convicts, the very best the Selected has to offer."

Rotten asked, "With that Loop still running, aren't we all prisoners?"

"You have a point, I suppose. But then again," Rouse said, cool as ever, "it doesn't have to be that way. All you have to do is take the eye drops."

Rotten was tempted to tell Rouse where he could stick those eye drops.

Instead, he asked, "What do you want with me?"

"We want you to catalog Frye."

"Not gonna happen—"

"With your help, Barney, you can prevent others from dying."

"When did the Company start caring about the living?"

"As Head of JeneCorp, I will admit that we were careless in Chloe's launch and we take full responsibility in what happened—"

"Millions of people died, Tahr. . . "

"And they'll never be forgotten," Rouse said. "Their sacrifice will be duly noted in the next phase of the human evolution." He paused, waiting for a response from Rotten but only received a 'Fuck-Your-Evolution'-type of glare from him. "I can assure you, Barney, that the Company has *changed* and we should, and we will, hold ourselves accountable, starting with Frye.

Resentfully, Rotten asked, "Is this how you treat all your friends?"

"Barney," Rouse said with a more careful and deliberate response, as if he was reading from a script, "former Special Agent Frye stopped being my friend the moment he decided to take the law into his own hands. We can't have a loose cannon out there, claiming he's doing JeneCorp's bidding—"

"So, now, what? You wanna make an example out of him?"

"By cataloging Frye, we'll be able to stop other agents, like Frye, before turning rogue. The Company needs to restore order—"

"*Order?*" Rotten said with disgust and pointed at a blackened house across the street which was left in a pile of burnt rubble. "Take a look outside, Tahr. Does this look like order to you? This town was doing just fine before you sent your devil dogs after one of their residents."

"About that resident, the boy, Brett is his name—"

"How do you know his name?"

"Before his unfortunate demise, Noble collected a sample of Brett's blood. Our agents were able to retrieve the sample. With that said, the boy is no longer any use to us."

"No offense, Tahr, but. . ." he said, the anger rising in his voice, ". . . I don't believe you."

"Believe whatever you want, Barney, but know this: If you come back to the Company, you will be given a direct link to Chloe. Anything you want. It's yours."

"Tempting offer," Rotten said, "but no thanks."

A tense pause developed over the two.

Rotten witnessed a slight twitch in Rouse's eyes which he believed was caused by a piece of debris. The unusual movement caused Rotten to do a double take.

After acknowledging Rotten's interest in his face, mainly his eyes, Rouse paced toward the kitchen.

"I don't know how she did it," Rouse said, as Rotten timidly followed him into the kitchen, "how she managed to open up the *exact* doors at the *exact* time—frankly, I can't begin to wrap my head around *why* she did it, but she helped Darwin escape from JeneCorp." Rouse loosely surveyed the sink area, prompting Rotten to vigilantly keep him in his sight. "If you take a step back and really try to understand the reasons why she did what she did: *Why him?*" he asked, as he stood behind the island in the middle of the kitchen. "Why help out some low-life gutter punk who attempted to assassinate the President of the United States? It starts to make sense once you look at the people around him, in particular, *you*, Barney. Did you ever stop to think, with everything that has happened before and after the Freeze, the relationship between you and Darwin, or D," he said mockingly, "Darwin escaping from a highly-secured facility, Darwin's death, did she foresee this very moment, with you putting aside your differences to help out the Company?"

Rotten thought carefully about Rouse's suspicions about Chloe.

"If so," Rotten said with his body squared to Rouse, "then wouldn't that make her God?"

Rouse couldn't quite comprehend Rotten's question. With a nearly identical expression that he displayed earlier on his face, the one where all life had drained from behind his eyes, Rouse's head tilted to the side. The expression turned to the look of a confused dog. All of a sudden, his eyes twitched yet again, starting with the left one and then moving toward the right.

In a varying tone, he said to Rotten, "Then I reckon it'd be pretty nice to have God on your side, wouldn't it?"

Rotten's heartbeat increased, his chest subtly inflating up and down behind the black windbreaker. His eyes pulsed and dilated. The lower left side of his abdomen slightly stirred, causing his former boss to shoot an unsteady glance toward Rotten's waistside.

With his eyes moving up Rotten's body, Rouse said, "What do you say, Barney. . . "

Rotten seethed behind his barred teeth, "Let me tell you something about God— "

A gunshot *rang* out before Rouse could suspend disbelief!

The left side of Rotten's windbreaker fluttered upward from the blast of the gunshot.

Since his waist was level with the island's countertop, Rotten aimed upward in a thirty-four degree angle, causing the bullet to skim over the edge of the granite before striking Rouse in the upper abdomen. Rouse's body was violently whipped backward against the sink.

The blood, which wasn't a red color, but rather more of a milky, synthetic Rosé sauce, splattered over the kitchen cabinets.

Once Rouse was left vulnerable, Rotten revealed the left arm underneath the windbreaker.

The arm was much smaller and shorter in size, not like what Rotten visualized after he rose from the dead, but rather much thinner and weaker and sicklier, roughly the size of a child's arm, its short and stumpy fingers could barely wrap around the gun's handle, let alone the trigger—a gun of its size, known for its light weight and durability, weighed three times as much in his left hand, which was still growing, surely but slowly.

With his right hand, he grabbed the handgun from his left and smaller hand, switching grips. Once the gun was secured in his right hand, his good hand, the gun feeling as light as air, Rotten aimed at Rouse and fired three shots, the first two shots hitting him in the chest and then the last one striking him directly between the eyes.

Once more, in a violent, exaggerated reaction, Rouse's body drunkenly whipped around the kitchen, arms flailing from side to side, knocking around silverware and dishes. Never did Rotten lose sight of the moving target. Each shot carried weight, cold and calculated, precise.

Rouse lowered the smoky barrel to his side and with a firm strut, moved toward Rouse, who was lying on the floor. Milky blood oozed from each bullet hole, including the one between his glitchy eyes, which, not to Rotten's surprise, were moving back and forth, like a tremor.

While towering over Rouse's body, he said, "Didn't see that one coming, did you?"

Curious about the color of the blood and how it didn't look like any normal human blood, he kneeled down and closely inspected the strange liquid oozing from the holes. He ran his fingers through the blood and held his fingers to his face.

In the corner of his eye, he caught a tiny glimmer coming from the perfect circle in Rouse's head. He dug his index finger, as well as his thumb into Rouse's skull and pulled out what appeared to be a neural implant, which was partially damaged from the bullet, the electrical connecting pins parallel to each side of the implant were curled inward and appeared like the legs of a dead spider.

More curious, he grabbed Rouse by the jaw and turned his head to the right and found a label behind his left ear.

A barcode-like tattoo with several numbers underneath.

Disgusted by the sight of Rouse's print, Rotten flicked the small chip to the floor and uttered under his breath, "Some human evolution. . . "

By the time he made it back to the dam in Snake's Creek he was overwhelmed by a feeling of dread.

While standing at the top of the hill, he peered through the trees and saw a lifeless body lying on the ground outside the door to the dam's corridor. With gun in hand, he rushed down the hill; and when he arrived at the dam, he discovered M.J. lying on the ground. He couldn't find a pulse on either his neck or wrist. He was shot several times in the back. He pulled his eyes from M.J. and looked up at the door, which was cracked open. He could sense death inside, its breath like a cold stench forcing him to stay alert.

As he cracked open the door and stepped inside, he first saw the dead bodies on the ground. Each and every local from Padadock, like M.J., shot to death, except for John, Brett, and Ashleigh, whom he couldn't locate inside the corridor.

While cautiously stepping over the bodies, including Pullman's, who was also dead, his eyes crossed the stark shadow mimicking his every move.

His shadow.

The light beaming through the doorway cast a lanky shadow along the concrete wall, which left him in a still and studious state.

With all of the carnage surrounding him, he couldn't remove his eyes from his own shadow. A similar feeling suddenly came over him as if he had lived or was reliving this exact moment in time. Strangely, after the shock wore off, he wasn't the least concerned by all the death that surrounded him. His concerns remained neither elsewhere or nowhere; and yet, his concerns were drawn to his very own shadow, leaving him skeptical about whether or not he could trust it.

Behind him, he heard footsteps.

A JeneCorp agent approached the doorway.

"Put down the gun, Cat," the agent demanded. "It's over. . . "

Hovering over the agent's shoulder like a tiny dark cloud was a drone.

If Rotten made one wrong move, then the drone was ready to vaporize its target.

"*Hold your fire,*" said the voice in the agent's earpiece.

As the drone scanned Rotten's body, the agent stepped away from the door and ordered Rotten to exit the corridor.

Rotten brandished his gun and aimed at the agent's head and as he was moments away from shooting the agent, he couldn't move his trigger finger. A sharp, stabbing pain spread from the center of his forehead to the rest of his body. His nerves were on fire, as he was stuck in a painful yet paralyzed state. He attempted to pull the trigger once more, but each attempt shot streaks of pain throughout his entire body.

"Last chance," the agent said. "Put down the gun. . . "

"*Stand down, Agent.*"

The burning intensified through Rotten's right hand, causing him to loosen his grip over the gun and eventually, drop the gun. Perplexed by what was happening to him (*Was there a chemical agent in the air? A new type of biological weapon? A hypnotic trigger?*), Rotten felt as if he was no longer in control of his movements, in particular, his fingers, which somehow moved on their own.

The agent waved Rotten closer.

"Walk to me," he demanded.

When Rotten failed to follow through with the agent's demands, he felt a burning sensation in his legs. Without possessing any control over his own body, Rotten found himself mechanically taking a step forward. The pain was too much to bear. Rotten cried out, "All right!"

"Make it easy on yourself, Barney," the agent said in a more calm voice. "He just wants to talk."

Despite the pain coursing through Rotten's body as if the pain itself was an electrical current an image appeared in his thoughts: Rotten grabbing hold of the black hand of a sick man lying in his death bed.

Rouse?

The pain returned as soon as he cleared his thoughts.

"All right," he said, more weakly. "You win. . . "

After Rotten gathered himself and ignored the echoes of pain, he found his feet again.

By his own willpower, Rotten exited the corridor and followed the agent up a hill where he was greeted by three more agents from JeneCorp.

Each one was wearing an exoskeleton-type suit made from E'Raknish.

The agents were standing guard at the post in front of a helicopter where a familiar-looking man sat with a tablet-like device in his hands.

Rotten remained in awe by the agents' suits.

The other agent pointed to the helicopter and leaving no room for questions, said, "Walk."

Rotten walked toward the helicopter where, of all people, Vernon Hawks sat in the passenger seat inside the cabin.

In his hands, Vernon was holding a tablet with a template of E'Raknish attached to the camera like a web cam that was spit in two halves: One half was sleek and polished and bared similar characteristics to the template Rotten once wore inside his wrist; the other half, dull and corroded and didn't properly fit into the sleeker template.

Startled but not all surprised by Vernon's appearance given the toaster that he just whacked, he combed through his thoughts until a past image surfaced, this time bearing more detail: Two hands, both protected by chain mail gloves, reaching inside the crater along the hip of a statue of an elderly woman. Next to the statue: a chisel and a mallet and a glossy paperback of a romance novel, *China's Veil* by Frenchie Valentine. He panned up from the two hands, revealing Vernon, not Forsake, as first predicted, kneeling over Hilda's statue. Behind him was a team of JeneCorp agents, who were accompanying Vernon in his quest to locate the template, which, for three and a half years, had remained in a state of dormancy.

As he studied Vernon's face, Rotten said in disbelief, "You're supposed to be dead."

"Never underestimate the power of survival, Mr. Rotten," Vernon said. "Based on what I've learned about, of all people you should know dying isn't as easy as you'd hope it to be—"

"You don't know a goddamn thing about me—"

"I know you've been through the ringer."

"What are you?" asked Rotten, as the rage filled his body. "Some kind of robot?"

"Easy, Mr. Rotten," he said, reading a glowing scan of Rotten's body on the tablet. "I know you are upset. You have every right to be. You think I like being in this position? The short answer is no—" he made a quick note, "—by the way, *not* a robot, not even close to one. The techies at the Company call them 'prints.' And you just destroyed a very expensive prototype."

He glanced down at the modified tablet in Vernon's hands, which he assumed Vernon was using like some kind of joystick to control him.

"What the fuck is that thing?" asked Rotten, as he nodded the strange device.

In a child-like manner, Vernon showcased the tablet in his hands.

"This bad boy here allows me to control E'Raknish—and if you know a thing or two about E'Raknish, which *you* do, then let me remind you that, when E'Raknish is coupled to a host, it becomes part of the host's nervous system, and once it becomes part of the host's nervous system that means. . . " the excitement suddenly melted from his face as he looked at Rotten with a sinister glare, ". . . I can control anyone who wears E'Raknish. The only downside: it has a limited range. But I suppose in time these issues will be addressed. Like, for example, the prints. What gave it away?" Vernon asked Rotten but didn't allow him enough time to answer. "It was the eyes, wasn't it?"

The eyes are the windows to the soul, Rotten thought.

"What makes you think I wasn't trying to kill Rouse? The real one, that is—"

"Please, if you would, indulge me, Mr. Rotten," Vernon said over Rotten and nodded at Rotten's left arm, "how'd you managed to magically grow that new arm? It's the boy, isn't it? You got his blood inside you, don't you?"

"The arm fairy paid me a visit last night," Rotten said sarcastically.

"Right," Vernon said, smiling off any frustration he had with Rotten. "Of course."

Color rose into the upper corners of his face, as he grew annoyed by Vernon's presence. A part of Rotten—the bad part—wanted to pull that smile off his face and stretch it out until the flesh ripped.

He took a breath and asked Vernon, "If you can control me, then why didn't he stop me from killing this so-called print?"

Not wasting any more time, Vernon asked, "Why don't you ask him yourself?"

While holding the tablet screen-side up, a hologram of Rouse projected from the template.

Seated in the passenger seat across from Vernon was Rouse's hologram.

"Have a seat," Rouse said, pointing to the seat next to Vernon, "will you?"

Rotten didn't budge.

Instead, he glanced over at Vernon's tablet.

Vernon appeared almost giddy about using it once more on Rotten.

"He won't use it unless I tell him, Barney."

Hesitantly, Rotten sat down, eyeing the tablet as if he couldn't take his eyes away from it.

"You're wondering where he got the template, aren't you?"

"Not really," Rotten said, squashing any interest he had in the tablet.

"The stewardess on the plane," he said, "she used E'Raknish to crash the plane." He pointed at the tablet. "The very same E'Raknish you now see on Vernon's tablet. After a rather significant investment, JeneCorp obtained a template from the Government of the Democratic Republic of the Congo following the infamous Eco-Revolution." Based on their previous agreement, Rotten appeared almost betrayed by Rouse's comment. "You thought you were JeneCorp's only fail safe? In this line of work, Barney, you must have a backup plan to your backup plan. Or, if you really want to get deep, you can go one step further and say everything in this life happens based off a strategic sequence of events that occur at the right place at the right time—"

Rotten carried an image of Niles falling into a cave somewhere in the ass end of earth.

Before he could make sense of the image, he blocked it out; and by doing so, a shooting pain rushed through Rotten's body, leaving behind a heavy ache in the center of his forehead.

He closed his eyes, rested his eyes, and then opened his eyes once the pain tapered off.

Left with only rancor, Rotten said to Rouse, "Sounds like you picked up a thing or two from Clypt'O."

Rouse grinned.

"You're one to speak—"

"Where's the boy?" asked Rotten.

"By boy, I assume you're referring to Brett Barbary, correct?"

Rotten's lack of response was enough answer for Rouse.

"As I was saying earlier before you shot me down," Rouse said, "we're no longer interested in the boy. We already have what we needed."

"And his father?"

"Apparently," Rouse said and glared at Vernon, "they escaped before Vernon could use that device of his."

"Then, why all of this?" Rotten said, growing upset. "These people were innocent!"

"I had to send a message to you—"

"And what message is that?"

Rouse sharpened his eyes, each one shooting daggers through Rotten.

"*Don't fuck with us*," he said coldly. "As for the property you recently destroyed," the tone in his voice softened, despite maintaining a stern and icy demeanor, "let's just say we *anticipated* that your emotions would get the better of you. After all. . . " Rouse said, looking over Rotten's body, ". . . there's still a human somewhere in there. Now. . . " his tone hardened, ". . . it's time for us to send yet another message." He nodded at Vernon and called out to him. "Show him."

As Vernon tilted the tablet, which caused the template to arch outward and hold a still projection of the hologram, he said sincerely to Rotten, "Apologies. . . "

Vernon displayed for Rotten a video feed of Krystal Bawl being held hostage inside a tight space no larger than a walk-in closet. Her mouth was gagged. Both her hands were tied behind her back, as she sat restrained to a metal chair in the center of what Rotten identified as a storage unit where, circling Krystal, were dozens of work lights, casting very little to no shadows, which made it nearly impossible for Blot to travel.

"I hate doing this as much as you hate seeing her like this," Rouse said with a hint of sympathy in his voice.

Rotten wasn't buying any of Rouse's sympathy; in fact, he despised the phony-baloney man for even using such a politically charged word like *hate*. He wanted to crumble up the word into a ball and chuck it right between his phony holo-eyes.

"Let her go!" Rotten shouted out as hot rage boiled over. "She has nothing to do with this, Tahr or whoever the fuck you claim to be—"

"But she does, Barney," Rouse said, remaining calm. "She chose to get involved with you. She should've known that being with a man like you comes with its fair share of *baggage*. . . The blood is already on your hands, Barney. How many more people will it be?"

Fuming, Rotten sat in his seat, ready to take his rage out on anything that he could wrap his hands, or this case, his good hand around, Vernon being his most tangible specimen.

Rouse said, "A team picked up the pirate at a local clinic. Apparently, a passerby found her on the side of the road, unconscious. I can only assume that the knife who was hired to kill you knocked out Ms. Bawl and left her for dead—"

"She sounds like just another pawn," Rotten said, "another piece to your puzzle, right? She was never going to kill me, was she?"

"Well, it's a good thing she didn't. But, most importantly, Barney, it's a good thing she spared Ms. Bawl; otherwise, it'd be difficult to find someone remaining on this earth you do care about."

Rotten turned toward the screen where he looked closer at the bruise along the side of Krystal's face.

"More people don't have to die, Barney. You have a chance to stop this. Right now. Hell, you may even grow to like your old job. Beats repairing cars. So, what's it going to be?"

In the feed the armed agent was standing behind Krystal.

Rotten eyed the gun, held down in front of the agent's waist, hands crossed.

"He won't hesitate for a second," Rouse said, as his hologram leaned closer to Rotten. "All I have to do is give him the order."

"And you will release her if I do what for you?"

"Catalog Frye."

"Why do you have such a hard on for that piece of shit?"

"Accountability, remember. The part about Frye killing all those people—"

"Except D."

"Except D," Rouse repeated, confirming that the story about Darwin was all fudged to get a rise out of Rotten. "It's all true, and he must be held accountable for his actions. That right there is the truth, my friend."

As Rouse waited for an answer, Rotten glanced at Vernon, who had aged dramatically since he last saw him on that airplane. All he could think about was why—how he was able to survive a plane crash? Was he even on the plane when it went down over the Pacific? Or did he exit the plane shortly after Rotten stumbled his drunken self from the cabin? He was so pissed-drunk at the time that he could hardly remember the details, and even those details surrounding the moments before he became blackly drunk seemed tweaked, as if he filled in the blackness with fantastical scenarios. *I remember slapping that bitch of a stewardess across her pretty face before she brandished an E'Raknish strap-on and told me, "Now, the shoe is on the other foot"*—No, you didn't; in fact, you could hardly look the woman in the eyes. *I grabbed Vernon by the collar and attempted to escort him from the plane before takeoff, but* I remember, *he refused and said with a strange smile, "0.01"*—No. The blackness had a way of filling the mind with blackly lies.

"If you accept our offer, Vernon will accompany you to Death Valley where Frye's currently being held—"

"Fine," Rotten said abruptly, reading Vernon's face, his gestures.

He faced Rouse, who said, "Wise decision, Barney."

In the feed the agent removed the gag from Krystal's mouth and then released her from the restraints.

Before Vernon switched off the feed, Rotten grabbed Vernon's hand.

"Not so fast," he said, ready to crush Vernon's hand. "Until she's free. . . "

"Do as he says, Vernon," Rouse said.

The hologram froze as if it was left in a state of pause.

Moments later, the hologram spawned back life as soon as Rouse privately ordered agents to capture her entire release.

Rotten released his hand from Vernon and watched the agent escort Krystal toward the exit.

Once she stepped outside the storage unit, the agent ordered her to run off.

With her body shaking, her hand shielding the blinding light, Krystal stumbled away, at first clumsily, from the two agents. After she regained her strength, she sprinted away. Rotten didn't take his eyes off the feed until Krystal vanished into the milky glow of daylight.

"Happy?" said Rouse.

The emotion boiled over Rotten, who could barely bring himself to look at Rouse.

Before ending the conversation, Rouse asked, "How did you know about Mr. Acosta?"

As the anger flooded his face, Rotten said, "I knew the moment he looked into *Her* eyes."

Finally, Vernon switched off the feed.

"As soon as you arrive in Death Valley, you will be assigned your temporary living quarters where you will reside until the job is finished," Rouse ordered. "Don't make it harder than it has to be, Barney. We might not be able to see eye-to-eye right now. But, in time, once the emotions cool, I'm certain that we will find a common ground."

Rotten fought off the rising thoughts in his head.

The images.

His hand shaking Rouse's frailer hand.

"And don't you ever forget that your contribution will play a vital role in how the world perceives JeneCorp from this point forward. You decide, Barney: Do you want the world to look at us as the enemy? Or, do you want the world to look at us the stewards of a bright and prosperous future? Your choice."

The hologram deteriorated and then crumbled away like a cloud of glitter sucking back into Vernon's tablet.

Vernon placed the headphones over his ears and through the mouthpiece, ordered the pilot to take off.

The agents entered the helicopter and closed the doors behind them.

The pilot started the engine and once the rotary blades started to run, the helicopter ascended into the sky.

During the flight, Rotten nodded at Vernon, who was staring out the window, and said into the mouthpiece, "So. . . what the fuck's your role in all of this?"

"As you know, Rouse isn't going to be around forever—"

"You mean the *real*-life version?"

"Good eye," Vernon said, surprised. "How'd you know?"

"The fakes have a particular *sheen* to them, subtle but there."

As far as the voice, Rotten believed the fakes did a decent job at replicating a person's voice. He'd even go so far to say that they mastered it.

"He's grooming me to take over JeneCorp once he's gone."

"You?" While his voice trailed off, Rotten then said to himself: "*So that's what he promised you.*" He turned the remark back to Vernon: "A lot of responsibility, ain't it?"

"I'm up for the task."

"So, why you? What makes you so special to take the reins of a monster?"

"Honestly," Vernon said, sighing, "I don't know why he chose me. But I guess he must've seen something in me."

"After everything that he did to you. . . " Rotten said, as he recalled the moment when he, in fact, handed a photograph to Vernon on the airplane.

The images in his head didn't lie.

Rotten finished, "Why would you work for a man who tried to kill you?"

"The same reason you are," Vernon said and shared a connection with Rotten.

"I don't have any other choice—"

"But you do, Barney," Vernon said, more personably. "You'll always have a choice."

"So how much time does he have left?" Rotten asked, as he ciphered through Vernon's bullshit.

New cancer?

Agent 5?

The return of the deadly "mind virus," which was created by a massive outbreak of the Quidaquin Diet?

He could run through all of the diseases or viruses that commonly sprouted up like weeds in the summer, but he didn't have the energy to put much stock into the well being of a man whom he felt was exploiting his ingenuity for the sake of repairing his Company's image.

Vernon grinned at Rotten and for a moment, almost forgot about Rotten's excellent skills as a cataloger.

"Not long," he said. "His diagnosis doesn't look optimistic."

"Well, I hope the man suffers to his last breath."

"Not exactly the best attitude to show toward your old boss who's offering you a way out of all of this fucking mess."

Rotten said callously, "I don't care."

"Something tells me that someday. . . " Vernon said, as he studied Rotten more suspiciously, ". . . you will."

Below, John emerged from a cave along the side of a valley.

As he watched the helicopter fly away, he signaled to Ashleigh that it was safe to exit. After Ashleigh, who was holding Stash in her arms, stepped out of the cave, Brett was last to exit. The three, plus Stash, inched toward the edge of the cliff and together, watched the helicopter fly farther away from them.

John turned his sights to the dam below.

More than likely, he knew, everybody was dead; however, there was still a possibility that a few were still alive. And it was that notion which left John with no other choice than to return to the dam.

As the four made it to the dam, Ashleigh discovered M.J.'s body.

Teary-eyed, she handed off the cat to John, rushed over to M.J., and held him in her arms.

After John surveyed the carnage and was unable to find one single survivor, he walked over to Ashleigh, who was balling for the loss of her best friend.

"We can't be here anymore," John said urgently to Ashleigh. "It's too dangerous."

As Ashleigh clung to M.J., she didn't want to let him go. Yet, she wanted to hold him until she could no longer draw breath.

"Leave him," John demanded.

As he loomed over Ashleigh, she pulled out the necklace with the stoned hummingbird pendant that M.J. had made for her. She removed the necklace from around her neck and placed it inside M.J.'s hands and brought his hands to his chest. She kissed M.J. on his forehead, leaving behind a smudge of tears and saliva along his bloody head.

"Goodbye," she said, as the tears rolled down her face.

After Ashleigh said her goodbyes, the four of them, including Stash, hurried into the forest where they'd begin a new chapter of their lives.

BALANCE OF POWER (REDUX): BETA TEST
NOVEMBER 4, 2019
SWAGAHGALI, DEMOCRATIC REPUBLIC OF THE CONGO

WHILE the deadly Miner's Strike continued to wage in the city of Baklique in the Lazembe Province, home of one of the largest open-pit copper mines that had been recently shuttered due to the ongoing strike, a six-man crew consisting of two producers, two cameramen, one assistant, and a driven reporter, who worked for a digital media company, Loyal News, followed around twenty-three year old Musa Nkulu and his friend Jean Sifa throughout their daily lives as artisanal miners in Swagahgali, which sat along what was known as the Copper Belt located on the southernmost tip of the Democratic Republic of the Congo.

With a population estimated around three-million people, Swagahgali, despite its reputation for being a magnet for filmmakers due to its incredibly gritty location where critically-acclaimed films such as Goah's action-packed science-fiction thriller *A Caw Heard From The Grave* or environmental dramas like *Paperlung* and *The Human Corkscrew* or *Afriction*, directed by the great Calitori himself, king of Spaghetti Westerns, who filmed the cultish sci-fi flick a year before his death, were shot within a spitting distance of the crew's temporary residence, was known to rest directly underneath one of the richest mineral deposits in the world. What these artisanal miners sought was cobalt, a vital component in the production of various types of lithium-ion batteries. These rechargeable batteries were found in electric vehicles, as well as many consumer electronics, including smartphones.

Popularized by its in-depth documentaries and video exposés, Loyal News hoped to not only shine a spotlight on inhumane and often toxic conditions surrounding the mines, as well as a dire humanity crisis behind a rapid surge of cobalt mining—in some cases, carried out illegally—but also provide a one-of-a-kind experience for its audience, who may or may not be unaware of the very products (i.e. electric vehicles, smartphones) on the market, with the up-close and personal stories behind the people risking their lives to extract these vital components which powered up millions of lives outside Swagahgali, as well as cover the overwhelming health concerns many of the young Congolese men—and boys—faced while venturing into what could only be described as "hell."

Hesitant to share their stories due to their "distrustfulness" of modern day technology, Musa, Jean, and many others were displaced due to the mine expansion, which demolished their village and forced them to live in much worse conditions along the outskirts of Swagahgali, cut off from medical resources and amenities.

Desperate and barely able to provide for their families, Musa, Jean, and many displaced villagers were left with little-to-no source of income other than the meager wages they earned from venturing into these unsafe shafts that vertically stretched hundreds of meters deep into the earth in search of cobalt, which usually came in the form of a small nugget—and if scorching hot temperatures below weren't enough to underline the urgency of time, these artisanal miners only had minutes-worth of oxygen.

While documenting Musa and Jean's journey for a month, the Loyal News crew was given a firsthand look at the debilitating health effects, which were what local doctors believed to be results of toxic runoff from nearby mines, which contaminated the soil and water in and around the village.

In an impromptu meeting, Musa, a god-fearing man who had become rather close with reporter Francis Pascal during his stay in Swagahgali despite his initial doubts about the foreigner, introduced the crew to another artisanal miner, Patrick, and his family, including Patrick's four-year-old daughter Aali, who was born with a medical condition that increased the size of her head. Aali wasn't the only child affected by the pollution cast from the mines. There were dozens of children, like Aali, who suffered from birth defects, like hydrocephalus and other conditions, as well as malformations and congenital disorders.

The next day, after Francis met Patrick and his family, he began to question his dedication to the documentary and wondered who was going to profit from the artisanal miners' stories—Was Musa or Jean's story going to bring about change or practical solutions or, fingers crossed, wake people up from their digital comas? Or, was Francis simply exploiting one side of a monster that couldn't be destroyed, even if those who rose up against the monster sacrificed the one aspect of their lives that resulted in the price of conveniency? Considering the scrutiny Francis and his crew faced ever since they stepped foot in Swagahgali and a militia group which had recently seized control over most of the mineral territory in the surrounding area and started to pay closer attention toward the "foreigners"—and not the kind of attention neither Francis nor his producers desired—the cameras kept rolling.

And what they captured was, to say the least, a "groundbreaking discovery," or what miners referred to as "*fossiles*," which was French for fossils.

Equipped with a headcam provided by the film crew, Musa used the jerry-rigged contraption to re-enter the mineshaft, which was about the diameter of an air vent, where he lowered himself to the bottom of the shaft. There, while crawling his way through the furnace-hot tunnels, Musa met up with Jean, who came across what he believed to be the body of a human, possibly one of the villagers.

With very little tools at his disposal, except for the two most valuable ones given to Musa at birth, he assisted Jean in the excavation of the body.

As crewmembers from Loyal News watched closely to Musa's shaky feed on the monitors, the bones started to surface from the earth.

One after another, each brush of dirt, a ribcage, then a spine, then, finally, a skull.

Despite the bones being slightly scattered, the skeleton remained partially intact by what appeared to be a metal wire that kept everything together in one ornament-like piece.

Once it was confirmed to be the remains of a human, Musa and the others securely wrapped the bones in a blanket without ruining their integrity and then hoisted them to the surface by way of a makeshift pulley apparatus made from worn cable and rope.

Shortly after, Musa, Jean, and the last three artisanal miners returned to the surface where the film crew was huddled around the corpse's skeleton.

Musa touched the bones.

"*Il fait froid*," said Musa.

"Cold?" Francis said in question.

Musa instructed Francis to touch the femur bone of the skeleton.

"Bloody hell," he said, shaking off his stinging hand. "It's freezing."

The ground around the body, as the others explained to the crew, was also freezing, or *froid*, which to Francis and his crewmembers made absolutely no sense whatsoever.

Next to catch Francis's attention was what appeared to be a necklace worn around the neck of the skeleton. The necklace was beaded, faded and scratched, with the pendant of what looked liked the canine of a coyote.

In French, Francis asked Musa if he had seen the necklace before.

Musa, who couldn't recognize the necklace, was equally as per-turbed by it as Francis.

What was more intriguing: a strange wire-thin metal that ran along the entire skeletal structure, which peeled away from the bone like a scab. Musa tugged on the metal wire along the collar-bone and followed it toward the center of the skull, which was partially caved in. Carefully, he reached his fingers inside the hol-low skull and pulled out the diamond-shaped piece of metal roughly the size of a pea. The hub. The nervous system of wires were connected to the piece in Musa's hand and when he lifted it from the remains, the wire peeled from the bones and dangled below like a loose bundle of floss.

As though somehow bound together by the strange wire, the bones suddenly started to break and crack and eventually shatter all on their own, prompting one of the artisanal miners to blame Musa for his carelessness, despite, only moments earlier, he took part in hauling the remains up a shaft as narrow as a laundry chute.

Blame aside, Jean pointed overhead at an approaching storm. The clouds began to form and plump and darken from the bot-tom up in what the villagers warned was a "*mauvaise tempête.*"

"A bad storm," Francis emphasized to his producers.

While inspecting the artifact between his fingertips, Musa no-ticed a circular engraving along the side of the metal with a tiny swirl-like pattern.

"*Qu'est-ce que c'est?*" asked Jean.

Mesmerized by the artifact, Musa couldn't explain what he held in the palm of his hand.

But whatever it was, he knew it was power.

He couldn't explain his justifications, but he could feel its en-ergy humming against the dried flesh of his callused palms.

Musa wasn't the only one drawn to the discovery.

The other artisanal miners, thinking it might've been some kind of weapon or even jewelry, couldn't take their eyes from it.

Jean even attempted to snatch the artifact from Musa's palms.

In defense, Musa pulled his cupped hands into the safety of his body.

"Finder's keepers, eh?" Francis said, laughing.

Led by Musa, the artisanal miners hurried back home before the storm arrived and swore an oath to one another not to tell a soul about the artifact, which didn't sit well with several villagers who believed the artifact to be worth a lot of money, enough money to find a better home, closer to amenities.

Eventually, as the artifact revealed its true nature, those who knew about the discovery were well aware of its power and how it was more than priceless.

More than the Holy Grail, it was life and death and something else.

It was everything.

And if people found out about it, Swagahgali would be one of the most sought-after places in the world.

Maybe it already was.